2005

For Leigh —
with warm wishes —

3/4/08

Praise for Suzanne Morris' previous novels

Galveston

"Casts a spell!"

—Publisher's Weekly

"Imaginative gusto...feverish...the most seductive kind of fireside read."

—Harper's

"When I saw the pages dwindling, I truly regretted knowing that the haunting story was coming to an end...I'm really impressed with the book."

—novelist William Goyen

Keeping Secrets

"an intricate, meticulously plotted novel with well rounded characters."

—Houston Chronicle

"The plot is both plausible and fascinating. The ending is devastating and unexpected. You won't forget this story 10 minutes after you put it down.

—Gazette Telegraph, Colorado Springs

Skychild

"Morris captures the subtle pressure that social and professional conformity bring to bear on a troubled marital relationship...with telling authenticity."

—Publishers Weekly

"engrossing plot...highly recommended."

—Library Journal

Wives and Mistresses

"A fascinating multi-generational story full of intriguing twists and turns."

—Booklist

"A rich canvas of a southern family spanning the years from 1887 to 1960.... A book you have trouble putting down and one you don't want to finish."

—Eastern Washington Book Review Council

LOOK BACK WITH LONGING

Also by Suzanne Morris

Galveston
Keeping Secrets
Skychild
Wives and Mistresses
The Browns of Ashton Villa

LOOK BACK WITH LONGING

Book One of the *Clearharbour Trilogy*

A Novel

Suzanne Morris

iUniverse, Inc.

New York Lincoln Shanghai

Look Back with Longing
Book One of the *Clearharbour Trilogy*

Copyright © 2005 by SUZANNE MORRIS

iUniverse books may be ordered through booksellers or by contacting:

iUniverse
2021 Pine Lake Road, Suite 100
Lincoln, NE 68512
www.iuniverse.com
1-800-Authors (1-800-288-4677)

ISBN-13: 978-0-595-36653-8 (pbk)
ISBN-13: 978-0-595-67400-8 (cloth)
ISBN-13: 978-0-595-81076-5 (ebk)
ISBN-10: 0-595-36653-8 (pbk)
ISBN-10: 0-595-67400-3 (cloth)
ISBN-10: 0-595-81076-4 (ebk)

Printed in the United States of America

In memory of Robert H. Bonner,
my friend and first reader
AND
in honor of Dorothy and Mary Margaret Niland,
my dancing teachers

Acknowledgments

I owe my thanks to many people for help in writing this novel. Some are no longer living. I am pleased, nonetheless, to include their names here.

In the United States:

Susan Schwartz, my Editor, for guiding me through this and all my published novels with patience and equanimity; Karen Giesen, for proofing and copy editing; Dianna Walton and Karen Javellana, for reading and commenting on the manuscript; Frank Bowie, for explaining the day-to-day operations of a trust department; Wayne Skelton, for answering legal queries; Dorothy and Mary Margaret Niland, for help in researching acrobatic exhibition dancing; Leona Mellen, for sharing her memories as a dancing teacher; Eddie Bell Tillman, for sharing her experiences as a vaudeville performer; Donna Bonner Garner, for researching vaudeville history in the Lincoln Library, New York City; A. D. Deason, for answering queries on the history of the Dallas Majestic, and Pat Meyer for giving me a tour; Christina Avena, Las Casas Foundation, for giving me a tour of the San Antonio Majestic and Empire theatres; Robert Eason, Dallas Public Library Fine Arts department, for providing materials on Karl Hoblitzelle and his Interstate Amusement chain; the staffs of the Texas and Local History department, Houston Public Library, and the Houston Heights Historical Museum; my mother Ruth Page, who shared her memories of living in Houston Heights during the 1920's; and special thanks to C. G. Javellana, for the original jacket art.

In England:

Patrick Beaver, author and social historian, for tireless aid in digging out answers to research questions, without which the *Clearharbour Trilogy* could not have been written; Margaret and Michael Wetz, for their hospitality at Coldharbour Farm in Bodmin, Cornwall, on which Clearharbour Farm is modeled;

Lois and Duane Luallin, for their hospitality, and especially Duane who taught me how to drive the English way; and Elaine Vincin, my companion, who had the courage to ride in the passenger seat.

Contents

It is a picture of moments following one another and yourself in each moment making some choice that might have been otherwise.

—C. S. Lewis

PROLOGUE

November 30, 1959

Geneva stands on the front walk of 1207 Heights Boulevard, shivering in her wool traveling suit. She had forgotten how quickly the sky will turn from hazy blue to iron gray and the temperature will plunge, when the sharp swift blade of a cold front cuts through Houston. The house is for sale again, according to the sign, and luckily it is vacant: She will be spared asking permission to walk around the back of the property. How would she convince the owner of her wish to see a place she knew once upon a time, when no visible evidence remains that it was there?

It strikes her as ironic that while it was not by choice she moved to this address forty-five years ago, she wound up residing here for more years than anyone else, before or since. The house is in pretty bad shape at this point—the wood siding is all but bare of paint, and wears the fragile patina of age; the screen in the screen door has curled away from all four corners of the frame, as if offended by its disrepair; and the window shades have warped and turned the color of tobacco stains. Yet—at least from where she is standing at this moment—the house appears structurally unchanged from the way she remembers it, with the wide wrap-around porch, the bay windows in the two front rooms, and the oval window in the center of the second story, from which she once peered down to watch the sure-footed field of energy that was Tony Selby walk out of her life before she could fully appreciate what she was losing.

No sign exists of the lush gardens once here, over which she toiled for hours, her knees and back aching, sweat pouring off her forehead and upper lip, and trickling down between her breasts and shoulder blades. Snapdragons, begonias, impatiens, petunias and many another variety grew in this part of the yard where there was a good balance of light and shade; and a bed of roses grew in the sunny side yard. All the flowers she planted—but especially the roses—were a means of holding on to a memory, and forming what she hoped from time to time and against all reasonable odds, might be a bridge between past and future.

Apparently one of the succession of owners abandoned the challenge of growing grass in the front yard, for there are only a few brownish patches here and there, and the rest is bare earth, making the ground look like it has a skin disease. You were always up against the many thirsty trees with spreading branches: oaks and elms, and sweet gums with prickly pods that stung like spider bites under bare feet. She recognizes most of the trees in the yard today as having been here when first she came. They survived the 1915 storm in far better shape than she did.

She walks around the side of the yard now, her fingers vainly attempting to straighten her wind-tossed hairdo for which she spent an hour and a half at the beauty salon this morning, most of it under the hood of a too-hot hair dryer, watching the clock while flipping through a copy of *Silver Screen*—movie magazines the only ones available. And now her hair feels like a scouring pad. She wonders why she didn't protest when the beauty operator aimed that pink aerosol can at her. All those years ago when she arrived on the doorstep of this house, carrying her suitcase, she did not imagine she would ever put her hair through such punishment. Thick coppery waves massing down her slender back were a major source of pride then. When freshly washed and allowed to dry naturally—by the fireside on a day such as this, the tresses picking up flickering light as she fanned them out, or in the heat of summer sunshine—her hair was wild, barely containable. It was like Rapunzel's, Victor once said. It was—well, it was part of her undoing.

Glancing up at her old second story bedroom window, she notes the rotting frame. She spent the better part of one year gazing out that window from her bed, quietly marking the seasons by the changing colors of the leaves, then their scarcity and finally their disappearance, anxiety increasing within her as the view harshened, the icy bare limbs suggesting an obstacle course below. Was there ever a time when she lived in this house that there was not some cause for anxiety?

She feels a twinge of sadness about what's become of the house, but then there's always the chance some buyer will come along and restore it. Not so with Victor's studio, unfortunately, and as her steps continue, the cold wind, flattening her clothing against the contours of her figure and stinging her sheer-stockinged legs, seems to be trying to push her away: *How can you, of all people, come back here?*

Her heartbeat freezes in time as she reaches roughly the point where the studio would have come into view: a rectangular building with stucco exterior and a flat roof that would develop a serious leak long after Victor was gone and result in damage for which—with a twist of irony—she would wind up accepting blame. There was a door at one end, and a large window on the long wall running parallel to the fence, that Victor carved out when he converted the building from a smoke house, and through which the sunlight poured in on her as she posed for him: a warm caress on her face and shoulders and breast. She closes her eyes for a long moment, calling back that ticklish warming of elastic skin, lying in the archives of her youth. Perhaps it is not strange—though it seemed so at first—that while visiting her parents' grave today for the first time in many years, she felt a yearning to come here. After all, it is a grave site as well: here her innocence lies buried. "Why do you want to go?" Willa asked astutely from behind the wheel of her Oldsmobile. The man who bought the house from Geneva had the studio torn down, as if it were any ordinary ramshackle structure blighting the landscape. She was gone by then. And though Rodney informed the buyer of the building's historical significance, the man had never heard of Victor Calais the photographer, and believed the building posed a danger.

He was correct in more ways than one, Geneva supposed.

She gave some thought to Willa's question before replying, "Because I survived, I guess, because we all did." She had no better answer then, as she was operating on instinct. But now that she's here, she thinks maybe she's like a soldier returning to the battle field years later, having to some degree overcome aversion to the painful associations, and wishing to relive a few moments that, even if not happy, were at least…well…poignant. An awakening took place here; cruelly snuffed out, but an awakening nonetheless.

By now her face and neck and hands are aching from the penetrating wind. "You'd better put on your coat," Willa advised as she got out of the car. But Geneva didn't want to be encumbered by an overcoat designed for a much colder climate, with its heavy cape collar. Encumbered: now there's an interesting choice of words. She is already encumbered by the undeniability of the wrinkles in her skin, and her joints connecting one bone to another, beginning to ache from being out in weather like this as she tries to go back and walk around in the taut skin of her youth. Her body's instinct to recoil just now is not unlike the state of her mind and spirit in October of 1914 when her parents were killed and she came—was sent—here to live with her guardian, Cousin Anne. She had been here for more than three weeks when her parents were buried, a delay owing to the necessity of bringing up their remains along with those of sixty-five others, making positive identifications, then dispatching them to the town where they resided by the very same locomotion which led them to their deaths. *"Miss you, Darling, see you soon,"* said the postcard, arriving fortuitously on the day after the tragedy. Geneva was less than two months away from her 16th birthday. Until then she had led the sheltered life of an only child with parents of comfortable means. It would not be an exaggeration to say that she felt on the verge of hysteria, and remained so for many months, her only anchor Victor's attentiveness and that not lasting through the storm.

In three weeks a lot of messages can pass between two people of the opposite sex and years apart in age, especially when the younger one is a female shocked and confused—making 'positive identifications' could mean that her parents may not have been on that train, and any minute may walk through the door of their house on Caroline Street in Houston and wonder why she is not awaiting them—and the other measures out kind words between contemplative glances carrying the weight of his own feelings of regret and of being stranded. Then, at last, the deep hole separating them is closed up and they reach across to each other.

Did her eyes meet Victor's above the grave that day as they had already done on a number of occasions above Anne's kitchen table, she not knowing what those silent exchanges meant but somehow intuiting they were dangerous? Strangely, Geneva does not now recall Victor's presence at the burial; perhaps he stood apart, being a second cousin by marriage. She remembers only their disconcerting conversation on the way home, and this with the breathtaking clarity experienced by people who have lived for many years, when memories of events long past are suddenly unleashed by a sound or a smell or a photograph...or the return to a place. She is surprised to discover that this is not a bad memory, regardless of all it led to, perhaps because it was the first diversion from the awful reality of losing her parents, which struck her fully for the first time when she watched them being lowered into the grave.

How much time could it have taken to drive from Glendale Cemetery on the east side of Houston, north to the Houston Heights? Today it took Willa around 30 minutes, part of it on the freeway. In 1914, speed limits were much lower and roads were fewer and poor, so it probably took close to an hour in Victor's long-nosed, low-slung motorcar—oh yes, and perhaps even longer:

During the journey a tire went flat and Victor got out to repair it. Geneva was left sitting there with the high stiff collar of her black crepe dress scratching her neck, trying to imagine herself in the role Victor wanted her to play, and failing to guess that the course of her life would be altered by that truncated conversation as surely as when the excursion train carrying her parents high up in the Rockies came upon a defect in the railroad bridge. *"I wonder if you'd consider modeling for me...."* As Victor pumped up the tire, Geneva's answer swelled in her throat.

Oh yes, the two graves are inextricably linked.

As she walks farther back in the yard to fix the studio's exact location, her heartbeat is speeding ahead of her as if it knows where to go even if she doesn't, and why not? Didn't it live there for—how many?—six, no, seven months, until all but the building itself came tumbling down around her? She just wants to stand there for a minute or two, that's all. But there is no way to be sure as she looks up and down the long grassy fence line, for all the reference points have vanished. The small brick cottage that used to stand on the other side of the fence, facing Yale Street, has been torn down and replaced by a Sinclair gas station. The garage—what was left of an old carriage house—that used to shelter Victor's motor car, and later her own succession of vehicles, has been torn down, replaced with one which is larger and sits at a different angle on the lot, looking a little awkward, as if knowing it was an afterthought.

Geneva is disappointed. Just locating the place where Victor worked seemed such a modest desire when she came here. Yet his studio and all that took place inside may as well have been an illusion, like the photographs he made.

She checks her watch. It is time to go. Time, too, is an illusion: you never have as much of it as you think you do, and then it's gone. Next stop is Houston Municipal Airport, back on the east side of town—Willa's a saint, spending the tail end of the Thanksgiving holiday driving her best friend from one end of town to the other, and back again. By five o'clock Geneva will be on a plane headed for home: a long, truncated journey. *But that's what life is.* And memories are the point of every beginning.

PART I

1914–1915

CHAPTER 1

On the day appointed for the burial of Dorothy and Henry Sterling, their daughter Geneva Louise rose very early, walked quietly into the hall bathroom without disturbing her two roommates, closed the door, and forced herself to look into the mirror and say the dreaded word: *"Orphan."* How appropriate, she thought, that the word began with the mouth forming a circle, for, like every circle, this one had no end.

Orphan. For this she had been brought into the world. What promise her parents had held, having waited so long—she'd heard the stories; they were both in their thirties by the time she was born. *"Why am I named Geneva?" She asked her mother at the age of six. "It is the name of a town in Switzerland where we spent a pleasant holiday in the spring of the year you were born. We'll take you there someday."* Numerous picture books were on the shelves of glass-fronted bookcases, with snow-capped mountains and villages springing up from deep valleys. And there was a painting in the dining room, of a flower market in a city square, bright colors enclosed by spreading trees. People carrying baskets. Geneva waited and waited, imagining herself filling a basket with flowers. Money was being saved. Next summer, provided the war in Europe was over, she was to have been taken there, part of a grand tour.

Geneva turned from the mirror. Whether or not the war was over next summer, she would not be going to Switzerland. The painting had been placed in storage. She wished never to see it again.

She endured the early part of the funeral conscious of the self-possession her parents had expected of her. *"Step outside yourself when in public during times of despair, and force your thoughts away from personal things,"* said her mother. For this accomplishment she imagined them peering down at her approvingly from heaven. She must always, always behave in a way that would have pleased them, she thought now. It would be a way of keeping them with her for the rest of her life. For a moment or two she felt truly comforted by this vision of the future. Then, the preacher's startling words at the conclusion of his sermon flung her back into the present. "Though we mourn, we must accept God's will in calling Dorothy and Henry home." Geneva wrung her hands, the storm of emotions inside her all but impossible to mask. "*We all belong to God*," her mother was fond of saying. How vividly this memory came to her now, when she had hardly paid attention, hearing it so many times. Now, under the threat of the preacher's words, it seemed a simple yet all-encompassing statement of faith which inferred that God loved all who belonged to Him. How, then, could it be that God willed destruction on her parents? Not to mention the others on the tragedy-bound train, or, for that matter, victims of all kinds of catastrophes down through the ages? And what of those loved ones who were left behind? Geneva was invited to accompany her parents on their trip to the Rockies; she could have missed a week of school and made it up. Did the fact she chose instead to stay at home—albeit with their blessing—mean it was God's will to make her an orphan?

This last provoking question had just evolved in her mind when Anne thrust a hymnal into her hands, opened to the closing hymn. The organ swelled with somber chords. Light rays filtered through a stained glass window, leaping like pink and purple flames upon the page. Geneva did not sing.

Later, as the burial service at Glendale Cemetery was nearing the inevitable point when her parents would embark on their final journey together, into the grave, Geneva found her mind being drawn to that place she had forbidden it to go today: imagining them on that fateful night. They would have reached for each other—she was sure—at the first terrifying jolt, the row of train carriages snapping like a string of beads and spilling into the dark abyss, end over end....

There were spots before Geneva's eyes. The ground was rising beneath her feet. Her mind struggled to climb back, hand over hand, to clutch the solid ground of their lives together: *It is six-fifteen on a weekday evening. The intoxicating summer scents of fresh-mown grass and blooming Ligustrum flood her mother's music room. Geneva sits near the window as her mother's long slender fingers trip and thunder over the keys of the Baldwin, her head of dark hair now lowering near her arched wrists, now tilting back on her swan-like neck, eyelids closing over her green eyes in rapture. Now her father strolls past the window in his white linen suit, four-in-hand tie, and straw boater, arriving from his job at*

Houston Lumber & Paint Company. Geneva rises from her chair and goes to the front door. Through the fancy cut work of the door glass she can see his figure on the porch, divided like sections on a map. She closes her hand around the smooth brass oval knob and turns it. She is enfolded at once in loving arms clothed in linen, damp with perspiration. He hands her his hat—the straw still warm from the sun beating down on it. The music stops. Her mother appears with a smile.

There were no words spoken in this memory, only music and fragrance, and the soul-stirring presence of love and consistency. Held in its folds, Geneva regained her composure. Yet too soon came the intrusion of Reverend Stone's solemn voice, leading everyone in the Lord's Prayer. *"…Thy Kingdom come, Thy Will be done…"* Geneva had long since memorized the universal prayer, yet only now did she truly hear the words contained in it. If the preacher's appalling statement in the pulpit were true, then, had she unwittingly prayed for her parents' death every time she repeated the Lord's Prayer? Hot bile rose in her throat and her stomach roiled. This could not be right. Yet, how else explain it?

The service was over.

Reverend Stone began dismissing everyone, and those who had not greeted Geneva earlier did so now. She could not concentrate on their words of sympathy for keeping an eye on the preacher. If she did not speak to him now, when and where would she do so? Reverend Stone was mopping the perspiration from his thin sallow face: a result of his exertion, surely; the temperature outside was no more than 40 degrees. Now he was smiling benevolently and nodding his head at her parents' dear friends Walter and Mary Hunnicutt. Now the crowd had dispersed and the preacher was bidding farewell to Anne, bestowing on her the same benevolent smile. The moment was close at hand, and Geneva struggled to compose her question in a way that seemed respectful.

She was distracted by the approach of a diminutive woman wearing a smart dress of midnight blue with a high lace collar and elbow-length sleeves. On her hair was a tall hat of midnight blue, with a stiff black plume on one side, adding inches to her height. It took Geneva a moment to recognize Madame Linsky. Day after day, year after year, the dance mistress looked the same as she instructed her pupils at her Main Street studio: her black hair with cobwebs of gray pulled into a severe knot at the nape of her neck; her sturdy figure draped in a black jersey, a straight broadcloth skirt with a slit up the side, and black stockings covering her muscular calves. The only variation in this attire was at spring recital, when she wore a plain black dress with long sleeves and a high neck, and nothing on her head. Today she appeared like a proud bird who had strayed outside her natural habitat. Geneva struggled to reconcile this strange image with more familiar ones.

"*Ma chère,*" said Madame Linsky gently, her arms opening to embrace her pupil, her dark eyes filled with such tenderness that it was hard to believe those same eyes bored through her pupils from the moment they took their places at the *barre,* searching relentlessly for the smallest error in posture, in turn-out, in the curve of each hand as ballerina arms opened simultaneously down the line.

Out the corner of her eye Geneva saw with alarm Reverend Stone's retreating figure. Pulling away from Madame Linsky and excusing herself, she called, "Reverend Stone, Sir, I beg your pardon—" When the preacher turned, his slightly piqued expression was chilling.

Slowly, as though gathering patience, he said, "Yes—?"

Geneva was at a loss. She opened her hands. "Sir, I—I do not understand how you can—how it can be—that the death of my parents was God's will," she stammered, the blood beating in her temples.

The preacher was silent, his face immobile. Geneva knew that she had overstepped herself. She was not raised in the church. She did not know the rules. Reverend Stone had come here today as a favor to Anne, and now she had insulted him.

Geneva was aware of Linsky's utterance behind her shoulder: "*Quelle horreur!*" followed by a string of French words in a voice so low that Geneva could pick up nothing more than the staccato tone. She understood only the few phrases her dance mistress used on the studio floor, and the one phrase she could make out clearly, she had never heard before. *Quelle horreur!* Was Linsky condemning her for blasphemy? For disrespect to an elder? If so, she may dismiss her from the study of ballet—the joy of Geneva's heart, and the one thin thread by which she held on to the life she led before her parents were killed. *Madame Linsky's wooden crucifix looms high on her office wall as she sits writing at her desk below: "Dear Madame Sterling"—no—"Dear Madame Calais, it is with regret that I inform you Geneva is no longer welcome to study at Elvira Linsky's School of Dance...."*

Anne, a heavier version of Geneva's dark-haired mother, looked especially formidable today in a tailored black suit with a three-quarter length jacket, slightly flared at the hips, an ankle-length skirt, and a black hat with an exceedingly broad brim. She shifted her bulk toward her ward's right side and looked up at the preacher. "Excuse the child, please, Reverend Stone; I'm sure she's not herself today," she apologized, all the while pressing a finger hard between

Geneva's shoulder blades. "And by the way, I'm sure Geneva would be very glad for the church to have her mother's piano as a token of our thanks," she continued in a fawning voice. "My cousin Dorothy taught piano lessons, you know, but unfortunately Geneva doesn't play."

The word 'unfortunately' was grossly unfair. Her mother expressed no disappointment when, after a year of squirming restlessly on the piano bench, she begged to study dance instead.

Reverend Stone smiled. "We are most grateful, Mrs. Calais," he said, with a respectful bow of his head. Glancing at Geneva he added, "And I trust Miss Sterling will appear each Sunday morning both to hear her late mother's fine instrument being used to the highest purpose of all, and to see my comments of the morning in a broader context." What 'broader context' could there possibly be? Geneva wondered bitterly.

"Oh, I can assure you she will be there," said Anne, with a sideward glance and a thin cold smile at Geneva.

Geneva resented being conversed about as though she were absent when she was standing right there—something her parents never did—nor was the veiled reference to her parents' failure to raise her in the church lost on her. Yet even this did not wound her as deeply as Reverend Stone's suggestion that her mother's piano was now to be put to better use than when she was alive. And he was standing not ten feet from the grave in which he had just buried her.

When Geneva turned back toward Madame Linsky, she had vanished. *"Dear Madame Calais, It is with regret…."* Needles pricked at Geneva's chest.

As she and Anne walked together to Victor's motorcar, parked at the cemetery entrance, Anne explained, "I checked, and the piano would ruin if it were left in storage for a long period of time because of the dampness. So naturally when Reverend Stone mentioned they need one at the church, it started me thinking…."

You might have asked me first! Geneva thought with fury. Yet even if they were not approaching the motorcar, Victor standing alongside with the doors open for them and the engine making such a clatter she would have to shout to be heard, she would not have dared to criticize Anne. The hard pressure of her guardian's finger lingered between her shoulder blades. On the day of her parents' burial. Anne's help over the past three weeks, in making room for her in her family's home and arranging today's service, had seemed sincere enough. But no. *She does not like me,* Geneva realized. *This is the beginning, the way it will be from now on. Cousin Anne is all that stands between me and the rows of narrow beds in lonely, impersonal rooms smelling of disinfectant, where freedoms are usurped; and she wants me to remember it.*

Yet Victor, she noted, was smiling as he handed her through the door. Somehow, though she did not know him well, she felt that his kindness today, as well as over the past three weeks, was sincere. That she suffered a severe case of lightheadedness when Victor looked at her was her business to overcome. Her parents would expect it. If he were to guess the effect he had of scrambling her nerves, he would think her foolish indeed; and now, especially, when his smile rose above the ashes of kindness she may have hoped for on this occasion, she could not bear to think he might ever think her foolish.

CHAPTER 2

Victor Calais had always spent more time on the road than at home, and up to the time Geneva's parents were killed, he had seen the Sterling family on few occasions—the most recent of these, three or four years earlier at some relative's funeral. He recalled Geneva's long, wavy red hair, and her erect posture that made her appear taller than she was. He did not remember her face.

Then, suddenly, she was living under his roof.

Victor liked to rise early, dress for the day in duck trousers, a work shirt and boots, and cook breakfast. Ordinarily he was the only one up and about until he knocked on Anne's door to say the meal was on the table. A few mornings after Geneva moved in, she appeared at the kitchen door wearing her house robe. Her green, wide-set eyes registered surprise. She expected to find Anne at the stove. Victor offered her sausage and eggs and biscuits; grits were bubbling in a pot. "Thank you, but I'm too nervous to eat," she said, bringing a dainty hand to her waist. Victor remembered this would be her first day to attend Heights High School, and later she had an appointment with her trust officer at the bank—a thoroughly disagreeable man who'd come by to check on the suitability of her living arrangement. Victor poured her some cocoa and sat across from her as she drank it. "I know it's hard, changing schools and all," he said with feeling. He would have added, 'after what you've been through,' but thought better of it. She looked at him above the rim of her cup, her eyes pleading in a way that made him think of a small injured bird.

From that morning Geneva often came to the kitchen before anyone else, and though Victor sensed she liked being there with him, she never stayed long or said very much. He surmised she was not sleeping well, and little wonder.

Victor naturally began to study her features: the curve of her forehead and the small apostrophe at the center of her hairline around which her hair swept up like wings; the narrow bridge of her nose perpendicular to high cheek-bones; and the way her chin tapered to a narrow tip beneath her mouth. She would make an interesting model, he thought. He'd been intrigued by art pho-tography for some years, but for lack of time, or a subject which interested him, he had never attempted it.

Besides, as Geneva sat there under the bright kitchen light, morning after morning, what Victor found most fascinating of all was the varying tones in her skin and hair. In his thoughts he would separate them, as if preparing a palette of oils. As a young boy he'd dreamed of being a painter one day; he showed some talent at sketching, and he had a good eye for color. Life inter-vened, however. His father died when he was 12, and he had to help support his family. He got an after-school job sweeping the floor at Bullard Camera Company, and four years later bought his Bellieni press camera. Happily, though his vocation turned him from painting, it often took him to cities where there were museums and galleries. Now he found himself thinking idly of what his favorite painters might do with Geneva. Monet, for instance. Granted, he was primarily a landscape artist, and the figures in his paintings were secondary, providing a focal point and giving the viewer an idea of scale. Still, with his genius for painting light, Monet would capture the translucence in Geneva's complexion and the multiple tones in her hair. Or, Guy Rose? Maybe. Like Monet, he had a gift for flushing light through his paintings. The red-haired girl in *The Blue Kimono* came to mind. It was easy to imagine Geneva as one of Renoir's rosy, youthful female figures, too. And he wouldn't mind seeing what Frieseke could do with her compact body and long limbs, though Frieseke was fond of cool blue and mauve pigments. Geneva's colors were amber and copper and ochre and red—blazing, combustible colors. Oh, for the skill to paint this girl!

Victor loved talking about painters he admired, but there was no one to do it with. He knew that Geneva's parents were well-traveled, and maybe she was too. One morning, hopeful of putting her at ease and satisfying his own wish, he asked Geneva who was her favorite artist.

"I'm afraid I don't have one," she said. "There was a painting on our dining room wall—" she began, then her eyes dropped; her voice drifted off.

Victor would like to have known more about this painting, but he recog-nized he had scratched the surface of a poignant memory. Tactfully, he went on, "I like the Impressionists best of all. Their vivid colors, and...and how their paintings may seem raw...unfinished...yet they're not; they're fluid, shimmering with life—take you by surprise—. And imagine the audacity: they were the first to paint outdoors, instead of in the studio!"

"Is that why you like outdoor photography?" she said, her eyes warm. He was flattered that she made this connection, allowed that his work was creative.

"Yes. Not that I'd mind working in a studio some," he hastened to say, seeing the drawback of her thinking otherwise. "I made a living with studio photography when the girls were little, so I could be nearby for Anne. It's just that I disliked the phoniness, people wanting me to make them look perfect, rather than the far more interesting way they really looked. *"Have you ever heard of art photography?"* he almost said. But Geneva was excusing herself. And when she was gone he was glad he hadn't opened the subject quite so soon. He realized what he'd really wanted, after a few mornings in the kitchen with her, was to somehow chase away her grief.

The idea of Geneva in an art photograph wouldn't leave Victor. One late night he rose from his cot in the studio and dusted off a book with a long piece on Julia Cameron—to his mind, the best of the art photographers. If he could find just the right angle—no, more to the point, just the right expression on Geneva's face, something that revealed her, then maybe....

The next night, when the children had gone to bed and Anne was in the living room with her sewing basket in her lap, he asked for her consent. He first tried to explain art photography. He didn't get very far before she bent her head down to search for a spool of thread, giving him notice to spare her the details. Anne liked every idea reduced to its simplest terms. Odd how this quality in her personality annoyed him just now, whereas he'd always thought it provided balance in the life of a dreamer like him. Curtailing his description, he said, "It'll take some time to develop my skill. It's very difficult to do well."

"In other words, it'll be some while before it pays off. What will we live on in the meantime?" Anne inquired, not looking up.

There she went again. Yet she had opened herself to reproach. "I've put a little money by. There's a benefit to my having stayed on the road so much lately," he told her, "other than the fact that it has kept me out of your hair."

Anne glanced up at him, her face suffused with guilt. Victor had a fleeting sense of hope, which left him feeling foolish when her eyes hardened and she looked down again. It was a little over a year since the stillbirth of their son. Both were devastated. Victor had never loved Anne more than he did then, or wanted more desperately to console her. He knew only one way to do this. Nor had he given up on having a son of his own. When she told him shortly afterward that she wanted no more children, his blood froze. *"We'll be careful." "We can't be careful enough."* His unwillingness to accept this only increased her withdrawal from him. Hoping if he left her alone, she'd miss him and come around, he gave in and took more assignments. When he was home he slept out in the studio most of the time. The trouble was, Anne was never much of a talker, and sleeping together had been their only form of intimacy. When out on the road, he missed that. When at home, he could not watch their children at play without longing for the mother who bore them. But the more time that passed, the more resolute Anne became, and though sometimes Victor's frustration got the better of him, it was happening less and less often because his feelings had begun to harden as well. Indifference in bed was the worst form of all.

"I'd have to get you to sign a release, and Geneva too, I guess," he said.

Anne shrugged, unrolled the spool of dark blue thread. "But don't take up all her spare time. She ought to learn how to cook at least. It seems Cousin Dorothy didn't teach her anything practical," she said.

"Don't tell anyone yet. I haven't made up my mind for sure," Victor said.

Afterward he puzzled over Anne's apparent lack of concern for the risks involved in his working closely with the innocent young girl for whom she was responsible. Did she trust him that far, despite their estrangement? Or did she think it unlikely that Geneva would become attracted to a man more than twice as old as she was when she would soon be the appropriate age for young men to come courting? Whatever Anne reasoned, hurting Geneva was the last thing Victor would do. He suspected he felt more responsible for her than Anne did.

Came the day Dorothy and Henry Sterling were buried.

Glendale Cemetery was old and shaggy, filled with lichen-crusted tombstones. A long-accumulated gloominess hung over it, and a thickness of moss-draped trees shut out much of the natural light. Standing a bit apart from the crowd, Victor watched Geneva, concerned she might break down. Yet her composure seemed invincible in the firm set of her full bottom lip as she stood there in her ankle-length black dress, her abundant waves pulled back in a tight knot with a wide band of black crepe laying on them like a shroud, yet with tendrils escaping and curling around her temples as if too energetic to be confined even on this solemn occasion. Her eyes were intent on some point far in the distance. Was she reflecting on the past? Or contemplating the harsh realities of her future? Anne may be right that Geneva had been "spoiled and coddled." But she possessed the inner resources necessary to survive even worse than those two hulking coffins with funeral flowers listing on top disappearing slowly, slowly, now smoothly on the cables, now with a quick jolt, down and down....

Victor knew now what he wanted to bring out in Geneva's photograph.

By the time the burial service was over, he was eager to ask Geneva to be his model. Yet this was hardly the appropriate time. He realized suddenly that he didn't know when the time would be right. A week from now? A month? Yet he felt as he had felt that morning in the kitchen, that modeling for him would be good for Geneva.

When they were ready to leave, Victor knelt down and cranked up the engine of his second-hand motorcar, setting it to cough and sputter as it always did when started. Benjamin—the only child they brought along; he alone could be trusted to keep quiet and be still—had sat in the back seat of the car during the burial, and now made a fuss when Victor told him to scoot over so Geneva could get in. "I'll sit with Benjamin. Geneva can sit in front," Anne said agreeably. Luckily Geneva didn't hear the exchange, having been detained by the couple named Hunnicutt, her parents' close friends.

On the way home Victor noted Geneva pulling her black handkerchief through her fingers, back and forth, over and over. He heard her breath catch now and then. *"It's alright honey; go ahead and cry,"* he wanted to say. He would have drawn her near, put her head on his shoulder. Yet such tenderness, coming from him, might offend her.

Geneva did not utter a word until they were driving down Washington Avenue, within a few blocks of Heights Boulevard. Then she turned to Victor and asked with a shivering breath, "Do you ever go to France? I—I understand from Kathy that your work takes you to Europe sometimes."

Her voice was tight, as if squeezed up in her throat; nonetheless, Victor was pleased that she was attempting to talk to him. He imagined showing her photographs he'd taken in France, out in the studio. "Yes, I've worked in France a number of times, though not since war broke out. Too dangerous, with a family at home." He had worked in and around Paris mostly, photographing public buildings and street scenes and gardens, for the International News Service. On one assignment he took a train to Giverny to photograph the gray-bearded, portly Claude Monet painting in his garden. When he was done the master shook his hand warmly. Monet's hand was meaty, rough, a workman's hand. To Victor it felt almost holy. From that encounter came his enchantment with

Impressionism. He was at the point of telling Geneva about meeting Monet, when she spoke again:

"Do you happen to speak French?"

Victor glanced her way. Did *she* speak French? He hoped she wasn't looking for him to converse with her in that language. His pronunciation of the few words he knew was embarrassingly poor. While in France he used a translator. "I can say 'please' and 'thank-you,' and ask if there's a room available. Not much else," he admitted. "Why? Do you? Speak French?"

"No," Geneva said with a sigh. So she could not look to Victor for help. Not wanting to appear disagreeable, she went on, "but my dance mistress is a native of France. Madame Linsky trained in Paris and Vienna, and toured this country as a ballet soloist, before immigrating." She would have gone on to say that Linsky taught with Elizabetta Menzeli at her *Conservatoire de Choregraph Classique* in New York City, before coming to Houston where she became the first teacher of classical ballet in the city. However, just in time she caught herself. Kathy was 11 and Virginia was 8, yet neither had been given lessons in ballet or piano, or anything of the sort—maybe Victor couldn't afford it—and Geneva's mother did not approve of boasting. She turned to gaze out the window, thinking of the day she first entered Linsky's small office. Linsky's voice was lyrical and fluttery as bird wings, yet her standards were as rigid as the wooden crucifix hovering behind her: *Your daughter has the body of a dancer, Madame Sterling. She may have possibilities. Geneva! Dancing is very hard work. I do not tolerate laziness in my pupils. Vous comprenez?*

The meaning of those two French words was obvious, and there was only one answer. But what had Linsky said today? Geneva found herself looking to Victor again, in desperation. "It's just—there's a phrase. I thought you might have heard it." She wished she had caught more of what Linsky said.

"Well, give me a try," Victor offered.

She sounded it out: "'*Kell-or-oore.*' Sort of." She felt embarrassed; it sounded ridiculous.

"Victor mouthed it silently, then shook his head. "One word?"

"Or as many as three, I guess," said Geneva, then shrugged. "Maybe I didn't remember it exactly right." Though she'd never forget its searing effect.

"Was it your dance teacher, said it?"

"Yes," she said. "But it doesn't matter," she quickly lied, not wanting him to ask her what prompted it.

By now Victor was convinced that Geneva was trying to get her mind off her sorrow, and so he ventured, "Have you ever heard of art photography?"

Geneva shook her head. Yet as Victor opened his mouth to explain, Benjamin grabbed the seat back, hoisting himself up so his head was between them. "I have! It's where you—"

"I was talking to Geneva, son," Victor interrupted him, perhaps too sternly. At 13 Benjamin felt awkward, his legs and feet long and clumsy, his body not yet begun to fill out. He was thin-skinned, too, and it was clear he was not happy about having given up his room to three girls. Benjamin sat down. Victor would deal with him later.

He weighed his next words to Geneva. To say that an art photograph probes deeply into the personality of the model was too forward. "It's more than a picture; it tells what a person is like," he ventured.

"I see…" she said, with no hint of disapproval in her voice.

"I wonder if you'd consider modeling for me in your spare time," Victor said, aware that his heart had leapt out with the words.

Modeling…for me. Amazed, Geneva looked across at Victor's profile. She was aware—not for the first time—that he was handsome in a rugged sort of way, his nose high-bridged, blunt, as if chiseled from stone; a lap of strawberry blond hair across his forehead. She remembered her awkwardness with him in the kitchen. "But I don't know how."

"I can show you what to do," he promised.

Then with a *Wop!* the right front tire blew. It rumbled as the air spewed out and the motorcar zigzagged like a spooked horse, requiring all of Victor's strength and concentration to regain control, steer it to the side of the road, and stop—luckily, before another car came along. He sat there collecting himself for a minute. "Well thank goodness," Anne swooned, a hand on her heart. Victor got out, removing his jacket and rolling up his sleeves, to put on the spare.

He remembered hurting Benjamin's feelings then, so he poked his head inside and said, "Give me a hand, son?" Benjamin scrambled out.

Geneva sat thinking. She did not feel equal to what Victor was proposing, and besides, how would she ever relax around him? The two of them out in his studio, where, according to Kathy, his children were not allowed to go. Did he regard her as more than a child then? If they were alive, would her parents approve?

Anne spoke quietly from behind, "Helping Victor might get your mind off things, Geneva, and surely you have nothing against giving him a hand for a little while." After a pause she added, "Between you and me, I doubt he'll stick with art photography for long. It's nothing more than glorified studio photography, and he'll soon want to get back on the road."

Anne's wish to bring Victor's idea down to size was not lost on Geneva. What could this mean? Her parents never spoke disparagingly of each other. She wanted to leap to the defense of the man who was kind to her, who gave her cocoa in the mornings and talked to her gently. She also heard Anne's implication that, without being prodded, she would take advantage of the situation she was in, and never offer anything in return.

By the time Victor got back into the car, Geneva had made up her mind, though not without some reluctance. What if she failed him?

CHAPTER 3

Geneva spent the Christmas holiday with the Hunnicutts in San Antonio, all their grown children and grandchildren coming in from other cities to join them. For this Victor was thankful because he was sure she'd get through it a little better if she were among long-standing friends. Otherwise, it gave him some time to prepare for indoor photography, which he had not done in years. The old reliable Bellieni press—still his favorite outdoor camera though by now he owned several others, more expensive and up-to-date—was like an extension of himself by now. He felt awkward working with the hulking Watson, and impatient with the need to have a hood draped over his head every time he took a shot. He needed a stock of new light bulbs, film, and a couple of new lenses. He soon discovered that a mouse had eaten through one of his light cords, and had to replace that. Benjamin begged to be taken out on a field trip—he'd been wanting to learn outdoor photography. Victor was too busy.

Victor and Geneva worked three days in a row before school started again. Then, given the demands of her homework assignments and ballet classes twice a week with daily practice in between, they were left with a few hours on weekends—not as much as he would have liked. He told her at the beginning not to dress any special way, that they'd worry about costuming later. Except on Sundays she appeared in school clothes: plain blouses of gray or dark blue starched poplin with long sleeves and high collars, and dark skirts. On Sundays she hurried to the studio after church, skipping lunch—claiming she wasn't hungry—wearing the same black dress she'd worn to her parents' funeral. She wore her hair tied back with a modest black ribbon. All that drabness made Victor long for color. He put aside all his studio props—the small gilt chair; the pedestal with a vase of artificial flowers; the gold tufted settee—and posed Geneva before a plain velveteen curtain. She stood out dramatically.

Yet, to his chagrin, he found that for all her willingness to cooperate, she was disappointingly false in front of the camera. For the first two or three sessions he overlooked it. Obviously, she was nervous. But day in and day out, the face he viewed from behind the camera was a frozen mask. If he drew close to shift her chin, or her shoulder or waist, he could feel her muscles stiffen at his touch. He was always saying, convivially, "Just try and relax, think of something pleasant." To no avail. He would like to have stood behind her and massaged her neck and shoulders for a bit, but he was afraid she would think he was being too familiar. One day, growing impatient, he said, "Look, now, just take a few deep breaths for me. We're not going to get anywhere until you relax." As he walked away he heard her intake of breath. "Again," he said, "Come on now." When he took his place behind the Watson and had a look, her bottom lip was quivering. He could not bear it if she cried. Quickly he pressed the button, releasing the shutter. "There, that's much better," he lied. "Oh, good!" she said, with a sigh of relief. He told her that was all for today. "See you bright and early next Saturday."

Afterward Victor sat down at the table, the back of his neck aching from the tension. What had he gotten himself into? He counted up. Four weekends wasted—no, three, because weekend before last his sister Ida came down from her farm near Huntsville to visit. Ida was the only other member of his family who lived in Texas. The rest of them were still in Massachusetts. Ida married late, and foolishly. When her husband died last summer, he left her in so much debt it seemed she would never see daylight again. Those long sessions at the kitchen table, listening to Ida's tale of woe, made his mind fuzzy and left him in no mood to work.

He thought how near Geneva had come to tears today. How would he break the news that he was calling it quits? He'd give her some more time.

The next Saturday passed with no sign of progress. Then on Sunday, before they started to work, while Victor was adjusting the studio lights on the tripods, Geneva asked to see his photograph of the Galveston storm. "Kathy said it made you famous."

The original used to be tacked up on the studio wall, but eventually Victor put it away in an envelope to make room for others. The walls of his studio were covered with photographs; photographs were heaped on the work table as well as the tops of all the cabinets. Boxes of them lined the walls. He was always going to take time and weed them out, but he never got around to it. He found the Galveston picture in a drawer, slipped it out of the envelope and handed it to her. He had a sudden, inexplicable wish for her to admire it, as if no one had ever seen it before. The photograph was his pride and joy. It captured the vortex of a high wave just as it crashed on the beach down near Murdoch's. The wave foretold all the violence and devastation swiftly to come, and Victor had known as soon as it began to come to life in the dark room that it was the most powerful picture he'd ever taken. Within a couple of weeks it had appeared on the front page of every major newspaper across the country. It was his first big break in photography. And the oil strike at Spindletop came right on its heels.

Presently Geneva looked up from the picture, her eyes bright. "It makes me feel as if I'm right there, as if the storm is happening this very minute," she said. It was exactly what he had tried to get across in the picture, and he smiled warmly and nodded. "Did you live in Galveston then?" she asked.

"San Antonio. Friday's *Express* mentioned there was a bad storm out in the Gulf. I just had a feeling in my bones; that night I couldn't sleep for it. I took my Bellieni press and caught the first train headed that way on Saturday morning. By nine o'clock I was on the beach. The wind was so violent, I nearly blew away. Afterward I stayed around town for a while, got a few more pictures, then I left in a hurry because the streets were flooding—waist-high in some places. By Saturday night I knew I was lucky to have gotten out," he told her.

Pretty soon he was behind the Watson, the drape pulled over his head, viewing Geneva through the camera lens.

"If not for that storm, I wouldn't be here," she said pensively. Victor didn't know what she was talking about, but to his delight, her face was relaxed. Quickly he changed to another lens, to bring her in a little closer. "Hold it just there, please." He released the shutter. Then he came out to move one light a few inches back. "How do you mean?" he asked.

Still thoughtful, she said, "My father's mother—she was pretty well up in years, a widow—and his two brothers were killed in the storm. One was a bachelor, and the other was married. His wife and baby were also taken." She looked at Victor, her face registering regret as if she were just now appreciating the magnitude of that loss. If he could capture that—

"Of course I don't remember them at all, I've only seen pictures—I was not quite two years old when the storm came. But Mr. Hunnicutt said the next time he saw my father, his hair—it was red like mine, though I have no memory of that—had turned completely white."

The sheer potency of the statement turned the tables on Victor, brought the storm home to him in a new way. And now he imagined Geneva's parents afterward, drawing up a new will, listing Anne as Geneva's guardian....

She went on, "Just think: They woke up that morning believing it was an ordinary day, never dreaming it would be their last. Just like my parents." She paused, then in a quavering voice, she asked, "Why do so many terrible things happen, Victor? Do you think it's God's will? That's what the preacher said at my parents' funeral."

Victor was astonished. He hadn't been listening to the old windbag. How cruel and unfeeling of the man. And now, owing to Anne's strict rules, Geneva had to sit Sunday after Sunday with him pontificating in the pulpit. The perplexity in Geneva's face cut him to the bone, and gave him an inkling of the anger and bewilderment that must be bottled up in her. No wonder she had trouble relaxing. He struggled for something helpful to say. "Would you like to go to a different church? I could talk to Anne," he offered.

Geneva shook her head. "We didn't go to church very often when my parents were alive. My mother was raised a Roman Catholic, but she left the Church when she became engaged to my father. He was a Presbyterian, you see, and not allowed at the communion rail."

"Well that doesn't seem very Christian," Victor remarked.

"No. And her father Dr. Rundell—he died long before I was born—practically disinherited her for it. Catholics are real strict, you know. Madame Linsky goes to church every morning before coming to her studio, and she has a crucifix hanging on her office wall. It's so...stern and, and forbidding...as if she means for it to drive home her high standards for her pupils, as if we needed reminding—" her voice dropped off; her cheeks reddened. "Oh dear. I'm talking way too much. My parents would be embarrassed."

"No, it's alright," Victor said gently. He had no idea where to go with this conversation, however. He smiled, went back to her opening statement. "Well, I'm glad it turned out that you're here with us."

Geneva didn't reply, which said enough about Anne's chilliness towards her to make Victor's stomach cringe. Granted, Anne had a terrible childhood, and she carried a lot of scars. Dr. Rundell was quite well off, and he lived in the Garden District in New Orleans. Anne's family lived in the poor part of town. He treated them like dirt. But that could not be laid at Geneva's feet. Victor used to rally to Anne's side when it came to her grudge against the Rundells. But that was before she began taking it out on Geneva.

He went back to taking pictures, pausing in between to have Geneva stand at a different angle so he could get her profile, then adjust her shoulders just a bit. As he worked, he was relieved to note that she remained relaxed. Nonetheless he kept trying to think of some way to help her. At length he said, "You know Geneva, you've got your whole life in front of you. One day you'll look back on this period, and it won't seem to have lasted very long."

A look of recognition flashed in her green eyes, then a determined look settled on her face. A glimpse of what he had seen at the cemetery. Just in time he got a picture, then she said, "I never thought of it that way. Every day I feel like I've awakened in somebody else's body, not mine," she said.

Victor's eyes grew wet. "I think I understand what you mean," he said quietly, glad enough to be concealed behind the camera.

"The only time I feel like I'm myself is at ballet, and when I'm…here," she admitted, the last word coming out on a breath. She looked down at her hands and apologized softly, "But there I go again, talking too much."

"No, I want you to talk to me," Victor encouraged. The more she confided in him about things important to her, the more relaxed she would become around him. He should have realized it from the first, tried to bring her out. Besides, the more she said, the more convinced he was that she was a person of depth. The more he liked her. "I have an idea we're going to do some great pictures together," he said brightly.

Geneva looked straight into the camera, smiling to herself. Victor took a picture, thinking with satisfaction that she had a greater range of facial expressions than he had imagined. This one session was worth all the weeks of waiting.

As Geneva left the studio, Victor suggested, "Next time, how about letting your hair just fall loosely around your shoulders, and let's try some different garments. Would that be alright? Just for the pictures?"

CHAPTER 4

Freed from the shackles of mourning dress—even if only during the brief hours she worked with Victor—Geneva felt that his encouraging words were being set in motion, that she was gaining at least a foothold on a future less weighted with heartache. *She would be alright one day.* If she felt a twinge of disloyalty on Friday nights when she put away those invariable dark colors and thought of the brightness of Saturday, she soon overcame it. Her parents would not have wanted her to live the rest of her life in a sink hole of grief. She had no doubt they would have approved of her modeling for Victor, her rescuer.

The pace of their work was dizzying: now she was standing in profile beneath the studio eve, rain pouring down inches away, her bare feet freezing; now she was bathed in studio light, Victor's thumb slowly rotating her chin; now, a quick-change artist in her room, garments flying from the closet, landing on the bedroom floor, two pairs of eyes in freckled faces watching, amazed; now she was hurrying down the stairs, out the back door and across the yard. She wore all her costumes—even practice pantaloons—plus bright boleros, ruffled waists, afternoon dresses dripping with lace. Her hair was strung with pearls; twirled into a psyche knot; whipped by an oscillating fan; lifted like a drape in Victor's fingers and hooked behind her ears. When she fell into bed on work nights and closed her eyes, a kaleidoscope of the day's images lit up her mind. Often, the last was of Victor's hands composing her: large hands with long fingers, and a gentleness that stirred her in a way that was new to her; that made the part of her he touched spring suddenly to life.

School lessons—even history and literature which had always engaged her—seemed dull. Dancing remained a challenge, but Linsky's dictatorial instruction, which Geneva once took in stride, seemed harsh and demeaning compared to Victor's patient entreaties. Viewing the results as he developed one picture after another—hundreds of them in those feverish weeks, most later discarded because in them the eye of the camera had not transferred the picture in Victor's mind's-eye—she found that being both the focal point of his work and the partner who viewed it with him, whose opinion he sought, was all but intoxicating. She had not dreamed she would become so important to him.

One day he admitted, "This is the most fascinating kind of photography I've ever done. Too bad I can't make my living at it, yet."

Yet was a word fraught with promise for future modeling sessions. Geneva clung to it. "My parents believed people should be able to do what makes them happy, provided it is not at the expense of others," she said.

"I think so too," Victor said, then after a reflective pause, he asked, "Are you happy, Geneva?"

The question surprised her, made her heart feel exposed. If she felt happy, it wasn't the same as before her parents' death; feelings of happiness were no longer right on the verge. They had to work their way up from the heaviness of loss, and they never quite rose above it. She measured her answer carefully, and, feeling a little embarrassed, she turned her head away as she spoke. "When I'm working with you, I feel happiness is out there—a possibility."

Victor gazed at her for a few moments, amazed at how her words resonated with the picture that had been coalescing in his mind for a while: a young maiden peering out a window with an air of expectancy, as though the window were a crystal ball revealing her future. And now he knew it was to be done in profile—Geneva's right side, he thought—rather than front on.

They started to work. Eventually he discovered the right costume among all the many garments Geneva posed in: a gauzy flesh-colored Grecian tunic, knee-length, the skirt and sleeves opened up the sides, like a drape; and a wreath of flowers in her hair. He knew it was perfect the first time he viewed it through the lens of the camera. Yet he was far from accomplishing what he wanted. The quality of the picture must be soft and ethereal, but so far all his efforts proved either too fuzzy, or too harshly defined. The trick was to back off from the focus just the right amount, but that was not as easy as it might seem. Julia Cameron had a genius for that. He had more respect for her work every time he stood behind the camera, hoping when he released the shutter, he would have the picture he was determined to get. And he would always have a strong feeling that, even if this were not the one, maybe the next would be, that it was within his grasp.

Geneva expressed curiosity about all the places Victor had been. She especially enjoyed hearing about his travels overseas. He was sad to learn about her ill-fated plans to tour Europe next summer. He wished he could take her there, and photograph her in the maze of London streets and on the wide boulevards of Paris. He would take her to the art museums and galleries. He often found himself describing a specific painting he admired.

Victor spoke so vividly, Geneva saw each painting through his eyes.

One day he said, "You'd love the paintings of Degas. He paints ballerinas, as you may know, and often he works from photographs of his models. I expect he'd be glad for the chance to paint you."

She could not help being flattered by the suggestion. "Did you ever think of being a painter?" she asked shrewdly.

He admitted he had, and explained why his dream never came true. "What would you like to be? A professional ballerina like your teacher was, I'll bet."

Geneva was surprised he remembered that detail, related to him during the drive home from the cemetery. She told him soberly, "I don't think I can now."

So he had guessed right. "Why not?" he asked.

"Madame Linsky told my mother there aren't many opportunities for ballerinas in this country. She wanted me to go to Europe and study a while, then try out in a touring company. She says the ballet masters over there are much more strict than she is—though it's hard to imagine anyone more strict than Linsky."

"So you'll have to wait until the war is over," Victor reasoned, thinking with regret of her moving far away, then imagining himself going to see her.

"I doubt that will make any difference," she said. In fact she felt relieved that the war allowed her to put off asking her trust officer for permission to spend the money. She was almost certain he would refuse. "It would be much too expensive. My parents weren't even sure they could afford it, though my mother intended to take a letter of introduction from Madame Linsky next summer, when we went over there. But now that my parents are—" She stopped short; she still had difficulty completing that sentence. Momentarily she said with a slight tremor in her voice, "—are gone, Mr. Scarborough says I have to conserve every penny because they did not leave me well off."

Victor knew that Henry Sterling was the Sales Manager at the company where he worked; surely he made a good living. Victor felt like stomping up to the bank, grabbing Scarborough by the lapels and demanding he let loose of that money. Hadn't Geneva lost enough already? Yet maybe the money really wasn't there. He didn't know anything about her estate. And if Victor crossed the banker, he might make it just that much harder for Geneva. Maybe he would wonder why Victor was so interested when he wasn't even her blood kin. Maybe he would find out Geneva was modeling for him and put pressure on Anne to put a stop to it, maybe threaten to withhold money for Geneva's allowance or even her ballet lessons, if she didn't. Then what would he do?

What indeed?

The question forced him to take a hard look at himself. He could hardly wait for Saturdays when Geneva appeared at the studio door, and he dreaded Sunday nights when she walked out and he knew he'd have to wait a whole week before they could work together again. During that time he thought of her constantly and had a deal of trouble not revealing it in his face when the family was around.

What was worse, he could see that Geneva was falling for him. Sometimes her eyes would meet his, maybe as he touched her elbow or her waist, and he could see that she was aware of him in ways she felt she ought not to be. It aroused an almost unbearable tenderness in him because she had no idea of the danger of that kind of awareness.

Victor's own words to her about her future came back on him now: "*You've got your whole life out in front of you.*" Geneva was 16 years old. He had a responsibility to protect that future he assured her was coming. He must put a stop to this. He would finish the picture he was working on, but he would not begin another.

For several weeks he tried to bring himself to prepare Geneva, but every time he was at the point of doing so, he would see them riding home from the cemetery that day, Geneva pulling her handkerchief through her fingers in despair. As if in retribution, every night when he went to bed and shut his eyes, his mind exploded with new ideas for pictures. One night he dreamed he was photographing Geneva nude. Strangely, the dream did not wake him up with a throbbing in his groin. In it they were both as dispassionate as a painter and his hired nude model, and what was even more strange, he never actually saw Geneva's body unclothed. He just knew that it was. He also knew it was the best photograph he'd ever done. It was a wonderful, sensuous dream from which he awoke feeling rosy. He could not help wishing it could come true.

But it could not. Finally one Sunday in March as they completed their work session, he realized time was running out. "I've just about got the picture I want," he said.

"What will we do next?" Geneva asked with enthusiasm.

He braced himself. "I—this has taken longer than I thought. I need to get out on the road again, bring in some money," he said. In fact he'd taken enough short assignments on weekdays in and around the Houston and Galveston areas to keep from depleting the bank account, but he couldn't tell her that.

Geneva understood he had to make a living. "Still, we could work when you were between assignments, couldn't we?" she asked.

Victor shook his head. "The problem is, I'll probably be away on a lot of weekends, plus it takes time to develop the pictures I take outdoors. Sometimes I wind up going back for more. One thing I've learned, art photography takes a lot of concentration; you have to keep your mind on it all the time."

"I see…." Geneva said quietly. She looked away from Victor as he helped her on with her coat. He forced himself to return to the dark room where he stood holding the edge of the counter, his eyes shut tight, until he heard the door open and close. Well it was done. Geneva was better off. Victor felt bereft.

All week long, Geneva hardly slept. By the following weekend she felt so despondent that she could hardly talk to Victor. Yet the fact he was taciturn as well seemed to prove he was as miserable as she was. Surely he would find a way for them to continue. If he really wanted to, he could find a way.

Yet in two weeks, on a chilly Saturday morning as Victor helped her off with her coat, he said, "We won't need a session today." Her heart froze. "I finished the picture last night. It's in the dark room. I'll get it." His voice was tight, and he looked fatigued.

While he was away, Geneva folded her arms and stared blindly out the window, wondering how it could be that this was over. *"God's will,"* she thought bitterly.

Victor brought the photograph and handed it to her. "I've entitled it, *Maiden at the Window.* I hope you like it," he said. He retreated to the table and began sorting through the clutter of photographs unseeingly, his heart pounding. He was very pleased with the result, but he knew that if Geneva failed to appreciate it he would be crushed. He cautioned himself that their separation might be easier on both of them if she did not like it, but it wasn't much help. Her eyes were now focused on the most vulnerable part of him.

By now Geneva had seen herself in so many photographs, she had long since gotten over worrying whether she looked good or bad. She hardly thought of the model as being herself. Sensing Victor's anxiousness, she studied the photograph carefully: Peering out a sunny window in her thin tunic, her hair a shower of waves around her shoulders and down her back, and crowned with a ring of flowers, the maiden appeared impregnated with light, as though the sunshine had been poured into her. Behind her, in the shadow she created, stood a small gilt chair on which a pair of ballet slippers waited, their ribbons spilling to the floor. The significance of the ballet slippers—which Victor added very late in the project, obeying an impulse—was lost on Geneva.

She struggled for the right word to describe her reaction to the photograph. Finally she said, "It's very good…provocative."

Victor looked up from the table, his eyes blazing. "You really think so?"

She came close and handed the photograph to him. "Yes I do."

He gazed at the picture fondly. He knew the risk of baring his soul to Geneva, nonetheless he was so touched by her approval that he could not help himself. "She is the person I see, when I look at you through the camera," he admitted. Their eyes met. Geneva saw the yearning in his face. For the first time in her life, she had a delicious sense of her feminine powers, and used them: "We could still find a time to work, whenever you're home. I'll give up one ballet class a week," she offered.

Victor hesitated. Then he said resolutely, "I couldn't ask you to do that." He laid the photo aside. Geneva walked back to the window. Victor had grown tired of her, she realized; he didn't want to work with her anymore. She felt betrayed.

Victor did not know what to do with her now. "You've been wonderful, a real professional," he said, standing behind her.

His farewell speech. She folded her arms angrily. She hated him.

She felt his hand on her shoulder, and flinched. "Don't!"

He moved around and stood between her and the window. His eyes were filled with pain. "I've made things worse, haven't I? You look so lonely, Geneva. It breaks my heart."

"Whether or not I am lonely is nothing for you to be concerned about," she told him, scornfully.

His eyebrows clenched miserably, he said, "Don't you understand why I have to go away?" Her eyes dropped. "Geneva, look at me."

She obeyed him. "I'm going away because I—" he paused, "—I just have to, that's all. You'll understand one day."

"No, I won't. That's what everybody says, when you lose someone. But it isn't true," she said. And as much to her surprise as to his, she began to sob.

Geneva never cried in front of anyone. She was embarrassed, and wanted to be left alone. She held out her arm as a shield.

Aware that he was crossing the line, yet desperate to soften the blow somehow, Victor reached out and pushed Geneva's arm away. "Come," he said, and took her in his arms. She stiffened at first, but then she sank into his embrace. She seemed slight and fragile, the way he imagined an angel would be. Yet he could feel the soft womanly peaks of her breasts against him. "I'm so sorry, please don't cry," he murmured. The apology only made Geneva more distraught: Victor thought of her as a child to be consoled then left behind. She sobbed harder. He stroked her hair and kissed her forehead. "You don't know what you are asking, if I stay," he said. "It isn't right."

She looked up at him, hope rising. "I don't care, oh, please don't go!"

Victor thought bitterly of Anne's rejection. Was it so much to ask of life, just to be wanted? He took Geneva's face in his hands and looked into her eyes. "No, I won't ever leave you," he promised.

Instinctively, she raised her mouth to be kissed. Yet she had never been kissed on the mouth by a man and she was not prepared for the lips that found hers and eagerly explored them, the tongue that worked its way inside. The vague physical stirring that she felt every time Victor touched her as they worked now gathered in a force swift as an undertow deep in her abdomen. She caught her breath. "Yes," she said, "Oh Victor!" Her hands clutched the back of his head.

He looked into her eyes for a long moment, then, his heart taking a great leap, he walked to the window. There he paused and turned to her again, uncertainty in his face. She nodded and reached out her arms. She knew nothing of what was in store. All she wanted was for him to come back and hold her some more in his comforting arms, to keep on arousing those sensations in her body that were a part of that comfort.

She watched him turn to lift his long arm and pull the curtain across the window where the maiden once looked out upon her future.

CHAPTER 5

Round and round it went in Geneva's head: The girl she had become. The odd crimson shape on the blanket in the floor that first time, her body a tree struck by lightning. The guilty system of counting days on a calendar thereafter. The turning away from the picture in the gilt frame beside her bed, because the smiles on the faces of the two people in it would vanish if they knew the girl their daughter had become. Averting her eyes from Anne, for fear of revealing herself. And more. *"But what if she discovers us?"* *"She hasn't set foot in my studio since we moved in. I have the only key."* *"But what if there's an emergency—one of the children gets hurt?"* *Anne was crossing the yard in a panic, her skirt lifted. Reaching the door." That's never happened yet."* *"But if it does."* *"We'll have time to grab our clothes. I'll say we were back in the dark room, developing a picture."* Oh, it was wrong, terribly wrong, and reckless. Yet the headiness of knowing Victor waited for her behind the studio door, his arms held out tenderly. The eagerness of his kiss, matched by her own, that led them again and again down to the blanket on the floor, that made her believe his promise that one day she would find pleasure there because she was loved. Wanting nothing more than to be adored. The girl she had become.

"I'd like to try some nude studies," Victor said one day.

The first thought to enter Geneva's head was that he would never have made this suggestion if she had never lain down beside him naked, just as she was doing now.

"No, I couldn't do that," she said, all the while tugging at the edge of the blanket to cover herself, for she had never, ever felt so naked.

Victor raised up on one elbow and looked down at her, tufts of strawberry blond hair forming a soft halo on his shoulders—how it had intrigued her at first, that men had so much hair on their bodies. "Why not?" he asked.

Fearing he would find a certain irony in her words, she nonetheless could not avoid speaking her mind. "It just seems indecent."

Seeing his eyes cloud with injury, she wished she could recall the hurt she had inflicted; but the fact remained, she would not, under any circumstances, agree to this.

Victor was aware that he was asking a lot of Geneva. Still, the word *indecent* was uncalled for, suggesting the kind of salacious photographs sold from behind shop counters, their treatment harsh and lewd. After having worked with him for all those weeks on the *Maiden at the Window,* and having seen the result, did she really think he would stoop to that kind of photography? "What makes you think I'd ask you to pose for something 'indecent'?" he implored. "Let me tell you about this dream I had—"

She interrupted, "It's not you I'm worried about. It's other people who would see those pictures," she said, amazed that the obvious could escape him.

"Hold on! I wouldn't sell any photograph against your wishes," he assured her, "besides, what I really want is the experience, because I believe it will make me a better art photographer. Think of art students working with nude models—male and female—as part of their basic education."

"But nude paintings are not done just in art school,"Geneva reminded him. How appalling. She had not used the word 'nude' more than once or twice in her entire life, and now here she was, carrying on a conversation in which it was the main idea in every sentence, and she was the object.

Victor brightened. "That's right, my dear, and some of them come to be regarded as masterpieces. They hang in the great museums of the world."

Geneva knew she had talked herself into a corner. Nude was nude, however, and the very idea of posing for hours and hours, the eye of the camera feasting on her body...then knowing that regardless of Victor's intentions, the pictures would be *out there somewhere,* certain to ruin her reputation if anyone identified her—"I'm sorry, but I just can't let you do it."

Frustrated, Victor looked away for a moment, and Geneva thought with a sense of relief that he'd given up. In fact, the more she resisted, the more determined he was that she see the value in what he was proposing. He faced her again. "Let me ask you this: if I were a painter, would you pose for me nude?"

Geneva studied Victor's face, in which the pain of his long-ago giving way to the dictates of life was more obvious than he thought. Poor Victor. Yet, she wagged her head. "I don't know, Victor. I never thought of myself as being a model of any kind, until you asked me. But now…well…it isn't that I don't trust you—you understand that, don't you?—it's just, this doesn't seem right."

What was 'right' or 'wrong' when it came to art? Unless you just couldn't accept the possibility that it *was* art, Victor thought glumly. He wondered if she'd really understood what the *Maiden* was all about. He lay back on the pillow. "Think no more about it, then. I'll try to figure out something else."

Geneva was frightened by the note of disillusionment in Victor's voice. Obviously he did not want to 'figure out something else.' And what if this led him to stop caring for her? He had promised never to leave her, and though she believed he was sincere, was she not leaving him, in a sense, by stopping him cold in the path he chose for their work? Still covering her breast, she sat up and looked over her shoulder at him. "*If* I agreed, how many would you do?"

Victor's eyes flickered. "I—I don't know. Just a few, probably," he said. "I want to try again at superimposing one image on another, for instance—you remember me trying that early on? But I couldn't get it to turn out right."

Geneva remembered. She was supposed to be a young girl dreaming of being a ballerina, but the ballerina supposedly in her head looked like a bizarre headdress, perched above her ear. She wished now that Victor would superimpose clothing on her body while he was at it. "Well alright then," she said, laying her head on her knees. *And now this. If her parents were alive, they would surely disown her.*

She felt the soft pressure of Victor's hand on the small of her back. "You won't be sorry, I promise. I love you," he said sweetly.

Victor had declared his love many times since that day they first laid down together. He had also told her of Anne's abuse, and she understood his longing to know that she returned his love. Yet in truth she struggled because she didn't know if what she felt for Victor was love, whether caring for him and needing him desperately were the same thing. Lately when she wasn't thinking with scarlet cheeks of how frightfully disappointed her parents would be, she often found herself reflecting on the love between them. They had no reason to feel guilty, if you didn't count the disapproval of the Roman Catholic Church, or of Dr. Rundell. They loved each other completely and without shame. Geneva had grown up believing true love was always like this and that someday she would experience it for herself. She never once thought she might fall for a man she had no right to love. Maybe love and guilt were like oil and water, and could not exist together. Maybe that was why she couldn't ever say *I love you* to

Victor out right, but must wait for him to coax her into it by saying it first. She looked around. "You too," she said, and consoled him with a smile.

Victor reached for his pants. "Let's get to work," he said cheerfully.

"Alright," she said. Still she wondered, if he had never made love to her, would he have suggested she pose nude? Yet now she would feel small asking him. "Victor, listen, you must promise me you will never show these photographs to anyone else, under any circumstances."

"You have my word on that," he said, then added, "Though you may change your mind after you see them."

The notion of having what she had become paraded before her eyes brought her to the edge of panic. "I don't want to see them!" she cried. "Just do them and get it over with."

"Get it over with." Just like Anne treated him in bed, he thought, wounded. "Fair enough," he said. *Geneva will change her mind*, he reasoned.

Geneva thought uneasily of the release she had signed at the beginning of their work together, a simple printed form giving Victor the right to sell any photograph he made of her. *But Victor would never go back on his word,* she thought.

CHAPTER 6

Fairleigh, near Bodmin, Cornwall.

Jane Tremont caught her image in the corner of her grandmother's looking glass: the narrow hips and small breasts; the flat white complexion and pale blond hair and steel blue eyes. She had no illusions about being a great beauty, and made no apologies about what some regarded as a certain deficiency in her nature. Jane now had only one object in life.

Folding her arms she leaned back in the tufted velveteen chair at the foot of her grandmother's great four poster bed, the impatient sound of her tapping foot subsumed in the carpet. She felt no sympathy for the wheezing figure lying there with wrinkled, ashen face. Grandmother's hands, with knuckles like white marbles, clawed at the counterpane, showing her desperation to hold on to life as her lungs greedily sucked up the air. God, how horrid to be that ancient!

In the far corner of the room sat a nurse, in crisp collar and ruffled cap, ready to spring into action for her patient. Nurses were provided 24 hours a day when Grandmother was ill—she frequently had some indisposition, which, for some baffling reason, she always managed to overcome—but the old woman must have Jane there too. She fancied Jane cared for her, but she was quite wrong. Unfortunately, at the moment Jane had nothing more interesting to do than sit at the foot of the purple damask-draped bed, else she wouldn't be here.

She had already parted the heavy draperies covering the huge windows of the room, and now she peered through the gossamer white curtains, over the rolling grounds surrounding her grandmother's gloomy house with its high, dark-paneled walls and heavily carved, overwrought furnishings. The

Brookhurst estate lay beyond, its manor house composed of airy, sunny rooms filled with garden flowers. Unfortunately it was now slightly out of Jane's reach. Not that money was the problem. Her father could buy Brookhurst ten times over, if he wished. There was no man wealthier than William Tremont in Cornwall, and few in all of England. A pleasant thought, buying Brookhurst, and nowadays who could say? Lord Edward might just be willing to sell up.

But of course it wasn't Brookhurst Jane really wanted. Brookhurst was simply the pretty package in which the real prize was wrapped: Lord Edward's son, Anthony Edward Selby—Tony, to his friends. Tony *dearest*, once upon a time, to her. For whom she had longed desperately during most of her life it seemed, while he went away, first to Eton, and then to Oxford—both by longstanding family tradition—touring with musicals in summer. Tony's younger sister kept her informed about his life. Poor lumbering, awkward Nell. How deliciously worshipful of one she used to be! How useful!

Of course, it was thanks to their despicable mother Lady Cynthia—former variety star—that Tony was a dancer, which made things awkward. He was quite accomplished, she'd heard, though she had never seen him perform. In her mind, once they were married—and they had planned to be, all her dreams come true at last—he would settle down to work at Selby Mines. Which her father could also buy ten times over, if he wished.

Then came that August day in the clearing in the Brookhurst wood, just after war broke out. God, wasn't it hot that day, the two of them riding in the trap with a picnic hamper strapped behind! Jane had felt particularly free and *ready* as Tony flicked the reins and the horse trotted faster and faster, kicking up dust, the breeze catching her bonnet and folding it back, her dress of soft white lawn hugging her breasts and thighs. Did Tony know he was only minutes away from having her? Or did he not guess until later, when they lay kissing deep in the primitive wood, where all around them bracken grew to jungle height; the elms and oaks and beeches formed a canopy high as the dome of St. Paul's Cathedral; and the nearby brook splashed noisily over the rocks? Tony's favorite place, the Brookhurst wood. Until that day.

One could easily see the broad belt of trees all the way from the house and the stable, but of course one would never guess what was going on within. Privacy was assured. Tony must not know what she was thinking or feeling as her fingers urged his hand up beneath the white dress, up the inside of her thigh, past the top of her stocking; must not guess her desperation to increase her hold on him. Oh, how conjecture had been keeping her awake nights! Tony might meet a show girl while on tour, or meet a girl while away at Oxford. All those fine young Oxford men, there were plenty of girls in town to keep them company. Or now that the war was on, Tony might go soldiering, and meet a foreign girl. Their engagement had not been made public as yet. Oh God, she remembered the trail of perspiration between her shoulder blades and her wobbly knees when Tony asked for her hand in marriage one month earlier in Father's study:

For one brief moment Father's face, with his piercing, hooded eyes, bore a tortured look like a face in a Goya painting. Jane braced herself for him to explode in anger, ordering Tony to leave, and then to do God knew what, to her. Yet, amazingly, his countenance cleared. He folded his hands over his chest, drew back his chin and observed, "Good match for you, isn't it, *Master* Selby. If it's what Janey wants, then I won't stand in your way."

As soon as Tony had collected his hat and gloves, and left Fairleigh, Father said to her amiably, "Well, at least we'll have a title in the family now, won't we? *Lady Jane.* Has a nice ring to it." Then he added with a sly smile, "And you'll go to your groom as pure as any bride ever did, won't you?"

Jane's cheeks were flaming; she lowered her eyes.

But then that day in the wood. Things happened rather hastily once they began, Tony's face slick with perspiration, his small moustache brushing her neck, dead leaves crunching beneath the picnic cloth where they lay. And the last thing before they discovered those two little eyes burning through the thicket of trees and bracken was the rupture within her.

There was blood. Yes, she was sure of it, for as they both stirred to look in the direction of the shuffling which alerted them, her eyes grazed the red irregular shape on the back of her dress. And she thought, just for a delicious instant: Yes, blood. And, of course, luckily, her stain was on Tony also.

Afterward, everything went awry. Not just Brian Potts having got an eyeful. What she said to Tony in her panic, as they rode home, changed everything. Tony's look of utter disenchantment burned in her mind like the eyes of Brian Potts, peering at them in the wood. Her actions later were unavoidable. She alone fully appreciated how vicious her father was. She could not afford for him to find out what she and Tony had done together in the wood. Her grandmother, that shrunken soul now lying nearby, had listened to the tale of Brian Potts on that doomed August day, horrified especially after Jane intervened to twist the details just a bit. Pray, what else could she do?

Burning eyes and blood, these were the things Jane dreamt of at nights since then. Now she saw them imprinted on the curtain in her grandmother's room. The blood would save her from the burning eyes. The time would come to bring Tony back. No matter how far away he went, or how utterly he despised her, Jane could turn things round in her favor.

For now, she must simply go on paying that beastly Brian Potts. Two letters already—barely intelligible—suggesting he might need a little more. "...*to keep moveng. There's them that's atter me you know, and the story cold change.*"

CHAPTER 7

Tony Selby stood near the edge of the vast wood plank floor of Madame Linsky's Main Street studio, the black blades of two ceiling fans whirring high above, the mirrored walls reflecting images of girls in pale practice pantaloons and ballet shoes laced high up their calves as they dispersed and took flight from the auditorium like a flock of exotic birds.

Only two remained, and at first sight Tony thought Martha Houghton the more promising of the dancers Madame Linsky selected—no, *selected* was hardly a strong enough verb to attribute to Elvira Linsky, whose English was laced with a French accent and embroidered with French phrases, and whose voice had the authoritarian quality of an operatic soprano. Linsky had *ordained:*

"*Mesdemoiselles Martha HoughTON and Geneva SterLING, remain after class to audition with Monsieur SelBEE, s'il vous plait!*"

Tony had specified dancers having a well-rounded background. And whereas, according to Madame Linsky, Geneva had given up hard shoe and acrobatic lessons several years ago to concentrate on ballet, Martha was currently enrolled in all three. The dancers were around the same height—their foreheads even with his collarbone, he estimated—and similar in build. He noted that the blond-haired Martha hurried to reach him before Geneva, who appeared slightly annoyed. Aggressiveness was a valuable trait in show business, and therefore this may be yet another point in Martha's favor.

Since moving to the States from England seven months ago, Tony had auditioned prospective partners in every major city between New York and this, his mother's native town. By now he had encountered several dancers who would have made excellent partners. The trouble was, Tony wanted more than excellence. He wanted *magic*. More than could be found in Irene and Vernon Castle, and Fred and Adele Astaire combined. He had already auditioned three in Linsky's Thursday hard shoe class, and one in acrobatics. If Tuesday night ballet did not yield a partner, there was nowhere to go but West.

When he took Martha in his arms, she smiled cordially and tilted her chin. Unhappily it was the only spontaneity she exhibited during the entire time they churned around the floor, hovering well below the floating melody of a Strauss waltz. Though Martha was by no means incapable, her movements were stiff and forced. Worse, the longer they danced, the more she reminded him of Jane Tremont, whom he hoped never to set his eyes on again, nor was he likely to for, thanks to her, there was an increasingly small chance he would ever again set foot in England.

The music stopped. "Thanks awfully," Tony said with a rather apologetic look. Martha repaid him with a haughty glance, then walked past him with ballerina poise. He was reminded of the hard line of Jane's mouth and her cold blue eyes, the last time they were alone together; engaged to be married, they were, and yet she looked for all the world as though she had never seen him before in her life—but there he went again, dredging it up. *"Take it from your mother, my dear, as soon as you find a partner, you'll be too absorbed in the present and the future to dwell on the past."* So one hoped....

He turned to Geneva. To his dismay, as if she hadn't a moment to spare, she had changed into street clothes: a dark green calf-length skirt with kick pleats, a high-necked blouse and a belted sweater. Earlier he thought she may have pretty red hair and lots of it, if it were uncoiled from its knot and allowed to fall loose. But now it was covered by a most unbecoming dark felt hat with the brim turned down. The green eyes which peeked out from under it were anything but encouraging.

Something—he was not sure exactly what—prompted him to ask the pianist for a little tango music. While the woman looked through the stack of sheet music on top of the upright piano, he turned to Geneva. "Is that alright?"

Geneva had never actually danced the tango, though she'd seen it performed from the sidelines of the Rice Hotel ballroom one evening while attending a reception with her parents. "I guess I can manage, as long as we don't do anything too complicated," she said.

"Just follow me," Tony encouraged, though her uncertainty did not inspire confidence. With a nod to the pianist, he opened his arms to Geneva. Down the scale rolled a minor chord, followed by the first of the crisp, unforgiving tango notes. Hips forward, shoulders back, and one, two, one-two-three....

By the time they had traveled all the way down the floor once, and Tony had twirled her under his arm and caught her tightly for the return, the curves of their bodies fitting together hand-in-glove, he knew he had found his partner. Yes, he knew even before—with a devilish grin—he began improvising a punctuated series of dashes and spins, low dips and deep, dramatic back bends, to which her movements responded with grace and fluidity. Geneva was an intuitive dancer. She knew what he was going to do almost before he did. It was as though he were a song she had never heard before, and yet she knew where the melody was going. His mind was reeling. For weeks, he'd been developing an idea: two grimy chimney sweeps, vying for a spangled red hat that would somersault in the air high above their fevered steps and grasping, greedy hands. Only it just now came to him that throughout the dance, the hat would never, ever touch the floor. Yes! That was the unique piece, missing until he danced with Geneva Sterling. It would take two dancing, juggling geniuses, by golly, and hours, weeks, months of slaving, but their act would take the vaudeville circuits by a storm—

The music stopped. They faced each other, panting from exertion. Then, obeying an impulse, Tony knelt on one knee and waited. Geneva read his signal, leaned one hand on his shoulder, hiked up her skirt hem and lifted her leg in an arabesque behind him. Their free arms lifted to form an arch. When they peered into the mirror, their faces together, stardom was immediate, like the flame from the strike of a match. A thousand people were on their feet at once, cheering and whistling above the fierce clatter of their applauding hands. The critics heaped on praise thicker than syrup on an ice cream sundae.

"When shall we begin?" he asked.

Geneva looked at the nimble, brown-haired young man with a small moustache. She had been wondering all along: England had been at war since August. With a face and figure noble enough to lead a regiment into battle, what was Tony Selby doing in Houston, Texas, looking for a dancing partner? What led him to believe just because Madame Linsky instructed her to try out with him, she was ready to pack her bags and leave with him at once? As if he were the only young man to ever ask for auditions among Linsky's pupils, though admittedly, he had the rare polish and style of a professional. "I'm sorry, but I can't. If you'll excuse me—"

Two deep brown eyes crimped together beneath a widow's peak. "Perhaps I could call on you tomorrow?" Before she could refuse, he rushed on, "You see, I have every reason to believe our prospects as a team are unlimited—you must have felt it also," he persisted. His eyes searched her face.

It was easy enough to imagine it while they were caught up in the moment, dancing. Yet it didn't change anything. "I'm afraid I'll be busy tomorrow," she said, not unkindly.

Tony believed Geneva was simply trying to conceal her reluctance. "I—while I realize that the risk of failure in show business is very high indeed—well, perhaps you have heard of my mother Cynthia Fournier?" he asked.

Your mother wouldn't approve of me, and neither would you if you knew I was involved with a married man, posing for nude pictures—"I'm sorry, but I don't believe—"

"Yes, of course. Eh—from the early 90's, just when vaudeville was becoming *family* entertainment. She was quite popular over here, before touring England, where she met my father. End of career. At least for a while. Your parents will remember her."

"My parents are dead," Geneva said evenly. Six months had passed. While she had not overcome the loss—perhaps one never really did—she had at least become able to speak of it without stumbling over the words.

Tony frowned. "I'm dreadfully sorry."

"Yes, thank you—well, I really must go."

"But my point was this: My mother is well connected both with Broadway producers and the big-time vaudeville circuits. Since returning to this country some years ago, she has done a good deal of expert scouting. She is in the position to use her influence, so you see our prospects are quite—"

Geneva could hardly keep up with the fast-talking young man, and his British accent was, well, a bit disarming. Still—"Mr. Selby, I'm sure they are, but I have another year of high school."

"Oh but, what I have in mind could easily require a year of preparation in the meanwhile. May I call on you tomorrow so that we might talk a little about an idea I've worked up that I think—"

"No, I'm sorry, but I am truly not available," she began, and something, she did not know exactly what—though it was, at least in part, his face, in which whole kingdoms were collapsing—prompted her to add, "just now." At which point hope sparked in Tony's eyes, like the embers of a fire when stirred just before dying. She wished him good luck and turned to go. It was nearly nine o'clock and she still had homework to do.

His business card was at her elbow. "Should you have a change of heart."

A few minutes later Geneva left the studio and walked one block over to board the streetcar. All was quiet—it usually was this time of night with the shops shut down and the awnings rolled up. There was no point in dwelling on what had taken place on the studio floor, yet as her shoe heels clacked along the boardwalk, the tango music, low and provocative, began to prowl through her mind with the stealth of a cat; and pretty soon she and Tony were doing it all over again: the mad dashes with hips together; the corkscrew turns; the sudden breathtaking pauses, feet arched on tiptoe; then back down the floor again. She paused, realizing her steps had fallen into the tango rhythm. She resumed walking, more slowly now, thinking of the way Tony expressed himself. He spoke rapidly, yes, but at the same time so very eloquently, his words flowing into one another like the perfectly executed steps of a dance. She'd never met anyone like him before....

Geneva had reached the corner where the streetcar stopped. She removed the card from her handbag and read by the faint glow of the street lamp: *TONY SELBY-DANCER. #6-A, The Beaconsfield, Houston, Texas.* The words seemed all lit up by bright lights, as though they appeared on a theatre marquee. Right alongside hers? Was it possible?

But of course not. In less than two months Victor had completed three nude studies, and was working with great exuberance on a fourth. "This is going to be the most original piece I've done, even better than the *Maiden*," he had boasted at the start: Geneva a fairy nymph, kneeling to cup her hand around a blossom in a field of wild flowers, her body bare except for a pair of translucent wings superimposed on her back. After several sessions, Victor admitted this was the most difficult composition he had ever attempted. Yet finally, last Sunday, he said he was very close to achieving the effect he wanted. And he was already thinking about the fifth in the series. If she began working with Tony, she would be forced to quit modeling, for it would consume most of her spare time. Victor might object.

Yet, how could he? She thought mutinously, when he had sworn she ought to go to Europe someday, where she might have a future as a professional ballerina?

Still, if she gave up modeling for Victor, she would have no excuse for being alone with him in the studio. Then something else dear to her would be lost. She longed for Victor to hold her now, the hours between tonight and Saturday morning stretching out like years. Yet...the sad fact was that, regardless of how she and Victor felt about each other, there was no future for them except to just continue what they were doing. Assuming of course that Anne never found out—something Geneva worried about constantly, even though Anne was totally indifferent, and had never even asked to see evidence that she was really modeling for Victor.

"*I have another year of high school,*" she had excused herself to Tony. Now the words came back to haunt her, for after graduation, what would she do? Her hopes of studying ballet in Europe dimmed as the war became more and more entrenched. Besides, John Scarborough frequently reminded her of her reduced circumstances: "*Two pairs of shoes in three months? And what's this? A dollar and ten cents for one pair of gloves?*" She would probably enter college and become a teacher, or take a business course. With no prospects of marriage, she had to earn her living somehow...

...of course, people got paid for going on stage, and some of them quite handsomely from what she had read. Again she heard the music, felt the rhythm overtake her steps...and one, two, one-two-three.... "*My mother is well connected....*" She'd gone to ballet class this evening expecting nothing out of the ordinary, and now she had stars in her eyes. Imagine, going on the stage....

Hearing the *clang-clang* of the approaching streetcar, she slipped Tony's card inside her handbag and fished around for a token. In those few seconds she made up her mind: no doubt Victor would finish the fairy nymph this weekend, and as soon as he did, she would tell him she had a chance to go on the stage. She would leave it to him to figure out how and when they could be together. For the first time, she felt she had been wise to allow Victor to take the series of nude photographs, for now he could hardly refuse to accommodate her wish.

CHAPTER 8

Late on Wednesday night while Geneva lay across her bed, studying for a history test, Anne knocked lightly on the door. Speaking softly to avoid disturbing her daughters' sleep, but with a firm edge to her voice nonetheless, she instructed her ward to come down to the kitchen.

Kathy bounded up from her pillow, her brown eyes wide and luminous as if she were being offered a lollipop. By now Geneva had a fair idea of what to expect from her roommates. Virginia looked up to her as if she were an older sister, and though she was too timid to say much, she often watched with fascination as Geneva did ballet exercises using the foot rail of her bed as a makeshift *barre*. On the other hand, Kathy was mean-spirited. Geneva was certain it was Kathy who occasionally rifled through her dresser drawers, and pulled a dress off its hanger in the closet, leaving it heaped on the floor. (Naturally she denied any such misdeeds.) Just now Kathy's delight that Geneva may be in trouble was written all over her face. "You're supposed to be asleep," Geneva admonished, hoping to conceal her fear that Kathy's instinct was right. Kathy eased down on her pillow slowly, all the while fixing Geneva with a sullen stare.

Geneva put on her robe and slippers, and soon she was hurrying downstairs, the blood throbbing behind her temples, her hands trembling on the rail. *Victor was sitting across from Anne, his face drained of color. The photograph of the fairy nymph lay on the table between them....*

When Geneva paused with trepidation at the kitchen door, the room was rather dark, with only the single light above the table burning. On the blue-checked oilcloth table cover was a sheet of ruled stationery with some notations on it—a sight which made Geneva's neck and spine go rigid with dread. Anne's reading glasses lay on top, and a pencil lay alongside. Anne was still dressed in her street clothes: a dark blue ankle-length skirt and a cotton shirt-blouse of a lighter shade of blue, with a high collar and wide cuffs on the sleeves. She was pacing back and forth in the shadows, her head down, her arms folded under her large bosom.

Geneva braced herself. "Yes ma'am?" she said meekly.

Slowly Anne turned to Geneva, the dim light between them picking up the somber expression in her eyes and the tight set of her full lips. There was a strange lifelessness about her, thought Geneva, as if she were a plaster figure being turned on its pedestal. "Let's sit down," she said. Geneva eased obediently into the chair across from hers. Now that the two faced each other at close proximity, Geneva noticed there were dark patches beneath Anne's eyes. *I was very upset to learn that you and Victor—*

"I'm going away for a spell. Leaving in the morning," Anne said. Her eyes veered off for a moment, then she focused again on Geneva.

Geneva felt warm all over, as if her blood had been frozen like a creek in winter, and now was thawed and surging through her veins. "Where?"she asked.

Anne took a shallow breath. "You've heard me speak of Aunt Flora, down in Florida. After Mama died, she came up to New Orleans and took me and my two brothers home to raise."

Geneva had not realized that Anne had any brothers, and she said so now, distressed that she still did not have full command of her voice. Soon Anne would be wondering why she was so nervous.

Anne shrugged. "Well, neither of them amounted to a hill of beans." Her older brother introduced her to Jim Rothby, a drinking buddy. Jim, who went off on a trip after learning she was pregnant, and did not return. But that was none of Geneva's affair. "Anyway, my aunt is ill, and I'm going down to look after her. I've been making a list of things that you and Victor will need to take care of. I don't know how long I'll be gone," she said.

Geneva noticed that in between each phrase Anne took short breaths, as if she couldn't get enough air in her lungs for a single deep one. Anne would do well to reduce her weight, thought Geneva. "Yes, I understand," she said.

"I really need to do this," Anne said with gravity, "Aunt Flora's like a mother to me." Her eyes grew misty. She picked up her reading glasses and put them on. Her eyes dropped to her list. Geneva noticed shiny gray strands along the center part of her dark hair. Victor had said that Anne was 37, two years older than he was. Tonight she seemed much older.

It occurred to Geneva that Anne feared her aunt was terminally ill. While she didn't have much use for Anne, she could not help pitying her now. There was no greater tragedy than losing someone you love. "I hope everything turns out alright," she said in an effort to be kind.

Anne looked up at Geneva, her face blank as if the remark had caused her to forget what she was about to write down. Momentarily, she said, "Oh. I'm sure it will." Then, her demeanor softening, she continued, "Poor Aunt Flora. Suffering from overwork most likely. Works herself to a nub; forgets how old she is. She used to own a boarding house there in Fort Lauderdale. Rented rooms mostly to citrus farm workers—not those who just hired on as pickers, you understand, but those who worked there all the time. Upright folks. I helped her, up until I got married." Had Anne been inclined to speak of Victor, she would have explained that's how they met: He'd gone down to take pictures of several farms there, and her aunt had a vacant room which she agreed to rent him on a weekly basis, until a permanent lodger came along. Victor stayed there several weeks, and when he left he took Anne with him, a wedding ring on her finger. They were married in Aunt Flora's private sitting room. There were no secrets between them. *"He's a good, responsible man,"* said Aunt Flora. *"You're lucky he came along."*

Now Anne handed the list to Geneva, who at this point was puzzled. If Aunt Flora wasn't all that sick, why was Anne going down to help? But then, maybe she was trying to calm her fears by speaking positively. "Victor will do the cooking, but I'm depending on you for most everything else," Anne said.

According to the list, 'everything else' ranged from ordering the groceries and collecting the laundry, to filling lunch boxes, and making sure Virginia and Kathy got their lessons, polished their shoes and washed their hair on Saturday nights. There was nothing on the list about Benjamin. Of course, he was pretty self-reliant at the age of 13. And besides, Anne must have realized he would refuse to take orders from Geneva. That he despised her was quite apparent. He never looked at her eye-to-eye; he hardly spoke to her. If she came through the door behind him, he let the door slam in her face. A thoroughly disagreeable person. Victor said it was because he had to give up the large upstairs bedroom when she moved in, with its double windows and view of the shady yard. "He'll get over it," Victor said. Geneva wasn't so sure. She tried to ignore him.

Geneva felt overwhelmed with the list of responsibilities before her. How would she do all this, and still have time for Victor? And as to Tony Selby's offer, that would have to wait till Anne's return because she'd need her permission to team up with him, and she certainly would not broach the subject with Anne, without first speaking to Victor. Geneva felt boxed in, all her plans gone awry. What if, in the meantime, Tony found another partner?

Now she realized she'd been staring at the list for quite a while, lost in her thoughts. Quickly she looked up. "I think I can manage."

"I hope so." Anne sat back in her chair and brought a hand to her forehead, closing her eyes for a few moments. This, on top of her overall unhealthy look and her shortness of breath made Geneva wonder if she, too, was under the weather. Before she could inquire, Anne continued, "Now, Mr. Kaplan delivers the groceries on Thursdays, so be sure you leave the list inside the screen door, before you go to school.

"And on Fridays, have the laundry basket on the back porch by seven o'clock. Mrs. Hart will pick it up and return the clean clothes on Monday."

Geneva had washed and ironed her own underclothing from the start, and since the time Anne complained about the number of blouses and skirts she added to the laundry, she had taken care to wear things more than once whenever possible. She had never even seen the laundry woman. "Guess I better get everything ready on Thursday night," she said. After dancing. After homework.

Anne gave her a pointed look. "You'll find out what's involved in running a household, that it's not as easy as you think," she said, then immediately regretted her sharp tongue. It was not her intention to berate Geneva tonight, not when she was asking for her help. Besides, it seemed she was always criticizing her, during what little time they spent together; and yet, all things considered, she couldn't really fault the child for anything on her own. It was just her uppity mother all those years, and then to be saddled with Geneva when she died. The odds of Dorothy and Henry losing their lives in the same stroke had seemed negligible when Anne signed the agreement. Yet, on the other hand, the child may as well learn that for most women—and she was sure to be one of them, since her parents didn't leave her well off—life soon became all drudgery. Dancing lessons? Modeling for photographs? You looked around one day and realized you'd lost your looks and become nothing but a fixture there to give pleasure to your husband, keep house and care for the children—. Anne stopped herself. She could feel her blood pressure mounting. This was no time to let her thoughts get off on that. Besides, her children were everything to her. She thought of Benjamin: her favorite, as was always the case between mother and son. With his slender features, his sloping nose and eyes set close together, he bore a striking resemblance to his father. And, like Jim, he was mysterious; she never knew quite what he was thinking. It was Jim's mysteriousness that had attracted her so. Would Benjamin one day attract women in the same way? If so, at least he had been taught to be responsible.

Now Anne felt a pang of remorse for putting Benjamin first among her children. It seemed guilt rushed at her from all directions now that she'd made her decision. She loved her little daughters, too. "I'd take all my children with me if I could," she confessed to Geneva, bringing her arms around her bosom as if she were drawing them close. "I've never been away from them much." Suddenly her bottom lip was trembling.

It came to Geneva now that for much of the time they had been sitting here, Anne had talked to her openly, as though she were a good friend. She was not quite sure how to take this, and wondered if it would resume after Anne returned. Or was it just that she was in a melancholy mood tonight, and Geneva happened to be available to talk to? "I understand," she said, not knowing what else to say.

Laying a hand on her chest, Anne rose from her chair and peered down at Geneva. "I doubt that you really do," she said, not unkindly. "It's hard for a woman in this world, Geneva. I expect your mother failed to teach you that—" Her voice broke off. She shook her head. "Please don't think I meant that as a criticism," she begged. "Men—" she moaned derisively, then, her eyes still fastened on Geneva's, she warned: "Just watch yourself."

Around Victor? Geneva thought, alarmed. But no. Surely Anne wouldn't be going away if she even dreamed there was any danger of the two of them becoming involved, let alone that they already were.

Anne knew by Geneva's confused look that her attempt to summarize some hard lessons about life had been clumsy, but at least she had imparted a message that would make the child think. She removed her reading glasses, folded them and put them in her skirt pocket. She noticed her fingers were swollen; her wedding ring was tight. She'd have a dickens of a time getting it off now. "Maybe we ought to both turn in," she told Geneva.

When they left the kitchen Anne was satisfied she'd done her duty by Geneva. Yet later, as she laid her weary head on the pillow, she realized she ought to have looked into having Victor's name put on with hers, as Geneva's guardian. If anything happened to her, Geneva would be sent to an orphanage. Well, nothing was going to happen, that was all there was to it. Besides, it was too late to do anything about it now. Her train left at 8:15 in the morning, and she wasn't about to delay, not for Geneva, not for anything.

CHAPTER 9

On Thursday night when Geneva came in from ballet class, the children were sitting around the table in the dining room, getting their lessons. Benjamin, seated next to Virginia, was pointing his finger at the arithmetic problem before her. "Look at this! Three times seven is not 18! How many times will it take you to get it right?" he barked. "I'm trying!" she cried, her bottom lip pushed out. Kathy chimed in smugly: "If she has this much trouble with multiplication tables, just wait till she gets to long division!"

This wasn't the first time Geneva had witnessed Benjamin and Kathy ganging up on Virginia as they studied. Benjamin made straight A's in school, and Kathy was a better than average student, while poor Virginia struggled. It was cruel the way they further demoralized her. "I'll give her a hand in a minute," said Geneva. "Is your father inside?"

"He's washing the dishes," said Virginia, a look of relief on her face.

When Geneva walked into the kitchen, Victor glanced around at her. "I saved you a plate," he said, "it's in the oven." She thanked him. She put her hat, handbag and the tote bag in which she carried her ballet things on a kitchen chair, reached for a cup towel and a plate, and began wiping it dry. Conscious of the children just on the other side of the door, she measured her words carefully. "Will we be able to work this weekend?"

No sooner did he tell her he didn't see why not than the door swung open and Virginia peered in. "Are you coming, Geneva?" Geneva and Victor looked at each other. She wondered if he was thinking what she was: until Anne returned, the children would beat a path to the studio door whenever they had a question or a problem. Their risk of being discovered had multiplied by three.

When Geneva came home from school on Friday, she was dismayed to find Victor's motorcar pulled out on the drive. He was loading up his kit bag, several cameras and a tripod. Kathy and Virginia were standing nearby. "I got a job down in South Texas," he told Geneva. Noting her crestfallen look, he added, "It won't take me more than a week or so, and the pay's good."

Victor didn't like leaving Geneva to fend for herself, but this opportunity had come just at a time when he needed to do some hard thinking, and he could always think more clearly when he was out on the road alone. Yesterday morning he drove Anne to Grand Central Station. As he pulled up to the curb, she said coolly, "You needn't go inside. I'll be alright." He pulled her suitcase from the back seat, opened the car door for her, and gave her a hand as she stepped from the running board down on the pavement. He missed her a little then, thinking how much they all depended on her. "Give my respects to Aunt Flora," he said. Anne took her suitcase. "I'll be sure to do that," she said, and with a quick upward glance that held no warmth, she said, "Goodby, Victor."

There was no reason to be surprised by the chilliness of her departure. Yet there was a queer note of finality in her voice that made him say, "You really don't want to come back, do you?"

"I guess it doesn't much matter what I want," she said. Then she added, "The children...." and her voice caught. He watched her cross the pavement and become lost among the pedestrians heading into the station.

Victor drove away feeling as bruised as if Anne had just turned away from him in bed. He found himself wiping a tear from his eye. He was surprised to find that she could still hurt him that much. It wasn't that he loved her anymore, as a wife at least. He had not felt that kind of love for Anne since the day he promised Geneva he would never leave her. He thought of that day now. He had never made love to a virgin before, and he was unprepared for the way it touched him that she put her full trust in him. Reaching out her arms as he stood uncertainly by the studio curtain. The pain she went through for him. He was not prepared to put her through that pain, and when it was over and they both lay back, panting hard, he felt bad for having done it, and swift to follow was a deep sense of protectiveness toward her. He felt that, in the most significant way, he had married Geneva, that her bloodstain on the blanket signified the bond between them. No. There would never be anyone else in his life but Geneva, he was sure of that. Now he just felt overwhelmingly sad that after 13 years of marriage to Anne, it had come to this. And he realized suddenly that he was worn out with so many months of watching it happen. Anne had

been grateful for his rescue, but she had never really loved him, he thought bitterly.

Yet the reality of divorce was daunting—he'd thought of it many times. He'd
have to give up his children, earn enough to support two households. And who
could guess what sort of reprisal might be in store when Anne found out he
intended to marry Geneva? Beyond that, what would John Scarborough do?
He had a lot of authority over Geneva's life; too much, in Victor's opinion.
Before today it had not seemed necessary to hurry about things, especially
since Geneva had another year of high school. *Yet Anne did not want to come
home.* Well, by God, he'd have it worked out so that when she did, he could tell
her he was ready to call it quits.

He needed time to think things through before bringing it up to Geneva.
Though he had no doubt she would marry him, there would be many sacrifices
on her part, marrying a divorced man with children to support. Geneva was
mature beyond her years in many ways, and had all the determination necessary, he was sure. But she was still a tender young girl with little experience of
life. He would need to help her along just like he did with modeling.

All this was in his mind as he drove home from the station yesterday. Then,
early this morning, came the job offer.

Unfortunately, as soon as Benjamin came home from school and discovered
he was leaving, he put up a fuss to go along. Victor had been putting Benjamin
off for some time now. He couldn't help feeling guilty. "I'm sorry, Son, but I
can't take you this time," he said. "I really will do it one day, I promise. Hey,
what's the rush? Look, here's your allowance for the week." He placed a nickel
in Benjamin's hand. He started to double that, but it would seem like a bribe so
he didn't.

"Your promises don't mean anything," Benjamin said, and walked away, his
head hunched down between his shoulders, his hands two fists in his pockets.

And now Geneva was put out with him. He wished Kathy and Virginia were
not standing here. At least he could hold Geneva in his arms before he left, to
reassure her. And maybe he could do with a little reassurance too.

Within a few minutes, he was handing her a wire loop which held his house
key—seldom used—and the key to his studio. He kissed his daughters, gave
them their allowance of two pennies each, then cautioned them to mind
Geneva. Both girls hopped upon the running board to ride as far as the street.
Victor cranked up the car engine, climbed aboard and backed down the driveway, waving goodby through a cloud of shell dust as the engine sputtered and
the motor car shimmied. Victor didn't spend much time looking after his

motorcar, Geneva observed. She feared he might have a break down out on a lonely road somewhere. She missed him already. Why did he have to take a job now? But maybe he needed the money. She watched until he'd rounded the corner, the car engine having found its equilibrium and settled into a rhythmical clacking.

When Geneva glanced around, Benjamin was staring at her from the back steps, his eyes two hard knots of resentment. She put the keys in her pocket.

On Monday afternoon when Geneva came in from school, three lunch pails were lined up on the kitchen hutch—the high school day was longer than that of the lower grades. She intended to make a pot of vegetable soup for supper. She put on Anne's apron and stood before the sink, peeling fresh new potatoes and carrots. She didn't mind cooking when Anne was not around to make her nervous. *"Hurry up and get the potatoes in a bowl, the gravy will be stone cold by the time we sit down to eat."* Geneva's mother was a fine cook, having been taught by the family cook in New Orleans. Those same hands that played a Bach piano concerto with vitality and brilliance also kneaded dough for bread and chopped vegetables for soup. Peering through the window above the sink and across the shady yard, Geneva remembered the enticing aroma of her mother's soups. What were the spices she used? Basil, oregano…and wasn't there something else? Cayenne? Yes, just a pinch. Though Anne had not planted a kitchen garden this year—"I'm just not in the mood," she said indignantly when Victor asked why—her cupboard shelves were stocked with vegetables and fruits from previous seasons: tomatoes and green beans (which would be used in tonight's soup), cucumbers, pickled peaches, plums and apples. When it came to spices, however, Anne used nothing more exotic than salt and pepper.

The sight of Benjamin emerging from Victor's studio stopped Geneva's ruminations cold. She stood paralyzed, a potato with a spiral of skin hanging loose in one hand, a paring knife in the other. Even before it registered that he had stolen the keys from her top dresser drawer, her thoughts leapt to the forbidden pictures. She did not know where Victor kept them, only that they were well concealed. As Benjamin crossed the yard toward the house, his hands in the pockets of his overalls, his pace easy—*I'll go wherever I please!*—she tried to compose herself. Even if he had not discovered the pictures, he might become suspicious if she appeared upset. She emptied her hands and wiped them on her apron.

When the screen door banged shut, her shoulders jerked. Benjamin walked in and headed for the door leading into the hall, ignoring her. "Wait just a minute," Geneva said.

Pausing, he gave her an insolent look. "What do you want?"

"What were you doing in the studio?" she demanded. Her heart seemed to be knocking against her breastbone.

Benjamin shrugged. "None of your business."

"But your father left his keys with me."

He took the key ring from his pocket, held it up, then tossed it on the table. "Here, you can have them back. I'm through with them."

"The point is, how did you get them in the first place?" she asked. Not true. The point was: what had he found when he used the key to the studio?

"Kathy told me where they were."

Kathy was in the room when she put the keys away. Geneva would have to deal with her next. She could not fathom why Kathy risked getting in trouble for Benjamin. Except when the two were ganging up on Virginia, he treated her with disdain. "I'm going to tell your father about this."

Benjamin raised an eyebrow. He looked much older, and a great deal craftier than she would have given him credit for. "I wouldn't, if I were you," he said evenly.

Geneva's knees wobbled. "What do you mean?"

"If you do, I'll do something worse to you," he swore, and walked out.

"I'm not afraid of you!" she cried. But of course she was.

On her way up the stairs to find Kathy, another possibility occurred: At the bottom of a drawer in the dark room was the calendar on which check marks noted her "safe" days. It was better to keep it there than in the house, where Anne might find it. What if Benjamin had found it? Would he guess its purpose?

By the time Geneva opened the bedroom door, she felt sick to her stomach. Apart from her concern about what Benjamin may have seen, she had no idea how to handle defiant children. Kathy was sitting in the middle of her bed. Virginia was up on her knees beside her, brushing Kathy's hair. "Why did you give your brother the keys, without asking me?" she demanded of Kathy.

Kathy's eyes widened. "He said he wouldn't tell."

"Well obviously he did. But answer me, why did you do it?"

"He said you couldn't tell him what to do. He promised me a penny."

"I wouldn't do that for a penny," said Virginia balefully.

"I know it. You're a coward," said Kathy.

"That's enough," Geneva warned. "Kathy, your father will be disappointed."

Kathy gave Geneva a fearful look. "I'll be extra good, if you give me one more chance." Geneva considered this. It would be nice to have Kathy on good behavior. Yet she could not report Benjamin without reporting Kathy. "We'll see," she capitulated. Oh, she hated this!

She was obsessed with looking around the studio to see if anything were amiss, but she dare not tip off Benjamin about her concern. Happily she remembered the stack of clean towels that needed to be taken out there. The next morning, in full view of the children, she took them. To her relief, there was no sign that Benjamin had been inside. Then again, what did that prove?

For the remainder of the week, as far as she could tell, Benjamin and Kathy both behaved properly. To her mind, Virginia was the only one of the three who showed any promise of growing up into a decent human being, and to show her approval Geneva began teaching the girl a little ballet. Wearing her cotton petticoat and stockings, one hand resting on Geneva's iron bed rail and the other arm opened out, knees bent, Virginia would sink ever-so-slowly down to her out-turned feet. Recalling how much Linsky's praise meant to her on the rare occasions she received it, Geneva praised Virginia extravagantly. She soon found that she enjoyed teaching as much as Virginia seemed to enjoy learning. In the daytime it helped keep Geneva from worrying about Benjamin.

Yet every time she shut her eyes at night, Benjamin's threat echoed in her thoughts: *"I'll do something worse to you."* Her imagination went wild: Benjamin was peering at her naked body. He was telling Anne about the pictures. Anne was telling Mr. Scarborough. *"Mrs. Calais wishes to have you removed from her household, and I have no alternative but to…"*

CHAPTER 10

Very late on Friday night, Geneva was startled from her troubled dozing by a knock on the bedroom door. Her nerves in a stew, she sprang up and looked wide-eyed in that direction. With the door cracked and the hall light shining dimly behind him, Victor was looking in at her, smiling. Hot tears of joy sprang to her eyes. Benjamin's spell was broken. No one could harm her as long as Victor was here. He motioned for her to come. Giving no thought to her robe or slippers, she hastily stole past her sleeping roommates.

Victor met her at the foot of the stairs, and they held each other. All week he'd been cooking on a camp fire and sleeping outdoors. He smelled of timber and smoky wind and dark, grainy soil and damp green leaves: a combination of scents that made him seem to have sprung from the earth's womb, and which awoke in Geneva a strange, primitive sexual urge. "Did you miss me?" he asked.

"Oh yes, you'll never know," she cried.

This was what it would be like to come home to Geneva, for the rest of their lives, Victor thought jubilantly. "You're all I've thought about," he said.

"There's something I need to tell you about. Benjamin…"

"Not now," he pleaded, one hand swiftly moving up under the tail of her gown and inside her thigh, creating a wild rush of excitement through her body.

"Where is the key to the studio?" he asked.

"In my handbag. Wait," she said. She flew upstairs to retrieve the key ring, and down again.

Outside they sped to the studio, giggling as though bewitched by the bright moon above, her legs locked around his waist, his manhood already straining beneath his clothing; and within seconds of locking the studio door they were naked on the floor. When Victor's flesh entered Geneva's, she felt as if shooting stars were erupting in her groin and flying heavenward. "Victor, Victor!" she cried, and all the while his pleasure-filled refrain rang in her ears: "Yes, baby, yes!"

Afterward he raised up on his elbow and cupped a hand around her face. "Say you love me, Geneva, say it!" His chest was still heaving.

"I love you, I love you, I love you!" She said, turning her face from side to side, making him chase her lips then letting him kiss her. She was completely enraptured. Victor was all there had ever been, or ever would be, in her life.

After a pause, Victor said, "I've made a decision. I'm going to divorce Anne and marry you, if you'll have me. I'll speak to Anne as soon as she comes home." His eyes searched her face.

It was the last thing Geneva expected, and immediately her thoughts fled to dealing with his children. "But your children already resent me," she said, and told him all about what Benjamin and Kathy had done. "He just used Kathy, I think," she said, still not feeling exactly right about telling on her.

"Benjamin would have needed a map to find those pictures," Victor said. "And even if he found the calendar—which I doubt—he wouldn't have made any sense of it, at his age. Don't worry, I'll speak to him. This is partly my fault," he admitted.

"What do you mean?" she asked.

Victor told her Benjamin wanted to learn to be an outdoor photographer. "Time and again I've put him off. We had a trip planned when we learned your parents had been killed. Then, at Christmas I was too busy getting the studio ready for us to work together, to go off with Benjamin."

"And all the time I thought he was just mad about having to give up his bed-room! Why didn't you tell me all this before?" Geneva demanded.

"Frankly I wish he'd forget about the idea. For Pete's sake, Geneva, he can do so much better! You should see the essays he writes. He'll graduate a year early, and his teachers are sure he can get a college scholarship."

Geneva could think of nothing to say. For all Victor's reasoning about Benjamin, it struck her that there was something in him that went far deeper than mere resentment, something in his personality that made him dangerous.

They lay there silently, the room in darkness except for the band of moonlight stealing around the edges of the studio curtain, which enabled them to see each other. Victor was troubled that Geneva had diverted the subject away from his marriage proposal. Maybe it was just what she'd been through this week; yet he could not help wondering if that was all there was to it. Anxiously, he said, "But you didn't answer me. Surely you've thought about our future."

"Yes, but I—I just didn't think we could ever marry. And after this week, I realize how much misery children can inflict," she said.

Victor felt somewhat relieved at her answer. Yet all week long he had been feeling guilty that he would soon be living apart from his children, and now he felt caught between them and Geneva. "You won't have to be around them much," he assured her, yet hoping somehow things could work out one day. Were they doomed to live the rest of their lives with anger and resentment casting a shadow over their happiness?

But they needed to talk about the immediate future now. And he was glad in a way that he had caught her off-guard, for he could assure her before the enormity of what they were about to do put a barrier in front of him. "Anne and your trust officer will put up a terrible fight at first—there's no doubt about it," he said frankly, "but remember, when it comes right down to it, no one can keep you from marrying me," he said boldly.

To his dismay she did not immediately respond. Turning to face her profile, outlined in the dim light, he added, "If…if it's what you want."

Geneva nodded thoughtfully.

This wasn't exactly what Victor had envisioned. Still…"Once we've gotten through that, I'll have to work most all the time to provide enough money for all of us to live on. But I figure, once you're out of high school, you can go on the road with me," he said, then added brightly, "We could see the entire country while we're at it! I've often thought of doing a series about seeing the country from a motorcar.

"And—here's the best part—eventually, there's nothing to keep us from living in Europe. The war can't last forever. Just think! Your dream of studying ballet will come true."

Geneva envisioned herself living in a rented room somewhere, finishing high school. And after that—well, while she wanted to travel, being on the road all the time did not seem very appealing. But that wasn't the worst of it. "'Eventually' might be years from now," she said. "Just look how close we came to being dragged into the war when the *Lusitania* was blown to smithereens. My history teacher thinks it's going to get a lot worse before it's over with. And besides, I can't stop studying ballet while I travel around with you, then pick it up when we move to Europe. It doesn't work that way, Victor. I'd lose everything I've gained in training."

"I see," Victor said quietly. He had not realized this. He felt all his plans were slipping through his hands like grains of sand.

The coolness in Victor's voice was the same as when Geneva refused to pose nude for him. She was terrified of losing him now. No matter what, she could not bear that. Hastily she raised up so they were facing each other. "I've been wanting to tell you that I've had an offer to go on the stage," she said, "though not until after I graduate, of course."

As Victor looked on in astonishment, Geneva told him about auditioning with Tony Selby. The more she went on about the talent of the young British dancer, and how they danced together as though they'd been doing it forever, the more jealous he became. Clearly the man was attractive, exciting. If Geneva went on the stage with him, how long before she fell for him, never mind dancing? Did she not realize the risk? Or, did she? Was it what she truly wanted? Was it over for them already?

She was saying,"If we marry—" and here her gaze dipped slightly from his, causing the "If" to feel like a punch in Victor's stomach—"I'll be earning a living too, on the stage, so the burden won't all be on you. It's no more than my mother did for my father."

This offer, though generous, and possibly sincere, struck Victor as hopelessly naive. He didn't know much about show business, but he did know that most of the money went to the big producers and a few star performers. And the British dancer, for all his talent and connections, may not turn out to be among the lucky ones. Yet that was the lesser of two points. "But don't you see, it is not the same thing? If you go on the stage, we'll never be together because both of us will be on the road all the time, going in different directions."

To his despair, Geneva looked away. Her shoulders slumped.

"Maybe you just don't love me after all," he said quietly.

She looked at him angrily, her green eyes flashing. "Or maybe I'm—I'm just not ready for all this. You never promised me anything, and now you come home tonight and expect me to—I never thought I had any right to love you, Victor. I've got to look at everything differently now. I need some time."

"Alright, that's fair enough," he said truthfully, though he had the most awful feeling it wasn't going to happen like he hoped, that he'd been a fool ever to think it was. Maybe Geneva would be better off with her British partner; maybe he ought to tell her that right now. But he couldn't bring himself to do it. She'd have to make the choice.

"Shall we work tomorrow?" she asked plaintively.

He shrugged. "I—I guess so. If you want to," he said. He really wasn't in the mood now.

"You need to finish the fairy nymph," she said in a conciliatory way, so that he would know that she cared that he finished, for his sake even if not hers.

"Yes, alright."

They left the studio and quietly slipped back into the house, both feeling torn and uncertain.

CHAPTER 11

Victor had been home less than a week when the telegram came. Frightening things, telegrams, more often than not conveying bad news. But Geneva had already received the worst of all possible telegrams, and by the time she had signed the receipt, found a nickel in her pocket for the Western Union boy and sent him on his way, she knew what this one said. Aunt Flora had died, and Anne was summoning her family down for the funeral. She would be taking this hard, Geneva realized, and she could not help pitying her. It was amazing how a heart-to-heart conversation with someone you didn't like could force you to feel more generous toward that person. Then the obvious struck her: Anne would soon return. *"I'm going to divorce Anne and marry you...I'll speak to her as soon as she comes home."* Victor was withdrawn from Geneva last weekend as they worked, and whether or not it was his way of pressuring her for an answer, she went away from the sessions missing him, and feeling guilty. Would things get worse when Anne returned? Suddenly she thought of Anne's scorn—soon to be faced if she agreed to marry Victor—and was terrified.

She carried the sealed envelope out to the studio and knocked on the door. This week Victor was developing negatives of the fairy nymph, superimposing the wings on her body, which itself was superimposed on the background of a field of spring flowers which Victor photographed on the steep banks of White Oak Bayou one early morning when the dew still lay on the grass. It was the most complicated part of the whole project, and she would not have interrupted him if it were not urgent.

As she stood waiting at the locked door, she could not help hoping that Victor's face would light up when he saw her there; that he would close the door behind her and take her in his arms. Yet when he answered the door, his eyes registered only mild surprise at seeing her.

He was wiping his hands on a rag. She could smell the peculiar combination of putrid odors that emanated from the dark room when Victor was processing a photograph. "Sorry to interrupt," she hastened to say.

"It's alright. I was just cleaning up," he said. After a pause, the motion of his hands stopped. With his eyes fixed on hers, he added hoarsely, "I've finished the photograph."

Pride in his accomplishment radiated from Victor's face. And defiance, too, Geneva thought. He was too proud to beg her to share in his joy. He may be giving her an opening, however. If she managed to cast aside her aversion to seeing her nude figure in the photograph, and say, *"I'd like to have a look at it,"* would he smile, and take her in his arms? Still, her dread made her hesitate too long. He noticed the envelope clutched in her fingers. "What's this?"

She handed it to him. "I'm afraid Aunt Flora has died."

He nudged a corner of the rag down inside his back pocket and walked deeper into the studio, unsealing the envelope as he went. Feeling stung that he had not invited her in, she hesitated for a moment, then decided to follow him. Soon he had come to a halt and was unfolding the telegram. She stood at his elbow and read: URGENT. ANNE HAS TAKEN ILL AND DIED. COME AT ONCE. FLORA BARTELLE.

Victor's body seemed to slide down in a heap. It was a moment before Geneva realized he had sunk into the small gilt chair used as a prop in the *Maiden*. The telegram was shaking in his hand. She was rubbing the nape of his neck, the shock of the words sending her back to that evening in her mother's music room.

Walter and Mary Hunnicutt had come from San Antonio to stay with Geneva while her parents were away. Mrs. Hunnicutt sat at the Baldwin, her wrists arched above the keys. Her halting efforts at *By the Light of the Silvery Moon* brought a number of apologies to her lips (she usually sang while Geneva's mother played). The doorbell rang, and Mr. Hunnicutt answered. When he returned, his wife glanced toward him. Suddenly the music stopped, and Geneva noticed her wrists drop as though having collapsed with exhaustion. Geneva turned to look at Mr. Hunnicutt. He was holding a telegram....

Suddenly Victor looked up at her, his face purple.

"Go and get my children, will you?" he asked, his voice tight.

She hurried outside and across the yard, her mind suddenly blank as to their whereabouts. Then she remembered Benjamin was up in his room. Kathy and Virginia were next door, playing. She looked across the fence and saw a knot of children around the tire swing in the neighbors' back yard. She called to Kathy and Virginia. When they turned to look, she said, "Your father wants you in the studio. Hurry."

She rushed into the house and up the stairs, and banged on Benjamin's door. "Benjamin, it's Geneva."

A few moments passed, then he said, "What do *you* want?"

His insolent tone infuriated her. Then abruptly the realization struck: *Benjamin's mother is dead.* Only then did she absorb the awful truth. She was thankful the door was between them. She did not want to face him. "Your father wants you in the studio right away," she said. She turned and fled. When she reached the landing halfway down, she heard his door open.

Soon they were all together in the studio. Victor's eyes and cheeks were wet. Geneva's absence had released his tears. He knelt down, stretching his arms around his children. In a soft, nasal voice, he struggled to explain the incomprehensible: "Your mother is—she's not coming—"

"She's dead, isn't she!" Benjamin cried.

Geneva stared at him, shocked at his perception. Was there some mystical bond between mother and son that articulated Victor's unspoken words for Benjamin? But of course, tragedy was written all over Victor's face.

Kathy and Virginia were staring at each other in confusion. Then Virginia pushed out her lip at Benjamin. "No she's not!"

Benjamin thundered, "Yes she is, stupid!" Before anyone could react, he was out the door, his barefoot figure in faded overalls racing headlong across the yard. Victor clutched his daughters to him, and they all wept. Geneva felt the loneliness of being an outsider.

Glad enough to have something to do, she went upstairs to pack a suitcase for Kathy and Virginia and one for herself. This took some doing as it was close to laundry day, and clean stockings and petticoats and drawers were scarce. And they must wear dark dresses on the train. As she plunged her hands into the row of dresses in the closet to select them, it occurred to her that before they left town Victor would need to ask a neighbor to notify the various schools that she and his children attended, or they'd be considered truant. Mrs. Crawford across the street would probably be glad to help. The Crawfords were among the most prosperous people in the Heights. Mr. Crawford was a lawyer, who owned a large interest in the textile mill, and was instrumental in building the water works. Their house was one of the grandest houses on the boulevard. Yet they were down to earth and friendly.

When the packing was done and the dresses were laid out on the bed with clean stockings alongside, she lumbered downstairs toting the heavy suitcases. As she unloaded her shaky arms in the front hall, her breath rushed out, making her aware of how tense she had become. Pausing a few moments to collect herself, she thought how silent the house had become. It was as if Anne's death were a shroud draped over it. In Geneva's home on Caroline Street there was a longcase clock in the front hall. After she learned of her parents' deaths, the striking of each hour brought a cruel jarring of her nerves, as if to remind her they were not coming back, that life as she'd known it was now part of the past. Here there was no clock in the hall, and time seemed suspended.

They would need food to take on the train. She went to the kitchen and gathered freshly ripened peaches and plums, a wedge of cheese, a jar of peanut butter, some of Anne's pear preserves, and a fresh loaf of bread from Norregaard's Bakery.

Geneva was slicing bread when Victor walked in. Through his eyes, red from crying, she looked painfully young to him. Her figure seemed feathery and insubstantial, perhaps because always it had been Anne standing where she stood, the universe of her kitchen seeming to revolve around her, as if her existence held planets of jars and pots and bowls and pitchers in place. Curiously, this image did not give Victor a sharp sense of the loss of Anne, nor did it flood him with tenderness for Geneva. He felt a strange sense of detachment, as if he were on a photography assignment. Since absorbing the first shock of Anne's death, his heart rent in two by the shattering effect he knew her death would have on their children, he had been more bewildered than anything else: *What illness could have taken her life so quickly?* He had not lost sight of his desire for a future with Geneva, but neither had he forgotten that his children abused her during the week of his absence. Now with Anne gone, if Geneva became his wife, she must accept the burden of helping him finish raising them. She may be inclined to go off with her British dancing partner instead. But Victor was far from being able to figure out how to deal with this now; it seemed an issue of overwhelming proportion. All he could concentrate on were the days ahead in Florida. He did not know how his grieving children would behave toward Geneva, and he had neither the strength nor the will to be vigilant about protecting her feelings.

Geneva was just at the point of reminding Victor about the need to notify the schools, but before she opened her mouth, he asked in a hoarse voice, "Will you stay here and look after things?" She thought of her suitcase waiting in the hall. *He has no desire for my presence on the journey,* she thought glumly.

Admittedly, however, there were numerous details which Victor could not look after while in Florida. Another telegram would come: *"Please put in the obituary that Anne's funeral will be next Tuesday at Heights Methodist."* She acquiesced, "I'll make a list—I assume Anne will be brought home for burial?"

Victor shook his head. "We never got around to buying a cemetery plot here, and besides, she would want to be buried in Fort Lauderdale. That was really her home." Geneva nodded, and resumed slicing the bread. In spite of her effort to maintain a sense of perspective, her throat swelled from her regret at being left behind.

Victor walked to the stove where the coffee pot sat on a burner, the question of how Anne died overtaking him again. "Appendix," he said suddenly.

"Pardon?" Geneva glanced up. Victor seemed to be looking through her.

"I had a cousin. His appendix burst when he was 14, and he died. The only warning was a stomach ache. It could have been her appendix."

Geneva nodded. She, too, had speculated about the reason for Anne's sudden death. Her shortness of breath when they talked right here in this room on the night before she left, plus the fact that she was overweight, made it seem likely her heart was to blame. Now she wondered: was Anne's reflective mood that night, and her moments of distraction, caused by a premonition of her own death, rather than Aunt Flora's? The maudlin thought sent a shudder through her. "Aunt Flora will know," she reassured Victor, then asked, "Did you want some coffee?"

He blinked a couple of times, as if his mind were returning from far away, then he lifted the lid of the pot. He sniffed, then pressed the lid down again, and looked at Geneva sadly. "Stale."

"I can make a fresh pot," she said.

He pressed the lid down on the coffee pot. He had to get there. He had to find out what killed Anne. He looked at Geneva. "It's too late," he said.

In that moment Geneva sensed his eyes held her at a terrifying distance.

At five o'clock Geneva carried the wicker hamper of food and accompanied the four sad figures as they crossed their side of Heights Boulevard to stop on the grassy esplanade and wait on the streetcar. Benjamin wore his Sunday suit. His hair was combed neatly and his lace-up shoes were polished to a sheen. He stood tall and stern, slightly apart from the others, as if his grief were somehow deeper and more noble than theirs. Nowhere had Anne's place as the mother of Victor's children seemed more sharply defined than in her absence among them now. It was as if someone had cut her image out of the family photograph. *"I'd take all my children with me if I could,"* Anne said, *her bottom lip* trembling, *"I've never been away from them much."* And now the children would never see their mother again.

When they heard the clang of the streetcar, Victor turned to Geneva and, with a faraway smile, murmured goodby. She remembered his distant look in the kitchen. *"It's too late."* Abruptly she realized that her worst fear since Victor first made love to her was coming true: she was losing him. It was like being overtaken by a high wave in the surf. "I'll look after things," she promised hurriedly, and her eyes filled. With all her heart, she wanted to say, *"I love you, Victor, and I'll marry you."* But the children were there.

The streetcar arrived. Geneva knelt down and hugged each girl. She managed a sympathetic nod at Benjamin. As the four picked up their suitcases and boarded, Geneva felt stranded as never before. And it was all her fault. She would have to wait until Victor returned and hope she could repair the damage her reluctance had done. Why had she not realized that love was simply wanting never to let go of someone? *God grant that the wait will not be long.* As the streetcar trundled off, she walked back to the house, trying to bolster her spirits, telling herself how helpful she could be by staying home and organizing things. By the time Victor and the children returned from Fort Lauderdale, she'd have the pantry stocked and the house spotlessly clean; and if it was night, a light shining in the window. Victor would be glad to see her. He would need her more than ever now. It would not be too late. *Please, God....*

That evening Geneva sat alone in the kitchen making her list: *notify church, notify schools, obituary to the papers, locate insurance policy.* Let's see, was that everything? Oh yes, find Anne's Last Will and Testament. She started to write this down, but the hand that held the pencil froze in the air, her vision blurring as she looked across at the pot of stale coffee on the stove. Anne alone was her guardian.

"Notify Mr. Scarborough," she forced herself to write down. Then, a feeling of revulsion overtaking her, she hastened to scratch it out. This matter can wait till Victor comes home, she thought.

CHAPTER 12

Geneva soon found that in submitting Anne's obituary to the *Houston Post* she had laid a trap for herself. At four o'clock on the day after it appeared, she walked through the door with opaque glass upon which the name John Scarborough was lettered in fine gold leaf, and sat down across from him. With her immediate future hanging in the balance, she would have given anything if Mr. Hunnicutt still occupied this office, as he did until a few months before the death of her parents. It was Walter Hunnicutt who drew up her original trust agreement. When he retired John Scarborough inherited not only his position as head of the trust department, but several of his clients, including herself, unfortunately. *I'm afraid you are unlikely to find Mr. Scarborough very sympathetic,*" Mr. Hunnicutt warned her on the day he accompanied her to meet him, a few days after her parents were killed.

She received his summons during second period this morning. All day long and through three tests her stomach churned. She was certain Victor would apply to be her guardian no matter how things stood between them, but she was unprepared to sit here alone and present his case.

Though the office was comfortably large and tastefully furnished with mahogany wood and leather upholstery, John Scarborough's personal effects reflected his thrifty, austere nature. His walls were adorned with a few desultory drawings, and a framed certificate with his name engraved in imposing black Gothic letters. Apart from his writing pen set with marble stand and silver plaque—*"In appreciation for 25 years of outstanding service"*—the only item on his desk at any given moment was one of imminent use: today, the familiar brown folder with STERLING, GENEVA LOUISE handwritten on the tab. Outside the door a nervous-looking stenographer sat before a typewriter with a sheaf of papers waiting nearby. Her furious pecks on the keys were followed at intervals by the grind and ping of the returning carriage.

Today Mr. Scarborough wore his dark blue suit with pin stripes, one of two summer suits Geneva had seen him wear. The dark color made his bald head and gaunt face look unseasonably pale.

"Fine way to inform me of Mrs. Calais's death, thank you very much!" he complained. "First thing this morning the bank president called me in to ask if I'd looked into the arrangements, and I had no idea what he was talking about."

"I—I'm sorry," Geneva stammered. She should have realized he would be offended. She could never have guessed the bank president would bring it to his attention, embarrassing him.

"Granted, it was Mr. Calais's obligation to inform me."

"It—it all happened so fast; I'm sure Mr. Calais never thought—"

"Then you should have had the courtesy to inform me, shouldn't you?"

"Yes. Sir," Geneva admitted uneasily.

Mr. Scarborough drew his chin back. "What did you think? That you could keep me from finding out? Go on living there indefinitely?"

A tight lump gathered in her throat. She was lucky he was unaware she modeled for Victor, or his case would have been closed before she ever set foot in this office today. Anne had not met with Mr. Scarborough since the day he stopped by to introduce himself and say the check from the bank for Geneva's part of the household expenses would be mailed on the first Monday of each month. "I did submit the obituary, sir," she reminded him quietly.

"Alright," he said. He sat back in his chair and began speaking in his normal tone of voice. His sentences were stiff mountains: starting low, peaking in the middle, then plunging toward the end. "In any case, a note of sympathy went out to Mr. Calais this morning on the bank letterhead. In it I assured him that we would immediately proceed to find other living arrangements for you."

You assumed my presence would inconvenience Victor, she thought woefully. And perhaps it was understandable, for Mr. Scarborough had no way of knowing that, from the beginning, Victor cared more for her than Anne.

Now Mr. Scarborough reached in his pocket for his steel-rimmed reading glasses and hooked them behind his ears. He opened the folder before him, quickly surveyed the notes on the sheet of paper on top, then peered at Geneva above the rims of his glasses. "You've heard of Faith Home, I presume?"

Geneva knew the terms of the trust, and though this question was strictly academic, since Victor would become her guardian, nonetheless she cringed at hearing it. "Yes, I have," she said, her voice tight.

"Good. I'm fully satisfied that it meets the criteria set forth in the trust, and it's located not far from where the Calais family live. While residing there, you can finish school at Heights High. You can also continue with ballet instruction, of course," he said. Fortunately, funds for Geneva's ballet lessons were set aside in the trust, or no doubt Mr. Scarborough would have curtailed them upon her parents' death in order to economize her expenses.

On and on he droned, his tone of voice ranging up and down. "Now, I stopped by earlier today and made arrangements with the director Mrs. Shields. Fortunately they have an opening, a room with two other young ladies whom Mrs. Shields assures me are of good character."

What would Mrs. Shields think of my character? Geneva wondered.

"As it happens, they're repainting the whole wing where you are to live, but Mrs. Shields says you can move in by Saturday, or Monday at the latest."

The statement brought Geneva near panic. It had not occurred to her that Mr. Scarborough would physically uproot her even before Victor returned. She imagined him coming home to an empty house: Finding the banker's letter—she'd leave it along with a note of her own in the center of the kitchen table, so that he would spot them immediately—he would hurry to the telephone and call the bank, to demand a hearing.

Or, would he, with the papers already signed and sealed? *Victor was standing in front of the coffee pot, staring at her distantly.* "It's too late."

Mr. Scarborough had closed the file and removed his glasses. He was looking at her oddly. She quickly gathered herself. "As—as a matter of fact, Victor wants me to stay on with—with his family," she said.

With a look of surprise, he countered, "Well, I'm afraid that's out of the question. Judge Miller won't allow you to become the ward of a man who is of no blood kin, who travels around from one job to the next like a *gypsy*." Here he paused as if to be sure the effect of his description hit home. "No doubt he would expect you to supervise his children, while he traipses hither, thither, and yon. Have you thought of that?"

You would never guess how much, Geneva thought with irony. Still, until now she had no reason to assume he had formed any opinion of Victor's lifestyle, let alone, a poor one. "But you see, Victor intends to hire a live-in housekeeper," she assured him, and was amazed and troubled at how easily she invented a conversation she and Victor never had.

"Oh he does, does he? And what's to keep him from up and hauling the lot of you to some other town?" he asked. "Look how often he has moved his family before. He does not own that home on Heights Boulevard, you know."

"Yes, but Victor's children like the Heights. They know their neighbors, and they have friends at school. I'm sure he'll want to stay there, for them—"

Mr. Scarborough wagged his head, his pallid complexion reddening. "What Victor Calais does with his children is neither here nor there. Mrs. Calais was your only viable link with that man. I'm quite sure your parents were appreciative of that, else they would have named *him* your guardian as well, now wouldn't they?" he remarked, his near-invisible eyebrows raised, his thin mouth closing in a hard line.

And Geneva thought how easy things would be right now, had her parents only named Victor as well as Anne. Yet Anne was designated her guardian shortly after she married Victor. Her parents hardly knew him. She started to say this, but she was not sure what effect it would have. Her eye resting on the folder, closed in finality, she was gripped by a terrible sense of desolation. Her life was not meant to turn out like this: with her belonging to no one, having no home of her own, sent first one place then another, dumped like cast-off clothing when she became an inconvenience. She was *more* than this, her life *meant* more. She must not let him do this to her. "Please, Sir, if—if you could just give the situation a chance to work out. I've been through so much upheaval already."

John Scarborough shook his head. "Unfortunate as that is, Geneva, no judge would base a decision about your future merely on your feelings."

She could think of no other means of appeal, and to her consternation, she began to weep. She opened her handbag and fumbled for her handkerchief.

John Scarborough waited politely for Geneva to take hold of herself. Her parents had been dead for over six months now, he thought, and she had yet to face harsh reality. Too many years of being spoiled, that was her problem. Except that a banker never divulged his private business to a client, he could certainly tell her a few things about accepting less than you deserved in life. Had he not worked harder than anyone for this bank, looked out for its interests above all? Never missing a single day of work, never slacking up like others did, always finding ways to be more efficient and save the bank money, no matter what position he held. And humbly accepting the few niggling raises given him over the years, not for the merit of his work—no indeed!—but simply to accompany his transfer to a higher department. Yet, what did he get for his loyalty, when all was said and done? Passed over for the bank presidency, that was what. Entombed in the trust department for the rest of his working life, nego-tiating with clients who always received far more than they were entitled to. And didn't old 'glad-hand' Horace—who was two years his junior, and who climbed to his position on the backs of others—enjoy having him under his thumb? *"I suggest in the future, John, you pay more attention to the obituary sec-tion in the newspaper,"* he said this morning. In fact he usually read the obituar-ies carefully, but just in the past few days he'd had far more serious preoccupations, and had let the newspapers stack up.

By the time Geneva returned her damp handkerchief to her handbag, she had begun thinking of Judge Miller. She recalled he was a kindly man. If only Victor could appeal to him directly—

"Now look. I wonder if you realize just how fortunate you are. Your par-ents—" raising a hand—"though granted, of modest means—provided for you in all circumstances. And as to your future—" His voice at the top of its pitch, abruptly fell silent, his eyes veering off, his expression becoming veiled as if he had just recalled some detail he failed to look after. *Victor was saying to Judge Miller, "Sir, Geneva has become an important part of our family...."*

"Well, let me put it this way: as long as you exercise good judgment and prudence, you will not suffer hardship," Mr. Scarborough continued, in a san-guine tone. That's a lot more than can be said for some people in your shoes, now isn't it?"

Geneva knew from Mr. Hunnicutt that the "some people" he referred to included himself. *"John grew up the hard way. The bank gave him his first job as a mullet, when he was 14 years old, and he has been there ever since."*

"Now, I'll arrive at nine o'clock on Saturday to accompany you—"

"Begging your pardon, sir," she interceded, "But I'm sure Victor would appreciate the—" She started to say 'courtesy' but revised the sentence. *"John has a long memory, so be careful not to get crosswise with him...."* "—the oppor-tunity to make his case before the judge. In your presence, of course."

John Scarborough swivelled around to gaze thoughtfully through the win-dow at the huge *Owl 5-cent Cigar* sign painted on the side of the Binz Build-ing—at six stories, it dwarfed most of the buildings around it, including the bank. He was loathe to admit to himself that Geneva had made a clever argu-ment. Nevertheless, he could hardly afford for old Horace to view his haste in this matter as a breach of etiquette. After all, he had become dependent upon this disagreeable job in the most desperate way. And now that he thought about it, it may suit his purposes very well for a man who was seldom home to become Geneva's guardian. And providing a housekeeper was on duty, Judge Miller just might....

Turning back to Geneva, he capitulated, "I *suppose* we owe Mr. Calais the courtesy of a hearing."

Geneva let out a breath. "Thank you, sir," she said. It sounded like a prayer.

As he put on his reading glasses, reopened the file and reached for his fountain pen to make a notation, Geneva felt lightheaded. She was going home! Yet only now, when she'd come within a hair's breadth of being snatched away, did the house on Heights Boulevard actually *seem* like home. She daydreamed about Victor's return: There would be fresh flowers in the living room and the pleasant aroma of coffee brewing in the kitchen. She would be waiting at the door in her soft peach dress with ruffles down the front and a ribbon around the waist—one of Victor's favorites....

After a while, as Mr. Scarborough continued to write, his head bent in concentration, she noticed how uniform were his pen strokes, and how often he paused to read over his words as if to be sure he did not leave out a single detail. She had never known anyone as rigid and narrowly focused as the man seated before her. It seemed the bank was his whole life, that he was as much a fixture as the dark wainscoting and polished wood planks of his office floor. Yet he must put on his hat at the end of the day, descend the cold marble staircase and go home. Geneva had no idea where he lived, but she imagined his quarters were small and sparsely furnished, rather like she imagined Linsky's apartment on Lamar Street. There would be a narrow bed, a chair, table and lamp, all rigid and colorless in design. Bare walls, except perhaps a pen and ink drawing of some unpopulated scene on murky paper, with a severe black frame—like the ones on his office walls. No photographs of family for, she had been told, Mr. Scarborough was a bachelor with no living relatives. No cat or dog to stroke, for surely he was much too miserly to own a pet. She imagined him eating a supper of no meat, a boiled potato, and stringy vegetables (he was skin and bones with a prominent Adam's apple that bobbed above his bow tie when he talked), then lowering the window shade and retiring early.

Abruptly John Scarborough looked up. Geneva had already caused him a deal of wasted effort, and now he'd hit a snag. There was nothing about interim living arrangements spelled out in the trust. "When will Mr. Calais be back? You can't stay there alone indefinitely, you know."

"Shortly after the funeral, I suppose," she said, though she wasn't exactly sure when that would be since she hadn't heard from Victor at all. *Burial will take place in Fort Lauderdale,* she wrote vaguely in the obituary. Anxious to present Victor in a favorable light, she added, "I'm sure he'll want to see that Anne's elderly aunt has someone to care for her, though. She was ill when Anne went down, you know."

"Well, if it's no more than a few days—a week at most—I suppose it's alright. But if it goes on any longer, it will be my duty to—"

"I'm sure it won't," she cut him off, imagining a desperate telegram: *"Please come home at once. Am in danger of being placed in an orphanage."*

As Geneva emerged from the oppressive granite walls of Houston Bank & Trust and stepped out on the pavement, the blue sky above had never seemed so vibrant, and the breeze on her face was as welcome as Victor's tender kiss. How she longed for him! Wouldn't he be proud of the way she had handled—dare she use the word? Yes, *handled*—the balky banker! Happily she recalled a stipulation in the trust that she had scarcely thought about before: Should she marry before age 18, she must wait until age 25 for the bank to surrender the balance of her funds, just the same as if she had never married. But, happily, once she was married—no matter what her age—that was the only control over her life that John Scarborough would be able to exert. He could no longer put her through what she endured today.

For a few minutes after Geneva left, John Scarborough sat drumming his fingers on her folder. Odd how the thought had just come out of the blue as he spoke to her. With the anticipation of a child filching a piece of candy from a jar at the confectionary, he put on his reading glasses, flipped to the back of her folder where the list of assets of her estate were to be found, and moved his finger slowly down the column.

CHAPTER 13

Victor's return home on the following Wednesday was the lowest point in his life aside from the hours of reflection, sitting alone at Aunt Flora's kitchen table following her description of Anne's death, which of course, for the rest of his life, he would never put aside, that description redefining what he was, for all time: a murderer.

When Geneva's anxious telegram came on Monday night, he folded it carefully and put it in his pocket, a sense of folding her away into some pocket in his heart overtaking him. He had already found a guardian for her, and he was sure John Scarborough would approve. He wired back to Geneva to expect him home on Wednesday.

They came in on the 5:15, their last stop having been in New Orleans at noon. All of them were worn out and listless. By the time they got their baggage off the train, made their way through the Grand Central lobby and hired a jitney, it was nearly dark. Victor didn't want to go home, didn't want to walk inside the house he had shared with Anne. More than anything he didn't want to face Geneva, and he held on to a shred of hope that in his absence her confusion about marrying him had been resolved and she would say, "It's alright Victor. Actually I had decided it isn't what I want."

When they turned off Washington Avenue and started up Heights Boulevard his stomach began to burn with anxiety, but he was clutched with sadness too. Up and down the street, dwellings ranged in grandeur from those on the order of the Cooley house with its ornamental tower and double galleries, and the three-story Crawford house, its vaulting roof line split into fanciful geometrics with a turret and gabled windows, to the more modest dwellings like the one his family lived in. In the dusk of twilight the scene looked like a photograph taken without sufficient light. The trees growing along the esplanade and in the yards cast deep shadows on the ground. All of the houses seemed farther back from the fence line than he remembered, as if they had receded in his absence. He had always liked living on this street. Everything had always seemed so permanent on Heights Boulevard....

As they approached number 1207, he saw that the yard was neatly trimmed. Now the jitney came to a stop at the foot of the walk. The sight of a lamp burning in the living room window very nearly broke him up. Anne had never intentionally put a light on for him, but Geneva had. In the square of light the porch looked neat as a pin, and there were pot plants placed along the porch rail that were not there before. Where had the plants come from? And who had trimmed the grass? He remembered with a stab of guilt that he hadn't left Geneva any money. For all his concern she might have starved to death. He started to shiver. He did that a lot lately, as if he'd been on assignment somewhere in the Tropics and picked up a disease. The shivers would come on him suddenly, sometimes in the night, sometimes in broad daylight, a thumb running down the slats of a shutter; then, just as suddenly, they'd leave him. He would see the receding figure of Anne, wearing a dark dress and a scolding look, as if her spirit had plunged through the barrier separating the dead from the living, to shake a finger at him.

Once they were standing on the pavement he knew he couldn't go in the house yet. He'd never have guessed the studio, with all its happy associations, would be a better place for him to talk to Geneva, but it sure couldn't be any worse than in the house she'd fixed up so nicely. Feeling in his pocket for the key, he remembered handing the lone house key to Geneva before they left. It seemed that many years had passed since then. He turned to Benjamin who in the past two weeks seemed to have grown even more remote, more sullen than before, though he perked up a little when he found out what they were going to do next—whether because he was glad for the diversion or because he liked being in on a secret, Victor wasn't sure. The girls couldn't be trusted to keep quiet about it long enough for Victor to break it to Geneva. "Son, take my suitcase in, and ask Geneva to meet me out in the studio, will you?" The small flame of triumph in Benjamin's eyes did not escape Victor.

Benjamin did not know the true story of how his mother died.

As Victor rounded the house he heard Geneva's voice from the porch: "Welcome home! Where's your father?" Even though he knew what he was about to do was right, was the most decent thing he could do for Geneva, he felt like the lowest kind of coward.

Lately Geneva had bought groceries on credit at Kaplan's. For tonight's supper there was a pot roast with carrots, onions and potatoes; corn on the cob; and a pan of biscuits, fresh from the oven. It had taken her three batches of biscuit dough, plus a consultation with Mrs. Crawford on Sunday afternoon, to learn how to make biscuits rise in the oven. Mrs. Crawford was patient and serene. Her complexion was flawless and her hair fell in a natural wave of light brown over her forehead. Geneva felt drawn to the soft-spoken woman. As they talked, she seemed eager to hear all about Geneva's mother. She, too, was interested in music and literature. These pursuits were actively encouraged by the Houston Heights Woman's Club, of which she was a member. She said she had often invited the late Mrs. Calais to attend their meetings, but she declined. Geneva was not surprised, for Anne was limited in her interests.

When Benjamin delivered the message, Geneva took off her apron and fluffed out the peach ruffles on her bosom. She hurried through the back door, hoping with all her heart that Victor's eagerness to see her alone was like the eagerness of the night he returned from his job in South Texas and she rode his hips across the yard, her legs locked around him.

The studio door was ajar. When she stepped across the threshold Victor was not waiting to take her in his arms. Her heart sinking, she walked inside. Victor was sitting at the table heaped with photographs, his back turned to the door, apparently lost in thought. "Victor?" she said. When he slowly turned in response, his expression looked so utterly broken that a terrifying thought lodged itself in her mind: *In spite of everything, he still loves Anne; even now, when she is in her grave, he loves her, longs for her to be back here in her place, for everything to go back to the way it was….*

"Come, sit down," he said. "I need to talk to you."

As she did so, sinking ever so carefully into the hard chair across from his, her instinct told her what was about to happen, that she was going to lose him, had already lost him, it was just a matter of hearing him say it. *"It's too late."* She fought down the instinct.

Though Victor had intended to get this over with as quickly as possible, he found he could not bring himself to say it right off. "Thanks for taking care of things while we were gone. Everything looks real nice."

Encouraged that he had noticed, she smiled. "Wendell Crawford mowed the grass, and his mom gave me some tips on making biscuits. I've got supper—"

"Nice folks the Crawfords," he interrupted. And he should have been thoughtful enough to alert them that Geneva would be here alone while he was gone. "Anne thought a lot of them," he added.

Geneva felt a sting from Victor's diverting the conversation to Anne. Nonetheless, she said, "Oh, they did her, too. And not only the Crawfords. The telephone has been ringing, and there's a stack of letters," she told him. Tactfully, she added, "People have been asking about, you know, how it happened—and of course, I didn't know."

Victor stared at her blankly for a time. "Her heart," he said finally. In a way that Geneva could not fathom, he was telling her the truth.

So it was exactly as she imagined. She nodded in understanding. "Ah, well—I—I'm sorry, Victor," she said. Even if he still loved Anne he would have to eventually overcome his grief and move on. And Geneva was right here, loving him, ready for marriage—should she say so? No, not yet. "Is Aunt Flora doing better?" she asked.

Again Victor looked bewildered.

"I mean—has she recovered physically? I—I told Mr. Scarborough I was sure you would not leave her until you found someone to look after her. I knew that you would feel responsible."

"Aunt Flora's alright," he said quietly.

"That's good," she said. "From what Anne told me that night before she left, Aunt Flora has a strong constitution."

"Oh yes, she is…very strong," he said, a forlorn look in his eyes.

There was an awkward silence then as Victor struggled to say what was on his mind. Finally Geneva could bear it no longer. "Well, I guess you knew from my telegram—and John Scarborough wrote you a letter, too, but never mind, he is willing to approach Judge Miller with you about being my guardian. At first he wasn't, but I persuaded him." Her coy smile was met with a pained look on Victor's face. "*It's too late.*" Her heart began to pound and she felt dizzy. She brought a hand to her chest. She rushed on: "Victor, I know I was unsure of my feelings before Anne's death, but I realized even before you left for Fort Lauderdale—I wanted to say so, but the children were there—" her eyes dropped—"and maybe it would have been inappropriate—that I love you with…with *all my heart.*" Her voice trembled through the last phrase. When she looked up, Victor's eyes were moist. She had touched him. "And…after a suitable period, of course, I would be happy to marry you if—if it's what you want." He had said these exact words to her when he was uncertain, she remembered, and this haunted her.

Victor cleared his throat. "That's what I need to talk to you about," he said, his voice thick. "You see, I've done a lot of thinking too and I—" He couldn't say it. He looked out in the distance, his eyes swimming. "I've decided to take my children and do some traveling. We'll leave as soon as school is out and we can get packed up."

"*You can't stay there alone indefinitely—*" I see," she said, assuming 'packed up' meant suitcases and perhaps a hamper of food. "Well alright if that's what you need; knowing you, I can understand that. But if you'll at least get the question of guardianship settled before you go—"

He looked at her. "I don't know that we're coming back."

The words were rocks thrown into a shallow pond. "What do you mean?"

"I mean…as difficult as it is to say this, I mean that it's all over for us."

Geneva looked beyond his shoulder at the shimmering figure of the *Maiden,* standing before the studio window, gazing out upon her future. "*I promise I won't ever leave you.*" She dropped her head. "You're just angry that I couldn't make a commitment to you earlier, you're just—just *punishing* me." She did not realize she was crying until a tear dropped on the table in front of her. If he left her she would die.

"No, no, it isn't that at all," he said gently. He wanted to reach across and touch her hand. He didn't do it. "I've just come to realize that I don't—" he took in a swift breath, then swallowed hard. "Geneva, all I have to offer you in marriage is to raise my kids and wait for me to come home from a business trip. Day in, day out. Year after year. That's all it will be. You're too young and—more important—too talented, to waste your life like that. You'll be old before your time." "*I don't want any more children.*" "*We'll be careful.*" "*We can't be careful enough.*" "You've already had one offer," he reminded Geneva, though he could not bring himself to say any more because he envied the British dancer in the worst way. Still, he knew he must at least bring up the offer.

"But I'd rather be with you," she pleaded, "and I wouldn't mind your going away, as long as I knew you were coming back. These two weeks—it's all I've thought about, the moment you would walk through that door. Dreamed of it at night."

Victor was shaking his head. He had dreams too, of blood-soaked bed sheets and a voice moaning in pain. He started to shiver and made fists of his hands. No. He wouldn't be married again. He managed a deep intake of air. The shivering stopped. Anne's figure receded. "I'm sorry," he said.

Geneva felt anger rising. "You promised you'd never leave me!"

"I know, and I'm sorry. But believe me, it's best this way."

"For whom? You realize what will happen to me now?"

He wagged his head. "No, it isn't as bad as that," he said, and his eyes shone bright for the first time, a strange brightness like that of the sun sinking on the horizon at the end of the day. "I've spoken to Ida. She came down for Anne's funeral."

"Who?"

"My sister, Mrs. Ruekauer. You remember, she came to see us one weekend a few months ago. She's willing to come and live here, to be your guardian. I'm going to talk to Mr. Scarborough."

Geneva remembered the woman now. They hadn't exchanged ten words over that weekend, but she'd often found herself staring at her, for her looks were compelling: a large woman, not fat but muscular, with a thick neck and boxy hands. She had dark hair and her eyebrows came to a sharp peak in the center, giving her face a threatening look. Underneath, her eyes were wary, distrustful. She smoked cigarettes, one after another. They fouled the air. "I remember you said she was bitter," Geneva reminded Victor. *How could he leave me with such a woman?* she thought with aversion.

"Yes, but I think coming here, getting back on her feet again, will improve her attitude. You see, she's putting her farm up for sale. She can probably pay off her debts and have a little to put by, with the proceeds. Here, she'll have a home, and she can look after you. Not that you need looking after. But just in a legal sense. She's a good, responsible woman, Geneva—

"And did I mention she's a trained nurse? Though it's been a while since she practiced because she lived so far from town. It will be easy for her to find work here and that will help her too."

"But Victor, don't you see? *You* belong here, and your children—what about them? You can't just put them in the car with you and trudge all over kingdom come, with no home for them to come back to. They are not *gypsies*." Geneva fell silent. She felt unspeakably cruel for invoking John Scarborough's degrading word.

"All my children need is for me to love them, take care of them," he said coldly. Love for his children was the only safe form of love he knew about.

"Alright then, but if you'll just become my guardian, you don't have to commit to anything else until…until some time has passed and…your mind is more clear. That's the least you could do, Victor."

He was backing out on the street in the motor car, Geneva beside him, the children behind them. She was smiling across at him, squeezing his hand, trusting him with her life. How easy it would be, to give in. But it wasn't fair. "My mind has never been more clear," he said sadly. He rose and walked heavily to the studio door. He put his hand on the knob and gazed down at it. "I hope someday you'll understand," he said.

"Victor, I love you and I know that you love me, too!" she cried. "Please, don't go!"

He did not answer, but walked through the door, leaving it open.

In the days that followed, word got around the Heights that Victor and the children had returned. Neighbors and friends from Anne's church came by to pay their respects, and many of them brought food. Mrs. Crawford baked a cake and she and Mr. Crawford brought it over. They stood out on the porch with Victor, talking in hushed tones. Often when Victor wasn't greeting people, Geneva would see him from the kitchen window, walking back and forth to the studio, emptying the contents. As he hauled boxes and boxes of pictures and negatives out to the trash, she wondered: how many of those trips were to throw *her* away? In so many ragged strips of photographic paper? Was the bright bolero in this heap? Were her bare feet on a January day in that one?

But then one day, when she was up in her room, trying hard to focus her thoughts on her study notes for her English Literature comprehensive, she heard a knock on the door. "My dad wants you out in the studio," Benjamin said.

Could it be, Victor was having a change of heart? She flew to the door and opened it. Benjamin was still there, his arms folded in front of him, a smug look on his face. "We're leaving next Saturday, and you can't come."

Geneva kept her eyes level with his. Though she did not want him to know it, his hatefulness still made her cringe. And it was yet another reminder of how far Victor's children were from accepting her. Since their return, Kathy had rarely spoken to her, and Virginia had refused her offer of a ballet lesson. "Mama didn't hold with dancing," she said uncomfortably, her eyes downcast.

"Thank you for the message, Benjamin," Geneva said coolly. She brushed past him and down the stairs. He may be in for a surprise in a few minutes.

Victor was crouched on the studio floor, in the process of wrapping his cameras in thick cushions made of old quilt sections, before looping them around with sturdy string and placing them inside a crate. The walls were bare. The curtain across the window was open. The sunlight poured in, reminding her of its pleasant warmth on her chest and arms when she posed there. Oh, what she would give to have those days back again. "You wanted to see me?" she said.

Victor looked up; their eyes met. The longing on Geneva's face brought him right to the edge: *"Geneva I'd like for you to come with us after all."* But it only took one glimpse of the picture ever-present in his mind—brief as the snap of the shutter—to return his perspective. He reached around and picked up a large brown envelope. He held it out to her.

Geneva was crushed. He had not had a change of heart. "These are all the pictures of you that I completed," he said. "I was going to put them in storage along with the others I'm saving, but then I thought you might prefer to keep them."

Prefer. Was his offer a way of honoring her wish to conceal the nude photographs? Her fingers closed around the envelope, lingering but briefly—he had not even let go—before she realized that in this envelope was their only tangible link to each other, that if she allowed him to keep the photographs, one day when his mind was clear he would remember how, in the end, she trusted him with the most vulnerable evidence of their work together. He would remember then that she had entrusted her virginity to him, had in fact been willing to entrust everything to him, even her life. Then he would realize that they were bound to each other. And he would come back. Her eyes held his. "I want you to keep them," she insisted, her hands locked behind her.

With a shrug, Victor laid the envelope aside. He would probably never look at the pictures again because it would hurt too much. That creative urge which had lived in him for all of his life and had finally inspired them, was dead. Ironically, the one who least appreciated that part of his nature had taken it to her grave.

For three days after Victor left, Geneva's spirits were so low that she could hardly rise from the bed. She scarcely ate a bite, and became weak and dizzy. Luckily her new guardian was too busy unpacking crates and arranging her newly-arrived furniture to take notice. Geneva could not afford for Ida to guess the truth. She hardly knew her. On the fourth day she went to the dresser and withdrew Tony Selby's card from the top drawer. Her hand was shaking as she held it. At the bottom of the card was his telephone number: Preston 583.

With the sound of Tony's ringing telephone she felt a sense of exhilaration that she would not have thought possible. Just hearing his crisp British voice would be reassuring. A new start. *"Why, Geneva, of course I remember! Is it really you?"* *"I've been thinking over your offer and...."* A Mexican woman answered the telephone, evidently the housekeeper. Her English was not very good. Yet the message was clear enough. Mr. Selby and his mother had left a few days ago on a tour of the West. They were not expected home until around the end of the summer. She would be happy to take Geneva's name and telephone number. Geneva told her no thank you. What was the use, when obviously Tony had already found a partner, and was touring the vaudeville circuits? She tore the card into tiny pieces and threw them in the waste basket.

Victor was gone ten days when Geneva realized her May period had not come. Her first instinct was to rush to the calendar and check the number of days since her last period, for in all the tumult which began after Anne's death and lasted until—until—had it ever ceased? She had not kept a mental note. Was it possible Victor had left the calendar behind? Or had it been in one of those boxes he toted out to the trash? Remembering that he left the studio key in a kitchen drawer, she hurried to retrieve it, then rushed across the yard. How far it seemed to the studio. The ends of the earth. At the door she hesitated. She did not want to go in there. At last she forced herself. With the curtain pulled back, daylight engulfed the studio, exposing every corner. The blankness of the room turned her stomach over. Not a stitch of furniture, not a photograph, nothing to show that Victor once worked in here. She hurried into the dark room and opened the drawer where the calendar used to be kept. It was empty.

CHAPTER 14

Waiting, waiting, waiting, day in and day out, for the sound of Victor's motor car coming up the drive, or maybe a letter: *I cannot live without you and I'm coming back.* Geneva did not tell anyone, but if Victor didn't hurry she would be forced to tell, and when John Scarborough found out, she knew what he would insist she do, though she wouldn't, not for anything; no one was going to take this child growing inside her, it was all she had; she would take a gun and shoot them if they tried, run away where she could never be found if need be. With all her might, she willed Victor to reason that she might be in trouble and rush to her side.

Then, on a mid-August morning Geneva awoke to the sound of pelting rain and the house frame groaning as though in pain. She glanced at the window. The sky was dark and menacing.

As she rose from the pillow, she felt slightly dizzy, but that was not unusual of late. She sat on the edge of the bed for a few moments, to steady herself, then dressed in a white blouse and red poplin skirt with a notched waist. She went downstairs to the kitchen to make a cup of tea and see what the morning *Post* said about the weather. Ida was an early riser and always brought the paper into the kitchen. Hopefully this morning it landed on the porch.

On the table Geneva found a note from Ida: "Telephones are out. Mr. Crawford is coming over to board up the front windows. I'm going out to buy provisions." Geneva realized a great deal had taken place before she got up this morning. She thought of Ida now. *"If you don't know how to look out for yourself by now, then it's time you learned,"* she had told Geneva as she hauled her black Remington typewriter into the roomy second parlor, which, like the parlor, faced the front of the house and had a deep bay window. This would be her office. Ida was among the founders of the Huntsville chapter of the Society for Women's Suffrage. She spent hours at the Remington, pounding out essays and news bulletins for the state-wide Society, all the while puffing on *Lucky Strikes*. She often traveled back and forth to Huntsville in her small Ford. Geneva wondered if Victor knew of Ida's work as a suffragette, and if he realized how little interest she would take in the life of her ward.

She picked up the newspaper and read the headline story with a feeling of unease: A storm was heading for Galveston, packing even higher winds than the storm of 1900.

The tea kettle was singing. As she turned off the fire, she became aware of a strong turbulence in her body: a cramping like the groaning of the shelter where her unborn baby lived. She feared this was like a storm signal, but there was no one she dare ask. She could only hope it would subside. Soon it did. Relieved, she made her tea and carried it into the parlor and sat down in Ida's platform rocker. She wrapped an arm protectively around her abdomen. She realized her heartbeat had grown rapid. She tried to relax.

Mr. Crawford and his son Wendell had just begun nailing retaining boards over the two bay windows in front. They were wearing galoshes and slickers. Behind them the weather raged. Geneva waved through the window, and Mr. Crawford waved back, then put a board diagonally across. *Thwack! Thwack!*

Geneva often wished that she lived with the Crawford family, though it wasn't their fancy house she longed for. The handsome furnishings Ida brought from her farm—cherry wood tables topped with alabaster; couches and chairs with velveteen upholstery and lacy antimacassars; figured carpets and sheer window curtains—made this house fancy enough for anyone, especially compared to the hodgepodge of plain furnishings that belonged to Victor's family. It was just that the Crawfords seemed so happy. Apart from Wendell, who worked as a clerk in his father's law office, there was a jolly young son named Joseph. Ida had cleaned and dressed a bad laceration on his knee one day when he fell down, the only occasion on which Geneva had seen her employ her nurse's training. Geneva stood by handing Ida the dressing and tape and scissors as she needed them. Afterward, Mrs. Crawford baked them a three-layer chocolate cake with peaks of white icing, to show her gratitude.

Most of all Geneva wished she lived with the Crawfords because Mrs. Crawford's gentle and kind ways reminded her of her mother.

By the time father and son left the porch with their tool box, rain was coming down so hard, and the sky was so black, when Geneva looked between the crisscrossed boards she could not see past the curb. Soon small limbs, flower stalks and roof shingles were chasing down the block as if to see which could get somewhere first—

There came another cramping deep in her abdomen. Frightened, she imagined Victor being instinctively drawn to Galveston, to photograph the storm. And afterward, rushing to Houston Heights to see how she and Ida had fared. But then harsh reality struck: the 16-foot granite sea wall—erected since the storm of 1900 to protect the island from destruction—would likely ward off the promise of another dramatic photograph.

Should she see a doctor when the storm was over? Yet, how could she, until Victor came back? The doctor would report to Ida, and Ida would report to John Scarborough.

Geneva obeyed an instinct to go up to her room and lie in bed. She had her own furniture now, retrieved from storage after Victor left: a high-back bed made of oak, heavily carved, passed down from her grandmother Rundell; a matching dresser and night tables; a floor lamp, two table lamps and a rocking chair. It had saddened her to see her parents' household furnishings, lovingly chosen each and every one and scrupulously cared for, now jammed together in a designated area of a cavernous warehouse. One day she would have her own home, and would surround herself with the things which had belonged to them.

As she walked through the parlor to the front hall, it was as if the wind were racing in her ears, upsetting her equilibrium. Her eyes blurred. She steadied herself by clutching chair backs and table edges along her way. Her abdomen felt heavy, as if she needed to pick it up and carry it in her arms.

She had climbed as far as the landing halfway up the stairs, gripping the rail with both hands, when the front door sprang open and Ida darted through it in a wildly disheveled state, a bulging shopping bag on each arm. The wind screamed through the open door like a deranged patient tearing down an asylum corridor.

Ida did not notice Geneva on the stairs. She dumped her bags, which sent canned goods rolling out over the floor. Then she pushed with all her might to force the door shut. She turned and leaned against it, blowing out her breath, her raincoat dripping on the floor.

It was in that moment Geneva had the dreadful feeling that a dam was breaking inside her: a thin stream escaped through a fissure and traced down the inside of her leg. She broke out in a cold sweat. This could not be normal. She suddenly realized she would need Ida's help. But that would mean confessing her pregnancy to Ida. How could she do that? Yet if it meant saving her child, she would. She held her legs tight together. "*Ida!*" she cried. Her eyes blurred like windows lashed with rain.

By this time Ida had retrieved the spilled goods and was toting the bags to the kitchen, her wet footprints glazing the hardwood floor. She did not hear.

Geneva could not make her voice any louder. She dare not go up to her room without Ida knowing she was in trouble because Ida might stay downstairs for a very long time. She crouched on the stair landing, gripping the rail. She was conscious of the stream widening, spreading over the insides of her legs.

Blessedly, Ida soon returned. She was holding a letter. "Geneva, where are you?"

"Up here! Ida—"

Ida looked up. "I've got the mail, put it in my pocket on my way out this morning, nearly forgot all about it. Letter from Victor, finally. It's a wonder it didn't get soaked. Ford's at the corner of Washington Avenue, water logged. Thought I'd be killed. I'm through with cars."

"What are you doing up there?"

Thank God. Geneva pulled herself up a bit, licked her dry lips. "Does—is Victor—coming h-home?" she asked.

"Victor? Naw. Off to Europe, to cover the war—no surprise. Probably there, by now. Left the kids in Massachusetts."

Not coming... Geneva thought confusedly, but the first of the big waves was cresting and before she could gather her senses, it smashed against the shore. She cried out, the stairway below swimming before her.

"What's the matter with you?"

As soon as the wave subsided, she gasped, "I—I am—am *expecting!*"

Ida's mouth fell open. She rushed up the stairs, hiking her wet skirt hem up to her knees.

"It's a hell of a note," she complained moments later, switching on the bedroom ceiling light and two lamps, then hurrying to the bed where Geneva lay, grabbing her skirt hem and throwing it back. "Open your legs, hurry!" she demanded, forcing her two knees apart like a pair of rusted scissors. "Oh merciful heaven, it's already a lake!" She snatched the pillows from under Geneva's head, closed her knees and shoved the pillows beneath them. "I'll be back!" She bolted from the room.

Please God, let Ida help! Geneva held on, jaws clenched against the onslaught.

Ida returned with a pile of linens and a pair of shears, huffing, puffing, hair escaping its jet comb and making raven wings above her temples. She drove several towels up under her ward, then removed her shoes and yanked her stockings down. "How far along?" She began to snip up one cold viscous leg of her teddy, then across the front, and down the other leg. Geneva was shivering.

"About three months, I—th-think."

Ida peeled the under garment away from the shivering, goose-bumpy legs. She took a sheet and made a tent over them. "I'll put some water on to boil. You must try to relax, breathe deeply. I don't know how much I can do."

The lights went out then.

"Oh, this is a hell of a note!" Ida swore in the darkness. "I'll have to bring a kerosene lamp. Damnation! Why didn't you warn me of this before now?"

Geneva's hand closed around Ida's wrist like a rope around a pier. "Save me! I am *dying*."

Ida pulled free and leaned close to Geneva's face. "I doubt it. Hold yourself together, girl. You got yourself into trouble, didn't you?"

Ida groped her way out of the room, swearing as she bumped the corner of the dresser, hurling complaints in her wake. Geneva's hair stringing wet, her teeth rattling like window glass, she gripped great wads of sheet as the wind howled and the waves crested and broke in her body. The reminder of her sin, carried in Ida's words, forced Geneva's thoughts to the ever-forbidding image of Linsky's crucifix. *Dear God, have mercy, forgive me all my sins and save my baby and me....*

Came the kerosene lamp, a beacon in a harbor across the roily sea, and by its light Ida leaned near and inspected her. The two lumps of her knees made shadows high as tidal waves upon the wall, and the shadow of Ida's hulking shoulders moved among them like a ship, its captain navigating the way to safety. "When was your last period?"

"April. I—I think."

"And when was the last time you let a member of the male sex sweet-talk you into being a fool?"

The curtain of the studio was rent in two by the wind, and there she and Victor lay, plotting the course of their future with their bodies. "M-May."

There was a pause in which calculations were made. Ida's shadow rose erect, and her black-eyed gaze, calm as the eye of the hurricane, rested on Geneva's face: "Who's the father?"

Geneva gripped the sheets more tightly, her eyes blurring, her mind struggling to imagine the consequences of answering her question. Victor was in the war. The children were in Massachusetts. Her mind could focus no better than her eyes. Her whole body seized up as another wave of pain engulfed her. "He can be made to take responsibility, you know. Tell me," said Ida.

No. Geneva turned her face aside. She would write a letter to Massachusetts: _Please Forward_. Victor would come home. Then they would face Ida and John Scarborough and the rest of the world, together.

"Well, are you going to tell me?"

"N—no. I—I can take care of it." Victor could be here before John Scarborough could make her do anything. _Please God!_

Ida was beginning to put two and two together. Geneva's reluctance on the subject for one thing; and the timing of all this, on the other. "Um-hum…. Was it, by chance, my brother?"

Dear God….

"Tell me, girl, or I give you my word, I won't help you."

Geneva felt Victor had delivered her into the hands of a monster. Terrified as never before in her life, she cried, "Help me, I beg you! You are a nurse!" The calm eye narrowed on her face.

Ida was somewhat amazed at how her threatening words had rushed out; it was partly from the shock of coming safely through a storm, only to find an aborted birth on her hands before she had even caught her breath; partly from a growing intuition about the father that sent anger rising in her like thick, bitter bile, at the thought of how—if she were right—once again she had been manipulated. She didn't give a tinker's damn for Geneva Sterling, but she did care for her vocation, and she would never stoop to neglect a patient. Patient! Virtually dumped on her doorstep was what it amounted to.

Ida gave the girl grudging credit for not backing down. "So it is him," she said slyly. Again, Geneva looked away. Ida uttered a dry laugh. "I might have known he'd do something like this to me."

Geneva looked at Ida. "He—he didn't know."

"He might have guessed! _Men!_" Ida spat, leaning down again, her wet, saturnine face gleaming like molten wax.

"Help me!"

"I'll do what I can. You won't help by becoming hysterical."

The eye having passed over, the storm exposed its broad back side. A swell, mightier than any preceding it, crested then plunged toward the tattered shore of Geneva's body. She bellowed in pain. Her fingernails embedded themselves in her palms; her jaws locked together.

As the tide ebbed away, Ida spoke. "There—oh!"

The catch in her breath between the two words brought Geneva up on her elbows in fear. "What has happened?"

Ida calmly gathered a towel from under her. "Nothing, child. Lie down. I'll be back." But Geneva could not move. She was paralyzed by fear. Her hair fell in ropes around her shoulders. Ida pressed down on her chest until she collapsed on the pillows. She carried the towel from the room.

Inside Geneva the wind ceased howling and the waters grew still: the storm weakened by its own recklessness. Geneva knew long before Ida returned that her prayers had been in vain. The child had washed from the shelter of her womb on the last violent wave of an incarnadine sea. God's will? Perhaps. Yet there seemed a terrifying randomness in the storm which struck her, not unlike the randomness of the storm raging outside, or that which destroyed Galveston in 1900, and her father's family along with it. Not unlike the randomness of her parents' train spilling into the dark abyss.

What she felt then was that God was a vast fulcrum of indifference. Her mother had been wrong. Reverend Stone had been wrong. *We are alone.* There in the stillness and the dark, that was what she felt.

Ida stood above Geneva now. The girl had suffered enough at the hands of the male gender, she reasoned, and no doubt had learned her lesson. Who could say? This experience might encourage her to join the cause one day. Ida decided to be generous—something that never came natural to her, and especially after having been married to a useless man who poured her life savings into an oil well as useless as he was. "You're lucky. You can go on now, as if nothing had happened. Your secret is safe with me."

Safe with someone who might have let her die? Or, had she been bluffing? If they lived together for the rest of their lives, Geneva would never trust Ida with another secret.

Using warm moist rags, Ida washed her as one might cleanse a body in preparation for burial.

CHAPTER 15

In terms of damages, it wasn't much of a storm, Tony Selby concluded two days later. He and his mother were returning home after their extended tour out West which included a month-long stay with friends recently moved to San Francisco. They had been worried by newspaper reports all the way from Los Angeles to El Paso.

Inside the busy lobby of Union Station they bought a *Houston Post*, and read that electric power had been restored and telephone lines were open. Outside streetcars were running and automobiles were splashing through puddles of water that reflected like mirrors off the sun. On the way home from the station they saw showcase windows being reset at Kiam's clothing store, and it looked as though the numerous fabric awnings with the store name in blazing letters had been torn to ribbons. The vast number of electric signs twisted in their frames, their missing letters forming odd words, was the most dramatic evidence of what had occurred, that plus all the tree limbs and other debris still being hauled away on the backs of mule-drawn wagons.

Tony and his mother were grateful to find that the eight-storied Beaconsfield, flanked by tall shade trees that surely posed a threat, had sustained no significant damage. Happily this supported the claim that the apartment house was hurricane-proof: These walls could sustain winds up to 150 miles per hour, his mother had been told when she moved in. As soon as Tony had bathed and put on a fresh suit of clothes, he paid a call to Madame Linsky, to inquire as to Geneva Sterling's address. From there he went directly to 1207 Heights Boulevard, to renew his appeal made last spring. After searching from coast to coast and finding but one dancer with whom success was written in the stars, he had resigned himself. If Miss Sterling refused him again, he would drop the idea of team dancing, and register for the upcoming term at the Rice Institute—a Johnny-come-lately school perched on a bald prairie; the only seat of higher learning in town—to complete his engineering education begun at Oxford, and terminated by circumstances beyond his control. Or, more to the point, dashed under the heel of Jane Tremont—one year ago this month.

Geneva was upstairs in bed resting when she heard the doorbell ring. Ida was not at home. She rose from the bed and took slow and careful steps toward the head of the stairs, a hand pressed against the teetering boulder of her abdomen. The doorbell rang repeatedly, conducting someone's growing impatience through the electrical wires attached to the ringer. She could move no faster, and was about to give up trying when, passing the small oval window on the upper landing, she glimpsed the back of a man's figure clad in a smart brown suit and bowler, advancing briskly down the walk toward a shiny Packard parked at the curb. Opening the door and hiking one foot on the running board, he turned to look toward the house, as if hoping someone might have come to the door by now. Tony Selby. So he had not found a partner after all. Somewhere deep in her spirit Geneva felt a sudden bright burst of hope. It was gone as quickly as it came. She moved aside from the window so that she would not be seen, and listened for the sound of the motor running. When she looked back again, Tony was gone. She remembered the tango music rolling up her spine, their long measured steps punctuated by sudden stillness; her pinpoint turns under Tony's arm, and deep back bends over it; remembered her arabesque behind his kneeling figure at the end, her hand resting on his shoulder; remembered knowing he was going to say, "When shall we begin?"

He wouldn't want me now, she thought.

PART II

1916–1918

CHAPTER 16

By September of 1916 Tony Selby rarely thought of Geneva Sterling anymore. He was about to enter his second year at the Rice Institute—though it may as well have been his first, for he'd spent last year compensating for the difference in structure and curriculum from that at Oxford, and the fact that he had not retained as much as he might from his year of study there, given all the upheaval which swiftly followed. Though Tony could not have claimed to be happy with his life, at least his mind was busy enough to ward off painful memories of the past in England, and he was glad, too, to be doing something to please his father who had suffered more mightily than he had, at the hand of Jane Tremont and her father. His letters were filled with the frustration of his failure to track down Brian Potts.

One Sunday afternoon, Tony and his mother were relaxing under the broad beamed ceiling of her living room. Having earlier attended worship at Trinity Episcopal—as they did on occasion since it was located near the Beaconsfield, and the Episcopal Church was a cousin of the Church of England—they'd returned to eat a leisurely brunch and change clothes. Tony wore a pair of flannel trousers with suspenders, and a striped shirt with the collar removed and the sleeves rolled up above the elbows. His dark-haired mother wore a royal purple silk kimono which brought out the violet cast in her deep blue eyes—the kimono was a gift from Tony last Christmas. Holidays were sad and lonely for them both, and they did their best to keep their chins up by lavishing gifts on each other. Tony had opened the windows overlooking the balcony, and the thin curtains rustled in the pleasant breeze. Newspapers and magazines were strewn about and china tea cups cluttered table tops.

Tony was thumbing through the Summer issue of the *New American Review,* a popular magazine which made him think of *Country Life,* the English magazine of similar ilk which was always on hand at Brookhurst. Feature stories of general interest and thought-provoking essays filled the pages of the *New American Review;* a good many illustrations and the occasional photograph appeared as well.

On page 39, he came across a photograph that made the hair stand up on the back of his neck: A young girl peering out a sunny window, her figure clad in a gauzy tunic; masses of wavy hair cascading down her back. On a gilt chair behind her in the shadows lay a pair of dancing shoes, their ribbons spilling down. The photograph, which covered the entire page, was just slightly out of focus, giving it rather an other-worldly quality, as if the girl were a trick of the imagination, rather than real flesh and bones. Tony drew slightly back from the photograph and studied it for a few moments, then brought it closer again. There was something about the young girl that was remarkably like—no. Geneva Sterling was a serious ballet student, not a photographer's model. Of course, he had met her only once, and hadn't got a good look at her hair, thanks to the hat she was wearing; still…. Blinking, Tony looked on the facing page and found the caption: "*Maiden at the Window* is the first art photograph to be published by Victor Calais." Not much help. Luckily the photograph accompanied a feature article about the life of the photographer, however. Tony turned back to its beginning, on page 37. His eyes quickly grazed the columns describing the career of Victor Calais, searching for the name he dare not hope to find. Then there it was: "Geneva Sterling…a second cousin by marriage…was the model for *Maiden at the Window.*" Tony felt as if he'd been grabbed by the chest and squeezed hard. He returned to the photograph. Yes, of course…. It bothered him that he had to see Geneva's name before he could be certain it was she. In those few minutes they'd danced together, he felt he'd become intimately familiar with her features: the curves of her figure beneath his hands, the angles of her face as he twirled her beneath his arm; and at last, the dance done, the face which stared back along with his in the mirror. *Art photograph.* Well. Tony supposed he must credit the photographer with creating an image that transcended reality.

So this was why she could not dance with him, he realized. "*Just now,*" she had said, which gave him hope at the time, but which he came to realize was futile, as days became weeks and weeks became months.

"Look here, Mother—it's Geneva Sterling!" he said abruptly, springing from his easy chair. "Now we know why she couldn't dance with me." Cynthia looked up from her newspaper in surprise. As Tony passed the magazine into her delicate ivory hands, he suddenly felt the dark tango rhythm stirring in his bones, as if he had danced with Miss Sterling but yesterday. He began to pace back and forth before the sculpted onyx fireplace, his hands driven down in his pockets.

Cynthia was now gazing with interest upon the photograph. So this was the mystery partner, the one with whom not another single dancer from coast to coast, during months and months of auditions, could compare. Admittedly Geneva Sterling was a stunner. Yet she had become a sore spot with Cynthia. She had never understood Tony's obsession with her, which, from the high color of his face and the luminous quality of his eyes just now, seemed to have a grip on him even yet.

Alright. Cynthia did not get where she was in the business by letting opportunities slip by. She read the article carefully to see if it might present an opening.

Finally in the second column, she found it. She looked up at Tony. "Did you notice from the article, the photographer has gone to Europe to photograph the war? He was interviewed while stopping in New York, en route."

"No, I didn't read much of the article. When was this?" Tony asked anxiously. *He was pressing his business card against her elbow. A tendril of damp hair escaped her hat….*

Cynthia narrowed her eyes, digressed a few paragraphs, and read aloud: "'Mr. Calais's wife died suddenly in May of last year—' how dreadful—'and he and his children traveled throughout the summer, before he went overseas.'" She did some calculating. "This had to have been in the autumn of last year."

Tony said nothing. Cynthia watched him pace back and forth, his face grim. Behind him, above the mantelpiece, hung an original painting by Maxfield Parrish of two translucent angels treading hand in hand down a beach under a star-flecked night sky: a glorious painting commissioned by a grateful client whom she managed for a while, and worth hundreds of dollars. Cynthia was known as "the guardian angel of show business."

"Well, are you just going to let it go?" she asked at length.

Tony stopped pacing and looked at her. "What do you mean?"

"Geneva Sterling isn't modeling anymore."

In a stony voice, he said, "So? I gave her my business card. She has had over a year to contact me."

For a few moments Cynthia struggled over whether to press the point further. When Tony arrived from England in 1914, he was pale and shaken, his spirit all but broken by the debacle with Jane Tremont. She was so sure she could help him pick up the pieces of his life and start over. Of course she had failed to anticipate he would become fascinated with one particular girl and set his heart on her as his partner, his idealism winning out over his professionalism. How could she urge him to run the risk of Geneva Sterling rejecting him a second time? She could hardly bear the thought he may be in for still another disappointment. Yet, watching him day in and day out as he attended classes at Rice, just barely going through the motions, she knew what she had known from the time her son was a small boy: He was only truly alive when he was dancing.

Cynthia took in a breath. "Maybe she assumed you found another partner."

Indeed, by now Geneva could be married, with a child, thought Tony. Still, there was no denying that seeing her photograph made the magic they created together seem as palpable as though they were looking at themselves in the mirror at this very moment, panting from exertion. And knowing the photographer was out of the way…well…. "I suppose I could telephone her at least," he said.

Yet, according to the Houston directory, there was no one named Sterling living on Heights Boulevard. Then Tony remembered Geneva's parents were dead. How sad she had looked when she told him this. So presumably she lived with some relative. Could it be she had moved by the time he called on her after the storm? Even left the city? He remembered feeling the eyes of every neighbor on him as he walked away from her porch in futility. He would not call on her again, unless he knew she was there and would receive him.

Thus he sat down to write Geneva. The obvious way to begin his letter was to say that he'd seen her photograph in the *New American Review* and found it positively enchanting, for that was the truth, and it should put her in an agreeable frame of mind. "Dear Miss Sterling…" he wrote. Yet on second thought—he sat back, pen poised in the air—to use the word 'enchanting' or any other superlative would not do, for it was more a compliment to the photographer than to Geneva herself. So he sat there for a while, trying to think of an alternative. Then suddenly it struck him: if not for Victor Calais monopolizing Geneva's time to make that photograph, he would not be sitting here right now, struggling over a way to rekindle the sense of anticipation he was sure she felt that night at Linsky's studio. She wanted to dance with him as much as he wanted to dance with her, he was certain of it! Nothing would have stood in their way. By now they would be well on their way to playing the *Palace* in New York City—the absolute pinnacle of success for any vaudeville performer. Instead, Calais had finished with Geneva, and gone on his merry way, oblivious to the fact that if not for him she would have her name in lights by now, along with his—oh, hang it all! He was getting quite heated up. Best thing was to forget about the bloody photograph and just to ask simply if Geneva might be available to dance with him by now. May he call on her to discuss it?

He wrote the letter and mailed it on Monday.

A month passed and she did not reply. Yet nor was his letter returned. So at least it was likely she had not moved away. He wrote again, and still again, taking the opportunity to tell her more about himself and his credentials as a dancer, repeatedly asking when he might call on her. None of his letters were returned; none were answered. Tony was growing more and more intrigued. He imagined Geneva sitting inside the house, reading his letters wistfully, her defenses—for whatever reason they existed—gradually breaking down.

Finally in April—the U.S. had just got into the European war—came a letter with Geneva's return. Tony could hardly catch his breath as he tore open the envelope. "Dear Tony Selby, I regret I am not available to dance with you, though I do appreciate your offer. I will be entering the Rice Institute in the fall, in hopes of becoming a teacher. Cordially, Geneva Sterling."

A wicked smile crossed Tony's face. He had neglected to mention in his letters that he was studying at Rice. He wouldn't let her escape him again. She was going to dance with him. Showing his mother her letter, he said, "I shall bide my time until September."

That night he began putting down in a notebook his dance centering around two chimney sweeps. And in the days that followed he spent every spare moment working out steps on his mother's balcony.

CHAPTER 17

Tony found it was not easy to distinguish Geneva from the other coeds when the fall semester rolled around at Rice, for by now military regulations had been imposed, and these included the wearing of regulation U.S. Army uniforms by all students. Then on the morning of the 25th of September, as he stood at the edge of the quadrangle gazing around hopefully, he thought he may have spotted her emerging from the Liberal Arts Building, carrying her books in the crook of her elbow. Eagerly his eyes swept from the oval shadow of her face beneath the broad hat brim, down to the symmetrical curves of her breasts under the tight-fitting, high-collared uniform shirt; to her slender waist and round hips clad in a long drab khaki skirt which partially concealed a pair of high lace-up boots. Tony couldn't be positive, but she was turning now and would soon be lost in a sea of military garb and campaign hats. "I say, it's Geneva Sterling, isn't it?" he called. When she paused and turned in his direction, his heart raced. He hurried towards her.

The sun boiled above the bare quadrangle that day. Geneva's hat squeezed like a vise around her head, and her high shirt collar was like a noose around her neck. What an appalling shock to find that Rice would be a veritable Army post by the time she began classes, with uniforms, drills, and fitness programs; and—most nefarious of all—an underlying message that it would be unpatriotic to speak in opposition of the war. Not that she didn't support the brave soldiers fighting overseas—she'd been outside the day poor Mr. and Mrs. Crawford returned from seeing Wendell off at the train station. They waved to her, their expressions conflicted with a certainty their son was doing what was right, yet an almost unbearable burden of worry. Baby Joseph clutched a small American flag in his hand; a full-sized version hung from the front porch. And now Geneva spent Wednesday afternoons in the Goggan building, packing comfort kits to be dispatched to all the Wendells in the trenches—her way of putting her sentiments into action. But Rice was an institution of higher learning, where freedom of thought and debate about important political issues should never be inhibited.

She had just left her United States history class, where the pupils were grumbling about the loss of academic freedom, when she heard her name spoken in a distinctly British accent, and turned to see Tony Selby a few yards away.

She had never expected to see Tony again, and now that he was walking toward her, she felt embarrassed by the way she had treated him. For a long while after the storm, she was reclusive, feeling the stain on her character was obvious to everyone she encountered. Following graduation, Ida urged her to take a correspondence course from a business school, and she complied because at least it would stop John Scarborough's frequent inquiries of what she intended to do about her future, and yet allow her to keep to herself. She had just begun the course when Tony's first letter arrived. As she read the words, he seemed larger-than-life as never before, impeccable. She could not face him. And there was more: *"I've decided not to return in September. Sincerely, Geneva Sterling,"* she had written to Linsky after the storm. She had not put on her dancing shoes since May of 1915. She was completely out of condition then, and Tony was sharp enough to notice this if he called on her. It was best to ignore his letter. He would soon get the idea.

Apparently undaunted, he continued to write, citing his accomplishments as a dancer, which began at the age of 12 when he played one of the lost boys in *Peter Pan* on the London stage. He also told her—with obvious affection, and perhaps to assure her of his good character—about his father and sister living in England. And he spoke fondly of their home in Cornwall, called Brookhurst.

Over the course of his letters, she often found herself thinking wistfully that Tony Selby was just the kind of person, from just the kind of fine family, her parents would have approved of her knowing. After she finally began dancing again, she could not help wondering: *Is it possible…?*

Then he wrote that his parents had been legally separated for years, and he had seen very little of his mother until the autumn of 1914, when he "came to the States to pursue a dancing career." Autumn of 1914? The question of why he chose to leave when his country was at war—which had occurred to Geneva on the night they met—seemed all the more significant, now that she knew of all he left behind. And inevitably she wondered: as the war raged on, how long before he would be conscience-stricken and go home to join the armed forces? It was just as well she had not teamed up with him. She wrote him her refusal.

"May I have a word with you?" Tony was asking now.

They sat down on a vacant bench under the cloisters, where a pleasant cross-current of air gave slight relief from the haze of heat.

Tony studied her for a few moments, his eyes so admiring that her heartbeat quickened and she smiled. "I must say, you look quite fetching in a uniform," he said playfully.

"Why didn't you tell me you intended to enroll here?" she asked.

"Actually this is my second year," he admitted uneasily, running a finger around the inside of his collar.

Geneva didn't know what to make of this. All the time he was writing to her, he was a college student. Was he going to ask her to go out with him? She could hardly imagine sitting across from him in a restaurant, or lounging under a tree on a picnic cloth. "I thought you were a dancer all the time," she said.

"And so I am. But I'd already begun the study of engineering at Oxford, before I came to this country, and then my career as a dancer became…well…stalled, shall we say."

Geneva was amazed. It was right at the tip of her tongue to ask the question that had nagged at her. But she did not want to appear to accuse Tony of shirking his duty, for that was hardly the point. "If you don't mind my asking, from your letters, you seemed to be very—well—happy in England. And studying at Oxford! What made you decide to come over here?" she said.

Tony realized he should have expected the question. Still, he owed her no explanation. His eyes level with hers, he said only, "Things don't always turn out as one would hope."

"Yes, how true it is," she said slowly, realizing now that something terrible may have happened to him, just as it did to her. She felt sad for Tony. A tendril of hair blew across her cheek, like a spider web. She brushed it back.

So she's been through a rough patch too, Tony thought. It occurred to him that perhaps Geneva had wanted to dance with him all along. Could it be that someone in authority—her guardian, perhaps—urged her instead to enroll in college? "I say, Geneva, what made you decide to become a teacher?"

"I've got to think of my future," she said, practically. "I'm not well off, you know."

He didn't believe it was as simple as that. "Then why did you wait so long to answer my letters?" he persisted.

Geneva hesitated before answering, "Your letters confused me. I'm sorry," she said quietly, and looked down at her hands.

So he was right. If he could just convince her to take a chance with him. Boldly he said, "Look here, there's no use beating about the bush. I've composed a little dance that I think would be perfect for us. And I—I wonder, would you allow me just to show it to you? If you don't like it, just say so, and I shall never trouble you again."

'A little dance.' Could Tony write dances as well as he performed them? Geneva wondered, intrigued. A few minutes then. Perhaps she owed him that much. "Alright."

Tony's face lit up. "Let's see, where shall we meet? How about at Madame Linsky's studio; that is, I presume you still have connections there—?"

"Yes, I do," Geneva told him. He would be surprised to know that his very first letter was to credit, for it reawakened her desire to study ballet, a desire that grew so strong, she was compelled to take the painful step of apologizing to Linsky for her abrupt departure, and confess the truth in hopes her teacher would take her back. Late one evening she stood in the shadows of the Main Street studio and watched as the last of the pupils in her old Thursday night advanced ballet class descended the stairs and came out on the pavement. How lithe and carefree they looked! How springy their steps! She did not want anyone to recognize her. Finally she braced herself and walked up the stairs to speak to her teacher.

By the time she arrived at Linsky's office door she was shivering with fright, and the first thing she saw, even before her teacher looked up from the small journal she was posting, was the wooden crucifix looming above her desk. Geneva's knees went weak. She felt the eyes of the crucified figure burning through her, felt the weight of her sins as never before. She should not have come. Linsky would not forgive her, let alone allow her to return.

Suddenly Linsky looked up, a startled frown on her face, her eyes piercing Geneva like swords. "Madame Linsky, I—" Geneva began, and burst into tears. Soon she felt Linsky's firm clutch on her shoulders from behind, ushering her to a chair. "Sit down, and tell Linsky what has happened." Geneva told her of the affair with Victor and the ill-fated pregnancy, sobbing all the while. At the end Linsky appeared a bit shaken, and Geneva feared she would order her to leave. Yet she nodded thoughtfully and said with gentleness, "You will survive this heartache and go on, *ma chère*. In the meantime you need to be dancing."

Now Geneva said to Tony, "I teach a morning primary ballet class, and Linsky gives me private lessons two nights a week in return. Come over on Tuesday night. I finish at nine."

"Splendid! And perhaps Madame Linsky would remain to observe."

As they rose from the bench, Tony said, "Oh yes, I've been carrying this around for days, thought you'd like an extra copy." He shuffled through his books and withdrew the Summer issue of the *New American Review*. Geneva need never know what agony he had gone through, knowing Victor Calais's photograph had robbed him of his heart's desire. He should have liked to tear it into pieces when it was all said and done. But then, how could he destroy a photograph of Geneva? After he found out she would be at Rice, he decided the solution was quite simple: he would give it to her.

When he handed the magazine to Geneva, she seemed puzzled. "Your photograph inside—*Maiden at the Window*—surely you knew about it!"

Geneva stared down at the magazine, all the blood draining from her face. It was as if Victor had walked up and put his hand on her shoulder.

"Here, look, it's on page 39," said Tony, flipping the pages over.

The sight of the *Maiden* robbed Geneva of breath. "*...I won't ever leave you....*" *His eyes on hers, Victor was closing the studio curtain.* She was glad Tony could not see her face right now. She struggled to find her voice. "Ah yes—no, I—I didn't know about it," she stammered.

"Fancy that! I should have thought Mr. Calais would have seen that you were provided a copy. Of course, he was about to ship out overseas, so perhaps it was impossible."

Geneva did not know how Tony knew that Victor was overseas, then she noticed that the facing page was filled with text. And she noticed the caption: "The first art photograph to be published...." She must find a way to end this conversation without revealing herself, then get away. Finally she looked at him and said stiffly, "Mr. Calais was a very self-centered person. Such a courtesy would not have occurred to him."

"I see," said Tony. So Calais was a conceited bloke. He might have guessed. "Well I trust he paid you handsomely, before he got away," he said.

"No—no, it wasn't like that. I did it as a favor to my guardian, his wife. He was just experimenting, you see. He took hundreds of photographs," she said, then after a pause she added, more to reassure herself than for any other reason, "But this was the only one he thought might ever be published." Or was it? She wondered, suddenly alarmed. She needed to think this through. Quickly she reached for her books. "I've got a class on the other side of the quad."

"See you on Tuesday night," Tony said cheerfully.

"Yes," she said absently.

As Geneva hurried across the campus, she saw herself on that day long ago when Victor called her into his studio just before he moved away, and offered her photographs to her. *"I want you to keep them,"* she said. By refusing them—how near that envelope had been, right on the tips of her fingers!—she had desperately hoped they would provide a link between her and Victor that would one day bring him back to her. All this time she had believed the photographs were locked away in storage. Yet he published *Maiden at the Window*. Did he lay it aside, knowing she liked it, and therefore assuming she wouldn't mind? Or did he take her refusal to mean she was permitting him to publish all the photographs, even the nude ones? Surely not. He knew how she felt about those nude studies. Yet she had no way of being certain. Was it possible he would publish the four nude poses while in Europe? After all, he was very proud of them. He might convince himself that it would be alright to do so, way over there, as long as he didn't identify her as the model—surely he wouldn't identify her! But no, none of this seemed likely. He would be going from one battle field to another, in war-torn countries. He probably left the others in storage, just as he said. Still, the war would be over one day, and Victor would return to the States. When that day arrived, she must somehow contact him and retrieve her photographs, then destroy them. That was the only way to be sure they would never bring her any harm.

CHAPTER 18

Tony hired Linsky's pianist Myra Brinkerhoff to play the accompaniment for his number, entitled, *Dance of the Red Hat.* He provided her with a notated copy of the song he'd selected: Scott Joplin's *Magnetic Rag.* Now as Myra looked over the music, and Linsky and Geneva took their seats at the edge of the floor, Tony took his place in the center. He wore a striped jersey over his rounded biceps and chest, a pair of knickers, knee sox and lace-up dancing shoes. In the firm grip of his fingers was a brown bowler with a juggler's ring sewn inside. He cautioned Geneva and her teacher that the success of the dance—part pantomime, part acrobatic stunt, part suspense tale—would depend upon the ability of each partner to control this article. Tony would play both parts in this demonstration: Good and Evil. As he introduced the story of a good but feckless chimney sweep who finds a spangled red hat one night, only to have it swiped from his hands by his evil partner, the studio floor disappeared, the silhouette of a vast skyline rose in the background, a spotlight flashed on him, and the brown bowler became bright red, sprigged with diamonds, potent with energy. Linsky and Geneva were among an audience of hundreds, brought to the edge of their seats.

Now he nodded to Myra, and the eight-bar intro pulsed across the keys.

Tony's agile figure moved through the steps with an assurance that suggested the juice of his creative mind was coursing through his bloodstream into his limbs, and within moments Geneva was wondering which part—Good, or Evil?—Tony envisioned for her. *I bet I was Evil,* she thought. She was possessed of a yearning, electrifying as the spangled hat, to get out there and dance with him. Her feet twitched; her hips moved to the ragtime beat.

She was amazed at Tony's ability to switch from one part to the other, pantomiming both with equal vitality, his countenance dissolving from Dr. Jekyll to Mr. Hyde and back again. Yet even more impressive was his ability to toss the spangled hat in the air, then calculate how many beats of music it would require to float down within his reach. He must have rehearsed this process hundreds of times. *This time, he'll miss!* her thoughts raced, breathlessly. But he never did until the end, when he blundered intentionally. The two chimney sweeps watched forlornly as the hat floated down between two building roofs, taking all their dreams with it.

Tony turned to the audience, folded his hands modestly before him, and bowed his head. He was bathed in sweat. The stripes of his jersey undulated with his exhausted breath.

"Bravo!" Linsky cried, applauding, and Geneva echoed her unabashed praise. Yet like the hat, Geneva was inevitably brought down to earth. She was back in the Goggan Building on a Wednesday afternoon, surrounded by mountains of supplies that would be divided and subdivided into hundreds of thousands of comfort kits—woolen stockings, tooth powder, safety razors, tobacco, bath towels, wash cloths, heavy cotton underwear, combs, tan shoe polish, safety pins, hand soap, hard candy, pencils and paper—articles without flash and glitter, articles that brought home the overwhelming magnitude of the war. The government was prepared to dig trenches for a very long time. How long could Tony avoid going home to fight?

Now he complimented Myra on her excellent rendering of Joplin's tune. Her bespectacled face reddened with pleasure, from her chin to the roots of her brown curls. He pulled a handkerchief from his pocket and mopped his face. "Suggestions, anyone?" he said, including all three parties in his gaze. No one could think of any way to improve on the *Dance of the Red Hat*.

Then suddenly Tony was looking directly at Geneva, as though there was no one else in the room. It was the moment she had dreaded since she agreed to watch his demonstration. She heard the piano lid close. Out the corner of her eye, she noticed Linsky discreetly heading for her office. She rose from her chair and went to where he stood. It was all she could do to keep from pleasing him by asking, *"Which part do I play, Good or Evil?"* Breathlessly she said, "I must tell you in all honesty, the dance is even better than I expected—"

Tony's brow lifted in delight. A smile teased at the corners of his mouth.

"I—it's just—" Her eyes dropped.

"What?" he prodded.

She summoned the courage to look up into his anxious face. "With the war on—" she faltered. "One day you might go home and join up. I can't take a chance on being...stranded." Again.

She could not help hoping Tony would at least try to understand her view. Instead, his face froze with insult. His brown eyes burned through her. After a few moments he turned on his heel and walked away.

Slowly Geneva walked toward her teacher's office, a storm of emotions overtaking her. She knew it had been wise to refuse to dance with Tony, and the fact he made no argument seemed to bear this out. Yet his abrupt departure, after the mesmerizing, spine-tingling spectacle of his dance, left a vacuum of energy in the air. It was as if someone had suddenly died in the room. She felt shocked and bereft.

As soon as Geneva walked into Madame Linsky's office and sank into a chair like a stone, her teacher knew the worst had happened. Aware of Geneva's reservations about dancing with Tony, nonetheless she had hoped—"I take it you refused *Monsieur Selby?*"

Geneva nodded tightly, and turned sideways in her chair as if to ward off a blow. Linsky wanted to shake her shoulders and shout, "*Je ne comprends pas! You may never have another opportunity like this!*"

Yet she understood that Geneva was only trying to survive, for life had dealt her blows similar to those the young girl had suffered. How happy she had been, growing up in Paris with her elder brother Edgar, and two loving parents! Then, when she was but a few years older than Geneva was now, Paris was overtaken by Prussian forces. Her father, a professor at *L'Ecole des Beaux Arts*, suffered an accidental cut on his hand from a shard of broken glass. This led to a fatal infection in his blood, simply for the lack of proper medical treatment. Her mother died within five years, never having recovered from his death. Not that she lost her faith—*au contraire!* The crucifix on her office wall hung above the bed her mother died in. But her mother lost *la joie de vivre,* and when illness befell her, she had not the will to survive. Two years later Linsky's brother Edgar fell ill and quickly died. She married soon thereafter to Gustave, a ballet master—a marriage in name only, for many years now. How she adored Gustave! But, after a year and three months, he left her when a lover who earlier rejected him had a change of heart.

Linsky never spoke of these personal things, not even to Geneva, for they still brought unbearable sorrow. Still, the fact that they had both struggled to overcome adversity formed an unspoken bond between them, and now Linsky felt almost as though Geneva were her daughter. She must not allow her to mistake survival for life—two very different propositions indeed!

At last she said reasonably, "If *Monsieur Selby* did not know his own heart, would he have dedicated himself so completely to this dream? Besides, *ma chère,* what if he does eventually do as you fear? He will come back from the war—God grant,"—crossing herself—"and you will resume. *Rien de plus facile!* The war cannot last forever."

Geneva turned to face her teacher. In the four days since she met Tony on the Rice campus, every conceivable outcome of dancing with him had crossed her mind, and this was among them. "Yes, but once the war is over, Tony may decide to resume his career in England, rather than returning here. His father and sister are there, you know, and from his letters, he feels very close to them."

How sad, Linsky thought, that a young girl as lovely and talented as Geneva believes she can never be first in a young man's heart. "*Ma chère*" she said, "could it be that you are afraid to trust any man after the photographer?"

"I don't believe so," she told Linsky now, thinking of her father: among the most trustworthy of men. "But I don't want to be dependent on Tony Selby, or anyone else. Oh, if only I could live my life like yours—I admire you so much!" she said earnestly.

"But *ma chère,*" Linsky cried, lifting her eyes to the heavens, "I did not begin to teach until I could no longer perform. It was through performing that I developed my skills as an instructor. If I were your age, a man like *Monsieur Selby* would not have to ask me twice, *certainement!*"

Geneva considered this, then shook her head. "I'm already a year late starting to college. If all this fell through, I would have wasted even more time."

"And you explained all this to him?"

Geneva shrugged. She told Linsky what she had said to Tony. "He looked very angry—as if maybe he knew I was right—and walked away."

"Ah, I see…," said Linsky slowly. She sat there stroking her chin, her eyes lowered. Abruptly she looked up again. "But you cannot be sure what he was thinking, no?"

"No," Geneva admitted.

Linsky leaned forward in her chair, her dark eyes narrowed. "Then let me suggest this to you: if you really want to dance with *Monsieur Selby*—" She paused, with an inquiring look.

"Oh yes, I do," said Geneva. And all the more so since he walked away, she realized now.

"Write him a letter and tell him what it will take to change your mind."

Two days later, having purposely avoided running into Geneva on the Rice campus, Tony was amazed to find a letter from her in the stack of mail on the marble table in his mother's foyer. His fingers shaking, he tore it open. *"I was wrong...."* "Dear Tony, I have been troubled since Tuesday night, for it was obvious I injured your feelings, and I did not intend to. Yet any girl would be reluctant to make the kind of commitment you are asking of me during a time of war. And in all fairness, your letters suggest that your love of England runs quite deep, and your ties to your family are strong. So naturally I would have to assume that at some point you would be compelled to put these things first, before the rewards of a career on the stage. If I just had some guarantee that nothing could get in the way of our dancing together, then I could follow the dictates of my heart—I truly want to dance with you. Always, Geneva."

Tony walked into the living room and sank down in a chair, thinking. The letter was not all he might have hoped, though Geneva admitted what he had always known was true: she wanted to dance with him. By 'guarantee,' did she mean, 'promise?' Or did she expect something more concrete? Well, she would just have to take his word on it, he thought, bristling. Yet, on the other hand, the sordid mess he left behind in England, while frightfully embarrassing and painful, was not his doing. Why not just tell her the truth and be done with it?

He sat down to write: "Dear Geneva, As I am in hopes that we are about to embark on a career together which will require the utmost trust on both sides, I feel it is only right to address your concerns in full. I shall begin by explaining my reasons for leaving England three years ago...."

First he gave her some background on his life-long acquaintance with Jane Tremont: how they grew up on adjoining estates, and she was his sister's chum; how his pity for her for being abandoned by her mother, and raised by a tyrannical father, had gradually turned into love. Next he told Geneva of the picnic that began so innocently in the wood on that August day shortly after they became engaged. Then he paused. She may be offended by his admission that he and Jane had made love in the wood. Yet, how could he tell her the story and leave that part out? So...he must put it delicately: "We who had known each other for many years knew each other physically that day." He reread the sentence. It read like a passage from the Bible. Alright. He went on.... "Riding home, Jane was nearly hysterical. She said she had seen Brian Potts about, that he worked at Fairleigh a couple of summers. She was convinced he would talk about what he had seen. 'It will get back to my father,' she said. 'You must pay him to keep quiet, whatever he wants, do you hear?'

"Jane's fear was understandable," he wrote, "William's brutish, vindictive nature was well known. Upon divorcing him, his wife Francine fled the country out of fear of reprisal! Still, on that day William was 200 miles away, visiting one of his factories, in Coventry. I told Jane I would not invite blackmail, but that by the time William returned, I'd have Potts cleared out, so she needn't worry.

"To my amazement, her blue eyes turned cold and menacing. 'When it comes to money, my honor isn't worth much, is it?' she said.

"As we rode on a little further, I felt shaken. I tried to reconcile such cruel injustice from the girl I thought I knew very well. I decided she was just upset and didn't mean what she said. Once inside the Fairleigh grounds, she demanded I stop the buggy. She leapt to the ground like a fool, twisting her ankle," he wrote. *He was watching in disbelief as Jane limped across the ground towards her grandmother's house, a small crimson stain on the back of her dress. He wondered if she realized it was there.*

"It was the last time I would see Jane Tremont.

"By the time I caught up with Potts in the Brookhurst stable, I could barely contain my fury. I ordered the little runt to collect his wages from the Steward's office, and told him I would be sure he never found work in the district again.

"Potts had a smirk on his face. He made an obscene remark about Jane's character, said that 'as an Oxford man,' I ought to be able to figure things out for myself. Then he began to laugh.

"I knocked him down," Tony wrote simply. *He was grabbing Potts up, battering him until he was barely conscious, and the whole side of his face was bleeding....*

Tony's forehead was bathed in perspiration as he remembered, his free hand clenched in an angry fist. He stopped to mop his brow and take a few steadying breaths, then continued writing:

"Late that night, William Tremont came to Brookhurst, demanding a word with me in the presence of my father, his face purple with fury. William is a tall man, with a broad back and a way of hunching his shoulders and thrusting his head forward on his neck, that makes one think of a predatory bird. We went into Father's study to talk. William's aging mother had summoned him home, he said. It appeared that Brian Potts stopped by Fairleigh that evening to report he had seen me force myself upon Jane in the Brookhurst wood. Jane—quite upset indeed—supported his claim to her grandmother, saying that, in hastening away from me, she had bruised her ankle.

"'Is this true?' my father asked, his eyes wide with shock.

"I told him it was not.

"Father told William very firmly that my word was good enough for him. 'We'll just see about that,' William said, and stormed out.

"Next morning, a letter was delivered: Provided that I agreed to leave the country within 48 hours, William would consider the score settled, and 'the matter a private one between the two families.' If I should refuse to leave, however, he would have me brought up on charges of—" Tony paused, his pen remaining in the air. He licked his lips. He could not force himself to write the word. Luckily he was near the top of a page. He discarded the page and rewrote the paragraph, putting a period after the word 'charges.'

"Brian Potts, who could have been forced to tell the truth to authorities, had vanished. No doubt, with plenty of brass jangling in his pocket, from Jane.

"Lawyers were consulted. A search was instituted. Meantime, I was advised to leave my home and my country, and go somewhere that communications were apt to remain open, for no one could say how far the war in Europe would go now that it had begun.

"Thus, in a state of disbelief, I sailed to America. Months later, a letter came from Father with some news of the investigation. Potts had volunteered in the armed forces under a false name. He was now serving on the Western Front.

"There will be no bringing him back until the war is over," Tony concluded, then sat looking at the regrettable sentence for a few moments. That was the hold they all three had on him now, the hold that kept his life in limbo.

"I only pray to God that Potts will survive with his mental faculties intact. Only then will my name be cleared.

"It hardly need be said, Geneva, that I shall not, under any circumstances, return to England to join the Armed Forces. Yours sincerely, Anthony Edward Selby IV."

As Tony put out the light and went to bed, an unexpected sense of peace filled him. Who would have thought that writing it all out in sequence would be a restorative? For the first time he actually felt confident that the whole unfortunate matter would be resolved one day.

The next morning at breakfast, feeling refreshed after his deep sleep, Tony placed the letter beside his mother's plate. "Would you mind looking this over, just to be sure the language isn't too harsh?"

It was a sunny morning with just a hint of autumn in the air, and they were dining out on the balcony. Cynthia wore a satin house robe of rose red, which enhanced her creamy complexion, and her hair was wrapped in a matching turban. Cynthia knew of Geneva's letter to Tony, but she was not quite sure how he intended to reply.

Tony watched her face intently as she read. To his dismay, as she progressed through the pages, her countenance grew increasingly dark.

Finally she put the letter aside. She was thoroughly shaken. Tony was about to ruin everything. "Cut to the phrase which begins, "I shall not, under any circumstances, return—"

"What on earth?" Tony demanded.

Cynthia pleaded, "Darling, she won't understand. She doesn't know you well enough. She may even think you're lying ."

Tony's eyes were blazing; his cheeks were red. "You mean, you think she'll believe I—*I* actually did what Jane accused me of?"

Cynthia gazed at him, her eyes moist.

Tony sat there utterly dejected, trying to comprehend his mother's reaction. Finally it came to him that her very first words described the situation precisely: for all he had sought after Geneva during the past two and a half years, for all his conviction that they would create magic on the stage, she hardly knew him. Finally he shrugged. "Alright," he said thinly.

Cynthia went to Tony's side and put her arm around his shoulder. She was aware she had dealt him a blow, but the thing now was to get them started dancing. Handing him the pages, she said gently, "Save your letter my dear, and show it to Geneva one other day, when she knows you better."

CHAPTER 19

As rehearsals got under way, Tony's sexual attraction to Geneva created a diversion which he'd failed to anticipate as he composed the dance, when Evil was a mere stick figure in his notebook rather than real flesh and bones. There were times when he could hardly concentrate. For instance, during one acrobatic stunt, in which they both reached for the imaginary hat—they had deferred using a real one—and wound up hooked together when Geneva's arm slipped through his suspender, his sense of the dance dissolved in the warm press of her buoyant breasts against his chest, and her mouth coming within an inch of his. And when Evil mounted his back in order to reach higher than he and, straining to catch the descending hat brim, her legs locked round his neck, sent him turning helplessly round the stage, struggling to free himself and retrieve the hat, it wasn't the hat he wanted to capture in his embrace but Geneva. Worst of all—or, so at times it seemed, best of all—each acrobatic stunt which linked the madcap chase had to be practiced over and over. Rehearsals ran long past the hour of ten, when Myra Brinkerhoff closed the piano lid. As soon as she walked out the door, Tony felt awkward being alone with Geneva. *"She hardly knows you,"* his mother had warned him. He'd better take it easy.

Geneva's magnetism for Tony did not live in her body only. Her growing absorption in the dance drew him likewise, plus her dedication to live up to her bargain no matter how long the hours, how hard the work. And her patience. Sometimes he spent three quarters of an hour figuring out why a certain series of steps refused to work according to plan. Geneva never failed to keep her eye on what he was about, and often made helpful suggestions. Sometimes 16 musical bars' worth of steps had to be painstakingly broken down by half measures. They'd do a step, then stop; he'd concentrate, she'd wait; then another step, and so on. She never so much as shrugged her shoulders or frowned. Now he knew with certainty there was at least one redeeming feature of the debacle in the Brookhurst wood. But for it, he would not be dancing with Geneva Sterling.

He would have asked her out long before an advertisement for the *Majestic* caught his eye that Sunday in early December, except that he feared she would refuse him because he was already taking so much of her time. The *Dance of the Red Hat* had displaced not only her Tuesday night ballet, but her Thursday night as well, plus Saturday mornings. And they were seriously considering the idea of discontinuing classes at Rice for the spring term, to free up their daytime hours. This plan did not please her trust officer, who apparently still had the outdated notion that vaudeville shows were lewd and vulgar, and not suitable entertainment for decent people.

Then the *Majestic* notice: Lead dancers from the ballet corps of the Grand Opera House in Milan, Italy, were the week's headliners. He'd never seen this ballet troupe, but one could always count on Karl Hoblitzelle's Houston *Majestic* for first-rate entertainment.

The following Tuesday, with a certain thickness in his chest, Tony invited Geneva to be his guest for the Saturday evening performance. They had just finished rehearsing, and were both toweling off their sweat. She wore a pair of snug knee shorts, specially made for her by Linsky's dance costumier, and a jersey top. Her hair was wringing wet, and a fringe of curly red bangs were plastered against her forehead. She looked quite fetching.

Perhaps Geneva was more surprised than reluctant, but as she did not immediately reply, he stammered, "It's—it's always helpful to see other dancers perform, and so naturally I thought—"

"Oh, absolutely!"

He exhaled a breath and his face broke into a grin. At such times as these, he did not mind being transparent. It came to him that one day he would be popping the question to this girl, and he wondered if he would still be so awestruck by her that he would stammer.

"Splendid! And of course, as you know, one wears formal attire. So, can you let me know within the next day or two, the color of your dress?"

"Why, yes," she said, and suddenly she looked exceedingly pleased.

All of which convinced him his timing was perfect.

On Thursday evening as he arrived at the studio, he chanced to meet Geneva coming out of the Adele Gregory Fashion Shop on the ground floor, its show windows occupied by empty-eyed female mannequins, wearing garments suitable to the war-time mood and privations: monochromatic tailored suits made of wool, serge, and broadcloth, with long lapels and belted waists; hats with high rounded crowns and gently rolled brims. He took Geneva's detour as a flattering sign that the coming Saturday was important to her.

As they climbed the steep stairs to the studio, she complained, "I've looked all over Houston, and everything on the racks is patriotically drab."

"Quite," he said.

"I'm not spending any money on clothes like that; I might as well wear my uniform Saturday night."

"Ah, yes...." said Tony, hoping she wasn't serious.

When they reached Linsky's door at the top of the stairs, she turned to him. "I'm afraid the best I can do is a dress from last year—I wore it to a reception for Rice coeds who had been accepted for the fall," she told him. She started to add that it was the first new dress she'd purchased since Victor left, but stopped herself just in time, her face reddening: how quickly a slip of the tongue could ruin everything. "It—it's nothing fancy...just plain green...."

How beautiful her eyes were, Tony thought, caught in the glint of the small light above Linsky's door. "I daresay, green will never be plain when you wear it," he observed.

Geneva blushed. So this was what it was like to be courted by an earnest young man, she thought with a thrill. She felt young and hopeful for the first time since the storm. And she had a feeling it was only a taste of more to come. Her involvement with Victor had cost her this simple form of pleasure for a very long time, and could well have deprived her forever.

When Geneva opened the door to Tony two evenings later, his eyes widened admiringly at the figure standing before him in jade green satin with long fitted sleeves on her slender arms, and a valley of lace down the front. She wore her hair in a knot, with a rolled band round her forehead, matching her dress. He paid her the compliment she no doubt expected, and then after a long moment during which she looked at him quizzically, he remembered to hand her the box containing the bouquet of roses.

They were standing before the hall mirror when he draped her soft woolen shawl about her shoulders, and the reflection of their faces together in the warm glow of light reminded him fondly of the first night they danced together. His heart was reeling. Geneva would have been worth twice the wait.

Tony had purchased the best tickets available—second row, center, the mezzanine—and they followed the crowd past gilt-encrusted mirrors and up the broad marble lobby stairs, then took their seats under a vast sculpted ceiling as ornate as a wedding cake. Tony had read that Karl Hoblitzelle spent a quarter of a million dollars building this monument to show business. Suddenly he was saying to Geneva, "I believe one day I should like to own a theatre."

As Geneva smiled at him admiringly, he wondered where he got such an extraordinary idea as that, and why he dared to say it out loud. Being with Geneva was doing things to him, making him feel alive again, making him look far into the future as he once had done, making him hope.

Driving home, Tony knew that he was going to kiss Geneva, for she had given him many encouraging signals as the evening wore on: the several times she sniffed her flowers, closing her eyes with pleasure; those times during the show when her eyelids dropped, then opened slowly on his profile next to hers; the special smiles and silent looks they exchanged between acts; all of which meant that neither of them was giving the show the attention it deserved.

Tony's shiny black Packard cruised smoothly down city streets, plunging around corners and stopping on a dime. Quite a difference—thought Geneva—from Victor's homely motorcar, which had to be hand cranked, then groaned and sputtered as he aimed it toward its destination. Odd to realize that whereas for a time she had wished to hide herself from view, tonight she was proud to be seen stepping out with Tony Selby, having people along the aisles of the *Majestic* stare admiringly at the handsome couple, sitting beside him in his fancy automobile. Victor would never have provided her with an evening like this. She would have spent her nights at home, cooking and helping his children with their lessons, while he traveled around making a living, she thought smugly. Then she remembered that was exactly his reason for leaving her behind, and she felt contrite for a few moments, until she remembered the storm.

They crossed to the 400 block of Heights Boulevard, just eight blocks from her house. Geneva wished the evening would not be over so soon. Should she invite Tony inside, offer him a cup of tea? Chocolate? She felt nervous suddenly. Would he kiss her when they arrived at her door? "You drive awfully fast, Tony," she observed breathlessly.

Indeed, by American driving customs, Geneva was correct. His mother was always after him to slow down. Yet behind her comment he sensed a shyness about what was coming, and this evoked feelings so tender that he slowed down just a bit. "Have you got a sweetheart?" he asked, certain of her answer.

She did not look at him as her lips parted. "No," she said, softly, "you?"

"No." They exchanged a smile. This was going to be the greatest night of his entire life, Tony thought. *He's going to kiss me*, thought Geneva, and swallowed down a dry place in her throat. She wondered if he could hear the swift beating of her heart.

They arrived a 1207 Heights Boulevard.

As they began the stroll from the car up to the porch, Geneva felt Tony's arm curl around her waist. She smiled up at him. When they stopped outside the door, Tony drew her near and lay his hand upon her cheek. They looked wonderingly into each other's eyes until that moment of the miracle of their lips coming together.

Then suddenly Geneva's hands were pushing against Tony's chest. Her eyes were wide with alarm. "No, please," she begged, "I have to go." Her trembling fingers struggled to open the door, then closed it swiftly behind her. Tony stood staring at the door, too shocked to even begin to analyze what had come over her.

He turned and walked to the Packard, feeling crushed as never before. He thought of the *Dance of the Red Hat*. Its magic was gone. He was uncertain he could even continue with it.

Tony was just stepping off the curb when Geneva recovered her wits and opened the door. She called his name, then watched him turn slowly to look: a lone silhouette from which an oval of pleated white dress shirt stood out as an indelible emblem of her rejection.

"I had a wonderful time," she said, knowing even as she uttered the words that her desperate attempt to smooth over her irrational behavior would have been better left undone; it only cheapened her. She was deserving of Tony's failure to answer, or even tip his hat before stepping inside the Packard. The head lamps flashed on; the engine roared like a reproachful voice, and he sped off into the night.

Geneva dragged herself upstairs to bed, her fingers still wrapped around the nosegay of tiny white roses with satin ribbons: the first flowers she had received since her father presented her with a bouquet for the Father and Daughter Banquet, just months before his death. Only a few hours ago, she had secretly vowed to keep Tony's flowers forever. But how could she now? She laid them on the table beside her bed and sank down on the pillows, not even bothering to change out of her dress.

She remembered Madame Linsky's suspicion that she was afraid to trust another man, after Victor Calais. Until she pushed Tony away tonight, her stomach sick and her brow clammy, she had not believed her teacher could be right. Yet, what other explanation could there be for the fact at the very moment when Tony's lips approached hers, Victor's hand reached out and closed the studio curtain?

CHAPTER 20

Working, working, working. It seemed to Geneva that Tony drove them as never before, as if the *Dance of the Red Hat* were a weapon with which to punish her, as if he just wanted to bring it equal to his idea of perfection, then take it on the vaudeville stage and be done with it. Perhaps he never intended to see her again, after that. His impatience with her errors multiplied them. In the early part of January they began working with a real hat, and she quickly developed a problem with wrist control, tending to toss the hat in a curve to the right. Uncorrected, this meant certain death to the dance. Hard as she tried to avoid the unfortunate curve, it happened over and over and over again, and each time the hat came down yards from its intended destination, all her blood drained down along with it. On one such occasion, Tony observed with humorless irony, his hands on his hips, "That would be roughly the third row of the parquet circle." By now she had dropped out of Rice—as had Tony—and persuaded Ida to sign a release for her to go on the stage, both moves strongly opposed by John Scarborough. Having put so much on the line, she must somehow succeed. She came to dread rehearsals, which always left her twice as exhausted as they used to, because she knew she was failing. She felt indentured to Tony and his dance.

They never spoke of what happened that night after the *Majestic*. Every time she thought Tony was about to broach the subject, she froze inside. How she wished she could reverse her mistake, but what could she say, without making it worse? *I just can't imagine what came over me!* would not do, when she most certainly could; only that was none of Tony's business.

On January 11th, 1918, the city awoke to one of the coldest days in its history—14 degrees Fahrenheit—and, for the first time in Geneva's life, the ground she lived on was covered with a mantle of snow. She barely had time to peer out her bedroom window at the snow-covered rooftops when the telephone rang and she hurried downstairs to answer.

"Geneva? Tony here," he began, his voice punctuated by static on the line. "I've checked with Madame Linsky and she's closing shop for the day, owing to the weather. We'll have the studio all day. I shall stop by for you round nine if it's alright."

She didn't like the way he had reset the schedule for the day—usually their work started at five on Friday evening. She would like to have stayed home today, curled up in a chair by the fire. Still, how could she refuse Tony, when she obviously needed practice? It was a little past seven now. "I'll be waiting," she said.

Geneva was determined to enjoy what little free time she possessed. She treated herself to a bracing breakfast of hot oatmeal sweetened with honey, and topped with a dab of butter that was the last of the week's supply. Like sugar and many other desirable foods, butter was now rationed. Then she quickly wrapped up in her heaviest coat, coiled a wool scarf around her neck, put on her thickest woolen gloves and cap, and pulled on a pair of boots that reached nearly to her knees. She stepped out on the front porch. Up above, icicles hung from the eaves from one end to the other, like a string of crystal beads. She walked as far as the front steps. The icy air made her nose and cheekbones ache. The snow had silenced the morning and made it so still, it was as though this place and everyone in it were not real but a representation, the work of a fine painter. On the broad canvas there were no streets in any direction to separate one row of houses from another. Snow lined the stark limbs of trees and fence rails, and laid like dollops of ice cream on shrubs and wood piles and parked vehicles. Geneva's spirits were light, as if she'd left the burden of her troubles behind when she entered the painting. Then suddenly she remembered Victor's unfulfilled desire to be a painter. She forced the intrusion from her thoughts.

Across the street at the Crawford house, snow powdered the imbricated shingles of the pitched roof, slipped down from the high point of its turret, and lodged in all the angles where its many gables jutted out. Over by their fulsome magnolia tree, its deep green leaves adorned with snow blossoms, Mr. Crawford and young Joseph were building a snowman, their movements laboring to a creep inside thick wool cocoons. Imagine, a snowman! She was aching to join the fun, aching to be a part of that happy family who lived across the street, instead of being the ward of a jaded guardian whose one preoccupation was the harsh injustices of life. Not that they didn't get along, since they had things out: *"Tell me the truth, Ida: would you have refused me help if I hadn't told you who the father was?"* Ida's eyebrows, two sharp peaks of insult. *"A fine thing for you to ask—"* *"But would you?"* *"Of course not. But you should have had enough sense to put yourself in the care of a capable doctor. What if I could not have saved you? In the middle of a storm, the telephone lines dead?"*

Still, Ida wasn't much fun, that was all there was to it. Just as well she was far away in Washington today, among the hundreds of suffragettes hovering like woolen shawls over the Congress as the Susan B. Anthony Bill came to a vote.

After a few minutes Geneva trudged across the street to admire the Crawford snowman. Joseph was a chubby little fellow, and with the thick wrapping of wool added to his figure, she wondered he could bend over to scoop up the snow. He let her lift him up to put the hat on the snowman—an old brown felt Alpine hat with a faded green feather. When the hat was on, Geneva and Mr. Crawford cheered for the finished snowman. Lowering Joseph to the ground, she wondered sadly, as she had many times, if her child had been a boy, or a girl. She was determined to have other children someday. A houseful. All as rosy and cheerful as Joseph.

By the time Geneva spotted Tony's Packard cruising up the street, she had gone into the house several times to warm up her hands and face; yet always she was drawn out again, fascinated by the snow. Once they finished practicing and returned home tonight, it would be too dark outside to appreciate it, and tomorrow it may no longer be there. The Packard moved so quietly it seemed to glide up to the curb on skates. Tony killed the engine, got out and stepped up to the walk without a word. His face was drawn. He looked exceedingly fatigued. So why didn't he just stay home and leave her alone? One day would not have mattered. He was just trying to prove a point.

"It's my first snow," she said reprovingly.

He glanced at her with mild surprise, as if he had hardly noticed the snow. "I suppose we could knock off early, if you really want to," he said indifferently.

"No, of course not," she said. "I'll just go inside and get my handbag."

Moments later as Geneva descended the icy stairs, her feet nearly went out from under her. She braced herself on the porch rail. Respecting the very real treachery of this weather for the first time, she took careful steps up the icy walk. Tony was looking out over the street—lost in thought?—his arms folded over his chest, his back turned: the perfect target. Overcome with wickedness, she laid her handbag aside, quickly scooped up some snow and formed a ball. Just as she hurled it at him, he turned. The snowball smacked him right in the face. "Whoops!" she cried, and then she began to laugh—he was the most comical sight she had seen in a very long time; probably all the more so because of his disagreeableness.

Brushing the snow off his face and shoulders, Tony looked angry enough to take a swing at her. But suddenly his expression cleared, and a diabolical smile crossed his lips. Her heart sped. She was making for a hedge under the eave of the porch as fast as her snowbound feet could carry her, when his first snowball hit her back with the force of a rock. "Ouch!" she cried, and as she dived behind the hedge, another slammed her. "Hey, give me a chance!" she yelled.

"Why should I?" he asked, smugly. "This will teach you to pick a snowball fight with a Cornishman! Where I'm from they have *real* snow, with drifts as high as the rooftops."

Geneva thought of all kinds of retorts to his insolent statement, the most biting one being to ask why he didn't just go back home again, if he liked it so much. Yet she sensed that might be a sore subject. His letter pledging he would not go back to join up was terse and direct, and didn't leave room for discussion. She didn't want to start a real fight today. She just wanted to have fun. She was busily squashing snow between her frozen hands, but there wasn't much of it under the hedge, and all the while, snowballs were crashing all around her as though shot from a cannon.

A meager snowball in hand, she stepped out a little and peered around the hedge. Tony was not there. Then she heard a squish-squish-squish, and realized he was relocating. But where? "Hey, show me where you are, coward!" she cried, and a snowball whacked her forehead. Smack! Another hit her shoulder. *Where is he?* Then she saw a snowball hurling toward her from behind the Packard. Just in time, she ducked. Taking advantage of his pause to gather ammunition, she headed for the broad knobby trunk of an oak tree near the curb, and hid behind it. She had to be careful not to trip. Its huge roots stuck up from the ground like arthritic fingers, no less treacherous for today's layer of snow. Bewildered by Tony's continued inactivity, she gathered snow furiously, then hurled one snowball after another toward the Packard, thinking she was getting pretty good at this, too bad she could not do as well with the hat. Whop! Whop! Whop! No response.

Then as she positioned her hand behind her shoulder, to hurl still another, a larger hand grabbed her wrist; a strong arm shut around her waist like a trap door. "Let me go!" she demanded, squirming. To no avail. Tony was laughing with glee. "I win!" he cried, triumphantly.

"By whose rules?" she challenged, laughing.

"Mine," he chortled, and then he turned her to face him. His smile vanished and his eyes leveled on hers. Before Victor could intervene, before she could even get her breath, her chin was between two fingers of Tony's gloved hand and she was eagerly accepting the warm invitation of his lips on hers. Immediately after he released her, her sense of relief that she had responded to him was profound. She was alright. Everything between them would be alright now. And she was also pleasantly aware that their kiss had been different from others in her experience: it lacked the guilt that accompanied every kiss in Victor's studio, the constant fear that the door might spring open, exposing their sin to the world. The press of Tony's lips on hers was as pristine as the snow surrounding them.

In the car, he pulled his English "rug" over her lap. Who needed it? She thought. She felt warm all over right now.

Tony sat behind the wheel staring ahead. She had struggled in his arms and he had held her still and kissed her. "I should not have done that," he said dolorously.

Let's do it again! She wanted to say, but propriety allowed only the quiet admission, "It's alright." *I didn't mind* would have been just as proper and much more encouraging, she argued belatedly in her head.

They were saved further discourse along the slick roads leading to the studio, for concentration was required to avoid collision with vehicles operated by people unaccustomed to such conditions, some of these hauling sleds behind—or rather, large cheese boxes converted into sleds—with young children for passengers.

Finally they reached Main Street and found it practically deserted. Very few vehicles were in sight, and no pedestrians at all. No patriotic flags snapping in the wind today; no one willing to hoist them. A lone streetcar glided down the center as if on skates. The Sweeney, Coombs, and Fredericks Building had snow sprinkled over its fancy cone-shaped tower. Snow whitened the awnings on the upper windows of Foley Bros. dry goods store, and lined the rail on the third floor balcony of the Binz Building. Her father's office had been located high up on the sixth floor of the Binz Building, and there she had first ridden in an elevator. She would never forget clutching her father's hand as she felt the disconcerting rise of the floor beneath her feet. Up and down the street today, everything was cloaked in white and clutched in stillness.

Now Tony was parking diagonally in front of the studio building. He switched off the engine and looked at her. "Just say the word, and I promise I shall never bother you again. God knows, you have given me every signal that you don't wish me to."

Geneva shook her head. "I just wasn't ready that night after we went to the *Majestic*, and I didn't know it until—until too late," she said. "And today—well, frankly, you did surprise me," she told him. She almost pointed out that he was in an even worse mood than usual this morning, but restrained herself. "You seemed kind of troubled when you arrived, preoccupied." That was the truth.

Tony did not entirely believe her explanation about that night she rejected him. Still, he put it aside for now. Miserably he said, "Last night I received word that someone I knew in England—a soldier—was killed in the last battle of Ypres."

Oh, why had she not guessed? She touched his arm consolingly. "I'm so sorry. A close friend?"

The presumption gave Tony a moment of pause. So absorbed was he in the shambles of his life that he felt quite disconnected from what people in normal situations were experiencing as the war dragged on—the loss of lovers, husbands, sons, and—yes—close friends. He overlooked the fact that his loss, that of one of the most despicable people he knew, and yet by far the most necessary to his rescue, was singular; no one would suspect the peculiar nature of his heartache. His eyes grew moist. "I—he was of some importance. To me and my family."

Geneva's eyes were so laden with sympathy and concern just then, Tony came very near confiding in her the whole story of Brian Potts. But just minutes ago he forced a kiss on her, and the kiss trapped him—far more so than her. He remembered how his mother turned pale, reading the details of his letter intended for Geneva. *"She may even think you're lying—"* What if, in the course of his story, Geneva thought: if Tony overpowers me now, what might he do in the future? Perhaps he really did force himself on Jane in the wood.

Finally, Tony turned from her and exhaled a frosty breath. "As you may have guessed, something rather unfortunate happened before I left England."

For a moment Geneva considered his wording...*something rather unfortunate.* It sounded ominous. Did he mean he left England in some kind of trouble? But she sensed—or perhaps was eager to believe—that if so, it was not of his making. "Something to do with the soldier who was killed?" she asked.

He drew in a breath. "Yes, but I shan't talk about that right now. The thing is, I find it difficult to trust people anymore." He looked at her now, his eyes haunted. "Geneva, if I ask you a question, will you promise to tell me the truth?"

She nodded uneasily.

"In the months we worked together, up until that night at the *Majestic,* I had come to believe that wherever you were, it was safe there…" he admitted, then with a frown, he added, "…that you wouldn't suddenly change, and become someone I didn't know. Then, that night, you seemed to have changed a great deal. It's alright if it was just a matter of not being ready when I kissed you—I apologize for rushing you. But I sensed it was something more. You seemed almost panicked. And I'd just like to know, is there someone else, Geneva?"

Jane paced up and down before her tall bedroom windows at Fairleigh, smoking one cigarette after another. God, how she hated the snow! How it sneaked down during the night, thick and heavy, covering everything…possessing it; bringing cold silent suffocation. And the bare trees, standing so still; their limbs like fingers waiting to seize her.

With angry stabbing jolts, she tamped out her cigarette in the porcelain tray that once belonged to her mother and now sat on the table beside Jane's canopied bed. She walked to her chest of drawers and opened the top drawer, at the back of which she had placed the packet of small envelopes. As she thrust her hand past the cambric handkerchiefs and stockings, her heart skipped a hasty beat—a fact which in the next moment infuriated her. There it was, however, safely hidden beneath the pair of fawn kid skin gloves with embroidered cuffs, from Paris. She withdrew the packet and stared at it.

The last of the threats from Brian Potts had been sealed and ready to post when he was blown to bits. His commanding officer, poor fool, sent her the sealed envelope with a note of sympathy. She'd saved all the threats, realizing that if Potts were ever forced to tell the truth, they might be turned to her advantage, proving to Tony the extent of her fear of Father, and gaining his sympathy. But now, with Potts dead, Tony would never come back again.

What to do? Burn the threats, or keep them? If Father discovered them, she would have hell to pay. Yet, how could she destroy them, when they may be her only lifeline to Tony?

She slipped the packet back into place and closed the drawer.

CHAPTER 21

As Tony and Geneva went through their steps on that snowy day in Linsky's studio, Tony humming the Joplin tune as their accompaniment, what had just taken place was never far from Geneva's mind. Knowing that Tony had secrets to keep made her feel less guilty that she could not be completely open with him about her past. When he'd asked if there was someone else, she had thought of the warmth of his lips on hers and her body pressed against his. She told him in all honesty, "No, Tony, there's no one else." She felt relaxed and confident now. To her relief and, obviously, Tony's, her wrist control was improving.

On the last Saturday in February, after their first time of rehearsing the dance all the way through, Geneva was amazed to hear applause coming from a corner of the room. Linsky was never here on Saturday. She turned to look. A woman of striking appearance sat on Linsky's high stool. She wore an exquisite pearl gray frock with black piping on the hem and lapels of the long double-breasted jacket, the overall tailored look relieved by a lacy jabot at her throat. Her hair was swept up under the domed crown of a black hat with a sloping brim. On her feet were a pair of high-heeled pearl gray walking shoes. From behind Geneva's shoulder Tony said, "It's time you met my mother."

Soon Cynthia was taking Geneva's hands in hers. "Do call me Cynthia, my dear," she said warmly, a charming hint of Texas drawl lingering in her voice in spite of her many travels and her years of residence abroad. "I must say, from what I've seen so far, Tony was right in refusing to settle for another partner." With a sanguine glance at Tony, she added, "I'm sure my son has told you, you have to be the best. I don't book my clients in eight-a-day houses. The competition is fierce."

Geneva was grateful Tony had not introduced his mother before she observed the dance. Miss Fournier—no, Cynthia—was very intimidating. And obviously her approval was conditional. *"From what I've seen so far...."* Abruptly Geneva realized Tony was smiling, clasping her hand.

"Now I must get to work, and let you two continue," Cynthia said crisply. Watching her sweep grandly out the auditorium door, Geneva felt the helpless sensation of being swept up in her orbit. She and Tony were a professional team now. They had a manager. They were headed into a very serious business, and obviously Cynthia intended that they start at the top.

On Monday evening Tony reported to Geneva that his mother had spoken by telephone with Celia Bloom, Karl Hoblitzelle's booker in New York City. Mr. Hoblitzelle's Houston *Majestic* was but one of his chain of Interstate Theatres, forming the southern link of the Keith-Orpheum circuit. Since the U.S. entered the war, he had been serving as Field Service Director of the Red Cross, while retaining close oversight of his business operations. He agreed to see *Dance of the Red Hat* the next time he stopped in Houston, around two weeks from now. *I'm not ready,* Geneva despaired. But she would have to be.

Three nights later, as the couple finished a grueling rehearsal at 11 o'clock, Geneva was surprised to see Cynthia breeze in, looking as fresh as if she had just stepped out of a tub of bath salts. "I've just received confirmation that Gaspard-Spritz in Providence, Rhode Island will decorate your hat," she reported with an obvious sense of triumph. She explained that Gaspard-Spritz was one of the few renowned jewelry makers that had not converted to manufacturing munitions for the war.

Cynthia did not linger. Before she left she placed a small box inside the palm of Geneva's hand and looked into her perspiring face with twinkling blue-violet eyes. "I see that Tony's wearing you out, Darling," she said. "But it will be worth it, once you're out on stage...it's nothing short of a love affair between you and the audience!"

As Geneva opened the box, she felt annoyed that Cynthia thought Tony was a harder worker than she was, but for the moment she kept silent. Inside the box was a tiny golden guardian angel pin, nestled in a cloud of velvet. The gift seemed to suggest that she knew her son liked Geneva a lot, and was hoping she would not let them down so the romance might continue. Geneva thanked Cynthia, but assured her that she was used to hard work as a ballet student.

With a lift of her brow, Cynthia darted her eyes at Tony, then bid them both goodnight.

When Cynthia was gone, Geneva turned to Tony. "I hope I didn't offend your mother. I really did appreciate the pin, but—"

Tony threw back his head in laughter. "I daresay you are a worthy match for Mother any day."

At seven o'clock on a frigid Friday morning, Geneva stood on the dancer's dream of a smooth maple wood apron at the foremost section of the *Majestic* stage. Her costume was a feminine rendition of Tony's: a white jersey, brushed with soot, a pair of faded black trousers cut to mid-thigh length, and black fishnet hose. Heavy stage make-up covered her face and neck, and her hair was plastered to her head and concealed under a beat-up billed cap. While Tony explained Myra's truncated arrangement of *The Magnetic Rag* to the pianist, Geneva shivered with cold—naturally the hall was not heated for auditions—and noted their props were all in place. At center stage was a set of low two-sided stairs—their makeshift chimney—with a ragged broom propped against it. A bouquet of fake flowers that Evil would offer Good in retribution waited behind the curtain mask, occasioned by the fact that a few days ago Tony decided to write a deadpan coda to the dance. That coda was not yet fully integrated in Geneva's mind, and she hoped she wouldn't blank out and forget about it this morning. Last and most important: sitting inert near the footlights was their practice bowler, by now so tattered and worn that no one would consider it worth fighting over. A pity they had not at least covered it with red satin, she thought suddenly.

Driving here, Tony had asked her, "Are you nervous?"

"Just a little," she replied, forcing a smile through the heavy coating of grease paint and lip wax. She reached up to touch her guardian angel, pinned to the inside of her jersey. She had vowed to wear it every time she went on stage.

"So am I. It's perfectly normal," he said. That was reassuring, yet over the past few evenings of protracted rehearsals, followed by sleepless nights, and enough black coffee this morning to make her head feel as high as the hat they would soon be tossing, Geneva had grown increasingly anxious about her lack of professional stage experience. If she failed today, Cynthia would very likely insist that Tony find another partner—

As if on cue, Tony squeezed her hand and brought it to his lips, smiling across at her. She smiled back. They felt easy with each other now, and often found themselves clasping hands. Their evenings together ended with a parting kiss. She was grateful Tony was sensitive enough not to rush her beyond that.

Now she gazed out over the auditorium, with its cantilevered balconies and ceiling fans, and long carpeted aisles. Today it seemed twice as huge as on that night when she sat in the audience with Tony; and, with the house lights up, the atmosphere was as harsh and unromantic as the conclusion of that evening.

When Tony was ready he came to stand beside her and clasp her hand, which only increased her anxiety because there was nothing separating her from potential disaster except the arrival of Cynthia with Mr. Hoblitzelle and his house manager. Within seconds, Cynthia appeared at the head of one aisle and swept down, a commanding vision in a slender royal purple suit and matching tri-cornered hat. Several times since meeting Cynthia, Geneva had tried to imagine growing up with such a formidable mother. Tony said she much preferred life in London, where she and his father met and where they lived in the early years of their marriage. She grew disenchanted in Cornwall, "with lawn parties and boring guests for tea." Cynthia's impatience with country life did not seem surprising now that they were acquainted. Geneva wondered: Did Cynthia hold her children to her breast and sing them lullabies? Surely not.

Now the two men followed Cynthia down the aisle. The younger-looking man, with slicked-down hair and wearing a neat double-breasted suit, carried a rolled-up drawing: Tony's rooftop scenic design, over which he had toiled between rehearsals. The design was as detailed as an architectural drawing of a grand building. In a way Tony was lucky for his detour into the study of engineering. Few dancers could design their own stage sets, let alone with the specifications necessary for a scenic company to build them.

Soon the three sat down. There was some low talk, and a ripple of laughter from Cynthia, which made her seem in league with them. Then a male voice said briskly, "Alright, let's see it.—Burt!" The foot lights beamed up.

As Tony crouched behind the double stairs and Geneva stepped behind the curtain to await her cue, every possibility of a way she might fail raced through her mind. The intro was played. Tony began his brief solo, in which his benign facial expressions and happy, leaping steps combined to cue the audience as to his character. Then it was time for Geneva's entrance. She took a deep breath, then assumed the devious countenance of Evil. Her face felt like hardened wax.

The first time she tossed the hat, it went high up toward that phalanx of pulleys and scaffolding that reach into oblivion above a theatre stage, its dark color blending into its surroundings. During the one or two seconds—they seemed an eternity—when she could not spot it, her heart began beating so hard and fast, it would not have surprised her to see it explode in the air like a firecracker, and rain down around her shoulders. If only they'd covered the hat in red satin! But now it reappeared—*Got it!* One down. She did quick breathless pirouettes across the stage, the words *Charles F. Thompson Scenic Company* stenciled on a huge crate at the back, going by in a blur, Tony at her heels. From that moment forward, she counted backwards the number of times her hands must come in contact with the hat brim to save it from sinking prematurely to the floor and taking their dance with it. Twenty-two, twenty-one, twenty.... On ten, she was reaching up from her position on Tony's back. Her perspiring knee slipped a couple of inches down his spinal cord, throwing off the position of her hand by the same distance. All the while, the hat was speeding toward her. She knew that she was going to miss, and there was never a moment when she more appreciated the genius of Tony's spellbinding dance, more grieved its ruination. Then, with no more than the first joint of her index finger, she seized it, and managed a firmer grip. She was so amazed that for a moment her mind went blank. Thankfully, by now the dance was so thoroughly ingrained in her consciousness, her feet remembered where to go.

Near the end when she fled the stage, the hat finally lost to both chimney sweeps, she was so relieved there were no more tosses that, while she remembered to come back for the coda, she left the fake flowers behind. She had to double back. But this took no more than two beats, and then she was humbly offering them. Soon Tony was pressing her down, flat on her back, closing her hands around the rejected flowers. She raised her shoulders. Looked balefully toward the audience through thick black mascara now mixed with sweat, and making rivers through her grease paint. Good knelt down and moved Evil's billed cap from her head, to cover her face; stood straight and brushed his hands in finality. Then he stepped over Evil's slain body and left the stage. The End. All was silent as he returned, and helped her up for a bow.

Even the breath-stopping suspense of waiting to catch the hat was not to compare with the suspense of waiting to hear a verdict from the judge and jury in the auditorium. Then: the ring of applause, and someone cried, "Bravo!" All she could tell through the pounding in her ears was that it was a male voice. She looked at Tony. He was grinning, his chest heaving from exertion. She was never so proud of anyone in her life. The footlights blinked off.

Now the two men were enthusiastically shaking the dancers' hands. Up close, the younger man looked no more than a boy wearing a suit with padded shoulders and eye glasses. "Karl Hoblitzelle, pleased to meet you," he said, then introduced the curly-headed, affable-looking house manager, Mr. Bremer. "I think we can work something out, don't you, Eddie?"

As the others talked jovially of the cities that would be along their tour, Geneva thought with wonder: the worst part was over! They were actually going on the stage! There would be performance after performance in theatre after theatre. Nothing would stop them now. After so much heartache, she was at last glimpsing a future that burned so brightly, she could scarcely peer into its many glistening facets. Yet, inevitably she thought of the bright lights flooding her naked body in Victor's studio. She glanced at the convivial face of Cynthia as she talked easily with her colleagues, and all she could see was the frozen expression that would overtake her lovely face if she knew of those photographs. Would Cynthia risk managing her son and his partner if she knew there was the possibility Geneva would one day be a profound embarrassment? And what would Tony say, if he knew? *They must never know,* she vowed.

She must be sure that a letter awaited Victor as soon as he returned from the war. She was sure that Ida would know the address of his relatives in Massachusetts, though she must not let on to Ida the reason she was writing him. Yet, what if he went from Europe to someplace else, rather than coming home? What if the likelihood of meeting with him to retrieve her photographs grew ever more remote? She must get word to him now. But how would a letter reach him when he was moving around all the time? And for that matter, if it did, how would his reply reach her, when she was about to embark on weeks and weeks of travel? Ida may get nosy and open it. It was the last thing she wanted.

Geneva felt utterly dejected now. She would have to delay writing Victor until a time when she would be home for an extended period. She found herself wishing the most terrible thing: that the war would not be over sooner than that.

CHAPTER 22

Ida Ruekauer stepped up and dropped her 5-cent token in the box, then took a seat near the back of the crowded streetcar between a woman holding a sleeping girl-child with an enormous pink hair bow, and a young man wearing knickers and a jersey with the letter H emblazoned on the front. It was awfully hot for the end of April, and Ida was sweltering in her tight corset, dark gray suit and high shirt collar. But she had learned long ago, if you wanted to stare eyeball to eyeball with a man, you had to look like you meant business. And she intended to do just that with John Scarborough.

Naturally, the annual statements from Geneva's trust account were forwarded to her, as guardian. And being married to August Ruekauer had taught her to pay careful attention to such things as balance sheets and financial statements. All the money she had accumulated in her 33 years—scrimped and saved from her earnings as a nurse—was gone after four years of marriage to a fool with a serious case of oil fever. A sweet-talking drummer from Shreveport, Louisiana, all he wanted was her money. She made the mistake of letting him invest it.

She had told Geneva all about what a fool she made of herself in a heart-to-heart talk after the storm; but to what end did she impart her wisdom? Had Geneva shown any curiosity about how her own money was being looked after? Had she sat down and taken note of the amount of interest being earned? Paid attention to the value of those railroad stocks, or oil and gas royalties accumulating from year to year? Not that they amounted to much. Still, it was the principle. When the most recent statement arrived from the bank, just after Ida returned from Washington in January, she looked over it, then gave it to Geneva.

After barely scanning it, she looked up at Ida with those innocent green eyes. "These things are always the same," she said. Then she left to rehearse with her dancing partner. And now they were touring the vaudeville circuits.

But were those statements always the same? Something about the last one kept nagging at Ida until she pulled it out and gave it a thorough looking over. It was a few minutes before she realized what was different: there should have been an item referred to as "miscellaneous asset—valued at $1." She was sure she had seen it on the previous statements.

Nonetheless, to double check her memory, she pulled out the earlier statements—what a mess, everything dumped in a box in the closet under the stairs; that's how Geneva kept her records. Eventually she found the statements from 1914, 1915 and 1916. Sure enough, that item appeared on every one, and now Ida realized something else: it was the only line item that was moved from one place to another on the page, a little closer to the bottom, each year that rolled around. Now, wasn't that interesting?

No matter what it was—maybe a piece of costume jewelry, or a folding fan, or a pair of opera glasses, or her father's favorite cuff links—it should have been there, even if it had nothing but sentimental value.

By the time the streetcar was heading down the middle of Main Street, Ida had reasoned she was probably wasting her time; there was bound to be some explanation. But at least she would get the satisfaction of showing that banker he'd better watch his step around her.

Inevitably—and not without some resentment—Ida began thinking of Geneva, living the glamourous life of a show girl, nothing in her head but the sound of applause, night after night. And obviously, there was plenty of money to be made, too. Look how Tony Selby and his mother lived—apartment at the Beaconsfield, the most fashionable residence in town; driving around in a shiny Packard automobile. Geneva would be smart to set her cap for her dancing partner. And from the look in her eyes when he picked her up to take her to the train station, she was thinking along the same lines. They'd wind up married before long—nothing to stop them; Geneva was 18 years old. The money from her parents' estate would come to her in a lump settlement on her wedding day.

Then, where will I be? Ida asked herself. Living in a small apartment, paying storage on her houseful of furniture; struggling to make ends meet, with no hope of putting anything away for the future. Some people got it all, while the Idas of the world stayed behind and cleaned up the messes they made. When Victor asked her to come to Houston and serve as Geneva's guardian, she had assumed the arrangement would last until Geneva came of age. It would have been worth her while then, having a nice place to live for five or six years, paying half the rent and sharing all the expenses. Ida knew she could get steady work in Houston as a nurse, and still have time to work for the Cause—not that any of her so-called "sisters" really appreciated her efforts; one day she'd grow tired of it and quit; let the others find out just how much she did.

Of course, she ought to have guessed Victor was up to something—what man isn't? And a beautiful girl like Geneva, right under his nose. Modeling, ha! She would have caught on a lot sooner if she'd paid attention to Geneva that weekend when she came to visit Victor. But all she could think of then was her money troubles. Ida hoped one day that Victor would come back so she could give him a piece of her mind. Of course, she would not inform him of Geneva's miscarriage; that was up to Geneva—Ida had given her word to keep it a secret, and she never went back on her word.

Meantime, here she was, looking out for Geneva's interests. As she stepped down on the pavement at the corner of Franklin and Main, and walked the short distance to Houston Bank & Trust, threading her way among businessmen in their suits and ties and straw boaters, and women flouncing by wearing hats and gloves and carrying shopping bags, it occurred to her that she might wind up getting some poor stenographer in trouble, for making a typographical error. She actually paused in her steps. She could just see John Scarborough making up those statements. (His handwriting was abominable; you could hardly read his signature.) He'd forget something, then squeeze it in where he found a place. Maybe change his mind; scratch through it; move it again. Then hand the whole mess to the poor girl who made a fraction of what he did. And for hours that girl would screw up her eyes, trying to read it. What if John Scarborough fired her over this? If he was like most men, he would blame his errors on someone else, as long as he could get by with it.

But on the other hand…. Ida decided to obey her first instinct.

She looked up at the imposing entrance of the bank, with its Corinthian columns and high, brass-framed doors, with the U.S. flag hanging above on a brass-knobbed rod. Like all the many buildings up and down Main Street, block after block, as far as the eye could see—the retail shops with their bright awnings, show windows and electric signs; the office buildings and hotels—the bank was a monument to the male species. Every position of authority was occupied by a male, who felt he was getting no more than he was entitled to.

She stepped inside and walked to the rear of the large lobby, with its vaulted ceiling and teller cages where customers waited in line, and so up the broad marble staircase, her heels clacking noisily.

She was soon sitting across from the banker behind his frosted door, opening her handbag, looking at him levelly. "I've come to see you about a discrepancy on Geneva's most recent annual statement—an item appears to be missing."

No response but a tic at the edge of his mouth; a slight narrowing of his eyes.

She lined up the statements before him. "Where's the 'miscellaneous asset' that appears before 1917? And for that matter, just *what* is it?"

Their eyes met and held for a long moment. Then he reached for his reading glasses, his face drained of what little color it had.

CHAPTER 23

The audition with Karl Hoblitzelle won *Sterling & Selby* a seven-week trial run, to begin at the Houston *Majestic* in April. They would be billed as an "Interstate Exclusive," though of course one must realize—as Tony certainly did—that the translation for this lofty term was that no one else on the circuit would bet on these two nobodies until they had proved themselves. Still, his mother managed to get them third place on the bill, when Tony would have been satisfied with any place at all their first time out, even closing the show.

In the interim they continued rehearsing, and he spent every spare moment making minor but time-consuming changes on his skyline scenic design, so that Charles F. Thompson could construct it in time for their opening night.

And now that performance was behind them, along with—God be thanked!—cheers and applause and two curtain calls. Tony's mind was clear for the first time since...well...since he set sail for America. Brian Potts was dead. And a terrible blow it was; still, at least Tony need no longer live in a state of limbo. Granted, he was likely to outlive William Tremont, at which time he would jolly well return to England, and Jane be damned. But William was a robust man in his 40's. One could not simply mark time for 20 or 30 years, waiting for William to die. No. The future was bright, starting here and now. And, he realized with no small thanks, there was more in his favor than ever there had been in England: Geneva was at his side.

The weeks traveled swiftly by—San Antonio, Oklahoma City, Wichita, Little Rock, Fort Worth. After the show closed on Saturday nights, there was time for a quick wash, then the troupe members quickly boarded the sleeper jump along with scenery crates and luggage, and headed for the next town. Though Geneva sat beside Tony on the train, he was lucky to kiss her cheek good-night before she fell asleep on his shoulder. He was always much too wound up to sleep, and besides, he carried the box containing the priceless red hat in his lap, not willing to stow it in a crate or even on the luggage rack above his head. The heavy crinoline hat was covered with bright red satin and glittering with enough paste diamonds to put the audience's eyes out. At the end of each impeccable performance, Tony was humbled by imagining the number of things that might go wrong in the next performance, or the next. Having any harm come to the red hat was certainly not going to be one of them.

Often, as he looked out upon the darkened landscape speeding by the train window, the pleasant floral scent of Geneva's perfume in his nostrils, he imagined fondly what it would be like to have her soft red hair resting on his shoulder in bed, her slender arm lying lazily on his chest. His dearest hope was that he would find out one day. Yet, while she had given him no reason to feel reluctant about any further advances, after that snowy day in January, neither had she encouraged him. Perhaps she expected him to make the moves. Well that was fine with him, yet sometimes of late—since they had left on tour—when he took her in his arms, he sensed a slight hesitation before her lips met his, which made him fear she was not falling in love with him, as he hoped.

On non-travel nights, a late supper followed the last evening performance. Geneva would sit patiently at his side in a smoke-filled diner, picking at the heavy war-time food—canned meat croquettes and mashed potatoes or rice, swimming in gravy—while he quizzed the other members of the troupe, his mother often joining in. Thankfully, theatricals loved nothing more than talking shop. And once he had got them past the gossip along the circuits of who got booked at the *Palace,* who broke an arm in Chicago, who got bumped in San Francisco, which act split up because they could not get along, and so forth, he might just learn something of their experience in houses where they had worked. Oh yes! Once voiced to Geneva, the dream of owning a theatre someday had grown steadily in Tony's mind and heart, and now that he knew he would be making a life in the States, the dream seemed to have taken on solid form.

There was nothing to prevent him. This he repeated to himself, over and over again.

From what he had learned so far, American theatres in general had clean dressing rooms of adequate size and decent stage floors. This was quite a change from Britain, where although even the provincial auditoriums were as posh as any in the States and some in London were obviously superior, backstage was often no more than a rabbit warren, poorly lit, with no dressing rooms for the rank and file performers. One must arrive in costume. Often stage floors were uneven, the wood planks craggy. Tony was determined that the performers who worked his theatre would regard it as the most desirable of all. No detail must be overlooked. He was hungry for any tidbit of knowledge.

One night in Fort Worth, he had an especially helpful interview with the husband and wife who led a five-member acrobatic team, *The Flying Rondolets,* which had only just joined the troupe, replacing an act that failed to go over. Geneva seemed to be listening with unusual absorption, and afterward Tony turned to her, his enthusiasm on the verge of spilling over: *How would you like to be married to a theatre-owner someday?*

Abruptly she rose from her chair. Her face quite piqued, she asked, "May we go, please?" Tony realized she must have been waiting for an opening.

As they left, Tony spotted his mother at a table at the other end of the diner, waving farewell. She and Geneva shared hotel rooms along the circuit. It had been one of the major selling points to persuade Mrs. Ruekauer to sign a release for Geneva to go on the stage, and it was awfully sporting of his mother, since she could afford to stay in a private room.

Soon they were walking along the boardwalk, their arms linked. Tony had an uneasy feeling that for some reason, tonight had been the culmination of whatever was troubling Geneva, and everything was getting ready to fall apart. "Something wrong?" he asked meekly.

It was a while before Geneva answered. Each time they finished a performance and stood before the audience, taking their bows with panting breaths, she was more in awe of Tony. The other acts on the bill—from comics to vocalists to jugglers and animal acts—could surely be replaced with similar entertainment anywhere along the circuits. But Tony's *Dance of the Red Hat* was nothing short of spectacular. The depth and diversity of his talents, more than anything else, would propel them into a long and fruitful career on the stage. And obviously Tony thrived on the life of a performer. From morning till night he seemed to be in a constant state of exhilaration—whistling a tune as he walked with springy steps; talking endlessly, and with great animation, about the business.

Unfortunately, Geneva had discovered she did not share his enthusiasm. Yes, she lived for those heart-racing times when they were out on the stage, giving their all in a performance; and there was nothing to equal the feeling of triumph when it was all over, and they were basking in cheers and applause. Cynthia had not exaggerated when she called it a 'love affair' with the audience. But this made up a very small percentage of any given day. Otherwise, life was abysmal. It wasn't so much the late night train journeys between bookings or the dreary hotels where they stopped—Tony had warned Geneva that life along the circuits was far from glamorous, that only the headliners could afford to go first-class. It was that they spent most of their time around show people, the majority of whom were not intriguing as Geneva had supposed, but, on the contrary, boring and small-minded. Her parents would have considered them 'common.' They thought of nothing but themselves, and as they felt constantly threatened by every other performer, they were always gossiping, and cutting one another down.

Yet this wasn't the worst part. Those who had children either left them far away in someone else's care, for weeks on end, or dragged them along from one city to another. Why should these people be given children, when they didn't even care about them? Was that part of God's will too? She wondered bitterly. But no. This, too, seemed random, like the death of her parents and the loss of her child in the storm. Tonight the wife of the couple Tony was interviewing—until long past midnight—held an exhausted baby on her lap. The poor child would doze off, be rudely awakened by someone's loud voice, whimper miserably as the mother shifted him around to quiet him down, then doze off again until the next interruption. *Give me that child and I'll take him to bed,* she wanted to scream. Did Tony condone this sort of thing?

At last she spoke up, "How do you feel about raising children?"

It was not at all what Tony expected to hear. Was she thinking about having *his* children? He wondered in amazement. If so, then she'd gone much further in her thinking about their relationship than he would have dared to imagine. He would have to sort this one out, and soon, but for now, since he'd given very little thought to the subject of children, his only resort was to answer Geneva in the context of his sister Nell's little boy. Nell had married Moreland West, the manager of Selby Mines, a few months after the war began; their son Gerry was born in 1916. Now that Morey was away at war, leaving her with time on her hands, she wrote many letters to Tony. Most were about the child. Tony had often spoken of them to Geneva. Innocently, he said, "Why, I suppose it must be fun, at least part of the time. I always enjoy hearing about little Gerry's latest antics."

"I mean—" Geneva persisted, her voice shrill, "—do you think it's right the way people in vaudeville treat their children?"

Tony was beginning to get her drift. He chose his words carefully. "I must confess, I never really gave it much thought, but I suppose it's rough on the kiddies," he admitted. "I suppose it might be wise to wait on children until one has performing out of one's system," he said, then added, "Though I realize things don't always work out that way."

"But what would you do if things didn't 'work out that way?" she pressed.

Tony was nonplused. "I—I don't believe one could say, unless one was actually faced with the problem," he told her.

"Yes, that makes sense," she told him on a final note, suddenly realizing she had let her emotions drive her too far in this conversation. Though Tony had not spoken of marriage, he behaved as if he envisioned her being by his side always, and the longer she knew him, the more it seemed right to her that she should be. Yet she did not want to appear to be encouraging him at this point. After all she had done to disgrace herself, she would not make a mockery of what her parents considered the most sacred of all commitments by entering into it dishonestly. If she married Tony before those embarrassing photographs were destroyed, then she must tell him they existed. How could she bring herself to do this?

On the morning they arrived in Dallas—the final gig on the tour—Cynthia announced to Tony and Geneva that her brother had offered them the use of his vacation house on Oyster Bay, for the month of June. "Good show!" said Tony. To Geneva he said, "Wait till you see it: huge three-story clapboard house, with wide galleries and a terrace overlooking the sea. We can go bathing and take long walks about the grounds, and go bicycling. What fun!"

Geneva tried to hide her distress. She was counting on returning home for a while after this tour, so that she could try somehow to get a letter into Victor's hands. Could she send him her forwarding address at Oyster Bay? But a month probably wasn't long enough for his reply to reach her. And where would they go from there?

Cynthia was already answering her unspoken question. She had managed a pre-casting audition, around the first of July, with the famous Broadway producer Charles Dillingham. "It's for a brand new musical, *The Daughter of Basin Street*. W. C. Handy is writing the score," she said brightly, "and if the audition goes well, the role of the lead dancers is yours for the asking."

"You don't say! Geneva, just imagine!" Tony said ecstatically. At once, he and his mother began talking about the particulars.

So there would be no extended period anywhere, thought Geneva. Unless it would be in New York City, if the musical went over....

Cynthia noticed Geneva's reluctance. "I'll admit it won't be much of a vacation on Oyster Bay. You'll be slaving away out on that terrace most of the time," she apologized. Then she added briskly, "But right now we've got to keep pushing, keep people in the business talking about *Sterling & Selby*. When the war's over, young men will be coming back, new partnerships will be established, and old ones revived. The competition will increase then."

Geneva gave thought to her guilty hope that the war would last for a while. For now, she certainly did not want to appear to be a slacker. "Oh, absolutely," she said.

After closing in Dallas they returned to Houston, to pack up for the trip East. There was a stack of mail waiting at the Beaconsfield. The bulky letter addressed to Tony from his father was near the bottom, the envelope practically consumed with postage. Lifting it in his hand, he had an odd feeling.... Usually his father was not given to many words, nor did he have time for chatty news letters while running Selby Mines with a drastically reduced war-time staff—Cornish tin mining activity had not been this vigorous since the market opened up in Malaysia towards the end of the last century, and by now he was minus the help of his son-in-law. So something serious had prompted this lengthy missive.

Tony opened the envelope and read through the pages with increasing amazement, his eyes often blurring with emotion. It was the best of news; it was the worst.

Cynthia walked into the room, wearing a satin kimono with a bright green and gold floral pattern, her dark hair loose about her shoulders, her feet bare. At the sight of him, she said, "You've gone pale. What is it?"

Tony looked up from the letter. "It's all over. William is dead," he murmured, the rest having got stuck in his throat. He handed her the letter.

CHAPTER 24

For most of that night, Tony lay awake thinking. The anticipation of returning to England was so richly potent that the end-of-May heat and humidity which scarcely let up here in Houston, even at nights, evaporated in his mind along with the ocean separating him from home. He imagined himself and Geneva walking arm-in-arm up the Brookhurst drive under a broad clear sky, the gravel crunching under their feet. They would feel the bracing breeze of late spring on their faces, hear the soft rustling in the new leaves of ancient trees. The granite wings of the house where he'd lived for most of his life would enfold the happy couple in their shadow like welcoming arms; and from inside would be heard the barking of dear old Angus and Kenegy. The two Old English Sheepdogs were as big as ponies, but Geneva need not fear anything from them except perhaps having her face licked with doubled exuberance! And finally, Tony would feel his father's firm handclasp, and see the deep love in his keen blue-gray eyes. *"Father, allow me to introduce Geneva, my wife...."*

Convincing Geneva to be a part of this rosy picture may not be easy, Tony realized. They had not yet spoken of marriage under any circumstances, and accepting his proposal now would call for her to sail to a foreign country directly engaged in warfare, and be prepared to do so within a matter of days. That would call for an awful lot of trust. So he had jolly well better explain to her just why he was being forced to break his promise, first of all. He was glad for the letter he wrote to her months ago, yet did not mail. *"Show it to her one other day, when she knows you better."* Now was the time.

He turned on the bedside lamp and withdrew the letter from the drawer in the mahogany night stand beneath. As he read the date, he remembered it was written before Brian Potts's death. He rose from the bed and sat down at his desk. He rewrote the first page, changing the date, and the last, to bring matters current, excluding William's death. Then he read through the entire letter. The wisdom of his mother's advice was clear—parts of it were pretty shocking. Yet, now that Geneva knew him intimately, she would overlook that, he was sure. He turned out the light and slept till the morning sun pricked the window curtain.

A few hours later, bleary-eyed, Tony pedaled his bicycle all the way to the north end of Main Street, over to Washington Avenue, and thence across White Oak Bayou and out Heights Boulevard. He rarely cycled since coming to the States, whereas in England—and particularly while studying at Oxford—it was practically his only mode of transportation. There was nothing better for increasing blood circulation, shaking out one's mind and focusing energies. And imagine, he would soon be cycling along the Cornish coast! Hopefully, with Geneva alongside him.

As he reached the edge of her yard, he saw her sitting upon the porch in a wicker chair, her hair pulled back with a gaily-colored scarf, her head bent in concentration. He parked the bike at the fence and walked to the foot of the porch. Only then, looking up and reaching for a glass of lemonade, did she spot him. Her face lit up with such pleasure that his confidence soared.

"What brings you here?" she asked, but before he answered, she raised up an odd assortment of papers from her lap. "I've just been going over my finances. Cynthia warned me that $560 won't go very far after you pay all your expenses, and she was right. I'm practically broke and I still have to buy some new clothes for our vacation."

His mother had refused her commission for this first tour, which helped, but in spite of Tony's objection, Geneva insisted on reimbursing him for her half of their bill at Gaspard-Spritz, and for the services of Myra Brinkerhoff. While Tony respected her for paying her own way, it made him feel that she was determined their romance should not supersede their business arrangement. Just now it threatened his confidence all over again.

He kissed her hello, then removed his straw hat, pulled out his handkerchief, and mopped his perspiring brow. Perhaps the shadows beneath his eyes tipped her off that something was amiss, for she frowned and asked, "What's wrong? We're not going to Oyster Bay?"

Would that it were as simple as that, he thought dismally. He sat down and took her hands consolingly. "Something quite unexpected has happened," he said, then hesitated. He had planned to tell her of William's murder, then show her the letter; but now that her eyes were focused on his, those two deep green pools of innocence made him wonder if such a plan would be too harsh. Should he hand her the letter without preamble? No, that may be even worse. Oh well. He tightened his grip on her hands. "There has been a murder in England," he said, his voice husky. "The man who was responsible for my leaving is dead at the hand of his daughter."

A look of bewilderment spread over Geneva's face. Yet quickly she said, "But I thought the soldier was responsible, the one who was killed at Ypres."

"Yes, that's part of it, but there's more," Tony said, aware all at once of how difficult it would be for Geneva to follow his tale with all its dangling plots. "The daughter was my fianceè, you see," he digressed, and now Geneva's eyes blazed as though he had struck her a blow. Dash it! He rushed on, "I don't love her anymore—you must believe me. Even before I met you, I realized I was a fool for having fallen in love with a person like her."

To his great relief, Geneva's face relaxed. He pulled the folded letter from his pocket, realizing his hand was shaking. "Here, I should like for you to read this. It will help you to understand all that I must tell you."

Geneva gave him a wary look, as though she had an inkling of what was coming. He wished to God he had simply handed her the letter when first he stepped upon the porch, rather than predisposing her mind in any way.

As she unfolded the letter and began to read, every muscle in Tony's body was clenched tight.

The text was fresh in his mind; therefore he easily kept pace with her as she laid aside one page after another on a small wicker table nearby. As her eyes moved across the page where he alluded to making love to Jane in the Brookhurst wood, he held his breath. To his relief, her face did not turn red with shock, or close up in judgment, as he had begun to fear in spite of himself. Tony let out his breath.

When she reached the page which began with William's threat to bring charges against Tony, she looked up at him, her eyes wide. He waited for her to speak, trying to discern what she was feeling. If she voiced even a slight suspicion that William's charge was justified, he would leave her porch and never look back. Yet finally her eyes returned to the letter, revealing nothing. Tony went and stood at the edge of the porch. He was bathed in sweat and his heart was pounding. In this moment he felt more than ever aware of what a bizarre sequence of events his life had become. He gazed through the summer haze toward the remarkably ornate house across the street, with its pointed turret and gables. Not a hint of breeze stirred the leafy trees in the yard. A plump little lad was frolicking with a spotted puppy out on the grass. His gurgling laughter rang in the air. The puppy's tail wagged in delight. A pleasant-looking woman stood high on the deep porch, beneath fancy lattice work, watching. The simple scene stirred Tony's heart. How was it that life for some people continued day after day, year after year, so *normally*?

Presently he heard Geneva say in a gentle voice, "I'm sorry, Tony."

He turned to look at her, and at once he knew from her face that she understood the torture he had been through. The love he had felt for her before today was nothing compared to what he felt now. His eyes grew misty.

She was asking quietly, "Do you think Brian Potts was lying about the sort of girl Jane was?"

Jane's hand was closing over his own, guiding it towards the inside of her thigh—Yet there was blood. "Yes, he was just trying to provoke me," he said with conviction, though his voice was tremulous. "There is no question that Jane was a virgin."

Geneva's eyes searched his for a long moment. Finally she nodded. Tony realized he could no longer put off telling her what he dreaded. He took in a steadying breath. "I'm afraid, as matters stand, I must return to England for…for a while."

"But why? I realize William Tremont's death makes you free to go, but—"

"I am called as a character witness on Jane's behalf—"

Geneva frowned in perplexity. "You? After she betrayed you?"

"I know it sounds strange," he admitted, running a hand over the back of his neck. "You see, her defense counsel believes that if I tell of that day in the Brookhurst wood and all that Jane said and did afterward, her almost hysterical fear of William's reprisal will support her claim in this trial that he was frequently violent, that his murder was an act of self-defense," Tony said. Each time he thought of Jane raising a gun and taking aim at her father, he found it difficult to imagine such a violent act, even though—as his father had written—the act followed a bitter quarrel.

"I see…."

"And frankly, I shall be glad for the chance to clear my name," he said.

"But, from your letter, William Tremont didn't bring charges—"

Tony shook his head, and gave her a hard look. "I mean, that people who knew me suspected—as you did—that I left England to escape military duty."

Geneva's eyes dropped. She folded an arm across her abdomen. Presently she looked at Tony again. "Well, surely you won't be away for long."

Tony braced himself. "I'm afraid there's a complication. You see, with the war on, my father is short-staffed at Selby Mines. He is in rather desperate need of my help. I shall have to stay until the war is over."

Suddenly Geneva thrust forward in her chair, her face red. "But you swore you would not return to England because of the war," she cried.

"Surely you don't think I could have foreseen William's death!" he retorted.

Geneva was shaking her head. "The point is, you said you were sure, and you could not have been, with so much hanging in the balance!" She brought a trembling hand to her chin. Her face was white. Her voice as hard and cold as flint, she added, "I'll leave it up to you, Tony. Do whatever you feel is right. But if you go away, don't expect to come back after the war and pick up where we left off because I won't—I won't be waiting." Her voice broke on the last word. She folded her arms and looked off into the distance.

Tony was at a loss now. It was reasonable that Geneva would be angry at his having to go away, but he had thought she would understand once she knew the reason. Was she right? Ought he have allowed for the possibility that something totally unforeseen would develop? He did not know. But he knew now that he could not ask her to marry him and go with him to England, for it would seem a last resort, rather than the first thing on his mind. He had never expected to be torn between the two people he loved most in the world. Yet there it was. He tried to think ahead. One could only speculate how much longer the war would last. Perhaps a few months? A year? Staying in England to help his father was not worth losing Geneva. Nothing was worth losing her. Quietly he said, "Very well. I—I don't know the date of the trial as yet, but I probably could be back in time for the audition with Dillingham; anyhow, I shall certainly try," he said at last. *How shall I break this to Father, when he has been through so much?* He thought, a vacuous feeling at the pit of his stomach.

Geneva looked at Tony's bleak expression. *He'll be miserable if he stays because he doesn't think it's right. Yet he owes me this!* Perhaps she ought to tell him right now why she had such an aversion to his going away and leaving her behind. But no. Her mind was too scattered to tell him about Victor right now. If he questioned her very much, she would wind up telling him things she didn't want him to know. Besides, she did not want Tony's sympathy. She only wanted him to live up to his commitment.

Yet.... She thought of Victor, ignoring her pleas that he not leave her, as if she didn't matter at all. And Tony was willing to put her first, even before the needs of his own father.

She suddenly knew that she could not in good conscience force him to do this. She felt dizzy, half-nauseated. *I am to be left again.* "No, I'm being unfair," she said finally, "you go on, your father needs you more than—" She could not finish the sentence.

Tony knew her words came at great price, and yet there was no sign of resentment in her voice. Overcome with gratitude and love, he did not wait to see if her next words would be, "*I will wait for you.*" He went near and took her hands again. "This need not mean a separation for us," he said tenderly.

Geneva looked at him uncertainly.

"I beg you to come home with me, as my wife," he said, the words a kite, swept up by the wind, and relying on her hand to hold fast to the string.

CHAPTER 25

Tony's proposal of marriage brought such a conflict of reactions to Geneva's mind that she could not readily find her voice. Quickly he said, "Would you like some time to think it over?" She could only nod. "May I call on you tomorrow morning, then?" Would that give her time to sort things out? She did not know. She nodded again. He kissed her goodby and turned to go.

As he wheeled away on his bicycle, waving to her, Geneva thought yearningly: *He believes I will say 'yes,' and I could say 'yes' and be gone from here in a few days. A whole new life.* With a sigh she leaned back in her chair and sat quietly, to compose herself. Soon she was lost in thought. She had known she wanted to marry Tony for many weeks now, not only because of the way she felt when they kissed or whenever he clasped her hand or slipped his arm around her shoulder, but because she admired him very much as an artist and as an individual. He would be true to her; of this she was certain. And all she had learned in the past hour or so only made her believe in him more.

How odd to realize that there was nothing whatever to tie her to Houston, Texas—it gave her a giddy sense, as if she were floating. Once married to Tony, she was free to go to the ends of the earth if she wanted to, and take her inheritance with her. Oh what a tantalizing thought: to be out from under John Scarborough's thumb for good! The only person she would miss was Madame Linsky, but she knew that Linsky would send her off with her blessings. *A whole new life. Yes!*

Perhaps best of all, apart from the sheer joy of being married to a man she loved, she would acquire a family. From what she knew of Lord Edward and Nell, they were decent people who would share in Tony's happiness and accept his bride as one of them. And Nell's son Gerry would be a special joy, to occupy her until her own children arrived. As a family they would endure the privations of the war, and as a family, they would rejoice when it was over—

Yet, unfortunately it was not that simple.

For weeks, the prospect of laying the ground work for retrieving her photographs from Victor had preoccupied Geneva's every waking moment. If she stayed behind, the time she needed to accomplish this would be at her disposal. Still, the idea of saying goodby to Tony was almost unbearable. Might she go with him to England, and hope by virtue of being nearer to Victor's location, her chances at getting the photographs would improve? But no. First of all, even if she could find Victor, she would have to lie to Tony in order to meet with him. Besides, in all likelihood the photographs were up in Springfield, Massachusetts.

All the rest of the day and through a long sleepless night, Geneva tried to think of some way she might yet go to England with Tony. Write to Victor and ask him to forward the photographs via the mail as soon as he could get his hands on them? Good heavens, she could never trust them to the mail! And what if they did arrive, and someone else opened the envelope by mistake? Perhaps she might tell Linsky of the photographs, and ask permission to have Victor write his reply to the studio? Then Linsky could—No, she could never tell Linsky of the photographs, let alone bring her into the mess they had created. Just forget about the photographs then, and trust in Victor's discretion? For at least an hour Geneva held stubbornly to this idea. But in the end, the fact remained, in doing so she would not be true to herself or to Tony.

The following morning at nine o'clock, Geneva watched from the porch as the Packard pulled up to the curb and Tony alighted. She had decided they would do their talking out here, for they would have no privacy in the parlor: Ida was across the hall, tapping away on her Remington. As Tony stepped upon the porch, he looked so anxious that Geneva was again tempted to answer him *Yes*. How could she break his heart, when he had already suffered so much?

Soon he was taking her hands in his. "Well, what do you say?"

After some hesitation, she began, "Tony, I'm sure you'll agree, this has all been very sudden—"

The look of dread which gathered on Tony's face made her hasten on, "You know, as I lay awake last night, thinking, I tried to imagine what my parents would have advised me to do." This was not a falsehood. Temporarily putting aside the matter of the photographs, she had given careful thought to how they would likely have counseled her. And this proved sobering, though granted their advice would have come in a very different context—she would have heard it while safe in the bosom of their love. As she went on speaking, she was surprised to find the heat of tears behind her eyes. "Oh Tony, I wish you had known my parents; they were so wise, and they thought carefully through every major decision, and discussed things till they agreed—"

Tony smiled kindly. "To have raised a daughter as fine as you, they surely must have been very wise indeed. I wish I had known them, too."

Only I disgraced them, she thought guiltily. "Yes, well, I think they would have suggested that, since you and I have known each other we've lived a very unique existence—nothing but work, and weeks on the road. We haven't had time to just be ourselves and get to know each other at a leisurely pace." She paused, took in a breath, and squeezed his hands consolingly. "I believe with all my heart that we are right for each other, Tony, but I think they would have urged me to wait until after the war before I made a decision."

Tony's expression had turned to gloom. "The war can't last forever," she reminded him, "and surely, if our love is real, it will be even stronger for the separation we've endured."

Slowly, as Tony absorbed her words, his face brightened. He clutched her hands to his heart. She could feel its swift beating beneath her fingers. "May I take this as your promise not to see—see other men while I'm away, but wait for me? And I—I—well, I promise I shall never look at another woman."

"Yes, I promise, Tony," Geneva said with feeling. His pledge meant as much to her as hers to him. She remembered how she bristled at the news he had been engaged before he left England. Well Jane was now a part of the past, and was certainly no threat. But from now on, she did not want to think there might ever be a risk of Tony putting another girl before her in his heart.

Tony folded her in his arms and they kissed. Still holding her, he pulled away just a bit. "Oh, I'll miss you so much! Every day will be a torment! Are you sure you wouldn't just—"

She pressed his lips with her fingers. "Please, Tony—I'll miss you too, ever so much! But we can do this, I know we can. And afterward, we will be sure that things are—are *right* between us in—in *every* way."

He released her. "There's so little time," he said, grimacing. "I must leave here within a matter of days." She wanted to keep him with her on the porch, to listen while he told her of all the many things he must do before leaving; she wanted to be a part of his leaving, even if she could not go with him. Then before she knew it he was reaching in his pocket and handing her the key to his automobile. "The Packard is yours. I shan't be needing it, obviously, and Mother doesn't drive."

A car! Geneva could hardly imagine herself owning a car. Granted, with men away fighting the war, many women were driving nowadays. And last summer her Red Cross supervisor had begun teaching her to drive so that eventually she could make runs to and from Camp Logan, which was a short distance from the Heights. Still, by the beginning of autumn, she and Tony had started dancing, and that was the end of the driving lessons. Abruptly she had a thought: "But why won't Cynthia keep the car and hire a driver? She'll need transportation."

Tony gave her a forlorn look. "Mother will be traveling most of the time, scouting, and helping other performers while I'm away."

Geneva had not given a thought to how Tony's leaving would disrupt all of Cynthia's plans, and now she felt contrite. She gave Tony a grateful kiss. "I'll finish learning to drive while you're away."

"Ah no, we shall have your driving up to scratch before I leave," he said firmly, and led her straight down the porch stairs and out to the Packard.

Three days later—unluckily the first day of heavy rain since they returned from their tour—Geneva and Cynthia walked with Tony across the slimy concourse of Grand Central Station, to say farewell. Cynthia was dressed entirely in black, as if the journey to the train station were a funeral procession. Her eyes were heavy from crying. She had hardly spoken on the drive over.

They were immersed in a sea of soldiers draped in drab green rain capes, embracing wives, mothers, fathers and children—all preliminary to saying farewell, for how long was anyone's guess. Cigarette smoke loomed above the aromas of coffee and doughnuts spread out for soldiers on a long serving table. Women wearing crisp Red Cross uniforms and encouraging smiles stood behind the table. Geneva had read in the newspaper that there were 25,000 recruits training at Camp Logan—easy to imagine on a day like today.

Each time she heard a thunderclap, she dreaded still more the moment she must slide behind the wheel and drive Cynthia south to the Beaconsfield, then turn around and drive north all the way to the Heights—which seemed the opposite end of the world!—without wrecking the Packard and injuring herself and others. Despite Tony's cocksure belief to the contrary, she was not prepared to drive in the busy downtown streets of Houston, in the middle of a thunderstorm. How annoying he was, forcing her into this.

Then he was crushing her in a hug and kissing her goodby, his warm embrace in a damp mackintosh dissolving her complaint. "Keep safe! Oh, I'll miss you!" she cried, her voice barely audible above the noise. Cynthia hugged her son closely, her eyes shut tight as her cheek rested briefly on his shoulder. Geneva saw her mouth form the words, *I love you.* She realized that apart from regretting the fact that all her plans for Tony had collapsed, Cynthia must also be grieving for the loss of her son's companionship. Geneva felt sorry for her, though it seemed odd to feel sorry for someone as invincible as Cynthia.

Soon, his eyes misty, Tony turned to walk toward the platform, and at once he was swallowed up in the crowd, his bowler a round brown dot vanishing among the over-sized campaign hats. Geneva felt a terrible wrenching inside, and a bitter sense of powerlessness. The war was a mighty machine that would consume whatever and whomever it needed to keep itself going. Well, at least working in the family tin mining business would exempt Tony from active duty, Geneva thought bracingly. Then a chill came over her as she thought of the dangers Tony would encounter crossing enemy-infested waters, and her heart echoed her parting words.

Minutes later, with steam hissing, its wheels groaning like iron legs gathering speed, and its whistle wailing with all the sadness of wartime goodbys, Tony's train lurched forward and chugged away.

After a long moment, Geneva sighed in resignation and turned to Cynthia. "I guess we may as well go."

Cynthia gave her a dolorous look, and nodded.

Outside thunder rumbled relentlessly and lightning seemed to stab the tops of buildings as the gray clouds continued emptying. With the Packard head lamps beaming on the wet pavement, Geneva gingerly maneuvered her way through the tangle of vehicles and pedestrians around the station, up Franklin Avenue, then turned right onto Main; all the while she gripped the steering wheel with white-knuckled hands, her stomach cringing.

Presently, Cynthia observed with bitterness, "Oh, what a miserable farce."

A puzzling remark. But Geneva dare not obey instinct and take her eyes off the street long enough to glance at the expression on Cynthia's face. "Tony's leaving?"

"No," she said with a mirthless laugh. "William's murder. I must admit I never dreamed even Jane would go that far, to get Tony back," she said.

Geneva was amazed at the conjecture. Yet even if true, what difference did it make? For the moment she was too distracted to point this out. They had reached the busy Capitol intersection, in front of the fancy wrought iron-covered promenade of the Rice Hotel, and the traffic signal was changing. Geneva carefully eased down on the brake, so as not to go into a skid. There. She let out a breath. Pedestrians criss-crossed the street hurriedly, under rain-pummeled umbrellas. Now she looked at Cynthia, and saw her deeply troubled expression. "But Tony hates Jane. He would not have gone back, except for the war," she reasoned.

"I know, my dear. But you see, Jane knows that too," Cynthia said evenly. Then her eyes hardened. "She's dangerous, Geneva. Don't ever make the mistake of underestimating her—Look, the signal is changing."

Geneva's chest tightened. She faced the street again, eased up on the clutch and pressed the accelerator, trying to concentrate on the foot coordination—still so awkward to her. A car pulled close behind and the driver honked rudely. Geneva's shoulders flinched. Cynthia glanced behind them. "Perhaps you could drive just a little faster," she said. Geneva felt she was being pushed toward the edge of a cliff. She did not want Cynthia to know how inept she felt. The other car pulled around, spewing water along the side of the Packard like an ocean wave.

Cynthia reflected, "I remember when I learned Tony was to marry Jane. I was distraught. I wrote him, begging that he reconsider. I wrote to Edward, begging him to reason with Tony. They both ignored me."

Geneva could not imagine anyone ignoring Cynthia. "But why?"

"Quite simply, Jane manipulated them. She's an expert at that, and always has been," she said, then paused as though to allow the remark to sink into Geneva's mind. At length she continued, "You see, Jane and my daughter are around the same age, and as children they were playmates. Nell has never been very confident of herself, not like Tony. Jane was lovely to look at. Cool...and...self-possessed. Nell all but worshiped her.

"I began to discover certain words in Nell's vocabulary that a child her age had no business knowing. And a book—*Sexology*—I have no idea how Jane came by it, but she loaned it to Nell. Nell tried to conceal it, but I found it.

"Nell was always doing favors for Jane. Lying to cover for her. Going to Fairleigh when I had forbidden her. Tony was away at Eton all this time....

"Nell did not want to go away to school, and I'd always been content for her to attend Bodmin schools. But I was about ready to send her away, just to get her out from under Jane's influence. Then Jane—blessedly, I thought at the time—went off to finishing school in York. They were both 14."

After a pause she went on, "It was a couple of years later that I—" then her voice skipped a beat, before she said, "—returned to Houston to live." Geneva felt there must have been volumes of information in that slight hesitation. During those weeks on the Keith-Orpheum circuit, when they slept in the same room, Cynthia never veered toward personal subjects in conversation.

She always talked shop. But then of course, they were both too exhausted to talk about much of anything. Perhaps someday Cynthia would tell her what prompted her separation from Tony's father.

"By the time Tony proposed to Jane, she was back from school, and had convinced everyone—except me—that she had outgrown her devious ways.

"I wish I could say that I had enjoyed being proven right."

They had arrived at the Beaconsfield. Gratefully, Geneva pulled to a stop at the curb, and caught her breath. Cynthia was gazing off into the distance, speaking softly, as though to herself, lashes of rain on the window reflecting in shadow streaks down her face. "Jane's father was ruthless; power hungry—the kind of man easy to figure out," she said. Then with a prescient glance at Geneva, she added, "But Jane is unpredictable. That's why she frightens me. I only hope she'll hang for his murder."

Geneva could think of nothing to say. The Beaconsfield doorman in a green uniform with gold epaulets and buttons approached the car, the handle of a huge umbrella gripped in his white-gloved hand. Unexpectedly, Cynthia gave Geneva a quick, desperate hug. "We'll keep in touch, my dear," she said. Then her eyes filled and she added staunchly, "Until Tony returns." Geneva nodded. The door opened. Geneva watched the two figures huddled under the black umbrella, hurrying up to the entrance door with its shiny brass fixtures. Reluctantly, she pulled back into the traffic.

CHAPTER 26

By the time Geneva arrived home, she was not feeling as brave as she had felt earlier about Tony leaving. The drab scene that had surrounded them at the railroad station made it seem as if the sad farewells of soldiers going off to war would never end. Apart from this, as she thought of Tony speeding toward the place where he and Jane had grown up as neighbors, and where Jane would return if she was found innocent of William's murder, Geneva wondered if Cynthia's grave concerns about Jane could really be dismissed. *If only I could have gone with him today, to be by his side constantly,* she lamented.

She parked the Packard on the driveway—she wasn't very good at maneuvering it inside the garage, and she didn't feel like bothering now. Her back and neck were already aching from the tension of driving home. As she hurried toward the screened-in back porch under the shelter of her umbrella, she noticed a light shining in the kitchen. Good. Ida must be at home, and she needed to talk to her. She shook out her umbrella and left it in a corner of the porch, then hung her drenched rain coat and hat on a hook, remembering sadly the press of Tony's damp mackintosh against her when they kissed goodby.

Ida was sitting at the kitchen table with a cup of coffee before her, her invariable cigarette sending up clouds of smoke. With so much dampness in the air, the odor was especially repulsive to Geneva and redoubled her feeling of gloom. *Tony is off to England and I am stuck with her.* Ida seemed lost in thought. "Do you have an address where I can write to Victor?" Geneva asked.

Ida looked up in surprise.

"I want to inform him of the child we lost," she lied.

"Ah well, it's about time," Ida said. "Learning to stand up for yourself—that's good. Too bad things turned out the way they did with your stage career. But as I've told you, never trust a man to keep—"

"Yes. The address—?" Geneva interrupted.

Ida took a drag off her cigarette. "You write Victor care of his agent in New York. I've got the address on my desk," she said, the words coming out in a haze of smoke. She put out her cigarette and rose from the table.

With the address in hand Geneva went upstairs, changed into a lounging robe, turned on the lamp beside her bed and sat propped on the pillows with pen and paper. The rain had slowed down to a drizzle, and the cool breeze coming through the nearby window carried the musty smells of wet tree bark and leaves. She must carefully measure her words to Victor, for someone else might get hold of the letter and read it before it reached his hands.

"Dear Victor...." As she formed the letters of his name with her pen, her cheeks grew hot; she had the same heart-sickening sense of his coming near that she experienced when Tony showed her the photograph in the *New American Review*. She thought of Victor packing up his things and running far away, out of her reach, oblivious of all the heartache he had caused her, not to mention the impact he was having on her future with Tony. She found herself striking out 'Dear' almost savagely.

Yet, she dare not be abrasive, for then Victor might be disinclined to answer her. After many attempts that wound up in the waste basket, she settled on, "Victor—I trust you are safe and well. There is something I would like to discuss with you. Please let me know an address where I can write to you direct. Always, Geneva." Looking over the short letter, she decided to put the 'Dear' back in place, the better to fool him into thinking she felt no animosity.

The following morning Geneva went to see Madame Linsky about the possibility of helping her teach while Tony was away. The sun was shining so brightly, it made yesterday's rainy farewell seem almost like a bad dream. Except that it was very real, as was the pitiful entreaty she placed in the mail on her way to the studio.

Madame Linsky greeted Geneva with a tight hug and a wet kiss on each cheek. "So! The famous stage personality has returned to visit her old teacher," she said, then scooped a stack of certificates and framed pictures off the chair across from her desk. "As you may notice, my souvenirs have not been taken down and dusted for a very long time. There now, sit down, *ma chère!*"

Geneva noticed that only Linsky's crucifix remained in place, as though it were a compass; and if it were taken down—even temporarily—she would lose her direction.

As Geneva took her seat, a bittersweet memory came to mind. It was on the night they opened at the *Majestic*, and Linsky—wearing a dressy frock in a deep wine color, its hem hiked up on one side and held with a satin rose—was presenting Geneva with a scrapbook bound in Moroccan leather, in which to post clippings from her stage career. So many blank pages waiting to be filled…. "Tony has returned to England till the war is over," Geneva said sadly.

Linsky frowned. *"Mais non! C'est regrettable!"* she swore.

Geneva hastened to explain, "It wasn't his doing at all—the reasons are…well…complicated—but in any case I promised to wait for him." After a pause, she added, "We're very much in love," and her eyes stung with tears.

Linsky gave Geneva a bracing smile. *"Très bien!"* Tony is a very lucky young man." She reached across and took Geneva's hand in hers. "Now, what will you do in the meantime? Return to college?"

Geneva shook her head. In January the Rice students had shown the good sense to stage a violent protest riot, knocking out a power plant. President Lovett was forced to suspend military regulations. It was all over the newspapers. Still, that was months ago, plus a seven-week vaudeville circuit ago, and she could no longer see herself as a college co-ed, even with her views vindicated. "I was hoping I might help you with your teaching load. And I could resume training in ballet, if you have the time."

To her despair, Linsky's eyes held regret. "I have something to tell you also, *ma chère*. I am sure you will remember Martha Houghton…."

"I remember Martha,"Geneva said, without pleasure. After graduating from high school, Martha had moved to California, to study at the Denishawn School of Dance. Her own life in ruins, Geneva felt envious when she saw the write-up in the newspaper, with Martha's picture above, a supercilious smile on her face. That was the last Geneva heard of Martha.

"Recently, Martha wrote to say she has married an attorney. Dixon is his name. They are moving here from California, and he will open a practice.

"I have decided to offer my school for sale to Martha. If she is interested, I will insist on training her for a full year, beginning in September—" she frowned helplessly "—so you see, I will have no need of an assistant."

Geneva was crushed. And envious. Well she remembered Martha strutting around with her nose in the air, believing her talents far exceeded everyone else's. And now she would be Linsky's successor, though she could never fill her shoes. Yet how could she question her teacher's good judgment? "What will you do after you sell the school?" she asked.

Linsky settled back and folded her arms. This she had thought about a great deal over the past few months. She felt a strong yearning to visit the graves of her parents and brother in Paris, and to travel around the country revisiting all the places of her youth. And she was not getting any younger! "I am going home to France. *Mais naturellement*, my plans, like yours, must wait until the war ends," she said. "Still, I have not been home in many years, and I wish to go there before I die," she added, her eyes blazing. She realized she could say no more without becoming emotional.

It was time Linsky got something she wanted, Geneva thought. Following the example of the adored figure that hung on the cross above her desk, she had asked very little for herself, living frugally, devoting herself to work. Geneva thought of Linsky's custom to begin every single day with a walk to the Church of the Annunciation to kneel in prayer. Perhaps she prayed for the opportunity to go home to France. "I am happy for you," she said with feeling.

"What a shame things cannot work out differently," Linsky said.

Geneva did not want her teacher to know how disappointed she was, how much she had counted on her continuing to be here, year after year, running her school. Linsky was Geneva's compass. "It's alright. I'll find something," she said, then managed a smile. "We'll write to each other when you are in France."

"Yes! How I enjoyed your letters while you were on tour. Some I read to my pupils. *Quel un exemple!*" Linsky exulted, her voice deep.

Yet, must it come to this? Linsky despaired, falling silent. Regardless of the fact that Martha had an excellent background in the study of dance, she had always disliked her air of superiority toward her peers. It troubled her that even while Geneva was right here in Houston, and available to help train her beloved pupils, Martha instead would be assisting her. *Non*, this would not do! Somehow—. Abruptly she said, "I have not yet made the offer to Martha. *Vraiment*, I am concerned for her personality, that she will be unable to temper the strict discipline so necessary in teaching with *encouragement, tu comprends?*"

Geneva nodded emphatically, the appalling thought of Martha unleashed on her Tuesday morning primary ballet pupils having crossed her mind.

"—Though I was hoping, with some training—So! What do you think of this idea? I wait until the war is over to sell my school. Assuming your plans do not change, well and good. But if anything should alter them, perhaps you might buy the school? Perhaps you and Tony might even settle here, eh? Then you might operate the school together. Make it famous!" Linsky said brightly, though admonishing herself all the while that this surely was the height of wishful thinking.

Geneva was amazed. Her imagination took flight. The school might be connected to a theatre someday. Tony's dream come true. And she need not wait to have the children she wanted so desperately, because she and Tony would not be traveling the vaudeville circuits. "I think it's a wonderful idea—oh, I can't wait to tell Tony!" she cried. Then it occurred to her that Tony may insist they live in England. "But if Tony and I do not buy the studio, and in the meantime, Martha gets busy doing something else, you will wind up without a buyer," she pointed out to Linsky.

Linsky shrugged. The longer Geneva sat across from her, the more intolerable became the idea of selling her school to Martha. "*C'est la vie!*" she said melodically, lifting her chin bravely. "I am not totally dependent on the proceeds. My needs are simple, as you know." She paused, then added forlornly, "It is only that one enjoys imagining one's tradition continuing, eh?

"So! It is only vanity, after all, and not so very important," she declared.

"But it *is* important." Geneva cried, thinking what a shame it would be for the school to simply dissolve, and on top of everything else, Linsky not getting a penny for it.

"Well then, you will come back and teach for me, and we will see what the end of the war brings, *oui?*"

After her visit with Linsky, Geneva left the Packard parked at the studio and walked from there to John Scarborough's office a few blocks away. She had dreaded telling him of the interruption of her stage career, and planned to put it off for a few days. But now that Linsky had made her an offer, she was eager to meet with him. Knowing she had a plan for her future—a practical one—would reduce his satisfaction in believing he had been right to disapprove of her dancing with Tony.

Before John Scarborough had a chance to open his mouth after Geneva finished telling him that Tony had left, she rushed on, "Madame Linsky would like to retire and return to France when the war is over, and she has offered to sell her school to—to me." She decided to leave Tony's name out of it for now, because he would only warn her that Tony may not come back as he promised.

John Scarborough was glad to hear the British boy was out of the picture. He saw the years ahead: Geneva's annual statements scattered hither, thither and yon—hadn't Mrs. Ruekauer remarked on her sloppy record-keeping?—all the way through 1924, when the balance was paid off. Geneva would never look back and notice that slight discrepancy in 1917. Such a small thing really, and whether or not it would ever pay off for him and Mrs. Ruekauer was a matter of speculation. But, some young dandy—British or otherwise—in love with Geneva, and determined to impress her, might look more closely….

Of course, he had never anticipated having a partner, and Mrs. Ruekauer might double-cross him one day—the question often went round and round in his mind at night, as he struggled to fall asleep. But so far, there was no sign her attitude was changing. And now that she knew of the unfortunate situation with his brother Fred, he had not only her cooperation but her well-deserved sympathy. Imagine, after all these years of being quite content to be alone, finding someone who had suffered from life's injustices as he had, someone his equal in intellect, with whom he could really converse.

Well, today things were certainly going in their favor. Still, he doubted Geneva had looked at the practical side of purchasing the school, and with this problem he could not help her except to show her how to negotiate terms with the seller, which as her trust officer he was bound to do. John Scarborough was never to be charged with dereliction of his duty. The fact that Geneva could not enter into a legal contract until age 21 need not be a problem. Mrs. Ruekauer would sign the papers if need be. Yet—"What will you use as capital for paying off Madame Linsky, tell me? There is a bank policy against investing from the principal of an estate the size of yours."

Geneva was at a loss. Tony would have plenty of money to buy the school, but she did not want to tell John Scarborough this. "Madame Linsky and I will work something out," she said vaguely.

"Well and good, but you would be wise to get something down in writing just as quickly as possible," he advised Geneva.

It seemed to Geneva that he was questioning Linsky's integrity. "I have no doubt that Linsky is as good as her word."

"Oh, is that so?" John Scarborough asked, reddening. How hopelessly naive Geneva was. Mrs. Ruekauer was right about that. His eyes rolled up to the ceiling, then came to rest on her. "And suppose someone comes along with ready cash? Have you thought about that?"

He would never understand Linsky's idealism, her love for her school, and why she was determined for Geneva to have it, or risk having no buyer at all. "As I said, Madame Linsky is as good as her word," she repeated firmly.

"Ah then, she ought to be more than happy to put her word down in writing, shouldn't she?" he persisted, tapping the desk with his index finger. "Give me credit for learning a few things in 40 years of banking, young lady. Only a fool would enter into a verbal agreement and expect it to hold.

"Now, if you will excuse me, I am expecting another client," he said.

Geneva bid him good day and left. Let him think what he would, she was not about to insult Madame Linsky by taking his advice.

That night Geneva sat down to write to Tony about Linsky's offer. Hopefully the letter would reach him soon after he arrived home, and he would answer her quickly. Of course, war-time mail schedules were very erratic.

In fact two months lapsed before she received Tony's answer; in the meantime, she received a letter he had written aboard ship, in which he described an idea of a dance in which the two of them portrayed characters from playing cards. Tony would be a foolish, clumsy Joker, who had fallen hopelessly in love with the Queen of Hearts, played by Geneva in an enormous crinoline skirt. How lost he must feel, with no prospect of dancing in the near future, she thought sadly. It seemed unlikely he would be interested in owning a dancing school.

Following this letter were two more, written from Brookhurst.

Finally he wrote, "I must say the idea of purchasing a dancing school and one day connecting it to a theatre is quite intriguing. Unfortunately, the financial picture here is a bit uncertain, I've found. Still, I shall be exploring it in detail over the weeks ahead, and may know more afterward...."

It was the last thing Geneva expected, having always believed the Selbys were quite wealthy. Of course, if she and Tony married, her inheritance could be used to purchase the studio—surely there would be enough to cover it. Still, a queer instinct overcame her that she had better speak to Madame Linsky about working out terms for her to purchase it alone.

CHAPTER 27

On Tony's first full day at home, he went to Falmouth to meet with Harvey Muldrum, Jane's barrister. It was the kind of grayish day that often befalls the Cornish coast in early summer, when the air is chill and the color of the sky blends with that of the sea. Mr. Muldrum's chambers were suggestive of his venerable status in the profession, with mahogany walls and polished brass fixtures, thick figured rugs and a huge bay window of mullioned glass looking out on what today was a strangely monochromatic view. Tony sat in a deep leather arm chair and gave his lengthy statement, which a clerk recorded. The story he was once at pains to recreate now unfolded in a voice clear and concise—an unexpected benefit to having laid it all out before Geneva months earlier, breaking its grip on his emotions. Muldrum leaned back in his chair, listening, a look of utter inscrutability upon his face; his heavy jowl lapping over his stiff collar, his hands—incongruously small for a man of such large proportion—folded over the dark blue vest covering his enormous girth.

Afterward the barrister shook Tony's hand and thanked him. The ceiling light, which was designed like a great sea lantern with frosted glass, glowed on his bald pate. As he ushered Tony out of his office, he said discreetly, "In a case such as this, one must guard against overstating evidence that would seem to give the defendant credibility."

Tony was not sure exactly what Muldrum meant by that remark, but he gathered that he was unlikely to be called to the witness box, after all.

On his way through the outer office, he chanced to see a woman passing through the gate, rather in her 40's he thought, who bore a striking resemblance to Jane: the small, boyish figure; the flat complexion; the mouth turned down in a scowl. The hair peeking out from beneath her hat brim was—like

Jane's—light blond, though it appeared stiff, as if it had been frequently dyed. The woman was accompanied by a hefty middle-aged man, with dark hair and a moustache. Both were stylishly dressed. They conversed very softly, as though exchanging confidences, on the way in to see Muldrum.

Tony suspected the woman was Jane's mother Francine Tremont, whom he had not seen since he was a small child. Shortly the receptionist confirmed this, and said she had returned from Italy for the trial. *That will be Jane in 20 years,* thought Tony with a shiver, *that is, if she goes free.*

That night Tony and his sister chatted softly as Nell rocked her son Gerry to sleep in the nursery. Owing to the war, Nell and her husband Morey had not yet purchased their wedding cottage, and now she and Gerry were living at Brookhurst while Morey was away on the battlefields of France.

Tony began by telling Nell about his visit with Muldrum. As he talked, Nell met his eyes with the blue-violet gaze of their mother, whom she closely resembled except that her figure was plump. Tony watched Nell lovingly hold Gerry on her shoulder, stroking his hair and his back as she rocked to and fro.

When Tony finished, Nell rose and carried Gerry to the nearby crib, all the while speaking to him: "Are we ready to be tucked in, Darling? Mummy loves you ever so much, and hopes you will have happy dreams!" Nell had a lovely lilting voice—well suited to motherhood, Tony thought now. Little Gerry gazed upon his mother as if she were the most fascinating person in the world. This was the first time Tony had witnessed his sister putting her child to bed, and he found it very touching. Was this the sort of leisurely, happy exchange Geneva longed for with her children? One day when they were married she must have what she longed for, Tony thought warmly, imagining their child cuddled against her soft bosom.

Tony was aware that while Jane was awaiting trial in Bodmin Gaol—this when he was en route to England—she had asked Muldrum to contact his father and beg that a member of the Selby family visit her and receive her apology. Nell offered to represent the family. Tony was curious as to what transpired during Nell's visit, and when she sat down again he asked her to tell him about it. Nell said she had found Jane's cell comfortable-looking enough, furnished with a small bed, writing desk and reading lamp, and upholstered chair—prisoners awaiting trial could have their own furnishings brought in. They could also wear their own clothing, and Jane wore a slim skirt of black flannel and a long black sweater with a belt around the waist. "She paced nervously up and down, smoking one cigarette after another. She urged me to tell you and Father that an apology would appear in the *Bodmin Guardian* immediately after the trial.

"Then abruptly she stopped pacing and turned to face me. Her cigarette was dangling from one side of her mouth, and a sort of indolent smile was tugging at the other. 'Don't worry Nellie, they won't hang me,' she said."

Tony laughed sharply. "Assuming you had been losing sleep over her prospects?"

"Hardly! Though I must admit I do pity Jane in a way…having William Tremont for a father. I remember as a child, quaking in fear if I happened to be about when he would come home to Fairleigh. Of course, he never threatened me in any way. It was just, one always sensed an explosion about to occur."

"And Jane—was she frightened of William then?"

"Not as much as one might have expected, I should think. She used to boast that she knew how to work him."

At the trial, Jane appeared to Tony to be amazingly composed. Once, while in the witness box, she caught Tony's eye with a pleading look, however. *"Christ, I wish I'd never met you!"* she had said on the way to Fairleigh from the Brookhurst wood. His blood boiled. He looked away and thought longingly of Geneva, who had redeemed his life of Jane's destruction.

Jane was correct. She would not hang for William's murder. The main witness for the prosecution was a servant woman who claimed to have seen and heard the entire quarrel between father and daughter. She stated that, rather than acting in self-defense, Jane had deliberately provoked her father into striking her, as she stood near the drawer in his study desk where he kept his fire arm. The defense discredited the witness by proving she had been caught-out lying to previous employers, and falsified her references before she became employed by the Tremont family.

Jane's mother gave the most cogent testimony to William's violent nature, claiming that he had brutally beaten her and Jane, and spoken to them in the most abusive terms. She probably won the case for her daughter, though her testimony did make Tony wonder: Why did Francine leave Jane at the mercy of her father? Surely any decent mother would have remained in a marriage—no matter how bad—in order to protect her child as best she could.

Strange lot of people, the Tremonts. But it was none of Tony's affair. He was done with them forever. At the close of the trial, Jane looked round the court room, a wondrous, triumphant smile breaking on her face. Again, Tony averted his eyes. He and his father and Nell hurried from the crowded, airless chamber, and returned to Brookhurst. By the first of August, Jane's public apology had appeared, and she was back at Fairleigh with her chronically ailing grandmother. Francine Tremont, he supposed, was back in Italy.

Whereas Tony once felt stranded by being forced to leave England and live in the States, now he felt stranded by being so far from Geneva. He was desperate to stay in touch constantly, to be reassured that her feelings for him would not flag in his absence. Once a week he began a letter to her, to which he added a few paragraphs every night until the end of the week, when he would post it. When he received her letter about the idea of taking over Linsky's dancing school, he would have been willing not only to move permanently to the States, but to put aside any plans for their returning to the stage, if she truly wanted this. Yet by that time, certain comments by his father had suggested the financial picture of Selby Mines may be a bit shaky. And as he explored the situation further—as he promised Geneva he would do—he became not reassured but truly alarmed.

Before the war, Tony had taken no active part in the business. He wrongly assumed that the funds borrowed to modernize the mines and Brookhurst as well, when his family moved here from London in 1901, had been paid in full before August of 1914. Now he learned that shortly after he was banished to America, the earlier loan balance was wrapped into another loan of considerable proportion, to handle the influx of war-time business. This was done at the behest of Morey, the firm's business manager.

One night as Tony and his father stayed up very late poring over figures—not for the first time, by any means—Tony reached a troubling conclusion: "It's going to be a bit of a job, staying afloat after the war with all this debt."

Lord Edward had silvery hair, a high forehead and a strong, jutting chin. He rubbed his chin thoughtfully now. "Obviously, we'll have to tighten our belts, shut down some of the sites reopened in 1915. Still, there will always be room for a few well-managed mining companies in Cornwall."

But when Morey was about, Selby Mines was not prudently managed, Tony thought bleakly. Yet he could understand his father's reluctance to face facts: Selby Mines was practically his whole life.

Tony's grandfather had inherited the Brookhurst estate, but very little money. He made his first fortune in the 1840's, speculating in mining shares. Eventually he opened Selby Mines and made another fortune, then closed down—by a stroke of luck, or shrewdness—before the great slump of the 1890's, which put so many mining companies out of business. He was an old man by then; the farms on the Brookhurst estate had always provided adequate income, and earlier revenues from Selby Mines had secured the wealth of the family. Unfortunately, he had built this wealth on the backs of his miners, for whom wages were minimum and working conditions, poor. He was slow to replace old, outdated equipment, and often turned a blind eye to much-needed improvements. As a result, though Selby Mines somehow managed a decent safety record, it was not held in respect by its employees. Nor was the Selby family well-regarded in the community.

It was much to the shock and dismay of Tony's mother—who was then aswirl in London society, and already had Tony enrolled in dancing instruction, drama lessons, and piano—when his father elected to return to Cornwall and rectify all this, by reopening Selby Mines. He soon provided the latest, most advanced equipment—one of his first projects was to convert steam-powered mine pumping engines to the use of electricity. And another, of which he was justifiably proud was the building of a large change house, where the miners could wash and exchange their wet, dirty underground clothing for clean dry surface clothes at the end of the work day, leaving their work clothes to dry by hanging above steam-heated tubes. This saved them walking the long distances home in wet clothing.

The sinking of a new shaft was always preceded by a great ceremony: Tony's father in top hat, holding a silver shovel; a photographer hired to record the event. Afterward the employees were treated to a festive lunch, and each employee was given two shillings as a gift. His father often paid doctor's fees when their children were ill. He replaced leaky roofs on their houses. Of course, it was all to the good of the company when his employees stayed healthy, and their attention was not diverted by worry about paying their bills. The business prospered, and the Selby family name gained high respect in the district. Selby Mines was one of the few mining companies that had remained family-owned, and his father was immensely proud of this.

While Tony was growing up, his father tried to inculcate his love for the mining business in his son. If he had his way, Tony would graduate from Oxford, come home and begin preparing to take over one day. But eventually he realized that turning Tony's thoughts from the stage was hopeless.

Naturally, he was gratified when Nell married a man who was interested in the business. Morey was a burly, plain-spoken Cornishman with dark hair and light blue eyes. He was the son of a miner. His father had been killed in a blast at East Pool. Morey was a natural-born salesman; he knew how to negotiate with the miners, and had all the practical skills taught by the Camborne School of Mines, from which he graduated.

Morey was less than two years older than Tony, and in some ways, was the son his father wanted. The fact that he had turned out to be a poor business manager aroused not only Tony's guilt, but also a feeling of profound responsibility. He suddenly knew that he must remain in England until Selby Mines was out from under the burden of debt, or until the business was sold—the latter prospect much more to Tony's liking. He could not say this to his father outright.

Tony could hardly bear to have to say it at all.

One evening in September, shortly after his 23rd birthday, he reluctantly knocked on the door of his father's study.

When he went in, Lord Edward was seated at his writing desk. He removed his reading glasses and turned towards his son, an expectant look on his face, as if he thought perhaps Tony may have thought of a ready solution to all the problems laid out in the papers before him.

Tony had the most awful feeling that with the words he was about to utter, he was sealing his fate, that he would never be able to return to Geneva, or even if he did, she would not be waiting. He walked to the fireplace, lifted a pine cone from the basket inside, and gripped it hard, letting the prickly points dig into the inside of his hand. With a glance round at his father, he said, "I have decided to remain after the war…and complete my studies at Oxford."

Lord Edward's face brightened. "Splendid, my son! Dancing is out of your system by now, I expect." Yet they both knew that wasn't the point of his staying at all, and only pride kept them from admitting it to each other.

Later that night, his heart aching, Tony wrote to Geneva, "I have some hope—vain though it may be—that by staying in England I can exert some influence on the future of Selby Mines. I should like very much to sell up while the picture looks rosy. On the other hand, if I go away, when Morey returns I doubt this idea will even be opened for discussion. Both my father and Morey are devoted to the business and its faithful employees. Please know with what terrible regret I write this, and that I pray your love will be patient as mine must be, and wait a little longer before we can be together."

By the time Tony posted this letter—the shortest he had ever written to Geneva, and the hardest one to part with—the Spanish Influenza had swept through England, and he was forced to add a sad paragraph: "Nell's young son Gerry succumbed to the flu-pneumonia at half-past six this morning. Nell had been constantly at his sickbed for the four agonizing days of his illness. He died in her arms. As you can imagine, we are all taking this very hard. How I wish you could be here, for I know your presence would be of great comfort to us all. Until that time comes.... Ever devotedly yours—"

CHAPTER 28

Geneva was increasingly concerned about the deadly Spanish Influenza. Brought into Houston by the troops passing through Camp Logan, by September it was spreading claw-like through the civilian population and quickly growing to epidemic proportion. On the day in October when the notice appeared in the morning *Post* that the city was officially placed under quarantine, Geneva telephoned Linsky—who had read the news also and was about to pick up the telephone and call her—and offered to drive to the studio and post a sign on the door. Fortunately, not one case had yet appeared among their pupils, but the frightening possibility had raised the question: should they keep the studio open, or shut down for the duration? Geneva was grateful to have the decision made for them. "*Au revoir, ma chère*," said Linsky before hanging up. "*Au revoir*," Geneva wished her in return, feeling a little awkward about her pronunciation as she always did when attempting a French phrase. But *au revoir* was worth the attempt. Surely it was the most endearing phrase in the entire French language.

Main Street was eerily deserted for nine o'clock on a weekday morning. Geneva felt a headache coming on as she drove along, and her throat was dry. She felt oddly detached from herself too, as if someone else were sitting behind the wheel of the Packard while she observed their hands on the wheel from far away. Yet, according to the papers, elderly people and very young children were most vulnerable to contracting the Spanish Influenza. Geneva presumed her symptoms were those of a mild cold. And no great surprise. Since mid-summer she and Linsky had been very busy getting ready for the new dancing year: interviewing the parents of prospective new students, placing orders for dancing shoes, conferring with the costumier and choosing the fabric for this year's practice attire. Linsky and Geneva had agreed that, contingent on her plans with Tony, after the war she would buy the studio, making installments out of proceeds from the receipts until she and Tony married and could use her inheritance, if need be, to pay off the balance. The knowledge that she had taken matters in hand and acted on her own gave Geneva a glorious feeling of independence. She had written Tony to explain the arrangement, "Don't worry, the studio can still be ours if we want it…."

Lately Linsky seemed to have withdrawn a little in spirit, as if she had turned her face towards her long-awaited trip to France. She seemed pleased when Geneva offered to take on a heavier teaching load than either had anticipated, including both day and evening classes. As a result Geneva had been driving back and forth to the studio twice on many days. *How could I have gotten along without the Packard?* She thought. Which reminded her to check the gasoline gauge. Once again, it was veering towards "empty."

When she pulled to a stop in front of the studio, she noticed a purple wreath hanging on the door of Adele Gregory's Fashion Shop below. Thoroughly unsettled, her instinct to avoid taking a breath for fear of catching a flu germ, she hurried upstairs with her homemade sign.

By the time she got home, she was feeling the weight of fatigue that accompanies a cold. Ida was in San Antonio, at a state-wide conference of suffragettes. She'd been reluctant to go because so many soldiers were stationed there. Geneva wondered if she should alert a neighbor that she was not feeling well. But no—it was just a cold. She took two aspirin, went up to her room and turned on the gas heater, then cracked the window just an inch or so.

Climbing in between the covers, Geneva fell into a deep sleep. When she awoke hours later, the room was in darkness. Her throat felt as rough as corncob; her body burned like a furnace. She needed to tell someone she was ill, for she may have the influenza. Yet when she lifted her head from the pillow it spun in pain as though she had been struck with a mallet. Groaning, she burrowed into the covers. Soon she was shivering so violently that her teeth chattered. Her last coherent thought was terrifying: *I could die, and no one would know.* Then it was as if she had tunneled down into a strange new world like that of *Alice in Wonderland:*

Dancing, dancing, would Tony never stop dancing? Round and round and round they went, the bells on the corners of his Joker's hat tinkling afresh with every step, the sound hammering in her head, the stage lights burning hotter and hotter; she was on fire. Round and round, the Queen's stiff crinoline red heart wadded up in her chest and scratching it raw; round and round, while she begged for the dance to end. But Tony's bright red joker lips went on smiling, his arms holding her ever more tightly, for they must keep going round and round or the dance would be ruined, he said; her head throbbed harder and harder. Tinkle, tinkle, round and round, the contents of her stomach sloshing in a cup, she would vomit up the crinoline if he did not, please oh please, stop the dance, it was coming, coming—

When the Queen of Hearts rose like the moon from her cold slimy crinoline, the Joker had vanished, and all she could do to escape her own effluvium was to scoot along on her stomach until she reached the edge of the stage, yes, a few more feet and her fingers would grasp the edge, and then—

Henry, look at the poor dear!

One on either side, glowing white, her parents enfolded her in their cloud-soft imbricated wings and flew her to the mountain top. There she lay on her back, looking into their faces etched in bright light, while soft cloths, warm and moist, coursed up and down her arms and legs and over her body. They were not dead, of course, it was all a mistake. Not having actually seen their bodies, she had always suspected it might be.

Where have you been?

We were here all the time. Didn't we say we would see you soon?

But when she reached out and embraced her parents, her arms sliced through them like a knife through butter, came back and crossed over her chest. She opened her eyes and they were gone. She called out to them but they did not answer.

And now Victor sat by the window, wearing eye glasses, reading a book. She had to get her pictures. But when she struggled to go to him, her legs would not move. She called out to him, but he did not answer....

Victor was on his third reading of *SUMMER,* a new novel by Edith Wharton, which he had discovered while passing through Springfield on his way here. Not that he was much of a reader; but his sister-in-law had a copy, and one night he just glanced over the jacket text and naturally found himself intrigued. A young orphan girl named Charity Royall...being raised by her guardian, an older man...falls in love with a young man engaged to someone else. Her virtue is compromised.... By the time he read the book through once, he knew that he had found his story.

After leaving Houston to travel with his children that summer of Anne's death, Victor had discovered that rather than getting his bearings again, as he had hoped, he was retreating deeper and deeper within the walls of his guilt. Day and night the specter of Anne, writhing in pain in her blood-soaked bed, beyond all help, haunted him; her eyes burned through him, condemning him. *"I told him I wasn't going through this again, but he wouldn't listen. When I go back and tell him what I've done, maybe he'll stay away from me,"* she told her Aunt Flora, who tried in vain to talk her out of what she was determined to do.

Aunt Flora had cried so much that her wrinkled face looked like a dry creek that finally had received a good rain. She reached across her kitchen table to pat Victor's forearm. "You are a good man, Victor. Anne knew it too," she said. But Victor knew better. He was a murderer. In those early days of working with Geneva, when he struggled over his feelings, knowing he should not touch her, he reached out for Anne as though she were a life line. And she gave in. He was a murderer.

Knowing his children needed him, and being anxious to attend to those needs as best he could, nonetheless he felt increasingly detached from them and knew he was letting them down. He had not worked in months; he could not bear to look through the lens of a camera. Then came the offer from the Consolidated News Service to photograph the war in Europe. They would pay handsomely for shots showing the might of the Allied Forces, through hulking cannon and uniformed generals doing troop inspections, and neat tents lined up in army bases with American flags posted at the front. The stuff of liberty bond campaigns. The stuff that expunged any doubt that the Allies would be victorious. Victor took the job readily, believing that being forced to get back to work would help his perspective so that he could get on with his life.

Now in retrospect he wondered how he could have failed to realize that the horror of Anne's death was soon to be played out before him on a daily basis and multiplied by the number of soldiers being slaughtered on the battlefields. How could he have believed the one terrible image in his mind would be dredged away by another so similar? He wasn't in Europe a week before he began to feel that in going there he had contracted his punishment, and that the lock on the gate of his prison was not being able to convey through his pic-tures the horror that he saw, to make them count for something. He was con-demned to have it live inside him, like Anne's death. *Murderer.* There were times when he wanted to call it quits and go home. But deep down, in some perverse way, he wanted to serve out his punishment. And so he kept going, moving from one place to the next as fighting broke out. Now and then he would get his hands on a newspaper from the States, weeks out of date of course, and he would find himself drawn to the entertainment pages. He felt sure Geneva had taken the young British dancer up on his offer after he left. He never found their names as part of any theatre bill, but then so seldom was he able to search that he realized the chances were slim he ever would. Tossing the old newspaper aside, he would tell himself that leaving Geneva was the one right thing he had done. He remembered loving her once, but he hadn't been gone very long before it seemed that loving her had been over with a lifetime ago. That Anne's death had destroyed his ability to feel love, though not the bittersweet memory of having felt it, seemed another way his punishment was meted out. Then again, Victor did not truly feel any sort of emotion anymore. When it came right down to it, he felt dead inside, as if all he was doing was going through the motions of life, like a machine someone had turned on and left running.

Then one day last year he chanced to meet up with King Vidor, the famous film maker from Galveston, with whom he had crossed paths occasionally back in the States. King Vidor was serving his country in France. During several conversations in a Paris bar in which he mostly listened to this great craftsman talk about his work, Victor felt the first stirrings of life again. One night when the weather was clear, as he walked from the bar out on the pavement, he gazed up at the moon and the stars. He remembered how pleasant that sight used to be when he slept outdoors while out on the road, how it filled him with hope and a sense of well-being. It seemed to him now that all the galaxies were looking down with despair as warring mankind besmirched their view.

That was when Victor knew that as soon as the war was over, he was going to become a film maker. Not one who made films retelling stories of valor about the war—no, not a chance—but one who told stories about the beauty of life. Once the idea took hold, he thought of scarcely anything else. And naturally he was soon led to reflect on the art of the Impressionists, how fresh and filled with life it was. The masters of Impressionism were quickly growing old and sick, and dying. He had heard that Monet's eyesight was practically gone; that Renoir's hands were horribly disfigured with arthritis. Still they painted, of course, for they'd as soon be dead as to stop. Yet before long the masters would all be gone. And already there were new movements, new trends to supersede the style they perfected. What if Victor could take Impressionism into another sphere, put it in motion on the screen?

Soon Victor wrote to Benjamin to see if he wanted to go in with him, making films. Whereas Kathy and Virginia had established friendships in Springfield and were happy there, Benjamin was as much a loner as ever. And he was about to graduate from high school. Benjamin took him up on the idea at once, said he wouldn't mind learning to write for the screen in fact. Victor felt like he was finally getting a chance to make up to Benjamin for all his neglect, starting from when Geneva moved in with them and continuing to the present. He'd never seen such excitement in Benjamin's letters as he found in them now. Sometimes three or four would reach him at once. He and Benjamin planned to move to Los Angeles after he came home from the war. Victor had made enough money to get them by for a while, and to get them started in the business.

In the meantime Victor gathered all the information on technique that he could get his hands on—not that there was much to be found except in Paris, and it was written in French of course. But he would buy it anyway, and find someone to translate it for him. Benjamin often sent him clippings he found in American papers and magazines: D. W. Griffith on the making of *The Birth of a Nation;* King Vidor, on qualities he looked for when choosing actors for the roles in his films; Lillian Gish on her experiences as a screen actress. He felt more and more eager to begin this new experiment, surely the greatest one of his entire career. All he was missing was a focus for his energies: a story to film.

Then came Geneva's letter. He was amazed to hear from her after all this time. That was all he felt, just amazement, and curiosity: What could she have to discuss with him? And anyway, wasn't she traveling all the time on the vaudeville circuit? The way he moved around it was impossible for her to write him direct. He would have to wait until he went home, and contact her.

As soon as Victor photographed General Pershing in the Argonne, he knew the war would not last much longer. Let them hire someone else to take the victory shots. He was sick of it all. He was going home.

Upon returning to the States and arriving in Springfield three weeks ago, he found Benjamin waiting impatiently. He gave him the money to go out to Los Angeles and find them rooms to rent. Then he placed a long distance call to Geneva. No one answered. For days, he kept trying. Maybe Geneva was gone on a tour, but at least Ida should be there. In the meantime, he discovered the novel *SUMMER*. After one reading he was making notes on how he would handle certain scenes, for instance:

On a summer's day, Charity is sitting at one end of a canoe, while her lover rows down a narrow stream between high, overhanging trees. The view of the lovers is infinitesimal at first, but then, the camera eases in a little closer so they are more clearly focused each time they appear between the trees; first, the dark provocative look in her lover's eyes, then the light shining on her face, gazing at him with trust and longing, her hair falling around her shoulders. And maybe a double exposure: the spirits of her dead parents looking down sorrowfully, to suggest she is on her way to trouble....

Quite naturally, he envisioned Lillian Gish in the role of Charity, though he doubted he could afford to hire an actress as famous as she was.

Finally, still unable to reach Geneva or even Ida, he became alarmed. According to the newspaper, Houston had a severe epidemic of the Spanish Influenza. He caught a train to Houston, and when he arrived at 1207 Heights Boulevard, he found the front door unlocked. He looked inside, and called out, but no one answered. Feeling more and more fearful, he went upstairs....

He found Geneva lying in a heap on the bedroom floor. The stench in the room all but took his breath away. Terrified that she was dead, he checked for a pulse. She was alive alright, but burning up with fever, so there was the fear of losing her yet; the frenzy of getting in touch with Doctor Robinson and getting her cleaned up. She'd gone to bed fully clothed, her shoes on her feet. Everything was stiff with dried vomit—her long hair, the front of her dress, her underwear and petticoat, her shoes and stockings; the bed covers she pulled off the bed as she went over, and the rug on which she lay.

And a day later Ida came home from San Antonio, shivering, pale, greeting him with a hoarse demand: "What are you doing here?" Not exactly the kind of greeting he expected from his sister after three years. She looked ill though, with the flu, he feared, and maybe that was why she was short with him.

"Geneva wrote that she wanted to talk to me. I thought she had gone on the stage."

"She did, but it didn't last long. Her partner went back to England. She's teaching now."

"That's too bad. I mean, about her stage career," he said, though instinctively he felt somewhat gratified that apparently romance had not developed between Geneva and her partner, as he once thought inevitable.

Ida shrugged in a disparaging way, then she said guardedly, "Why does Geneva want to talk to you?"

"I don't know. I came here and found her out cold, with the flu."

Ida teetered on her weight for a moment, her eyes opening wide, then narrowing to a squint. "I'm going to bed."

"Yes, I think you'd better." He helped her to her downstairs bedroom, the one he once occupied with Anne.

For days after that, Victor hardly slept. He did nothing except climb the stairs to Geneva's room and come down again to Ida's, caring for both women, with Dr. Robinson checking in as often as he could. One of three doctors in the Heights, with flu victims from one end of the neighborhood to the other, it was a wonder he didn't collapse. And when Ida got better, and Geneva was out of danger and resting comfortably, her face composed, he would sit across from her bed and just slowly take in the sight of her. It was like viewing a fine painting, marveling at how the artist had used certain kinds of brush strokes to bring out the play of light on the contours of her face and hair. And he observed Geneva at all different times of day—with the morning sunlight shining through the window; in the evening by the lamp light—so the sight of her was always slightly different than before, always fresh and new. He understood why some artists—Claude Monet came readily to mind—painted the same subject again and again and again, from various angles, at different times of day.

The thought that Geneva might have died had he not walked in when he did chilled him to the marrow. He was thankful he'd obeyed his instinct and come. Maybe saving Geneva's life was a sort of redemption for Anne's death. It was comforting to believe so. Inevitably he wound up reflecting on those days with her in his studio. Hadn't they been together for just a brief period? But now hundreds of memories, tender and poignant, came back to him; it seemed as if they must have worked there and made love there over a very long period of time.

Why had she written him again, after three years? He felt sure that she must have realized by now he did her a great favor by leaving her. Otherwise she would have never had the opportunity to go on the stage. For how long? he wondered. Couple of years, probably. And the fact that her partner returned to England—to join the Armed Forces, no doubt—was no fault of Victor's. Though the word, 'discuss,' had a business-like ring, the tone of her letter was warm enough. Could it be she just wanted to say she had forgiven him for leaving, and tell him all about what she had done since he left?

Then one evening he opened the copy of *SUMMER* he had acquired and began to reread it, sitting across from Geneva's bed. Suddenly he looked up and imagined Geneva as Charity Royall. But no, he would need to hire an experienced actress. He went back to the book, but soon paused in reading again. According to King Vidor, one sign of a great actress was the ability to assume a variety of facial expressions. Victor knew from experience that Geneva had this ability. Again he returned to his reading, casting the thought aside because Geneva had no training in drama. But soon he was thinking about the story's uncanny similarities to her situation, which had drawn him to read it in the first place. Who, then, could feel what Charity was feeling better than Geneva? And surely her time on the stage had prepared her for performing in other ways. On top of everything else, there was the fact that

Geneva had contacted him at just this point in his life, and that her illness had brought him home. Could it be, the forces that drove them apart and all that happened during their long separation were leading them back to each other after all? The thought sent a thrill of anticipation through him. Whereas he had nothing to offer Geneva before, he had something spectacular for her now.

Victor took in a breath of air, suddenly feeling free and pure as a climber who reaches the mountaintop. He knew that he was cleansed of his sin, that the years of punishment had not been his imagination, but real. And immediately he realized he had never stopped loving Geneva, but rather his love for her had been held captive along with the rest of his emotions.

And now she was moaning, stirring in the bed. Hastily he laid his book aside, removed his reading glasses and went to help.

Geneva watched as Victor approached, her eyes struggling to bring him clearly in focus. "You're all tangled up in the covers," he said. The noise of his voice hit her ears like a blow, and she clapped her hands over them.

"Guess you've been dreaming again," he said, a little more quietly. Gently he unwrapped her legs and brought the covers up over her chest.

And so she was dreaming of Victor's presence now. She would touch his face and he would vanish like her parents. She raised a hand and laid it on his cheek. It felt warm and stubbly, with the solidity of bones underneath. She began to shiver; her stomach reeled. Victor was back. She raised her arm and aimed her hand to slap his face, but her hand went limp before it reached him. He picked it up, closed his eyes and kissed it. A tear spilled from his eye and ran over her fingers.

CHAPTER 29

Geneva had a vague sense of Dr. Robinson's solemn presence: the cold stethoscope on her chest, his large hazel eyes shifting left and right, the taste of alcohol from the thermometer in her mouth. He turned away. "She's improving," he said to Victor. His weight lifted from the bed.

She had never felt so exhausted. She slept. She awoke. Slept again. Time was a swirl of waking and sleeping, punctuated by a spoonful of bitter quinine, or warm broth or oatmeal, or buttermilk—more foul-tasting than quinine—offered by Victor's hand.

She was certain he had returned her pictures and she had put them in the drawer beside the bed. Time and again she meant to check to be sure they were still there, but then she would fall asleep again.

As she began staying awake for longer periods, she wondered in a detached way why Victor was here and where Ida was, and whether she would be able to make it in time for ten o'clock acrobatics. Yet something nagged at the back of her mind, some reason why she couldn't go. Then she remembered that the Packard was nearly empty of gasoline.

Abruptly she awoke and saw Victor in the chair reading. Behind him the sunlight poured through the window. She raised up on the pillows. "Please go to the Texaco station and fill up my car. I've got to go to the studio."

Victor closed his book and removed his eye glasses. She was quite sure he had not worn eye glasses when he lived here, and she could not remember him being a reader. He came to the bed and smiled down at her. What had she said to bring a smile to his rugged face? "You aren't going anywhere for a while."

Engulfed by fatigue, Geneva sank back on the pillows. "Then call Madame Linsky and tell her I am sick," she begged. "I am her assistant. She is depending on me."

He did not answer, but sat on the edge of the bed and took her hand. She did not want him to hold her hand. She pulled it away.

"I don't think you understand how ill you've been, or how long. And…well…a lot has happened," he said, his eyes tender.

"How long have I been ill?" she asked anxiously, for even though the sun was shining, she realized it must have been longer than just over night.

"You were ill when I got here two weeks ago."

She was astonished. Ninety-two soldiers dead at Camp Logan, she remembered the headlines now. Keeping extra distance between her pupils during class, watching for listlessness, coughing, any sign of the flu. Ida reluctant to go to the meeting in San Antonio because of all the soldiers there.

"Is Ida home now?"

"No, she recovered more quickly than you did. The Red Cross called. She's out nursing other flu patients."

She struggled to follow him. Ida was in San Antonio at a meeting of suffragettes. So she'd come home, gotten sick and then recovered, and in all that span of time Geneva was oblivious to anything going on around her. She felt she had been sick for a year.

"Others haven't been so lucky," Victor said with gravity, then studied her face before continuing. "Mrs. Crawford died a couple of days after I got here. I saw them carry out her body—a heart rending sight. Mr. Crawford is pretty bad off. They've sent a telegram to Wendell."

She could not take this in. Nothing bad ever happened to the Crawfords. Nice Mrs. Crawford reminded Geneva of her mother. She showed her how to cut the shortening into the flour, her wedding diamond flickering on her finger. Mr. Crawford and Wendell, in their rain slickers, nailed boards across the window to save her from the storm that Victor led her into. Young Joseph Crawford built a snowman with his father…

…which brought back the memory of Tony, kissing her in the snow. And now her memory plunged forward through the next six months like the sleeper jump speeding between the towns on the vaudeville circuit, stopping at one memory, then the next, and the next. A post card arrived from San Francisco: *"I've discovered the new Sarah Bernhardt—Sonja Vitalé. You must hear her sing! Ever yours, Cynthia."* But all these memories seemed long ago, as though the bout with the influenza had purged her of a huge chunk of her life.

"We almost lost you, too. It was touch and go," Victor said quietly.

Geneva supposed she ought to thank him for looking after her, but she thought of the other time, when he had not.

"Do you remember vomiting, falling off the bed?"

She stared at him, bewildered.

"I found you on the floor. I was afraid you were dead."

She remembered the stench of vomit now, and her parents washing her body with soft cloths, warm and wet. But of course it had been a dream. "Who helped me up?" she asked, then realization struck. "Who bathed me? Ida—?"

Victor's hands opened apologetically. "Ida wasn't here."

Geneva turned toward the wall. She despised the thought that Victor had seen her naked body, had *touched* her! He would never, ever touch her again. She turned to look at him. "Why did you come here?" she demanded.

The way she had turned to the wall, as if she thought that instead of attending to her limp febrile body in a loving way, he'd stolen some lascivious pleasure when she was unaware of it, plus the shortness of her tone just now, as though she were interrogating him, made Victor's blood freeze. "I—I got your letter. I didn't know where to tell you to write, so I decided to wait until I got back to the States. I called you long distance from Springfield, but there was no answer. I called again and again. I'd read in the papers about the flu down here, and I got scared, so I just caught a train."

Geneva screwed up her eyes in confusion. Victor had gone overseas to cover the war. "But the war isn't over—or, is it?" She asked then, looking up at him wonderingly. Tony was coming back. It seemed too good to be true. He had not been away so long, after all.

Victor was relieved by the softening in Geneva's demeanor, eager to believe he had misread her earlier. "Well, virtually. I took pictures of General Pershing and his troops arriving in the Argonne," he said, then, warming to the opportunity to converse with her again—how much he had enjoyed that once!—and eager to share with her how he felt about that stirring moment, he went on, "I took a shot of the General. I wish you could have seen him, Geneva. His face under that billed cap—*unsparing* is the only word for it—and the fingers of his right hand, clenched tight. And I thought, it's going to be over soon, yes, it's written all over his face! Pershing will wrap things up. So I saw no reason to stay any longer.

"Besides, I've got plans and I was eager—"

Suddenly, as if she had not heard a word he said, Geneva leaned over and pulled out the drawer next to the bed. She peered inside, then closed it and looked at him with acute consternation. "I can't keep things straight. Did you bring my pictures?"

"Your pictures?" he asked, puzzled.

"You know the ones I mean."

"No, I left them in Springfield, in storage there. You said you didn't want them."

She was beside herself. "Oh but I do. It's why I wrote. I intend to destroy them."

He felt she'd struck him a blow to the chest. How could she destroy the best work he'd ever done? "I didn't guess that, no, I didn't guess that at all," he said unevenly, shaking his head.

Now she remembered her shock when Tony handed her the *New American Review*. "You didn't bother to tell me you published the *Maiden at the Window*," she said. "Why did you do that without even informing me?"

Visions of Geneva as Charity Royall hung by a thread in Victor's confusion. He had saved her life. Why did she keep attacking him, twisting everything he did into something selfish and terrible? "I—my agent urged me to publish something recent before I went overseas," he said. A thin smile crossed his mouth. "I think he thought maybe I wouldn't come back," he said softly. Geneva's expression remained unchanged. "And I thought if there was anything I wanted to publish, it was the *Maiden,* something you and I did together," he said, remembering the tenderness he felt as he withdrew it from the envelope. "But I was gone long before it was due to come out, and frankly I never even gave a thought as to whether it did, the way things were over there. You can't imagine."

"You didn't publish any others, did you?" she asked, her tone threatening.

He hesitated. "You mean, the photographs of you in the nude? No. I promised you I wouldn't."

"Well. That's one promise you kept, anyway," she said coldly. He watched helplessly as she laid back on the pillow and closed her eyes, shutting him out. As he left the room and closed the door quietly behind him, he was trembling all over.

Geneva slept, then awoke in the late afternoon, that time when it is neither light nor dark out the window and leafy shadows dance upon the walls. Often at this time of the evening when she was growing up on Caroline Street, she would peer down from the dormer window of her bedroom and watch for her father to approach up the block, strolling home from work. The memory brought despair. Life would never be that good again.

She thought of Linsky now. Her mentor disapproved of self-pity. *"You need to be dancing,"* she wisely counseled upon Geneva's return from her year of tragedy. How exhilarating! Suddenly Geneva could hardly wait to get back to her pupils, filing into class to the roll of the piano, one by one, arms out, backs straight, downy hair growing at the nape of their necks. *"Good morning, Miss Sterling." "Good morning, Melinda." "Good morning, Miss Sterling." "Good morning, Sheila...."*

The door swung open and Victor brought in a supper tray, smiling uncertainly. Since this morning he had been puzzling over Geneva's anger that he published the *Maiden*. He could not for the life of him remember promising not to publish it. And now she wanted to destroy the nude photographs, as if she didn't trust him to keep his promise not to publish them. He must somehow talk her out of this. "I thought you might be up to some solid food," he said. "And about the pictures..."

"Did you ever reach Madame Linsky?" she interrupted anxiously. Victor's eyes shifted away from hers. He left the tray on the dresser and sat down on the edge of the bed. A simple question, and his reluctance to answer told her more than a hundred words: The worst had happened.

"Linsky is dead." She said it for him.

He nodded sorrowfully.

Linsky in her little apartment, day after day, year after year, allowing herself few luxuries, waiting to go home to France. Walking to Annunciation Catholic Church every morning to pray. The crucifix above her desk like a guiding light. And this was how her faithfulness was rewarded.

Victor reached into his pocket and pulled out a news clipping. "I saw this and saved it for you."

Geneva unfolded the clipping. *Houston's Renowned Dance Mistress Elvira Linsky Succumbs to Flu-Pneumonia.* She was 67 years old, it said. There was a photograph of her, taken some years ago, for in it her hair was quite dark, showing none of the gray it gradually accrued. Otherwise, she had changed very little. There was the same proud forehead and high cheek bones, the look of severity that had fooled Geneva until her life fell apart and she needed a friend.

Geneva began to sob.

Victor took her hand in his and rubbed his fingers back and forth over her wrist. He wanted so much to console her. Maybe if he could get her to talk about her good memories. "When I saw Madame Linsky's picture, I remembered you used to complain about how stern she was, although it was obvious you admired her a great deal. When she would praise you during class, you'd talk about how much it meant to you. You would just glow, you were so proud!"

Geneva paused to catch her breath, but she said nothing. She just stared solemnly at some point in the distance. Victor reached inside his pocket and gave her his handkerchief. As she dried her eyes, he went on, "Ida told me you were teaching now. But when you mentioned you were teaching with Madame Linsky I was surprised, and wondered how it came to be."

Slowly Geneva looked up at Victor. "Linsky befriended me after you left," she told him. And then she told him about the storm.

CHAPTER 30

Slowly her eyes journeyed along the contours of his profile: past the forehead and brow, the sorrowing eyes and sunken cheeks; past his bare chest and the prominent bones of his rib cage, over the folds that draped his loin, and down the length of his legs to his nailed feet.

It was not to dwell upon the image of Christ crucified that Geneva had taken a seat near the front. She intended to sit near the back, in case she needed to leave before the memorial service was over, for she was still somewhat giddy and weak. Yet she was among the first to arrive, and as she walked into the sanctuary, she noticed that the last few rows had been roped off. Then a kind old man with a flower in his lapel offered her his arm. He conducted her down the long center aisle like the father of the bride, and deposited her one pew away from the forbidding holiness of the chancel, within view of a small table filled with unlit votive candles. "You'll have a very good view from here," he said, patting her arm. She smiled at him politely, then removed her coat and neck scarf, and sat down, tugging on the fingers of her gloves. She had become ill on an October day, when the weather was balmy; and now—her first time out of the house—winter was in the air. It was the 8th of November, 1918.

She had never been inside Annunciation Church before, though its towering steeple with the golden cross had cast a long shadow over downtown Houston for many years before she was born, and it stood within blocks of her house on Caroline Street. She found the sanctuary even larger and more grand than she anticipated. It was in such a church, in New Orleans, that Geneva attended the funeral of her grandmother Rundell, a gentle woman who outlived her tyrannical husband by some years. Apart from that occasion, there were few times when Geneva had entered a Roman Catholic church, but she knew the language of the architecture and the names of many of the accouterments from listening to her mother.

After Geneva got settled in her seat, her eyes had circled the high barrel-shaped ceiling above, frescoed with sainted figures against the background of a blue sky and celestial clouds. Then, inevitably, her gaze fell on the crucifix. She wondered now if she would ever escape its power, whether, no matter where she was for the rest of her life, there would always be that figure in a crown of thorns hovering above her, reminding her of her failings.

How she dreaded the day she would return to the studio, and walk into Linsky's little office, seeing the emblem of her faith mounted on the wall, yet knowing her teacher would never again sit beneath it. And then, what? Though Linsky wanted Geneva to have the school, she had no means to buy it out right. Nor was she certain of her future as a teacher, for that would depend upon what she and Tony decided together. Everything would be in limbo until the end of the war. Not just *virtually* the end, as Victor put it. How many times in the last four years had it seemed the end was near? Every time some new victory was won by the Allies, hearts leapt with hope, only to be crushed.

She wondered how long Victor would stay. Had she been fully recovered, or even had Ida been about, perhaps he would have packed his bag and left for good that night she told him of the storm.

"I had not the good sense to see a doctor, but waited for you to return."

Quivering, helpless, he sank in a chair and covered his face. *"No, no, God, please, no!"* He moaned. She spared not a single detail, but dug each one into him like fangs, aware that she was making him suffer, and feeling at times an almost perverse sense of righteousness.

As the story progressed he looked up, his face wintry with despair, his eyes fixed on hers. And when finally she came to the end and her voice fell silent, he literally staggered toward the bedroom door, threw it open and rushed out. She heard his heavy, uneven footsteps on the stairs, and then she heard the front door slam shut. She lay back on the pillows, exhausted, a sense of emptiness overwhelming her, almost like she had felt right after the storm. *Telling Victor did not bring my baby back.*

Since then Victor had hardly uttered a word as he attended her sickbed. He had not apologized, nor would it have changed anything if he had. Seldom did his eyes meet hers. She believed he was not sleeping much, for he occupied Benjamin's old room down the hall, and she often heard floorboards creaking in the night, and knew he was pacing up and down, up and down. In the daytime he looked like the ghost of Victor, as if her unburdening had sucked the life out of him.

Now the tinkling of a bell interrupted Geneva's thoughts, and she looked around, surprised to find the sanctuary filled. The ropes had been removed from the back pews, and these, too, were occupied. The priest was advancing up the aisle in his robes, his hands folded piously at his waist. He was flanked by two altar boys with closely-cropped hair, their faces glowing angelically.

The priest came to a halt, knelt on one knee before the cross, then rose and turned to the congregation. He had a kindly face. He explained in a soft, reverent voice that the service would begin with selected Scripture readings, followed by the lighting of individual candles by those present, for the deceased members of Church of the Annunciation, and their families—he explained this process in detail, how each name would be called and anyone so inclined could approach the table holding the candles. Finally he said the service would close with the celebration of the Mass. He did not say that only Roman Catholics were invited to kneel at the altar rail; perhaps in this situation he felt it would be unpastoral, and only hoped those who were not permitted would remain seated. For the first time, and doubtless because of the unassailable quality of this place and the potency of the rituals to take place here tonight, Geneva felt the full weight of her mother's decision to leave the Church in protest of this rule, and realized how hard a decision it must have been.

As the readings progressed, Geneva felt increasingly uneasy about hearing her teacher's name spoken, and wished she had not come. It would be like learning of Linsky's death all over again. She was growing a little woozy at the thought. Yes, she realized now that she ought to have stayed home. But being seated near the front, she could not leave without disrupting the service.

And now the names were being called, in alphabetical order, with the crisply definitive ringing of a bell between each one. For Geneva, this created almost unbearable suspense. She clenched her hands a little more tightly each time. People—many with tear-strewn faces—made their way up the aisle, bowed to the cross, reached for a match, lit a candle, then returned to their seats. "Beatrice Corcoran...Doris Anne Evans..." *"The child has the body of a dancer, Madame Sterling...."* "Nancy Helen Fields...Miles Foster..." *"You will survive this heartache and go on, ma chère. In the meantime you need to be dancing."* She could not do this..."Amy Fidelia Grose"..."*Could it be that you are afraid to trust any man after the photographer?...*" "Philip Jackson..." "*...one enjoys imagining one's tradition continuing....*" "Wilfred Jones..." "*C'est la vie! It is* *only vanity, after all...*" "Darlene Koppelle...William Leed...James Franklin Lemont...

"...Elvira Christina Linsky...."

Geneva held her breath until the bell had been rung. And so it had been borne, and was over. She exhaled; her hands relaxed. She rose so abruptly, the blood rushed to her feet and she had to steady herself by gripping the pew in front of her. She moved the short way up the aisle to the table, and there, putting a match to the wick, she watched the flame flicker uncertainly, then gradually assume the shape of a tear drop. *Au revoir, ma chère....*

When she stepped away from the table, she spotted Martha Houghton—no, Dixon, it was now—coming forward. She was relieved that apparently Martha did not notice her. She did not want their eyes to meet in a sharing of this moment. Though perhaps it was selfish, she wanted to hold the moment within the privacy of her heart, because Linsky meant more to her than to Martha, or anyone else. She returned to her seat with a studied attempt to avoid all familiar faces.

Not until the memorial service was over, and everyone was outside, did Geneva realize how many of Linsky's pupils were in attendance. The wind was cold and biting, and no one wished to linger. She exchanged tight hugs with one pupil after another, leaning down to reach the little ones, pressing their cold little cheeks with hers. How grateful she was that they were alive. How terribly fragile life was! She caught sight of Linsky's pianist, Myra Brinkerhoff. A wool head scarf covered her curls. Myra had kindly telephoned and left a message with Victor about the details of this service. Soon they were hugging each other, both of them in tears. Myra took off her spectacles and dabbed her eyes with her handkerchief. "Will you take over now?" she asked, hopefully.

Geneva suddenly realized that was exactly what she must do, at least for now. Why had she complicated matters in her mind? Just see about paying the rent and keeping things going, perhaps until they could have a big spring recital. Linsky would like that, she knew, and the thought of it rescued her flagging spirits. "I'll see what I can do, then get in touch with you," she promised.

Myra walked away. Geneva hugged her coat around her and headed toward the Packard, parked down the block. Her breath puffed out on the icy air. Then she saw Martha coming toward her on the arm of her husband. He looked considerably older than Martha. She had stopped by Linsky's studio one day, and the three of them chatted in the office. Linsky admitted that she would retire in a year or so, and Geneva was considering taking over in her stead. It seemed of little interest to Martha. She boasted of the palatial home she and her husband—*"He's an attorney, you know...."*—were building on Montrose Boulevard.

Now, drawing even with the Dixon couple, Geneva greeted Martha, expecting to be introduced to her husband. Instead Martha gave her a tight nod, drew closer to him, and hurried past. Her husband did not even look Geneva's way. How very odd. She had mistaken Martha's eagerness to show off the prosperous man to whom she was wed.

CHAPTER 31

That night after Geneva told Victor of the loss of their child in the storm, he walked through the Heights under a quickly darkening sky, up one street and down another, his mind a blur of disbelief. The one thing he thought he had done right had been perhaps his greatest mistake of all. Had Geneva only realized her period was late before he left, and told him, nothing would have taken him from her side. He imagined it now: Geneva standing in the door of the studio while he packed up his cameras, her arms open, palms lifted: "My period is late." Just four words and everything would have changed. With proper medical attention early in her pregnancy, the child she carried might have survived. They would have been married when the baby came. Right now it would be nearly three years old, sleeping contentedly down the hall. Yet even if Geneva lost it regardless, she would not have gone through the ordeal alone. He would have attended her as lovingly as he had done these past weeks as she recovered from the flu. That was what he regretted most of all, that she went through it all alone. Her eyes flashed with lightning as she recounted the story. The details flew at him like wild debris in the storm which had raged outside. It was as if it had only just happened. At one point she said, "You just cast me aside, as if I were nothing to you. And you never looked back." No wonder she hated him. He hated himself. He could not even find his voice to apologize because no apology would ever be enough. He felt twice a murderer.

As he walked aimlessly, his hands locked behind him, it seemed to Victor that his life was nothing but an endless trail of mistakes. The only thing that ever came out right, or did anyone any good, was whatever he captured through the lens of a camera. Could it be that Geneva wished to destroy the best pictures he had ever done in order to hurt him? And if so, did he not deserve it?

The thing for him to do was to go back on the road, forget about motion pictures altogether, because that would inevitably bring him into close contact with women. He would fall in love again, and wind up ruining someone else's life as surely as he had ruined Anne's and Geneva's. *Murderer, murderer.*

He thought of his children. Last week, he received a note from Benjamin with the address of a boardinghouse in Los Angeles. He was eagerly awaiting his dad's arrival, pricing out equipment they would need. He said he had found a good deal on a 35 mm Bell and Howell camera. Well, Benjamin would be better off if he went out there long enough to help him get settled in, then went away. He could hang his hat there in that boarding house with Benjamin—he had to have a home base somewhere—and he would support Benjamin until he could make his own living. He was lucky his daughters didn't need him around. They got on very well with his brother and sister-in-law. Kathy had asked for money to go to college in a couple of years; he'd promised to provide it and he would; and Virginia was taking piano and organ lessons and doing well at it—she had played for him several times in the few days that he visited there. He had paid for all those lessons and he would go right on doing it. At least no one could say that Victor was irresponsible about supporting his family.

The moon was full now. Victor had come to the foot of a street, a narrow little street that was unfamiliar to him. Thick limbs of bare, skeletal trees formed an arbor across it, closing like a cage above him. By the moonlight shining through he could see the few small cottages on either side of the street. There were no lights on in any of the dwellings; they seemed deserted. He turned and walked back to the corner. Fifth Street, according to the sign. He had walked many more blocks than he realized, and wound up at a dead-end. He was going back now, to pack up his things.

As he made his way down White Oak to Heights Boulevard, his steps slow and dispirited, he noticed lights blinking off here and there in the houses that he passed. How simple life could be for some people. A man grew up, fell in love, got married and had a family. In the mornings he went to work; in the evenings, he came home, his family waiting. He sat with his wife and children around the supper table. Later in the evening he went to bed with his wife at his side, both of them content to be there, and if a person were walking down the street all alone—just as he was doing now—he would see the lights blink off in the house where he and his family lived. All at once, that seemed to Victor the most beautiful life any man could have. And knowing he would never have it made him desperately sad.

When he got back, he went into Benjamin's old room and began stuffing his clothes inside his bag. Then he saw *SUMMER* on the bedside table, and picked it up. All at once, he hated it. It was a cruel trick of fate that he had discovered it. He was tempted to tear the pages right out of the book; he had the binding turned backwards…

…and then he saw his meticulous notes all over the margins—*"medium shot," "iris-in."* He turned the page: *"close-up of her face," "dissolve," "begin new sequence here?"* And another: *"Try an f/22, depending on the sunlight," "fade-out."* How hard he had worked, feverish with ideas because the story had awakened something in him that he thought was dead, painted bright colors in his imagination after the endlessly drab muddy gray landscape of Europe; made him believe he could portray something beautiful about life up there on the screen, something that would make people forget the devastation of war, at least for that period when they sat in a dark auditorium, the pictures flickering across the screen like a beautiful dream.

Was it right to deny Geneva the opportunity to be Charity Royall, just because of his failures? How did he know she wouldn't take to the idea, with her stage career over, and without employment now that Linsky was dead? Maybe she would be grateful for a new start. Not that he believed there was any redeeming what they had together before he left; no, not at all—how naive had been his dreams, brewing while he sat at Geneva's bedside. But maybe they could go on together, on different terms, working as partners. He could get a room for her out in Los Angeles. And after the shooting of *SUMMER*, she could go on acting in other films if she wanted. It might be the beginning of a glamorous career for her because, if his hunch was right, she would be a natural as an actress. Offers would come from all directions.

But the inescapable fact was that Geneva hated him, and would despise any idea he put to her. There was no hope of changing that…unless…unless…he told her the truth about Anne's death. The thought filled him with dread. He'd intended to carry that story to his grave. Besides, even if he could bring himself to tell Geneva the whole truth, maybe it would backfire, and she would hate him all the more. But if not…. Could he take the risk? He'd have to take some time to consider all this. And now that he thought about it, she was pretty upset about Madame Linsky's death, and that memorial service was coming up soon. It might be less of a strain on her if he let things be until it was over.

The house was quiet when Geneva returned from the memorial service. Exhausted, she climbed the stairs to her room. She found that Victor had turned up the gas heater and folded down the bed covers, and lit the lamp. She wished he would not do thoughtful things for her; wished he had not been the one to nurse her back to health. All this made her feel beholden to him, just a little. Nothing would undo the pain he had caused her, or restore her loss. In the morning she intended to tell him he might as well go. She did not want to feel she owed him anything when he walked out the door.

She changed into her sleeping gown and crawled into bed. She had not been there long when she heard a soft knock at the door. "Come in," she said.

"I've been needing to say some things since…well…since we talked," Victor said quietly. Geneva raised up on the pillows and switched on the light. He pulled a chair over near her bed and sat down heavily, then looked across with pleading in his eyes. "Every time I think I'll tell you that I am sorry for what happened, I wind up saving my breath," he said, his voice thick with emotion. He looked up at the ceiling and squinted for a moment, fighting tears. "Truth is, that's just not enough, when you've ruined someone's life."

"You didn't ruin my life," Geneva said defensively. "It was bad for a while. But I got over it—to the extent anyone could—and I went on."

He nodded. "But I'd like you at least to understand my reasoning at the time I left, that I wasn't just casting you aside. And if I'd had any idea your period was late, I—I would not have left for anything."

He paused and took in a breath. Geneva waited for him to continue, her expression unchanged.

Haltingly, he said, "I've never told anyone this before—I told my children the same lie about Anne's death that I told you." He swallowed. Then, his voice shaky he began, "My wife—she bled to death…following an abortion. I didn't even know she was expecting our baby." He forced himself to continue the story Aunt Flora told him: how she begged Anne to change her mind, to no avail; and how Anne disappeared late one night, and came home in the wee morning hours in the back of a cart, pale as a ghost. How the driver did not even help her into the house, and Flora went out to bring her inside, bundled her up and put her to bed. How Aunt Flora's doctor was called in when she started to bleed, and labored valiantly, but could not stop the hemorrhaging.

At the end their eyes met. Geneva's hand was clapped over her mouth.

She could not comprehend this. Aunt Flora was sick. Anne overdid, and died of heart failure. Her mind returned to that conversation they had on the night before Anne left. Dear heaven. She had known full well she was heading into danger. No wonder she was in such a maudlin frame of mind. There was scarcely anything more risky to a woman than abortion. *"I really need to do this."* But Anne had three children depending on her. How could she have been that selfish? Perhaps it would be understandable, had she been tied down with a dozen children or more; had she been destitute, or married to someone who abused her. But no. Anne was heartless and vindictive. She wanted to spite Victor, and used her unborn child to do it. A poor innocent child....

Geneva never thought she would wind up pitying Victor, but she did. Helplessly she told him, "I'm sorry. Not just for you, but for Benjamin and Kathy and Virginia."

Victor nodded. His mouth trembled.

"But don't call yourself a murderer! Anne was the murderer."

Tears sprang to Victor's eyes. He looked so painfully lost. And...worn out. She thought of him, hauling his camera all over Europe, seeing death and destruction everywhere he looked, while carrying this heavy weight of death along with him. "Come here," she said. She took him in her arms and held him as he wept. "It's alright," she said soothingly, "it's alright."

It was late Sunday afternoon before Victor could bring himself to tell Geneva about his plans. He cherished her forgiveness almost too much to do it now, for what if she agreed to her part, put her whole heart into the film—as he knew she would do—and then he failed? He would be letting her down all over again. Yet, how could he not ask her? If he succeeded without her in the role of Charity, he could not bear to think she might see the film someday, and wonder why he hadn't cared enough to give her a chance. "I'm going out to Los Angeles to make a motion picture—the first of many, I hope—and I want you to have the leading role," he said at last.

When she replied with a look of astonishment, he quickly conveyed the tragic story of Charity Royall so that she could see what he meant when he claimed that she was perfect for the part, that no one else could bring the same depth to the role as she. He was quick to point out that in the end, Charity's legal guardian married her to give her child a name. As he voiced the phrase, *married her,* he wondered if Geneva could read the message of hope in his heart. For hope to rise in Victor was as natural as a bird raising its voice to sing.

For Geneva, regardless of how the story came out, reliving the experience of being abandoned by the man whose child she carried was abhorrent. She wondered how Victor could fail to see that portraying Charity Royall would only bring her misery, and for a moment she felt angry. But she was through punishing Victor. So she simply told him, "I've fallen in love with my dancing part-ner. When he comes back at the end of the war, we're going to get married." She almost added, "It's why I want to destroy those pictures—I don't want him to know about them." But again, that would seem terribly cruel, at a time when Victor's feelings were obviously tender.

Victor's countenance fell. It was the last thing he expected. At length he nodded in resignation, and the ghost of a smile crossed his mouth. "I'll be leav-ing in the morning," he said quietly.

CHAPTER 32

When morning came—Monday, November 11th—Geneva was awakened by a series of loud popping noises. As she lifted her head from the pillow, Victor dashed in and threw up the window sash.

"What is it? What's that noise?" she queried, resting on her elbows.

Victor swung around, grinning. "They're firing the guns at Camp Logan. The war is over!"

She threw off the covers and raced to the window. The sky in the direction of Camp Logan had taken on an orange cast. The firing continued to rip through the air. It sounded like two armies in combat. How odd, she thought, shooting guns to mark the end of all the shooting.

"And me without a camera," Victor said to himself.

To Geneva he sounded more amazed than regretful. He kept looking out the window mesmerized, as if viewing a fireworks display. She clasped her arms to ward off the morning chill and stood gazing at his profile for a long moment. He'd had a shave, and he was dressed in work clothes and boots, just as though he were about to walk out to the studio. Only he wasn't. She remembered John Scarborough calling Victor a gypsy long ago. She felt sad all at once for his rootlessness. Well, maybe he would settle down in Los Angeles.

He turned to her. "Let's go out and see what's cookin'," he said.

She hastened into her robe and slippers, and they hurried downstairs and out into the chilly air.

The crowd congregating in Heights Boulevard was clucking with joy, but while Geneva was certainly thankful the war was over, she could not ignore all that had been lost. It was a mixed blessing, like having escaped a house that burned to the ground with all one's possessions in it. Even civilians had not been spared because soldiers, prepared to die for their country, unwittingly spread death from the camps of Europe to the military posts in their homeland, in the form of the Spanish Influenza. If not for the war, Madame Linsky would be alive, and there would have been no table at Annunciation Church aglow with candles. Mrs. Crawford would be alive, too, as well as many thousands of others all over the world.

There were so many people on the boulevard, you could not make out the esplanade dividing it. Flags were flying; cowbells, ringing. A few women had turned kitchen pans into makeshift drums, and were banging them with spoons. Neighbors were hugging neighbors, laughing and crying together. Dogs were barking and circling, their tails wagging. Mr. Wald from over on Ashland Street had just gotten off his shift at the Southern Pacific shops. He hurried amongst the frolicking people with his lantern, a self-appointed town crier: there would be parades downtown on Main Street, starting at 6:30, he croaked. Geneva and Victor became separated.

She heard a fiddle tuning up to play, and then someone grabbed her elbow from behind. She turned to find Dr. Robinson, who had attended her along with many other victims of the influenza. The serious, cogitative expression he wore with his stethoscope was transformed into a wide grin. His large eyes seemed to strain at their sockets. Before Geneva could catch her breath he had thrown an arm around her waist and they were among those dancing to the music of the fiddle and the beat of the makeshift drums.

As they danced, she spotted Victor carrying little Joseph Crawford on his shoulder, wearing his sleeping gown and house robe, and clutching a teddy bear. She thought of Wendell, who would return from the war to visit the grave of his mother—one patient Dr. Robinson could not save. And what would become of the family now? Yesterday Mr. Crawford approached Victor while he was outside burning dead leaves. He said that as soon as Wendell came home, he would put their home up for sale. "We need to escape the memories," he said, and went on his way, his shoulders sadly hunched.

By the time the merriment adjourned, the bright pink and lavender stripes of daybreak were infringing on the orange cast of the sky. Victor came to put his hand on Geneva's shoulder. "I guess I'd better be on my way pretty soon. It will be hard getting out of town today," he said, the earlier, end-of-the-war happiness in his voice now missing. She nodded. They turned toward the house.

As they walked inside and shut the door behind them, she felt panicked. Victor had come, and now he was going, and still, she did not have her pictures. "Victor, please—I want my pictures back!"

He looked at her helplessly. "To destroy them? But if you had ever just looked at them—"

Quickly she cut in, "Maybe destroying them is what I need, to put all this behind me." That there was a reason far more practical, and pressing, she did not admit. She had no idea what effect this information might have on Victor, and there was no time to reason it out.

But really they are my pictures, Victor thought mutinously. He shrugged. "Alright. It may be a while before I get back to Springfield, though."

Geneva could hardly bear the thought of prolonging her wait. Besides, surely it would not be long before Tony returned, complicating matters. "Could you not go to Springfield, before you go to California, and bring the pictures here?" she begged. When she saw Victor's look of consternation, she realized how much she was asking. She capitulated, "I suppose you could send them to me by registered mail, if—if necessary." She still felt an aversion to having them placed in the mail, but if she made things too hard, Victor may become even more resistant.

"No," he said stubbornly. "Benjamin has been out in California a month, waiting for me. I'm always putting things before him, and I won't keep him waiting any longer."

Geneva had not realized Benjamin was waiting for Victor. And she knew that 'putting things before him' really referred to all the times he had put her first, before Benjamin. She felt very small just then. Victor had devoted a whole month to saving her life and nursing her back to good health, and she had never even thought to ask about his family. "Alright, I understand. But you will let me know when next you go back to Springfield?" Once again fearful of entrusting her photographs to the postal service, she added, "Maybe I could even meet you halfway, and pick up the photographs." Even as Geneva made her plea she wondered how she could manage that, for she did not know where she and Tony would be at that point. Suddenly it dawned on her that if Victor waited very long before returning to Springfield, she and Tony may be married by then. All her hopes of having the matter resolved beforehand would be gone. *"Tony, there's something you need to know about…."* Oh, how she dreaded telling him.

"I'll let you know," Victor said quietly.

Geneva let out a breath of resignation. For now she would simply have to hope for the best. At least Victor knew what she desired, and how strongly. Yet she could see from his face that his pride was deeply wounded. She would have never believed that when they finally came face to face, to have this conversation, she would wind up caring about his feelings. Placing a hand gently on his arm, she said, "I appreciate all you've done for me in the past month, Victor. You'll never know."

He looked deeply into her eyes. "I'm glad I was able to help," he said with a forlorn smile.

Geneva offered to fix breakfast for Victor, but he refused, claiming his stomach was too jumpy. He went upstairs to pack his things. As she lit the stove to warm up the pot of coffee he'd made earlier, she heard the weight of his footsteps crossing the bedroom floor above the kitchen. Her throat swelled. *He never meant to hurt me,* she thought tenderly.

They soon found that the pre-dawn mayhem of Heights Boulevard was nothing compared to the mayhem of Houston now that the sun was up. They had arrived between parades. People in uniforms—mainly Red Cross, U.S. Army regulation, and Houston Fire Department—were wandering among civilians, trampling on confetti and streamers pitched out of high office windows in an earlier parade. From somewhere came the oom-pah of a band rehearsal, and still, the loud popping of guns relentlessly split the air. Bed sheet banners abounded: *"Down with the Kaiser," "Long Live the Allies," "November 11, 1918—The End of All Wars."* The banner declaring there would never be another war struck Geneva with great force, for if it were true, then perhaps all that had been given was not in vain.

The ten-minute drive to Union Station took more than an hour today. But within a short time after they arrived, Victor secured a ticket on a train for El Paso, leaving in less than five minutes. Then he was hurrying across the concourse with her following behind, her hand stretched out, holding on to his hand as they threaded their way among the throngs of people there. On numerous occasions when Victor spotted an opening and angled left or right, she ran square into him.

Finally, when they were a few yards from the platform, a woman's narrow French heel pressed the center of Geneva's right foot with the concentrated heft of a stone mason engraving a piece of marble. She cried out, grabbing her foot, and Victor turned, his eyes wide.

"You alright?"

No. My period is late. "Yes." Her eyes swam with pain both physical and emotional.

She intended to follow Victor a few more feet, but now his arm went around her rib cage. He hugged her closely for a very long moment, and she hugged him back, drawn, in spite of everything, to the warmth of his body next to hers. She closed her eyes and his mouth met hers. Just that quickly it all came back, that day in the studio when Victor kissed her and then closed the curtain. It felt good not to be angry with him anymore.

Watching him make his way through the crowd toward the train, she thought of Tony and was seized with guilt for that parting kiss.

More than an hour later, as she drove the Packard up the driveway, exhausted and sad, she saw the postman leaving the mail in the box. She parked the car in the garage, then circled back to pick it up. Among the envelopes was a letter from Tony, posted some five weeks earlier. Well, that was nothing unusual with wartime mail.

Her sense of guilt about Victor's parting kiss sharply renewed, she opened it to read, "Dear Geneva, I feel very sad as I write this. I shall not be able to return to the States as early as we had both believed...."

CHAPTER 33

So soon did Tony's letter arrive after Geneva's disheartening talk with Victor about the return of her pictures, his opening sentence brought a sense of relief that there would now be more time for her to get them back and destroy them. Yet how much longer would it be? A few months would be perfect, she thought hopefully. Yet, as she sank down in a chair on the porch and read Tony's long explanation, she became increasingly grim. It seemed to her the problems facing his family were staggering. If a buyer could not be found for Selby Mines, or if Lord Edward refused to sell, it may take many years for them to work themselves out of debt. Would Tony remain in England until then? And if so, would he eventually beg her to come overseas and marry him? This left her bewildered, though not overwrought with emotion. Tony loved her. Of this she was certain. And she was well-experienced at waiting. In fact she paused in her reading to marvel at how well she was taking this latest setback.

Then came the news of the death of Tony's nephew Gerry—a totally unexpected end to his letter. Her eyes blurred with shock. Another innocent victim of the war, if ever there was one, and the child was not yet three years old. That Tony longed for her to be there with his family through this heartache brought bitter tears to her eyes. If only she could have gone to England with him....

After a while she composed herself and sat thinking ahead. For the first time in her life, she had a solid alternative when things did not turn out as she had hoped. How encouraging that was! She needed to figure out a way to assume ownership of Linsky's dancing school, and do it quickly.

Yet now John Scarborough's advice came back to her:

"You would be wise to get something down in writing."

She went inside and reread Linsky's obituary. No longer blinded by despair, she found herself questioning certain areas. For instance, "Mr. Claud Henckel of New York City, a friend from many years ago and executor of her will, journeyed to Houston immediately upon learning of her death, to conclude her affairs. In accordance with Madame Linsky's will, all proceeds from the estate are to be donated to the Catholic Church."

Linsky had never mentioned this *friend from many years ago*. Was he a dance master? A former lover? More to the point, had he sold the school while she was recovering from the flu? Yet, on the other hand, how would he have found a buyer within less than a month after Linsky's death? Of course, he may have sold it to an established school listed in the telephone directory—there was the Giezendanner school, over on Harvard in the Heights; Monta Beach was down on Prairie; and McMillan's Academy, on Rusk. And there were others. Linsky's pupils would not settle for any of them; they were far below her standards. But would Mr. Henckel know this? Yet she somehow doubted that he could have acted that quickly. It occurred to her she might persuade Ida to sign the purchase contract for now and arrange to begin paying off the contract from receipts, as Linsky had suggested. If some hired professional were in charge of Linsky's estate, like a lawyer or a trust officer, probably he would not settle for anything except the full amount in cash. But Mr. Henckel was a longtime friend. If he knew of the terms agreed upon between Madame Linsky and her assistant, would he not wish to honor them?

"You would be wise to get something down in writing."

The next morning at ten o'clock Geneva drove down Main Street to Linsky's studio. Just a normal weekday morning of moderate traffic and pedestrians going about their business, after yesterday's euphoria. Yet, the sight of yesterday's proud ribbons and confetti, now limp and dirty, littering streets and sidewalks, was a little dispiriting. *"Get ready for a shock when the boys come home; it will not be a pretty picture,"* Victor had said. He had seen first-hand the price of victory, paid in the currency of maimed young bodies and minds. For many, dreams of the future would be left unrealized; plans delayed until after the war would never be fulfilled. Hopefully hers with Tony would not wind up in this category.

Soon she was parking in front of Adele Gregory's. It was uplifting to see the "OPEN" sign on the door, and to note the absence of the purple wreath hanging there: it made it seem an eternity since she drove down here to post a sign on the studio door, feeling the onset of flu symptoms. And it was a comforting reminder that life went on even after the greatest of catastrophes. After fishing inside her handbag for her studio key, she began the long journey up the dark stairs, trying to steel herself for the reality that Linsky would not be in the studio to greet her. Then, halfway up, light swept over her. The door at the top was standing open.

In that moment, all hope abandoned her. Yet, she quickly reassured herself that the landlord may be about, and could tell her how to contact Mr. Henckel, or at least, explain the means of assuming Madame Linsky's lease.

As she walked through the doorway and into the hall, the pungent smell of turpentine wafted toward her. Somewhere, a hammer was pounding. Paint buckets, a saw horse, and a series of drop cloths spattered with assorted colors of paint lay in her path. Signs that a new tenant was moving in, or that the landlord was preparing to offer the space? She hurried toward the sound of the hammer. Passing the auditorium along the way, she glanced inside. More signs of painting, but otherwise it looked unchanged. The mirrors were still on the walls; the piano was in its place, a drop cloth covering it. She had no time to analyze what this meant, or to obey her mind's wish to dwell on the memories provoked by the scene. She hurried on in search of information. The hammering continued.

Soon she was standing at the door of what used to be the small dressing room. The wall at one end had been knocked out, to take in a large closet that used to be next door. Chunks of plaster were all over the floor; white dust covered the marble window sill and clouded the air. Just inside was the source of all the hammering: a lone workman, his overalls and cap layered with dust, was nailing a board in place.

"Excuse me, sir," she said.

The man looked around, then pulled down the dusty bandana shielding his nose and mouth. He was gray-haired, with a gray stubble on his face. His eyebrows hitched together as if this had not been the first interruption of the day, he asked, "What can I do for you, miss?"

"Can you tell me who is moving in here?"

"Don't rightly know. I work for the building contractor. He's over at the lumber yard right now, be back in an hour or so."

"I see. I was…associated with the dancing school here. Maybe you knew of Madame Elvira Linsky, the dance mistress? She died in the flu epidemic."

He shook his head. With a flat look he said. "So did my wife."

"Oh, I'm sorry to hear that," she said, instinctively bringing a hand to her throat, wondering how many conversations with strangers over the next few weeks would wind up like this one. "I left some things in a cabinet that used to be against the wall that has been knocked out. Do you know where the cabinet was taken?" she asked.

He shook his head. "As I say, you'd have to ask the boss."

"Yes…well I'll just wait around if you don't mind. In—in the office."

"Don't make no difference to me," he said, and lifted the bandana back to his face.

Walking in that direction, Geneva realized that from all evidence these rooms had indeed been let to a new tenant, and very likely to another dancing school. *Losing the studio lease doesn't necessarily mean I've lost the school,* she told herself. But where would she relocate? Suddenly she wondered if Mr. Henckel had removed all the personal effects. If so, where had he taken them? Her black jersey and skirt didn't matter so much, though her ballet shoes were expensive, special-ordered like those of all Linsky's pupils from London, England. More important, what about such things as business records? These would be necessary to a prospective buyer.

The door to her teacher's office was closed. Geneva paused before opening it. Regardless of the present state of the room, the very essence of Madame Linsky would be there, distilled inside four walls. She dreaded walking in as she had dreaded the voicing of Linsky's name during the service at Annunciation. Finally, she forced herself to turn the door knob.

The room was dark. She fumbled for the switch on the wall, and when she found it and turned the ceiling light on, naked walls stared back at her. Inevitably her eyes went to the spot where the crucifix belonged. There a faded cross shape remained, as if its significance were so great it could never be entirely removed. Geneva found this oddly comforting. Reassuring, too, was her presumption that Mr. Henckel had taken the crucifix and put it safely away. It occurred to her that maybe the crucifix had been buried with Linsky. She would have liked that, Geneva surmised; in fact, it hardly seemed she could go to her grave without it.

Apparently someone had been housekeeping. In one corner was a large waste basket, heaped with trash.

Doubting that business records were left behind, Geneva nonetheless sat down in Linsky's chair. As she did so, the image of Madame Linsky lowering herself into that chair, her hands gripping the arms, was so vivid in her mind that it almost took her breath away. *I am here,* her thoughts traveled to Linsky, as if her teacher's spirit would be comforted by this knowledge. She began pulling out desk drawers; first, the lap drawer. It proved empty. To her surprise and delight, however, in the top right hand drawer she found the ancient accounts receivable ledger, with its faded binding and metal screws—probably the only one Linsky ever owned. It was like discovering a long-lost photo album belonging to one's ancestors; she felt a mystical connection to it. She took it from the drawer and opened the front cover. The first sheet was devoted to the roster of pupils' names and addresses. Following this were the individual account sheets, all filled out in Madame Linsky's spidery script. Geneva lightly turned the pages, wishing all the while she could turn back time. Just weeks ago, Linsky sat right here, making the last of these entries.

Where was the corresponding ledger for payables? She wondered, and opened the drawer below. To her surprise, she found several bills of sale, stacked haphazardly. Suddenly certain of finding the explanation for all which had eluded her, Geneva flipped through them. And what she found made her cheeks burn: the locksmith, hardware store, paint store, flooring company and lumber yard all had one thing in common. They were made out to Madame Linsky's School of Dance, Martha Dixon, Proprietress. Geneva leaned back in the chair and closed her eyes.

"…I intend to return to France. Geneva is considering taking over my school. Perhaps you and Mr. Dixon will one day enroll your children here…."

Martha was passing Geneva in front of Annunciation Church, nodding tightly while her husband looked the other way.

Geneva bent her head over the desk again, and feverishly checked the dates. The oldest of all—from the locksmith—was dated October 20th. Martha must have contacted Mr. Henckel as soon as she had read the obituary. Geneva felt dizzy with rage. She could not stay here any longer. She yanked up the accounts receivable ledger and rose to her feet. Dear Mr. and Mrs. Bessemer…. As you know, Madame Linsky intended for me to take over her school one day and your daughter Melinda was among the most promising pupils in morning primary ballet, which I taught for Madame Linsky. I am opening a small school…. Dear Mr. and Mrs. Walters…. Dear—

Yet…if this ledger vanished, Martha would not have to investigate very far before she found out who had taken it. And Martha's husband was a lawyer. Geneva could not risk it. There were 92 pupils listed on that roster. At least she could take down a few names.

She had a fountain pen, but no paper unfortunately. She began retrieving crinkled scraps of paper from the waste basket. Then she spotted a familiar envelope, then another, and still another: her letters written to Linsky during her vaudeville tour. These were not yours to throw away, Martha Dixon! She yanked them out. Her curiosity aroused, she set them aside and kept digging.

Farther down were Linsky's framed certificates and pictures that once hung on the wall. *Nor were these!* She put them aside and kept digging. More wadded up papers. And finally, at the bottom of the can, the first article to be disposed of: Linsky's crucifix.

At first Geneva could only stare, as if seeing it for the first time. Then as she reached toward it, she thought, *I never expected to touch it.* Soon she was closing her fingers around it, tenderly lifting it out. No friend of Madame Linsky's would have thrown this away, she thought bitterly. Mr. Henckel, perhaps in a rush, must have left all personal effects to Martha's discretion.

Geneva continued gazing at the figure of Christ on the cross in her hand. The crucifix no longer seemed forbidding. In fact, having been taken down and cast aside, it seemed all too vulnerable; the suffering figure, all too human.

She sat down again and quickly thought through what she was doing. If the contractor returned and found her perusing the ledger, copying information, he may later report to Martha. She wasn't afraid of this, particularly. But if he found her removing items from the office, he may not believe the truth: that they had been discarded. He may stand in her way. And if she left without taking Linsky's treasures, they were all doomed.

Geneva had no idea how soon the contractor would return. It could be any moment. She would have to forgo copying names. Linsky's treasures had to be saved. Hurriedly she placed the crucifix inside her handbag, and slipped her letters in. She rose from her chair and gathered the framed articles in the crook of her arm.

Geneva knew she must find a way to continue Linsky's fine teaching traditions, and be a credit to her. But she had been robbed of all the means of doing so. She had no fees to collect, to provide the money; no studio; no piano—thanks to Anne. And for the first time, as she entered a new and scary phase of her life, she had not the encouragement of the friend who used to occupy this sparse little office. To Geneva this seemed the greatest loss of all.

At the door she took one final, lingering look around, her eyes resting at last on the spot once occupied by the crucifix. Then she turned out the light.

PART III

1922–1924

CHAPTER 34

It was at *Le Café des Etoiles* in Paris, on the 20th of May, 1922, that Tony first had an opportunity to see a performance of acrobatic exhibition dancing. Tonight's performers were a couple from the *Folies Bergere,* reputed to be the best acrobatic dance team on the circuits. As Tony sat in the smoke-filled cafe, waiting for the show to begin, his expectations were high that he was about to behold a crystal ball through which he would view the future of *Sterling & Selby,* to resume—he hoped with all his heart—after an interruption that had stretched out four years, far longer than he could have imagined.

Even though his *Dance of the Red Hat* was thoroughly imaginative at the time, it seemed rather naive now, for the new decade had ushered in a mood of cynicism—no doubt as a result of the war. One needed a keen edge, something dramatic and dangerous. Hard to believe he once envisioned himself as a love-sick Joker, twirling about the stage with Geneva in a huge skirt as the Queen of Hearts. It just wouldn't do now, with women wearing bobbed hair and short, clingy dresses, their brightly painted lips balancing cigarettes.

The show was late, which frustrated him. One could not depend on schedules being kept in a little night spot like this. He drummed his fingers on the table and ordered another drink. How he craved a cigarette now, with everyone about him puffing away. Always prone to smoke in times of stress, he had been doing so steadily since he returned to England. Recently, facing the happy prospect of returning to Geneva's side, he swore off the habit. He only hoped Geneva was looking forward to his return as much as he was; frankly he was becoming a bit uneasy about this.

In the years since he bade her farewell, not a day had passed that he didn't wake up in the morning thinking eagerly of the moment he would take her in his arms again; and he always checked the morning post immediately, hoping to find a letter from her. He was encouraged by her willingness to be patient when she learned he could not come home at the end of the war as planned. Since then, he had kept her fully apprized of how matters were developing at home, and the tone of her letters suggested she perfectly understood his prolonged absence. Yet, while he received a brief letter from Geneva in early March, he did not hear from her in April or yet in May, though he had written her several times. Still, preparations were under way for her Spring recital—always a busy time—so perhaps that would account for her lapse in writing. Or so he hoped.

In the past four years Tony often felt he was taking two steps forward, and one back. When Morey returned from the war, Nell had not begun to recover from the loss of their son Gerry; she spent hours sitting in the nursery, weeping at the side of his crib. She hardly slept, and lost all appetite. The weight she lost—more than two stone—lengthened her face and made her body sag. How lovely she used to be when plump and in the pink of health! Now she looked like walking death. Whereas Tony had assumed Morey would return to work at Selby Mines immediately, and he would be off to Oxford in the autumn, instead he and his father urged Morey to devote all his time to helping Nell get past the tragedy, perhaps do a little traveling about, and then locate a house to buy, where they might start afresh. Morey had his faults, but one certainly had to credit him for his devotion to Nell. In June of 1920 they moved into Camellia Cottage in Launceston—a lovely Edwardian house to which some previous owner added a second story with two bed-chambers and bath. The house was surrounded by steep lawns, huge trees and scads of camellia bushes. Shortly after—thanks be to God!—Nell gave birth to a healthy son named Guy. Only then did Morey return to work for Selby Mines. Thus it was not until Michaelmas term that Tony re-entered Trinity College.

As often as possible, he traveled home at weekends; and he spent every long vac at home, just to keep abreast of the business picture. All the while they awaited Morey's return to work, Selby Mines had done nothing more than hold its own. Even though on occasion Tony made discreet inquiries about the possibility of selling up, none of the offers were handsome enough to retire the debt that weighed so heavily on their shoulders. Once Morey came back to work, a little progress always seemed to be taking place—enough to keep Father from losing heart. Tony decided that when he finished his exams in May of this year, and had some time at his disposal, he would try once again to find a buyer for Selby Mines. If he failed—which seemed more than likely—he would just have to be content that he had discharged his duty as best he could, and write to Geneva that he was ready to return. He resisted the temptation to write and tell her of this plan, for he could give her no specific date of his arrival. If by some miracle a buyer was found, Tony knew he would be wise to stay around until the sale was fully consummated, and there was no telling how long that might take. Tony's final months of study at Oxford, beginning in January of this year, were so demanding of his time, he did not get home except on one occasion, in February. Thus did he lose a sense of how things were progressing with the family business.

Finally, after sitting his last exams, he went home to Brookhurst. Soon after his arrival, he sat down across from Lord Edward in his study. "We had a strong showing for the first two quarters, much better than expected," his father reported, the leather wings of his chair framing his fine head. "Bankers are content. Secret is to keep the business coming in, and expenses down. Morey's working harder than ever. Doing the business proud."

Unhappily, last year was lackluster to say the least. Tony suspected the influx in business this year came about as a result of a very small mining operation, near Redruth, shutting down. In any case, unlike his father, Tony was not convinced that two strong quarters or even several more presaged the end of troubles for Selby Mines. Not in peace-time. Not with the cost of doing business constantly on the rise. However, he also realized—and with mixed emotions—there would be no convincing his father to sell up now.

"I suppose there's nothing to keep me from getting on with my plans, then," Tony said.

Lord Edward reached for his pipe, filled it with tobacco, then glanced across at him as he lit it. "Will you be returning to the States?"

"I plan to." Depending upon Geneva....

"And to show business?"

"Yes, hopefully," Tony said.

The notion of running a dancing school with Geneva in Houston may have worked at one time, but no longer. Around the same time that thief Martha Dixon absconded with Madame Linsky's school, Mrs. Ruekauer became disgruntled with her work for the women's suffrage movement, and began nursing full-time. Taking advantage of the opportunity, Geneva converted the second parlor into a studio. The Geneva Sterling School of Dance had steadily prospered. However, ultimately Geneva wanted a family and Tony wanted a theatre. No dancing school in Houston, Texas, no matter how prosperous, would yield the kind of profits required to purchase or build a theatre. And after what Selby Mines had been through, Tony had a strong aversion to borrowing heavily. What they needed was a dramatically successful season on the vaudeville and variety circuits, by which they would rise to headliner status, and several more for which they could command the highest pay, and—if they were very lucky—some break along the way that elevated Tony's status to that of producer. He knew very well that he could be a capable producer, but one didn't just walk in and begin. One needed to cultivate friends and contacts in the business. And how would one accomplish this, except by being in the thick of it? Never had Tony been more grateful for his mother's fine reputation and many acquaintances. Her help would be invaluable, especially at the beginning....

"You're not thinking of settling in the States for good, I should hope?" his father asked now.

"No sir, I shall be back," Tony said, "though I'm not sure exactly how soon." He had come to realize over the past four years that he would not be content to live permanently in the States. He must somehow persuade Geneva to live in England.

"Bringing Miss Sterling with you, I trust?"

"I certainly hope so," Tony said, and found himself grinning. Yet, again he thought uneasily of Geneva's failure to write him lately.

"Jolly good! We shall all look forward to her arrival," his father said. Then after a pause he began tenderly, "And, my son—" He hesitated for a long moment, taking a draw on his pipe, before continuing hoarsely, "Thanks awfully, for coming home, helping out. Staying so long. All of us pitching in, sacrificing, helped us attain the position we're in now, I daresay."

Tony had not the heart to say he was doubtful their position was stable. He would have to put it out of his mind, for there was nothing more he could do.

"And you were wise to complete your studies at Oxford. It isn't just a matter of family tradition, though that's important enough," he said, lifting his brow. "Thing is, one never knows when an engineering degree might be useful."

Tony could not imagine anything worse than spending the rest of his life over a drafting table.

Up to now, Tony had not allowed himself the luxury of dreaming up dance routines because he had to focus all his energies on passing his exams. Yet, the necessity of doing so was never far from his mind.

At Christmastime last year he'd spent a brief holiday in London, and while there he heard rumors about a new dance form called acrobatic exhibition dancing. The idea had originated from the circus, and was reputed to be rather dangerous. Very few teams were even attempting it, and none were performing on the circuits as yet. Tony was intrigued. During the train ride home from Oxford after exams, he caught up on his reading. In the most recent issue of *Dancing Times,* a notice appeared about an acrobatic exhibition team currently performing in Paris. Now, upon leaving his father's study, he went into the library where he'd left the issue, and thumbed through it again. According to the notice, the act would close on Saturday of this week. This was Thursday—he'd have to leave at once, in order to get over there in time to see a performance. And depending upon his impression, he might mention it when he wrote to Geneva that he was finally returning to the States.

Thus was he drawn, two days later, here to the smoke-filled *Café des Etoiles.*

Alas, finally watching the dance progress—it was half an hour late beginning—his only source of amazement was how easily pleased the audience proved to be. They swooned and applauded for every acrobatic lift. This was the problem, he soon realized, or one of them. It was a series of lifts, loosely strung together by some not very convincing ballet steps by the girl. Geneva would make her look positively amateur! And the boy—well, he was far too big for her. Every time he put his muscle-bound arms round her rib cage, one thought she was in danger of being crushed to death. And for all those lifts: twirling arabesques, backbends high above the boy's shoulders, windmills—all good ideas in theory of course—the boy was slightly off in his rhythm, a little late every single time, which drove Tony positively mad; he wanted to tell him to get the lead out and quit missing the beat! Oh, it was dreadful all round.

When they took their bows, the audience cheered and whistled like trained parrots. Tony got up and made his way among the tables and out the door, thoroughly disappointed and craving a cigarette as never before. All of which put him in a very bad mood.

Outside a fine misty rain was falling. Still, he had no wish to be cooped up in a taxi all the way back to his hotel. What he needed was a good brisk walk. He pulled up his collar round his neck and drove his hands into his pockets. As he strolled along, he stared dejectedly at the cobbled wet pavement before him....Which, now that he thought about it, was quite interesting on the *Place de la Concorde.* Slick from the rain, bathed in the soft penumbra of gas street lights above, the swirling pattern reminded Tony of ocean waves. One could not tell where the odd wave ended, and the next began. By Jove, it was mesmerizing, a vast continuing—

But that was it! If one could do the sort of acrobatic stunts that he had seen tonight...only making them flow into one another, so that the audience could never distinguish when one began or ended...threaded through by a dreamy adagio melody—. Or no, something more original...a story, yes! A heartbreaking tale, casting a spell. A villain with the darkest motives, and a beautiful, trusting maiden....

Tony stayed up all night in his Paris hotel, feverishly composing the dance; now up on his feet, his hands making motions of a lift, now sunk over his notebook again. Crossing the English Channel on the ferry early on Sunday, he continued writing. At midnight on Sunday he fell into bed exhausted; four hours later he rose again, and started trying out new variations on what he had done. By six he was out on the terrace, working on sequences of steps. By Monday noon he had everything written down. He was on fire with excitement when he sat down to write to Geneva. "Darling, I'm coming back! And I have written the most haunting, death-defying dance for us; it shoots right for the heart, and will drive audiences positively mad...."

Two days after he posted it came a letter from Geneva. With a chill, he thought of her long silence. He tore her letter open with shaking hands. "Dear Tony, It is with sadness that I write this letter, and believe me, I have given a great deal of thought to what I must tell you."

Tony sank into a chair and leaned forward, gripping the letter tightly. He did not take a breath. "As you know, I have been faithful to my commitment to wait for you, and I believe I have been more than patient. Yet after so long a time, I've come to realize that my love for you can no longer be sustained. And without this, there is no basis for continuing to anticipate a future with you. I am not saying you are necessarily at fault, Tony; you know best where your duty lies. Still, I hope you'll understand that in view of all this, I feel I must put an end to our relationship."

Great tears welled up in Tony's eyes. He read on, "Having held out hope that you would return one day, I have put off expanding my school far longer than I should. Currently I have sixty pupils, and 27 on my waiting list, with little hope of ever working that list down. Therefore, I have made an offer on a piece of property out on Milam Street where I will build a school. I'm now in the process of applying for a loan—a tricky situation for a woman, I must admit. It is good to do something decisive at last, and it is very exciting to think I've come this far as a teacher. Mine remains the only school of dance in Houston that truly lives up to the standards established by Madame Linsky. I know she would be proud.

"And I'm sure you will wish me well...."

"Tony, please know that in return I wish you all the best as you go forward with your life in England. I'm sure the ties that bind you there are very strong. Regards to your family. Always, Geneva."

Tony sat back and touched his trembling fingers to his forehead, trying to collect his thoughts. Geneva had not said that she had fallen in love with another man. Thus, far more bruising were the words that she no longer loved him, when there was no one to blame for stealing her affections, no adversary to fight. He alone was to blame, for asking more than she could give. Why had he not realized?

Should he write her again? Send a cable, saying his letter was on the way, begging her to reconsider? No. He would wait, and see if she replied to his letter posted two days ago. Perhaps knowing he was coming home, and that he had composed the most exciting dance for them that he would ever write, would rekindle her feelings. He would hope and pray. It would be the longest wait of his entire life.

CHAPTER 35

"Name this child."

"Sidney James Younger."

Voicing the name, Geneva thought soberly, *This may be the closest I ever come to motherhood: babies carried in Willa's womb. Imagine me a godmother!* Only for Willa and Rodney would she go through this ritual inside the great and venerable walls of Christ Episcopal Church, Houston, and take on the responsibility that was beginning at this moment on the last Saturday morning in May of 1922; only for Willa and Rodney, from whom Geneva kept no secrets about her ambivalence toward God and His Church; from whom, in fact, she kept no secrets at all.

Geneva knew of Willa long before they actually met. She'd had a fast reputation at Central High, where Geneva was enrolled when her parents were killed. Willa Frazier was one of those girls your parents forbade you to mix with: tasty fodder for lunchroom gossip. A tall, willowy, brown-haired rich girl, with sexy, tilted eyes, she sneaked cigarettes, lied and cheated through every class, filched the key to her father's Pierce Arrow, then drove like hell until she wrecked it. She got people's attention by doing things others only dreamt of, and if they came too close, she lashed them with her sharp tongue. If not with her fingernails: Boys found that out if they mistook her recklessness and tried to go too far. That she was a foundling, adopted by wealthy parents, was the tale people spun around her; and it was partially true. That she was tortured by questions ignored, no one guessed. *"Who is my real mother? If you don't tell me, I'll run away and find her myself."* Her adoptive parents heard it enough times as she grew up; they ought to have known she was serious.

Then along came Rodney, a real estate broker who was a few years older than Willa, with a boyish smile and dark red curls and a steady personality. Rodney was not afraid of Willa; saw right through her anger and fell in love with her. In turn she fell in love as fiercely, uncompromisingly, as she did everything else, but not without vanishing long enough to find the answer to the question which had haunted her entire life, before she married him. Geneva knew none of this at the time, but she soon would because the newly-weds would make their home in the old Crawford house.

The house had been vacant forever, it seemed by then. Its yard was over-grown; its paint was peeling; its overall demeanor was sad and wistful. Geneva often thought, in fact, that if houses could weep from loneliness, for lack of footsteps and laughter up and down the halls, this one certainly would. The Youngers soon set to work transforming it with paint and varnish and hard work, and love. The first chance Geneva got, she baked them a cake and took it over, explaining that such hospitality was in the tradition of the late Mrs. Crawford. Naturally she went on to tell them all about the Crawford family, and this led to her picking up a paint brush to help—she knew the newlyweds were busy and didn't want to slow them down, yet she was drawn to them for how easy they were with each other, how affectionate, and she didn't want to leave. This was how she came to know Willa and Rodney Younger.

In less than a year after they married—October of 1921—James arrived, long-limbed and auburn-haired; and Geneva went speeding to St. Joseph's Infirmary to see him every day, in the roadster for which she had traded the Packard after the war. Geneva gloried in her role as "favorite aunt."

These across-the-street neighbors, as close as blood kin, plus the 60 pupils who made up Geneva's dancing classes, had gradually filled her life. And on a day-to-day basis her life could not have been much better. Not until lately had she told herself that it was enough, because not until lately had she come to believe it might be all there was. The offer she made on a piece of property out on Milam Street was the first bold step she had taken toward a future that was a natural outgrowth of this life: that of a spinster dance mistress, like Madame Linsky. When her mortgage loan application had been approved, subject to her signature with Rodney as cosigner, he brought the papers over and went through them carefully with her so she would understand exactly what she was getting into. Sitting alongside him at the dining room table with the papers spread out before them as orderly as pieces of fine china set out for a festive meal, she'd felt a surge of pride and certainty. Finally, she would have the stu-dio she and her pupils deserved.

Yet later that night in bed, and on many nights to follow, she lay there with the text drifting across her mind:...*the balance to be paid in equal installments beginning September 1, 1922, and the final installment being due and payable on August 1, 1942.* She saw her life no longer as a succession of individual days, but a solid block of time, from which she would emerge middle-aged. Linsky's words upon seeing Geneva headed earlier for exactly the kind of future she was now to have, came back to haunt her: *"But ma chère, I did not begin to teach until I could no longer perform.... If I were your age, Monsieur Selby would not have to ask me twice, certainement!"*

When the sale closed on June 8th, there would be no more hope of resuming what she and Tony had begun before the war. Probably there would be no hope of ever seeing Tony again. But perhaps there never really had been. Four years....

Geneva knew exactly the point where her love for Tony and her hopes for their future had finally become so brittle with age, they snapped like old bones. Long ago he had written to explain very reasonably that only by returning to the stage for a while could they ultimately have what they both desired. Geneva was touched that he took seriously her wish for a family, even if he did not say he shared it. And she was certainly willing to help him fulfil his wish to own a theatre someday. Thus did she continue teaching in the cramped quarters of her second parlor, though every year that she held her school back from growing, she grew more frustrated.

Tony would come home one day, she consoled herself, so she must be patient and make do. He could not be blamed for all the delays.

Finally, in mid-March of this year came a letter saying that Tony would take his last exams in May. Geneva's heart leapt. The very next sentence would read, *"I shall be coming home as soon as I finish."* Instead he spoke only of all he must accomplish by what he called, "May term." "...but at least I can see daylight at last; I only wish I could say the same thing for Selby Mines." He ended by asking if she had chosen a theme for her spring recital, but did not say that this would be her last one, as soon they would be dancing. Dizzy with regret, she started to write back and ask if he was coming home after May. But suddenly she rebelled. Wasn't it all too obvious? Tony was in no hurry to return—just as she had predicted years ago, when she feared he would go home during the war and not return when it was over—and whether he realized it or not, he was using the business as an excuse. *Things will never be good enough for him to leave.* She thought of how many years they had been apart: the stacks of letters filling two dresser drawers, all the times he had said how much he missed her and could not wait until they were together again. What a fool she had been.

Furious, she fired off a letter outlining her suspicions, and concluding, "If you can't see your way to coming back as soon as you graduate, then don't bother coming at all." Completing the last sentence, she looked up and stared at the blank wall behind her writing desk. A strange feeling of detachment came over her. She had her school. She had Willa and Rodney and James. She had a good life. She suddenly realized it really didn't matter very much if Tony came back. Not that it wouldn't be nice, just that she felt no more passion for the idea. *I don't love you anymore*, she realized.

Quickly she revised the last page of the letter, telling him not to bother coming because she would not be waiting. And she ended with the five word sentence she never expected to write.

When she actually saw the words on paper, she felt frightened. Loving Tony had been a part of her life for so long, waiting until they could be together had been so much a part of that love, that now it was as though she'd lost a limb like one of those poor soldiers in the war she'd read about, but still had a strange sensation of feeling where it once was connected to her body.

Out of a need for assurance that she could not have explained, she hurried across the street to show the letter to Willa.

Willa had just put James down for a nap in the upstairs nursery. She poured Geneva a cup of coffee, and the two sat down in the sunny living room.

Geneva waited anxiously as Willa read the letter carefully, putting each page aside as she went on to the next. Finally she came to the end. She looked up at Geneva, her brows knitted above her long slanted eyes. "You know how I dread the thought of your moving away. But…are you sure you don't love Tony anymore, that you're not just angry?"

"I—frankly I don't know what I feel anymore, Willa," Geneva said uncertainly, and her eyes grew wet. What could the absence of passion mean, except the absence of love? "Maybe I've been on my own too long. But the prospect of Tony coming back just doesn't excite me the way it used to. Maybe I need to move on."

"What will you do now?" Willa asked, puzzled, as if she could not quite fathom Geneva not waiting around for Tony anymore. Maybe it had become a part of her life too.

"I'll keep teaching, of course. But I won't stay where I am," Geneva said hotly. "I'm the best dancing teacher in the Houston area, and look where I teach! I can't get more than six pupils in one class, so I have to teach three times the number of classes, and I still can't get everyone in—oh, I'm sorry, Willa. I didn't mean to take this out on you."

Willa was nodding.

Geneva sniffed. She thought of all the crushing blows Tony had received, and she felt guilty for the way she lashed out at him in her letter. "Look, maybe I'll hold on to the letter until I'm not feeling so angry, and see if I want to rewrite it. But it won't change anything, and in the meantime I'm going to have Rodney start looking around for a piece of property...."

"Sidney James, I baptize thee in the name of the Father, and of the Son, and of the Holy Ghost. Amen." The Priest dipped his hand in the basin and dispatched rivulets of water from James's forehead into his hair line. James screwed up his face and bellowed. Willa smiled at his spirited reaction.

At the conclusion of the baptism, everyone emerged from the church and into the warm sunshine. Geneva was holding James, his white christening gown spilling down to her knees. Feeling a sudden rush of gratitude for the simple rituals of life and the sense of newness they created, she clutched her new godson to her breast and kissed his forehead. "I love you," she said, "and I'm going to be the best godmother you could ever have!"

On Monday a letter arrived from Tony.

CHAPTER 36

"Darling, I'm coming back!" As Geneva read Tony's opening sentence, she was startled to realize that their letters had crossed in the mail. Behind his words was the certainty that she loved him and would be waiting. "And I have written the most haunting, death-defying dance for us…" he continued with the bold enthusiasm that was so emblematic of Tony's nature, it was as if he was standing right there. Her cheeks flaming, she read the second paragraph:

"*Chimaera* is the story of an avaricious collector who discovers a monarch butterfly, beautiful beyond his wildest imagination. At once he devises a plan to capture her, becoming more and more demonic as she eludes him…." He went on to describe the new acrobatic exhibition dance form that was catching on in Europe and had obviously captured his heart, and to describe some of the lifts he had in mind for *Chimaera*. It was just like Tony to compose a dance so dramatic and challenging that the page before her dissolved, and all she could see was the aging dance mistress she would be 20 years hence; the dowdy spinster with her long fading hair curled up in a knot, who had settled for an existence of staid certainty, rather than taking a risk on the thrill of a lifetime.

When her anger had finally subsided, and she rewrote her original letter to Tony, it seemed only fair that she tell him she no longer loved him so that he would move on with his life, because she was determined to go on without him: regardless of how she felt about Tony, once the idea of owning her studio took root, she was so driven that the very idea of reopening her school one more year in the cramped second parlor became abhorrent to her. Now, if she wrote to say she'd had a change of heart, she would be doing so because she was drawn to Tony's *Chimaera,* rather to him. With just a few words, he had the dark, riveting spectacle of the dance whirling in her head.

As she took the remainder of days to make up her mind—11 in all, before the date of closing on her dream come true on Milam Street—Linsky's words echoed in her mind again and again; filled her with fear that if she refused Tony, she would be making the biggest mistake of her life. Finally she decided that if things did not work out, she could still come home and buy a piece of property. What was a few months, give or take, when you were obligating yourself right into middle-age?

And if she fell in love with Tony all over again, nothing would stand in the way of their future: her nude photographs had been destroyed by the hand that created them.

On June 7th she wrote to Tony, "I trust by now you've received my letter. However, I am willing to give *Chimaera* a try...." She walked across the street and apologized to Rodney for having put him to so much work only to wind up backing out. Rodney, being the person he was, forgave her at once, and he and Willa and Geneva drank a toast to the future of *Chimaera*. From the glowing faces of her best friends, Geneva realized they had known this was right all the time. Which made it seem all the more right to her.

Feeling giddy after a glass of Cabernet, she thought: *It's time to cut my hair.*

At five o'clock in the evening on June 20th Geneva paced anxiously along the platform at Union Station, wearing a short silk floral-print dress with a drop waist and a long string of pearls that she had purchased for the occasion. *I am fortunate that at this moment in my life, I need not worry about those loathsome pictures,* she thought. Some months after she and Victor parted, he wrote that he was going to Springfield, to visit his daughters. *"I'll get the pictures out of storage, but I see no reason for you to destroy them. They are mine, and I will do it."* She was flooded with relief. Victor included a return address on his letter—an apartment building, apparently, called the Mercury Arms. She considered waiting a few weeks, then writing to ask him to confirm that he had carried out her wish. After all, how could she forget how devastated he was when he found out she wished to destroy the fruits of his labor? It was as if she had asked him to murder his firstborn child. Yet, to insist on confirmation would imply she did not trust him; he was undeserving of this. Finally she wrote, "I am deeply grateful that you honored my wish, and were kind enough to let me know. Yours always—" Having put the whole matter behind her, she felt truly free for the first time in years; and her love for Tony was more intense than ever. With all her heart she wanted to write to tell him she was coming to England to marry him. Yet, the future of Selby Mines remained in question then, and Tony was enrolled at Oxford. He might be glad that she was coming, but he would probably wonder what had suddenly prompted her; and his father would no doubt consider her appearance an intrusion. She felt stranded.

Now that she was minutes from coming face to face with Tony, she wondered if the inability to put her feelings for him into action at that pivotal point had begun gradually to erode them. Or, rather, to make them dormant? Hopefully she would soon know the answer.

When Tony stepped from the train, in a gray pinstriped suit and gray bowler, a mackintosh looped over one arm and a bouquet of yellow roses in the other, it was—Geneva thought with relief—as if not years, but days, had passed since he left. How perfectly natural and warming to her heart it was to raise her hand and wave, and see him spot her in the crowd and grin.

This is right. Yet, as he came nearer she noticed that his complexion seemed inordinately pale in this climate of heat and humidity, like someone who had just been released after an extended hospital stay. His brown hair and small moustache were speckled with gray—not much gray, just enough to remind her that he would soon be 27 years old. He handed her the roses, and said rather uncertainly, "Well! Hullo, Geneva." Four years since she last heard his voice. She had forgotten how distinct was his British accent. It sounded odd now, terribly misplaced. Then they were hugging, a little clumsily, and she felt a pang of guilt. He had come all this way, for such a lukewarm welcome. Still, she found herself relieved that he did not try to kiss her. He held her away and smiled, his eyes crinkled with longing. "How good it is to see you!"

"You too!" she cried. After a very long pause in which they stood looking at each other, at a loss for words, she said, "I've had my hair cut." Immediately she realized her stab at conversation sounded foolish, because he would not understand what a milestone this had been in her life, how it symbolized her readiness to take a risk on the future.

"You don't say?" Tony said doubtfully. "But I suppose one can't get stuck in time, like Miss Havisham," he assured her, and watched as she removed her hat pin, reached for the edge of the peach-colored cloche that matched her dress, and whisked it off her head. She smiled and shook out her short waves for his approval. He only frowned.

"You don't like it," she said, crushed.

"Ah no, it's very fetching, just takes a bit of getting used to."

"I'm having a switch made," Geneva confessed. She'd sat high up in a chair in the hair salon, watching 14 inches of what used to be her pride and joy drift to the floor, a feeling of being stripped naked overtaking her.

"Fancy that! Well I dare say, you shan't need it any time soon, since your hair will be covered with a black jersey cap."

Geneva gave him a blank look.

"For *Chimaera*, of course," he said, and after a beat or two, they both broke up in laughter, for it was so like Tony to be completely absorbed in his new dance. *Tony is back*, she thought happily.

Cynthia sat before her dressing-table mirror on a satin-tufted bench, stroking her lashes with mascara and fighting down a feeling of unease. When Tony wrote that he was coming back, and that Geneva had agreed to dance with him, she had clasped the letter to her breast in joy. A successful tour over here, followed by another in England, would wind up with a proper wedding at the end. What could be more inevitable?

But then there was that unfortunate appearance by Jane at a party Tony attended, which he reported in a letter shortly before he sailed. Until then, except to mention old Mrs. Tremont's death at Fairleigh a couple of years ago, Tony had not written a word of the Tremonts since reporting the outcome of Jane's murder trial in 1918. Cynthia had become hopeful that her fears were unfounded, that they had heard the last of Jane. But no longer. How much better if Tony and Geneva could be married before returning to England! Yet the tradition of marrying in St. Petroc's Church was too entrenched in the Selby family for Cynthia to promote that idea with any success.

So after the wedding bells ring, what shall I do? she asked herself now, summoning back her optimism that the bells really would ring. She reached for a delicate flesh-colored silk stocking, smoothing it carefully over her foot and up her leg. Of course if Tony had his way he and Geneva would go on touring for two or three years at least, and in that case they would need her. But sooner or later, they would settle down and Tony would buy a theatre and produce his own shows. With the right breaks he may make enough money to swing it. Or if not, Edward would probably loan him money from the estate. Edward had plenty of money, that was sure, and he was generous. So, at some point, Cynthia would simply have to figure out what to do with the rest of her working life.

She wished she could do something other than scouting. After more than a decade, she was worn down by the traveling, the eight-a-day, fire trap, small-time houses where she just might discover an act of genius on the stage; of pot-bellied producers' offices, filled with leather and cigar smoke and myopia; of charging with her discoveries to the top of the bill. If not for Tony, Sonja Vitalé would have been Cynthia's swan song, the perfect exit. Undiscovered until Cynthia came along, the diva was now booked regularly at *The Palace*, while her gift of a Steuben glass font, held up on the delicate wings of angels, sat on Cynthia's dining table at this very moment, filled with hyacinths. How had the angel motif gotten so far out of hand? Cynthia was fortunate to have inherited more money than she could spend—the quarterly statements from the brokerage in New York always astonished her. There was never a shortage of performers down on their luck, and as word got around, she had acquired her nickname, "the guardian angel of show business." Whenever she received a gift from any business associate, she knew what its theme would be before she unwrapped it. Apart from the Steuben glass font there was the Maxfield Parrish painting above the mantelpiece; and the mirror through which she now viewed her face was surmounted by a magnificent gilt angel whose wings formed the mirror's frame. Tonight's toast would be offered with angel-held champagne goblets of etched glass—an original design, signed by the artist. Unfortunately, the truth underlying all these extravagant gifts was that Cynthia had no real friends anymore, only grateful business associates.

She reached for her rouge pot and smoothed a little color on each cheek, then dusted her face lightly with powder. Forty-six years old! Crow's feet around her eyes, slack skin around her mouth and chin. What a surprise to find that showing one's age was not a gradual process, but rather as sudden as an accident. She had always been a woman of considerable beauty, and this had proven useful. It was her looks, more so than her talent, that had taken her from First Place in a contest at Tony Pastor's 14th Street Theatre in New York City, to the top of the bill on the vaudeville circuit, and from there to London's West End, by the time she was 18. Returning as a talent scout years later, she had to dazzle producers and booking agents, forcing them to take her seriously.

But now the new fashions, just at a time when nature was taking its toll. She had never imagined how hard it would be to lose 10 pounds: living on poached fish and steamed vegetables, while Selena's dinner rolls and desserts were the envy of everyone on the sixth floor! Months of enslavement to floor exercises, just to wear dresses that exposed a little knee.

Of course, there was Oyster Bay. Richard was after her to sell some of her stocks, and buy a place near his; sit back and enjoy the view. The trouble was, her older brother was always trying to run her business, and they could not be together more than an hour without getting into an argument.

No, what Cynthia truly wanted was simply to go home, and view these years as a party that was now over. *Could it be so bad?* she asked herself, as she painted her lips coral and ran a comb through her short marcel wave. After all, she and Edward had loved each other. Most of their arguments were over issues that no longer mattered. She recalled now, when Tony was born, she could have held her son in her arms all day long. Yet, her status in society required that she hire a wet-nurse to feed him; and a nanny, who spent more time with him than she did. Round and round they went, but Edward won. One night, they returned from an evening at the theatre to find Tony crying his heart out in the crib, while Nanny sat in a rocker not two feet away, snoring. Cynthia fired her on the spot, and refused to hire another. Then there was his education. Tony was sent to Eton at age 12. Edward had applied for his admission there on the day he was born. Yet by the time Tony was six years old, she knew he was born to dance. Round and round, they went. Again, Edward won, though Cynthia still managed to get her son back and forth to London for the expert training she insisted he have.

Though Nell would be loath to admit it, she was raised more like an American, simply because she was female, and Edward deferred to Cynthia's judgment. She gloried in feeding Nell at her breast. Later, she dissuaded Edward from sending Nell away to boarding school—not that it was hard to do. Father and daughter thrived on being together. They still did.

How she missed her daughter, even though they never got on well. Trying to develop a little self-confidence in Nell when she was young, Cynthia arranged for lessons in violin and piano; back and forth to London they went, Nell sulking all the way. Finally, Nell protested to her father, and that was that.

Poor Nell, losing little Gerry to the Spanish Influenza. Cynthia had never seen her grandson, except in the photograph Nell sent—how she treasured it, sitting in its small gilt frame on the table beside her bed. She ought to have been there to help Nell through the loss of that child. Yet, for Cynthia, going home was impossible.

Her big mistake had been in accepting an invitation for an encore tour, five years after they moved to Cornwall. But Edward ate, drank and slept Selby Mines. She was lonely, hungry for the excitement of the stage. Hungry to be noticed and admired. Then came—amazingly—an invitation from the King to perform at Sandringham. The tour which followed was inevitable, as was perhaps the brief affair that took Cynthia by a storm along the way and lasted one week. The man was not particularly handsome, but he was charming, and sensitive enough to know a lonely woman when he saw one. She was smart enough to know he was using his advantage, but flattered and reckless enough not to care. She had no illusions that it would last, either, for like her, the man was married. His wife and three sons met him at the station in Brighton, the last stop of the tour and where they made their home. Watching the four of them walk away down the platform, laughing and talking as if nothing had happened, she thought: *he won't tell his wife, and there's no need for me to tell Edward either.*

What folly to believe she could carry such emotional weight around with her for the rest of her life. By the time Edward greeted her at Bodmin Station, she was so weighed down with guilt that she could scarcely breathe and had to confess. *"I had an affair in Edinburgh. He was a vocalist. It didn't mean anything. I'm sorry."* If Edward had yelled at her, or even struck her. But no. After looking at her with astonishment, he simply turned and left the room. A permanent wall went up between them. No, she could not go home again.

She stood now and glanced at her figure in the short lacy slip, then removed the dress she would wear tonight from its hangar—a chemise of lime green beads with a scalloped neck and hem—and stepped into it. How heavy it was, to be so slight in design….

When she heard the doorbell ring, tears sprang to her eyes. Tony was here at last, and Geneva was on his arm! Swiftly her feeling of unease returned, however: *"Jane showed up at a party at Lanhydrock last night,"* Tony had written. *"Someone tapped my shoulder, and I turned and there she stood, in a gown of dark blue beads, cut to the bone, looking for all the world as if she expected me to throw my arms about her.*

"'I've been renovating Fairleigh since Grandmother died,' she said. 'It's all done now. I assure you, the gloomy trappings of the past are quite gone. So refreshing! Makes one feel like a brand new person. Perhaps you'll come and see for yourself before long.'

"I could have told her I was sailing for America within the week. But I just turned and walked away."

There was no doubt in Cynthia's mind that Jane was looking for an opening. She must direct all her thoughts and energies to being sure she didn't find one.

CHAPTER 37

During the eight-day voyage across the Atlantic, and the long train journey once he reached the American shore, Tony tried to prepare himself for Geneva to greet him coolly. The discouraging tone of her letter asking him to come left him almost as demoralized as he had been when she broke up with him earlier. Somehow he must win her over, but how would he begin? When would it be permissible for him to take her in his arms and kiss her? Until a short time ago, he had not anticipated being at such a dreadful disadvantage when they finally came face to face, or so bereft of confidence. By the time his train crossed the Houston city limits, he could scarcely get his breath.

Their first few moments together were so awkward and out of rhythm, Tony feared he had been foolish to come; Geneva's feelings had gone too far away ever to be retrieved. But then, later, with a sparkle in her green eyes, she was suddenly flinging her hat off her head, and shaking out her short waves, like a proud bird showing off her colorful plumage. Though he couldn't actually say he was thrilled with her bobbed hair, he was deeply touched and encouraged that she wanted to please him. By the time they left the station and headed for the Beaconsfield, they were both feeling more at ease. Yet he would not dare to try and kiss her. Long ago he had learned not to rush Geneva.

Over the next few days, as they plunged into the herculean challenge await-ing them, weather conditions in Houston seemed to conspire against him. How could he expect Geneva to become romantic when any physical exertion left them both dripping with perspiration? Even the whirring fan in the high ceiling of her second parlor was little help in July. What he would give for another snowy January day! He would never forget the flame of that kiss, melting her reluctance. Perhaps she expected him to force a kiss upon her now. But he would wait a little.

Tony's practice get-up was a tight-fitting jersey with a scoop neck, an old pair of knickers, and lace-up boots with rubber soles. Geneva wore an old-fashioned knitted bathing suit with a sleeveless top, and trunks that reached around four inches down her thighs—much shorter than her trousers for *Dance of the Red Hat,* and revealing a very fetching pair of legs. She had only to walk in the room and he felt a strong physical stirring. Was it possible that, in spite of the withering heat, she was feeling a mutual stirring for him? If so, she did not show it. They began each morning with basic lifts, his hands round her hips from behind, his line of vision from her slender neck—exposed now, with her short hair—down to the small of her back. Geneva must virtually lift her own weight, relying on the strength and resiliency of her muscles, and there was always a moment just before she flexed her knees deeply in preparation when Tony thought if only she would just slightly turn her face, showing him her profile, he would swivel her hips round and kiss her. But no. Her back was a wall. Soon she would be high in the air: 12 inches in the beginning, then 15, then 18, and more. Tony calculated that before long, the ceiling would be too low to accommodate them, and still—how frustrating!—he had yet to kiss her.

He had all but given up looking for her signal when finally it came, most unexpectedly. As they must develop elasticity between their bodies, in order to avoid the disjointed movement that characterized not only the first, but most of the teams Tony had observed by now, they did an exercise he called the "push-pulls." At least twice a day, they stood facing each other, around a foot apart, and with her hands resting on his upturned palms, they moved their arms back and forth at the elbows, somewhat like the motion of a platform rocker. This exercise went on for ten minutes or so, per session. Naturally they could not just stare at each other, but looked elsewhere—up at the ceiling, down at the floor, past each other's shoulders towards wall mirrors or windows, while her hands were cradled in his palms, moving back and forth. Late one afternoon, he noticed Geneva gazing vigilantly upon his flexed muscles. Which of course drove him positively mad for a kiss. Suddenly, perhaps because neither of them was concentrating any longer on the exercise, their sweaty palms slid right past each other and Geneva fell slightly forward, grabbing his biceps to brace herself. She looked up at him and waited, her lips curled invitingly. In the least precipitous, most unromantic circumstances imaginable, two heads with perspiring brows and dripping wet hair came together, their mouths meeting in a salty kiss. They stood back and laughed at themselves, and then they were kissing again. They had come full circle, Tony thought with glee. One day he would again propose marriage, and this time Geneva would say yes.

Emboldened as never before, he found himself scrubbing many of the lifts he had spent hours composing—how timid they were, just variations on things that he had seen others do, none with the originality he expected of himself. He devised more and more daring lifts that would add to the drama of the dance. There was nothing of which the two of them were incapable.

Sooner than either of them expected, it was time to pull out the acrobatic pad, transfer the lifts from the paper on which they were scribbled, and work on the connecting tissue of *Chimaera*, to make all the parts into the whole, and to make that whole into the dance Tony had dreamed of.

For Geneva, acrobatic exhibition dancing was any graceful ballet step, any acrobatic stunt, lifted high in the air and turning, turning, turning. A magician's spell, a sleight of hand, it changed in less than the blink of an eye; all the while she was twirling, twirling, twirling, a bolt of velvet unfurling, an adagio line from the stirrup of Tony's hands to the back of his shoulders and higher, higher; a windmill, a weathervane, an arabesque, turning, turning, turning; a bow and arrow, the figurehead on a sailing ship, cartwheels and splits, turning, turning, turning, higher and higher, then lower and lower, a corkscrew whirling around Tony's body down to the floor, and there without a pause, she was flowing into the next lift, and turning, turning, turning.

It was a grand illusion, accomplished by way of spills and tumbles, bodies sliding on oily sweat; grasping hands, poked eyes, gouged ribs, missing, missing, missing, trying again. A second too soon, a second too late; an inch too far; an inch too little. It was the shape of her fingernail embedded deeply in Tony's skin, resulting in ten half moons, clipped away and discarded. It was a crop of new bruises traveling each morning to Sylvan Beach, where the height of two bodies stacked on top of each other met no resistance except the sun, baking relentlessly, for hours and hours, on tired backs and aching limbs. It was not wanting to go there. It was missing her pupils—the memory of their faces sometimes almost bringing tears—as the summer pushed forward like a fist.

And it was sliding down, being stopped just in time, the collector's groping hands saving the butterfly's head from embedding in the grassy shore. It was wondering if any dance could be worth this much, just for the spectacle, for the applause. It was the certainty that keeping ten red hats in the air at once would not have been as hard. It was absolute madness, exhaustion unparalleled. It was fear of falling, which she dreamt of at night, and woke herself bolting straight up in the bed.

But it was Tony Selby at his brilliant best. Since their first, sweaty kiss in her second parlor—that pleasurable kiss which finally convinced her she had never stopped loving him—she had realized her heart was repeating the same beats as before, when she marveled at the genius of his *Dance of the Red Hat*, at his ability not only to write it but to perform it and pull it out of her as well. If she could dismantle what she felt for Tony just as they dismantled every acrobatic stunt, lining it up by its parts to learn it, she could easily arrive at the conclusion that she loved every individual quality that made Tony who he was. And that was what kept her going through the horrendous work-outs, day after day after day.

At last, his eyes lit up like Christmas morning, Tony described *Chimaera's* magnificent climax, more daring than any lift ever attempted by an acrobatic dance team. "It is the moment when the evil collector triumphs over the butterfly; a heart-stopping, four-part lift exemplifying her pain. Now she is perched high, hands across her breast; her hips resting in the collector's hands. Now her body latches tight into the fetal position. Now her body jack-knifes and arches over his hands." A pause, a wicked look. "Now comes the ultimate test—he flips her in the air."

"In the *air?*"

"Quite!"

The time between the spring of Tony's hands and the moment when he caught her was falling into the black pit of the dream. The greatest danger, he admitted, was that of a broken pelvis. Three or four times into rehearsing this four-part torture routine, winding up, upside down, clawing at his ankles, Geneva saw Tony as having become the collector, using her for his own purposes. How dare he demand this of her. She was incapable. She hated him. She would show him that she could do this, by golly.

But the worst was yet to come, she learned as the chilly fall weather blessedly arrived, and they rented Munn's Auditorium where the ceiling was high. There were the butterfly wings to be worn on her back—not lighter than air, billowing panels of color, stirred by a backstage fan, as she had surmised, but the product of an Oxford engineering degree. The wings were two folding fans, hung upside down, to be opened at strategic points in the dance by tugging on two small finger rings, and lifting her arms. They were a masterpiece of two black crinoline frames and multicolored panels of China silk, sprigged with flashy sequins. They cost three times the price of the spangled red hat, but never mind. They were every dancer's nightmare costume-come-true.

In late November, when they had mastered the dance, and Cynthia had approved, they made a publicity photograph: the butterfly posing in an arabesque, standing high on one shoulder of the collector, her wings opened in all their glory, her bruises covered by a black body stocking and a pair of black fishnet hose. When *Sterling & Selby* viewed it together, Geneva suddenly felt protective of their accomplishment, and resented the booking agents who would not understand what it took for those blacks and whites and shadows to appear in their particular order on a sheet of thick glossy paper. They would not realize they were looking at a miracle.

CHAPTER 38

Karl Hoblitzelle's new Houston *Majestic* on Rusk Avenue transcended the opulence Tony remembered so well from his earlier theatre, and created a world of fantasy: when the lights went down on the gilt-encrusted Italianate villa garden scene which flanked the proscenium on each side, it was as though the domed ceiling of the auditorium had been rolled back, and one gazed with amazement at a vast Mediterranean night sky, with twinkling stars, a moon rising, and wispy cloud formations drifting lazily across. As he watched a demonstration on the morning of the walk-through rehearsal, Tony could not help feeling envious. How could anyone ever top this?

Securing a spot for *Chimaera* on the all-star bill for the *Majestic's* premiere was among his mother's greatest triumphs, for by the time *Chimaera* was ready, the show was booked. It took several negotiating sessions to finally arrange an audition with Karl Hoblitzelle, just a week before the show. Upon seeing the dance, he said without hesitation, "We'll make a place for it."

Not until the day of the performance was Cynthia able to learn the order of the bill and advise Tony and Geneva. Unfortunately, *Chimaera* would close the show. Geneva despaired that after all those months of slaving, *Sterling & Selby* would not have the full attention of the audience. Most of them would be thinking of the crush they were about to encounter at the hat check stand on this frigid January night, when overcoats, scarves, and furs would add to the general confusion behind the window in the lobby. Tonight's performance was sold out—all 2500 seats.

Geneva kept her concerns to herself. She didn't want to appear ungrateful to Cynthia, and as for Tony—well, all week long he had seemed preoccupied. When she asked what was troubling him, he only shrugged and said, "It's nothing." She didn't believe him. Was he worried about their opening performance? Or, was it bad news from home? She always half-expected this, even though he had maintained since he arrived from England that his father was optimistic about Selby Mines. If the picture had changed of late, surely he would tell her eventually. In the meantime she would not pry.

All too soon the *Majestic* premiere was nearing the end and Geneva was taking her position behind the curtain. From out front she could hear gales of laughter, though she could not make out what George Whiting the comedian was saying to provoke it. She tested the rings for resistance, then had a sudden horror that one might come un-threaded, rendering the wing as good as broken even before the butterfly was captured. Now she heard enthusiastic applause for Mr. Whiting, followed by a pause. Now he said something else; the audience roared with laughter again, and then they cheered him. She counted four curtain calls, each one increasing her dread. She was going to fail. *Relax. No one will be watching.* Except, of course, Willa and Rodney—one from the sixth row center, the other from the mezzanine—Rodney having purchased two of the odd seats still available as of a week ago when they found out *Chimaera* would be on the bill. What a comfort to know they were here.

Now Geneva looked toward Tony, waiting offstage in his deep purple Cossack shirt and leather leggings, his fingers wrapped around the pole of his outsized hoop: the illusory net with which he would stalk the butterfly that was beyond his wildest imagination. He threw her a kiss. She was struggling to break her heavily-painted, trembling mouth into a smile when she heard the foreboding toll of the bell that signaled the beginning of the dance and set the mood. Once…twice…three times. She faced the back of the stage and forced herself to breathe deeply. Behind her, the curtain was slowly parting. *No one is watching.* Then came Rachmaninoff's *Vocalise,* a bittersweet dream swirling around the senses, Tony's perfect choice of music for the beginning and the end; delicate as the wings that slowly, provocatively, opened. Or, were they opening? She could not tell. It was as if her arms were disconnected from her body. But then she heard an audible swoon. People were watching, after all. But soon their attention would wane, she reasoned through single, then double pirouettes across the stage. Her feet were like two sticks, preceding her body. Then she spotted Tony, crossing the stage in leaps and turns, his spicy cologne wafting toward her, his net held aloft in pursuit of the innocent butterfly, unaware of his aims. Now he changed tactics. Putting the net aside, he came to romance her. In that fleeting moment when Tony's eyes met hers, the hard lines of mascara coming to high points on his brow, making his face diabolical, he was all evil; she pitied the harmless creature she portrayed, stalked and captured for its beauty, its movement destined to be stilled forever.

One after another, they flawlessly executed the lifts, turning, turning, turning. She could hardly believe how well it was going, higher and higher; how the audience responded with increasing applause, as though somehow they knew that every lift was more daring than the one before it. Now her foot was in the stirrup of Tony's hand; now she was riding on his shoulder, and now up in an arabesque, and two…and three…and four. Open the wings, that's right. Tony was a genius, she thought reverently; wings closed, and lower and lower, turning, turning, it was too bad no one would be watching when it was time for the four-part—

Then it was time. Hats, furs, claim tickets occupied their minds. Then she was perched above Tony, his hands around her hips. The music stopped for four beats. Geneva imagined she could hear the audience breathing. Then, a great minor orchestral chord, the sound of every stringed instrument plunging low. Wings opened. Closed. Three parts to go. Now, hands across her breast. Two beats. A lunge into the fetal position, and two, and three. Then the jack-knife—*was he there? Yes!* Now, the drum roll, and a deep breath, go! On an intake of breath, her body spun in the air.

But then she was falling.… Everything went black.

A clash of cymbals, and Tony seized her at the hips. All the breath flew from her body. The audience went wild. From somewhere far away she heard Tony's voice: *"Open them!"* Oh yes, the wings. She tugged. They opened. Had she ruined the dance by her delay?

But there was no time to worry, for the long passage from one of the composer's wild piano concertos had begun and they were into the next step, right with the music, turning, turning, turning, the wounded butterfly desperately attempting to escape the collector now shadowing her every step. The audience was dead silent. Their attention was moving past the organ concert at the end, calculating the quickest route to the lobby and the hat check; perhaps many had already left their seats. The dance was simply too good to have been sacrificed. Cynthia should have held out for—

It was over. Standing above the slain butterfly, the collector held away from himself a torn piece of purple China silk, signifying that he had destroyed the very prize he had won. Now, sorrowfully, he was releasing it; now it was drifting down over her body as he left the stage in despair, and the final bars of *Vocalise* closed around her like a shroud.

They were clasping hands, bowing to the black void between the glaring lights, the audience cheering, whistling, applauding, going wild for *Chimaera*. Bless Karl Hoblitzelle! He had given the dance the only place on the bill that would do it justice; and in return it delivered the grandest finale he could have dreamed of for his new *Majestic*, with its dramatic night sky hovering above.

Geneva could not make out what Tony was saying above the cheers from the audience and her ringing ears. She glanced at him. "What?"

"I said, do you love me?"

So this was what had preoccupied him all week long. Knowing Tony, he must have been counting on a triumphant performance to provide the perfect moment to propose marriage, for it was coming, she was certain, even as she cried, "Yes, I love you!"

Tony grinned broadly as they sank into another bow. Geneva waited, as perhaps she had always waited somewhere deep within her—even from the night they first met and danced the tango in Linsky's studio—for the moment to arrive when Tony would ask—

"Will you marry me?" He was rising again.

"Yes!"

Now they were both grinning. The traveler curtain thundered across the stage before them. Tony was so eager to take her in his arms and kiss her, the butterfly wings narrowly escaped being crushed. They kept kissing till the stage manager warned them back into the wings, with grease paint and mascara sliding down their faces. The music of the huge pipe organ was booming loud enough to burst right through the atmospheric roof.

Cynthia was waiting at the stage door. When Tony announced that they were to be married, her eyes filled; she threw her arms around them both, and Geneva thought that she read on Cynthia's lips, "*Thank God!*" It was good that she was pleased. One could never guess what Cynthia was thinking. It had always seemed queer to Geneva that she had mothered two children. Now it seemed amazing that she was to be her mother-in-law.

"I have some more good news. Just before the show, I got confirmation on a five-city trial run, after you finish here, at $300 a week," she said.

"Splendid!" Tony happily swung his mother around, kissing her cheeks.

"Put me down!" Cynthia protested, laughing. "You open at the Kansas City *Orpheum*," she told them breathlessly, "and from there you play Denver, Salt Lake City—let me think—San Francisco, and Los Angeles."

Tony was hugging Geneva close, his chest swelling with pride, while hers contracted in despair. Any good vaudeville act would eventually wind up playing the West Coast, would wind up in Los Angeles. But the news struck Geneva's ears with the solemnity of the bells tolling for *Chimaera,* because it reminded her that although she need not tell Tony of the pictures, there was the other secret that she had to confess. Would he be understanding when he learned she would not come to him as a virgin on their wedding night? Or was he one of those men who lived by a double standard? In any case, she dreaded voicing the words, and watching his face as she did so.

CHAPTER 39

When finally they parted on Geneva's porch at two in the morning, having been treated to a midnight supper at the Youngers' with a bottle of champagne to toast the betrothed couple, Tony and Geneva agreed that he would return at ten o'clock, to discuss wedding plans. They kissed, and went on holding each other. "I love you," he said, with special male tenderness in his voice and his eyes, as if he were anticipating their wedding night: *Don't be afraid; trust me to treat you gently, and with patience.* The trouble was, Geneva had seen that look before on another face. She felt cheap, disingenuous. Had the hour not been so late and the two of them not so exhausted, she would have confessed right then.

Soon she was tossing and turning on her pillow, devising different means of explaining her affair with Victor in a way that would gain Tony's sympathy, including—how she despised her cowardice!—playing up Victor's seducing her, yet omitting his obvious reluctance on the first day they made love. Must she tell Tony of the ultimate price she paid, that day of the storm? Surely she must, for she hoped to have children with him someday, and the miscarriage may have significant impact on how her physician advised her during pregnancy. In that case, might she vilify Victor for his failure to consider the possibility she was pregnant when he left her behind?

By the time she met Tony at the door, bleary-eyed, she knew she would simply tell the truth unsparingly, rather than twist the details in her favor. She didn't want to live with her guilt for what amounted to fabricating lies.

Ida was at home this morning, puttering around in the kitchen in her house robe before getting dressed to go out on a new nursing case. Geneva discreetly slid the parlor doors closed, and sat down at the opposite end of the sofa from where Tony sat. He smiled and reached for her at once, but she held up a hand. "Wait. There is something I must tell you before anything else." And thus she related her lengthy tale, beginning on the day of her parents' burial, when Victor asked her to model for him, and watching closely the changes in Tony's expression as her story progressed. By the time she finished telling him about the storm, his cheeks were bright with anger; his eyes were two boiling pots. She hastened to digress and say, "I am as guilty as Victor. I knew he was reluctant to get involved with me, but I overrode that; I was reckless—"

Tony interrupted with a fierce wag of his head. "You were a 16-year-old girl who had just had the rug pulled out from under your life. You can bet Victor saw you coming!" he swore. She opened her mouth to protest—"And left you carrying his child, the filthy lecher!

"I should have guessed something like this, the day I gave you that magazine with your photograph inside, and you told me he was thoughtless, self-centered. I daresay! I swear to you, if I ever set eyes on him, I shall give him reason to curse the day he laid a hand on you."

Geneva thought of Tony's violent tale of slamming Brian Potts to the Brookhurst stable floor. Would Victor be any match for Tony, if it came to that? With horror she imagined two bloody faces and banged up bodies, lying on the ground. How would such a conflict end? With one of them dead?

The last thing she had expected was for Tony to disallow her right to take responsibility for her part in the affair with Victor. It was as if he considered her weak-minded or helpless. She told herself that he didn't mean it that way; that he only hated to see her hurt because he loved her. She was tempted to tell him the secret of Anne's death. He might then understand why Victor would not—could not—come back to her, after burying his wife. But that was a private matter, divulged in confidence. She would not repeat it behind his back, even to Tony. He would simply have to accept the person she was now, partly shaped by her affair with Victor. Oh, she hated that they had to begin this way; it robbed all the magic from her memory of Tony proposing on the *Majestic* stage as they took their triumphal bows.

She had no idea where the conversation would go from here. But then Tony was reaching across the sofa, clutching her in his arms. She could feel his heart thundering against her breast, and she, too, was trembling. He cradled her face in one hand and looked into her eyes. Poor Tony! She had never seen his brown eyes more sad. "I do love you so awfully much, and I can't bear to think that anyone would hurt you," he said.

"Yes, I understand," she said, her voice quavering. And then they were kissing desperately, his hands slipping down her body, going places they had never been before. *Because you need to know that I love you, as never before,* went her thoughts, wrapped up in her own growing desire. There was nothing to stop them. Then suddenly an alarm sounded within her. They were to be married soon; she did not want to rob what should be saved for marriage, for that was what she had done with Victor. Immediately a chilling question arose: *Knowing what you know about me now, would you respect my wish to wait?* She found herself pushing at him. "Hold on!" she cried.

Panting, Tony threw her an injured glance and composed his hands.

"I need to ask you something," she said, catching her breath. "Just say so, if you think I have no right to ask this. But…is it worth—can we just wait? To—" she faltered, "—to make love, until after we're married?"

Tony paused to consider this. He saw no reason it should matter whether they were married or not. That is, unless she thought he may leave her one day, like that blackguard Victor Calais. Surely, after all his years of fidelity, she could not think that. Still, he had to ask, "Do you not trust me?"

"Of course I do," she said tenderly.

"Well I think what's important is our commitment to each other," he said.

"Yes, me too. I just want to do everything right, this time," she pleaded.

Again he paused. He did not understand Geneva's reasoning, but nor did he want her to believe him incapable of such restraint. At last he said resignedly, "Well then, so be it." Suddenly he thought, *my God, where's the sense of joy we had last night, that propelled me out of bed this morning? We shan't either of us ruin this, I won't have it. There has been too much heartache already, for us both.* He willed himself to regain his sense of humor. "But I warn you, Geneva Sterling, never has a groom more hotly pursued his bride than I will you, once we're married."

She smiled coyly. "As you may have guessed, the bride will be as eager."

Tony felt a little easier now. "And by the way, I thought I came over this morning for us to begin planning our wedding."

"So you did," she agreed.

Cynthia was already working on a variety tour to begin in April, so they set a tentative date of June 2nd. The service would be held at St. Petroc's Church in Bodmin, Cornwall. Marrying in Tony's church was a concession Geneva readily made, given what she had just put him through.

It seemed such a perfectly reasonable idea to Geneva, nor had she any guilt, either for keeping the pictures from Tony's knowledge or contacting Victor behind his back, not after the explosive way he behaved when she told him about their affair: just a telephone call. She still had the number Victor had given her, and the address of the boardinghouse where he lived. *"Tony and I are getting married in England this spring. Knowing those pictures have been destroyed means so much. I feel free to go on with my life...."*

And then, if Victor admitted he was unable to bring himself to destroy the pictures, after all—a frightening possibility that her bruising conversation with Tony had opened in her mind; it was amazing how being put on the defensive filled you with self-doubt—she would simply say, *"I'm coming over. Please have the pictures ready."* Then she would have to figure out some way to do that without Tony being aware. But what if Victor had never taken the pictures from storage? She thought uneasily. Well, she would have to deal with that problem when and if it arose.

As they made their way along the tour, heading ultimately for Los Angeles, the notices for *Chimaera* were stunning and made nice additions for Geneva's growing scrapbook. Said a critic in Denver, who had no respect for acrobatic exhibition dancing in general: "But ladies and gentlemen, these are dancers! What a pity there is no place for such imaginative work, except across the vaudeville stage, or squashed between two acts of a frivolous revue."

Consequently, *Chimaera* was the main feature in advertisements all the way from Texas to the West Coast. What if Victor saw the advertisement, and appeared at the stage door of the Los Angeles *Orpheum* on the day they opened, ostensibly to wish them well, but really to size up the man who had bested him for her affections? She thought of Tony's anger. She certainly hoped not.

As their train sped toward Los Angeles, she became increasingly worried. She must call Victor at the first opportunity, to save herself from being distracted during a performance. If ever there was a time when she and Tony could not afford a less than perfect performance, it was now. Armed with *Chimaera's* glowing reviews, Cynthia was angling for a try-out at the *Palace*, before they sailed to England. Playing the *Palace* in New York City was the envy of every vaudeville act in the business. Geneva would rather die than ruin the opportunity for them.

Over the week they played the Los Angeles *Orpheum*, she was relieved that Victor never appeared at the stage door. There was no listing for him or Benjamin in the telephone directory, but there was a number for the Mercury

Arms. She called this number repeatedly, from an instrument in the most obscure location in the hotel: a small corridor behind the dining room, near the swinging doors of the kitchen. She soon grew to hate sneaking off furtively. Still, somehow she could not give up. By Wednesday, the only thing saving her from the distraction she feared was to convince herself that Victor had left Los Angeles. And he had promised to destroy the pictures long ago. She had it in writing. Why had she created all this worry for herself?

On Saturday, their last day in Los Angeles, she decided to try to reach him once more. After all the failed attempts, she was startled when a man answered. The manager was out of town right now, he said. He was passing by the front desk when he heard the telephone ring. She asked if he knew Victor Calais. He said that he knew who he was. Her heart took a leap. "But I haven't seen him lately. The young man who lives with him is around, I think. I could mention you called."

She assumed he was referring to Benjamin. Now she did not know what to do, and there was no time to think about it. In a few minutes they would be leaving for the matinee. "Just say that Geneva Sterling called, to say hello." She had to repeat her name, and spell it slowly, while he wrote it down. By now she was standing on one foot, then the other. A busboy wheeled a trolley around the corner, heaped with used plates and cups and cutlery, from luncheon. The man said something. She could not hear above the clatter. "Hold on," she said. After the kitchen door swung open and shut behind the busboy, she asked the man to repeat himself.

"And where shall I say you can be reached?"

"Oh yes. At the *Orpheum*," she said, then quickly added, "Thank you very much." She hung up before the man had a chance to pursue her with more questions. She rushed down the stairs to pick up her things.

Afterward, she wondered if she had done the right thing, and where Victor had been lately. Why had she not thought to ask how long since the man had seen him? Days? Weeks? Months?

Thankfully, all three Saturday performances went smoothly. As they were leaving the theatre late that night, a guard at the stage door handed Geneva a telephone message. Tony and Cynthia were standing on either side of her. "*My father took a job in Singapore four weeks ago. B. Rothby.*"

Vaguely Geneva wondered why Victor took a job in Singapore, and what happened to his plans to be a film maker. Yet at the moment she was more perplexed by the name 'Rothby,' which was slightly familiar, but why? A few moments passed before she remembered where she had heard it before. Growing up she had the impression that Benjamin was not Victor's son—probably from overhearing her parents talk. She had no idea of the circumstances, however, until Victor told her that Benjamin's father walked out on Anne as soon as he learned she was pregnant. "Jim Rothby was a no good scoundrel," Victor said. So Benjamin had reclaimed his natural father's name. How very odd, when the man abandoned him before he was born. *B. Rothby.* Not *Benjamin*—she noted—as one might sign a message to a person who used to live under the same roof. She thought of him now, stealing the key to Victor's studio, having a tour, then walking past her in the kitchen, bold as could be. How terrified she was that he had found her nude pictures. *"We're leaving on Saturday, and you can't come."* How hateful he was, how spiteful. *B. Rothby.* Did he still carry a grudge against her, after all these years?

At least the unfamiliar signature on his note was convenient for her now. "Friend of my parents," she said to Tony and Cynthia. "I just thought, as long as I was here, I ought to say hello."

And now she was forced to live with the fact that she had lied to Tony. *But at least that will be the end of it,* she thought.

CHAPTER 40

In between the West Coast tour and her departure for England, Geneva met with John Scarborough to arrange for the closing of her account. Tony had offered to accompany her, but having put up with the man for all these years, alone, she felt it would be appropriate to be alone when she terminated their association.

Upon receiving the news that she and Tony were soon to be married, Mr. Scarborough's eyes flickered; his mouth grew hard. After a long pause, he said doubtfully, "Well, I must say, this is all very sudden indeed." He rose from his chair and stood by his sunny office window to look out toward the Binz Building, his hands clasped behind him, his gaunt profile turned towards Geneva. "An Englishman...hmm. Let us hope this fellow can provide for you. You never know about foreigners, and all this business about titles, well, it doesn't mean money in the bank, now does it?" She could see his bottom lip curling upward.

He knew how long she had known Tony Selby. How dare he suggest her fiancé was some slick talker, taking her for a fool. Though she owed him no explanation, she could not resist assuring him, "All that belongs to me is to be set aside in the marriage contract." She felt a little false just then, having boasted of a document she resented for its inherent suggestion that she and Tony dare not trust each other."*That's just the way it's done in England, when there is a landed estate to be inherited,*" Tony apologized, then assured her once the details were settled, they could both forget about it.

Now, in order to further drive her point home, she continued, "I'm going to take all my documents in my steamer trunk, so that Tony's lawyers can get started on the contract as soon as we arrive. Tony felt it would be wise."

Abruptly Mr. Scarborough turned to face her, as if she had surprised him. After some hesitation he said, "Oh, but surely they won't need anything but the most recent statement. I'll be happy to have my secretary—"

Amazed at his cooperativeness, Geneva interrupted, "Thank you, but I've already gathered up all my statements and packed them, along with everything else I could think of that they might need, just to be thorough." She would not have him know how much time she spent rooting through boxes until she found all those annual statements. Nor would she admit that the process made her appreciate the modest size of her estate—a fact he was always harping on. Comprised chiefly of the proceeds from a life insurance policy, the sale of the house on Caroline Street, a savings account, some railroad stocks and oil and gas royalties, the settlement would be around $30,000.

Mr. Scarborough's mouth opened. He cleared his throat. "I see...."

He sat down again. Geneva reached inside her handbag for a slip of paper with the name and address of Tony's lawyers, and handed it to him. "They will be sending a formal request for an inventory of the assets of the estate," she said, "and their transfer to me once the marriage takes place on June 2nd."

John Scarborough reached inside his pocket for his eye glasses and put them on to read. Presently he peered at her above the rims. "You may inform Messrs. Braxton, Muggeridge & Smythe, at 36 Caxton Street, London, that everything they need must be spelled out, to the last tittle and jot! Nor will I release one red cent until I have indubitable proof of the marriage," he said. "The bank auditors have their rules, you know."

"I'm sure they do," she said calmly. That he regretted relinquishing control over her account was obvious, and came as no surprise. Geneva suspected he viewed all his accounts the same way.

"And where can you be reached in England, in case the bank has a question?" he inquired, removing his eye glasses.

Geneva hesitated. After spending one night in London, she and Tony would leave on their variety tour, returning on May 15th for a booking at the London *Coliseum*. After which they'd be on their way to Cornwall.

"I'm afraid I'll be moving around a lot. If you need an answer quickly, suppose you contact the lawyers? Otherwise, I'm going to ask Ida Ruekauer to forward my mail to the Selby home," she said.

John Scarborough leaned back in his chair. "So, Mrs. Ruekauer will continue living in the house on Heights Boulevard, is that it?"

"Actually, I haven't had a chance to talk to her yet," Geneva admitted.

Mr. Scarborough's near-invisible eyebrows shot up. "Oh, I see…." he said with gravity, as if her remark had shed some light on a significant quandary in his mind. Just what it might be, Geneva could not fathom.

"I've been away so much, and when I'm here, Ida is usually gone," she explained. "She is in great demand as a nurse, you know."

"Tony and I hope she will agree to stay until we've found a house, and can arrange to have all my things shipped over. Of course, we'll pay half the rent in the meantime."

"Yes, of course," he said, then added thoughtfully, "I suppose then she'll be obliged to find a much more modest residence to rent."

"I suppose," said Geneva, though in fact she was not so sure. One day last fall she had come home from rehearsal at Munn's Auditorium, where she and Tony finished perfecting *Chimaera* during the cold winter months—to find Ida entertaining a caller in the parlor. She introduced Jacob Lowerby, a Canadian investment broker and former patient. Were his distinguished looks and smooth manner the reason for Ida's nice dress, and the special touches of rouge and lipstick on her face? This, along with Ida's having left the crusade for women's suffrage—apparently with no regrets—made Geneva wonder if she had become more open to opportunities for romance, perhaps even remarriage. "I'll be home mostly for the next few days, and I'll be sure to speak to Ida before we leave," she told John Scarborough.

He gave her a queer look, then said absently, "I'm sure she'll be appreciative."

When Geneva rose to leave, she was so thankful that she would never again have to deal with the man, she felt quite generous suddenly. "Thank you for doing an excellent job with my account, all these years."

He shrugged. "I only strived to follow the principles set down in the trust," he said.

She was annoyed that he could not accept a compliment. "Yes, well I do wish you…and the bank…every success," she told him, nonetheless determined to end on an amicable note.

"I have no doubt the bank will enjoy continued success. As for me, I am retiring in less than two years, and moving away."

Perhaps this news should not have shocked Geneva, but it had always been so easy to imagine Mr. Scarborough returning to his meager rooms at the end of a workday, eating a plain meal and going to bed. It was impossible to envision his off-time stretching into full days, one after another. What would he do with himself? Go fishing? Golfing? Plant a garden? She could not believe he had ever learned to enjoy leisure activity. She could not imagine him wearing anything except a business suit and bow tie. Finally she said, dubiously, "I hope you'll be happy."

"I only hope to be useful," he said reproachfully. "Good day, Geneva."

Closing the door behind her, Geneva wondered idly: 'useful' to whom? For what? She'd never know. It seemed to her a little sad that after her association of nearly a decade with Mr. Scarborough, there was not a drop of genuine warmth on either side as they said farewell. If only Mr. Hunnicutt had remained her trust officer, they would have parted with a warm hug. In fact, he and Mrs. Hunnicutt would have had her and Tony over for dinner, so they could meet her young man. She admonished herself for having lost contact with the Hunnicutts years ago: a consequence of guilt over her affair with Victor.

She descended the stairs far down to the safe deposit department in the basement, her heels clacking on the marble. As she searched through her safe deposit box to retrieve her baptismal certificate, she ran across her mother's wedding band. She slipped the ring on her finger and held her hand away to look at it. The ring seemed to encircle her own deepest convictions, instilled in her by her parents: marriage was a simple joining of two hearts and two lives. There in that airless room, she missed them with a sudden, acute sharpness she rarely experienced anymore, as if all the painful memories of their deaths, safely deposited here, had been released when she opened the steel box. She would not be walking down the aisle on her father's arm. She would not see her mother watching from the front pew, happy tears glistening on her cheeks. How unfortunate it was, when she knew they would have liked Tony, and welcomed him as a son-in-law. She removed the wedding band and looked inside at the engraving: *Dorothy and Henry—July 9, 1889.* There was just enough room to add: *Geneva and Tony—June 2, 1923.*

She felt especially glad that she had insisted she and Tony wait on sexual relations until after their wedding. How pleased her parents would have been that she had finally redeemed her mistake with Victor.

Geneva's farewell to her pupils was nine months behind her by the time she packed her bags for England, and it was handled at a safe distance, more or less—she wrote a letter and had it printed, then sent out copies in hand-addressed envelopes which inevitably brought a poignant memory of each pupil as she wrote out parents' names. She received many replies wishing her well.

On the eve of her departure, there was but one farewell remaining, the one she dreaded most of all. Since Tony and Cynthia were to come for her in a taxi at 5:30 on Sunday morning, to catch an early train for New York, the Youngers invited her over for a farewell dinner on Saturday evening. Stepping out on the chilly porch just before five o'clock, she noted the welcome sign of spring in the shiny new green leaves sprouting from old tree limbs. She would miss the Houston Heights, she thought longingly.

As Geneva crossed the street, she was reminded of the many times she had made this short walk, how she had counted on her friendship with Willa and Rodney and James. Whether her path ended in a festive holiday meal or a quick cup of coffee with Willa on a busy morning, her heart was always warmed by the love that filled the Younger house, swelling from the spacious rooms of the ground floor to the tiny nooks and cosy window seats of the high upper stories. Could the love of the Crawford family have become so absorbed into the walls of the house that it would pervade every family who lived there down the ages? Geneva liked to think so, and she hoped that such all-encompassing love would pervade the home she shared with Tony and their children.

The tasty food and wine, savored in the glow of candlelight, enhanced the sharing of memories with Willa and Rodney, and made Geneva more than a little sentimental. Still, as she left just before seven o'clock—her steamer trunk had already been dispatched, but she was not quite finished packing her train luggage—she managed to remain composed through Rodney's tender brotherly hug and warm wishes. But then she gathered her godson in her arms for one last time. She kissed James's fingers, his forehead, his hair, breathing in his little-boy scent as if it were fine perfume: *Never to forget.* Would he remember her next time they met? She must send him presents and cards and letters galore, to be sure he would. He patted her cheeks and looked at her solemnly. "Gee go bye-bye?" He had called her "Gee" since he began to talk. Her tears spilled forth. Reluctantly putting him down to accept the offer of Rodney's handkerchief, she promised, "Yes, Darling, but I will come back one day to visit, and maybe your mommy and daddy will bring you to visit me in England sometime."

James worked the word 'England' around on his tongue, but found it beyond his ability to utter.

Willa walked with Geneva out on the darkening porch, its lattice blooming with jasmine. Geneva closed her eyes and breathed in the sweet fragrance one last time, then looked at Willa. "Well—" she said, helplessly.

A tear rolled from Willa's eye. Her voice gravelly, she said, "You are my best—my only—friend. I will miss—" her voice broke off. She drew her lips together.

Geneva knew it was much easier to go away than to be left behind. She held Willa's hands and looked into her eyes. "We'll always be best friends. No matter how far away we are from each other," she assured her. Then with an attempt at levity she added, "Even when we're old and gray-headed—"

"And wearing bifocals—oh, how I dread wearing bifocals," said Willa.

They exchanged a quick grin, unable to imagine the day ever coming when they would be that old. "We'll write to each other at least once a week," said Geneva.

Willa sniffed. "I'm no good at letter writing, but I'll do my best."

There was nothing left to say. They went into each other's arms and held on tightly, four cheeks wet with tears. *To have such a friend as Willa,* thought Geneva with awe. *You would only need one such friend for all your life....*

Crossing the street, she turned to throw Willa a kiss. Her friend returned the gesture. Geneva felt she would never forget the sight of Willa standing there alone, slim and long-limbed, the shadows closing on her face and figure. Presently Willa hugged her sweater around her, pivoted in her T-strapped shoes, and walked inside.

CHAPTER 41

Victor had felt just fine when he arrived in Singapore. Well, just a little off maybe; he didn't have much of an appetite, and when he did sit down to the table hungry, three or four bites and he felt full. But then, the ship had encountered two violent storms in the South China Sea, the second of them less than 16 hours out of port; so no wonder his digestive system was touchy. He thought uneasily of the many weeks ahead, of heat and humidity in the crowded city, of frequent rains and relentless mosquitoes. There was a time when such a prospect would not have bothered him. Yet the offer was generous—compiling photographs for a history of the Rahban Steamship Company, to commemorate its 50th anniversary. He'd be developing some new photographs, and restoring a number of old ones. Couple of months' work, maybe three, and the pay was $2500, plus expenses.

Three weeks in, the copywriter quit, and after a little negotiating, Victor got Benjamin hired as a replacement. Benjamin was a good writer, and this was his first decent break. Victor still felt guilty about letting him down in Los Angeles. He'd told him flat out, as soon as he arrived, that making films wasn't for him after all. "I can't seem to get the idea to come together," he admitted.

Crestfallen, Benjamin said, "But what about *SUMMER?* When you wrote to me, I checked it out of the library, and read it twice. I've been sketching out some scenes for it. I was going to show you."

Victor wished he had not mentioned the idea of making that film to Benjamin. He doubted the boy was capable of writing a screenplay for a major film, just yet. Victor had not realized he would get so carried away, and it was all his fault. The least he owed Benjamin was the truth. "But son, I knew only one girl who could portray Charity Royall as I envisioned her, and she turned me down."

Benjamin knew Victor had been in Houston. He put two and two together. His eyes grew stormy. "*Geneva?* What do you want with *her?* She's no actress. There are plenty of girls out here—"

Victor raised a hand. "I'm sorry. I'll stay around, help you get your feet on the ground good, and then I think I'd be better off back on the road."

Benjamin pouted for a few days, but eventually he seemed to get over his disappointment.

During the next couple of months, before he took another assignment, and thereafter whenever he was in Los Angeles between jobs, Victor taught Benjamin all he could about still photography, because if Benjamin could both write fluently and make good pictures, he could always earn a good living. Magazines were using photographs more and more nowadays, whereas before the war, when Geneva posed for him, the idea was in its infancy. In his spare time Benjamin still worked at learning the craft of writing for the screen and Victor didn't discourage him. Maybe someday he could do that for a living, but in the meantime he had to be practical. Secretly Victor thought it was a crying shame that people so often wound up selling out their real dreams for the sake of practicality. Few people were lucky enough to avoid it.

Benjamin was grateful, and even though he seemed to have a perpetually sour outlook on life for some reason, the two of them got on very well in California. When Benjamin decided to use his real father's name professionally, Victor felt wounded. Jim Rothby's name wasn't worth carrying on. But Benjamin thought the name sounded 'erudite'—as he put it. "He never gave me anything, so what's wrong with me taking the least that he owed me?" the boy said. Victor could not argue with that. He could easily sense that Benjamin was trying to define himself as a person, and that was probably a good thing.

By the time Benjamin got to Singapore, Victor was deep into the work, digging through crates and boxes of old photographs, yellow and brittle and faded; getting a preliminary idea of how all this was going to come together. He felt reasonably content in his little office, high up in the Rahban headquarters on the waterfront, though it was always a little damp, and noisy with the windows open. He didn't like the food in Singapore—he had always been one for plain beef steak and potatoes. But he was too busy to think about food very much anyway. He could go for hours on black coffee; otherwise, rice and tea seemed to sit better on his stomach than anything else.

Seeing Victor, Benjamin said worriedly, "You've lost a lot of weight, Dad. And your coloring—have you seen a doctor?"

"Good heavens, no! I'm swell," Victor assured him. Actually, he had moved his belt buckle over a notch, but he was surprised he'd lost enough weight for it to be noticeable. A feeling of uncertainty overtook him, which may have done so earlier had he not been so busy. It wouldn't do for Benjamin to travel all the way over here, then be worried about him, however. "It's just the food over here. I've got to get used to it. You look great yourself!" he said, and clapped his shoulders vigorously. How bony and small those shoulders were for a young man his age. "You could stand to put on a few pounds, though," Victor told Benjamin good-naturedly. *It's just the food,* he repeated to himself. What else could it be?

That night it came a pounding rain, and Victor stood at the window of his hotel room, looking out. It was as if the rain were a veil, separating him from the rest of the world. *I'm going to die in Singapore.* It went through his head just like that. He didn't take to the notion of dying all the way around the world from home. But then, where was home? First, it had been wherever Anne was. Then, just for the amount of time he nursed Geneva through the flu, home was where she was—though that was mostly wishful thinking. Home was no particular place anymore, Victor realized, and he felt depressed. Then he told himself that Benjamin's worry had just spooked him. He was fine.

Within a couple of weeks, he began having mild stomach pain all the time. He went on working. Benjamin sat in a corner of the room, contentedly pecking away on his typewriter, which he had brought all the way from the States. One day Victor was looking over a few paragraphs that Benjamin had written about Sir Harry Ord, and his part in the way the Rahban Steamship Company developed, when a bolt of pain blind-sided him. He dropped the paper from his hands and doubled over.

They took him to a British hospital, a good place, connected with the medical school. Nurses wore white wimples and aprons. Everything was clean and white, from the thin curtains fluttering over the windows, to the gauzy mosquito bars around all the beds. Kind of made you think of heaven. Victor's bed was down at the far end of a ten-bed ward, by a window. There were only two other fellows in there, and within a day or so, all but his bed was empty.

The doctor said it was inoperable cancer, far advanced, why had Victor not sought medical advice before? He had a handlebar moustache, salt and pepper gray. British people always liked to lord it over Americans, show them the error of their ways, Victor thought. "I don't believe in mincing words, and I always tell the patient, rather than have a relative do it," he said. Victor had two or three more months at most, he said, and all they could do was administer morphine, try to keep him comfortable. The doctor gave him a firm squeeze on the shoulder and said he'd be looking in.

Odd, how calmly he took the news. But since that rainy night of Benjamin's arrival, he had never quite dismissed the idea that something was wrong. So in a way, he had been preparing himself.

By and large, Victor's mind was at peace, for the work was virtually done. Benjamin could finish up. Lying there alone, he toyed with the idea of suicide before the pain became unbearable. He imagined walking out of the hospital, and getting a gun, taking it out in the open somewhere. But some people believed suicide was an unpardonable sin. He didn't like thinking about the fires of hell, especially when he was this close to finding out what the next life was all about. Victor had always just thought the good Lord loved people, and that was all there was to it. It was one reason he enjoyed photographing people truthfully, bringing out what was really inside them. It was too bad he had never become better informed about the hereafter. He supposed he could ask for a chaplain to come. But he didn't want somebody giving him one slant on a subject nobody seemed to agree on.

Besides, he needed to figure out what to do about his photographs of Geneva in the nude. They were in his camera case, back at the hotel. Long ago, he had picked them up from Springfield, just as he promised her. But as soon as he took them out and looked at them again, he knew he could not bring himself to destroy them. They were even better than he remembered. There was about them a mystical quality. He had captured not Geneva herself, but a vision that went beyond her, as though she had stepped out of herself. How hard he had strived for such a quality, yet at the time he was too close to the work to see that he had achieved it. Still, he had made a promise. He must destroy them.

He'd gone back and forth like that, struggling over what to do. Finally he decided just to put off dealing with them. There was a piece of lining in his camera case that had come unstitched a long time ago. Just far enough to slip something behind it. There the pictures would be safe and dry as he traveled.

Now he decided to ask Benjamin to bring him his camera, tell him it was for no other reason than that he just wanted to have it with him. Benjamin would understand that, for he was sentimentally attached to his typewriter.

For several days Victor kept the camera case nearby, considering what to do. In that time he never once took Geneva's pictures out from behind the lining to look at them, for he knew that if he did, he would be a wreck from then on. Should he tear them up? No, that was the savage way, what you did when you were angry. He would treat them with reverence. The thing to do was ask the nurse for a pair of scissors, and one night when all was quiet and dark, he could remove the photos, keep them face down while he cut them up into tiny pieces, and later ask the nurse to dispose of them. Then he could write to Geneva of what he had done, so she would know that he kept his promise.

How he wished Geneva were here right now. Just seeing her face, having her touch him, would make him better.

Every time a nurse came in, he thought about the scissors. All the time she was changing his linens, or filling his water pitcher, or just before a morphine injection, provided the pain hadn't gotten so bad he couldn't think straight—*"Just a little sting, Mr. Calais. There we are."*—he thought of the scissors. But he could not bring himself to ask.

Finally he made up his mind what to do. One evening he said to Benjamin, "Son, I'm going to write a new will. I hardly remember what the first one says. Your mother and I had it drawn up after Virginia was born, if I remember right.

"I want you to write this down, then take it and typewrite it, bring it back and I'll sign it. We'll have a nurse witness it."

Benjamin always had a hard time through those hospital visits. He had never reached the point in his life where he made friends, and it seemed obvious now that he never would. Though he was a nice-looking young man and had no trouble getting dates out in California, he rarely took a young woman out more than twice. He always said they bored him. He didn't see his sisters often, for they lived too far away. Nor did he get along with them whenever they were together—they'd gotten kind of narrow in their thinking, over the years. Victor was Benjamin's only close friend.

Benjamin had a pained look on his face now, as he pulled a small notebook and a pencil from his pocket.

Victor explained, "I've already given you more than I've given your sisters—more of my time, for one thing. Now I want to set this up so there won't be any reason for conflict to develop."

"I won't start anything," Benjamin said defensively.

"I'm sure you won't. Still, write this down: whatever cash value is in my estate, I want to divide equally among you. I think that's in the old will, too.

"As to all my cameras, and my photograph collection—" he paused and looked at Benjamin, who was still scribbling. He felt guilty, for this was not going to seem fair. "I want them to go to Geneva Sterling."

Benjamin looked up, his eyes filled with shock inside the round wire frames of his glasses. "But I would have thought you'd want me—"

"I'm not finished yet, son. I never paid Geneva for all those hours she spent posing, and I learned more from the work we did together than from any other single experience," he said. After a pause, he added, "Much of it, I've passed along to you." And though this was true, it seemed gratuitous to point it out to Benjamin and he wished he could take it back.

Benjamin shrugged. "But I still don't see—"

"Besides, you need to keep your load as light as you can, for you will always travel a lot, I'm sure. My things will just be a burden. Believe me, I know what I'm talking about. Besides, I have something special in mind for you." Victor paused to get his breath. The pain was starting to bear down. "I want to sign my pay from Rahban over to you. You may need to have a paper drawn up for me to sign. Check on it, will you, soon as you can? Put together with your earnings from the company, it will set you up pretty good for a while."

Benjamin nodded, but his mouth was drawn down. "I still don't see why you want to give Geneva anything, the way she let us down."

Victor was in too much pain to hang on much longer. He had to get Benjamin's promise. He clenched his teeth for a minute, tried to get his breath. "I'm depending on you to carry out my wishes," he said, his voice barely above a whisper. Times like these he wished he could step outside his body, pick it up and ram it against the wall till he killed the pain.

As Benjamin sat huddled over his pencil, Victor took a picture in his mind: Benjamin closed up around his life. What a shame....

Finally he said, "Alright, then."

Thank God! "Send the nurse in, will you? I need a shot in a hurry."

Benjamin sprang from his chair, his eyes wide, the notebook spilling from his lap. Victor gripped the bed covers and clamped his jaw tight. Sweat popped out on his brow. Sometimes he thought of the pain as a huge bear, hibernating inside him; and now and then it would stir, then settle down again. He needed to—what? Oh yes, write Geneva, and tell her where to find the pictures among all his things. Or, did he? She would first look through all the photographs, and when she didn't find the ones she was looking for, she would figure out they were hidden somewhere, that he had given her everything in order to conceal what she didn't want anyone to know. Besides, where could he write to her at this point? Houston Heights? England? Victor's eyes blurred with pain. His thoughts were starting to twist and warp out of shape...Geneva married...British partner...

The nurse pulled back the mosquito bar. *"Just a little sting, Mr. Calais...."*

It wasn't long after Benjamin got everything signed that Victor's condition quit spiraling and took a dive straight down. They increased the dosage of morphine. For a while it made him violently ill for a few minutes after every injection. But then it settled down. There were shorter periods when the pain hibernated. *"Just a little sting now."* Then oblivion. He still had his wits some of the time. There was a basket of flowers on the table beside the bed. Had Geneva sent them? The mosquito bar moved aside. *"Just a little sting, Mr...."* He was looking at the flowers. In the center, a red rose was opening slowly, provocatively. Inside was Geneva's face. He slept. Pain awoke him and he yelled out, lost his breath. *"Just a...Mr. Calais...there..."* He sank down in a well of contentment. He could see Geneva through the white gauze, across the South China Sea, with the baby on her shoulder. He was swimming to them, but he was so tired, all his muscles aching from the strain. His stomach cramped up; water filled his nostrils. *"Just a little..."* He slept. When he awoke, Geneva was leaning over him, wiping his brow. He had never seen her look more beautiful. Ah yes, the *Maiden* in oils, his dream of a lifetime come true: huge in proportion when done, swallowing up one studio wall. Her complexion was dewy, her cheeks faintly blushed. Her green eyes focused her love on his face. "I've come to take care of you," she said soothingly. He reached up and touched her mouth. *"No, put your hand down Mr. Calais, steady...."* Her mouth was moist and yielding, the texture and color of a ripe plum, yes he'd gotten that just right. *"Just a little...there...are."* The sunlight poured through the window, kissing the *Maiden's* face and shoulders, and making bright swirls in her abundant coppery waves. The master saw how he painted the light and, smiling, his rough hand taking Victor's, said it was just...*"a little sting...."* And the soft rounding of her hips under the thin tunic...and in the background, the little chair, with her ballet slippers waiting. All there. He turned from his masterpiece.

"Victor, please, don't go."

He reached up and closed the curtain, knowing that he never would.

CHAPTER 42

✿

Geneva suffered a severe bout of seasickness that persisted for the entire eight-day voyage on the *USS Olympic*. Neither the tablets prescribed by the ship's doctor nor the bottle of Mothersill's beside her bed were of any significant help. Subsisting on beef broth and soda crackers, she rarely left the state room she shared with Cynthia, and was grateful when the ship finally docked at Southampton.

As Geneva walked with Cynthia toward Tony's state room a few doors down, she noted a uniformed attendant standing with Tony outside his door. Presently Tony gave the man a tip, and he touched the bill of his cap and walked away. Tony slipped a piece of paper into his breast pocket.

"Ah, there you are," he said to the two women, and came to relieve Geneva of the valise she was carrying and take her arm in his. "Steady?"

"Working on it," she said.

"What was that all about?" asked Cynthia, gesturing toward the retreating figure of the attendant.

"Oh, nothing important," said Tony absently.

Weak from hunger, her muscles slack from spending so much time in bed, Geneva felt somewhat like she had felt while recovering from the flu. Just now she was too absorbed in putting one foot in front of the other to give much thought to the message Tony had apparently just received.

During the train ride to London, she consumed three piping hot buttery scones, a huge glass of orange juice and two cups of coffee, brought to their first-class carriage by a steward in a crisp white uniform. All the while Tony gazed out the window pensively. Thinking of the message? She wondered. When she was finished eating, she reached for his hand. "Everything alright?"

He turned. "What? Oh, yes." Eyeing her empty plate he said, "Good Lord, did you eat all that?"

"I sure did, and it was heavenly. But I may never be hungry again."

Tony grinned. "I hope you will. We're dining at the Trocadero tonight, and the food is spectacular."

"You'll want to dress to the hilt, my dear," Cynthia piped up. The Troc is *the* place in London. You'll run into important people from the theatre."

Geneva wondered if she would be joining them. She hoped not. She and Tony were long overdue for a romantic evening to themselves. If Cynthia joined them, the outing would be given over to promoting *Sterling & Selby.*

To her relief, Cynthia soon said she would be dining with old friends in Chelsea this evening. She remembered being told how well Cynthia enjoyed her social life in London before her husband moved the family to Cornwall.

Soon they arrived at Victoria Station and made their way outside to the taxi halt. The sun was shining brightly. "Taxi!" Tony called crisply, his arm raised. In moments they were swooped away to the Hyde Park Hotel.

The streets of London were alive with automobiles, and crowds of pedestrians strolled in all directions on the pavement. Geneva stared out the taxi window fascinated, while Tony identified famous landmarks she had seen in picture books and on post cards collected by her parents in their travels. "Look, just there is Westminster Abbey," he said, and a few minutes later, "Up there—no, look to your left, Darling—the dome of St. Paul's Cathedral." Geneva delighted in the pulsing energy here, the wealth of promise yet to be articulated. Could it really be true, she was in London, England? Presently they drove into Knightsbridge, which Cynthia claimed was her favorite place: "I intend to spend one whole day at Elizabeth Arden's while you are on tour, getting the works," she said with relish. They whizzed by elegant shops with two-part names, By Appointment of His Majesty, strung like pearls down Brompton Road toward Harrod's huge department store, into which all the shops could have fit, with space left over. Abruptly the driver pulled over to the curb on the right—or maybe it just seemed abrupt because the driver's side of English cars was on the right. A doorman wearing white gloves, with gold epaulets on his shoulders, came to usher them inside. "Oh yes, good day, Mr. Selby, it's the Beaumont Suite, I believe; fourth floor, above the park. Right this way, please." Geneva stepped out on the pavement and gazed up at the venerable facade of the Hyde Park Hotel. With turrets and balconies and fancy ornamental stone work, the structure had all the dignity of an aging dowager with silver hair piled high atop her head; the ivy trailing down from window boxes like dark lace spilling from her high collar down her bosom. Tony had told her that his father lived here in his bachelor days, when the Hyde Park was a residence hotel. Lord Edward had arranged for them to stay in the two-bedroom suite as his guests.

Inside the Beaumont Suite, Geneva went straight to the room she shared with Cynthia and took a long afternoon nap. When she opened her eyes and raised up on the pillows, the lamps were lit and Cynthia was putting on a pair of elbow-length gloves, her slender figure aswirl with beaded spirals in tones descending from pale orchid at her breast to deep purple at her feet.

"Ah, good! I was hoping you would wake up before I left. I have great news—" she screwed up her eyes at Geneva—"well, great for the most part, anyway. A cable was waiting when we got here. You remember the producer Charles Dillingham?"

Geneva nodded. She and Tony were set to try out for one of his shows during the war, but they canceled when Tony was called back to England.

"Well, he saw *Chimaera* at the *Palace,* and guess what?" said Cynthia, her eyes blazing with triumph. "He wants you and Tony to be the lead dancers for a new musical going into rehearsals in July, called *Jackson Square.* In fact, he wants Tony to compose all the dances for the show. Our Tony will be working with George Gershwin, no less! What do you think of that?"

Geneva took a moment to absorb all this, then said uneasily, "But we'll have to sail back to the States." The very idea made her stomach queasy.

Cynthia gave her a sympathetic look. "I'm afraid so, dear, but it's the chance of a lifetime for Tony. Of course, he won't let me respond until he checks with you," she said. With a lift of her chin she added, "And it won't hurt Mr. Dillingham to wait a little. I might wind up negotiating a better deal."

Now Geneva realized the message Tony received must have been from Mr. Dillingham. It seemed odd for the offer to come to Tony, rather than Cynthia. But then, maybe Mr. Dillingham was not aware Cynthia had sailed with them. She went on speculating: Obviously Tony didn't want to discuss the offer with his mother. Maybe he wasn't willing to return to the States no matter how good the opportunity. Maybe while she was sleeping, Cynthia had pried the information from Tony, and now she was hoping for a little help persuading him. "I'm sure we'll talk about it tonight," said Geneva.

Cynthia reached for her mesh evening bag and slipped its dainty gold chain over her wrist. "Have fun, my dear," she said cheerfully as she swept through the door, the scent of her expensive perfume wafting behind her.

Geneva glanced at the clock. It was nearly seven, and their dinner reservation was for 8:30. She undressed and headed for the luxurious marble tub, for a long soaking bath.

At 8:15 Geneva stepped up to the parlor door, dressed in a Sally Milgrim original—thin coral-colored chiffon, with a drop waist and cap sleeves and a low bodice uplifted by the contours of her bosom; a matching headband with a beaded medallion in front. The frock cost a full week's pay, and she expected to be greeted with an admiring look from Tony. Yet, on the other side of the door, she heard his voice: "See here, Morey got Selby Mines into this, so he can just—yes, I suppose so…." he said bleakly. She gathered he was talking on the telephone to Lord Edward. She had an uneasy feeling the message he received aboard ship was from his father, rather than Charles Dillingham, and was urgent. She stood listening till she heard him say, "Yes, I'll see you round the 20th of May. Goodby." When he hung up the telephone, she knew very little more than when she first began to eavesdrop. She opened the door and walked in. Tony looked around, blinked, then gave her the compliment she had expected.

At twenty past eight they were stepping into the lift. There was plenty of time, Tony said; Shaftesbury Avenue was not far away. And indeed, as they descended the lobby stairs, a uniformed attendant spotted them. In moments a taxi door opened at the curb as if most of the surrounding population were not trying to hire a ride at this very hour.

Geneva felt a little guilty for her eavesdropping, and decided to wait for Tony to tell her what was going on at home. Yet during the drive he was silent, staring gloomily out the window, his hand closed around hers. "Your mother told me about Mr. Dillingham's offer," she said at length.

Tony looked at her as if he had forgotten it entirely until now.

"Whatever you want to do is fine with me," she assured him.

His eyes sparkled. "If we're lucky, *Jackson Square* will get us where we're going a great deal sooner than I imagined." He raised her hand to his lips and kissed it. His moustache felt like pin pricks through her gloves. "Of course, one never knows whether a show will go over."

"Well, if it flops it won't be for lack of great dance numbers," she said kindly, then after a pause she added, "One thing though, if I should get pregnant, I'll have to drop out." She studied his face anxiously.

"Absolutely," he said, and kissed her forehead sweetly.

The Trocadero was an elegant balconied restaurant of grand proportion, with a stringed orchestra and glistening chandeliers. Women in jewels and designer gowns and elaborate headdresses abounded. Just as they walked in Geneva spotted a woman wearing a remarkable full-length evening cape made entirely of black feathers. Regally she swished by a huge potted palm.

Tony was soon introducing Geneva to people he knew, telling them with great enthusiasm about *Chimaera,* and the upcoming *Jackson Square.* Wearing a black dinner suit with a white double-breasted waistcoat, and patent leather evening shoes, he looked like a model from *Esquire* magazine. This was the world where Tony belonged. How unfair for him to be burdened by the struggles of a tin mining concern 200 miles away, just at the advent of his career.

Later, as they awaited their dinner check, a dapper young man paused at the table. "Why, if it isn't Tony Selby!" he said. To Geneva's amazement, she was soon being introduced to the Prince of Wales. "Do call me David," he said warmly, his clear round eyes focused on her. "Tony and I were at Oxford together." He sat down to chat, his manner as friendly and relaxed as if she and Tony were neighbors out on the front porch.

Geneva was so disarmed by the Prince's conviviality, when he mentioned that he would try and catch their act at the *Coliseum,* she gave no thought to his unique status. "Oh, that would be wonderful, but I'm afraid all performances are sold out. Ella Shields is headlining," she said. The Prince and Tony exchanged a startled glance, then broke up in laughter. Geneva was mortified.

"Perhaps you and Tony will join me in the Royal Box, after your performance," he said, then leaned near and whispered, "I shall save you a seat." He winked at her, kissed her hand, then slipped out. Geneva was utterly charmed. As the Prince walked away it occurred to her that he was charmed as well. *I could have him,* she thought brazenly. *If I were one of those women who do such things, I could have him in my room tonight.* Suddenly she felt very far away from Houston, Texas. Then she turned to Tony, who was signing the check, and she felt guilty for her ruminations.

On the way back to the hotel, a fine misty rain was falling, and Tony sank into silence again. "What's going on at home?" Geneva finally asked.

He glanced her way, surprised.

"I overheard you speaking to your father on the telephone," she admitted.

A sigh. "Father asked me not to discuss it, I'm afraid," he apologized.

Geneva felt wounded. Lord Edward did not consider his son's fiancée one of the family. Perhaps it was understandable, since they had never met. Yet, surely Tony could have overridden his wish if he'd wanted to.

She turned to gaze out the rain-glazed taxi window. Theirs was among hundreds of boxy black cabs, all threading their way down the wrong side of the slickened streets, with horns wailing *bee-bah, bee-bah.* The city had lost its magic. It was a great noisy maze of thoroughfares encroached by brooding buildings and monuments. She felt Tony's hand squeeze hers, heard him say, bracingly, "Sorry. But don't worry, it will all come right."

The taxi came to a halt. A gloved hand was opening her door from outside. Tony took her arm in his and soon they were swallowed up by the opulence of the Hyde Park Hotel: huge urns of fresh flowers, beveled mirrors with gilt frames, and cloud-soft carpets on marble floors. Geneva thought back to the first-class accommodations aboard the *USS Olympic*, the first class train carriage from Southampton, the expensive dinner at the Trocadero. She wondered if they ought to be spending so much money.

So far, Tony had shown respect for Geneva's desire that they remain on this side of the sexual threshold until June 2nd, though admittedly, with Cynthia their constant chaperone there was little opportunity to test his resolve. Once they were standing just inside the parlor door of their suite, however, Tony's good-night kiss seemed to find no convenient stopping place. Had his preoccupation with matters at home built pressure inside him all evening, making him desperate for reassurance? But if so, why not just tell her what was troubling him, instead of expressing it with his roaming hands, for heaven's sake, propelling her instincts ahead to June 2nd? Finally she forced his hand from inside her low coral bodice, whispering with an edge, "No, Tony, please remember!" She gave his forehead a consoling kiss, swiftly crossed the parlor floor and opened her bedroom door, feeling well within her rights. They had an agreement. She shut the door behind her.

Cynthia was propped up in bed on a cloud of pillows, with a pink sleeping net on her head, her face glistening with night cream. She was perusing a copy of *The London Dancing Times* in which she had placed a very pricey ad for *Chimaera*. Geneva wished that she could talk to her about Tony's worries tonight; yet, while she had not been told outright, she gathered that Cynthia was not privy to matters of the family business. How awkward, marrying into a family where your in-laws were estranged, and you must take care not to open the wrong subject. *"I won't be coming to Brookhurst until the day before the wedding, Geneva; you understand, of course...."*

Cynthia put the magazine aside. "Was the evening a great success?"she asked. Geneva was tempted to say contrarily that it depended upon what you thought was important to achieve. "We're going to do *Jackson Square*," she said flatly, then headed for the dressing room to put on her sleeping gown. Perhaps by the time she came to bed, Cynthia would be asleep. She didn't feel like talking about show business; the subject seemed rather superficial just now.

Yet Cynthia was still awake when Geneva climbed into the bed next to hers. "Dear, there are times in every girl's life when there is no substitute for her mother," she said delicately. "Just before you get married is one of them."

The truth in that statement—coming so unexpectedly—plus the feeling of being set adrift by Tony this evening, put a knot in Geneva's throat.

"Still, you know me well enough; I always speak frankly," she said, "so if I can answer any questions about the wedding night, I'd be happy to."

Geneva's face went hot. She wondered if she should make up a question or two. Still, it would seem ungrateful to patronize her kindness.

Cynthia went on, "I was barely 18 when I got married, and I had little idea of what to expect. Edward was a good bit older, and experienced of course. Thankfully, he was patient and loving."

If Cynthia mentioned her husband at all, it was usually in a reserved tone one might use for a business associate. The intimacy in her remark, and the dreamy look in her eyes as she stated it, made Geneva feel awkward, although she was thankful to hear her future father-in-law described in such warm terms. "I don't have any questions at this point, but thank you. I'm sure my mother would have appreciated—" she began, and to her dismay, her voice broke. She laid her head on the pillows and stared up at the ceiling.

She felt Cynthia's hand close around hers. The two looked at each other for a long moment. For the first time, Geneva sensed real tenderness in Cynthia. Suddenly it was not so hard to imagine her as a nurturing mother.

"There is one other thing, Geneva—though perhaps I shouldn't bring it up," she said now. "Tony will never admit this to you, but he is still wounded by what happened with Jane Tremont, and he's a bit sensitive." She paused, then added, "I won't say anymore. Just try to understand."

Geneva was seized with guilt for having walked off and left Tony standing in the parlor a few minutes ago. How could she have been so cruel? "I will," she told his mother in all sincerity, and to her surprise, Cynthia's eyes grew wet. "You are good for my son, and I am so grateful—you will never know."

They squeezed hands again. Cynthia dabbed her eyes with a lace-edged handkerchief. "By the way, I have a feeling that Jane will find a way to meet you, once she knows you're in the district—to size up her rival. Don't let your guard down, even for a moment," she urged.

It seemed to Geneva there was something pitiful about Cynthia's perennial efforts to make things right for Tony, and being powerless to do so. If Jane had any sense of rivalry between them it was quite misplaced. Yet if Cynthia was still worried even after Tony had spent four years at home in England, living very near Jane's residence for much of the time, she doubted there was any use trying to convince her.

Geneva was far more concerned about developments at Selby Mines.

CHAPTER 43

Just how bad was it? Tony went over the question in his mind all through that night as he knew he would do for many nights to come, his father having tiptoed round the subject as it were, reluctant to force too much on him when he was weeks away from being able to deal with any of it. The idea of outside investors in Selby Mines was positively abhorrent to Lord Edward; he'd rather admit to failure, sell up what had always been a family business and be done with it. Only, the offer from Karforth Mining Group really was stingy at this point. Father knew exactly what to demand, but the velvet pen of diplomacy was needed all the way round, and that was where Tony's objective viewpoint and particular way with words would be crucial. For the bank was nervous after two rather disappointing quarters in a row, and had suggested profits might be better in the offing, and in the meantime, perhaps more collateral might be in keeping with the situation. Unless, of course, a sale took place. Bankers! Greedy monsters, the whole lot of them, who sat back and twiddled their thumbs with never a sweaty brow. If Tony had his druthers, Morey would have spent the past nine years toiling in a miner's cap with a candle on the front, just like his father before him. If Karforth bought Selby Mines, they would be wise not to leave him in the office with a check book.

Just how bad was it? No real threats from the bankers at this point, and Karforth interested. That was about all he knew until he could have a look at the numbers. On the one hand, he was eager to do just that, send apologies to Charles Dillingham if necessary, and stick by until the whole mess was resolved one way or another. On the other hand, he wished desperately to run the other way and never look back. *Jackson Square* offered an opportunity for making very important acquaintances in the business, one that might never come again—George Gershwin, for instance, was a genius, and a star on the rise without a doubt. Apart from that, Dillingham's offer was more generous than usual—he was reputed to be as tight-fisted as they came—and whether or not his mother could persuade him to increase it, if the play was a great success there would be much more money into the bargain. Whether it took a few years for him to be in the position to buy a theatre, or decades, Tony was determined that he and Geneva and their children would live entirely on his earnings, and never live off the estate no matter how wealthy it might become once they got out of the current mess. His family had always worked for a living. Only Morey sponged, by failing to earn the high salary he accepted. Even that was alright as long as they were making money, for Nell deserved all the benefits of his excellent pay. The way the Selby estate was set up, she received only a small legacy—not much more than the purchase price of Camellia Cottage—and a few of her grandmother's jewels. Tony inherited everything else.

Tony had long since figured out that he was neither as idealistic as his father, nor as practical as his mother, and therefore he constantly struggled somewhere in between. His mother, with her keen head for business, had been absolutely right. They should never have returned to Cornwall and reopened the mines 20 years ago. However, for a good many of those years—before Morey West came on the scene and married the boss's daughter—things did go better than anyone had a right to expect. Which, now that he thought about it, brought him to another troubling point his father voiced on the telephone: the Selby Mines employees, who were a great part of their prosperity, may be threatened by Karforth policies should a sale take place. The company was under new management since the war, people they did not know. They were not sanguine about the idea of retaining all Selby Mines employees, but promised "to give each consideration." When all was said and done, how many of those who had been loyal to Selby Mines for all their working lives would wind up unemployed?

The tour of the Provinces would begin tomorrow, and Tony was not looking forward to it. All the worries on his mind, and then, he was more than a little annoyed with Geneva. She had known when they returned from the Trocadero that he was troubled. How could she pretend to overlook his desperate need to make love to her? *She would not have turned away from Victor Calais,* he thought bitterly as he stood alone in the parlor of their suite and watched Geneva's bedroom door shut behind her. Now, tossing and turning in bed, he asked himself, *What can she hope to prove by behaving like a virgin until June 2nd?* Oh, he was being mean, and he knew it. He should not be this jealous, and frankly, before she left him stranded, he had not truly realized that the whole matter was eating away at him. More so, because she had never looked him squarely in the eye and said that she hated Victor Calais with all her heart. *Does she long for him still, sometimes?* Oh, stop it! He punched the pillow. At least if she had told him about their unfortunate affair early in their relationship, instead of waiting, he might have got used to it by now.

The tour had barely begun when Tony found his annoyance at Geneva evaporating, for she was a jolly good trouper. The White Star line had dispatched their costume trunk to the Bradford *Empire*, rather than the Birmingham *Empire*, which resulted in their being bumped on opening night for want of costumes, the exorbitantly expensive, impossible to duplicate, butterfly wings included. They lost their place as second on the bill, and were forced to open every show for the next three weeks, till another act was bumped. Being first on the bill spelled disaster for a dance like *Chimaera*, which demanded undivided attention from the beginning, and lost its grip among the stragglers milling about in the stalls. Apart from that, in many towns they had to relay via taxi between two theatres in one night, doing two shows at each—something unheard of in American theatres. Geneva took all this in stride, far better than he.

She was enchanted by the countryside, now in full bloom, through which their trains trundled between shows. Her face was plastered to the windows constantly, while others in the troupe slept or read the papers, and Tony pored over ideas for dances in *Jackson Square*, with nothing to go on except for the play's setting in New Orleans—an intriguing city he'd visited once, long ago—and a four-line synopsis in Dillingham's cable. He wanted a flavor of steamy nights in the French Quarter, of secret passions behind shuttered windows. Oh, the opportunities for deliciously daring acrobatic lifts!

On Sundays when they were off, they rented bicycles and pedaled up and down the winding lanes round villages and beyond, for miles and miles, over quaint stone bridges, past patchwork meadows, often stopping for Geneva to take snapshots of the most ordinary sights—pink valerian blooming out of nooks in railroad embankments; wild roses taking over an abandoned cottage, spilling through the paneless windows and climbing through holes in the roof, making the place look like a basket of flowers. "Oh Tony, I feel like I went to sleep and woke up in the Garden of Eden!" Geneva cried. He was ashamed to admit that years ago, he had stopped noticing the lovely sights Geneva was now happily discovering. And he could not count the number of times she would ask him for the name of a wild flower, and find him lacking.

"But my sister Nell is a gardener, raises camellias—didn't I tell you? She can name all the flowers in the fields. And she is an expert on all that grows in the Brookhurst wood." Whereupon Geneva decided to collect wildflower specimens for Nell to identify, hoping this might be a good way for them to become acquainted. Tony bought a huge woven bag for her to stuff them in.

When at last they returned to London, in the midst of trousseau shopping between shows and meetings with solicitors, Geneva insisted upon combing the bookstores until she found a huge picture book on the subject of English wild flowers as a gift for Nell. When finally they located the perfect volume, she turned to Tony with sparkling eyes. "Nell will just love this! Don't you think?" Suddenly he realized that Geneva had high hopes that Nell would warm to her straightaway, perhaps because she missed her dear friend Willa so much. Unfortunately, apart from the fact Nell was rather reserved by nature, with all the business worries plaguing the family, she was apt to be even more withdrawn than usual.

Which brought Tony round to the question once again: just how bad was it?

CHAPTER 44

At the end of the variety tour, Tony took Geneva home at last. Rather than traveling all the way to Bodmin by train, he arranged to have his Rover left for them at Exeter Station so that he could drive her to Brookhurst by way of Dartmoor Forest. He was eager to show her how the English countryside that so fascinated her began to look very different once you got as far west as Dorset, becoming wilder, more mysterious.

The road was a torturous thread before them with a high stone hedgerow hard on one side and bushy heads of wild rhododendron thrusting upward; the head lamps picked up the shifting green of the wind-blown trees that formed an arbor above them, an arbor so thick that at times it blocked out the quickly darkening sky. Down below, exposed tree roots raised up around the broad tree trunks like huge, grasping knobby hands. And on the other side of the snaking road, in brief clearings between the trees, one could see an embankment, perilously steep, leading so far down that one could not see through the gathering shadows where it stopped.

It was near the end of this drive that they had their first rain since Geneva arrived in England; not a steady drizzle or even a hard drenching, but violent, intermittent gushes that pummeled the auto roof as though someone had turned over a bucket above, and which made Geneva feel they were being ambushed. Nonetheless Tony drove at breakneck speed, and the Rover hugged the road like a dog following a scent.

It was long past nine o'clock when the rain stopped. Soon the Rover head lamps beamed on a long stone fence, shiny from the rain, then on the imposing Brookhurst gate with its archway above, crowned with a finial like an oversized urn. Tony applied the brake and tooted the Rover horn. The motor purred, marking time. A pot-bellied lodge keeper in work clothes and cap hurried out from his small cottage to open the gate, the wind lifting his shirt tail. Geneva noticed one small window in the cottage, four square panes giving off shafts of yellow light. How cosy.

Now the man waved Tony on, holding his cap on his head so the wind wouldn't tear it off. The tires crunched on the gravel as the Rover plunged down the long drive leading to the Selby manor house. Vaulting trees encroached on both sides. Geneva looked up at Tony's face. It was suffused with happy anticipation, like a soldier coming home from war.

She sat cuddled next to Tony with a rug pulled over her knees. Here it was, near the end of May, and she was freezing. She was a little nervous, too, which probably reduced her body temperature. As they turned into the broad loop at the end of the drive marking the main entrance of the house, she could make out little detail of the structure except for its grand proportion blotting out the sky. She could not help feeling a little disappointed that not a single light shone from the front windows. Just four little shafts of light would have been welcoming enough. But it appeared that the entire household had gone to bed.

Soon Tony pulled to an abrupt halt before a set of wide, shallow front steps. "Welcome to Brookhurst, Darling," he said with a smile, and kissed her cheek.

When Geneva stepped out on the drive, the chilly wind stung her cheeks like sharp claws, and blew her hair in all directions.

A single light now punctured the dark above the arched entrance way, as blinding to Geneva as a spotlight to a performer. Then from inside came the ferocious thunder of barking dogs. Parker the butler, an elderly man for whom Tony had great affection—he had been on the Brookhurst staff since Lord Edward's father was alive—emerged and made his way stiffly down the steps. "Good evening, *Mahster* Tony, good evening, Miss. I do hope you had a pleasant drive down. His Lordship is waiting in the study."

Had I been bringing Tony home for the first time, my father would have been out here on the front steps, and every light in the front of the house would have been lit, thought Geneva. She braced herself. Perhaps English hospitality was different from that in America.

All the while Tony assisted Parker in removing their things from the boot, the old man prattled in a tinny voice: "His Lordship was concerned, given the bad weather setting in. Of course, it isn't so bad as in March…frightful winds in March…sucked the loose slates right off the roof…did for a fact. Found them strewn all over the grounds." He took in an exaggerated breath and snapped the boot shut with surprising alacrity.

In moments they were walking across the stone floor of the entrance hall, where two Old English Sheepdogs waited, their tails wagging—Tony had warned her. Angus and Kenegy stood waist-high to Geneva. They circled her steps with affable curiosity, then let her pat their huge heads. How friendly they were, how welcoming! The dogs accompanied them all the way down the long hall to Lord Edward's study. Then, to Geneva's regret, Parker shooed them away.

Lord Edward's study was commodious, with honey-colored paneled walls, leather furnishings, and figured rugs on a wide-planked floor. Magazines and books mingled on table tops with bowls of fresh flowers and framed pictures. Hulking logs flamed behind the grate, giving off a woodsy pine scent. The room had the soft, faded atmosphere of having been put to use for many years by the same contented owner.

In the far corner, next to a bay window, stood a tall wooden secretary with the writing desk folded out, and glass-enclosed bookshelves above. Lord Edward sat before the desk in a tweed jacket with patches on the sleeves, working by the light of a small lamp. He seemed not to hear their approach.

"Good evening, Father! I've brought Geneva at last!" Tony said cheerfully. Lord Edward glanced around quickly, then finished a sentence he was writing, stabbed the paper with a dot, and laid his pen aside. Removing his eyeglasses, he rose from his chair and turned to face them. He was a little taller than Tony, and slender, with silver hair combed straight back from his forehead. To Geneva he looked frightfully imposing, distant.

He took her hands in his, looked into her face for a long moment. "Good evening, Miss Sterling. Welcome to Brookhurst," he said coolly then, his mouth curling slightly at the edges. Clearly he regarded this as no more than a duty visit, reinforcing Geneva's first impression made by the darkness of the house front. But then perhaps his attitude stemmed from his business worries.

"Good evening, sir, it's very nice to be here," she said politely. She would have been glad to excuse herself, leaving father and son to continue their discussion, begun via long distance. But Lord Edward dispatched Parker to bring drinks for everyone. He gestured toward one end of the sofa facing the fire. "Please, Miss Sterling, won't you sit down?"

Please call me Geneva, she ought to say, but she could not find her voice at the moment. She noticed a few wayward dog hairs on the floor near the fireplace, and found this oddly comforting.

As the drinks were brought, Lord Edward settled in a wing chair by the fire and lit his pipe. The tobacco oozed a sweet, cherry-like aroma. Geneva wondered if she should compliment the man on his home, even though she had not seen very much of it as yet. Thankfully, Tony spoke up, "Father, we happened to see the Prince of Wales at the Trocadero. He was quite taken with Geneva, came to our opening at the *Coliseum,* and had us join him afterward in the Royal Box."

"You don't say!" said Lord Edward.

"We invited him to our wedding," Geneva told him.

"Splendid! That's all for now, Parker, but do ask Mrs. Beasington to get a formal invitation off to the Prince of Wales in the morning, straightaway."

"Very good, Sir."

Encouraged, Geneva ventured, "And I thought we might include the King and Queen. Tony says they have been your house guests on occasion."

A doubtful look crossed Lord Edward's face as he puffed on his pipe. "Yes, but that was years ago, before the coronation," he said, then added obviously, "It takes a bit of advance notice to get on their busy calendars. What is it now—less than two weeks away?"

Absently, as if he couldn't remember the exact date. She should have checked with Tony about the King and Queen, and not extrapolated their good will from a passing remark he made on the train. "But of course, I should have realized. It—it was very kind of you to arrange for the engraving of the wedding invitations."

Lord Edward lifted his brow. "Oh, I should like to take the credit, but I'm afraid our housekeeper Mrs. Beasington made all the arrangements, with Liddell's in Bodmin."

"One can always count on Liddell's," said Tony, and winked at Geneva.

Are they both laughing at me? she wondered. Father and son chatted a little more about things going on in Bodmin lately, then the clock on the mantelpiece struck the hour of ten—it seemed to take an excruciatingly long time to do so, and all conversation was forced to a halt in the meantime. Afterward, Lord Edward turned to Geneva. "I expect you're tired after the trip down," he said.

And I do so need to speak with my son in private. "Yes, I am, a little." She glanced at Tony and caught the tender look in his eyes.

"Tony, if you'll ring for Parker so that he can show Miss Sterling up to her rooms—" Lord Edward instructed, then said to Geneva, "I do hope you'll find your rooms agreeable. They were my mother's rooms; she chose them when she came to Brookhurst as a bride."

"I'm sure that I will, thank you," Geneva said, wondering if his use of the word *bride* should be construed as a sign of his acceptance of her.

Upon leaving the study, she noticed a painting of a younger Lord Edward in a straw hat and blazer, standing with his children in the grassy foreground of a tall, narrow, stone building with three stories of single, arched window openings—a small church ruin, she assumed. Nell bore a striking resemblance to her mother, with long, dark sausage curls and a pale complexion. She had a chubby face and rosy cheeks. Tony wore a blue sailor top, plus-fours, and high stockings. His hair, cut straight across his brow, was much lighter than now—almost blond. His deep brown eyes were the life of the painting, so real, she could hardly tear her own eyes away from them. And he was almost too beautiful to be a boy.

Tony noticed the painting had caught Geneva's eye. "It's from a photograph taken shortly after we moved here," he said. Perhaps guessing her mistake about the building in the picture, and wishing to save her the embarrassment of voicing it, he said, "There, in the background, is an engine house, above a mine shaft. An engine house is designed to resemble a church, you see, so as to be a pleasing sight on the estate owning the mineral rights."

"That one is Wheal Beatrice in St. Agnes," said Lord Edward. "Still operating until late 1914, it was; one of our best producers of all time—both copper and tin," he added proudly.

Tony had never said very much to Geneva about the tin mining business, except for the fluctuating financial state of Selby Mines, and now she was surprised to find herself intrigued. "Is the engine house still standing?"

"Oh yes," Lord Edward replied, "the painting is queerly prophetic, as the artist deleted the smoke stack, and all the surrounding buildings, giving it a sort of ghostly quality." He paused, then mused sadly, "And that's all there is left, now, just the engine house, choked with vines. There are many of them up and down the coast, in varying stages of decay."

"Will you take me to see this one?" Geneva asked Tony.

Tony glanced at his father uncertainly. "I should think we can get away for a few hours tomorrow, take a drive along the coast?"

After rubbing his chin thoughtfully, Lord Edward said, "I suppose so. Oh yes, I'd quite forgotten, I heard from the vicar today. He is expecting the two of you tomorrow afternoon at four."

Tony had warned Geneva of the necessary interview: *"It's just a formality really, like announcing the wedding banns starting three weeks in advance."*

The study door opened, and there stood Parker. Tony's smile at Geneva was warm as a kiss. "Goodnight, Darling. Sleep well."

With Geneva following, Parker detoured around the figures of Angus and Kenegy, snoozing on the floor outside the study, then led her up a tall stairway of dark wood and spindled balusters, the cream-colored walls surrounding it stretching high as a castle, and covered with oil paintings of immense proportion—seascapes and landscapes, and portraits. How dreary the paintings were; but then there wasn't as much light as there would be during the day, with sunlight streaming through the big windows, she supposed.

Parker glanced over his bony shoulder. "I'm sure you will like Lady Cynthia's rooms, Miss. They overlook the terrace and the south lawn, so they have rather a nice view, and they get the full morning sun."

"They belonged to Tony's mother?" she asked, surprised.

Parker reached a landing and turned, his bony profile coming into view. Parker was much too old to be lugging people's suit cases around and climbing stairs, Geneva thought. "Yes, Miss. Lady Cynthia had them completely redone when the family moved here from London, some years ago."

"Lord Edward didn't mention they were hers," she said.

"No, Miss, he wouldn't."

CHAPTER 45

The next morning, when Geneva raised her head from thick feather pillows and emerged from the warmth of a heavy comforter, the room was freezing. Last night a cheery coal fire had greeted her from the gracefully sculpted cherry wood fireplace across from the bed, but the fire had died out. Someone had parted the drapes. She glanced at the bedside clock: 7:30. As she reached for her house robe she noticed a beverage tray on the small table in front of the fireplace, with a porcelain pot and accessories. Coffee, rather than tea, she wished, lifting the lid of the pot. Amazingly, it was—Tony must have alerted the staff—and apparently it was left not long ago, for it was steaming. This was real hospitality! She filled her cup and took a sip. The brew was strong and rich, just the way she liked it. She gazed around at the luscious walls and upholstery of the room: silk and velvet in soft mauve and cream, with accents of cool mint green. Last night's lamp light had not done justice to Cynthia's decor.

Parker had spoken of the nice view. Geneva took her coffee and stood before the window, her eyes circling the broad blue sky above, and the wide stone terrace below, from which swept a bright green lawn. Verdant flowering shrubs and trees defined the lawn's periphery into meandering curves. Parker was too modest; the view was magnificent.

Now a gardener in a floppy straw hat and baggy work pants emerged at the far end behind a push mower: last night's gate keeper? Maybe. The sight of him brought to mind a sharp summer-time memory of her father, mowing the lawn on Caroline Street. Over the years, as his promotions at Houston Lumber & Paint demanded increasing hours behind a desk, he relished the physical effort of yard care, and took pride in his accomplishment. The day after he was buried with her mother, Geneva watched a real estate agent drive the stake of a "For Sale" sign into the ground her father had tended. He might have been driving the stake through her heart. Only now, in view of this memory, was she able to fully appreciate the fact that Brookhurst, a haven for the Selby family for generations long before the time of those gathered here now, would remain so long after they were gone. This concept of timelessness was new and stirring to her; how wonderful it must be to grow up securely enveloped in it.

She had just poured her second cup of coffee when there was a knock at the door, and a lilting voice: "It's Tony's sister, Nell West. May I come in?"

When Geneva opened the door and stood looking in her deep green house robe, Nell was thankful it had been borne at last, the thing she had dreaded: *to be seen by Geneva.* She had stood at the door for quite some time before knocking, wishing her figure could be reduced by five stone, wishing she could disappear altogether. What a beauty Geneva was, just the sort of person Tony would fall for. Nell was painfully conscious of the plain brown broadcloth suit she wore over her buxom frame, and the pair of homely oxfords on her short wide feet. Whereas her straight hair was swept back severely into a tight bun at the nape of her neck, Geneva's short red waves were shiny and buoyant.

"I do hope I didn't disturb you. Tony thought you might enjoy a tour of the grounds, before breakfast."

"That would be lovely," Geneva said, "Come in, sit down. I'll just need a few minutes." Nell did as she was asked, taking a chair by the fireplace. Geneva hurried to the dressing room, leaving the door ajar.

"You must have gotten on the road early this morning! Tony said you live on the other side of Bodmin Moor," said Geneva through the door.

"Oh no. My husband has been in Camborne this week," Nell said. "I drove over yesterday afternoon, with our son, and somehow it got quite late. Father didn't like for me to drive home. Launceston is only around 15 miles from here, but the road is pretty treacherous at night." No sooner were the words uttered than she realized Geneva may feel slighted that she had not come down last night. In truth she had chosen to put off the inevitable for a little longer by turning in shortly after Guy went to sleep.

When Geneva came out, Nell noted with envy the clingy white sweater and gray skirt so becoming to her slender figure. "I should think we might begin with the walled garden, if you're agreeable," she suggested.

"Oh yes, that reminds me—" said Geneva. And before Nell knew it she was handing her a volume entitled, *Motley's Guide to Flowers of the British Isles.* "Tony says you are an expert gardener. I thought you might enjoy this."

How like Tony, saying something like that, always trying to build one up. And trying to make things work between them, obviously, putting Geneva up to buying her a book on flowers. Well, it simply wouldn't do. She was not the sort of person Geneva would want as a chum, someone attractive to be seen with. "Oh? I've had some good luck with camellias, but that's about all," she said deferentially, then opened the book and found the inscription on the fly-leaf.

To Nell—with all good wishes-In friendship, Geneva. She was caught off-guard by the words; they seemed overly familiar. They made one feel all the more awkward. Still. She looked up and smiled. "That's very nice."

Geneva nodded slightly. Nell sensed she might have expected a more effusive response. Oh well.

How handsome was the book, with all the colored plates, thought Nell as she carefully turned the leaves. It must have cost a fortune. Presently she looked up again. "How lovely, but it's quite an extravagance, I'm afraid." *Oh dear, that was not very subtle, was it?* she chastised herself. But money, money, money, was all anyone thought about nowadays. One had become infected by the subject. Still, Morey would see them through. Unlike Tony, who didn't care, and would run off to be on the stage.

She thinks of me as an empty-headed show girl, throwing away money, Geneva realized. How naïvely she had imagined Nell's pleasure as she handed three crispy £1 notes to the clerk at Foyle's. "I collected some wild flowers while we were on tour. Tony said you might identify them for me."

"Oh? Perhaps…. But I only know the common names." The edges of Nell's small mouth curled up slightly. "Thanks awfully for the book," she said.

You'll never open it again, Geneva thought.

The Brookhurst walled garden was a shimmering riot of color with an intoxicating floral scent, composed by the geometric design of gravel walks, and a long pergola at the far end. Bees burrowed into blossom throats, then looped the air as if drunk from all the nectar. Beautiful, colorful butterflies—many so great in size, it was impossible not to think of *Chimaera*—fluttered from one blooming plant to the next. What plant names Geneva could not recall, Nell readily provided. Up the stone walls grew thick clematis vines, with purple and pink blooms; and honeysuckle, sagging with trumpet-shaped blossoms. Down below: a carpet of calla lilies, snapdragons, stock, cyclamen and marigolds; pansies, sweet peas and petunias; daffodils, daisies, asters. There were plants with names Geneva had never heard: fox gloves, pinks, snow-in-summer, Venetian bells, busy lizzies. As they walked along, she swiveled on her heels again and again, amazed. It was the whole wild-flowered English countryside, tamed and brought to order.

Nell spoke with authority about why the plants were arranged as they were, what each needed in order to thrive. Nell knew a great deal more than she admitted. "I wish I knew how to grow flowers. Would you teach me, once Tony and I get settled down?" Geneva begged, for she felt now that she had never wanted anything more in her life than a garden.

But why? She could not possibly mean it, not when she can dance with my brother on the stage, Nell reasoned. The two of them would go up to London and live as her mother liked to live, and Geneva would never give another thought to gardening....

Soon they turned to the roses: "the pride of Brookhurst," Tony had claimed to Geneva. Rows and rows of bushes—their petals ranging in tone from pale and delicate to bright and boisterous—burst from the sunny center of the garden, like a chorus of glamour girls in a Ziegfeld production: wine, crimson, pink, magenta, yellow, salmon, peach, white, and many with petals of one distinctive color edged in another.

Nell said, "When we moved here from London, the rose garden was yet to be; a pond was here—round three feet deep, I should think. I barely remember it. My mother was afraid that Tony or I might drown, so she ordered it filled in, and the roses planted." *And the pergola built, and the wisteria planted, which now covers the whole pergola, end to end. But she never sat beneath it to have her tea, as she said she would. She could not ever be happy here, no matter what she did. A king's ransom in William Morris wallpapers; new rugs, new upholstery, curtains. But no. She just got bored and walked away one day. Poor, dear Father. It was so dreadfully unfair. She will never know how she hurt him....*

Nell glanced at her wrist watch. "Shall we go? Breakfast is served at half-past eight here, and it's nearly that now. Plus, Morey is hurrying in from Camborne because he and Father and Tony are to meet with some gentlemen on business, later this morning. We really mustn't keep them waiting."

With that bit of information, Geneva's hopes for a pleasant meal with Tony were dashed. Perhaps it showed in her face, for Nell capitulated, "Shall we take the long way back, round the front of the house? If we go now, it will not run us too awfully late, I shouldn't think."

They were soon coming to a halt on the front drive, the gravel crunching beneath their feet. Geneva gazed up at the graceful three-storied Georgian house of rose-colored granite, with a cupola at the central-most point of the roof. The morning light seemed a halo surrounding it. Stately trees clustered nearby, their numbers thinning in a wider and wider radius around the periphery, their shadows rippling over the ground as the breeze stirred them. Larches, sycamores and elms, sweet chestnuts and Corsican pines—Nell knew them all by name. Many were planted by her grandfather, she said, but others were well over a century old. The endearing sense of continuity rushed up in Geneva again.

"It must have been wonderful, growing up here," she remarked, her thoughts surfacing.

"Oh yes," said Nell, but thinking that the joys of growing up here did not explain by half what Brookhurst meant to her. Everywhere she looked, she saw little Gerry. This was the only home he knew, in his brief life, since they had not bought Camellia Cottage until after he died and Morey came home from the war. She braced herself. "One has a great many memories here. My first son lived here, you know." *But then, he was burning up with fever, crying in the night, "Mummy! Mummy!"—and I held him in my arms, but could not save him....* "He died here in the nursery, of the influenza."

During the pause before her last sentence, Geneva noticed Nell's face had grown pinched and red; she looked as if she would explode with emotion. "Yes, Tony wrote to me. I'm so sorry. Is it sad, being here?" Geneva asked.

Sad? But what if they should lose Brookhurst, somehow? Although surely that would never happen, even if everything fell through. But if it should, she could never return to the happy memories, either. Sometimes she feared she might forget the details of Gerry's face, the exact shape of his mouth and chin. But then she would come to Brookhurst, and she could just see him sitting at the breakfast table on his grandfather's knee, with a dimpled grin and big blue eyes—Morey's eyes. Geneva wouldn't understand. "Sometimes I am sad. But one must take the bad with the good, I suppose," she said, then rushed on, feeling foolish as she did so, but unable to stop herself, "especially for the sake of my son Guy. You see, it's very important that Guy should grow up knowing that he had an elder brother who was special...and loved...just as he is." She paused, then added helplessly, "One can't show him through pictures, thanks to the war." Of course, there was that snapshot of Gerry—an infant in his bonnet—in the back of a pony cart with his father, just before Morey went off to war. But it was not in sharp focus. Nor was that one of him by the Christmas tree in 1917, the one she'd sent to her mother, because she begged for a picture. She must ask for it back one day.

Geneva was nodding as though trying to understand.

"But at least I can walk about, holding hands with Guy, and say, 'Here is where your brother took his first steps. And in this room, he said his very first word—milk!'" Nell paused for a moment, her son's first word having come out just now on a wave of emotion. "'And there in the corner of the library is the chair where we sat together, looking at picture books....'" Her voice drifted off.

The silence they fell into was, if not companionable, at least unstrained. Geneva did not know what to make of Nell. Perhaps over time, they might draw a little closer. But for now, she could not imagine having the sort of heart-to-heart talks that had drawn her and Willa as close as sisters. She felt very lonely for Willa just then.

Presently she emerged from her thoughts to realize she was facing the stable, at the far east end of the house. Immediately in her mind's eye, Brian Potts was mounting a horse there on that misbegotten August afternoon. She turned her head slowly, following horse and rider from the stable across a wide meadow sloping down from the front drive, and so on, to the Brookhurst wood, where, at the end of that ride, the course of Tony's life changed. The wood—perhaps a quarter of a mile from where she stood—seemed of small proportion. But Tony had said it was deep, stretching to the outermost point of the estate.

"I suppose Tony has told you about what happened there," Nell said quietly from behind. When Geneva looked around, she added, "It was very difficult for my father."

She would not let Nell get away with that. "And Tony."

"Yes, though of course he went away. It was lucky people round here didn't know what had happened until much later, when Jane made a public apology to our family. What an awful brute her father was."

Was Nell placing all the blame on William Tremont, and excusing Jane's reprehensible behavior toward Tony? Geneva recalled Cynthia speaking of Jane's ability to manipulate Nell, when they were children.

Now Nell said with great feeling, "Since then, I have been especially thankful for the goodness of my own father."

"Yes, I'm sure you have. My father, too, was—"

But Nell interrupted, her voice hoarse with conviction, "And then, happily I married Morey, who is all that is good and kind in a human being." No one understood the sort of man Morey was, how he held her up; torn with grief about the death of their son, yet he held her, and was strong. Without him, she would not have survived. And then they had bought Camellia Cottage. *It will help us get over the pain, Nellie.* When Morey returned to work at Selby Mines, she missed him dreadfully for they had spent every waking hour together for many months. She took consolation in the profusion of camellias, and waiting for the birth of Guy....

"And quite the smartest man in the world—" she added fiercely, of Morey, then uttered a small laugh "—after Father, of course."

Tony would have disagreed, Geneva thought, at least when it came to the subject of business. Did Nell realize that Tony had expressed his opinion to her over the years they had known each other? Very likely she did. And this was her subtle way of reprimanding her brother, and setting his fiancée straight as well.

There, I have said it, thought Nell. It took more courage than one would have thought one possessed, and she felt proud. If Morey had made any mistake at all, it was in believing, unswervingly, in Father's dream. Tony had no right to condemn him for that. Besides, Morey would see things through to the end, which was more than could be said for her brother.

CHAPTER 46

Later in the morning, Geneva and Tony stood silently together on a craggy bluff, in the shadow of Wheal Beatrice. The sun blinked at them between swiftly moving clouds; the wind whipped around them and the sea roiled and crashed against gigantic slate boulders far below. Geneva felt they had walked into the painting on Lord Edward's study wall. Behind them stood the engine house—built of rough stone and covered with dark, greedy vines, it was as spectral as the artist had portrayed it. In spite of the roar of the sea, the ancient structure, long in disuse, seemed to exist in its own orbit, maintaining an eerie silence.

During the motor trip down the coast, Tony had told Geneva, "Selby Mines has been sold to Karforth Mining Group. They pretty much firmed up things with Father in the middle of last week, but he waited until I arrived last night to make a final decision whether to accept.

"Now we can go off to America without any worries."

Geneva was glad he had finally told her what was going on, and she realized that he and his father had preferred waiting until there was positive news. That was understandable, she guessed. Yet Tony was not jubilant, as she would have expected, given the fact that he had longed for years to sell the business. Had he changed his mind after all? She was about to ask when he said, "All that's left is getting the papers drawn up and signed."

So that was why he was not terribly excited, Geneva thought uneasily, remembering her ill-fated verbal agreement with Madame Linsky. She patted his arm and said encouragingly, "Well I'm glad to hear it, Darling."

Thence they drove on in silence until Tony parked the Rover at the edge of the road and they got out and climbed up the ragged path to Wheal Beatrice.

Staring ahead, Tony abruptly broke the silence: "I can't help feeling that I've let everyone down." His voice was tight, as if he'd been holding the admission back. Or perhaps he was only trying to compete with the noisy wind and surf.

"But how?" Geneva asked, her voice pitched high, her fingers pressing her wind-blown hair back from her face.

"I should have held out for a better deal. Should not have been so quick to settle," he said, then shrugged. "Not that it's less than adequate. Still…."

To Geneva, Tony had seemed the soul of patience for all these years. "I don't think you should feel guilty. After all, you deserve to get on with your life," she said.

He shook his head sadly. "That wasn't really why I buckled under. I was afraid Karforth would back out and leave us stranded," he admitted.

That afternoon they kept their appointment with the Vicar Sorrell. The two-storied vine-covered vicarage sat in a far corner on the grounds of St. Petroc's Church. The vicar's bicycle waited outside on the shady porch as though any minute a parishioner may call for aid.

The vicar's office was oppressive, with loden walls, high ceilings and darkly-upholstered club chairs. No sooner had Geneva and Tony sat down than his wife placed a dainty tea tray with doilies and Devonshire cream on a gate-legged table between them. Mrs. Sorrell was a tidy woman with honey-blond hair, hazel eyes, and a pug nose. Her proper smile as she poured the tea, then left the room and closed the door, suggested she had served tea to her husband's visitors for many years, and had cultivated this demeanor for the purpose.

The vicar's trunk was so long, he seemed to hunch above his desk as he looked over the documents there. "I noticed in the records forwarded to us that your name did not appear on the rolls of Heights Methodist Church until you were 15 years old," he said. He had a long, scholarly face, which seemed in keeping with the Cambridge University diploma on the wall behind his desk and the floor-to-ceiling shelves of musty-looking volumes surrounding him. Though he was not yet 40 years old, Geneva was sure, he occupied an enviable position. St. Petroc's Parish Church rose terrifyingly above the center of Bodmin. Second in line for the cathedral of the diocese, Tony had told her as they passed by the venerable structure on their way here. "Should one assume that you transferred there from the Presbyterian Church, where you were baptized as an infant? And if so, what, may I ask, prompted this change?" he inquired.

"Just a formality," Tony had said. Geneva's palms were sweaty. Reluctant to come here at all, she certainly was not prepared to undergo a quiz on her religious background. Should she tell the vicar that she was rarely taken to church, that Anne's preacher was hired to bury her parents because they had no church home? The word "gypsies" flew to her mind. No, it was none of the vicar's business. "My parents were killed in a—" her voice faltered and she glanced at Tony; they would not be at the wedding—"rail accident. My guardian, a second cousin, was a Methodist," she explained.

"I see...." said the vicar absently, his eyes dropping to the page before him, where he made a notation then looked to see what other questions he had written down in preparation for this interview.

Not a moment's pause to offer sympathy for the most tragic event in her life, one which had taken on new immediacy as she prepared for the ceremony that he would perform. Could he not figure this out? Yet, what could she expect after the Reverend Stone, who buried her parents? Men-of-the-cloth were all alike, she concluded, distant and arrogant, absorbed in themselves.

She gazed up at the formidable cross that hung behind the vicar's desk amidst the proof of his credentials. Made of shiny brass, with ornate tooling around the edges, it was sterile and safe, uncluttered by the figure of a suffering Christ to bring to mind the blood seeping around the nails and the crown of thorns. Not like in Linsky's spare little office. *She was wrapping the crucifix in soft cotton gauze and storing it in a box high in the closet, the feeling of its vulnerability still upon her.* No, this was all very neat and tidy, bringing to mind the more palatable thought of the lilies and sunshine of Easter morning. Not that Geneva had any idea of how the crucifixion was supposed to explain God, or convince you that he was any closer than he obviously was, still—

"And you were an active member of Heights Methodist?"

Had she not sat, week after week in her Sunday best, down the pew from Anne, the children fidgeting in between? Had she not suffered the incompetent pianist punishing her mother's Baldwin with hollow-ringing hymns? "Yes."

"Up until you came to this country?"

At last, she understood what this was all about. Cross the T's, dot the I's, fill in all the blanks. The Vicar Sorrell was another John Scarborough, only with his stiff shirt collar turned around. One small fib, and he would have her experience as a church member all tidied up, like the cross behind his desk, his duty discharged, his conscience clear. Never mind her faith, or lack of it.

"Of course, we've been on the road a great deal," Tony spoke up, saving her from replying. "But once we have settled in our home in England, I'm sure our attendance will improve."

Was he really? He had never once mentioned this to her.

When the vicar suggested the three of them stroll over to the church, Geneva knew that he was satisfied. She was more than relieved the interview was over, yet she felt cowardly for having failed to voice her opinion even once as her thoughts were churning. Of course, how dare she raise the vicar's ire? A hundred and fifty wedding invitations engraved beneath the Selby family crest, had been posted.

The door of St. Petroc's Church lumbered to a close like the door of a vault. Inside, Geneva looked around at the high granite altar above the chancel stairs, the towering columns and stone arches, the rows of stained glass windows—immense in proportion—depicting holy scenes. Surely there could not be a more gloomy place in which to be married. Ten times the flowers, coming from London, could not brighten it. Did Cynthia realize this as they sat making arrangements with the Knightsbridge florist?

Outside, shadows of huge trees danced on the window glass as if mocking Geneva for being shut up inside; and as the tall vicar stepped two up on the steep chancel stairs holding a Book of Common Prayer, and began familiarizing her with the lofty Thee's and Thou's of the Rite of Marriage, she could hear the joyful sound of birds singing. *This isn't real,* she thought. But of course it was real, and she would get through it somehow, in the elegantly simple bridal gown she had selected, carrying her bouquet of white peonies. Perhaps she should not have eschewed the fashionable silver helmet headdress, with flowers over the ears and tulle trailing behind, that somehow looked as if the bride should glide up to the altar standing in the prow of a gondola.

Blessedly, a few minutes later the vicar opened the vault-like door. They emerged into the fading daylight and said their farewells. Tony took her hand. "There's something I want to show you. Hurry, before the daylight's gone."

Soon they were walking past an old church yard, where, under the shade of ancient trees with thick knobby trunks, stood rows and rows of thin slate headstones, some of them leaning slightly forward, like feeble old men. Though busy streets encroached on every side, the trees filtered out all noise. How peaceful it felt. Like standing at the foot of Wheal Beatrice.

Tony must have ancestors buried here. But no, he was tugging her hand, heading beyond this, and not many steps later they came within sight of a structure, until now all but hidden by the hedges and trees. Exactly where it was in reference to the church yard, or the vicarage, or to the big church itself, Geneva could not have determined. It simply appeared, as though in a dream: a stone ruin, overgrown with vegetation. The four walls were intact, punctured by arched window openings, looking strong as a fortress. But there was no roof. It stood open like a font, the weary daylight sinking down into it.

"It's the Chapel of St. Thomas Becket," Tony said. "The roof has been missing since before I was born. I don't know what happened to it. I've always found the place intriguing."

Geneva was more than intrigued by the ruin; she was magnetized. "Let's go inside," she urged him forward. There was an overgrown path nearby.

"Well, I suppose it's safe enough; mind your step though," he said. They went along. "When I was an acolyte, I used to sneak over here sometimes with my fellows, and smoke a cigarette."

"I didn't know you were an acolyte."

Geneva's shoe heel caught in a thorny vine that crept along the path, and she nearly fell. Tony steadied her; knelt to untangle the vine. "Yes, indeed! All good English boys are acolytes, unless they can sing, in which case they are in the boys' choir."

Perhaps Tony was not speaking falsely to the vicar, after all.

They mounted a flight of crumbling steps and walked inside. The narrow stone floor was around 50 feet long, and littered with odd pieces of cracked molding that had come loose and fallen from window openings. Vines of all description grew up the walls like lattice work, and made leafy frames around the windows. Bright pink valerian blossoms sprouted from crevices. White pyracantha blooms spilled like a bridal bouquet through the huge, gaping chancel window. In its state of neglect, the chapel had all the charm and friendliness that its neighbor, St. Petroc's, lacked. Here, nature had redeemed what humans left to ruin. Had Geneva been inclined to admit as much, she would have declared to Tony that this was a holy place.

She twirled around. "Let's get married in here! We could cancel the flowers from London. I could carry a bouquet of wild flowers!"

Tony laughed, and came to lift her off the floor and circle her around. He nuzzled her neck with kisses. "I love the streak of wildness in you!" But then he put her down and held her shoulders as the vicar might hold a precocious acolyte. "But, dear heart, what would we do if it rained on our wedding day?"

With all her heart, she wanted to tell him she despised the huge, indifferent sanctuary, would as soon be married in a tomb. But to beg his family to break with tradition—or even bend it a little at this late date—would be disruptive, she knew. And with all the Selbys were enduring right now, it would be unfair.

What would they do if it rained? As they walked away, Geneva felt that it already had.

CHAPTER 47

Jane was ever amazed at how easy it was to manipulate people to one's purpose. Father used to say one simply must know what they need more than anything in the world, and—if possible—before they are aware of it. Had he not proved his point well enough, beginning one evening as the two of them dined at his townhouse in York? *"Janie, wouldn't you like some company overnight? A girl shouldn't spend the night of her 14th birthday alone." And all the while, one hand slipping under the table to gently cuddle her knee, then up a little farther, and farther still, she could feel his fingers splay....*

Jane must arrange to meet Geneva Sterling in order to determine how best to manipulate her, prevent the show girl from ruining her best chance at getting Tony back. After all, one kept one's eyes and ears open, and the future of Selby Mines was hanging in the balance. At a time like this, Tony needed a wife with plenty of money and a certain amount of status. Whereas she had both, Geneva obviously had neither, a fact which was easy enough to discern from the article about her and Tony in the Sunday *Times*. A former dance mistress in Houston, Texas—really, what could Tony be thinking? Oh, one might have thought her pretty, in a brassy sort of way—there was the grainy photograph of her sitting with Tony in the lobby of the Hyde Park Hotel. Which made Jane want to go for her throat. Tony belonged to her, and would forgive her and love her again. Still, she assured herself, Geneva was unlikely to present any real challenge. The real challenge lay in managing to get inside the same room with her.

Then there was that notice in the *Bodmin Guardian*—a meeting was to be held in the Bodmin Public Rooms, in a week's time, concerning the upcoming charity ball to benefit the Bodmin Orphanage. All those wishing to help were invited. Subcommittees would be formed. Signed by steering committee members, the Vicar and Mrs. Sorrell, Mrs. Morey West, and Lord Edward Selby, General Chair. Oh God! She had forgotten about that fancy dress ball. She had been contacted by the orphanage administrator months before, asking that she help to underwrite the affair. She refused.

The notice quite brought on a change of heart, that no doubt set Father whirling in his grave: *"You're going to give* my *money, to build a wing on a bloody orphanage?"* Well, Father was out of the way now: one day when Jane was away in York, Grandmother got it in her befuddled head that one of her many finger rings was missing, and flung open her dresser drawers in search of it, soon discovering Potts's letters and turning them over to Father. *"What's this, Jane?"* he *demanded, raising Potts' s letters in his fist, his face florid. "You lied to me, then spent my money to keep it quiet?" Before she could answer he knocked her so hard that she flew to the floor, bloodied her mouth. It was the first time he had struck her since before they went to Brighton. He flung Potts's letters on the fire, her lifeline to Tony curling up in flames.*

I will kill you, she thought, and only awaited the opportunity.

Jane began thinking about a sufficient sum, and then how to parlay this into an invitation to the Selby manor house. In the end, it proved a simple matter of placing two telephone calls. One to the administrator, *"I'm considering making a pledge, and shall speak to Lord Edward about it."* Then to Lord Edward, reporting this, and so on.... *A long pause from Lord Edward, in which she began to fear her scheme had failed. But then: "Well, yes of course, I suppose we might have a small affair for the committee. As I am sure you realize, such a substantial pledge would make all the difference to the success of the benefit this November."*

Unsaid: *"Or make no mistake, I should never invite you into my home."*

So here she was within two days' time, in the Brookhurst drawing room. "I'm a bit early, I shall just slip in and wait. Don't bother, I know the way," she had said very sweetly to Merton—heir-apparent to Parker the butler, his dottering old father—then brushed his cheek with her finger and watched the tips of his ears turn red.

Inside the room, Jane paused to feast her eyes. How she once loathed the fact that she might never be invited in here again, for she had always felt this room showed her looks to their best advantage. Thanks to her grandmother's penurious nature, Fairleigh had nothing to compare with this room, nor had all those costly improvements after Grandmother's death accomplished anything as handsome: the high arched ceiling and gilt frieze, pale lemon walls and silk upholstery; figured carpets of jewel tones over the parquet floor.

The doors opened and Jane turned. Nothing could equal the sheer deliciousness of watching Lord Edward walk in at this moment, wearing his dinner suit. For Lord Edward had only one reason to walk into this room on this night, at this hour, and that was because Jane had commanded his presence. *Take care not to reveal your sense of triumph, Jane. This is only the beginning.*

"Good evening, Jane."

"Good evening, Edward, how delightful to see you," she said, and went toward him smiling....

"If Jane wants to pay £750 to meet Geneva, then by all means, let her," Tony had said. Yet, just minutes before the dinner party would begin, he sent a message to Geneva by way of the housekeeper that he would be late. How could he leave her stranded, after years of building up Jane as an adversary? But for her reluctance to appear weak-kneed, she would have refused to go down until he was ready.

She stepped into a dress of beige chiffon, overlaid with a mull tunic and a drizzle of opalescent beads, then stood before the mirror and slipped on the matching headband with its enormous bow on one side. She stood back, hesitating. *I probably look too fussy for a small dinner party*, she thought. But it was too late to change again. When she walked out the door, evidence of her indecision about what to wear lay in the heap of discarded garments on her bed.

There was no one in the drawing room when she entered. She had not been in here before, and had thought to ask the housekeeper Mrs. Beasington for directions when she learned Tony would be late. The light, airy elegance of the room convinced her it was another example of Cynthia's taste. In the last rosy blush of daylight, the far end of the room appeared to magically dissolve into the walled garden beyond, as in the setting for a fairy tale.

Now, from the far left corner, Lord Edward strolled into view, forcing awareness of the high wall of pale yellow, spanned by a triple set of French doors. His hands were clasped contentedly behind his waist. It struck Geneva that he wore his home like a comfortable mantle on his shoulders; that he belonged here, and would never belong anywhere else.

Soon she spotted a pair of shapely feminine legs keeping pace on the other side of him. Jane Tremont, no doubt. Now Lord Edward nodded his head, as though agreeing with something Jane had said. Now he was opening one of the French doors, and stepping aside for her to enter. Jane had a small, boyish figure, and pale blond hair, straight-as-an-arrow and razor-cut. She wore a simple petal pink chemise with tiny shoulder straps, silver slave bracelets, and a thin silver band around her forehead. Geneva felt Jane had already won a point, for her surer instinct of how to dress for tonight's occasion. She was like a delicate rose that Lord Edward had snipped from a bush and brought in from the garden.

No sooner had Lord Edward introduced them, than Jane sat down on the opposite end of the sofa from Geneva, removed her evening sandals, and tucked her small feet up under her as if she were on a picnic. In the most formal room of the house. She reached for a mother-of-pearl cigarette holder. Apparently Merton was standing in for his father tonight. He lit Jane's cigarette, after which she drew up her shoulders and winked at him flirtatiously. Merton had brown hair parted down the center. His face relaxed into a natural frown, which he now fixed on Jane just for a moment.

Jane and Geneva took a long look at each other. Jane's blue eyes were hard, and her complexion had the chalky look of porcelain, prior to being fired in a kiln. She was chillingly attractive, like a corpse laid out for a funeral.

"We must call each other by first names," she said chummily. Her voice was delicate and sweet, but with a cold leaden undertone.

"If you like," said Geneva.

"So, you are the dancer I've been hearing about, or is it, acrobat?" She giggled suddenly, exposing innocent, little girl dimples on her cheeks. "I haven't seen anything on the stage for ages. I feel positively ignorant about what's 'in' these days." She narrowed her eyes. "Do tell me all," she begged, thrusting her chin forward.

For once, Geneva was ready. "Really, male impersonators are all the rage. You should see Ella Shields, with her boyish figure. I think you would appreciate her," she said, thinking how proud Cynthia would be to watch her in action at this moment.

But then, Jane threw back her head in laughter. "Perhaps *I* ought to try being a male impersonator. A moustache might help." She pinched up her mouth. "What do you think, Edward?"

Not *Lord* Edward. Simply, Edward.

But before he could reply, Nell walked in with her husband, wearing a shapeless gown of deep green silk georgette, with a pink camellia in her hair. Morey's beefy shoulders and broad chest overfilled his dinner jacket. He would have looked more at home in a small dark pub with a low ceiling, surrounded by miners having their ale and swapping stories. He was almost too polite as he greeted everyone, and then he quietly withdrew, rarely speaking.

Not until after the vicar and his wife had arrived, and the party was on the verge of exhausting both the subject of the charity ball and their first round of drinks, did Tony walk through the door. "Hullo everyone," he said, then came at once to Geneva's side. "Hi, Darling, sorry I'm late."

"High time," said Jane. "We were about to send out a search party." No one had raised the issue of Tony's delay, in fact. But Geneva had already learned that Jane was never content to have the group's attention diverted from her, and would frequently use a provocative comment to turn everyone's head.

Tony did not even glance her way. "I had a devil of a time running down Oliver Upsbridge," he said to Geneva, "but he says there are no offers on Clearharbour Farm at this point. He'll arrange for us to have a look at it."

Geneva felt guilty now, for having been annoyed with him. They had seen the sign posted on the Clearharbour fence as they drove out Castle Canyke Road this morning, and though the tall stone farm house was located far back on the property, through the trees, Geneva could see enough of the steep pitched roof and upper-story windows to have her curiosity aroused.

Lord Edward, overhearing Tony and perhaps at a loss for engaging the group in conversation, cut in, "Clearharbour has the best view round Bodmin, if you ask me. It may need some work, though. From what I've heard, old Mrs. Findlay was not up to looking after it, the last few years."

"Yes, it was rather going down when I used to visit her," said the vicar. "She's moved to Kent, to live with her nephew I believe."

Jane chimed in, "Oh yes, I remember old Mrs. Findlay…half blind, deaf, and crippled up with rheumatism. But still she must cling to life. What a frightful bore that must be!"

Everyone turned to Jane. She smiled in satisfaction and tilted her chin. "I've no intention of going out that way. I shall go out in an instant, like a candle being snuffed," she declared.

With a peremptory lift of her brow, and the proper smile that Geneva remembered, the vicar's wife remarked to Jane, "We should all be so fortunate, my dear."

"Unless, of course, you're talking about suicide," said the vicar thoughtfully, drawing back his chin, "in which case it is my duty to warn you of the danger of such thinking to your immortal soul."

Jane had no ready answer. Merton seized the moment of silence to announce that dinner was ready.

"Splendid!" said Lord Edward, with obvious relief. He rose from his chair. "May I?" he said politely to Jane, and offered her his arm.

As they walked out, Jane managed to catch Geneva's eye and smile triumphantly.

CHAPTER 48

✿

The next morning before daybreak, Geneva was stirred from her sleep by an urgent rapping on the door. She raised her head from the deep valley of pillows, confused. "What—who is it?"

"It's Tony. May I come in?"

She grabbed her house robe and went to the door. Tony was still wearing his dinner suit, though he had dispensed with his stiff collar and necktie. His eyes were purplish underneath, and his face was unshaven. He did not have to tell her that the sale of Selby Mines had fallen through. It was etched in his fatigued expression.

They sat down at opposite ends of the tufted floral love seat. Geneva tucked her frigid feet underneath her. After confirming her suspicion, Tony said, "Karforth had money problems apparently. Morey heard rumors in Camborne." He raked his fingers through his hair. "Well, it's all in the past." He rose from the sofa and walked restlessly over to the cherry mantelpiece, smoothed his fingers along the beveled edge.

"What will your father do now?" Geneva asked.

He turned. "There's a group of French investors. Father has put them off, for he hoped for a sale. But they are still interested, and they've big money to spend."

"Good!" she said, though somehow it all seemed rather desperate. It occurred to her that Lord Edward must have known of this situation during the party last night, but kept up a brave front for his guests.

"We live in hope," Tony said dispiritedly, and rubbed his stubbly chin. How strange that over the years, through all the months they had spent in rehearsals, and all the weeks on the road, not once had she seen him needing a shave. She felt a slight stirring in her heart.

"As a result, Father leaves for France on Sunday, to meet with the investors. Meantime, over the next four days, we will be drafting a formal proposal. Muggeridge is coming down from London tomorrow, to help. Then, he returns to his office, gets the thing typewritten. I go to London on Monday, pick up the proposal and see that it clears the bank. As soon as it's all in order, I send it over to Paris via courier service."

He gave her a pleading look. "The crux of the matter is, Father cannot get back here by the second of June. He has asked that we postpone our wedding till the 9th. I said I'd have to speak with you, first."

For a moment Geneva was too stunned to reply. Then the first and most obvious of the drawbacks came to mind. "But the invitations have already been mailed."

"I know. Assuming we can clear the new date with the vicar, everyone on the list must be contacted. And the florist in London, of course."

"Well…alright," she said slowly. Then another realization occurred. "But wait—we leave for Southampton on the morning of the 10th. We'll miss out on the Lake District, and spend our honeymoon aboard a ship. I'll be sick the whole time!"

Tony was nodding, his eyes luminous with tears. "I'm dreadfully sorry. I so wanted everything to be perfect, didn't want you to be burdened by any of this."

She took a moment to absorb his apology, then asked, "Is that why you wouldn't tell me anything for so long?"

His eyes dropped, then he looked at her again. "It wouldn't have been fair. None of this was your doing."

"But it wasn't yours either. Tony, this is the first time you've ever let me in on anything that wasn't already settled—well, at least as far as you knew. I never asked for things to be perfect. I only wanted to feel a part of what you were going through," she said, and then she fell silent, for a tear rolled from Tony's eye. Poor Tony. Now she'd made him feel guilty, and that was horrible, after what he'd been shouldering. "Oh, come here!" she cried.

He knelt before her. She kissed his mouth. She kissed his cheeks. She brought his head to her breast and kissed his hair. Her arms encircled his shoulders. "Oh, I love you so much! And everything is going to be alright."

Tony sniffed, and looked up at her, his eyes bright with adoration. He'd known since the day he told Geneva of the debacle in the Brookhurst wood that she was as strong and nurturing as any individual could be. He should have never listened to his father when he said not to discuss with her the mess they were in now. It was Geneva who would enable him to survive whatever came. "Yes, I rather think it will, now," he said at last. "I know that *I* certainly shall be alright." He kissed the tips of her fingers and the palms of her hands. "Your hands are freezing," he said, and rubbed them inside his own.

"I've been freezing since I came to England," she said, and they began to laugh, then smothered their laughter in each other's shoulder. He looked up. "Father's waiting. I shall leave you now, and you can go back to bed where it's warm." He rose to his feet, and she rose with him. She kissed him again, and held him close. She did not want to let him go, would not have minded in the least had he picked her up and carried her back to bed. That he didn't press his advantage made her want him even more. "I love you," she said, again and again, drunk with the sound of the words, like the bees looping above the flowers in the walled garden were drunk with sweet nectar. The more they kissed, the farther away June 9th seemed, then the week aboard ship, lost to Mothersill's and stomach tablets, then straight from New York Harbor into the demanding arms of Charles Dillingham.

"Tony," she said, catching her breath, "would it matter if our honeymoon in the Lake District was the week before the wedding?"

His face broke into a grin. "I've been praying that you would ask that question!"

CHAPTER 49

By Monday noon they were in London, and after leaving Geneva at the Hyde Park to spend the day with his mother, Tony hurried to Caxton Street and picked up the proposal from Craig Muggeridge. Craig peered above the rims of his eyeglasses with a sagacious look. "Lots of luck with this. Let me know if there's anything more." And of course, there was, Tony realized as soon as he walked into Barclay's Bank and found its officials pouting because the Karforth sale had fallen through, and they did not entirely trust the French investors. Consequently, what should have taken a matter of hours stretched into two full days, with Tony volleying between the bank and Muggeridge's office, trying to meet the ever increasing, niggling demands of the bankers.

What kept him from losing patience entirely, and telling them exactly what he thought of their greedy gnawing at the edges of his honeymoon with Geneva, was thinking up special ways he could make that honeymoon more memorable for them both.

Finally, at 10:30 on Tuesday night, having conveyed the last of the amendments to his father in Paris, Tony was past exhaustion; and having drunk at least 20 cups of coffee since noon, he could have climbed up the Pennines on foot. He went directly to the Beaumont suite, took Geneva in his arms and said, "I know it's late, but if you're up to it, we can still catch the 11:15 to York. It makes a lot of stops, I'm afraid, and takes rather a long time."

"Couldn't be worse than the sleeper jump. Just give me a minute," she said agreeably.

"How did it go?" Cynthia asked, worriedly. By now she had a general idea of what was going on—there was no keeping it from her, not with the week's delay in the wedding, and Tony's desperate run up to London.

"About as well as can be expected, I imagine," he told her.

Cynthia wished the happy couple goodby, smiling, hugging and kissing them both. When they were gone, her face turned grim. She folded her arms and paced the floor. Edward may very well wind up with nothing to show for Selby Mines. It wasn't the end of the world, certainly, as long as that *was* the end of it. She wished she knew more about the situation. More than anything she wished Jane would butt out. One more week, just more week, please God, she prayed, making a steeple of her hands and bringing them to her lips.

As their train pulled out of the station, Tony said to Geneva, "The bankers are satisfied; who knows about the French?" It was the last thing he would say about the whole affair. It wasn't that he did not have plenty to get off his chest—he felt somewhat like a kettle of soup, coming to a slow boil—but he positively refused to spend another moment of their honeymoon thinking about it, much less talking about it. And when Geneva parted her lips to speak, he pressed them with his own, then declared the subject out of bounds.

Geneva soon fell asleep with her head on Tony's shoulder. Still wide awake, he looked out the carriage window, all that had happened since their arrival at Brookhurst two weeks ago inevitably swallowing up his mind like the blankness of night swallowed up the view of the countryside. What if this fell through? French businessmen were known to be among the most obstreperous negotiators in the world. Still—one must hope for the best, and leave it to Father. After all, there were not that many Cornish mining companies left, and Selby Mines had the strongest assets of all. Oh Lord, now he was thinking like Morey! How he longed to be far away in America, with all this behind him. He looked down into Geneva's sleeping face, at the fringe of eyelashes above her cheeks. He closed his eyes and tenderly kissed her hair. *"Oh, I love you so much! And everything is going to be alright."* She was his salvation.

In more than five hours on the train, he never really slept, though he dozed fitfully. Once in York, he just wanted to be on his way—from here, the journey was miles and miles of steep uphill driving—but when they stopped at the garage, parts of the Rover he had reserved for hire were scattered all about. Greasy from one end to the other, the owner emerged from underneath, hitched up his pants around his protruding belly and said, "Hit's sommot in the steerin' column, Sir, keeps pullin' to the right, see; but I been 'ere since three o'clock, and I'll have it ready 'fore sun is op good. You an' the missus have a seat on the bench there, and I'll be done in no time a'tall."

"Very well," Tony said, with a helpless glance at Geneva.

The man disappeared under the Rover again. "Ah, 'twas a fine little eight 'orse power Rover took all the prizes in hill-climbin' op at the Coomberland County open last moonth. Did'ja hear about it? So I ses to meself, ah can' go lettin' this gent'mun take no substitute, no sirree, not if he's headin' over the Yorkshire Dales and into the Pennines."

When Tony turned to Geneva again, she'd covered her mouth with her hands, and tears of laughter were running down her cheeks. In spite of himself, he began to laugh, too.

Just at dusk on Wednesday evening, they glimpsed the lower end of Lake Windermere, unfurling like a silver thread through the shadows of green-black trees, with the mountains, gray-blue and vaporous, towering behind. On they drove, the Rover top down, the road following the lake's sinuous contour, the two of them enjoying the damp wind in their hair and breathing deeply of the intoxicating air. Soon they approached a high stone wall and a sign: *Welcome to the Ghyll Inn.* Tony took a sharp right and crossed the road, then immediately a hairpin jog to the left, at which point they started the climb up a steep, angling drive, passing mountain-size pines and spruces and fir trees on both sides. At the top, the vine-covered inn stretched three stories high, with pointed gables and wide bay windows on each floor. Tony and his family had vacationed here when he and Nell were children, and Nell had awakened one morning to find a ram, with great spiraled horns, peering curiously through her window, just inches from her face. Shrieking with fright, she leapt into Tony's bed. He smiled at the memory now.

Mrs. Twickenham the proprietress led them to the attic suite—the most spacious one in the inn—and opened the door. There before them was their own bay window, with a sweeping view of Lake Windermere and the mountains beyond. A log fire cheerfully burned in the small fireplace. In the bedroom, there was a huge wooden canopied bed that quite dwarfed the room, with a snowy-white comforter and big fluffy pillows. Nearby a candle burned in the candle stand, with a small volume of poems by the Lake Poets next to it; a pot of flowers sat on the window sill. It was perfect, just what Tony had hoped, and Geneva was obviously enchanted. He felt quite giddy all at once.

Mrs. Twickenham was Amazonian, with a huge bosom that tilted her posture forward. She had great frizzes of carrot-colored hair, a long, bumpy nose, and wide protruding eyes which ran like lascivious fingers over her attic suite guests, as if she wanted to keep an image in her mind that she could return to later, when she supposed them to be making love. "O' carse, as ya were dootifully in-farmed, we have no 'lectricity, nor central 'eat. But we do have runnin' water for yer bahth, just let me know when you need to have it heated op."

"Yes, thanks."

"An' if you like music, I can provide a wind-op gramophone from me own parlor, and me late hose-band's favorite Caruso recordin's. Some of 'em 'ave wee scratches, ya know, but not so much as to roon the sound."

"Yes, thank you, we'll let you know."

"Do ya desire dinner this evenin', in the dining room?"

A glance at Geneva. "Eh—no, I don't believe so."

"Could I bring op some tea? An' I made gingerbread this afternoon. Ya might ha' got a whiff of it downstairs."

Tony urged her toward the door. "Not just now, thank you."

"Well, toodleoo then," she said, then with a glance at Geneva's naked ring finger, she added, "Bein' on yer 'oneymoon, you probably won't, but if you do go'oot, take an ombrella. We're in for some rain 'fore night's doone."

Tony closed the door. Geneva started to giggle. "Come here, you!" he said. He closed his arms about her and nuzzled her neck. He could feel her heart pounding against his chest. "I love you," he said, then added, "And it is sommot of a coom-fort to me, noticin' there is a lock on the door."

"Well…" she said, and looked up at him invitingly.

"I want to take you to a place that I remember. Put on your best bib and tucker, and a pair of walking shoes. I'll change my shirt and tie, here in the sitting room. Hurry now, it will be dark soon."

Geneva was surprised that Tony would call for an intermission, or an 'interval,' as the British would say. "Alright," she said sportingly, thinking of her white wool pleated skirt and sweater set with pearl buttons, from Debenham & Freebody in Knightsbridge.

When they walked outside there were leaden clouds gathering faraway above the mountaintops, and thunder rumbling lowly. Somehow, in the confusion of the last 48 hours, Tony had managed to remember to bring his camera. He nabbed a fellow guest, to take their picture. They posed at the edge of the garden bed, midst hydrangeas and snapdragons and roses, with huge pale pink rhododendrons forming a backdrop.

From the main road they walked arm in arm, uphill towards Ambleside. Even from afar you could tell this was a substantial village; there were numerous dark gray stone buildings with stark, pointed gables. Yet it was positively minuscule in proportion to the round rise of a loaf-shaped mountain beyond: the ancient god of the village, napping with his shoulder against the sky.

In Ambleside their descent began, off the High Street, one block, then a turn and down another, and another, and so on, until at the end of Vicarage Lane, the Church of St. Mary's stood peacefully before them. It was as small and unpretentious as Tony remembered, and thank goodness, it appeared to be deserted.

He turned to Geneva. "Let's have our own private ceremony, here."

He had managed to surprise her yet again, and she was grateful to his nod of respect for her wish to be married before they shared a bed, the best he could do under the circumstances. "I'd like that very much," she said.

He reached up with his pocket knife and cut off a shaggy cluster of blossoms from the giant-sized rhododendron by the door. "Miss Sterling, may I present your bridal bouquet?"

Geneva lowered herself into an elaborate curtsy, and accepted it. Then she rose and hugged his neck. "Oh Tony, I do love you!"

He had never been so happy, nor so eagerly expectant. Inside, he deposited some coins in the collection box—what a clatter this made; he might have alerted the whole village they were here! He picked up a musty Book of Common Prayer from the stack behind the pews. They walked down and knelt before the small altar, gazing up at the simple bare cross. Geneva found herself thankful for the absence of the suffering figure on this evening, for she was filled with joy and didn't want pain to enter in.

For a few moments, she and Tony both felt a desire for silence. Then Geneva turned to him. "You know, Tony, I've just had the most amazing feeling: that Madame Linsky is smiling down on us."

"Then I know this is right!" said he. "I think we should name our first daughter Elvira, in her honor."

"Yes! Elvira Christina Selby. How lovely!"

With fading sunlight slanting down on them through the colored window glass, they spoke their vows from the prayer book, slowly and lyrically, often looking up into each other's eyes. At the proper juncture, Tony reached inside his breast pocket for Geneva's newly-engraved wedding band. He slipped it on her finger. Her face crinkled in delight. "I'm afraid the date by our names is wrong," he apologized. "Wrong twice over—it says June 2nd."

"What is today's date? I've lost track," she said.

"It is the 30th day of May, in the year of our Lord, 1923. I now pronounce us man and wife. What God hath joined, let no man put asunder."

They stood up and kissed, hearing wedding bells and the swell of the organ, as surely as though they were sounding.

Outside, Tony reached inside the pocket of his blazer, giving Geneva a wicked look as he did so, then showered his bride with rice. "What? Where did this come from?" she cried, laughing and ducking as he tossed a little more.

"Courtesy of the Hyde Park kitchen staff. I'm sure it's premium rice."

They were beginning the climb up the steep angling drive to the Ghyll Inn when they heard a clash of thunder, and rain ripped through the clouds. Tony raised the umbrella, and they strained their legs to climb faster. Inside, they scurried up the stairs past paraffin lamps glowing on wall pedestals, giggling all the way. A door on the first landing sprang open, and Mrs. Twickenham leaned out to see who was coming. Geneva flashed her wedding band, and the poor woman's bulging eyes widened most remarkably. Quickly she shut the door again, and Geneva and Tony giggled still harder.

When Tony unlocked the door of the attic suite, his heart was pounding to beat sixty. He lifted Geneva in his arms and carried her over the threshold.

Inside, the only light was from the flaming logs. He lowered her to her feet and they kissed each other eagerly, his hands hardly knowing where to go first, so grateful they were, at last, not to be restrained by hers. Yet, she pulled back suddenly and said, "Wait! I have a special gown. Give me a minute?"

"No, you shan't need a gown or anything else, trust me," he said teasingly, still holding her fast, his lips pressing beneath her ear.

But Geneva slithered free of his arms. She hurried into the bedroom, driven by her wish that this night be marked in her mind forever, bearing as little resemblance as possible to the day when Victor closed the studio curtain.

The bedroom door shut. Tony sank into a chair, thinking it was all ruined, the spontaneity he had counted on. Whoever was responsible for the tradition of a special gown for a wedding night ought to be drawn and quartered. It made the most intimate event seem more like a theatre opening. He sat staring downcast at the fire, impatiently drumming his fingers on the chair arm.

At last, he could sit still no longer. He called through the door, his voice husky, "I believe I'll just dash out and buy a bottle of champagne."

He was looking about for his mackintosh—where had he stashed it? Then he heard the bedroom door creak on its hinges, and he turned, the hair rising on the back of his neck. There stood Geneva, wearing her gown, wispy and thin, the soft light behind her revealing the delicious outline of her figure. How, he wondered, could her curves and angles, so long familiar to her dancing partner's hands, seem to his eyes so breathtakingly new?

She said not a word, but looked at him with luminous eyes. He understood, suddenly—and gratefully—that the gown had forced him to slow down and savor this once-in-a-lifetime unveiling.

She held out her arms and he went to her.

CHAPTER 50

Love in the Lake District was dizzying climbs and glorious descents; slowly up steep mountain paths on bicycles or on foot, then down again, with breathtaking speed, between fringes of dripping trees (it was always raining, or threatening to); up three flights of stairs to the attic suite, down into the haven of homespun linens to complete what was constantly beginning, ever new, always in need of replenishing.

Love was two pairs of eyes meeting over a candle-lit supper of grilled mountain trout—buttery crisp and spicy at the edges, soft and moist in the center—with a concertina playing in the corner. And Tony whistling its tune as they left the little restaurant in Grasmere and motored back to the Ghyll Inn in a great hurry to climb into the cycle again.

Love was opening the door at the top of the stairs and finding the splendor of the Lake Poets there. Lying naked before the fire, in the afterglow of love-making and sometimes just before, they let Wordsworth and Coleridge give rhythm and voice to what they were living: *"The budding twigs spread out their fan, to catch the breezy air; and I must think, do all I can, that there was pleasure there...."* Love was Tony's hands fanned out around Geneva's hips and the brush of his lips on her ear.

She would have been happy to stay forever, felt almost as if when they left, it would all disappear, having been nothing more than love's illusion.

On their last day, the sun toyed with the idea of burning through the gray clouds. They dressed warmly and went boating on the lake with a picnic hamper, courtesy of Mrs. Twickenham. While Tony manned the oars at one end of the boat, Geneva languished at the other, her nostrils filled with the wet wild evergreen scent, her eyes following the legions of firs and pines and spruces—interspersed with wild purple rhododendron—that banked the edges of the lake. Around noon they found a place along the rocky shallows to pull ashore, and discovered ham sandwiches and chunks of white Cheddar cheese; plump amber pears, their hips blushed with ruby; flat spicy ginger-bread bars, and a bottle of dry Chianti. The proprietress knew how to fix a honeymoon picnic lunch. They consumed the feast with mountain-air appe-tites, then lingered at the water's edge, sipping wine and gazing contentedly across the glistening lake at a witness of trees, mysterious and dark, and blue-black mountains beyond.

"I wish we could live in our little attic suite, forever," said Geneva.

Tony was wearing a straw hat with a roguish twist. He pushed his hat back and looked at her. "You're just a simple girl at heart, aren't you?" he said, admiringly.

"Yes I am."

"You'd love me, even if we were dirt poor, living in a little hut with a coal stove and a leaky roof?" he conjectured, a sad, wistful look clouding his face.

He could not have painted so vivid a picture unless he had been forced to imagine it. "I certainly would. Maybe even more," she said. She looped an arm through his and snuggled closer.

"I love you, Geneva," he said with a quiet solemnity that touched her.

"I love you, too, dear, precious Tony!"

"No, I mean more than that—I love what you are; love whatever it is that makes you able to love me enough not to want anything more," he declared. He gazed out toward the water again. "I only hope I can let you love me that much, if ever you need to…."

And so, tomorrow and the unavoidable return to all the problems he had left behind, were already staring at him through the trees. Geneva wished with all her heart to force away this invasion on their happiness. "Kiss me," she begged. They reached for each other desperately. Pretty soon Tony's warm fin-gers were hastily fussing with her skirt hem, then slowly stroking their way up her thigh. Suddenly it began to rain.

They grabbed the picnic things and scurried back into the boat. As they pushed off into the lake, it rained harder. Geneva struggled to raise the umbrella, then made a valiant, if futile, effort to cover them both, while Tony strained the oars against the water that rolled and clapped and pitched furi-ously. It rained still harder, and the gusty wind blew the umbrella inside out. Tony's hat flew from his head and they watched it sail across the lake and disappear. Then, through the icy fingers of rain, their eyes met, and they laughed at their powerlessness.

Clearharbour Farm found a place in Geneva's heart somewhere between her home on Caroline Street and their attic suite at the Ghyll Inn. In empty garden beds she saw roses, periwinkles, daisies, marigolds, asters, snapdragons—she would have seen more except that Tony was tugging her hand, eager to show her a huge double sycamore where he fancied a tree house for their children. A small conservatory with a pointed roof marked the entrance of the house, and as they walked through it, Geneva lined its empty shelves with blooming house plants. She saw her parents' longcase clock in the front hall by the stairway, saw her father pull out his pocket watch and compare the two time pieces. Their furnishings, so long in storage, only awaited *this* living room, *this* dining room. In the kitchen was an enormous, fierce-looking cast iron stove; and off this room was a small buttery that brought to Geneva's mind a play room for children on rainy days, and to Tony's, a study lined with books and recordings, easy chairs and a gramophone.

Upstairs were four bedrooms with sunny windows, and the largest of these offered a fine view of the faraway rooftops of Bodmin. Tony pointed out the steeple of St. Petroc's, towering above the buildings and treetops surrounding it. It did not seem so daunting when you were perched high above it, Geneva thought.

"Just think, all this, and it even has electricity and hot and cold running water!" Tony quipped.

As they stood looking out the window, there was no question in Geneva's mind that they belonged here. Tony wrapped his arms around her from behind, and said, "Assuming it's structurally sound (*Oh, please let it be! she entreated Providence*), it shouldn't take much, really—new wall paper, a bit of floor polish, and a good paint job. What do you think?"

She could hardly imagine what she would have done if he had voiced the least reluctance. She would spend her inheritance if need be. She would go without what ever was necessary, if only this could be their home. But perhaps this was not the time to allude to that. "Oh Tony, it's perfect! Do you think we can afford it?"

He kissed the bare nape of her neck and tightened his arms about her. "We shall see. I have a feeling, one way or another, it'll be ours."

CHAPTER 51

When Geneva and Tony arrived at Brookhurst shortly after tea time, Lord Edward—who had been home from Paris since morning—seemed to be forcing cordiality into his greeting. Geneva was sure the man must be exhausted. Immediately, he and Tony excused themselves and retreated behind the study door. Some problem had arisen, Geneva realized. With the bankers? The French? Poor Tony. Would the future of Selby Mines still be hanging when they boarded ship, three days hence? But perhaps it was only the details that needed working out. Considering the haste of the negotiations, there must be a great many of them. The trouble was, Tony anticipated contacting Oliver Upsbridge immediately upon their return. How long would this have to wait?

She stood alone in the hall, the dogs sniffing curiously at the unfamiliar scents on her clothing. After all those days in the unpretentious Ghyll Inn, Brookhurst seemed overwrought in furnishings and decor; its size disproportionate to the number of people who lived beneath its roof; the chunk of nature its granite bulk displaced, embarrassingly large. The ceremony to take place within the vaulting structure of St. Petroc's Church seemed superfluous, now that she had knelt with Tony in the modest Church of St. Mary's Ambleside. Her wedding band hung from a chain around her neck, concealed inside her blouse. There it would stay until Tony again slipped it on her finger.

She could hear trolley wheels roll across the hardwood floor of the formal dining room, and the clank of silverware being laid at table settings. Housemaid chatter was punctuated by the authoritative voice of Mrs. Beasington and the hoarse croaks of Parker.

With everyone busy except her, Geneva felt at loose ends. She considered opening the presents which, according to Merton, had been collecting in the drawing room over the past week. But when she walked through the big double doors and saw the splendid array of gift-wrapped boxes, sent by people whom she had never met, it seemed odd to open them without Tony. She decided to go up to her room, to see if she had any mail. As she climbed the stairs, she wished that she could turn back time, and be racing with Tony up the stairs at the Ghyll Inn. She felt homesick for their attic suite, especially when she thought of other guests occupying what had seemed, for all time, to belong exclusively to them. The thought of Clearharbour Farm cheered her. Except, what if, by the time Tony was free to contact Oliver Upsbridge, someone else had bought it?

As it happened, there were two letters awaiting her, one from Willa, and the other, from Ida. She opened Willa's first. "Dear Geneva. I have great news. We're expecting a new baby in December!" Meantime, they had purchased a small cottage on Lake Astoria, near Austin, Texas, and were fixing it up. "When we first saw it, Rodney said, 'Look what a quaint little place!' I thought it was ugly beyond redemption, and naturally told him so. But he was sure it had great potential, and I'm beginning to think he may be right.

"I'm too lethargic to do much these days, so when we're up there, I mostly watch Rodney work. James follows his dad around with a toy hammer (no severe damage, yet). We all look forward to you and Tony spending a holiday there with us one day in the future. The view is spectacular."

It could not possibly equal the view from the Ghyll Inn, Geneva thought contrarily. But how she missed the Youngers! And the realization that she would not be living across the street from them in December, on hand to hold their new baby in her arms as she had held James, made her feel that something of great significance would be forfeited. Geneva had not yet cleaved to Tony's family. In her heart the Youngers were still her closest relatives.

Now she opened the envelope addressed in the dark, slightly uneven strokes of Ida's Remington. Inside was a typewritten letter, and a clipping which fluttered to the floor as she unfolded it. She left the clipping for now. The letter was dated May 26th. "I write to you in haste, because I leave early tomorrow for Fort Lauderdale. The clipping is self-explanatory. I doubt many will attend the funeral—it has all been so hurried, due to the amount of time already elapsed. Benjamin is anxious to get things over with, and of course, there is a lot of business to tend to. I thought you would want to know—. Sincerely, Ida."

Flora Bartelle had died, apparently, which prompted Geneva to count up the number of years since Anne was buried: eight. It hardly seemed possible.

She retrieved the clipping and unfolded it. *WORLD-FAMOUS PHOTOG-RAPHER VICTOR CALAIS, DEAD AT 43.* No. She blinked, then reread the bold headline, but her eyes blurred at the four ineluctable letters separated from his name by a comma, a heartbeat. She leaned her head back and closed her eyes. No. *Victor was closing the studio curtain, and turning to her. Victor was nursing her through the flu, spooning broth into her mouth. "I'm going out to Los Angeles, to make a motion picture, and I want you to have the leading role." Victor was crossing the concourse of Union Station on the day the war ended, and then he was kissing her goodbye—*

At the sound of a knock on the door, her eyes flew open. "Who's there?"

"It's Nell. May I come in?"

Could Geneva have found her voice, she would have cried, "No!" Nell opened the door and peeked inside. "Could we have a little chat before dinner?"

She had not realized Nell would be here for dinner. "Come in," she said reluctantly. She put the clipping aside.

Nell was carrying Geneva's woven bag. At the moment, Geneva could not employ her mind to reason why. Nell sat down across from her, then frowned at her like a mother surveying the feverish look of her child. "Are you alright?"

"I—just a little tired." The headline had burned a hole through her brain. Victor was dead. *DEAD.* But how? When?

"I've identified all the wild flowers and tagged them," Nell said brightly. "And I must say, the *Motley's* was enormously helpful."

Oh yes, Geneva now recalled leaving the woven bag with Nell when they departed for their honeymoon.

"You may want to dry some of these, and hang them in your kitchen as a keepsake. There are detailed instructions in the *Motley's*, if you'd like to borrow it," she said, then smiled timidly at the irony in her offer.

Nell had put each wild flower into a separate packet, and now she began pulling them from the bag, one by one, delicately opening the wrappings for Geneva, like one opens a baby's blanket for an eager admirer. "This is Black Byrony…and here's Milkwort. And Meadowsweet.…"

On and on she went. Geneva did not know how to respond to her unexpected thoughtfulness. The wild flowers, which she had so proudly collected, were horrid things now, dried up and *DEAD…at 43.…*. Victor had been in Singapore. Did he die in Singapore? If Nell stayed much longer, she would go mad. "Nell, I have a bad headache," she said abruptly.

Nell's cheeks grew splotchy. She began replacing the specimens in the bag, her hands trembling. Even through her despair, Geneva was aware she had lost important ground with Nell in the effort to win her acceptance. "Perhaps tomorrow—"

Fretfully, Nell said, "I doubt I shall be available tomorrow. All these business matters…Morey is hardly ever at home, and poor Guy is growing quite cross. I've promised him a day trip to Kilmarth." She re-packed the last of the flower specimens, and rose from her chair. "Will you be joining us in a few minutes?" she asked. Her voice was brittle with injury.

Geneva's eyes veered toward the clipping. "No. I'm not hungry. I think I'll lie down. Please, will you make my apologies?"

"You really do look quite pale," Nell said with a contrite frown. "Have you taken anything?"

"Not yet, but I have some aspirin in my handbag." She did not, really, but neither did she really have a headache.

"Perhaps I could get them for you. Just tell me where your handbag is—"

"Please, Nell, don't worry about it," Geneva said stridently. She put a hand on her forehead. "Oh, I'm sorry, I don't mean to be so edgy."

Nell considered her for a long moment, then said, "All these business matters have put you out of sorts too, I fear."

Grateful to have an explanation provided her, Geneva said, "Oh, I'll be fine." Then she asked anxiously, "Nell, is everything going alright?"

Nell didn't really know the answer. She forced a smile: a shield to deflect criticism away from her husband. "Yes, as far as I know."

"Good, that's very good," Geneva said sincerely.

When Nell finally walked out, Geneva locked the door. She returned to the clipping from Ida and hungrily scanned the text. "…diagnosed with cancer while in Singapore…died in a hospital there a few weeks later, on April 20th. His stepson Benjamin Rothby…working with him since March…at his bedside when he died…accompanied the body to Fort Lauderdale, for burial." *Victor was sitting on the edge of her bed, his eyes tender, having brought news of Madame Linsky's death.*

When Geneva put the clipping aside, she felt old beyond her years; her relationship with Victor seemed a lifetime ago.

And then, inevitably, she thought of the pictures of her in the nude, and remembered Victor's reluctant promise. *"I see no reason for you to destroy them. They are mine, and I will do it."* But had he? Now for the first time, Geneva allowed that underlying her belief—oh, how eager was her belief!—that Victor had lived up to his word lay the certainty that, whether he destroyed the pictures now or later, they were safe in his hands as long as they existed, for he would never allow them to harm her. But now he was dead.

Benjamin was accompanying Victor's body home...going through his things...discovering her pictures?

Shortly after she put on her sleeping gown and laid down in bed, she heard a sharp knock at her door. A pause, then another. Tony's voice, gentle, solicitous: "Geneva. Are you better, Darling? Open up, it's me." Nothing more than he should expect given the week above Lake Windermere. Yet she couldn't talk to him now, let alone untangle her sadness for Victor and make love to him honestly; and he would never, ever understand that. She needed to be alone, figure things out. The question of the pictures loomed before her like a nightmare maze which she must find her way through. Tony was knocking again, more insistently, rattling the door. She was torn. She opened her mouth. Shut it. Let him think she'd gone to sleep.

Presently he went away. A tear ran down her cheek like a spear.

CHAPTER 52

By morning Geneva had acquired the headache she claimed to Nell, having been awake most of the night. When she opened her eyes, the draperies were parted; the room was filled with sunlight. She spotted the coffee tray. That was what she needed, to get rid of the headache: good, strong, hot coffee. She made toward it groggily, shivering in her bare feet and gown. But the coffee had plunged to the depths of room temperature. She looked at the clock: half-past nine. No wonder. There was no choice but to get dressed and go downstairs. If she were very, very lucky, perhaps the breakfast room would be empty by now and she could slip in and out again with her coffee. She was not ready to face anyone yet, especially Tony.

Unfortunately, she found Tony at the table, alone, the newspaper open before him. When he looked up at her, his eyes were dark underneath, as though he had not slept any more than she had. "Feeling better this morning, I trust? Nell said that you had headache, so I left you alone. Later, when I knocked, you didn't answer. When I tried the door, it was locked," he said, the last phrase catching in his throat. Now she saw last night from Tony's side of the door: standing there helplessly. Perhaps Nell passed down the hall, or Lord Edward, or even a servant, and saw that Tony had been shut out of her room. Eyes were dropped discreetly; nothing was said, but volumes were gathered in the silence. She felt enormously guilty.

"No. I didn't sleep well," she said. So desperate was she to withhold the one secret she hoped Tony would never have to know, she had spent hours searching her mind for a way to avoid revealing it. She might just assume the best—as she had done for years—that Victor had destroyed the pictures. But no. The three words: *What if not?* chased back and forth through her mind like a raw winter wind through a room with open windows. Should she contact Benjamin and offer him her inheritance? He may not even have found the photographs, so why tip him off to start looking? By the time the light of dawn made pale bars around the edge of the draperies, she had reasoned herself into a corner. If those photographs still existed, once she married Tony the entire Selby family would be subject to whatever consequences might result. She would have to tell Tony about the pictures. At least the business crisis had apparently passed, which would make it a little easier. Exhausted, she finally dropped off to sleep.

She picked up a china cup and saucer now, thinking of that first morning of her arrival, happily discovering Tony had ordered a coffee tray for her room. Her throat squeezed up tight. As she poured her coffee, cup and saucer played like castanets in her hand. She stirred a little sugar in, hoping to boost the effect of the caffeine. "I think I'll take my coffee upstairs, and try to get waked up," she said. "Maybe we can take a drive after while, when I get over this headache." Then they could talk. She remembered driving down the coast, standing in the shadow of Wheal Beatrice. Would he be as understanding of her troubling news now as she had been of his then?

"You'll never make it upstairs with that coffee still in the cup. Let me take it for you," Tony said coolly. As they walked through the breakfast room door, she remembered the clipping, lying in full view. Once Tony saw it, there would be no putting off telling him about the pictures, and in a context she would give anything to avoid. She wished she were dead.

When they passed Angus and Kenegy, lounging in the hall, the dogs looked up curiously, but did not stir. They must have sensed their master's dark mood. Geneva had a sudden urge to weep for the two puzzled animals.

As much as she had dreaded walking inside her room with Tony, she was not prepared for how quickly things got out of hand once the door was shut behind them. Immediately he spotted the bold headlines about Victor's death, handed her the coffee with a cold *So that was it!* glance, his jealousy ignited, and set about reading as she gazed out the window, down at the peaceful south lawn with its meandering curves, all the varying shades of green shimmering with life under the bright sunlight. How strangely fragile was the view this morning, as if it were painted on glass.

Soon Tony put the clippings down and looked at her icily: "And this is what caused your headache, and kept you awake all night?"

No. There's something I must tell you—The words formed a hard lump in her throat and stuck there.

"This man, who took advantage of your innocence when you were 16 years old, then walked away—leaving you with his child—is dead. This man, whom you have not seen, or heard from in—what—eight years? Correct me if I am wrong." He waited, a threatening look of expectation on his face.

What are you getting at? "No, I did see him once again," she said, her voice shaky. "He—he came home near the end of the war."

Tony grimaced, as if his line of reasoning had hit a snag.

"I didn't know he was coming."

"Still, you allowed him to cross your threshold—"

"I had the flu. I was alone. I had vomited all over myself, and passed out on the bedroom floor. He found me there, and—" she stopped herself, took a breath "—and took care of me until I was well."

She could see Tony's mind filling in the words she had left out....*soft cloths, warm and moist, coursed up and down her arms and legs and over her body....* "Oh yes? And what prompted him to come, may I ask?"

Dear Victor.... There is something I would like to discuss with you—"He wanted me to make films with him, but I told him that I was to marry you. So he went away." *And their lips were parting after a guilty goodbye kiss.*

After a considerable pause, Tony said, "Remember when we played the Los Angeles *Orpheum,* Geneva? That message from B. Rothby—friend of your parents, I seem to recall. 'My father is in Singapore,' he said."

Dear God.... "Tony, there's something I must tell you," she said, knowing she could not have chosen a worse moment. She spoke breathlessly. "There were pictures...nude pictures," she said, suddenly feeling more naked than ever before. Tony's face went ashen. His gaze upon her was as relentless as the eye of the camera during all those hours she had posed in the nude for Victor, her every instinct crying out in opposition.

Now, everything there was to tell rushed from her mouth in a torrent of words, including her fear of Benjamin. With every word, Tony's face grew more somber. Finally she took in a breath and admitted, "I was hoping, out in Los Angeles, to confirm that Victor had kept his promise to destroy the pictures. But I truly believed that he had."

Tony's brow shot up. "You *believed* him? Knowing the sort of person he was? Pray, when did Victor Calais ever show to you that he was capable of doing a thing he did not wish to do?"

She would not attempt to answer that. "The fact that he might lose his life never once occurred to me. But it changes everything. I can't ignore the possibility that the pictures still exist, that Benjamin may find them, and use them against me." She paused and let out a helpless breath. "Against us."

"Well, you are absolutely right there is every likelihood we haven't seen the last of them. But do you know what really troubles me, far more than those pictures, Geneva?" he implored.

She shook her head miserably.

"That you allowed him back into your life after what he did to you, and at a time when you had promised to wait for me."

She opened her mouth to protest—

"If it was so easily explained, then why were you not honest enough to write to me about it? Or, tell me, along with everything else, on the morning after I proposed marriage?"

"You were upset, and I—I didn't see that it mattered," she said, and she knew that he did not believe her.

"Do you know what I think, Geneva?"

She shook her head.

"I think the ties between you and Victor were much stronger than even I realized. It's why you locked the door last night; you didn't want me to intrude on your sorrow…or your—your *memories*."

He had gone too far, and he knew it by the stricken look on her face, yet he could not stop himself. On the banks of Lake Windermere, she had promised to love him through whatever came, and then last night, just when he needed to be assured of that more than ever, the French and the bankers at each others' throats, she locked her door. Yet, perhaps—"Unless you can look at me and say that Victor meant nothing to you, that his death left you cold."

She was outraged. "How dare you dictate how I should feel about Victor's death, or anything else!" she cried. "If, after all that has happened between us—" she said, her voice cracking "—you're convinced that I lied about my feelings for you, that I am not—not—*worthy* of your trust, then I'm really sorry for you.

"I—I can't, won't stand here and be interrogated any more. I want to go home. I need to figure—I want to go home." *I want my mother!*

It was the last thing Tony expected. He felt he had burst apart, like a tree split into logs for burning. He saw it all inevitably coming apart now, for his father, for Nell, for all of them, knew he could not hold things together any longer, not when even this—which he had counted on above all else—was crumbling before his eyes. "You're not going anywhere. It's much too late," he said, realizing at once that his desperate plea had come out more like a threat.

So that we might just go right on arguing until we stand before the vicar? She could see them, side by side before the altar, with smiles as phony as all the trappings surrounding them. And down the years, the threat of her pictures to his family creating still more resentment, if not disaster. No, she could not. "You just try and stop me!"

Tony could no longer separate his anger from his fear. "If you leave now, I never want to see you again. You're no better than Jane Tremont. Scratch the surface, and you're the same underneath—"

She was not even conscious of lifting her hand until she had slapped his face. His eyes widened and grew wet. His hands moved upward from his sides, trembled, then swung back again.

"Get your baggage together. I'll see that Merton is waiting with the car. Goodbye, Geneva," he said, and his voice broke. He walked out and slammed the door.

CHAPTER 53

At first it did not occur to Benjamin to simply ignore Victor's new will. Thousands of miles from home and dazed with sorrow over his father's death, he had all the arrangements resting on his shoulders. He hardly knew where to begin. The people at Rahban were nice. They helped with the documents that must be drawn up and signed, and they even paid to have the body sent home on the ship that would carry Benjamin. During the long weeks of the voyage, if the will crossed Benjamin's mind, it was in the context of all the arrangements still pending in Fort Lauderdale. He would quickly dismiss it, out of exhaustion—he had never been so tired in his life—and a feeling of detachment from everything on dry land, which had overtaken him soon after he sailed.

But then he arrived at Aunt Flora's house in Fort Lauderdale, where he and Kathy and Virginia and Aunt Ida were to stay until after the funeral—the old woman was generous to offer this hospitality, but there was only so much room so the other relatives stayed in a hotel. At Aunt Flora's he soon learned that his sisters had not only reviewed the joint will drawn up by their parents in 1908. They had also discussed their father's camera collection and equipment, and his photographs—most of which were in Springfield where they lived—and arrived at the conclusion that his photographs should be given to an appropriate museum, and everything else appraised and sold, the proceeds to benefit the church building fund.

"We assume you would agree that's fair," said Kathy. She had been married for a year to a preacher. She wore her long hair parted in the center, and braided into unattractive knots on each side of her head. This, along with her modest black dress and lace-up shoes, made her look at least 50, and repulsively moral. "Oh yes, and I assume Daddy had a bank account in Singapore?

According to the will, we each get an equal share of all cash." She glanced at Virginia, who was such a coward she could but go through life letting Kathy make her decisions for her. "We have decided to donate our part to the church building fund. If you would care to do likewise, it would be a fine Christian deed."

I would burn in hell first, thought Benjamin.

About that time Aunt Ida walked into the parlor where they were sitting. Apparently she had overheard Kathy's suggestion, because she exchanged a dry look with him. Ida eased herself into a chair in the corner, clutching a handkerchief in one hand. The rims of her dark beady eyes were red from crying.

"There was barely enough cash to cover the incidental expenses," Benjamin told his sisters. He had even dipped into the pay from Rahban which his father assigned him, though he was not about to allude to that money. "And as to the photographs and cameras and so forth—" he began, then paused, thinking of the new will folded up inside his suitcase. If the beneficiary were anyone but Geneva, he would have shown it to his sisters now. How could they be so coldhearted as to talk of selling their father's most valued possessions, even before he was buried? It suddenly occurred to him that Geneva would likely be just as quick to sell them. How convenient to reason, then, that as Victor drafted his new will, he had been in too much pain to think clearly; after all, by the time he finished he was desperate for a shot of morphine. "—Dad wanted me to have all the things connected with his work. He knew they'd mean more to me than anyone else."

Kathy's face reddened in consternation as she saw one of the stars disappearing from her crown. "How do we know you're telling the truth?"

"It's a hell of a note, fighting like this over your father's possessions," Aunt Ida croaked. "Benjamin's a photographer; obviously he can put my brother's things to use."

Benjamin had always considered Aunt Ida a strange old bird. He was surprised that she was taking his side. "You don't. You weren't there," Benjamin said accusingly to Kathy.

Virginia's eyes filled up. She cried, "You could hardly have expected us to travel all the way over there, knowing Daddy may—may have been dead when we arrived." She brought her handkerchief to her face, and hurried away.

"Now see what you've done," Kathy said petulantly and rose to follow Virginia. At the door she turned, lifting her chin. "And Aunt Ida, I'd appreciate it if you would avoid the use of profanity in my presence, and my sister's."

When all was said and done, Benjamin took only mild satisfaction in having concealed their father's will from his sisters, the kind of satisfaction he had derived from assuming his real father's name: he had taken for himself at least one thing that was rightfully his.

When he was ten years old his mother sat him down and told him Victor was not his real father, and explained that Jim Rothby had abandoned her before he was born. By the time he was 12, he was secretly planning to run away after finishing high school, to find Jim Rothby and force him to acknowledge him. *"You're a jerk for running out on me and my mother; and a fool, because if you'd stuck around, one day you would have said, 'Here is Benjamin Rothby, he's my son, and I'm proud of him because, by God, he can do anything he sets his mind to.'"* The words went round and round in his head, the anger knotting up in his stomach. But obviously he had to know a trade so that he could survive on his own. Though he begged his dad to teach him photography, time and again he put him off. And of course Benjamin could not reveal the reason he was in such a hurry, not when everyone expected him to go to college. Then his mother died, and time ran out. Stranded up in Springfield while his dad went over to photograph the war, Benjamin was more unhappy than ever. Springfield schools were more advanced than those in the Heights, and instead of graduating from high school early, he had to repeat a year to catch up. He spent most of his spare time trying to locate Jim Rothby via the mails. He got a map and wrote to him care of the general post office in every city of any size in Florida and the surrounding states. He remembered the names of several citrus farms his mother had told him about. He wrote inquiring if they'd heard of him. At the public library he got the names of shipping companies that plied up and down the Atlantic and went into southern ports. He wrote to them. No one seemed to have heard of Jim Rothby, and his letters to the general post offices were returned unclaimed. When Benjamin and his dad began preparing to go out to California and make films, he gave up the project of finding his real father as hopeless, a young boy's stupid dream. Yet all the while he had been writing out those letters one after another, he had become more and more infatuated with the name Rothby. His father didn't deserve such a name.

But Benjamin did.

Aunt Ida was the first to leave, boarding a train a few hours after her brother's funeral. Some distant cousins on her mother's side who'd moved to Central Texas after the war were expecting her to visit on her way back to Houston. As they said goodbye she told Benjamin she'd be relocating in Houston pretty soon, and she'd send him her new address. "What happened to Geneva?" Benjamin asked, taking care not to reveal anything in his expression.

"Marrying her dancing partner and moving to England. He's from a very wealthy family over there," she said, then paused before adding, "Some people get all the breaks, don't they? Well, good luck to you, Benjamin."

Sir Benjamin Rothby went through his head. He had never realized how much he and his aunt had in common. Had she been there any longer, he might have told her about concealing her brother's new will. She might just get a good laugh out of that.

CHAPTER 54

One morning in late June, Willa checked the mailbox across the street as she had been doing daily for more than three weeks, since Ida Ruekauer came to her door and said, "I've got to go to Florida to attend my brother's funeral." Not her brother Victor, obviously, for he was in California. It must have been another brother. Willa did not ask, and Ida did not volunteer any further information. But for the fact that Geneva's mail was still being delivered there before being forwarded to England, Willa would not have agreed to help Ida by picking up the mail. Ida had never been likable—always somber and taciturn, and fearsome looking: James hid behind her skirt that day Ida came to the door—and now that Geneva was gone, Willa had come to distrust the woman.

Due to Ida's busy nursing schedule, the house was often empty for long periods of time. Willa kept an eye on it for Geneva's sake, usually looking out her front window just before going to bed at night. Naturally there were nights when she looked over there to find the lights lit in the windows, indicating Ida had come home. On more than one occasion, very late, Willa spotted an unfamiliar male figure emerging from the shadows of the porch. It was none of their business, as Rodney pointed out, but it did seem odd to Willa that when Geneva was home, Ida rarely had visitors of either sex, even in the daytime.

Otherwise, Willa suspected that Ida was drinking heavily when she was at home. One morning when the two of them happened to pick up their newspapers at the same time, Willa called out good morning. Slowly her neighbor turned, then stared at Willa as if she had drawn a blank, her face pasty-looking. After a moment she mumbled something—probably said, 'morning'—then went inside and closed the door. Willa dismissed the encounter from her mind. But on another early morning soon after, a garbage day, a neighbor's dog got out of the fence and toppled a few garbage cans, Ida's included. Noticing the scattered contents as he left for work, Rodney stopped to reload them in the can. That night he told Willa, "I didn't know Ida Ruekauer went for hard liquor. There were two Canadian whisky bottles in the mess I picked up."

Now Ida was a heavy smoker, just as Willa herself used to be until she went through the tortures of hell to quit, while carrying James. This could be a dangerous combination, she reasoned, for what if Ida drank herself into a stupor one night, and became careless with a cigarette? She could burn the house down. And many of Geneva's things were still in there. Oh well, there was no use worrying about it when there was nothing she could do. Just keep an eye out, that was all.

Willa turned from Geneva's mail box—empty today—then retraced her steps home, thinking as she went how she missed her best friend. And writing letters was a miserable chore. Until Rodney came along, Willa had never cared whether her words or actions offended other people. Consequently, she had never developed the art of diplomacy. Now she regretted it. At least, if she were talking to Geneva face-to-face, she could tell by her expression if she had blundered, and apologize then and there. In writing letters, though, she may as well be blind. Sentences, paragraphs, pages must be rewritten time and again in case she put something the wrong way. Willa would never forgive herself if she injured Geneva's feelings while she was thousands of miles away.

It was ten o'clock. After checking on James, who was taking his morning nap, Willa poured a cup of coffee and sat down in her living room. She suffered no morning sickness with this pregnancy, as she had with James. But she often got very blue around this time, with Rodney at work and James napping and Geneva gone; and she would find herself drawn to gaze upon the picture of her real mother, hanging on the wall. All the while Willa was growing up, her adopted parents stubbornly refused to reveal her identity. Then at age 20 Willa discovered some clues in an old carpet bag in her parents' attic that eventually led her to the truth: an unmarried young woman from Galveston, named Serena Garret, died giving birth to her. Through this journey of discovery, Willa wound up with two of the dearest treasures she owned: Serena's diary, and a picture of her in a ballerina dress, posing in an arabesque out on a Galveston veranda in 1899. Rodney arranged to have the original snapshot enlarged and touched up as a present to celebrate their very first month as man and wife. Such was Rodney's intuitive generosity.

They hung the picture on a narrow wall between two tall windows, where it remained today. But Willa could not bear to have her mother surrounded by the dark woodwork and oppressive wallpaper that—from all appearances—had been in place since the house was built. So this room became the starting point from which she and Rodney would transform the entire house, painting the woodwork white, hanging cheerful new wallpapers, and replacing the heavy draperies with thin curtains that shuddered lightly in the breeze on such a fine morning as this.

Warmth and brightness; hope and promise, were the qualities Willa found in her mother's pretty face. She could not have had any idea that she would be dead within a year after she posed for that inspiring picture. Yet, gazing at it, Willa often imagined that Serena the ballerina *knew* tragedy would befall her, and if this was so, then maybe that sunny perspective meant that she was looking past her own life, to right now, when her daughter gazed at her, silently sharing her innermost feelings, that bewildering phrase she often heard in church—that all Christians were a part of the *communion of saints*—kind of making sense.

If she was even halfway decent at writing letters, Willa would write to Geneva, describing all these feelings. She was sure that, had her mother lived, she would love and admire Geneva. And the fact that Geneva was an accomplished dancer would have pleased her very much. Had she lived....

Sometimes Willa worried that, like her mother, she would die in childbirth. She'd think of all the bad things she had done, and fear that her punishment was waiting for the severing of the umbilical cord. If God granted undeserving people one last prayer, she would ask that her baby be a girl. She would name her Serena Garret Younger, and ask Rodney to please give her dancing lessons—.

The doorbell interrupted Willa's maudlin train of thought. Yet, upon opening the door, she could only blink at the figure before her, certain that all her thinking had led her imagination to play a trick. "Geneva, what are you doing here?" she cried at last, wondering where Tony was and why did she look like the world had collapsed around her feet?

Geneva broke up in sobs, and walked into Willa's arms.

Soon the two women were sitting across from each other, Willa with a firm grip on Geneva's trembling hands. "I hadn't cried at all. At least, not this morning...till you opened the door," Geneva said. "Oh, Willa!"

"Why don't you start from the beginning and tell me all about it," said Willa gently.

And so Geneva recounted her story in full detail, from the time she reached Los Angeles and found out Victor had gone to Singapore, to the time she sailed back from England alone. Finally she said with a sob, "Oh, there were so many times I wanted to turn back—I love Tony and Tony loves me; how could we have wound up abusing each other?

"But always, always, at the back of my mind: Tony's look of despair as I told him about the pictures. Plus the thought of how his whole family could be hurt by them if I married him and—" Her voice broke off. She sniffed. "I just can't take the chance. You know, Willa, Victor used to say that he always thought of the *Maiden at the Window* as looking out upon her future, like it was some wonderful thing waiting to happen. But he was wrong. Her future was sealed in those nude photographs." She started to sob again.

By that afternoon, feeling some relief at least, from having poured out her heart to Willa, Geneva was more clear-headed, and decided to write to Benjamin in Los Angeles: *"If you should discover any pictures of me in Victor's things, I would appreciate your sending them to me, as a keepsake. I think Victor would have wanted me to have them."* If Victor had indeed destroyed the pictures, then her letter was harmless. If not, and Benjamin had them, she hoped he'd get the message that if he dared to blackmail her, he would be implicating himself.

She felt less stranded when an envelope came with his return on it, though the letter inside was chilling: *"All this time I thought you'd gotten married and moved to England. So far, I have not run across any photographs of you. My father did weed out his collection on occasion, and may have disposed of them. Frankly, it would seem to me that if he wanted you to have anything that belonged to him, he would have remembered you in his will. B. Rothby."*

She almost wrote to Tony, to say what she had accomplished and make some effort to patch things up. But then it wasn't the pictures that started the fight. She still felt bruised by his anger and distrust. Why should she grovel at his feet? She would wait for Tony to overcome his pride, and write her an apology. Then she would go back to him.

CHAPTER 55

Geneva had a period in early July which started several days late, and lasted a little more than two days. *Dear Tony, I think I may be expecting....* No. She hadn't heard a word from him, and probably all her upset of late threw her off schedule and caused the period's short duration. It wasn't like not having one at all.

In August, five days passed after her period should have begun based on July, and still nothing. On the 6th morning she was sitting alone at the kitchen table, having poured herself a cup of coffee. Abruptly her instincts told her that to drink the coffee would send her straight to her knees in front of the toilet. That was when she was sure she was pregnant, or at least as sure as she could be without having seen a doctor. *If I am pregnant, everything will change,* she told herself soberly, pushing the coffee aside; *the quarrel between Tony and me will not matter. The pictures will not matter. Nothing will matter except the baby.* She took in a breath. A *baby!* She was filled with the joy of revelation, as if the sun were coming up inside her body. Tenderly she placed both hands on her abdomen. A *baby.*

She went to the telephone in the hall and started to dial Willa's number.

But then, Ida was between cases right now, down the hall in her room. She may overhear her talking. There was no point in Ida knowing until she was certain—at which time there would be no choice but to tell her. For now, she went across the street to tell Willa in person.

"Of course, I may be wrong," she admitted uneasily that afternoon as she handed Willa the key to the roadster. They were on their way to see Willa's specialist in Houston. Geneva was much too distracted to take the wheel.

Willa gave her hand a reassuring squeeze, then slid in on the driver's side. Soon they were backing down the driveway. Geneva was gazing at the wedding band she had slipped on her finger, her thoughts on the prospect of writing to Tony. *If I am pregnant.*

Of course, Tony might think she would never have written to him again, except that she was expecting. He might not believe how close she came to turning back after she left him, or how close she came to writing to him after she received Benjmin's letter, or the number of times since then that she had been tempted to write because, in spite of his obvious stubbornness, she loved him and could not imagine them going on like this forever. He might not believe the number of times she had tried to reach Cynthia—hoping she would confirm that the French investors and the English bankers had reached an agreement—just because she cared what happened to Tony's family. No one answered Cynthia's telephone. It was as if the woman had vanished into thin air, taking her housekeeper with her.

Dr. Latimer was a slender, light-haired man with a pleasant, if humorless, demeanor. At the beginning, he asked Geneva a number of questions about her health history, and was particularly observant as she recalled the loss of her first child. Nothing that she said brought any comment, though he did jot down some notes.

He wore a frown of concentration during the long and thorough examination which followed, and remained so quiet that she grew doubtful about her condition. Perhaps she was not pregnant, but seriously ill.

When Dr. Latimer finished, he offered Geneva his hand. She came to a sitting position, her eyes moving anxiously to his face. "You're going to have a baby, Mrs. Selby. Around the first of March." At last, he smiled.

Geneva burst into tears.

"Dear Tony,

WE'RE GOING TO HAVE A BABY! Willa's specialist confirmed it today. I am ecstatic, and I trust that as you read this, you are too. We must put our argument behind us, not only for the sake of our baby but because it had no basis in fact—please read these words again, Tony, *no basis in fact.* You were outraged over what you thought were my feelings. I was infuriated by your misapprehension. We were both wrong, but too close to the situation to realize it. What I will hold in my heart every moment as I carry this precious offspring of our love is the joy of our week on Lake Windermere when we conceived it.

So far, I'm doing very well, only a little nausea this morning and probably more in store, but that's normal. You will be amazed to know that I cannot abide coffee, and will resort to tea! On the way home from Dr. Latimer's in Houston, Willa remembered there was a sale on baby things at Kaplan's in the Heights. So off we went, and you'll be glad to know our baby now has a nice assortment of blankets, bonnets, booties and gowns! It's just as well, too, for my shopping days may be over until the baby comes in March. Given my history, the doctor has confined me to bed for at least the next month or so—possibly longer. He told me to settle either upstairs or down, and stay put. The bathroom is up here, and the view is nice, so here I am even as I write. Knowing I'd need a full-time nurse until you can get over here, I mentioned Ida's name to Dr. Latimer. He said that she has attended his patients in the past, and he considers her very capable. So I've given Ida the job.

Darling, it's growing late and I'm feeling tired, so I'll close for now. Ida promised to mail this letter tomorrow, and just now she came to suggest that I send you a telegram also, just in case. So I'm going to take her advice. By the time this letter arrives, then, you will know the situation. I love you more dearly than ever, and can hardly wait until we're together again. Always, Geneva."

CHAPTER 56

Waiting, waiting, waiting...

...the first 24 hours of which brought Geneva a sense of peace, for her letter and wire were, by way of rejoining her life with Tony's, reminding her of how many years their relationship was sustained by the written words they exchanged, and how fleeting was the quarrel that separated them. The next three days brought increasing anticipation, for Tony would surely not wait for the arrival of her letter, but cable his reply at once—what a blessing Ida thought of sending a telegram. Any time, night or day, the doorbell could ring, a Western Union boy could hand Ida an envelope with Geneva's name on it, and send Ida hurrying up the stairs: DARLING: BY THE TIME YOU RECEIVE THIS, I SHALL BE ON MY WAY.

After four days she began capitulating: Tony must have been away from home when her telegram arrived, or he would have cabled back by now, assuming he intended to. Could it be, he was waiting to see what her letter said? Surely not. And yet.... Or perhaps—though it seemed unlikely—he would come without telling her when to expect him, and if so, it would be two weeks, maybe less, from the time she sent the telegram before she heard the doorbell ring and his footsteps on the stairs. Oh, the thought of hearing his footsteps!

So keenly did she listen and hope as the days increased, she came to recognize the footsteps of different visitors. For instance, Ida's steps brought a heavy, even creak of the boards when her hands were empty; slightly slower if she was carrying a tray, but the same even rhythm nonetheless. Willa's steps were quick taps—five months into her own pregnancy term, her belly was rounded but she had gained very little weight. When she brought James, however, Willa's taps were considerably slower as James held her hand tightly and took one step up, then put both feet together before continuing. He frequently paused with a question, which brought a smile to Geneva's face when she overheard it: "Why can't Gee come downstairs? Why can't Gee come to our house? How long will she have to stay in her room?" And dear, kind Rodney. He had suffered an injury to one leg during the war, and though eventually he had surgery at Scott and White Hospital in Temple—she babysat James for a week so that Willa could go with him—and he hardly limped any more, he still had a slightly irregular gait when climbing stairs.

One morning, without telling Geneva beforehand, Rodney drove out to the Beaconsfield to inquire of someone—the landlord, maybe, or a neighbor—about Cynthia's absence. He didn't have to go any farther than the elderly doorman. Miss Fournier was out of the country at present, he told Rodney. And was to stop in New York and visit friends before coming back down to Houston. "Probably waiting for the hot weather to be over with," the doorman conjectured. "Wouldn't we all be grateful for an escape!"

Not until Rodney reported this to Geneva did she realize the extent of his concern for her situation. "Let's ask Willa to try calling once or twice a day, to see if Cynthia has come home," he suggested. Gratefully, Geneva wrote down the telephone number, gathering—as no doubt Rodney had done—that Cynthia would be able to explain Tony's delay in responding to her.

After Rodney left, a possibility occurred to Geneva that was so obvious, she was amazed she had not put two and two together before: Tony was with his mother. Surely the deal with the French investors was long since finalized, so he was not needed at home. Very likely he and his mother were in London, where Cynthia was trying to put him to work in some show or other—it would be just like her to coax him to move on with his life through the work he loved. The question was: why was Tony not notified in London that he had a telegram—and surely by now, a letter—waiting at home? Perhaps, then, Tony and Cynthia were not in London at all, but traveling, and could not be reached. Of course, that must be it. Looking for another dancing partner for Tony? Geneva could hardly bear the thought. She also despaired that after all this time, he still had not come to his senses about his part in their quarrel.

Whatever the case, she must try again to contact Tony. She considered writing to Lord Edward, then a chilling thought occurred: If Tony was away, he would have opened her telegram as soon as it arrived. Telegrams were not to be ignored. Yet if so, he had not bothered to cable back any words of reassurance. She would not ask his help.

She wrote Tony a brief note: *"Why have you not responded to my messages?"* She addressed the envelope to Brookhurst, noting: URGENT. PLEASE FORWARD. There. All she could do was hope for the best.

When Ida brought in Geneva's lunch tray, she handed her the letter. "I think Tony may be on the road. Would you please put this in the very next mail?"

Ida glanced at the front of the envelope, then looked up. "I don't think the postman has come yet today," she said, and hurried downstairs with the letter.

Afterward Geneva resigned herself to a few more weeks of waiting, until Tony's mail caught up with him. And who could say? Maybe her earlier messages were on their way to him at this very moment.

One afternoon she heard the doorbell ring and pretty soon Ida was bringing someone up the stairs—four adult feet, two leading the other two, and Ida's voice low and deferential. A soft, clipped male voice made her listen hard for a British accent, and her heart leapt when Ida peeked around the door. "Dr. Latimer's here."

And then he wanted to know why her heartbeat was accelerated, and reminded her it was important to keep her blood pressure in check.

To think that a little child growing in its mother's womb was the recipient of everything conducted through the mother's body, from nutrition to emotion. What a miracle! She was determined, for the baby's sake, not to let her failure to hear from Tony upset her.

And she held to it, with one exception. One day Ida walked in and asked, "What will you do if Tony ignores your messages?"

Ida was forcing on Geneva exactly the upsetting possibility she was trying to keep from her thoughts. "I—he wouldn't do that," she said, her breath short, her mind far away from the notion that she must remain calm.

"You ought to be considering other options, just in case he doesn't turn out to be the person you thought he was," Ida continued sagely.

Ironic how quick Ida was to judge, when she had been given the benefit of the doubt. Shortly after Geneva returned from England, Willa told her of her suspicion that Ida was drinking heavily. Geneva was shocked. In all the years they had lived together, she had never seen Ida take a drink. Yet admittedly, the combination of heavy drinking with smoking did pose a danger. One day when Ida was out on a case, Geneva checked every nook and cranny of the house; invaded Ida's closet and drawers—how furious she would have been! She found no whisky. The fact that those contraband bottles spilled from Ida's garbage were Canadian, suggested that her male caller was Jacob Lowerby, and he was the drinker. When Willa, still skeptical, voiced concern about Ida nursing

Geneva, she felt Willa was being unfair and told her so. "Ida may have many faults, but neither drinking nor poor nursing are among them," she said.

Her defending of Ida now colored her response. "I would think you would be more concerned about the fix you'll be in if he comes," she retorted.

Ida's jaw dropped. "Just what do you mean by that?" she demanded.

"If Dr. Latimer doesn't object, we'll probably leave for England as soon as we can," she told her, then recalled her shipboard nausea. Well, even if they must stay here until after the baby was born, Tony would look after her. Obviously, Ida would need to move out.

Ida shrugged. "Nothing new about me being out on a limb."

Geneva felt contrite. For years Ida had put up with the uncertainty of the future of her living arrangement, and had voiced few complaints. And now she was waiting on her hand and foot, 24 hours a day. "I'm sorry. Guess I'm on edge from being cooped up," Geneva said.

Cynthia arrived home in the late afternoon, feeling she'd been away forever. The apartment seemed strange to her eyes, as if it belonged to someone else. But there were the proverbial angels, staring back at her from all angles. Some guardian angel she was!

It was unusually hot for this late in the afternoon, in the early part of October. Besides, the apartment had been shut up for months and the air was stale. Cynthia removed her shoes—the ankle straps were tight from her swelling ankles—and burrowed the balls of her feet in the plush carpet. She took off her hat and gloves, placed them next to a stack of mail on the onyx-topped table behind the sofa, then walked through the living room, past the dining room, and over to the balcony to throw the windows open. For a few moments she stood there breathing in the fresh air, gazing out upon the vast open space dotted with trees and dwellings here and there, stretching far beyond Travis Street, which her balcony faced. Being in Houston was not like being in London—a maze of old buildings closing in; nor was it like being at Brookhurst, where memories were thick as the walls. There, that was better. She felt more at home now.

Everything was dusty, she noticed as she walked back into the living room, dust motes dancing in the rays of sun coming through the windows. Selena should have returned from Brownsville by now. But last Friday an uncle died—or was it a nephew? Cynthia could not keep track of Selena's many relatives. Anyway, she'd return next week, and put everything to rights.

What a thought, *everything to rights*. As if anything would ever be right again, as if she would ever again wake up in the morning without feeling sick at heart. Oh, if only she had stayed at Brookhurst! Even though it was clear her opinions were not welcome, she might have been able to ward off disaster. Instead, she returned to London, then sat in the hotel wringing her hands. But it was best not to dwell on it anymore. What was the use of coming all the way back home if she left her thoughts mired in England?

She must think of her future. She may well move to Manhattan. She had considered this when she first moved back to the States, before deciding on Houston. Her brother and his family in upstate New York were far enough away that he would not be too much of a nuisance. And several families whose friendship with the Fourniers went back to her parents' generation—established well before they migrated to Houston—lived in Manhattan. Cynthia's stockbroker and his wife were among them. She had looked up these old friends in the past month, and found she enjoyed their company more than she expected. Besides, there was so much going on in New York to keep one occupied, to keep one *alive*. She wouldn't need scouting to keep her busy. Sadly she remembered standing by as Tony cabled his regrets to Charles Dillingham just two weeks before rehearsals for *Jackson Square* were to begin. All the building-up she had done for years, to position Tony for a quick and sure rise to prominence in show business, down the drain. However, that was the least of the tragedies.

The telephone was ringing.

"It's Willa Younger, Geneva's neighbor. Could you please go over and see Geneva, right away? We've been trying to get hold of you for weeks."

Cynthia hesitated. As soon as she arrived at Brookhurst for what she thought was to be her son's wedding, Tony told her about the quarrel he had with Geneva and said that she walked out on him. He forbade her to have anything further to do with Geneva. And though her instinct was to find a way to negotiate things back to where they were, for she could not believe the situation was hopeless—not then, at least—how could she refuse him after Geneva had broken his heart? Yet, why was Willa calling, instead of Geneva? And sounding, well, almost desperate?

"Is Geneva alright?"

A very long pause. "You need to go over there. *Please*—"

"Doctor's orders," Mrs. Ruekauer said laconically, when Cynthia asked why Geneva would not come downstairs to receive her. That Geneva might be pregnant had occurred to her as soon as she assured Willa she was on her way, and hung up the telephone. However, she had counted up from the first week in June. Geneva would be more than four months along, and obviously would have contacted Tony weeks ago. Oh, what a thought! It might have changed everything. But there was no use entertaining it now.

By the time Ida opened the bedroom door and announced her arrival, then with a *Well, see for yourself* glance her way, turned to go, Cynthia was convinced Geneva was seriously ill.

"Cynthia!" cried Geneva. "I'm so glad you're here!" Cynthia was completely disarmed. For months, she had felt so angry at this child. But look how thin she was, and how sickly, her complexion. She went to her at once and hugged her lovingly.

Cynthia sat down on the edge of the bed, and took Geneva's hands. "Dear, if I'd known you were ill, I would have come much sooner, no matter—"

Geneva interrupted. "I'm not ill. I'm pregnant."

Cynthia's hand flew to her mouth. "Oh my God!"

"What do you mean? Is it so bad?" Geneva implored, her voice trembling. "I wired Tony as soon as I found out, and I wrote him, too, and when he didn't respond I wrote again. I thought maybe the two of you were traveling."

Cynthia was frowning, shaking her head.

"Then, what's the matter with him, Cynthia? He can't be that angry."

Cynthia's head was reeling. She needed to think. There had to be a way. She walked to the window and looked out over the treetops. It had grown dark suddenly. She felt as if she were standing at the edge of a deep black pit. She must put Geneva's condition first, above everything else. She turned to her. "Why are you confined to bed?"

"I—because of my history. Cynthia, there are things you don't know about me, things that happened long ago."

The memory of her son's distraught face prompted Cynthia to turn back to the window and say coolly, "Tony told me about it as soon as I arrived at Brookhurst and learned the wedding had been called off."

But now she thought of the wire Geneva had sent, realizing that its timing could change everything. "Tell me, when did you send that wire?"

"The morning of August 10th. Ida mailed the first letter on the very same day, and I wrote Tony again on the 22nd. So if he wasn't with you, why hasn't he answered?"

Cynthia continued looking out the window, thinking with glee, that would have been in plenty of time! Thank God! All this may wind up turning out alright! What was the solicitor's name—Mudworth...Mudge...Muggeridge!

That was it. She must get over to London. She would wire ahead to Tony that she was coming, and tell him to meet her there.

"Cynthia, tell me, what is going on?" Geneva pleaded from the bed. And when Cynthia turned, she was sitting up, clutching at the sheets. "Something has happened to Tony! Oh, Cynthia—"

Cynthia took in a hasty breath and walked over to the bed again. She gripped Geneva's hands. "I've got to tell you something which is going to be hard. But I want you to relax if you can, because it's going to be alright. I have it all figured out. Now, take several deep breaths—"

"Cynthia!"

"Do it!"

Geneva obeyed her, and laid her head back on the pillows.

"Good!" Cynthia said, and exhaled her breath. "Tony got married the eighth of September...to Jane Tremont."

CHAPTER 57

It was not like the shock of learning her parents were dead, or the shock of Victor's death—both of which had left Geneva in a momentary state of numb disbelief. No, too much time had passed since she wrote to Tony; too often she had awakened in the middle of the night, feeling the heat of his anger as though he were standing at the foot of her bed. She absorbed Cynthia's words at once, and she was appalled that Tony had ignored her, had even ignored their child—his own flesh and blood—to marry that *woman*—no, one could not confer adulthood on that self-centered, overgrown child. And for spite, obviously. She would never speak to him again, never let him near her child.

She became aware of Cynthia's grip on her arms, and of the blood pounding in her temples, but she did not realize that she had verbalized her fury until Cynthia cried, "No, it isn't fair to blame Tony! He cared nothing for his life, after you left him."

Then why bother to create more misery for himself? Why not just drown his heartache in drink? No, he was stone sober, getting his vengeance, that's what he was doing, Geneva thought.

Suddenly Cynthia's eyes widened. "Look at you—your face is scarlet! I'm going to bring Mrs. Ruekauer." She sprang to her feet.

"No, I have to do this myself. Just give me a minute," Geneva said, and forced deep drafts of air into her lungs. Forced her mind away from Tony; fixed her thoughts on knitted blankets and booties and gowns boxed up in the closet.

Cynthia sank down in a chair, closed her eyes, and brought a trembling hand to her forehead.

At length, Geneva said evenly, "I'm alright now. Go on...."

Cynthia kept her voice deliberate and calm. "I was in London at the time. I was not told until it was all over, and I was no less upset than you."

Now the consequences began converging on Geneva, like an after-shock. There would be no happy reconciliation. Tony would not be present when their child was born. *Dr. Latimer, my husband won't be coming over from England, after all.* She looked down at the wedding band on her finger. She would have no husband. Their child would be raised without a father.

Her mind swam back to Cynthia's voice. "...and everything was on the line—the business, Brookhurst, everything Edward possessed in the world."

Brookhurst. *Lord Edward was walking in the garden of a summer evening, his hands folded behind his waist; and now he turned toward the drawing room. One of the French doors slowly opened.* Tony had given Geneva to believe that Selby Mines alone was in jeopardy. He had never even hinted that everything his father owned was at stake. "But what about the French investors?"

Cynthia uttered a scornful laugh. "The bankers scuttled that deal. Edward had till September 15th to pay off all the notes."

Nor had Tony said there was a deadline. Only now was she beginning to appreciate the desperation Lord Edward, Tony, Nell, Morey—all of them must have felt. "And Jane just happened to be around...with all her money."

Cynthia nodded with bitter resignation. "But Tony would not have married her, no matter what, if he had believed that you loved him."

"But I told I him in my messages that I loved him. Yet he ignored me."

Cynthia leaned forward, frowning. "You can't really believe that my son received your messages. It's obvious, Jane took them."

Geneva sat straight up. "How can you be so sure?"

"Because my son would never have done that to you."

Geneva laid her head back. "That's just what you want to believe," she said dolefully, then took some more deep breaths.

Cynthia bristled as if Geneva had slapped her face. She let the remark pass without comment, however. "Didn't I tell you Jane Tremont was dangerous? Well, now you're seeing an example of her handiwork. Oh no, you can't lay this at Tony's feet. We'll get to the bottom of it, I can assure you."

Of course, one could not deny the basis for Cynthia's suspicion of Jane, Geneva reasoned. "In the telegram, I told Tony to expect a letter...so if Jane intercepted the one she would have intercepted the other. And then, knowing, without an answer, I would attempt to contact him again—Oh, Cynthia, I never thought anyone could be that vicious, even Jane!"

Cynthia swept up her hand as if it could sweep away the whole problem. "Forget about that for a moment. I believe we can have the marriage annulled, with or without proving Jane's guilt. I'm going to London, to see Tony's lawyer." She rose from her chair and began to pace, her arms folded in front of her, one hand clapping the other elbow. "Of course, I'll need to get some things together, first. Let's see…your receipt from Western Union will be helpful. And…" She pivoted on her heel and faced Geneva, her eyes fiery. "…far more vital—proof that you and Tony were together that week in the Lake District. Tony's signature on the registry where you stayed will do it. And receipts from places you went shopping, whatever. A letter from your doctor, placing the date of conception. Yes! And a deposition from you, perhaps even from the Youngers, and Mrs. Ruekauer, if necessary."

Up shot Geneva's blood pressure again. Her face felt like she'd opened the door to a hot oven and leaned in. The thought of having the most precious, intimate memories that could ever belong to two people transformed into a legal argument, perhaps even bandied about in a courtroom, was despicable. Perhaps she would be forced to endure it one day, but at this moment she felt she was being rushed headlong into a whirlwind of Cynthia's creation. "Cynthia, I need to think about this."

Cynthia came to the bed. "But time is of the utmost, dear," she pleaded.

"I realize that, but I think the baby and I have had enough excitement for one night…if you could come back in a few days?"

Cynthia let out a breath that seemed to expel all the momentum she had been building. "Just as you wish." She seemed hesitant to leave on that note, however, and quickly added, "Remember that Tony loves you deeply." Her eyes grew moist. She bit her lip. "And so do I." She gave Geneva a tight hug.

When Cynthia was gone, Geneva looked down at her abdomen. There was definitely a roundedness, the most beautiful proof of all that her child was growing, thriving. She thought back. Her child by Victor had not developed this far. The only signs of its existence were those of absence—of menstrual flow, of appetite, of energy. But not this time. Her baby was safe. She would keep it that way.

She began to carefully weigh her options. Assuming Tony had not ignored her, given some legal maneuvering, perhaps his marriage to Jane could be annulled. But, what then? Lord Edward would be destitute. He was 61 years old. After all he had been through, he may not survive such a catastrophe. And if he did survive, he would surely despise her as the woman who walked out on his son, then attempted to worm her way back through her child. Worse, he would probably despise the grandchild she brought into the world.

How could Tony ever really be happy, married to her in these conditions? Could he give her and their child his unqualified devotion? This was not the rosy picture of marriage and family that she and Tony had once envisioned.

On the other hand, what if the worst case were true, and Tony was guilty? She tried to imagine his reasoning. He could not have expected to ignore her for long. Could it be, he intended to acknowledge their child at some point, after he married Jane? In so doing, he would have the means to support the child, and he could consider his moral obligation fulfilled. *"If you leave now, I never want to see you again."*

But Geneva could hardly believe Tony capable of such underhandedness. Cynthia must be right. Jane was the guilty one. Yet…suppose Lord Edward was responsible? After all, everything he owned was at stake. Considering what she had done to Tony, would he feel that relieving her plight was worthy of his ruin? Oh yes—Lord Edward's guilt seemed frighteningly plausible, now that she considered it. But then, what about Nell? Morey?

Far into the night, Geneva alternately speculated on who the guilty party might be, and contemplated what she ought to do about the consequences to herself and her child; and so it was not surprising that the next morning, when Ida checked her blood pressure, she commented, "A little high."

Geneva did not want to get into a conversation with Ida. She wanted her to leave so that she could return to the struggle she had been locked in all night.

But inevitably, Ida asked, "Did Tony's mother bring news from England?"

The hurt was still too great to be contained. "Tony married someone else," Geneva said, and her voice broke.

Ida's eyebrows shot up. "Knowing you were expecting his child?"

Geneva composed herself. "He never received my messages."

Ida frowned. "But I sent them! You have a receipt from Western Union."

"It appears someone intercepted them, over in England," she said.

Ida let out a breath. "It's a hell of a note, isn't it? What will you do now?"

"I don't know yet. I have to think about it."

Ida looked at Geneva for a long moment. "I always thought it was a mistake for you to get involved with Tony Selby," she said.

Geneva's face went blank. "Why?"

"Because wealthy people don't marry for love. They marry for money. It's how they hold on to their wealth, and increase it."

After Ida left the room, Geneva realized she had said nothing to her about Tony marrying someone who was wealthy. Was Ida simply making an assumption? Could be, given her fatalistic streak. *"I always thought it was a mistake...."* And now she jumped to the conclusion that she had been proven right. Or, had she been eavesdropping while Cynthia was here, and made a slip? If so, she must not have overheard the whole conversation, for she made no allusion to the Selby family's money problems.

Geneva felt uneasy all at once—Ida may be nursing her for a much longer period than she had imagined. Should she dismiss Ida, ask her to move out, and hire someone else? On the other hand, she was doing an excellent job, as Dr. Latimer would agree. And in all probability, her nosiness stemmed from her ongoing concern for her future living arrangement.

It would not seem a sufficient basis for what amounted to a very harsh reprisal, Geneva decided, for if she dismissed Ida, Dr. Latimer might become suspicious, which could wind up costing Ida future jobs, and the poor woman had no other means of making a living.

Perhaps when all was said and done, Ida just happened to overhear part of her conversation with Cynthia as she passed down the hall on her way to the bathroom. Geneva was aware her voice had been raised higher than usual, as a result of her upset. From now on she would be more careful.

CHAPTER 58

✿

Geneva's decision to leave Tony's marriage intact and raise her child alone came very hard, and only after talking it over with Willa and Rodney, to be sure she was not overlooking anything that might persuade her differently. Her choice was not based solely on the cold enmity from Tony's family that she knew would lie ahead for her and her child, and probably would never be healed. There was also a notion—so strong that it sometimes startled her awake in the middle of the night—that the long, entangled legal act of breaking up Tony's marriage to a woman who was conniving and mean, and in all probability mentally unstable, might prove so upsetting that it would endanger their child.

Once she had set her course, Geneva felt at peace, and even—somewhat cautiously—looking forward to the future. She would reopen her dancing school, and eventually use her inheritance to buy a piece of property and build a new studio building.

She asked Ida to call Cynthia and say she needed to see her. It seemed only right that Cynthia be the first to know her decision. Immediately she began to dread giving her the news. This would break Cynthia's heart.

"You cannot force me to keep this from my son," Cynthia said, after listening to Geneva's explanation. Geneva was disheartened by her defiant tone, when—perhaps foolishly—she had counted at least on her understanding.

"I know that, but I beg you to let me tell him, when I feel the time is right," she said. She would certainly wait until after the baby was born, and maybe—for Tony's sake—even for a long time after. "Think what it will do to him, to be trapped in a situation he cannot change."

"He already is," Cynthia said, her tone acidic. She did not say, "*Thanks to you*," but Geneva heard it nonetheless. "Do you think it's fair to deny him the privilege of at least supporting his child?" Cynthia implored her.

"I don't want Jane's money," Geneva said scornfully.

Cynthia's eyes flashed. "Tony will not live off her money indefinitely."

"I didn't mean to infer that he would," Geneva apologized, thinking nonetheless how wise she had been in her decision to avoid a string of upsets. Even now her face was growing hot; her pulse, racing.

Cynthia reached for her gloves and drew them slowly over her hands. "This is the worst thing I have ever been through," she said darkly. "The nightmare just seems to go on and on."

When Cynthia shut the door behind her, Geneva wept, for the woman's trust and affection must now be counted among her many losses.

Ida accepted Geneva's decision without comment, but as she left the room, she paused at the door and turned. "Shall I inform Mr. Scarborough?"

"Why? By the time my baby is born, the trust account will be closed."

Ida hesitated, then said, "Just a matter of courtesy. He has telephoned several times, to ask if you were making plans."

Geneva had informed John Scarborough of her break-up with Tony, way back in June. And now he was aware she was pregnant with Tony's child, for when she canceled a routine appointment scheduled in his office in September, there seemed no point in hiding the reason. However, there was little left for them to discuss at this point, and she had not seen him since her confinement began. No doubt he would be glad when her birthday came in December, and he could wash his hands of her once and for all. Still, there was no reason to keep her decision from him, she supposed. "Go ahead and tell him," she said.

She was surprised when Ida told her, shortly after, that Mr. Scarborough would like to stop by. "Maybe he wants to talk to you about setting up a trust fund for your child," Ida suggested.

This gave her a very odd feeling that history might be repeated. After all, Mr. Scarborough would soon retire, as Mr. Hunnicutt had done early in Geneva's life, and if anything happened to her—No, she mustn't dwell on that.

Always a stickler for observing the proper decorum, Mr. Scarborough insisted Ida be present in the room. He sat stiffly by the window in his dark worsted business suit, his hat resting on his knees, his fingers, with scrupulously manicured nails, draped over the edges of the chair arms. "Might I remind you that what you propose to do is quite unacceptable in society?" he pointed out.

As if this had not been on Geneva's mind, night and day, along with other questions, such as, how would she explain this to her child? And when? "I intend to go on wearing my wedding band," she told him.

"And do you intend to inform the father, may I ask? After all, he does have some obligation to the child."

"I'm sure that I will, someday," she said.

John Scarborough appeared to consider this. Then he said, "I feel it's my duty to urge you to give up this child for adoption. For all these weeks, I had hoped you might reach that conclusion on your own."

The words brought an irrational feeling of panic to Geneva that this man—who yet held some control over her life—might force her to give up her child. "I'm perfectly capable of raising my child," she said, regretting the tremble in her voice. She refused to remain engaged in this discussion. She was about to ask him to go, when Ida rose from her chair in the corner.

"I'm under strict instructions from Geneva's physician, to avoid having her upset," she told John Scarborough sternly.

He raised a hand as if to ward off Ida's assault. "I'll show myself out," he said. Then he looked at Geneva. "Mark my word, you are making a big mistake.

"But then, when have you ever listened to my advice?"

Early in December, Cynthia came again to visit. She wore a copper-colored Chanel suit with a sailor collar and a knife-pleated skirt—a very smart ensemble, one Geneva had seen her in before. Only today, her matching cloche, with its narrow brim tacked up in front, accentuated two hollow cheeks and eyes dark with fatigue; the suit hung loosely at Cynthia's hips and shoulders. Geneva felt guilty, as she was largely to blame for Cynthia's unhealthy-looking state.

"I'll be moving to New York the first of the year," Cynthia told her. "I need a change, and besides, I think it will be easier if I'm not around…until you feel the time has come to tell the truth."

Cynthia's subtle inference that Geneva was betraying Tony preempted her wish to say she would miss her very much and find it hard to imagine her living anywhere except the Beaconsfield. Still, she was relieved that apparently Cynthia had decided to respect her wish to choose the moment to tell Tony about the baby. "I understand," she said.

Cynthia walked to the window and looked out. "Have you chosen any names?"

Though Geneva realized what lay behind the question, she put it aside for the moment. Choosing a girl's name had presented quite a struggle. She had not forgotten Tony's inspiration to name their daughter after Elvira Linsky. But now, whenever she thought of the name, she was reminded not of her teacher, but of the fact that those happy moments with Tony at St. Mary's Church in Ambleside had come to nothing. She felt proud of her eventual choice. "Emelye Rundell Selby, if it's a girl." She recited the unusual spelling of 'Emelye,' then said, "It's from Chaucer's *Canterbury Tales,* the one about the man who loves a girl named Emelye so much that if he does not see her every day, he will die.

"And Rundell was my mother's maiden name."

Cynthia continued gazing out the window. "That's very pretty," she said thoughtfully. Then her shoulders lifted slightly. "And?"

"Anthony Edward Selby."

Cynthia's shoulders settled again. "Thank you," she whispered as though uttering a prayer, then she sniffed and turned from the window.

She picked up her handbag and withdrew one of her new calling cards, then placed it on the dresser. She gave Geneva a brisk hug, and walked out.

Serena Garret Younger was born at four in the morning on Christmas Day, at St. Joseph's Infirmary in Houston—since the war, Dr. Latimer did not deliver babies at home. Around a week later, when Willa brought Serena to meet her future godmother, Geneva was enchanted. She held the auburn-haired infant against her breast. "Oh Willa, she's beautiful!" She kissed Serena's tiny curled fingers, then opened her cocoon of pink blankets and peeked inside.

Willa was perched on the edge of the bed, her eyes glistening with pride. "She's all legs. I think we've finally got another dancer in the family."

"So I see!" Geneva grinned at Willa, and lifted Serena upon her shoulder. Serena yawned contentedly and closed her eyes.

"And she'll have the best teacher in the world," Willa said fiercely. With a glance at the door, she lowered her voice and asked with gravity, "How are you?" Geneva had warned her that Ida may be apt to eavesdrop.

Geneva laughed. "Ready to be where you are!" All the months without exercise—Dr. Latimer had not relented from his position on her need for bed rest—plus the normal fluid retention of an expectant mother, left Geneva looking and feeling that she was carrying her baby from head to toe.

"Any regrets about your decision?"

Geneva shook her head, felt tears threatening.

Serena began to whimper, so Geneva handed her to Willa. She felt a twinge of envy for the Youngers, loving one another, being together under the same roof, reasonably sure of the future. It was no more than she had always expected out of life. And yet, one mistake when she was 16 years old had cost her any prospect of attaining it.

Willa sat down in the rocking chair, opened her blouse and brought Serena to her breast. When the baby was settled in the routine, Willa asked Geneva, "And how is Cynthia taking all this?"

"Not very well," she said, then told Willa about Cynthia's farewell visit. On a forlorn note, she added, "I doubt we'll be in touch very often once she moves. And that means I'll rarely, if ever, hear any news of Tony."

"Well, maybe it will make things easier," Willa said consolingly.

Truly Geneva did not think so, with their child reminding her every single day that she loved Tony still, and they belonged together.

Before leaving, Willa brought Serena for a goodbye cuddle. "Bye, little sweetie. Hurry back soon!" Geneva said, and as she kissed Serena's forehead, a feeling of certainty swept over her: *But Cynthia, I'm going to have a girl.*

The month of January blew in the coldest part of winter, with frequent, hard freezes. The bad weather often prevented Willa from getting out with the children to visit Geneva for days on end. Geneva had never felt so isolated, and she grew fretful. It seemed to her Ida was increasingly fatigued and washed-out in the mornings. And though she had never been talkative, she was now even more taciturn. All of which brought freshly to mind Willa's suspicion that Ida was a drinker. One morning near the end of the month, she said, tactfully, "You seem awfully tired, Ida."

Ida put down Geneva's breakfast tray with a poached egg, dry toast and hot tea—did her fingers shake just slightly as she did so?—then looked across at her. "Not sleeping lately. Don't know what's wrong, though maybe I just need a break. This is the longest case I've ever taken, and no relief nurse."

Glad for the opportunity, Geneva offered, "Why don't we hire a nurse to relieve you at night? I can ask Dr. Latimer for a name."

Ida thought about this. "I know plenty of good ones myself if it comes to that," she said, then asked defensively, "Why, are you afraid I'll let you down?"

In fact there were few ways Ida could let her down at this point. She had not driven an automobile for years, so when Geneva went into labor, Ida was to contact the Youngers. Either Rodney or Willa would drive her to St. Joseph's. Rodney had taken her roadster in for servicing, in case it was needed. Geneva's suitcase was packed and under the bed.

"Not at all. But there's no sense in your wearing down your resistance, making yourself sick—I mean, sometimes babies are late. It may be awhile."

Ida shrugged. "Alright then, I'll check around."

Geneva felt reassured. Probably Ida really was just exhausted, and she was just overly fretful. From the beginning, Ida had been an excellent nurse, and she still was.

Often Geneva put herself to sleep at night with comforting thoughts of all the careful preparations she had made. With the help of Rodney's lawyer, Robert Bowen, she had drawn up her will. Most important: her inheritance would be passed along to her child. Otherwise, in the will she acknowledged Tony as the baby's father. This had proven harder to do than it might seem. Not that she would begrudge Tony their child—assuming his innocence, of course. She had even written him a letter explaining the choices she made. She told him that she would always love him. The letter was in the hands of Mr. Bowen.

What troubled her was that, in the event of her death, Jane would become the child's stepmother. Appointing Rodney and Willa as guardians would have been an easy solution. But it would seem dreadfully unfair for Tony not only to learn he had a child whose existence had been kept from him, but then to be denied his right to bring it up when Geneva was no longer around to do it. She could have begged Cynthia to be the child's guardian. But first of all, she'd probably use that as leverage to tell Tony the truth right now. Besides, if Cynthia wound up with Geneva's child, she would only take it to England to be near Tony. And that meant being near Jane.

Though Geneva tried not to get snagged on the detail of guardianship, she often did, then lay awake telling herself that Dr. Latimer was confident of a normal delivery. She was not going to die in childbirth, for heaven's sake.

Wasn't it a pity, she thought while tossing and turning one night, how you could do only so much planning in life, and you had to leave the rest to—to what? Providence?

A strange feeling overcame her then—an alertness to the tranquil silence of the earth, wrapped up inside the vastness of the universe. How small and insignificant she felt, as if her life and all her fears were swallowed up.

She kept lying there, looking into the dark. After a while, she thought of Madame Linsky and the strength of her faith. Naturally this led to thoughts of her wooden crucifix: the two images were inseparable. Since putting the crucifix away for safekeeping, years ago, Geneva had rarely given it a passing thought. Yet now she felt a strong urge to have it nearby. It would be almost like having her teacher near. Unfortunately, unless she awakened Ida, she had no way of getting the crucifix. Though Ida had made inquiries, she had not yet found a relief nurse who was available on short notice.

Still, it was not yet midnight. Ida may be awake. Geneva reached for the bell on the night stand, and held it in her hand for a few moments. *Ida, I know you'll think me ridiculous, but I need to ask you a favor.* She stopped short of ringing the bell.

CHAPTER 59

In the very early hours of a morning in mid-February, long before daylight and sunshine would break through the stillness of the winter night and melt its icy glaze, Geneva awakened to a disconcerting realization: two weeks ahead of schedule, her uterus had begun the process of flushing her child from the safe universe of her body. She reached for the bell on her bedside table and began to ring urgently, reminding herself all the while that, according to conventional wisdom about first babies, many hours were apt to be required—16, even 20—to complete the process of birth. There was plenty of time to put her plans in motion and get to St. Joseph's. She paused in her ringing to listen for Ida's footsteps, but they did not come. She rang some more, remembering uneasily the night nurse scheduled to begin at the first of next week because Ida was exhausted. Remembering how close she came to ringing her bell one night a couple of weeks ago, for Ida to bring Linsky's crucifix. Would she have learned something vital, had she rung the bell? Though once, early in her confinement, she had rung the bell close to midnight when she tipped her water goblet over, and Ida had come at once, she had never rung the bell this time of morning before, to test out whether it would awaken Ida. *A lapse in all the careful preparations…*

However, there was no reason to work herself into a state of distraction, Geneva thought as, shivering in her slippered feet and unable to see past her own bulk to her shaky, distended ankles, she nonetheless made her way downstairs, grasping the cold stair rail. At the bottom, right around the corner, was Ida's bedroom. Geneva called out, but there was no answer. She turned the corner and found the door closed. A bar of light shone beneath it. How careless of Ida, leaving her door closed, yet it would explain….

Opening the door, she was alarmed to spot a whisky bottle—less than half full of amber-colored liquor gleaming jewel-like in the lamplight—on the table beside the chair where Ida sat sleeping in her street clothes, mouth agape, head flung back, snoring loudly. "Ida, wake up!" she cried sharply, again and again. But the woman was not to be roused from her snoring beyond a sleepy lolling of her stone-like head and a fluttering of her eyelids, regardless of Geneva's cries, or the frantic jostling of her shoulders which soon followed with a barrage of epithets Geneva had heard on occasion, but until that moment had never been angry enough to repeat. *"Are you afraid I'll let you down?"* Ida had asked.

She slammed Ida's bedroom door hard enough to make a skeleton rattle in its grave.

Now, outside in the hallway, a sharp invasive pain caused Geneva to suck in her breath and grip her belly, and wonder if anger could hasten the progress of labor…

…something she did not, above all, want to do. She must telephone Willa, for Rodney was at Lake Astoria. A hard freeze two nights ago had burst a pipe in their cottage and sent him there in a hurry, to deal with three inches of water on the downstairs floor. Wasn't it a pity how, just when you needed people the most, they could not be there for you in spite of the best-laid plans?

"Operator, connect me with TAylor 837, please." Willa's telephone rang and rang, causing Geneva to reason that since Serena had but recently begun to sleep all night, and Willa was exhausted from the weeks of being awake almost around the clock, she may not hear her telephone ringing in the hall. When, in fact, this proved to be the case, Geneva quite calmly signaled the operator again and asked to be connected with Dr. Latimer's home in Houston. "No, I do not know what his number is, and please will you hurry?"

"Is this an emergency, ma'am?"

"No, I'm in the early stage of labor." *Hurry up before it becomes one.*

The prudent thing would be to let Dr. Latimer know that he may be forced to make an exception and deliver her baby at home. Then all she need do was lie down and be still until he arrived…

…only Dr. Latimer's wife finally answered the telephone to report sleepily that he was at St. Joseph's, delivering a baby. And who was calling? Another pain seized up Geneva's insides, and she dropped the receiver. "Hello? Hello?" she could hear as the receiver swung like a pendulum on the floor, and when the pain had ceased, she lifted it to her ear. But Mrs. Latimer had already hung up.

She signaled for the operator again. "I think you had better send an ambulance to take me to St. Joseph's Infirmary," she said.

"Alright, honey, what's your address?" Geneva gave it to her. "Hold on." Geneva waited. She put her free hand on her bulbous abdomen. How enormous she was, her sleeping gown as big as a tent. In moments the operator came back on the line. "They'll be there in fifteen minutes or so."

Fifteen minutes. It sounded like an eternity. "Alright, but I'm going across the street to try and wake up Mrs. Younger—she's supposed to take me. We could be gone by the time the ambulance arrives." She hung up.

How many minutes between each pain? Geneva wondered, and reminded herself the thing to do was avoid getting into a state; after all, this was as different from the other time as the still silence of winter was from the churning, howling violence of a hurricane, coming three months into a pregnancy. Two weeks early was nothing to fret about. She would just walk over to Willa's and bang on her bedroom window, which, thankfully, was on the ground floor at the back of the house; she thought she could just barely reach it, and fortunately the window was located right next to Willa's side of the bed. Except if Willa had fallen asleep on the day bed in the nursery upstairs, which on occasion—Geneva just now remembered—she did. Well, there was no reason to work herself into a state over something that may or may not be true.

Only a fool would go outside in the freezing weather wearing slippers and house robe, so she made her way down to the hall tree near the front door and removed Ida's heavy coat from its hook—her own coat was unlikely to reach even halfway around her belly. She soon found the large woman's coat sleeves reached to her fingertips, and the hem brushed her ankles. It was like wearing a bear rug. The front door was only a few steps away, and she would be at Willa's within a couple of minutes. But, how hard she was breathing now! She felt exhausted as she used to feel at the end of a grueling rehearsal with Tony, who, now that she thought about it, ought to be here right now, driving her to the infirmary, instead of an ocean away.

She switched on the front porch light, then opened the door and looked out on the forbidding sight of drizzling rain. Five slick porch stairs led down to a slick front walk, which led to two widths of slick street, an esplanade yawning in between, all separating her from Willa's front gate, not to mention the staggering amount of icy grass which she must cover on foot, in the dark, across the esplanade and from the gate to the back of Willa's house. And her in a pair of felt house slippers, ten miles away from the upstairs closet where street shoes sat gathering dust. Here and there, the wind stirring in the trees shook little clumps of ice loose from the dead branches, and whisked them to the ground. How arrogant was winter, she thought suddenly, controlling its domain even in a state of inertia. But there was no need to worry. She would drive to Willa's and honk the horn. That, Willa would hear whether upstairs or down.

Geneva did not have another pain as she lumbered slowly back up the hallway, through the kitchen and out on her back porch. As she walked across the porch, she spotted her tall Wellington boots, which Tony had purchased for her with great ceremony, while in England. Right now, the boots were no more use than he was. Without help, she could not get them on her feet. Or could she? Maybe, just maybe.... She held on to the rail, worked off one house slipper by backing her heel across the wood planks, and slipped the foot down inside what felt like an ice chest. Good! Now, cautiously, the other.... Pretty soon the screen door was banging behind her.

Inside the garage she discovered that Rodney had put a blanket over the radiator of the roadster. Nearly in tears over this gesture of his thoughtfulness, she swept it aside and opened the car door. Her hulking torso just barely cleared the steering wheel. She moved the seat back as far as she could with her feet still reaching the pedals. She pressed the starter and sighed with relief as the car engine hummed encouragingly. Had Rodney been there, she would have kissed him. But her satisfaction that things were beginning to go her way was abruptly displaced by a great, quaking pain—the worst so far; the longest in duration. And when she finally recaptured her breath, she dreaded all the waiting still ahead, before she would be on the road to St. Joseph's: waiting for the honking horn to awaken Willa, then waiting for her to come sleepily to the window, wondering who could be honking in the middle of the night; then waiting for her to get dressed, and figure out what to do about James and Serena while she was gone from home. Maybe a neighbor could come, but that would take time, also, for all the neighbors were asleep.

Surely the ambulance would soon be here. She listened for the sound of the siren. Nothing. How long had it been since she told the operator to call? Her mind felt scrambled. She could not guess how long it had been, nor could she recall her exact words. Had she left the impression she didn't want an ambulance, after all? Maybe she should check with the operator again, but she was in the car now, and the telephone seemed miles away, and time was wasting. One cumbersome Wellington boot pressed the accelerator, pulled back a little. Not so fast. She'd never driven in these boots.

Before she knew it, she was heading down Heights Boulevard. Cruising close to the curb as if it were a supporting arm. St. Joseph's Infirmary was not more than ten or twelve minutes from here. Why had she not thought of this before? And there were no other cars out on the street this time of night, let alone, in this weather, so if she had a pain, she could simply apply the brake and let it pass. What would be the difference if Willa were driving her? Only her position on the front seat. "It's going to be alright, sweet Emelye," she found herself saying aloud. How lovely it sounded, this name she had chosen. How reassuring to speak it aloud! How odd, until now, she had communicated with her daughter only through her thoughts and the tender strokes of her hands. She patted her belly. "Just give Mommy a few more minutes."

Her fingers locked so tightly around the steering wheel that her knuckles were white, she drove slowly and with utmost caution down Heights Boulevard. But the blocks had never seemed so numerous: 900...800...700.... She sped up a bit, but slowed down again to safely negotiate the turn on to Washington Avenue. Look how far she had come, and without one bit of help! "We're going to make it, Emelye. Just hold on."

She was still enjoying her sense of triumph when she approached the place where Preston Avenue forked off to the right. Her car lamps caught the stripes on a barricade crossing it. It was closed for repairs. Her heartbeat fluttered momentarily. But there was another street up ahead...Elder...yes, she could see the sign now. Elder, the street on which a new hospital would soon rise—it had been in the papers—she realized with irony. And, now that she recalled, there was also a new hospital being erected on Ashland Street, a few blocks from where she lived. Heights Hospital, it would be called. Future tense.

She turned right onto Elder, went over a few annoying bumps, then began her left hand turn onto Preston. She felt marooned in the middle of the street, far from the safety of the curb....

Cautious as she was, this time the roadster went out of control. It careened diagonally across the intersection, as if the four wheels were on ice skates. She braced herself for the worst. It was Tony failing to catch her in the death-defying flip in *Chimaera*. It was her parents, in the sudden revelation that they were not going to live to see the other side of that railroad bridge. It was recognizing an utter inability to change the course of events, and it seemed to last forever.

When the car came to a thudding halt, she had a sense—though she could not be sure—that it was a result of one of the roadster's rubber tires bumping the curb at a particular angle. Her left shoulder had struck the car door. Thankfully, it was not a hard blow.

But now she was shaking with terror, and could hardly get her breath. She could not speak to Emelye. Her mind was scattered. How many blocks to St.

Joseph's? And in which direction? She had the feeling of being cut adrift in space, without borders on any side. She was afraid to restart the engine and keep going, but she could not stay here. She had a terrible, wrenching pain then. Her knees jerked up against the steering wheel, and she bit down so hard on her lip that she tasted blood. Afterward she realized that she had no idea how many minutes apart her pains were coming. She could be hours away from giving birth; she could be minutes away, seconds. She banged on the horn again and again. The sound was swallowed up in the cold vacuum of the winter night.

I can't do this! Her arms went limp. Moaning, she leaned her head against the steering wheel. "God, help me!" she cried. "Help me!"

It wasn't long—a few seconds perhaps—before she sat up straight again. She felt a curious sense of calm. From whence it came, she did not know. Then she remembered crying out—a prayer, she realized. She remembered that night when she felt herself infinitesimal, and in need of some sign of Linsky's presence, which she had talked herself out of by morning. She thought of Madame Linsky's steadfast devotion, her never-failing sense of peace. Was this the source of it, then? Just knowing that you were not alone? She had no time to question it further. Her finger was already on the starter button.

As she straightened out the roadster and drove cautiously down Preston, her hands trembling around the steering wheel, she felt that sense of calm ebbing away, and was desperate to recapture it. Prayers began to pour out like swift-flowing tears. *Please protect this child who has not sinned. Please bring her safely into the world. Dear God, hear my prayer.* She was unable to speak aloud. She simply formed the words in her heart again and again and again. She was still doing so when she reached the corner of LaBranch and Leeland, two blocks from the St. Joseph's emergency entrance. She could see the light above the door. "Thank God!" she cried, and pressed harder on the accelerator.

Then came an implosion of pain, like a brick wall collapsing inside her. She screamed out, her hands pulling the steering wheel to a sudden far left. The roadster spun around in the middle of the intersection and arrowed toward the utility pole inside the curb. Her foot pressing the brake was futile. The pole loomed closer and closer. This time there would be no stopping. As the roadster jumped the curb, Geneva laid over to the right and crossed her arms over her abdomen. *Please, God.* The roadster's right fender crashed into the pole, the force of it crushing the steering wheel into the side of her belly. Her breath sucked down in a fulcrum of pain. She closed her eyes and clenched her teeth.

She did not know how much time had passed when she raised up in the seat and looked around, disoriented. She felt all cold and wet underneath. She pressed her abdomen. "Emelye? Emelye?" She felt no pain. Only a still void. The truth came swiftly. *My daughter is dead.*

CHAPTER 60

Geneva looked up and around at a circle of white wimples, a grave mask peering down at her from each one. When she closed her eyes, they doubled. Or was it the other way around? A disembodied male voice came: "Push, Mrs. Selby, push now, hard!"

Push what? Where am I?

"That's it! Good! Hold on now, we're almost there. Once more—"

Your immortal soul is damned…cursing the Almighty at the top of your lungs…Willie McKee reported you.

I don't care. My baby is dead.

"That's it, Mrs. Selby! Great job! You've got a baby girl!"

A dead baby girl….

Geneva closed her eyes. A sharp cry ripped across the mountains of her knees. A wimpled face came near. "Don't shut yer eyes *now*, Mrs. Selby. Have a look!"

Geneva's eyelids fluttered at a tiny figure, with face rubescent and pinched, flexing her arms and legs, and howling ferociously. She raised up her head. "She's alive?"

"With a set o' lungs w'd put Gabriel's trompet to shame? Well, o'carse she's aloive!"

Geneva stretched her fingers to the arm of the tiny, screeching form. Flesh touched warm, pulsing flesh. "Emelye?" she whispered.

Then the tiny figure was gone. Dr. Latimer appeared with an uncustomary grin. Where had he come from? "Congratulations. Your little girl is a beauty…third one I've delivered since midnight. One of the nurses calls it 'the girls' night out.' They'll clean her up now, and bring her to you. You've got some bruises from the crash, but as far as I can tell, you're alright, just a little foggy. You rest now." He pressed her shoulder. Her whole body contracted in pain, and she moaned. "Oops! Sorry."

A wooden crucifix about the size of Linsky's hung on the wall facing Geneva's bed. It was the first thing she saw in the morning, and the last thing she saw before going to sleep at night. She could hardly escape it, unless her eyes were closed. Its purpose seemed to be to remind her of her unpardonable sin of blasphemy. Around 3:30 in the morning, Willie McKee had delivered a male patient suffering from severe chest pains to the emergency room. Returning to shut the ambulance door, he heard a horn honking erratically down the street. He ran in its direction till he came in view of a car crushed against a utility pole, one head lamp still burning. He climbed up on the running board and looked inside. He could see the dim outline of the woman's body. She was spouting maledictions that would curl a sailor's hair, he said.

Everyone at the infirmary seemed to be talking about the miracle, for rarely was a meal tray brought to Geneva or collected, never were her vital signs checked, never was Emelye brought in or returned to the nursery, that the miracle of God's grace was not mentioned. After all, if the debilitating labor pain which caused Geneva's accident had occurred even a block or two earlier, no one would have heard the noise of the crash, and both she and Emelye would have been dead by the time they were discovered because a child in the womb cannot survive its mother's death, and Emelye's mother was in a life-threatening state of shock. Geneva wanted to believe it was a divine miracle, but surely miracles were not the reward for such anger as she felt at having been betrayed by the God whose presence she had felt for the first time in her life; and to whom she had been praying up to the very last moment, to save her child.

Geneva cherished her daughter as much as any mother ever cherished her child. When she fed Emelye at her breast, their bodies forming an unbroken circle of communion, the eyes of mother and child mirrored the intensity of their love. Geneva would be content for all her days without another person in her life. She even felt a certain smugness that she would not have to share Emelye with Tony.

Still, she could not help feeling that her punishment was the clear memory of her hate-filled outpourings to God, when she had no memory whatever of being rescued and brought to the infirmary, or anything after that until Emelye was born, and she was reminded of this every time the wooden crucifix entered her field of vision. She would find it convenient at such moments to believe there was no God, that it was but chance that saved her and Emelye. But then she would think of the feeling that she was not alone, that had entered her spirit after her near-accident at Elder and Preston, and was kept alive through prayer for a few blocks down Preston Avenue; and she would wish for its return.

Then came Father Quanset. A newly ordained Priest, an assistant on the staff at Christ Episcopal Church, he was not—according to Willa—what you would expect when it came to a man of his station. Which was why, after hearing of Geneva's confusion, Willa had insisted on asking him to visit her friend. He was a rather odd-looking man in thick glasses, whose large head rested on his shoulders with barely enough of a neck in between to provide a place for his white clerical collar—surely the largest size available. Willa said he was a bachelor, yet he was well into his forties, judging by the amount of gray peppering his dark hair. Geneva wondered: why was he so late to enter the priesthood? What was he doing when he received his 'calling'?

Father Quanset listened attentively as she recounted the many losses in her life and all the unanswered prayers, which preceded the miracle of Emelye's birth. In fact, she talked so long that at one point he excused himself to go out to the nurse's station and telephone to cancel an appointment. At the end of her tale, in a thoughtful voice with the hard-as-granite *r*'s of a New England dialect, he responded, "It's hard to find a startin' point for faith, when things are that random, isn't it?"

"Random! That's it, that's exactly it," she cried, grateful that he had uttered the very word that seemed to describe the absence of order in the events that had shaped her life, not to mention her all-too-frequent inability to take a series of well-considered steps and wind up in the place she thought she would be. "Where was God when my parents were killed? Where was God when Linsky died from the flu, just months before she would have had the only real luxury she had ever asked for in her life—going home to France? Where was God for Tony and me when we knelt together at the altar rail of St. Mary's Ambleside? And now Tony is married to Jane!" she lamented. Earlier, as her story progressed, she had told Father Quanset all about Jane Tremont, how she betrayed Tony and later murdered her father, how she used her money to worm her way back into the Selby family when Geneva was out of the way, and, if Cynthia was right—and it seemed as likely as any other possibility—how she intercepted those messages that would have shattered her plans to marry Tony.

Father Quanset tapped a stumpy fingertip on his chin. "The Almighty did not seem to make an appearance in your life until you had given up," he suggested.

She found herself thinking this through aloud. "But I began giving up years ago—I think when the preacher who buried my parents claimed their deaths were 'God's will.' Then later, during the storm, I prayed so hard, and yet—*nothing*. I felt so alone. But I was pretty much resigned to it, you know, until I thought I'd lost Emelye, too, then—" Her voice broke and she fell silent.

"But you still had that same instinctive yearnin' for God that we all have—you were prayin' right before the accident."

"Yes, my prayer for help was instinctive, I guess. But it did not occur to me to continue praying until I thought of Madame Linsky."

He nodded understandingly. Then he folded two meaty hands across his chest. "I don't know why your parents happened—unfortunately—to be on that train when the bridge went out up in the Rockies. I don't know why things have always turned out wrong for you, though I'm sorry they have. But I'll confess to somethin' else: I don't know why God saved you and your daughter, either, when you know yourself not all prayers are answered in the way we'd like. It's possible you might see the meaning of it all one day—I've seen it happen often enough. But there's no guarantee of that."

Geneva felt profoundly disappointed. Well, at least Father Quanset did not look down his nose at her and speak in grave platitudes designed to ward off hard questions, like the other men of the cloth whom she had encountered.

He studied her face momentarily, then said, "'*Fear wist not to evade as Love wist to pursue.*'"

"What?"

He repeated himself. "It's from Francis Thompson's, *The Hound of Heaven*—my all-time favorite poem. About God bein' in constant pursuit, like a lover, who won't let go of you, or me, or any of us, no matter how hard we fight him. I've found everything in life squares with that, eventually."

"But, what if I had died in the accident? Where would my soul be right now?"

He knitted his brow. "That's a very good question, and there is really no certain answer to it. Some people would say you'd be in hell. Some people would say your spirit would just continue its journey, the same one you've always been on, but without the encumbrance of your body. I tend toward the latter philosophy, myself."

Geneva shrugged.

"I have a feeling you expected more solid answers from me."

She opened her palms. "Yes—no. I don't know that I expected anything from you. Willa was the one who insisted you come by. Not that I don't appreciate it."

"The Church doesn't have all the answers," he apologized.

Again, Geneva thought of Linsky. "Well then, where does that sense of peace come from, that helps devout people like Madame Linsky get through life? Can you tell me that?"

"I think I can. You had it almost right when you were on your way over here in the car, in the dead of night, and you suddenly knew you were not alone. Like the poem says, God will not let go of you, Geneva. Through all the trials we endure on this earth—and they are random, most of the time, because we are random individuals and we behave in random ways that affect others—he's still urgin' us toward accepting his presence in our spirit while we live on this earth, and his perfect presence, after we leave it. It's up to us individually: fight it, or let go and accept God's way of doin' things."

"So that's what Linsky knew?"

"I expect so, or at least, part of it. She must have been quite a remarkable human being."

"I've never met anyone like her, before or since. And I miss her all the time," she said, her voice thinning with emotion. She felt guilty now for not giving Emelye her name.

Father Quanset sat thoughtfully for a few moments, then said, "Puttin' aside matters of faith just for a moment, a question pops into my mind: What do you think the woman—Jane, is it?—what do you think she'd have done had your messages gone through, and she found her marriage plans down the drain?"

"I—I don't know; I never thought of that," Geneva said uneasily.

"Well! I must go. Shall we pray together?"

Why did the suggestion surprise her? "Yes, please."

He came to the bed and reached for Geneva's hands. His grip was warm and comforting. It was the first time that a member of the clergy had ever clasped her hands in his. She thought he would lead her in a confession. But instead, he offered thanksgiving for her life, and for the safe delivery of Emelye, and for the insights the miracle had provided. He prayed for continued growth in the Faith, for them both. "In the name of the Father, and of the Son, and of the Holy Ghost. Amen." They lifted their heads, and he smiled at her: a sweet, unpretentious smile.

After he left, Geneva looked up at the crucifix again. She did not feel unburdened of her guilt, but neither did she feel weighted down with it anymore. She realized all that Father Quanset had done was to help her put things in a different perspective. She felt a sense of yearning deep inside—though, whether for God, or for Father Quanset, she could not have said.

Later she thought over the priest's conjecture about Jane. He seemed to have concluded that she was not only vicious, but dangerous—just as Cynthia believed. Was he suggesting that, disappointing as it was, maybe things had worked out best for her and Emelye in the end? Now Geneva wondered, regardless of whether Jane actually purloined her messages or someone else did, what would she do when she suddenly found herself sharing Tony with his American daughter?

Presently Emelye was brought in for her feeding. As always, at the sight of her, Geneva's whole body went warm with joy. She cuddled her daughter tenderly, then opened her robe for her to suckle. It seemed to her then that Emelye instinctively sought her mother's breast not only for nourishment, but in the certainty that her mother was above all things her source of protection. In a fever of conviction, Geneva determined she would put off telling Tony about Emelye for as long as possible. "I will never, ever let any harm come to you," she promised her.

CHAPTER 61

❀

On Saturday Willa brought Geneva and Emelye home from the infirmary. Ida stood holding the screen door open. Passing through with Emelye in her arms, Geneva greeted Ida with a cool look. She was wearing a mouse brown dress with a pleated front and a crochet collar. Her hair was neatly combed and she was wearing just a dab of lipstick. She looked washed-out and fatigued.

"I'll carry that," Ida said to Willa, and took Geneva's suitcase and all the baby paraphernalia from her arms. She avoided meeting Willa's glance. It was Willa who had informed her of the consequences of her neglect on the night of Emelye's birth.

Before Willa turned to go, she cuddled Emelye's chin and kissed her cheek. Geneva thanked her for all she had done. "I don't know what I'd do without you and Rodney," she said, feeling the heat of tears. "Bring the children over later, so they can see Emelye. I miss them!"

As Geneva crossed the entrance hall, the smell of lemon oil filled her nostrils. She looked around. The downstairs rooms seemed uncommonly clean, as if Ida had spent the past few days with dust pan and mop, readying the place for important guests. The wood floor was polished to a sheen, the glass gleamed in the light fixture above, and there was not a speck of clutter as far as Geneva could see. It seemed forever since she left here. Her memory of the most remarkable night in her life had taken on a surreal quality, as though it were all a dream. "I can hold Emelye while you take off your coat," Ida offered quietly.

"No thank you," Geneva said stiffly. As she climbed the stairs, she could hear Ida's footsteps behind her. She remembered how she used to lie in bed and listen for the sound of footsteps on the stairs. She went into her room and laid

Emelye in the crib beside her bed, removing her bonnet and loosening the blankets around her. Ida put her things inside, then lingered in the doorway uncertainly. Geneva could not help gloating over the woman's anxiety just a bit. "I'll be down in a few minutes, and we'll talk," she said. She changed Emelye's diaper, then stayed with her until she was asleep. By then she felt exhausted and would have much preferred to lie down for a nap herself than to talk to Ida.

Ida was waiting at the kitchen table. Geneva sat down across from her. Just now she did not feel angry so much as she felt a dull sense of bitter resignation. Still, she demanded: "How could you?"

Ida looked at her levelly. "It was the first time I'd ever let it interfere, though I knew there was a problem...it's why I didn't stand in your way when you wanted to hire a relief nurse." Her eyes dropped. "Of course, some nights were worse than others."

"Determined by what?" Geneva asked, feeling anger rise again.

Ida looked up. "Oh, some nights I just got to thinking about things."

"What 'things'?"

Ida let out a breath. "The injustices of life. How some people have it so easy, and the rest of us have no security at all, nothing to keep us from living out our old age in poverty. You'll know what I'm talking about one day."

Geneva recalled Ida's husband squandering her savings. That was hardly any fault of hers, however. "Well, you won't help matters by drinking on the job," she said.

Ida sat back. "I guess you informed Dr. Latimer about how I let you down," she said.

"No. He was very busy at the hospital. The subject did not come up."

Ida's pointed brows lifted in surprise. Her eyes searched Geneva's. "But it will, when you go in for your follow-up appointment. And you'll tell him."

"Are you asking me not to?" Geneva said carefully.

Ida lifted her chin. "How can I?"

Geneva had fully intended to report Ida, not only for her own vindication, but to prevent Ida from abusing future patients. If not for the fact that Ida assumed Geneva had already told Dr. Latimer about her drunkenness, she would have been sure the reason for speaking of her worries about dying in poverty was to manipulate her into being sympathetic, and she would have resented it. As it was, she considered whether it would be right to destroy Ida's only means of support, after many years of an unblemished professional record. At length, she said, "Look, if you'll promise to immediately undergo treatment—"

Ida's eyes flashed with hope, but her pride extinguished it. "I was planning to, anyway. I know a place not far from here."

"Then I'll just say I gave you a night off because you were exhausted," Geneva told her. It occurred to her she may have already told Dr. Latimer that Ida was drunk. If he asked her between the time she was brought in and Emelye was born why she had arrived at St. Joseph's in such a state, there was no telling what she told him. So she would have to retract her story, blame it on delirium. "But Ida, as soon as your treatment is over, I want you to move out."

"Yes, I was going to do that, too," she said, then rose from her chair and left the kitchen, even then carrying herself with dignity, Geneva noticed.

Three weeks later Ida returned from her treatment, announcing herself cured. Indeed, her coloring was much improved, and she looked rested. "I've located an efficiency apartment downtown," she said. She did not offer Geneva her address, nor did Geneva request it.

Within a week, her furnishings had been collected by a moving and storage company, and she was walking out the door. After almost ten years of sharing a house, the farewell between the two women was brief and reticent:

Geneva was holding Emelye on her shoulder. "Good luck," she said, for she could think of nothing else to say.

Ida gave her one of those long, thoughtful looks which often preceded a word of advice, then said, "You ought to marry one day, for the sake of your daughter—if you can find a decent man. You'll find the going very hard, if you remain single."

There was a damp chill in the air that day and the sky was overcast. Geneva watched from the window as Ida retreated down the front walk and crossed over to the esplanade, to wait for the streetcar. Her thick figure was clad in the coat Geneva had borrowed on the night of Emelye's birth. Against a joyless backdrop of bare trees, Ida stood erect and held her head high.

As Geneva turned from the window, the happy thought occurred to her that after all the years of living here, this house had finally become her home. And Emelye's.

The weather was warming as Geneva contentedly arranged her parents' furnishings about the house, and even planted her first garden bed in a flush of optimism: two neat columns of rose bushes. She chose a sunny place within view of her second parlor dancing studio, which would be put to use again in the fall. She didn't resent the limited space as she used to—having Emelye in her life made up for every lack. Still, she was already looking forward to the day when she would build a studio elsewhere. And hopefully without a mortgage.

One day a Houston Police officer, Sergeant Dickerson, appeared at the door. A tall, trim-figured man, he seemed young to be in a position of authority, though his light blond hair was already thinning on top. His boots were polished to a high sheen, and his crisp white shirt and four-in-hand tie further suggested he took pride in his appearance. He held a pearl gray Stetson hat in his hands.

Remaining on the porch as they talked, he told Geneva that Ida Ruekauer had been reported missing by relatives she was to visit in the central part of the state. A wide search of the area had yielded nothing so far. "You may have read in the papers about the flooding rains up there lately," he said. As he spoke, he had a way of creasing his eye brows and looking down his nose at Geneva that suggested he was filled with cocky self-importance. She did not particularly like him. "We've talked to the neighbors around her current residence in Houston. No one seems to know much about her."

"Ida always kept to herself," said Geneva.

"So I gather…. We're tracing backward now, and wondered if you might have any clues as to what happened to the woman."

Geneva was baffled. She told the sergeant what little she knew, and suggested he contact Houston Bank & Trust. "Ida had an account there."

"One of the first things we did," he remarked. "No checks have cleared the bank dated after the day she was reported missing."

Geneva remembered Jacob Lowerby then. "He was a former patient, an investment broker. He came to visit on occasion, I believe."

As the sergeant wrote down his name, Geneva started to tell him about the Canadian whisky bottles, but decided to refer him to the Youngers.

He thanked her, and handed her his card. "If you hear anything else."

At the end of April Sergeant Dickerson stopped by to say that the police were presuming Ida dead, though her body had not been recovered. It was theorized that she left her train for some reason, had fallen perhaps—receiving a fatal blow—and her body was eventually carried away by flood waters.

Was it possible Ida had begun drinking again, her accident resulting from drunkenness? That she would come to an unfortunate end, and all alone, seemed to Geneva sadly in keeping with the way she had lived her life. And it was ironic that she had worried so about spending her twilight years in poverty.

On an exceedingly fine day in early May, Geneva carried Emelye out on the front porch and laid her in her portable crib to enjoy the sunshine. Before long, Mr. Hatch the postman approached. After admiring Emelye in her crib—Mr. Hatch had six grandchildren—he reached into his leather pouch and handed Geneva several pieces of mail. Right on top was a letter covered with English postage, her name and address written in Tony's neat hand. Geneva must have looked as stricken as she felt, for Mr. Hatch put his hand on her elbow. "You alright, Mrs. Selby? Here, have a seat."

"No, I'm fine really; thanks."

He touched the brim of his hat and walked down the porch steps with his pouch on his shoulder, but he paused at the sidewalk to turn and look back at her worriedly. She waved at him reassuringly, then looked down at the envelope again. *Dear Geneva.... Things have settled down here, at last. I think of you often and wonder, is there anything I can do for you...?* The stubborn question of Tony's innocence reopened in her mind. She tucked Emelye's blanket around her chest and said, "Well, sweetie, let's see what your father has to say for himself."

When she unfolded the letter, she found a small snapshot enclosed: Tony and Geneva standing in front of the Ghyll Inn, their arms about each other, broad smiles on their faces, and flowers and vines framing their figures. It was as if they had stood in that spot but yesterday. She could smell the chilly mountain air, pungent with rain. She could feel the rough woolen texture of Tony's blazer, where her fingers clutched his arm. She looked intently into Tony's face. She saw that same face, with its loving dark eyes, shortly after as they knelt together at St. Mary's Church to exchange their wedding vows, and still later when her petal-thin sleeping gown lay in a heap upon the floor and they were moving together toward the big poster bed, each anticipating the other, their rhythm as smooth as though they were dancing.

Surely Tony would not have sent this picture, had he ignored her messages, she thought with relief. Well then, was it to encourage her to remember their honeymoon with fondness? Could he really hope for that, in spite of everything?

She put the snapshot aside, and turned to the two-page letter: "Dear Geneva, I should have written to you in any case before long, but Mother confessed in a recent letter that she paid you a visit before moving to New York, and told you that I have been legally wed to Jane Tremont since September of last year, and the circumstances which brought it about...."

Legally wed. It sounded cold and miserable, which gave Geneva a swift moment of satisfaction until she read the next sentence: "We are expecting a child early in June." Despising herself, nevertheless she counted up the months; there was a minimum of time, from early September. Tony had no desire to share Jane's bed, she told herself stubbornly; he did so out of an obligation to carry on the family name....

"The prospect of having a little one to love and care for brings me comfort, but I fear that Jane is incapable of loving even her own child. When she was less than three months' pregnant, she took a fall while cycling and wound up in hospital casualty. Though she swore it was an accident, and I could not prove otherwise, I am not altogether convinced she wasn't trying to miscarry...."

Abruptly Geneva stopped reading. She felt sickly, faint. She had too recently come close to losing her child, to absorb Tony's report without a sense of physical aversion. How she pitied the helpless creature growing in Jane's body! She gazed down adoringly at Emelye, who was snoozing contentedly, secure in the love of her mother. Knowing how Tony would warm to her love for their child, it seemed more wrong than ever to conceal her from him. Yet, knowing of Jane's unbridled hatefulness, it had never seemed more wise. She returned to her reading.

"Jane begs me to promise I won't put the child before her. I promise her nothing. I think I could summon at least some tenderness for Jane, if she could show just one normal instinct as an expectant mother. Not love; I could never dredge that up again.

"All this is by way of saying, Geneva, that I shall always regret, more deeply than you could possibly know, having incited the quarrel that precipitated your leaving. I should like to think, without the pressures being brought to bear just then, I would have behaved differently.

"Were those decisions made, subsequently, the right ones? I suppose I shall never know with any certainty. They seemed the only solution at the time."

And now, if there is anything that you need or desire....

"I shall be going up to London after the baby is born, and probably will lease a townhouse for us to live in. I have an urgent desire to be productive, and I may take a part offered me in an Andrè Charlot revue, opening soon at the *Prince of Wales*. Once there, I am in hopes of hearing from you—have you reopened your dancing school? And how are your dear friends the Youngers? I shall send you a box number in London where I can receive your letters without fear of being discovered.

"I shall always love you, Geneva...."

Her eyes swam before the page, and she looked away. What difference did it make, now? What good would it do, to go on writing each other? Except…

…If there is ever anything at all that I can do for you….

"While I have no right to ask anything more from you, as you see from what I've written on the reverse of our picture, as far as I am concerned, we are bound by the vows exchanged in St. Mary's Ambleside. It is my own selfish desire that someday we might be together again. Forever yours, Tony."

She looked up, realizing guiltily she'd gone from the beginning to the end of his letter, looking for him to trap himself. *But he didn't! I should never have questioned his innocence, even for a moment, for I always knew it deep down,* she thought.

She lifted the snapshot from the table and turned it on the reverse side. *Wedding Day—30th May, 1923*

For just a few moments, Geneva fell victim to Tony's idealism—how could it have survived all that he had endured?—and longed to believe that what he wanted for them was still possible, if only they would be patient. But then she looked down at her peaceful child and she felt the fullness of joy. There were nights when she suddenly awoke, feeling the crushing impact of the steering wheel against the side of her belly. The fact that Emelye had entered the world without so much as a bruise seemed increasingly miraculous. She had hung Madame Linsky's crucifix on the wall above Emelye's crib, a constant reminder.

I have so much! she thought. It would not be right for her to spend her time wishing for what she could never have. All the same, what harm would there be in writing to Tony?

PART IV

1930–1931

CHAPTER 62

Tony had not intended to walk all the way to Trafalgar Square on that January afternoon, but upon leaving Craig Muggeridge's office after having delivered—at long last—the evidence needed to clench his case against Jane, he could not force himself down a flight of concrete steps to ride the noisy, crowded underground through the bowels of London. Wintry as it was—the trees bare of leaves, snow slush all about and the cold wind chilling his ears and nose and driving his hands deep in his pockets—he was compelled nonetheless to press on across St. James's Park, sorting things out in his mind as he went....

"You don't want to lay a hand on Mrs. Selby, Sir," Mrs. Briscoe warned, with a restraining hand on his arm. *"If I might make a suggestion, take pictures of Elizabeth's injuries, and I shall stand behind you all the way."*

Would he ever be able to get the picture out of his mind?

For Tony, the happiest moment of every day was when his sprightly, dark-haired daughter Elizabeth—whom he called 'Lizzie'—flew into his arms. Often in the afternoons she would burst through the doors in whatever theatre he was working, fresh from Queen's Gate School; and bound up on the stage. He'd lift her up and swing her round, both of them laughing. On days when he was busy elsewhere, usually in meetings, he would yearn for the evening to come, when he would open his front door at No. 3 Wilton Place to see her small nimble figure running happily towards him. But four nights ago, he had been out late rehearsing the dancers for *Moment by Moment*, a new musical premiering in two weeks' time at the *Duke of York's*. Around ten o'clock he opened his door, expecting to go up to Lizzie's room to kiss his sleeping daughter goodnight and tuck the covers about her. Instead, he was met by the sound of her shrieking, all the way from her mother's bedroom, and Jane screaming vulgarities all the while. Mrs. Briscoe was halfway up the stairs, her face distraught, her tidy frame wound round like the stairs on which she stood: "Thank God you've come! Mrs. Selby's got the door locked. I telephoned you, but—"

Tony took the stairs three at a time. With good reason, he never left Elizabeth alone with her mother. Now he realized how foolish he had been to believe that the child could ever be safe, no matter his precautions. Soon he was pounding on the door, threatening to break it down if Jane didn't open up. When she did, her cheeks were flush, her eyes wide and prurient. She was breathing hard, gripping poor Lizzie's riding crop. And across the room was Lizzie, crouched on the floor in her sleeping gown in front of Jane's dressing-table bench, her long dark hair tumbling about her terrified face. "Father, what is a slut? I don't want to be one of those! Please, help me!"

Horrified, Tony rushed towards Elizabeth, assuring her, "Don't worry, Darling, Father's here, it's alright." Yet as he reached his arms around her, she yelped in pain, and then he saw blood leaking through the back of her sleeping gown. His stomach pitched. With a murderous glance at Jane, he raised up the gown to find Lizzie's back striped up and down with red whelps. And all the while, Jane's anxious voice: "The way you spoil her! Look, she had got into my cosmetics. See the mascara on her lashes! Mark my word, by the time she's 16, you'll have lost all control."

Tony picked up his sobbing daughter as best he could without causing her more pain, and carried her from the room. Over his shoulder he threw Jane an icy threat: "Don't move an inch. I shall be back." No doubt she was already developing her strategy.

For nearly six years—the whole of Lizzie's life—Tony had been determined to divorce Jane and take their daughter away from her. Yet his lawyer Craig Muggeridge advised the utmost caution. Although traditionally in divorce cases, the father received custody of his children, the courts had broad discretionary power, and given the circumstances of his marriage to Jane—the fortune he gained which saved his family from ruin—he could very well appear in a court of law as nothing more than an opportunist who used his wife's money then grew tired of her and wished to be free. In consequence, he could very well lose custody of their child. He must have indubitable proof that Jane was an unfit mother.

Jane's bicycling down a steep hill towards a shingle beach while carrying Elizabeth in her womb was the reckless act which first prompted Tony to seek counsel from his lawyer. Yet, without positive proof that she was attempting to cause a miscarriage, Craig could only make note of the event and urge Tony to keep a close watch on Jane's actions, documenting everything. Which he did.

Jane never again tried to dislodge their child from her womb, and her verbal and physical cruelty—alternating with cold neglect—from the time Lizzie came into the world, were never extreme enough to tip the scales in Tony's favor.

How often had he clenched his teeth, listening to Jane's cloying apologies to Lizzie? They always convinced the kind-hearted child, who went to church every Sunday down the street at St. Paul's Knightsbridge, and heeded the words of Father Ogilvie about the importance of forgiving others. *"Mummy is sorry she became so upset when you were naughty. Look, she has brought you a brand new doll!"* Jane was idiotic enough to think she had bought back Lizzie's affection. But Lizzie already had every possession a child could wish for, plus riding lessons at the Cadogan School, ballet instruction from Miss Eileen Bellamy, and every possible moment that Tony could spend showing her that he loved her enough to make up for her hateful mother. No, the forgiving heart which beat in Lizzie's breast was what saved her from being completely disillusioned with her mother. Tony would stay married to Jane till Lizzie was grown, rather than risk losing custody and so condemn her to the whims of a psychopathic mother.

Just reflecting on those years now as he crossed the frozen, deserted park, made his heart pound with rage and his breath come out in short frosty puffs. But—God be thanked—it would soon be all in the past, for everything Jane did from the moment she laid that riding crop on Lizzie's back, including every perverted word she uttered in her own defense, would wind up strengthening his case against her.

Not least of which was that she overdosed on sleeping pills that night. Admittedly, if he, rather than Mrs. Briscoe, had discovered her lying in her bed unconscious the next morning, he would have walked out the door and shut it behind him. In any case, directly the ambulance sped Jane away to hospital casualty, he telephoned her psychiatrist, and based on the revelations he conveyed, arrangements were made for Jane to enter Ticehurst Hospital. By this morning, the psychiatrist had informed Tony that she was seriously unstable and would need to remain there for at least six months of rigorous treatment.

According to instructions from Craig, following Jane's release from Ticehurst, Tony and Lizzie were to move from No. 3 Wilton Place. The petition for divorce would be served on Jane there.

Now as Tony walked along, the happy thought occurred to him that Jane would be safely tucked away at Ticehurst at the end of April, when he was hoping Geneva would arrive for a visit. The Prince of Wales remembered seeing *Chimaera*—plus, no doubt, meeting its charming heroine—in 1923, and suggested its inclusion on the all-star bill of the King's Command Variety Performance, at the *Palladium* on the 22nd of May. It was a terrific honor, but while Geneva had promised to consider the offer, she was reticent to accept for Jane would be their constant shadow while she was here. Now, everything had changed. He could bring Geneva home to meet Lizzie. Best of all, he and Geneva could plan for their future, face-to-face.

Of course, he must exercise the utmost care lest Jane discover the nature of his ongoing relationship with Geneva, and thankfully he'd got plenty of practice at that. Boxes and boxes of her letters, sacred to him, were stored in Kenneth Owsley's flat. Even if Kenneth was a bit of a philanderer, as Tony learnt long ago after hiring him as librettist for *The Baron and the Texas Girl*, he had also proved a trusted friend. So, in came Geneva's letters to Tony's box at the Sloane Square Poste Restante, and from his fingers and the press of his lips, back they went into their envelope and into the box in Kenneth's attic. How Tony longed for the day he would have his own theatre, and an office where not only Geneva's letters, but his other possessions, would be safe. Sometimes, in a tiff, Jane would steal sheet music, or tear a page from his composition book with a dance routine outlined, or a telephone number jotted down. She always hotly denied it, of course.

Over the years, Tony had written to Geneva a great deal about his troubled marriage and, in particular, Jane's abusiveness towards Elizabeth. Her replies were always loving and solicitous. He often wished, however, that she would seem more confident in the future he envisioned for the three of them. Then he would not fear each time he opened a letter that it might begin, *I am engaged to be married.* It wasn't that Geneva seemed to have a busy social life; she was very involved in her successful dancing school. Not surprisingly, by now she owned a commodious studio out in Milam Street, of which she'd sent him a picture. She had also purchased her home at 1207 Heights Boulevard. This surprised him, and made him uneasy—granted, it was foolish to pay rent year after year, but why would she invest in such a large house unless she anticipated marrying and having children one day?

Tony suspected he had a rival for Geneva's affection in her priest friend Father Quanset. She spoke fondly of him in her letters. He had somehow got her going to church regularly, this when she had generally an aversion to men of the cloth. Tony didn't think much of them either, except for Lizzie's Father Ogilvie. Moreover, after a Saturday night at the theatre which ran into the wee hours, attending church on Sunday morning was not appealing to him. However, Lizzie dragged him from his bed. She was very bright, and especially inquisitive about matters of faith. Father Ogilvie respected her questions, and answered with candor. Tony gathered that Father Quanset was of the same ilk. What a relief, now, to be able to give Geneva some solid hope for their future together, before Father Quanset stole her from him.

Tony had urged his mother to accompany Geneva if she decided to come to London, at his expense. Sadly, he doubted that her pride would allow her to accept such an offer. Poor Mother! Her outlook was pretty bleak since the stock market crashed in October. Though she was not reduced to poverty by any means, she lost half of everything she owned in investments, and was being forced to make some difficult adjustments. Upon moving to New York several years ago, she had purchased a three-story brownstone overlooking Central Park. Though he had never seen it, he gathered from her description that it was huge and rather exquisite, with ornately carved woodwork, arched doorways and ceilings, and several Tiffany windows. A large staff of servants were required to maintain it and organize the lavish dinner parties his mother hosted. Lately she offered the brownstone for sale, and was looking for a more modest residence. Though she was quick to say in letters that some of her friends were worse off than she was, Tony could sense her spirits were exceedingly low.

Otherwise, there was the problem of her estrangement from Geneva. Even though Tony had overcome the pain of the past, and accepted responsibility for his part in it, his mother held a deep grudge against Geneva. How he deplored this! Yet all his efforts to resolve it were ineffective. Truth be known, his mother was pretty angry all the way around, and had been since he married Jane. She was devoted to Elizabeth and Guy, and often remembered them with presents and cards. But seldom had she come to visit her grandchildren, even in the days when she could easily afford to do so. Perhaps the sunny new outlook for him and Geneva would cause his mother to have a change of heart—

Suddenly he was within view of Trafalgar Square, passing the *Garrick* theatre. He glanced at his watch. He would have just enough time before his next appointment to rush home and dash off a letter to Geneva, telling her all about the events of the past few days which culminated in his visit with Craig.

Then up the way he noticed that the front of the old *William & Mary*—boarded up for years and entangled in some sort of complicated litigation which kept anything from being done about it—had a For Sale sign posted.

CHAPTER 63

❀

A full month passed before Tony had a look inside the *William & Mary*, there being no electricity in the building. Nor was there even yet, for when the authorities finally came to inspect it at the estate agent's request, they deemed it unsafe without being completely rewired. He was too impatient to wait any longer.

Tony had no memory of ever having been in the *William & Mary*, and a little preliminary research, conducted at the odd spare moment, suggested the reason: though it opened in 1858 and remained so except for the period from 1893—when a fire virtually gutted it—through most of 1896, after which it rose from the ashes according to the design of Frank Matcham, its real heyday was during those years when his family lived in Cornwall. Even though his mother brought him to London for instruction in dance and drama, and eventually to play in a production or two, he did not become acquainted with even a small percentage of the many theatres in the West End. During the war, the *William & Mary* was used for a servicemen's club, and afterward it fell on bad times, the management abandoning its tradition of quality productions in favor of low-grade flicks. About the time Tony returned to the States in 1922, it closed down.

Apparently the present owner had no interest in the performing arts, and saw the *William & Mary's* future as—heaven forbid!—a shopping arcade.

"Vandalism, you know, only way was to board it up," said the agent as he opened the crude hinged door in the plyboard front. Tony stepped inside, holding his lantern high. Immediately before him was a formidable bow-shaped entrance, comprised of six wooden doors—or what was left of them—inset with frosted glass. It appeared as though someone had started at the left-hand corner and worked his way all the way across, door by door, with a hatchet. There was scarcely a glass pane intact. The wood frames were badly scarred—perhaps unsalvageable—and someone had sloshed them with ghastly green paint, apparently before sustaining boards were nailed in place. Every bit of exterior wall he could see had served as a tablet for crude messages and drawings. He felt somewhat daunted by the extent of damages here—truly his hopes had soared higher than they should.

But then he swung the lantern down to have a look at the walkway to the entrance, and found he was standing in the center of a pair of entwined golden letters, *W & M*, set in a marble crest with a crown on top. A chill went up his spine. He suddenly felt he was standing on holy ground. He moved back, crouched down for a closer look, and ran his fingers reverently over the letters. Yes, there were missing pieces and broken places galore, but just imagine it restored to its original state! When he rose to his feet and looked up at the dark, gaping underside of the old marquee, he saw bright lights there. Yes, and now he saw the door frames ahead restored and varnished, with shiny brass handles and beautiful glass set in them once again. And inside…

…well, he was somewhat prepared for the musty smell and spongy feel of damp carpet in the long, narrow lobby; and the skittering sound of frightened mice, not to mention rodent droppings all about.

"Bad shape!" remarked the agent. "No good for anything, I imagine, except providing a space." Clearly the owner did not wish to sell to Tony.

He looked around. "I know—for a shopping arcade," he said, with irony. He did not want the man intruding on his thoughts. Notwithstanding the owner's serious case of myopia, Tony already felt this was his theatre. "If you'd like to wait outside, where the air is a bit more pleasant…."

"Righto. Place gives me the creeps, frankly. I could use a smoke."

Tony wished he had some way of prying up the carpet, to see what was underneath. Luckily, he soon found a long rip, and reached under one side with his hand. The carpet tore like parchment paper. He ran his fingers underneath, and rapped it with his knuckles. Hard wood! He could not have hoped for anything better. Of course it may not be worth saving at this point. Still, one never knew…. He picked up his lantern and walked along the walls of the lobby. Gun metal grey, with orange trim! This deliberate paint job was no more appealing than the green paint, sloshed on the exterior by vandals. Altogether, it was quite enough to make one nauseated.

Everything had been removed from the lobby, except for some old posters advertising moving pictures, scattered about on the floor, and a few outsized letters, apparently once used on the marquee. He looked up above then, and found an oval-shaped rotunda with a railed gallery, gun metal grey and orange again. He thought at first the rotunda was plaster, but then he noticed a couple of bare patches, one shaped like an irregular triangle, and he realized it was glass—yes, opaque glass, he was pretty sure. He could have swooned at the thought of its bygone beauty, hidden like a diamond in the ceiling of a cave; he could have wept that someone had the appalling taste to defile it. Oh, he was far less infuriated by the work of the vandals, than by that of the decorator.

The auditorium awaited. He walked through one of the solid doors leading to the stalls, and circled the lantern around. How small it was, how intimate. He recalled reading that the seating capacity was 750. He walked down one aisle, the stale air pressing against his diaphragm, the bottoms of his shoes sticking to something like dried syrup. One must dismiss the rude motion picture screen still hanging amidst threadbare curtains, and concentrate on the proscenium arch: A proud *W & M*, with the crown on top, marked the center, the arch continuing down like ribbons, to enclose the boxes on each side.

He need not risk sitting down in one of the decrepit wooden seats, in order to imagine it upholstered in plush velvet; and at this point, he didn't really want to see if he could get behind the stage. Odd to think, he had always imagined owning a theatre with at least eleven-or twelve-hundred seats, and doing lavish productions like *The Baron and the Texas Girl*. He was still amazed at its success. He did not expect it to go past the *New* theatre in Oxford, where it opened; instead it went directly from there to the London *Palace,* and lasted for 715 performances. He could only guess that his heartache at losing Geneva was conveyed to audiences as they watched Eva and the Baron, deeply in love, become hopelessly separated by the war. Writing the play reopened his painful wound, but at least it established his reputation in London, and brought him a great deal of money. Even now, it was earning him considerable royalties, especially on his love song *A Safe Place In Your Arms*. And the play also made the lovely and talented Helena Magden into a star. He would never forget her convincing Texas drawl. Gave her the part of Eva right on the spot; canceled the rest of the auditions.

Ever after Helena played the role inspired by Geneva, she occupied a tender place in Tony's heart. And in fact that tenderness wound up leading him closer than ever he came to breaking his vow to Geneva. Like his marriage to Jane, Helena's marriage to Kenneth was turbulent. And during one of their many separations, he and Helena—well, he could only be thankful it didn't come to that after all. Helena and Kenneth were together now and seemed to be happy.

Hopefully they would stay that way, for they had a young son, Jerome. No child deserved to live in a hostile atmosphere. How he loathed that Lizzie had been forced to do so....

Tony could not see lavish musicals here. This house was designed for serious drama—Chekhov, Ibsen, Shaw, O'Neill, Shakespeare. And comedies, too, on a small scale, where audience and performers could easily resonate. He looked up and about, feeling elated. But, what a fortune all this was going to cost! Luckily, *Pip & Pocket* was booked again for next Christmas holiday, the public always eager for a bit of Dickens. He and Kenneth had better get cracking right away on new music and dances. They needed to keep it fresh, year after year. And speaking of time—how long was he in for, with the *William & Mary*? He'd probably be an old man in his bath chair before he'd got it reopened, much less paid for.

He was still mulling over the enormous commitment ahead when he walked outside. The agent appeared. "Finished?"

Tony looked at the man, who could not have imagined how that simple word could be so fraught with meaning. He could walk away. After all, his dream was to own a theatre someday, not to begin with a renovation that would break the bank and turn his hair white beforehand. Yet, how could he, in good conscience, leave this battered, neglected work of art to some other buyer, who may well complete its destruction? In future, how could he bear to pass by a shopping arcade, knowing he could have saved the *William & Mary* from its cruel fate? "Yes, thank you. I shall be in touch if I—"

"Of course, sir. Good day."

The last few unspoken words of Tony's farewell robbed him of sleep every single night over the next week, whence he returned for another look, feeling surely he had come to his senses by now. It was no use. He was more in love than ever.

Soon Craig was preparing an offer. Probably there would be a lot of quibbling before it was all done—he left a little room to manoeuver. He was scared to death he would get it; terrified he would not. He made a list of all he would need to begin: old architectural drawings of the original design and of Matcham's restoration; photographs, if available; programmes; playbills; newspaper/periodical accounts of the reopening in 1896. Where would he find all this memorabilia? he wondered. He absolutely would not lift a finger until his offer was accepted.

Three weeks later, with only minor changes, it was. He had a fluttery feeling in his stomach. It was the biggest, most uncertain, risk he had ever taken. He hurried home from Craig's office, having promised to take Lizzie out for dinner, to celebrate. "Ribbons and curls and your prettiest dress," he had told her.

When he walked inside his study, to have a quick look at the post before having a shower, he found a letter from Geneva in the stack. He opened it eagerly. "Dear Tony, Since learning of your impending divorce from Jane, and knowing that the way is now clear for me to come to England in a few months, there is something I must tell you. And I find it particularly difficult, having waited so long...."

He looked up. *Oh God, she is married.* He braced himself, and returned to the letter.

"Tony, dear heart, we have a beautiful daughter...."

"Father, father, look at me! See what Mrs. Briscoe's done to my hair!"

Through a blur he saw Lizzie pirouetting through the doorway, sausage curls bouncing and a big pink hair bow on top of her head. *A daughter....* "Eh—yes, Darling, how lovely you look! But I'm afraid father is feeling a bit—eh—out of sorts just now," he gasped, and sank into his desk chair.

CHAPTER 64

On the train from Southampton to London, Cynthia stared pensively out one window while Geneva gazed out another, and Emelye—seated next to her grandmother with her ankles crossed lady-like—remained unusually still, determined that no strands of long dark-blond hair should escape the taffeta bow pinned securely at the back of her head, or wrinkles appear in her blue Easter dress—her favorite dress of all, with smocking across the front and a crisp white collar. "Are we almost there?" she would ask now and then, her brown eyes—Tony's all over in color and shape—wide with anticipation. But this question and its reassuring reply, usually coming from Cynthia, were among the few words to break the silence.

Not much given to praying in general, Cynthia nonetheless had prayed daily for nearly seven years that God would open Geneva's heart to inform Tony of their child, and that somehow—though she was furious at Geneva, there was no denying it—Tony could be free of Jane and he and Geneva could be reunited, with their children. Was the child a boy, or a girl? she often wondered. But no—the less she knew, the better, until the circumstances changed.

Then came Geneva's long-awaited letter: "*I have written to Tony that we have a daughter....*" Cynthia hastily replied, "Do bring my granddaughter to me. We will spend a few days getting acquainted, then sail to England together."

Cynthia had envisioned this child with the red curls and green eyes of her mother. What a surprise to find that Emelye was the spitting image of Tony at the same age. Upon seeing her, Cynthia had one of those sudden urges that overcame her now and then, to return to Brookhurst and be a part of her family again. Hard to imagine herself a gray-haired grandmother, telling stories to her grandchildren out on the terrace. But in fact she had recently stopped hiding the gray in her hair, and even put on a little weight; and stories were about all that was left of the life she had known. The money she lost in the stock market was really the last vestige of what used to be, and was no more.

Since the advent of motion pictures, vaudeville had been dying by pieces. Scores of headliners were out of work and out of luck—many asked the guardian angel for help, which she could no longer give. Even those who found work were pathetic, clinging to the past, performing their hearts out for audiences who had purchased tickets primarily to see the feature film on the bill. Live entertainment had become secondary, and over time, its quality suffered proportionately. Even the *Palace* had increasingly lower standards. Cynthia stopped going to shows long before she stopped receiving complimentary tickets in the mail; they were degrading; they made her sick inside.

Some of her discoveries had made the switch into pictures. Sonja Vitalé had done remarkably well. She always lunched with Cynthia when she came to New York. But she seldom came any more, being very busy in Hollywood, where she was under contract with Universal Pictures.

Cynthia felt wistful sometimes, especially when she thought of Tony's brilliant dances. They were the best of the best in vaudeville. But she was not one to look back over her shoulder. And besides, Tony's star was on the rise. *The Baron and the Texas Girl* was spectacular. The talent that Tony put together for that show was magical. Kenneth Owsley—a charming, red-headed Irishman who never thought of anything except music and sex—was one example. But Helena Magden! When she walked on stage, the rest of the world quite simply ceased to exist. Cynthia would have spotted her from a mile, just as Tony did. And now he was buying the old *William & Mary.* How exciting! Edward had taken her to the premiere of the restored theatre, John Hare in *A Pair of Spectacles.* It was her first outing after Tony was born. However, she was not inclined to allude to this when replying to Tony's letter reporting that his offer had been accepted, for the news was little more than a post script after the accusation: "I've just learned that Geneva and I have a daughter. I am doubly devastated to learn, also, that you conspired with her to keep this from me for all these years."

Little did Tony realize, that secret had burned a hole through Cynthia's heart. It was why she so seldom went to England to visit. She could hardly bear to be around Tony, knowing what she knew and especially as she witnessed his pain, living with that ghastly woman. Well Jane had not won, after all—though the battle was far from over. She could turn the tables, even yet.

One may fault Geneva for many things, but not for the way she was rearing her daughter. Emelye was inquisitive, but polite; lively, but well-disciplined, and, like Elizabeth, she was kind-hearted. Cynthia could hardly wait for Tony to see Emelye for the first time, and to watch her son's face when he did....

Geneva saw that they were on the outskirts of London now, chugging by little cottages with geraniums peeking from window boxes, and daffodils and daisies blooming in tiny gardens. Here and there, bright pink valerian blossoms sprouted between the stones of railroad embankments. Oh, the memories the sight of them brought back! Hard to believe seven years had passed. Unlike Tony who lived for the future, Geneva counted every day a blessing, for every day she awoke to the fresh realization that Emelye was in the world.

Then, astonishingly: *"I am divorcing Jane."*

Late one night shortly before they sailed, Geneva went up to the attic to collect the box of articles she would finally take to Tony: valentines Emelye had made for him and pictures she had drawn; thank-you letters for the presents on Christmas and her birthday, and many times in between. *"Look what Daddy sent from England, sweetie!"* Geneva would lie, feeling guilty. And photographs: Emelye in her christening gown, in Father Quanset's arms, with godparents Rodney and Willa on either side; Emelye in her recital costumes, and on her first day of kindergarten; her first snow, in January, 1926—all wrapped up in warm woolen, standing with Geneva by the snowman they had built; Emelye and Serena and James in swim suits, frolicking on the shore of Lake Astoria. Each time Geneva placed a new article in this box—each one precious, and modest in quality—she had asked herself: when would be the right moment to interrupt the quiet composition of their lives in order to crash in on Tony's: glamourous theatre openings and cast parties till three in the morning; luncheons with producers at the Garrick; dinners at the Savoy with West End stars? And all the while, somehow placating the ever more disruptive Jane and protecting Elizabeth from a mother who had tried to murder her in the womb. The possibility that Jane might harm Emelye was never far from Geneva's mind as Tony's letters recounted her cruelty to Elizabeth. This, more than anything else, was what always persuaded her to continue holding on to her secret.

There was but one occasion when Geneva felt a threat to Emelye's wellbeing. Last September, Benjamin wrote that he wished to come down and photograph Victor's studio for a feature article in the *New American Review*—the New York magazine which had published *Maiden at the Window*. She read between the lines for some sign he had found her nude pictures. *Is that the underlying reason for doing the article? Will he offer me the pictures in exchange?*

Or will he want money as well? What If I can't pay what he wants? He will publish the pictures somewhere, let the identity of the model be known, and people here will eventually find out. My dancing school will be in jeopardy, and along with it, my daughter's secure and happy life.

She wrote to Benjamin, setting a date and time.

She did not sleep at all on the night before their appointment, and in the morning she took Emelye across the street to the Youngers' and removed every trace of her existence from the downstairs rooms—toys, books, pictures, clothing—feeling glad as she did so that she had put off buying Emelye a back yard swing set until Christmas. There was no point in revealing to Benjamin the full extent of her vulnerability.

Then came the day. Not until Benjamin rang the doorbell did Geneva remember she had not removed her wedding band. She froze in her steps. The blood rushed to her knees. The doorbell rang again. She hastily stuffed the ring in her skirt pocket and opened the front door. She could hardly believe her stupidity, which condemned her to feeling all the more unsettled.

Benjamin's figure had filled out around the chest and shoulders, but otherwise, he looked much like the lanky boy she remembered, with his dark hair parted in the center and slicked down, and a pair of round eyeglasses on his narrow face. His camera dangled from his shoulder by a strap. Geneva's eyes veered down to his hands. He was not carrying a large envelope, as she had hoped. He greeted her with the coolness she half-expected.

Geneva had been inside the studio only once since Victor left, and that was a couple of summers ago—or, was it three?—when she was thinking of storing gardening tools there. She had opened the door, walked two or three steps inside, and glanced quickly around the room before her. As soon as she saw the dim square of the studio curtain covering the window like a ghost, her diaphragm squeezed up. *It's too far back in the yard to be convenient,* she told herself.

She felt that same apprehensiveness now as she waited for Benjamin to take a couple of exterior shots, then unlocked the door and showed him inside.

Unfortunately for them both, they found the studio interior utterly destroyed by mildew; its wooden beams were black with rot, and there was a putrid spongy glaze over everything. It looked like a 'haunted house' on Halloween. The stench was overpowering, and sent them scurrying outdoors.

"I—I'm so sorry," she faltered, "I guess the roof must have started leaking. I never dreamed it would be like that."

Benjamin reached for a cigarette. "Too bad," he said stoically, "I'd counted on showing where Dad worked in the middle part of his career." He lit the cigarette, took a drag, then exhaled out to the side, his eyes fixed on hers. "The exterior won't give a clue as to what went on in there, will it?"

What are you saying to me? She gathered herself. "No, I guess not."

They were walking toward the street now. Her cheeks were flaming. She had nothing to lose by asking about her pictures.

Benjamin looked at her with a puzzled frown. "Pictures?"

How thoroughly you must hate me. "Yes, I wrote to you once—"

"Oh yes, of course—*that*," he said, his tone the echo of a door closing far down in a long dark corridor. "You know, to this day, there are still boxes I haven't gone through. I'll keep it in mind, though," he said, and with a smile as arrogant as the brush-off he had given her, he dropped his cigarette on the ground, smashed it under his foot and walked away.

The train conductor announced Waterloo Station, and in minutes the station swallowed up the sunshine as the train made its noisy entrance and lurched to a halt. As they rose to their feet, the two women exchanged a significant look. Emelye was tugging on Geneva's hand. "Hurry, Mom!"

Tony spotted his mother and Geneva from far off, and hastened toward them, clutching a nosegay with pink ribbons, for Emelye. Though he tried, he could not see Emelye's small figure through the crowd. When finally he approached the group, she buried her face in her mother's skirts.

Since receiving Geneva's letter in which she told him of all the vicarious ways she had made him a part of Emelye's life, Tony had tried to see past the blur of his anger at being denied their child, and to imagine her. Yet his only reference point was that one glorious honeymoon week in Ambleside. He relived all those sacred moments with Geneva, knowing that although they were not aware at the time, Emelye had already made her entrance into their lives. As they sat that day on the banks of Lake Windermere and spoke of the depths of their love for each other, she was there; as they lay naked before the fire and read to each other the beautiful verse of the Lake Poets, she was there; perhaps even from that first night, minutes after Geneva's gown slid to the floor, Emelye was there. But there was one particular night that he recalled again and again. Sometime in the wee hours, the fire in their bedroom died out. Tony awakened cold, and naked though he was, he hastened out of bed to rekindle it. When the logs were flaming once again, he returned to bed. Geneva lifted the covers and reached out to enclose his shivering body in her arms; his chest and groin, warm from the fire, warmed her breast and belly. And as—inevitably—they made love, he thought, *wouldn't it be the most beautiful thing if Geneva were to be carrying our child, when we release each other?*

But of course, all of those memories gave him only a profound and grateful sense of Emelye as his own. He had no idea what she would be like, six years later, in person. He did not anticipate her shyness, for Lizzie was so outgoing—at least when Jane was not around—from having been raised in the presence of adults in the theatre. He did not want to begin by frightening Emelye. "These are for you," he said, holding out the flowers to the little girl whose face was hidden from him.

With urging from her mother, Emelye slowly turned toward him and timidly accepted the flowers. He saw then that she bore a striking resemblance to himself. His eyes flooded with tears. He could not find his voice. He reached for Emelye rather helplessly, and she dutifully came into his arms.

Watching Tony lift their daughter off her feet and hug her as if he'd waited a lifetime to do so, Geneva felt a sense of reconciliation in her heart that she'd finally done the thing that was right for both of them.

"Mommy, why is Daddy crying? You said he would be happy to see me," Emelye soon inquired. Geneva decided to let Tony answer that question.

He held Emelye away and looked into her face. "Sometimes joy comes out in tears. I am ever so happy to see you, Darling! We're going to have such a wonderful time together," he promised, and clutched her tightly again. But even as he felt her tiny rib cage in his embrace and her heart thumping against his chest, all his confidence about their future deserted him, and in its place was the specter of Jane's malice. The day when his family of four would live safely and happily together suddenly seemed frighteningly beyond his grasp. How he dreaded the clock ticking away, after Jane came home from Ticehurst and the petition for divorce had been served.

CHAPTER 65

All the morning at school, and during her riding lesson, Elizabeth thought of nothing but going home to meet Emelye. Imagine, a sister! For as long as she could remember, she had been praying that God would send her a sister or a brother. All her schoolmates at Queen's Gate had at least one or the other, and more often than not, one of each. Elizabeth could not understand why she had none. Then, suddenly, Father announced she had a sister her very own age, coming from America. It was the miracle for which she had prayed. Since then, she had knelt beside her bed every night, to thank God for his goodness. She promised to love her sister and be faithful to her, forever. Unfortunately, Emelye would be here for only a month, "this time," Father said. He would not explain why, but promised one day she would understand. Therefore, she must make the most of every moment. Luckily, Mummy would not be here to make Father cross, and to make everyone else unhappy and afraid—the reasons Elizabeth never invited chums to visit.

At precisely four o'clock, Elizabeth burst into the parlor, in her riding jodhpurs, her hair coming loose from its knot, her shirt tail coming out on one side—there was no time to tidy her appearance. She ran straight to Emelye, who was having her tea—how beautiful she was, like a princess!—and threw her arms about her. "Emelye, my dear sister, thank heaven you've come at last!"

Until a few weeks ago, Emelye knew that even though her father loved her very much, he could not live with her and her mother because, according to her mother, he had "important responsibilities" in England. From the small picture of her parents on Emelye's dresser, in which they stood smiling among vines and flowers on their wedding day, Daddy was the most handsome man in the world. And she never doubted he loved her because he always sent her special gifts on her birthday and at Christmas, and Easter and Valentine's Day, and often in between. She wrote him many letters, often enclosing pictures of herself so that he would know her when they met, as Mother promised they would "one day." Everyone at dancing and at school knew that she had a very handsome, important father. Then, a few weeks ago she learned that her family included also a grandmother who lived in New York, and even a sister her own age in England. Since then she had felt very confused. No matter how many questions she asked, she still could not make sense of it.

And now she felt overwhelmed, not only because Elizabeth seemed to know her already and like her so much, but also because she talked as if she were grown up. Emelye wished Serena and James were here.

After Elizabeth was introduced to Mother—curtsying, as you would do at the end of a recital dance!—and hugged and kissed by Grandmother, she invited Emelye up to her room to play with all her toys, and said that she hoped Emelye would sleep there tonight and every night during her stay. Emelye moved closer to her mother. "No thanks. I'd rather sleep with my mom," she said cautiously.

Elizabeth concealed her disappointment—she was well-experienced at this—and determined that Emelye must be given her most treasured possession: a cross made of Honiton lace.

Late that night, Tony invited Geneva into his study: a room reflecting his passion for the theatre. The tables were cluttered with trade papers and magazines. Books and sheet music lined the shelves, and walls were filled with colorful playbills and glossy photographs. The *Chimaera* publicity photo was nowhere in sight, Geneva noted. Tony probably kept it hidden from Jane. All the memorabilia seemed to date from his first musical, *The Baron and the Texas Girl*. Before the tall windows stood a small wooden desk, with a typewriter on top and a brass lamp with a green glass shade. A baby grand piano filled one corner. The sight of Tony's dancing shoes—placed side by side under the piano bench on the parquet floor—flooded Geneva's mind with memories of watching his feet as he demonstrated a step they would do together. Spotting the spiral bound notebook on the end table, near a lamp with the shade tilted toward the sofa, Geneva found herself imagining Tony sitting on the sofa with his stockinged feet propped up on the magazine table, composing dances....

In spite of the fact that her letter informing him of their child fully explained everything—including her foiled attempts to tell him of her pregnancy, and ultimately her reasons for keeping Emelye a secret—Tony did not write back to explore the issues with her, and his coolness toward her today suggested he had not forgiven her. She sat at one end of the sofa while he fixed drinks for them, and braced herself for his anger to erupt. She was prepared to check that anger if need be; it wouldn't get out of hand as it had before.

As Tony handed Geneva a glass of sherry, he said, "I suppose we may as well start by talking about those stolen messages."

Geneva preferred they begin by clearing the air between them. "You're angry with me, aren't you? You don't really understand my reasoning for all I did," she said.

Tony's brow lifted: Alright. He sat down at the far end of the sofa and looked at her. "I certainly understand your decision not to step in and break up my marriage. I'm not sure I am as appreciative as I might be—though I could not have saved Brookhurst, I could have got us back on our feet eventually," he said.

Lord Edward was walking in the garden on a summer's eve, his hands clasped behind him. No, thought Geneva, Tony was wrong about his father getting 'back on his feet' after losing Brookhurst. That home was his heartbeat.

Tony continued in an injured tone, "But when I think of all those years when I was completely open with you about my hopes for our future, and all the while, your letters kept from me the information I deserved most of all!"

"I was afraid of what would happen when Emelye encountered Jane!" Geneva reminded him. "I knew I would tell you when the time was right. And I did," she swore.

"You should have at least trusted me to figure out how to protect Emelye from Jane," Tony reproached her. She could have pointed out how often Jane abused Elizabeth, in spite of his efforts, but it would have seemed terribly cruel.

Tony took a sip of his drink, then said resolutely, "Alright, let's talk about those messages."

Geneva was loathe to mention possibilities that she knew Tony would resent. "Do you think Jane intercepted them?" she asked cautiously.

He shook his head. "It's very doubtful. All through August, we were both traveling back and forth to London, hammering out a marriage contract. But I have one theory—a receipt does not prove your wire was actually transmitted. You would have to have a signature from over here. And unfortunately, you've waited too long for any surviving record of that. I have already checked.

"I think Mrs. Ruekauer pretended to change her mind after paying the fee, and hurried from the telegraph office with that receipt. Either that or she diverted the telegram somehow. God knows, she could have had it dispatched to Australia for all we know, or delivered right to your home, and you'd be none the wiser. And of course she never mailed your letters. Keep in mind her heavy drinking by the time Emelye was born. I daresay she was hounded by guilt."

Geneva admitted she had never thought the receipt might be faked. "But if she didn't intend to send the wire, why suggest it in the first place?" she argued.

"It's obvious! She feared Willa and Rodney would do it."

To a point, his theory was plausible. But there were still two unresolved questions in Geneva's mind. "Would Ida really have gone that far just to protect her living arrangement? And besides, how long could she have expected to get away with it? She could not have predicted that you would marry Jane, or that I would decide not to interfere."

Tony frowned. "Yes, that's the thing that bewilders me. I'm sure the explanation is tied in with her disappearance."

"You mean to say, you think that was just a masquerade?" Geneva asked. She felt foolish suddenly that she had pitied Ida in the end, for dying all alone.

"I think it's very likely."

Geneva decided they may as well get the difficult part over with. "Or, let's face it, Tony, Ida might be innocent. She might have lost her life exactly as the police surmised. Someone over here just didn't want you to hear from me."

Tony knew exactly to whom she referred. How many times had he imagined the sequence of events: *"This wire just received for Master Tony, your lordship; I wasn't quite sure…." Father was reading the text, his heart sinking with every word. What to do? Geneva could hardly be ignored. And yet, she was to be the means of his complete ruination, the loss of everything he had worked for in his life, and all the while, Tony was so bitter towards her, he would not even speak her name. According to the wire, a letter was on its way. And if it was not answered, Geneva would write, perhaps wire Tony, again. Yet, Tony's wedding with Jane was less than three weeks' hence…. Supposing Geneva were ignored just long enough for the ceremony to take place? And then, afterward, he would tell his son of the problem, and allow that some responsibility must be taken for this American girl. There would now be sufficient money to support the child.*

Yet amazingly, after the second letter, coming close on the heels of the first, there was no further word from Geneva. The 8th of September arrived; Tony married Jane. A week passed, another week, and nothing. Perhaps Geneva had lost the baby—.

At this point, Tony's heart would cry out in protest. His father was an honorable man. How could he even imagine such calculating on his part?

Now Tony downed the rest of his drink, and said stubbornly, "If you're thinking my father concealed your messages, well you're just dead wrong."

He could tell from Geneva's face that she was not entirely convinced. How he regreted her doubt, would have done anything to dispel it—

"Alright. Who else may have been around? Morey? Nell?"

"I must admit Morey sprang to mind immediately I read your letter. But by then he had got a job with Tolgus Mines. They were keeping him on the road practically all the time. And Nell—well, first of all, my sister is no more capable of such deception than my father. Besides, Nell had no further reason to truck back and forth to Brookhurst with poor Guy, as she had been doing earlier in the summer, with Morey tied up in meetings there. No doubt she was tending the garden at Camellia Cottage when that wire was delivered."

"I'd still lay my money on Ida Ruekauer."

"But you're not absolutely certain Jane was not at Brookhurst when that wire came," Geneva pointed out, then added, "I've just been thinking…if we can prove Jane's guilt, it might strengthen your case for divorce."

Tony shook his head. "Jane sealed her fate that night she beat Lizzie with a riding crop. All that she did and said that night, she later admitted to doctors.

"I shall explain, but I'm going to need another drink," he said, his voice shaky. Geneva looked at him, bewildered, and handed him her empty glass.

Soon Tony was standing near his desk, gazing out the window at the quiet street, bathed in flickering gas light. At length he said, "There were things I did not tell you in my letter. One loathes writing such things down. But as you know, Jane always appeals for sympathy whenever she has got in over her head. She made a rather revolting confession…about certain liberties her father had taken with her."

At first, Geneva did not comprehend Tony's meaning. Once she did, she was reluctant to believe it. She stammered, "May—maybe she lied."

Still looking away, Tony shook his head slowly. "I think I'd suspected something since that day in the wood, before we realized Potts was staring. Jane was so—" he hesitated—"wise…about things she ought not to have known. But I dismissed it, for it just didn't fit. Then, with all that happened after—"

"You mean, didn't fit with her being a virgin?"

He glanced at her over his shoulder, then looked out again. "At that time, she was, in a manner of speaking." His voice became hoarse. "You don't want to hear anymore, how she went on and on to me about his...his coming into her bed at nights...*stroking* her...from the time she was 14."

"Yes, that will do," Geneva said quietly. She was appalled beyond measure, yet it struck her even then that, if Cynthia were to be believed, Jane had been wicked long before the age of 14; no doubt William's sexual violations contributed to her corruption, but they didn't create it.

Tony sat down again. When he looked at her, his eyes were moist. He spoke in fits and starts. "Pretty disgusting, isn't it? But here's what really drove me over the edge: Jane said that when...whenever she saw Lizzie and me together, she feared what happened between her and William might happen eventually between...us. And that she was...*jealous.* Not concerned for Lizzie's welfare, which might have suggested she was a reasonably sane person, with normal instincts. But, *jealous.* Do you know, Geneva, it made me so sick that I fled to the bathroom and vomited."

Geneva could only shake her head, wondering what was behind such a perverted notion. It was almost as if Jane actually welcomed her father's violations—oh, surely not! On the other hand, did she recognize his behavior as a sign of the tyrant's weakness, and gloried in the power it gave her over him? Who could guess what went on in Jane's head? The best Tony could do was try and forget about it. Gently she said, "Poor darling, it's alright. Come here...."

He remembered that morning at Brookhurst, when he'd gone to Geneva's room, the burden of Selby Mines dragging his steps. She laid his head on her breast and told him—in a way she had never done before—that she loved him, and that it was going to be alright. And it would have been, if not for his own idiotic jealousy. He suddenly felt more grateful than ever that, while the obstacles ahead were many, Geneva would be with him through them all. In that moment he forgave her everything.

When Tony laid down with his head in Geneva's lap, the warmth of his head against her groin stirred her. She smoothed the graying hair around his temple. How she loved him! "In spite of her mother, you've made Elizabeth a lively, generous child—well-adjusted. How proud you must be!" she told him.

He smiled sadly. "I've had a good deal of help—mostly from Father, whom Lizzie adores," he said, for it was true. And also he could not help being eager to put his father in a good light for Geneva. "And by the way, you haven't done a bad job with Emelye, either. One hasn't got to be around her long before seeing that she believes in herself. That's your love shining through, Geneva."

She would not have dared hope for that admission.

He touched her cheek. "Did you breast-feed my daughter?" he asked.

"Of course!" she cried, her face aglow. "For months—until I reopened my dancing school. So many times, I wished you could be there with us."

He smiled. "Next time." Tenderly she lifted his hand and pressed it against her breast. He sat straight again and clutched her to him, and then they were kissing. In between kisses she said, eagerly, "Do you remember, that last day of our honeymoon, how we rushed upstairs—"

"Chilled to the bone from our rained-out picnic—"

"Wet clothes clinging to us!"

"And we got naked and stood before the fire—"

"Toweling each other off with long, caressing strokes—"

"Inching toward the bed," he said, his hands running over her breasts, down her rib cage.

"Oh Tony, no matter what happened afterward, the memories of that week count just as much!"

Suddenly Tony forced himself to break away, admitting hoarsely, "If you got pregnant now, we could not dig out of the trouble we'd bring on ourselves."

Geneva nodded reluctantly. Sat back, catching her breath.

Tony remembered he had a surprise. "Still, where would you like to be living, once you and I are 'officially' married, and we can make love any time we please?"

The answer came quickly. "A place like Clearharbour Farm," she said longingly. "I've thought of it so often…."

It was exactly what Tony wanted to hear. "Unfortunately, I don't know that there is such a place," he said with mock sorrow. Then he grinned. "But not to worry. You see, Clearharbour Farm is ours, free and clear. Thanks to *The Baron and the Texas Girl.*"

CHAPTER 66

It could not be ignored, the chandelier in Tony's entrance hall, suspended above the black and white marble floor: an ice castle high up in the clouds of a fairy tale. Every visible part was covered with crystal; layer upon delicate layer, swirling spun glass concealed even its spine and members. At night, when the globes were lit, a galaxy of stars beamed from its tips.

The fanciful light fixture caught Geneva's eye every time she came through the hall and went up the stairs that spiraled around it, or came down. She made this journey many times a day, staying home between rehearsals, surrendering her daughter to Tony and Cynthia and Elizabeth for shopping trips, afternoon tea at the Ritz, visits to the London Zoo, the museums, puppet shows, parks and gardens: small payments against a six-year debt.

But this was the day of the King's Command Variety Performance. After the run-through rehearsal this morning, Tony had sent her home in a taxi, then hastened to get a haircut, and to pick up a new pair of *Chimaera* wings at Peake Scarab Costumiers. Cynthia was visiting friends in Stratford-Upon-Avon, the girls were playing outdoors, and Geneva was packing her bag for the theatre.

Now, as she affixed her tiny guardian angel pin inside the neck of her body stocking, she heard Elizabeth screaming frantically downstairs. She dashed from her room to the top of the stairs, from which the chandelier blocked her view of all but Elizabeth's oxfords pounding the marble floor. "Help, Geneva! A man has taken Emelye away! Oh, do hurry!"

Within seconds Geneva was plunging down the stairs and through the front door, querying Elizabeth as to which way they went. "Towards Brompton Road! Oh, do hurry!" she sobbed.

Outside Geneva jerked her head towards the busy thoroughfare, where vehicles sped by in a blur. More slowly her gaze retreated, following the quiet leafy Wilton Place back towards St. Paul's Knightsbridge at the opposite end, past three-storied townhouses with enameled entrance doors and iron fences, fanciful topiaries, and window boxes sprouting with flowers and dripping with vines. All the while her mind was arguing that Elizabeth must surely be mistaken. "Emelye!" she cried. "Emelye!" There was no answer. The street was completely empty in both directions, as though her daughter had been swallowed up by the pavement. She rushed back through the door and headed for the telephone in Tony's office. In moments she was on the line with the police. All the while she talked, Elizabeth hung on her skirts, sobbing. She kept a comforting arm around the child, scarcely able to believe what she was reporting into the receiver. As she hung up, she saw Mrs. Briscoe standing in the doorway, just back from the market, her eyes wide with alarm. Geneva could not stay here and wait for the police to arrive. She knelt down before the pale, quivering child. "You stay with Mrs. Briscoe, while I look for Emelye," she instructed, then hugged Elizabeth tightly.

Even before Geneva went out the door, Elizabeth began to pray. She could not believe that God would let someone take her new sister away.

London had never loomed so threateningly large or confusing to Geneva. She hailed a taxi at Brompton Road. Spurred by her dilemma, the driver dashed up and down streets and alleyways from Wilton Place to Piccadilly, and all around the fringes of Hyde Park and Kensington Gardens, Geneva's eyes two search lights at times blurred by a fog of disbelief; her hopes rising and falling around every corner. *Thank God, there she is! No. Wait—up there! But no....*

Finally the driver said, "Miss, if I were you, I'd go home and wait for the authorities."

When the taxi pulled up to the curb, Tony was waiting, his countenance bleak. They held each other. He said he returned from his errands to find a police car out in front of the house.

"Detective Inspector Chandler is waiting inside to talk to you. Elizabeth is pretty upset. She has gone up to bed now. She said she and Emelye had been playing "hide and seek." She was next door, standing behind a hedge, when she saw what happened. Apparently the man collided with Emelye on the front steps as he was coming out of the house. Elizabeth was able to give us a good description of him: tall, slender, with a small dark moustache and a goatee. I wondered if it might be Benjamin Rothby."

Geneva could not pierce through her gloom to follow his reasoning. "Benjamin—why?"

"There was a note found in the vestibule. It appears the man came here to blackmail you."

Within a few moments, Geneva was staring down at a cheap reproduction of *Maiden at the Window* on the magazine table in Tony's study, and beside it, the typewritten threat: By 7 p.m., £1,000 in £1 notes were demanded, "…or other pictures, bolder in nature, will appear in tomorrow evening's edition of *The London Gate*." The name of the tabloid had a salacious ring, as if what lay behind the gate catered to the sickest kind of voyeurism. So, finally, as she had long since feared, this was the future gazed upon so innocently by the *Maiden*. Only her fears had not included the abduction of her daughter: the worst nightmare there could ever be. Oh God, if she could only just wake up and find it was no more than a horrible dream! Tony was right when he said she was foolish to hope that Victor had been decent enough to destroy her nude pictures. She had now lost all respect for his memory.

The house quickly became a center of activity. With the help of Emelye's latest school picture, taken from Geneva's wallet, Scotland Yard began a search from one end of London to the other. The *Maiden* reproduction and the demand that she pay for the worst mistake of her life were whisked away to be dusted for finger prints, the paper and typeface analyzed. Uniformed officers, their jackets flashing bright brass buttons, paraded in and out of Tony's study, dispatched to various duties, while at least one officer stood by at all times; a special wire was attached to the telephone line, to intercept calls. *I have your daughter. Here is what I want you to do….*

With his snapping dark eyes above a pair of half-eye glasses, and his thin wavy hair parted up the side and swept into a wing, Inspector Chandler in his plain business suit resembled a dramatic actor in want of his sword and cloak. As he questioned Geneva about her relationship with Benjamin, jotting down notes as they went, Tony alternately paced back and forth before the window, and sank down beside Geneva to hold her hand consolingly. She could not help listening with one ear for the sound of the front door opening. Whenever she heard it she would glance toward the entrance hall, expecting Emelye to emerge. Finding instead yet another uniformed officer, her gaze would swing back toward the inspector and she would pray despairingly, *Please, God, bring my daughter home safely. Don't let her believe for a moment that she won't be found.* For that was part of this waking nightmare: that Emelye may not realize the immense effort being undertaken to find her, by, according to Tony, the most efficient police force in the world. An effort that would not fail, *Please God....*

"Mark of an amateur, losing his wits when the child surprised him," Inspector Chandler quickly surmised. Still, he said, he was not inclined to assume Benjamin's guilt. First of all, Geneva could not be certain Benjamin had discovered her photographs. Victor may have sold them before he died, and even if he was discreet about the identity of the model, someone may have made the connection from publicity photos of *Sterling and Selby*. (Geneva did not believe Victor sold the pictures, but this did not excuse his abominable self-centeredness which had wound up punishing the most undeserving victim of all.) Assuming, however, that Benjamin found the pictures after the photographer's death, there were seven years to be accounted for. Why had he waited so long to make use of them?

"You see, if Rothby—or Calais, whatever name he goes by—had no reason to believe you had sufficient means to make blackmail worth his while, and besides, it was obvious you'd suspect him at once if he tried it, he may have felt it would be a smart move to sell them."

"But how would he have known anyone in England?" asked Geneva.

With a lift of his brow, Inspector Chandler stated the obvious: "Journalists are free agents, and often travel about following stories. On the other hand, the photographs may have changed hands several times by now."

In a way Geneva wanted to think Benjamin was behind this, for surely he was not so morally corrupt as to hurt an innocent child, whereas, if someone else had taken Emelye, there was no telling what he was capable of....

Yet, if it was Benjamin, did he know by now whose daughter he was holding captive? Surely he did. There was no telling how much information he'd gotten from Emelye by now. She thought of how he had despised her for monopolizing Victor's time when they lived together. How he signed his message to her in Los Angeles, "B. Rothby," as if he'd never met her in his life. Now, having discovered the photographs, he was bound to have concluded that she was having an affair with his father when they were made. Was he apt to be especially abusive to Emelye, because he hated her mother? She willed herself not to begin dwelling on the worst possibilities. She prayed: *Oh dear God, don't let any harm come to my daughter, whoever's hands she has fallen into....*

"...Which brings me to my next question," the inspector continued. "Presuming Benjamin's guilt for the moment, tell me, Miss Sterling, when Rothby came to your home last year, did you mention your upcoming trip to this country?"

Geneva drew a complete blank, her mind far too stretched to recall two events that had nothing to do with one another at the time. As she struggled Tony spoke up: "I say, I believe it was in October that I wrote to Geneva inviting her over."

"That's right," she said, remembering. "Benjamin came in September."

The inspector looked back over his notes, tapping his pencil on his notebook. Presently he asked, "Do you know whether he was a staff writer at the time, or just contracting his services?"

Geneva thought about this. "He wrote to me on a letterhead, so I guess he was a staff writer."

He jotted a note. "By chance, did you notice on the letterhead if the *New American Review* has an office over here?"

She had not paid much attention, having been struck by the fact that Benjamin must have parlayed Victor's former association with the magazine into a job for himself. "All I remember is a street number on Park Avenue in New York. Oh yes, and at the bottom of the page, a drawing of a globe."

"Might there have been a name as well—try and remember," urged the inspector. "Some publications company. Globe publications, perhaps?"

Geneva struggled, shook her head. It did not ring any bells.

"*WORLD!*" Tony cried now. "Wait—I may have the answer right here!"

Geneva and the inspector stared mystified as Tony flew to the cupboard behind his piano, and began pulling out magazines. "The trouble is, these are not in any special order—here's one: Fall, 1929. Too early...." He searched some more, hurling the discards on the floor. "Summer—'28—dash it! Hold on, hold on. Of course, I loan things out, and don't get them back sometimes. But just—ah! Spring, 1930. Good!" He held up a magazine called, *WORLD of the ARTS* for Geneva and the inspector to see. He glanced at the editorial information inside, and noted it was a *WORLD* publication. Geneva and the inspector exchanged a look of amazement at his detective work.

"And look here, a globe!" Tony said, tapping it with his finger. He flipped over to the back of the issue and studied the text. "You see, they run a calendar of events for the arts, in New York, Paris, and London. It's the only reason I subscribe to the thing. But if I don't look at it within a month after it arrives, Mrs. Briscoe stashes it. And I've been so busy—yes—here it is." He handed the magazine to Inspector Chandler, who quickly put on his reading glasses and peered at the page before him. "22nd May...Command Variety Performance and...*Sterling and Selby*...so forth, so on. Excellent!" He flipped back to the editorial information. "Let's see...they must have an office over here. Yes, indeed. In Marylebone Road." He jotted down the address, tore it from his notebook, and thrust it at the officer standing at the door. "Get on this straightaway. See what you can find out about Rothby and the *New American Review.*"

Shortly afterward, Inspector Chandler pulled out his pocket watch and checked the time. Which forced Geneva to look up at the wall clock across from Tony's desk. Five-thirty. Just then, the sound of a door opening brought Geneva swiftly to her feet. She rushed to the study door. But Tony was ahead of her. "It's Mother, back from Stratford," he said quietly, and kissed her forehead. "I'll speak with her." The sudden soaring of hope, followed so quickly by a crash, made Geneva dizzy. She leaned against Tony for a moment.

When she returned to the sofa and sank down, her knees were trembling so hard they were banging one against the other. Then swiftly she heard Cynthia's desperate, "Oh my God!" and her feelings of helplessness ballooned. She closed her eyes, *Please, God,* then looked at the inspector.

He smiled consolingly, and removed his eyeglasses, squinting. "I can only imagine how difficult this is for you. I wish we could speed things up some-how."

Geneva asked the inspector if he had any children. "Two. A boy, 13 and a girl, 10," he said.

Geneva imagined them, the boy with the gangling body of a young teenager, the girl with eyes like her father's and a bow in her hair, safe at home with their mother as she prepared the evening meal, telling them that their father might be late, for he was on a case, his office had called. For them, it would just be an ordinary day.

She looked out the window. The sunlight was fading like her old *Chimaera* wings, left in the attic and forgotten until Tony's invitation came. Earlier the weather had been fair and warm. Emelye and Elizabeth were wearing matching plaid pinafores and short-sleeved blouses that Tony had bought for them at Selfridge's in Oxford Street—Elizabeth's outfit had long since been taken to Scotland Yard. Emelye had no sweater to ward off the evening chill—over here, the temperature plunged into the forties at night. And she had not eaten since lunch. Imagining her daughter cold and hungry and scared, her hopes dwindling as the hours passed, threatened what little was left of Geneva's composure. How could it be that Scotland Yard, with its vast manpower and resources, put to work less than an hour after Emelye was taken, had not been able to find her?

Now Cynthia came into the room, her face disconcerted, her eyes darting this way and that as if in search of some explanation to the horror confronting them. She sat down beside Geneva and clutched her tightly, then released her and gazed into her eyes. As she opened her mouth to speak, Geneva turned away and put a cautionary hand on her arm. Words of sympathy would prove her undoing. Mrs. Briscoe came to the door with a tea tray. Geneva looked up. Out the corner of her eye, she saw that the globes in the chandelier were now lit, and star light beamed on the illusion of the fairy tale castle.

"Now, Mrs. Selby, listen carefully," Inspector Chandler was saying. "This is how we will proceed from here…." Tony came in and sat down.

CHAPTER 67

Geneva walked out behind the curtain to wait, Tony's kiss still wet upon her cheek, his eyes following her from offstage. The way for her to get through *Chimaera* was to avoid those long-familiar associations which came to mind as the tragic story of the captive butterfly unfolded, the associations which had always helped her to enter into the spirit of the dance but would now lead her down another, terrifying, path.

For the few minutes left her, she fixed her mind on the reality that Tony now owned the *William & Mary*. Twice he had taken her and Cynthia on a tour, eagerly conveying his plans. When she and Emelye returned to England, the ruins of the *William & Mary* would be transformed into as fine a theatre as that which she stood in now. *Yes, think of the two of us, with Elizabeth and Emelye and Cynthia, walking inside on opening night....*

When the spotlight found her in the darkness of the stage, and she heard three foreboding bells—the cue to begin her solo—she envisioned a musician depressing three low keys on a pipe organ while a certain stop was pushed in. When the opening notes of *Vocalise* came tender as a lullaby from the strings of a single violin, she almost gave way. She clenched her teeth and forced her mind away from the innocent butterfly, whose magnificent wings were now slowly opening as the evil collector looked on. She immersed her thoughts in the glorious moments when morning is breaking, with the high pristine melody gently teasing the air; now swaying, now gracefully diving, as light spreads over the sky and the earth beneath, in the promise of a beautiful day:

Had they not given Emelye's abductor every reason to return her? Had they not taken the utmost care to avoid frightening him into some foolish action? According to instructions, a thousand £1 notes had been deposited in Carlisle

Street, on the slim chance that they would be collected. Emelye wandered off this afternoon while playing outside—all of London heard of it during this evening's broadcast on the wireless—and anyone who may have seen her would kindly contact Scotland Yard immediately. A reward was being offered. Though Geneva had helped devise the text, she neither listened to the broadcast, nor inquired as to the amount of the reward Tony was offering. How did one arrive at such a figure? How much would a stranger expect for rescuing a child? Perhaps Scotland Yard had guidelines. She did not want to know.

Emelye's parents, continued the news bulletin, would remain on the all-star bill for tonight's Command Variety Performance at the *Palladium*, with proceeds going to the Variety Artists' Benevolent Fund.

…turning…turning…turning. Tony's hands making a stirrup for her foot, then lifting her on his shoulder, and now in an arabesque, she was turning…turning…then swirling down Tony's body to the floor, falling in love expressed in a series of alluring pirouettes, ending in a swooning backbend over the collector's arm, and up and up, higher and higher, a windmill churning. As the collector with his outsized net romanced the butterfly, the police romanced Emelye's abductor with a London-sized net of trained professionals. Without a single word exchanged, clear signals had been transmitted over the air waves to a man almost certain to be listening: *here is your chance to redeem your mistake.* Of course, the thousand notes inside the brown paper sack were marked by the bank. Plainclothesmen hovered in the shadows of Carlisle Street. Others surrounded the *Palladium:* a bracelet of understated design, with the royal purple carpet for the Sovereign and his family cutting across the Argyll Street side, its single jewel. A clever man would not pick up the notes. He would not bring Emelye to the theatre. But he might bring her within a few blocks, and point her in the right direction, believing he could still make away. And if he were caught, the prospects later in the courtroom might be improved by his cooperativeness. *Along with his gentle treatment of Emelye. "No, he didn't hurt me at all."*

This evening Elizabeth had stolen downstairs alone, and paused outside the study door. Inspector Chandler was with Tony at the bank. Except for an officer stationed inside the front door, Scotland Yard had emptied from the house like an audience emptying from a theatre after singing *God Save the King.* With nothing to do but wait in the unaccustomed silence, Geneva had few resources at hand for occupying her mind, and she fell victim to guilt. "Emelye is being punished for my sins; you know, like it says in the Bible," she confessed to Cynthia, who was sitting with her arm around Geneva's shoulder.

Elizabeth burst into the room, barefoot, in her sleeping gown, her dark hair a wild mass around her head, her eyes puffy. "No! Father Ogilvie says that Christ took all our sins to die with him upon the cross. God would never bring harm to Emelye! He loves all his children!"she cried indignantly.

Perhaps she only repeated the unfathomable words of a kind Priest, not really understanding. But did it matter? This child, as upset as anyone else in the household, had retained a firm grasp on what was becoming increasingly slippery for the adults. How many times today had Geneva wished for the steadying presence of Father Quanset? Regardless of Madame Linsky's crucifix, which, for all of Emelye's life, had hung above her bed like an amulet, drawing her mother's eyes to it every night as she tucked in her beloved child; despite all their church-going of the past six years, and Emelye's perfect attendance pins for Sunday School, neither Geneva nor Emelye had developed such a faith. It was a gift, wonderful and mysterious. Based on innocence, or lack of experience? Geneva asked herself. But no, not with red stripes on your back, from your own mother's hand. If Elizabeth had been kidnapped, she would pray constantly. But would Emelye pray? Would she feel the sense of being uplifted by all the prayers in her behalf? Geneva would have given anything she owned to believe that Emelye was feeling the comfort of being enveloped by prayers. But all she could internalize was Emelye's helplessness, her rising terror as the hours passed: *My mother is not coming.*

When they left for the theatre, Elizabeth was sitting watch at the top of the stairs in her sleeping gown, in case Emelye might return during the show. As they walked out the door, Geneva looked back, a sudden longing for affirmation gripping her. The fanciful chandelier blocked Elizabeth from her view.

But now, knowing she was there made it seem all the more hopeful that somewhere, as the butterfly approached its perilous mid-air flip, and eventual cruel destiny, Emelye was nearing the theatre entrance, having been set free, *free*, and knowing that her mother was inside, waiting for her.

Emelye, can you hear my thoughts, guiding you to me?

She was falling....

Tony's hands broke her descent at the hips and he held her there, steadily, for the required number of beats, just as he had caught and held steady the burden of her mistakes since he arrived home this afternoon to find Inspector Chandler there. Her eyes met his. Their faces were immobile, without their usual registration: *we did it!* Could he imagine the depth of her sorrow for what she had forced him to endure?

Had she opened the wings at the strategic moment after the flip? Had she ever once opened the wings, since the beginning of the dance? She could not remember. Then it was suddenly over, and she could not remember having done the final steps. The bells were tolling one.... *An organ stop. Emelye is free.* Two.... The piece torn from her delicate wing was drifting down.... Three. Time stood still long enough for Geneva to think of the costumier snipping a large triangle of purple china silk, then hemming the edges to prevent it from unraveling. *Just a costume. Emelye is alive and free.* The *Palladium* roared with cheers and applause.

They were bowing, their faces like death masks. Four curtain calls. They dare not look at each other, either during the bows or between.

Are you out there, Emelye?

But she was not.

How utterly superficial, Geneva thought as she stood before the dressing room mirror, buying a new dress for curtsying to the King and Queen after the show. Made of filmy caramel-colored silk chiffon, cut on the bias, it had a simple neckline and short frilled sleeves, a tight bodice from which it shunted down to a snug fit at the hips, then softly flared between the knees and the ankle-length hem. She'd bought silk evening sandals with a golden T-bar and two-inch heels, and over the past week had practiced her curtsy several times in the whole ensemble. Tony liked it especially, so she planned to wear it a few evenings from this one, when they would celebrate the 7th anniversary of their wedding vows in Ambleside, by dining at the Trocadero.

But would they be celebrating?

Of course, they would. *Chimaera* was third on the bill tonight. Considering the maze of London streets, the show may be well past the interval before Emelye found the theatre. But never mind. If she had been released—*Please, God*—she would find her way. Emelye had no shortage of common sense...unless she was too upset to employ it. In any case, a London bobby on the street corner would very likely spot her. Or an adult would offer help. She could tell someone her father's full name, and the street where he lived. She knew the name of the theatre. No matter who she encountered, in all of London, she would be safe, would find her way, Geneva was certain of this.

She ran a comb through her short shingled hair, then laid the comb on the dresser top and sank down on the bench. She felt utterly drained suddenly. Always following a performance, there had been the combined feelings of triumph and relief to replenish the supply of energy exhausted before and during the dance, to keep her going for the rest of the evening. It would have animated her through the Royal introductions tonight. But not now. She had a vague recollection—it seemed years ago—of looking forward to meeting the King and Queen, and seeing the Prince of Wales again. Now she did not believe she could bear the kindness of the King and Queen, or the charming sympathy of the Prince who had kissed her hand at the Trocadero one night, and invited her and Tony to sit in the Royal box. She swiveled around to face Cynthia. "I don't believe I can do this."

"Of course you can," said Cynthia. "It's just part of the performance, remember. And the King and Queen will want to take the opportunity to—to—" at a loss, she waved a hand in the air.

"That's why I don't think I can do it."

Cynthia leaned forward in her chair and took Geneva's hands. "The evening is far from over, so just—"

But her sentence dropped off at the sound of noise in the hall: an uneven shuffling of footsteps, a lot of voices speaking at once. Too many people making too much noise when the show was not yet over. Both women looked toward the door, then at each other, eyes luminous with hope. Geneva freed her hands from Cynthia's. She walked to the dressing room door, and after a moment's hesitation, her hand squeezing the knob, her eyes shutting tightly, *Please, God,* she opened it. Looked out.

A parade was coming down the corridor, including several uniformed officers. And at the center was Inspector Chandler, carrying Emelye in his arms, his jacket draped around her shoulders, dwarfing her. Geneva had the queer sensation that her body had melted into a pool. Her arms were out before she bounded through the door.

CHAPTER 68

Happy as he was to witness Emelye and her mother reaching for each other that night in the backstage hallway of the *Palladium*, and no apparent injuries save the red marks across Emelye's cheeks and around her wrists from being bound and gagged, Inspector Chandler would accept no gratitude. "There are some awfully decent people waiting downstairs—a Mr. and Mrs. Bledsoe, from Spitalfields. You'll want to thank them," he said. "But go ahead, take a few minutes." He gestured for the other officials to clear out of the corridor, and stood at a discreet distance.

The news reached Tony in his dressing room, from which he now emerged with necktie dangling, shirt tail hanging, a desperate look on his face: *I shall believe it when I see her*. And then he did, wrapped around Geneva like a vine around a tree, both of them sobbing. Tears blurring the scene before him, he rushed toward them.

Midst the concert of hugging, kissing, weeping, swooning, and thanking God, that followed in the privacy of her dressing room, Geneva was altering the future: sharing her bed with Emelye at night, accompanying her to and from school in the day, and keeping vigil at the edge of the playground; the doors and windows of their lives locked at all times.

Now Tony was holding Emelye in his arms and looking firmly into her eyes: "Did the man hurt you in any way at all?" It had been Geneva's first question, before Tony arrived. And only when Emelye shook her head—as she did now again as Tony repeated the question—had Geneva allowed herself to be fully thankful for God's grace.

Geneva asked, "Did the man ask you your name?"

"No. All he said was that if I cried out or made a fuss, he would never let me go home. He kept saying that. I did not see how you would find me!" she said, and she began to cry again. Tony held her closely and stroked her hair. "We would never have given up till we found you, never! And it's alright now my sweet, you see, the man is gone and you're safe...."

All the while Geneva prayed that her daughter believed she would be rescued, her abductor was convincing her that she was completely at his mercy. She had never believed the instinct to do violence to another human being beat in her breast. Now she was cutting out the tongue of the verbal terrorist.

When Emelye was composed again she said that they kept going to different parks, and sitting for a while, then walking some more.

"Did you listen to the radio?" Tony asked.

"No," Emelye said. "We were outside."

"Was it dark when the man left you in the truck?"

"No. But it was dark in the truck. There were no windows," she said. So then he had already left her behind when the broadcast came over the wireless, Geneva reasoned.

"He told me not to try to get out, that he would be listening, and wouldn't let me go home, if I did," Emelye said now. "I waited as long as I could before I started kicking at the door, and Mr. and Mrs. Bledsoe heard me."

"Till you thought it was safe to make noise?" Tony prompted her.

"No, I had to go to the bathroom."

Tony's and Geneva's eyes met above the top of Emelye's head. *And what if she had not had to go to the bathroom?*

A few minutes later, leaving Emelye in the safe net of her grandmother's lap, Geneva and Tony went with Inspector Chandler to meet Joe and Stella Bledsoe.

While walking down a street not far from the London Bridge, they heard a noise—"A kickin', kickin', bangin'-round like," said Joe, an exceedingly skinny man with sunken cheeks and round, bulging eyes. They traced the noise to a delivery truck, parked at the curb and locked. Alarmed, they began tracking down the owner. They found him in a nearby pub, where he had been for around three hours. He appeared as surprised as anyone to hear the noise coming from inside his truck.

Mrs. Bledsoe was a stout woman with clear gray eyes, and a wide smile that exposed a mouthful of crooked teeth. She brought a hand to her chest. "Me heart stopped bea-tin' when we saw yer little gell. Face dirty, hair all tangled, eyes wild with fear—I'd never seen the like. Joe untied the scarf and took it out of her mouth. She sobbed, 'I want my momma!' I told her don' worry, dear, we'll find yer mum. I took her in me arms and she clung to me that tight, and kept sobbin', sayin' she wanted her momma; that's all she could tell us, at first. I told Joe, 'Did you hear the way she talks, Joe? I don' think she's English.'"

The story returned Geneva's tears, and Mrs. Bledsoe held her lovingly. "There, there, dear, I know how it is. We 'ave three boys and a baby gell."

Tony asked the couple to come round to Wilton Place in the morning, to pick up the reward. "Naw—why, if it were our lit'tul Jenny, we'd 'ope some'un would do wot we did," said Joe.

"But you see, we need desperately for you to accept it," said Tony, pumping his hand. "Perhaps you could buy something for your children."

It was nearly midnight when the four returned to Wilton Place. Through the door glass, Geneva could see the bright light radiating from the chandelier: *Welcome Home.* She recalled the eternity of waiting in the study, and that moment when she realized the chandelier had been lit because the daylight was quickly dwindling; the feeling of doom. If not for Elizabeth—

The moment she saw them coming through the door, Elizabeth crossed herself in a prayer of thanksgiving. Frightened as she was, had she not been certain in her heart that God would save Emelye? She fled down the spiraling stairs and ran to her, crying, "Sister! Sister!" She smothered Emelye with hugs, kissing her fingers, then dancing around her as if she were paying homage.

Emelye managed a wan smile. A realization hit Geneva with the cruel surprise of a finger sliced by a kitchen knife: *She is a little older, part of the innocence of childhood, destroyed.* She knelt down and hugged Lizzie tightly, then said, "Thank you for making me believe that God was listening."

Tony scooped up Elizabeth and held her close. "I've missed you so much!" he said, his voice thick with emotion.

It could easily have been Elizabeth in that truck, rather than Emelye.

On the second of June, Geneva, Emelye and Cynthia bid farewell to Tony and Elizabeth at the Southampton dockside. The parting was especially hard, as there were so many unanswered questions all around.

Inspector Chandler had stopped by on the night before to report that the exhaustive efforts of Scotland Yard had yielded one ambivalent clue—The *New American Review* folded at the end of March, a victim of the growing economic crisis. An official at the small *WORLD* bureau in London said they began laying off people at the first of the year. The inspector reasoned that if Benjamin was among those laid off, he may be desperate, perhaps embittered—which would establish a motive. The question was, how could he afford a voyage overseas and a bogus passport? Still, the machine on which the note was type-written was not one manufactured in England. There was no evidence that the photograph was reproduced over here. The length of cord used to bind Eme-lye's hands, and the ragged cotton scarf used to gag her, were probably picked up off the street or salvaged from a refuse can. The man left no distinguishable finger prints on any article, including the blackmail note and reproduction.

Apart from the unresolved issues surrounding Emelye's abduction, what of the problem of Jane's vindictiveness?

During a discussion of the subject late last night, Cynthia urged Tony, "As soon as the doctors say that Jane can go home, have Edward bring Elizabeth to New York, and leave her with me until the divorce is final. That way, you'll know she is safe, and you can concentrate on your own safety."

While Geneva welcomed Cynthia's plan for Elizabeth and hoped Tony would agree, her words of caution about Tony's well-being sent a chill up her spine. Before now she had not anticipated that Jane may try to harm him, her mind being fully absorbed with the vulnerability of their children.

Frustrated, Tony wagged his head. "We've got to face down Jane at some point. Sending Elizabeth away will only delay the inevitable. And rest assured, Mother, I can look out for us both."

The ship's whistle sounded. Geneva and Tony embraced like two dear friends rather than two people who were desperately in love, and whose part-ing left the raw edge of knowing they would be prevented from sharing each other's burden. In the presence of the children, there were no plans for a shared future. Jane could easily learn that Geneva had come over to dance with Tony. If so, one day she was bound to probe Elizabeth: *Did Geneva and your father hold hands? Kiss each other? Which room did Geneva sleep in?*

Inspector Chandler had strongly advised engaging a private investigator in the States, who would cooperate with British authorities in finding Emelye's abductor. He returned the threatening note and reproduction to Geneva, hav-ing reproduced them for their records. Tony was to wire the funds to pay an investigator to Geneva's account. But what sort of man made his living by doing the work outside the jurisdiction of the police? Geneva wondered. She imagined opening the door of a seedy little office, and sitting down on a dusty chair in a haze of cigarette smoke; pressing a wad of cash on the sweaty palm of a man who may be no more honest than the person she was trying to find. *It all started with certain...photographs.* She must force out the words, all the while the man undressed her behind his shifty eyes. All the same, bringing

Emelye's kidnapper to justice was what mattered. For this she could countenance anything.

Now Tony said, "Get the best private investigator available, and keep me informed on how things are developing."

"And keep me posted on—on things over here," she entreated.

He nodded, with a troubled sigh.

She could not leave him like this. "And I want progress reports on the *William & Mary*—I'm so excited!"

Tony said gloomily, "There's an overwhelming amount of work ahead, and the timing could not be worse. I wish I'd never got myself into it."

"No! You were its only hope for survival. And it's what you've always wanted. Just think ahead to opening night. We'll all be together."

He smiled *I love you.* He wanted, needed so much, just to hold her, to feel her softness against him and breathe in her scent.

Geneva turned to Emelye. She was unwrapping gift paper from a small article. "I do hope you like it!" said Elizabeth. "It's made of Honiton lace."

Emelye held up an exquisite white cross, around three inches in length and two across. "It's very pretty. Thank you," she said politely, with no sign that she understood the profundity of the gift, or appreciated it, Geneva noticed.

Elizabeth smiled, her face controlled. How many times had this child masked her disappointment when life dealt her less than she deserved? Geneva thought sadly. "It's beautiful," she told Elizabeth, "just like you."

"We need to go, or the ship will sail without us," Emelye said worriedly. She had a vague sense that she was not saying things right. It was like on the day after the man took her, when a little silver basket, filled with white roses, arrived from the King and Queen, and she just stared at the man in the fancy uniform who delivered it. But she could not help herself. She had been terrified since the man took her. At night, though her mother's arms around her would enable her to fall asleep, she would soon tumble into the strange man's arms, and she could hear her voice screaming until her mother awoke her. She hated London as she had never hated anything in her life, and she would never come back, not for anything.

Tony closed his arms around Emelye, then looked into her face. "You are very brave, and I am proud of you. Lizzie and I will miss you *so* much."

"When will you come and see us?" she asked, for she liked her father and her new sister very much, in spite of everything, and wanted to see them again.

Tony glanced at Geneva. "I really don't know, Darling. Perhaps you will come and see us again, before—"

"At my grandfather's house!" Lizzie cut in, desperately. "Emelye does not find London agreeable, Father. She told me so."

Tony glanced at Geneva helplessly. He kissed Emelye and smiled. "I love you," he said. "Take care of your mother."

After Geneva and Cynthia—each gripping one of Emelye's hands—joined the column of passengers boarding the ship, Geneva looked around and waved. In a few quick moments, the light had switched off in Tony's face; the shades were drawn. She knew he had not intended for her to see him this way.

Elizabeth frolicked at her father's feet, throwing kisses at Geneva and Emelye, the sunlight before her casting frolicking shadows behind. It seemed to Geneva that in these gestures were captured the most endearing elements of Elizabeth's personality: movement, vitality, generosity. *God preserve and protect her from her mother,* she prayed. She knew that Tony would stop at nothing to ensure Elizabeth's safety. But she also knew, in spite of all efforts, how miserably one could fail a child.

CHAPTER 69

❀

He arrived on Geneva's porch one sweltering afternoon at the end of July, wearing a pale blue linen suit and a four-in-hand necktie with bright splashes of color; white buckskin shoes and a straw panama hat. She had just about decided to ask for another referral by then, even though the Houston Police Chief—who had worked with him for years before he retired from the force in 1921—said he was the best in the business, worth waiting on while he finished another case.

"Miss Sterlin'? Cap'n Ezekiel Beekman, pleased to meet you," he said through the screen door, pulling a business card from his coat pocket. "I understand you been tryin' to reach me."

Geneva opened the screen door. "Please, come in."

The skin sagged beneath Captain Beekman's eyes, giving him a sleepy look; the skin on his neck hung in loose folds. He was portly, though not overly so. And Geneva noticed when he removed his hat that his hair was gray, with a few lingering traces of black. He followed her into the parlor, apologizing, his voice slow and deliberate. "Sometimes when you are on a case, you wind up takin' a detour. While investigatin' a husband's adultery last spring, I discovered he was much busier operatin' a ring of jewel thieves."

Captain Beekman's southern drawl and easy manner provoked a mental picture of a southern plantation and steamy summer air, intoxicated by the fragrance of blossoms weighing on ancient magnolia trees. Fleetingly Geneva remembered having imagined all private investigators being shifty-eyed characters of questionable motives. She felt a little foolish.

As they sat down in the parlor, she placed the evidence returned from Scotland Yard in his hands. She admitted, "When I was 16 years old, I modeled for some…embarrassing photographs. I was living with the photographer's family at the time…." She went on to tell Captain Beekman briefly of the event that had prompted her to contact him. When she finished, he said thoughtfully, "I got four children and nine grandchildren. The last thing I want is to frighten a youngster unnecessarily. Do you think your daughter is up to talkin' with me?"

Geneva appreciated his sensitivity. On the whole, Emelye seemed much better since their return home, though she still had occasional nightmares. She had been cautioned not to talk to her playmates about what befell her in London, and therefore Geneva's uncustomary vigilance on the playground was puzzling to the neighborhood kids, and sometimes led to cruel remarks aimed at Emelye.

She told Captain Beekman she had prepared Emelye for being questioned. But for the moment, she was at the Youngers', the only neighbors she was allowed to visit without her mother. "She's across the street. I'll get her."

"Never mind. For now, s'pose we see how far you and I can git?"

Like Inspector Chandler, Captain Beekman made pencil jottings in a notebook. His handwriting was a rapacious series of bold strokes across the page, its capital letters exaggerated in height. Geneva could hardly imagine anyone who talked as slowly as he did, writing as rapidly. After she had told him everything she could think of that was relevant to the case, including Inspector Chandler's reservations about assuming Benjamin's guilt, he raised his eyes beyond her shoulder, his gaze lining up with the spreading trees and flower market of her parents' beloved oil painting. "Alright. Let's assume Rothby figured he would deflect suspicion from himself if he blackmailed you in England 'stead of over here…. There you were, about to perform before the King and Queen in just a few hours. You'd pay in order to prevent a scandal. He was careful about fingerprints, just in case the plan backfired, and he may have reasoned it would be safer to have that picture reproduced and typewrite that note over here in order not to leave a trail of evidence in England. That works as far as it goes."

He looked at her now. "But then last time Rothby saw you, you were a dancin' teacher, livin' alone in Houston. How did he expect you to come up with a thousand pounds sterlin'?"

"He was counting on Tony coming up with the money," she said.

"Alright. But how would Rothby know he could count on Tony?"

It was a question that had never occurred to Geneva. After searching her memory, she said, "I may have told Victor that Tony was well-to-do at some point, and Ida Ruekauer knew for sure."

"Who's Ida Ruekauer?"

Geneva let out a breath. "Long story," she said. Notwithstanding the breeze of the whirring ceiling fan, by now Captain Beekman's brow was dotted with perspiration. The under-arms of his coat were a darker shade of blue. And Geneva could use a little cooling off, too. "Why don't you take off your coat," she suggested, "and I'll pour us some iced tea."

Later as they sipped their tea she told him Ida Ruekauer was Victor's sister—Benjamin's aunt by marriage—and explained that Ida also served as her guardian for some years. "Benjamin and Ida met up at Victor's funeral."

"Alright, good! I'll make a note to interview her," he said.

"Unfortunately, that won't be possible," she said, and told him the circumstances of Ida's disappearance. Then, out of deference to Tony, she qualified this: "Unlike the Houston Police, Tony doesn't believe Ida is really dead." So then she explained about the stolen messages, thinking that, until this very moment, she had never realized how complicated her life was.

Thoughtfully, Captain Beekman drummed his fingers on the table a few times. "I hope I haven't completely confused you," she apologized. "I really wanted to keep this as simple as possible."

Captain Beekman looked up. "It's been my experience that few things in life are simple. Everything we say or do has a bearin' on someone, or somethin', else. And it just keeps goin', like ripples in a pond." He smiled. "That, by the way, is what makes my job so interestin'. And makes my wife complain that I'm away from home too much."

I like this man, Geneva thought suddenly, returning his smile.

"Now. Did Mrs. Ruekauer know about your pictures?"

"Not that I'm aware of. Of course, she may have overheard me talking about them with my neighbor Willa. Ida did her share of eavesdropping."

Captain Beekman raised an eyebrow. "Any idea how Mrs. Ruekauer was doin', money-wise?"

"I think Ida got by alright as a nurse, but her late husband had squandered her life savings, and she was worried about dying in poverty."

Captain Beekman jotted down a note. "Alright. Can you think of anyone else that might have been involved with Rothby?"

Geneva thought about this. "He has two sisters, Kathy and Virginia Calais. They live up in Springfield, Massachusetts, as far as I know. But I don't know what their married names are, or even if they are married." She frowned. "Somehow I doubt they'd help Benjamin, because they don't get along with him very well. I remember Ida telling me that they squabbled about who should get Victor's things, when they were all down in Florida for his funeral."

Captain Beekman narrowed his eyes at her for a moment, then said, "But then you know what they say about blood bein' thicker."

Geneva realized he may be right about that. And if all three had concluded that she had an affair with their father, they surely regarded her as a common enemy. Since the day Emelye was abducted, Benjamin's words when he came to see Victor's studio and found it ruined had often come back to haunt her: *"The exterior won't give a clue as to what went on in there...."* She wondered if Captain Beekman had figured out she had an affair with Victor. If not, should she tell him? But no. He seemed to feel Benjamin's motive was established, whatever he had figured out about her and Victor.

When Captain Beekman finally closed his notebook, he said, "If I took the case, I'd begin by fillin' in the blanks about Rothby. Has he ever been in trouble with the law? How did he pay for that trip to England? Sold his stepdaddy's cameras? Hocked 'em? I'd start in New York City, and maybe go on up to Springfield, Massachusetts where his sisters live, dependin'."

Geneva told him she'd like him to take the case and asked about his fee.

"Twenty a day, plus travel expenses. I'll need an advance—say, a hundred dollars. And by the way, would you happen to have a picture of Rothby? Even an old one?"

"Unfortunately not," Geneva said.

She went to the secretary and withdrew her check book from the drawer. Tony had already wired £200 to her account. At this rate, she would soon be asking for more. Her income from the dancing school year barely stretched through the summer.

She was handing over the check. "Do you have any idea how long—?"

Captain Beekman looked at her with sleepy-eyed sagacity. "I understand how you feel, and I wish I knew. We got lots'a loose ends to tie up, though, and no tellin' where Rothby is by now." He slipped the evidence back into the envelope from Inspector Chandler and put it in his coat pocket.

Geneva thought mournfully of all the time wasted while she waited on Captain Beekman to finish his previous case. And he had admitted taking a detour on that one. She wished she had not told him about the possibility Ida was alive. What if he got busy looking for her, while Benjamin's trail grew even colder? And what if, after all that, Benjamin turned out to be innocent, and the real culprit was still out there?

Feeling a strong desire to hold her daughter in her arms, she hurried across the street to bring Emelye home.

CHAPTER 70

White is the color. Yes, definitely, white, Jane thought while climbing the stairs that late November day, when the house was all done. Four hours of grisly work; she had scarcely ever exerted that much, her rooms the only ones left untouched. White: the color of faces drained of blood, of burial dresses, and crosses above.

The color of piano keys prized from the board and candle wax drizzled in the cavities. And inside black lace-up dancing shoes as well. *You never danced with me.* White. The color of legal documents brought to the door, signed in her hand with disappearing ink.

White. The color of mummy's high stiff collar and hat, the day she fled. *"You're better off, Jane darling, he'll take good care of you,"* she said. And he did. White. The color of sleeping gowns and beds. At last, the veil pierced through: years and years of promising the Brighton holiday, the unlocked door between high adjoining rooms. And down below the Grand Hotel, breakers churning and smacking white against the shore in violent kisses. White was the color of the door she watched, waiting for the latch to move. Open, shut. Coming in. White. The color of legs, parted by sin. The color of teeth sunk in shoulder skin. A mere formality by then, the map of her body fully explored, summits claimed; valleys bored. But just a little pain—one must pay for the Brookhurst wood. Open, shut. Open, shut. Coming in. Coming in. *"He'll take good care of you."* And he did. For years. White. The color of bone behind his skin when she had had enough.

White cashmere wool for an afternoon spin in the white Mercedes, Jane thought then, with ten pearl buttons and long dolman sleeves, courtesy of Marshall & Snelgrove. The tag was yet affixed when she snatched it from its place, thinking ahead to white kid gloves, shoes and purse; a small white cloche to hug hot-ironed finger waves.

When she stood before the mirror, her dressing done, she formed a thin red outline round her lips and filled it in. *I shall be beautiful in death.* She drew close to the mirror and kissed her corpse.

Pulling on her gloves, she thought once more of white: the color of bridal flowers—lilies, peonies, chrysanthemums. Let him have Geneva as a consolation. And the little girl—the bastard child—what was her name?

Yes, her also, for I am taking the prize he thought he'd won.

Queen's Gate—such an easy mark. *Mummy is taking you to Brookhurst, to visit Grandfather, so do hurry! Mummy can hardly wait!* White: the color flashing through dense skeletons of forest trees, above winding roads and steep embankments. *I know just the place.*

The moment Tony tried his key in the door was the darkest yet. Jane was certainly within her rights to have the lock changed, with him and Lizzie two weeks' gone to a furnished flat in Great Russell Street, and the divorce petition served. And yet it was only yesterday he met a man here to have a look at the boiler, while Jane was at the hairdresser. His key worked then. Nor were all the window draperies shut, as they were now. If not for this he might have held on to the slender hope that spiriting Lizzie away from Queen's Gate was simply a ruse to demonstrate how easily his instructions to the school were defied: under no circumstances was Lizzie to leave the school with anyone except himself. He might have hoped that at this very moment, Lizzie was safe, and Jane was gloating about how she walked into the front office where no one had ever laid eyes on her, gave a false name, asked to see Lizzie's teacher on a fictional matter, and while Miss Freeland was being summoned to the office, enquired as to the location of the ladies' room; then disappeared.

When the headmistress called in a state of great alarm to report that his daughter was missing, Tony instructed Mrs. Briscoe to notify Inspector Chandler and ask that he meet him at the school, then hastened there.

Vainly he peered through the door glass of No. 3 Wilton Place now. He could not see beyond the vestibule. He rang the doorbell again and again, demanding that Jane open up. "Where does your wife keep her automobile?" the inspector asked quietly.

Soon after her release from Ticehurst, her doctor strongly advising that she continue therapy at home, Jane had gone on a shopping spree that included all manner of clothing, jewelry and accessories for herself, and new dresses, hats and shoes for Lizzie—whom she treated with uncustomary attentiveness until he and Lizzie moved out. And she purchased a fabulous white Mercedes sports car, long-nosed and narrow, with a convertible top and bright silver wire wheels. She was not supposed to be driving as yet, for she was taking some strong medication to calm her nerves.

Tony told Inspector Chandler where the garage was located. A sergeant was dispatched to question the attendant. "Let's try the windows," the inspector suggested then.

And in the end it was quite easy, for a basement window round at the back was slightly cracked, and they opened it all the way and climbed through.

All was quiet in the kitchen and scullery, everything clean and in tip-top shape, as it was yesterday. No one was about. They climbed the stairs and walked down the narrow servants' passageway leading to the main rooms.

When they opened the door at the rear of the entrance hall, the sight that greeted them brought to Tony's mind the assessment of Jane's doctor: *"There is an awful lot of anger pent up inside your wife, Mr. Selby. 'Calcified' might be the word that best describes it."*

The entrance hall floor was strewn with shattered glass, the priceless Waterford crystal chandelier above having been battered so violently that there was no crystal left on it at all. All its branches were contorted, and even its main column was bent like an elbow—one could hardly imagine the strength Jane employed, using God only knew what sort of instrument. Wires dangled this way and that, like octopus legs. Neither Tony nor the inspector could force any words through their sense of shock. They took crunching steps across the floor and looked fearfully up the spiral stairway. The wooden balustrade had received a succession of swipes, as though Jane had taken an ax, begun at the bottom of the stairway and worked her way up to the landing. There were burnt places in the carpet runner—likely from cigarettes—and zigzags of candle wax all over.

Tony started up the stairs, but the thought of Lizzie lying behind a door somewhere up there, seriously injured or murdered, cut off his breath. He swayed on his feet. Inspector Chandler was behind him. "I say, allow me to check upstairs, see if anyone's up there," he said with quiet foreboding.

Tony turned to look into the inspector's dark eyes, and blinked. Presently he nodded, found his voice. "Yes, I'll finish the downstairs."

Gingerly Tony opened the door to his study, terrified. But no one was in there, which gave him a moment's relief. Like the entrance hall, the room had met with destruction, with souvenir playbills, photographs and other memorabilia torn from the walls, their frames smashed. The upholstery had been slashed, and burned in places. The wood of his empty desktop was battered and deeply scarred; the green glass dome of his study lamp was shattered, its pieces strewn over the desktop, its slender brass base lying horizontally as if it may have been put to use as a weapon. The glass fronts of cupboards were shattered. Books and magazines and sheet music were heaped from their shelves and torn to ribbons; like the stairway, the piano had been hacked, numerous keys torn out, and white candle wax dribbled like a sugar glaze over a cake. Tony owned a pair of dancing shoes which he had long since put away in a cupboard because they had not proved a comfortable fit; he'd hoped to break them in one day, for they were frightfully expensive. They were sitting on the piano bench now—to capture his attention, perhaps? The leather had been slashed, the insoles torn out, and candle wax drizzled inside.

He looked quickly into the dining room and living room. Both were equally ransacked. No one was there.

When the inspector came out on the landing at the top of the stairs, Tony was waiting at the bottom, his heart pounding in fear. Lizzie was murdered, lying face down on the bed—

"No one up there," said the inspector.

Tony could only nod and sigh, his mouth too dry to speak. The inspector started down the stairs. "Find any clues?"

"Nothing. Just more destruction."

"Pretty much a mess up there too, except for the rooms which, I gather, belong to your wife. There is a crow bar, a hatchet, a broom, and a couple of kitchen knives lined up on the pillows of her bed, as though sleeping there. And also—equally bizarre—a red lip print in the center of the dresser mirror."

He reached the bottom of the stairs. "Oh yes, and this beside Mrs. Selby's bed—" he lifted a box of prescriptive tablets from his pocket. "None missing, according to the label."

"Medicine for her nerves," said Tony. "Should have been several days' worth missing."

He felt weak all over. He made for a gilt chair, one of two placed on either side of a table beneath a huge gilt-framed mirror. Like the chandelier, the mirror had been pulverized. He brushed shards of mirror and crystal from the seat, and sank down, then noticed blood was oozing from his fingers.

He had moved all of Lizzie's things to Great Russell Street. Rooms were small there, and many of his own things he was forced to leave behind. But he wanted her surroundings to be as familiar as possible. How thankful he was for that bit of foresight: he would never have to explain what had happened to all her things. She need never know of any of this. Yet, where in God's name, had Jane taken her? It was a repeat of the nightmare, waiting for Emelye to be found, only no one, not even Benjamin, could match Jane's propensity for violence.

The sergeant walked in. The attendant at the garage had reported that Mrs. Selby stopped by for her car an hour ago, alone, and said she was leaving town, taking a drive to York, and not to expect her back tonight.

The inspector squinted at Tony. "York?"

"I should not trust that if I were you."

Inspector Chandler looked at the sergeant. "All roads leading out of London, straightaway. They are half an hour at least, gone from Queen's Gate."

CHAPTER 71

On the Wednesday night before Thanksgiving, Cynthia went to bed feeling especially blue—nowadays sadness often took hold of her with a tenacious grip. Light snow was falling outside, and she switched off the bedside lamp and lay on the pillows, gazing at the frosty window through which, of course, she could see nothing except for a vaporous brightening in one corner, from the street light. Cynthia was living her life behind a frosty window, it seemed, with no clear idea of what was on the other side.

She ought to have accepted Geneva's invitation to spend the holiday in Houston. By tradition, Geneva and Emelye dined with the Youngers and their relatives, with their good friend Father Quanset rounding out the party. Geneva made the pumpkin pies for dessert each year. What fun it would have been, what a welcome diversion! It was the Thanksgiving Day tradition that Cynthia missed most of all, while living in England. And even all those years in Houston, she never made much over it because she had no family nearby. When Tony came—well, he didn't *get* it, being British, so it was no fun at all. But here in Manhattan, a houseful of friends—old and new—came every year. She could seat 30 at her table, with all the leaves added. Two roasted turkeys, a ham and a rib of beef were standard fare. Crystal goblets bubbled with champagne; romantic candlelight lit up the faces reflected in the mirrors. It was like a painting by Jean Béraud, come to life.

But for two Thanksgivings now, there had been nothing to celebrate, and very little romance in Manhattan. Many of her friends had moved away and fallen out of touch; others had simply fallen out of touch. In any case, she could no longer afford to serve such a lavish meal, nor did she have the help required. She employed one housemaid now, who came on Fridays to clean those few rooms still in use. Most of the house was sealed off like a tomb, with dust-covered furnishings rising from the floor like mummies. She often wondered what possessed her to buy such a huge house when she moved here. But, she had the money then, and was anxious to entertain as a way to keep busy and amused, and thereby avoid dwelling on the fact that Tony was married to a monster while Geneva secretly raised his child.

Over the years she filled the closets and cupboards of this house—how had she managed to acquire so much? In the past few months, she'd sold a few selected items—her original Maxfield Parrish for instance, though she loathed parting with it. Yet the sales gave her a sense of triumph that she had not experienced since the days when she would shrewdly close a deal with a vaudeville producer. Looking ahead to her move to a smaller place, she thought perhaps she'd own a little gallery someday, when times were better and people could afford to buy luxury items. She found just the thing in Greenwich Village: a sunny studio apartment above a small park. It had belonged to an artist who—sadly—died young and without recognition. Life there would be stimulating, with lots of interesting people around. The problem was finding a buyer for this house. How disappointing to arrive home from England in June, and learn that the realtor had not shown the house to a single prospective buyer. Since then only two had come, both backing off in favor of a smaller place with a lower price. Cynthia could go down only so far, with a mortgage to pay off.

Now she spent a lot of time separating things she intended to keep from those she must part with—perhaps the beginning inventory for her gallery? Yet storage costs in the meantime may well eat up all the profit. She had already filled several crates; in fact she was thus occupied when Geneva wrote to invite her for Thanksgiving, so it seemed the better part of wisdom to conserve the train fare—after all, with every day she lived here, her assets were dripping steadily away, like water from a leaky faucet—and go on preparing for the move that was out there waiting somewhere, sometime, on the other side of the frosty window.

By ten o'clock, she was sound asleep. And then the doorbell woke her, and soon she was standing inside the frigid front hall, wrapped in her robe and slippers, the telegram in her hand, her eyes consuming blocks of words: Jane and Elizabeth...auto crash in Dartmoor Forest. Jane killed instantly. Elizabeth hospitalized in Exeter, critical condition. Need you here desperately. Edward.

Cynthia flew up the stairs to her room and threw on the lights. She rushed to the telephone by the bed, lifting the receiver with quaking hands. "Operator, Western Union, please." After sending a cable to Edward that she was on her way, she asked for long distance, Houston. Geneva's telephone rang and rang and rang. Where was she, for pity's sake? Then she glanced at the clock and noticed it was 3:30 in the morning. When Geneva finally answered, with a sleepy voice, all Cynthia could blurt out was, "Elizabeth—!" She burst into sobs.

Geneva spent what was left of the night lying awake in bed, numb with dread, the road through Dartmoor Forest a nightmare zigzagging through her head. Grateful that Emelye had not yet asked to go back to sleeping in her own room, she held her sleeping daughter pressed against her breast as though she were a life buoy. She would not, *would not* accept that the God she'd come to believe in, the God who delivered Emelye safely from her womb, and later from Benjamin's clutches, would slap them all in the face now; would set the price of freedom from Jane as high as the life of Elizabeth. *Please, God....*

Early on Thanksgiving Day Geneva took Emelye and the pumpkin pies over to Willa's, then drove to Christ Church, to kneel in the pew and pray for Elizabeth's full recovery with the same focused determination she'd had when she drove herself to St. Joseph's Infirmary on that frosty night of Emelye's birth. At some point she felt Father Quanset's meaty hand on her shoulder and looked up into his solemn face. "What's happened?" he asked.

Struggling to maintain composure, she told him what little she knew, and that Tony had once driven her along that scenic but treacherous road where the auto crash took place, but what Jane was doing on it, with Elizabeth in the car, she would scarcely dare to imagine.

Father Quanset nodded in sympathy. "Someone needs to pray for the soul of the mad woman," he said humbly.

Geneva's stomach contracted into a hard fist. "I can't," she said in a leaden voice.

"It's alright. I will," he said, and knelt down beside her.

CHAPTER 72

For many weeks afterward, Tony lived in a daze. Always work had been his salvation, and yet he could scarcely concentrate for the memories that would explode in his mind. He found it almost impossible to make even a simple decision about the redesign of the *William & Mary,* and often left the architect at an impasse. He was fortunate to have composed all the new dances for *Pip & Pocket* while Jane was in Ticehurst, for he was forced to virtually turn the production over to Kenneth and his co-director. He would walk for hours at a time, and finally stop, look about, and wonder how he had got to the place where he was. He bought cigarettes for the first time in years, and at nights he would go home and pour a whisky. Then he would pour another....

Later he would go to bed, then lie there smoking, events playing out in his mind sequentially, unhindered by the interruptions of the day. The white Mercedes was speeding over the twisting, turning road through Dartmoor Forest. Now the auto was approaching the hairpin curve; now, with a sharp downward turn to the right on the steering wheel—Elizabeth had said little of the event, but confirmed this action on her mother's part—the car was pitching over the side and diving down, Jane and Elizabeth flung through the air like rag dolls. Now the auto was bursting into flames, Jane pinned beneath one of the silver wire wheels and burning with it.

More than four hours after Jane appeared at Queen's Gate School to spirit Elizabeth away, a woman's dire telephone voice: *Your daughter is here in St. Martha's Hospital, Exeter. She has a brain concussion and a number of broken bones. But it's the loss of blood from a gash in the forehead that concerns us most, for now. They're giving her blood transfusions....* Four hours. Given the drive between London and the place of the crash, that translated into at least an hour before Lizzie was found: whatever part of her consciousness was still functioning, must have been whispering that she was going to die, alone, that no one cared....

Now Tony was rushing down the hospital corridor; now opening the door to the room where Elizabeth lay with her eyes closed, her face whiter than the bandages in which she was wrapped. *"I'm afraid there isn't much hope, Mr. Selby...."* Now he was kneeling down beside her bed to weep and to pray and to pound his fists in anger.

Miraculously, Lizzie pulled through, and most of her injuries would heal, including a hairline fracture in her shoulder and several broken ribs. But one of her legs was fractured in three places. A surgeon was able to put it back together with screws and pins. The best they could hope for was that she would gradually be able to get about in a wheel chair, then on crutches, and eventually be able to walk without aid, he said. But the injured leg would not develop at the same rate as her good leg, so she would always have a limp—severe at first, perhaps improving some over time, but never completely going away. Nor would the surgical scar on the back side of her calf completely disappear. At nights Tony thought of coming in on the conclusion of Lizzie's ballet lessons, seeing her talents blossom a little more each time, the fluidity of her movements riveting his attention, reminding him of Geneva. He thought of his joy of teaching Lizzie to tap dance, in his study at Wilton Place. He thought of her riding lessons; she would have begun hurdle jumping after the first of the year. All of these activities which she had loved so well, and at which she strived so hard for excellence, would be a part of her life no more.

Most of all, he thought of her bursting through theatre doors, fresh from a day at school, rushing down the aisle, up on the stage and into his arms.

Six weeks in hospital, then she was released and sent to convalesce at Brookhurst, where his mother promised to remain for as long as she was needed. Tony was especially glad for this, because Lizzie's spirits were so very low. His mother was always good at bolstering people. His father's presence was also vital to her recovery. He sat with her and talked, or read her stories, while Angus and Kenegy luxuriated at the foot of the bed. Auntie Nell brought kettles of soup and homemade breads—among her specialties. Father Ogilvie came down from London every other week and visited for hours. Schoolmates from Queen's Gate and friends from Lizzie's other activities, and admiring adults from the theatre, sent cards and presents and boxes of chocolates. Emelye and the Younger children drew pictures galore to hang on the walls—once a week an envelope arrived containing new ones, plus a loving letter from Geneva.

Tony went down at weekends, always with a gift or two, hoping he would see a difference in the way Lizzie looked at him. For the light in her eyes that used to be there, just for him, was gone. That she did not seem pleased to see him broke his heart. She accepted his hugs and kisses, and if he said *I love you,* she would say it back. Now and then he would find her gazing at him, trance-like. "What is it? Something wrong?" he would ask. And her thoughts would have been so far away, it would be as if she had awakened suddenly, and was surprised to find him there. "Nothing," she would say. He would try all week-end to get through to her, encourage her to talk to him freely, as she used to do. But she excluded him from her thoughts and feelings. He would return to London on Sunday, aching with regret. It would take him all week to get over it, whence he would return to Brookhurst once again, with a smile on his face and a feeling of renewed hope.

She blamed him, of course, he thought at nights with his cigarette and whisky, and well he deserved it. For all her life, Lizzie had placed her trust in him. Then at the most significant point, he failed her by underestimating her mother's craftiness. Perhaps someday Lizzie would forgive him. He would never forgive himself.

CHAPTER 73

During the Christmas holidays Captain Beekman called on Geneva to update her on what he had learned so far: Benjamin had vanished from New York City leaving behind no criminal record, no outstanding debts, no evidence he had sold or pawned Victor's cameras, and no forwarding address. Her photograph was reproduced from a magazine page, so it was possible Benjamin availed himself of the printing facility at the now defunct *New American Review*. The typewriter used to typewrite the note was a Remington 1921 model, and the paper was common foolscap. Benjamin had never applied for a reference from *WORLD* Publications, and—as far as Captain Beekman could ascertain—he had not held a job since January 31st, when he was laid off. So either the person who paid for his trip to England, including the provision of a fake passport, was continuing to pay his living expenses, or Benjamin was getting along by free-lancing, which was more likely, and would enable him to move from place to place—which he'd be wise to do.

Victor's training Benjamin in photography had served him very well, Geneva thought with irony. And he still had her pictures, though by now he probably wished he had never laid eyes on them. She did not honestly believe that Emelye was in any further danger from Benjamin—whatever his designs, he surely would not dare to come near the place where they lived and chance being recognized. Yet at the same time, Benjamin's guilt had not been proved, so until the case was solved she would continue her careful vigilance. And in truth, she doubted she would ever again feel completely at ease when Emelye was out of her sight. Often she woke up at night remembering how naively she gave permission for Emelye and Elizabeth to play outside on that fine London day that turned into a nightmare. Which inevitably brought her to reflect on

Tony's naivete in thinking that he really could protect poor Elizabeth from someone as experienced at deception as Jane.

Captain Beekman had proceeded from New York to Springfield, where, posing as a collections agent for a mail order camera company, he called on Mrs. Kathy Maze, wife of Pastor Luke Maze of Light of the World Church, and inquired as to the whereabouts of her indebted brother. Her sister Miss Virginia Calais, the church's music director, resided in the parsonage as well, and was present during the interview. Kathy dominated the conversation, he remarked—which came as no surprise to Geneva—and her voice grew soft and tremulous as she claimed that neither she nor her sister had any idea where Benjamin was to be found, and they had no intention of being responsible for their brother's debts.

Though certainly there was a good possibility that Benjamin's sisters were helping him out, or at least covering for him, Captain Beekman found no sign that he had been in Springfield lately. He asked Geneva to search her memory for the name of any other party on this side of the Atlantic who might be aware of her pictures, and aware that Tony Selby had money to buy them. Perhaps, though not necessarily, someone who knew Benjamin.

Try as she might, apart from her friends the Youngers and Tony's mother Cynthia, Geneva could think of no one at all. Finally she said doubtfully, "John Scarborough must have gathered the Selbys were reasonably well off, but I feel certain he didn't know about those pictures."

"Who's John Scarborough?"

One cold, raw morning in January, Geneva crouched on her knees in the attic, searching through boxes while Captain Beekman sat by the cosy parlor fire, sipping hot cocoa and reading the terms of her trust, a copy of which was in the envelope Tony's lawyers had returned in 1923 when there was no need for the marriage contract they had been assigned to draw up. Captain Beekman was anxious to review her annual statements also, and while she had felt sure they were all in the envelope, those for 1917, 1918 and 1920 were missing. At a loss, upstairs to the attic she went, having little hope they'd be up there, and embarrassed that she could not locate three pieces of paper in her very own house after all the miles Captain Beekman had traveled to discover things so well hidden they might never have been revealed but for his imaginative persistence. As she searched, she was still mulling over those two snapshots he'd brought for her to see this morning, slipping them one at a time from his pocket:

Captain Beekman had stopped by Houston Bank & Trust Co. and asked for a forwarding address for John Scarborough. The bank provided him a post office box number in Joplin, Missouri. Captain Beekman proceeded to Joplin, where he discovered the former banker living with a twin brother in a big house, with a picket fence and shade trees. This when Geneva had said he had no living relatives that she knew of. Without revealing himself, Captain Beekman took a snapshot of the two brothers, sitting in a porch swing. John Scarborough looked strange to Geneva, wearing a baggy sweater, his shirt open at the neck. And without the stiff clothing she remembered, he looked less threatening too. Fred Scarborough was a heavyset version of his brother: baldheaded, with dim facial features; yet looking out with a sweet, vacuous expression. As she went on studying the picture, Captain Beekman said that John Scarborough had owned that house for 15 years, and until he retired, he employed a caretaker to live with his twin. Fred was mentally retarded, he said. Geneva could not help thinking there were ways John Scarborough was retarded, his nature lacking all compassion and kindness. Yet, obviously when it came to his brother—

"All this on a banker's sal'ry?" said Captain Beekman. "But look here—" He laid the other photograph face-up on the table: a large buxom woman, pausing to open the front gate. She was clothed in a dark dress, her hat brim casting a shadow over her face; yet her squarish jaw looked familiar, as did her build. "Miz John Scarborough, since August of 1924." Their eyes met above the picture. Geneva felt she had been socked in the chest.

That was when Captain Beekman asked, "Do you by any chance have a copy of your trust agreement handy?"

Eventually Geneva gave up her attic search and went downstairs. "I may not have sent all the statements over to England after all," she apologized, "I was in a rush, and the one they really needed was the most recent, from 1922."

Obviously vexed, Captain Beekman lined up the available statements and studied them far more carefully than she had ever done. Finally he asked, "What's this 'miscellaneous asset, valued at one dollar'? It appears up through 1916—not always in the same place. But it's gone by 1919. Course those missin' statements might explain. Which is probably what Tony's lawyers thought, and the reason they didn't make a note of it anywhere."

"I'm afraid I don't know," she said limply. "It's just a dollar."

"'Zactly my point. Easy to slip by someone who's not lookin' carefully."

Like me, Geneva thought guiltily. "What do you suppose it could be?"

"Could be nothin' more than a cheap piece of costume jewelry. On the other hand, it could be a stock certificate, a bond, anything."

"But the bank examiners would have noticed."

"Only if the statements Scarborough provided them matched those he made up for you. You see, he could have slipped this 'miscellaneous asset' into a file one day, nobody the wiser," Captain Beekman said.

For a few moments Geneva sat quietly, trying to take all this in. The idea that John Scarborough was leading a double life, supported by stolen assets from her account, was almost impossible to believe. And that Ida, the biggest man-hater in the world, was conspiring with him—But then Captain Beekman went on to say, "Frankly, accordin' to this, there's not enough in your parents' estate to justify stealin' from it. So if Scarborough's wife is who we think she is, what's goin' on? I found nothin' to suggest they were involved with Rothby."

"Should I tell the Police that we think we've found Ida Ruekauer?" Geneva asked.

Slowly Captain Beekman considered this. "What was the name of the investigator who came to question you after she disappeared?"

Geneva thought back. "Dickins. No, Dickinson. Sergeant, I think."

He shook his head doubtfully. "Can you describe him?"

"He was tall and blonde. A young man, but his hair was thin on top, like peach fuzz."

Captain Beekman's expression cleared. "Pete Dickerson, I bet."

"Dickerson—that's it!"

"I was there when he came on the force. Too big for his britches, if you'll pardon the expression. I wouldn't git in touch with Pete just yet. If there's anything goin' on here, he's not gonna look good for havin' dropped that missin' person case sooner than he should. And I think he's up for a promotion.

"Try to git a look at the bank's copy of those statements. But, be careful. Even though Scarborough's retired, he may still have friends at the bank."

Friends? Doubtless, everyone at the bank was glad to see him go. Not like Mr. Hunnicutt, for whom the bank threw a big party, that she and her parents—"Wait! My original trust officer—the one who drew up the trust and signed it—he might know what that asset is."

"I doubt he'd remember from all the way back in nineteen-and-two."

"But Mr. Hunnicutt and his wife were close friends of my parents."

Captain Beekman raised an eyebrow. "Oh, I see." He rubbed his chin. "They still in Houston?"

"No, they moved to San Antonio," she said. "I have an address and tele-phone number...but I'm afraid I fell out of touch with them, after my parents died," she said. She did not tell him of her shame.

"Try and reach 'em. Dependin' on how it goes, contact Dickerson."

Later when the long distance operator told Geneva that the number she gave was no longer in service, she knew it was just what she deserved. There was no telling where the Hunnicutts were by now, or even if they were alive. She had a vague memory of the Christmas and birthday cards that eventually stopped arriving.

Luckily, the operator found another listing, however, and soon Walter Hun-nicutt was on the line, his voice enthusiastic, though a little unsteady. "Well of course I remember you, Geneva! What a surprise!" he said.

"And how is Mrs. Hunnicutt?"

"Oh you know, my Mary's been dead over two years now," he said sadly.

Mary was tucking a blanket around her as she lay on the sofa, trembling with shock at the news of her parents' death. And no sign of Geneva at Mary's funeral, or even the courtesy of a sympathy note. She had disgraced herself. She could only say, helplessly, "I'm so sorry to hear that."

Hard to believe she had intended to question Mr. Hunnicutt via long dis-tance. She owed him a personal visit, at the least. "I need your help with some-thing...and I have a daughter—she'll be seven years old in two weeks. I'd like to bring her to meet you," she said.

"Well, say!" Geneva could almost see his face light up through the receiver. It brought a lump to her throat. "I'm always home—210 Washington Street. A few blocks from downtown," he said.

"Yes, on the river. I remember," she said. She'd spent Christmas there shortly after her parents were killed, immersed in the good will of the Hunni-cutts and their family. "How about this Saturday?"

"Fine, fine! Have you got a pencil handy? I'll give you directions...."

CHAPTER 74

Geneva parked at the curb of 210 Washington Street around one o'clock, and sat behind the wheel looking up at the house. Along the journey, Emelye had asked her what the house looked like. Now she was satisfied her description was reasonably accurate, though the house and yard surrounding it were a little smaller than she remembered. The dwelling was two-story, wood frame, raised up high and reached by a set of tall stairs, beneath which was a small stone terrace. It sat far back in the shadows of moss-hung trees—cypress, magnolia and oak. As they got out of the car, Geneva recalled the dampness of the air above the river. Cold and penetrating in winter....

Walter Hunnicutt greeted Geneva with a hug and a wet kiss on the cheek, as if they'd seen each other but yesterday. He smelled of spicy after shave lotion and talcum powder. He gave Emelye a courtly bow and took her arm in his as he led them up the stairs and inside. He was more slight in build than Geneva remembered, and he was now white-haired, with fluffy white eyebrows. His complexion was wrinkled and leathery—he confessed he stayed busy with a little vegetable garden most of the year, and still did all his own yard work. He led them all the way back to the kitchen, noting he didn't use the other downstairs rooms very much, not since Mary died. Geneva remembered that the kitchen was filled with delicious aromas of holiday food that Christmas, and the air rippled with the good-natured chit-chat and laughter of women as they prepared the holiday feast. She remembered that she was so heartbroken over her parents, she could hardly eat a bite when they finally sat down at the big dining room table.

Now, bereft of a woman's touch, the kitchen seemed kind of sad. The counters and stove were neat and tidy. A radio sat in one corner: a lonely widower's substitute for conversation over morning coffee. The air was filled with the scent of ripening bananas in a bowl on top of the refrigerator.

Walter Hunnicutt poured a glass of milk for Emelye and arranged Sunshine biscuits on a plate, while patiently answering questions. "Are you very old?" "Eighty-two, that's pretty old!" "Do you know my daddy?" "No, but I'd sure like to meet him." "He lives in England. He is busy putting on shows, and doesn't have time to come see us."

Once Emelye had settled down in the living room to play with the dolls she brought along, Geneva told Mr. Hunnicutt they would be moving to England sometime after school was out, to live with Emelye's father. She kept her voice low. She preferred that Emelye not know there were plans to move in the making until after her abductor was apprehended. Hopefully that would be soon. Hopefully Emelye would lose her fear of London then.

Mr. Hunnicutt brightened. "Why, that's wonderful! I saw your wedding band, but then—. Well, well, I'll say. Isn't that just fine!"

That Mr. Hunnicutt could care that much about her life was humbling. Perhaps his ties with her parents were too strong to be broken by her neglect. She realized suddenly that, but for her stupidity, the Hunnicutts may have been like loving grandparents to Emelye.

There was no need to tell him about the investigation at this point, she decided. To keep things simple, she said, "I've been going through my old records, getting ready for the move. I discovered there is an item missing on some of the annual statements for my trust. I'd appreciate your having a look."

After a few minutes of careful study, Mr. Hunnicutt looked up, his fluffy white eyebrows raised. "Where's that stock certificate?"

Geneva felt a tingling beneath her ears. "The only stock I know about is my grandfather's railroad stock."

He shook his head, frowning. "No, I'm talking about Houston Lumber & Paint. Henry took 200 shares in lieu of a big salary increase when he was made Sales Manager. Course it wasn't worth much back then, just a small local company. But we talked about his decision at length, because he and your mother liked to travel, and with a bigger salary and all...."

Yes, and money was being saved for a grand tour of Europe when she was 16, all her mother's earnings from piano lessons going toward it....

"But that stock was too good a long-term investment to pass up. Now it's gone. Somebody has been monkeying with these statements."

Suddenly nervous about the investigation that would be unleashed when she reported all this, she was compelled to ask, "Are you sure? I mean, it has been so many years."

"I'm positive. Listen, when you get old like me, you can't remember what you did yesterday, but things that go far back in memory are always at hand," he said. He paused for a moment, looked down at his hands, then faced her again. His voice a little softer, he said, "But there's another reason. You see, I strongly encouraged Henry to take that stock. And...after he and your mother were killed..." he swallowed, went on, "I felt bad thinking about how they could have spent that money traveling, had a good time. You just never know how long—" Mr. Hunnicutt's voice drifted off and his eyes grew wet, as if the tragedy of their deaths happened in the recent past. As a matter of fact, hearing him talk about it, she was beginning to feel it wasn't so long ago.

She reached across and touched his forearm consolingly. "I'm sure my father would not have taken that stock unless he was convinced it was the right thing to do," she said, then added contritely, "You and Mrs. Hunnicutt were so kind to me after they were killed. I feel terrible that I didn't stay in touch with you. And didn't even know about Mrs. Hunnicutt's death."

He sniffed. "That's alright, Geneva. Kids grow up, have their own lives to live. Learned that with my own. Not one of them lives in Texas anymore. Don't see very much of them, or my grandchildren."

Geneva had seen the framed photographs of grandchildren lined up on the mantelpiece in the living room when she took Emelye in there. Now she imagined the brown-wrapped packages arriving in the mail from out of state, *"Fragile—handle with care."* Not much of a substitute for having the grandchildren run into your arms.

Her mind returning to the subject of the stock, Geneva remembered Captain Beekman's reservations. "But would anyone risk stealing a stock certificate for a small company? How much could they hope to gain?"

Mr. Hunnicutt sat back. "Well now, that's a good point. But see, that little company had some huge lumber reserves," he said, "that's why I was sold on it, and by golly a few years ago I read where they sold out to a national firm—did you see that in the papers? I said to myself, well at least now Geneva has a nice little nest egg."

It was after three o'clock when Geneva finally drove away. As Walter Hunnicutt waved to her and Emelye from the porch, Geneva thought sadly of the 15 years she squandered, years when she could have held on to her parents through the continued relationship with their best friends. And now, despite all the farewell promises to keep in touch—if they came again in a few months, Mr. Hunnicutt would send fresh squash and tomatoes and green beans home with them—she realized she and Emelye would probably not get back to San Antonio before they moved to England. Then it would be too late. Another ripple in Captain Beekman's pond....

After that her thoughts turned to her stolen stock—how much would it be worth now? She wondered bitterly. Would she ever recoup what was rightfully hers? When and how did Ida get in on the deal? How dare John Scarborough preach to her about her meager inheritance, when he was stealing her future blind?

"As to your future...." A piece of memory bobbed up, like a chunk of wood rising to the water's surface.

She was trying to get it to click into place when she realized she'd missed a turn. It took an hour to find her way out of the most confusing city this side of London, with hardly a square block to be found. Now the early dark of February was swiftly closing in. She'd better concentrate on the road, and let the police handle this.

CHAPTER 75

God does not love me anymore, Elizabeth reasoned, *nor count me as one of his children.* At first she could remember very little of what happened just before her mother's auto went over the edge of the road, and sent them both reeling through the air; before the loud explosion that shook the earth, close enough to where she struck the ground that she could feel the heat of the flames of hell which followed. *Hell:* a word one must never say aloud, but which now formed an indelible picture in her mind. *God does not love me anymore.* She only remembered her mother's white-gloved hands on the steering wheel, suddenly circling to the right, as though she were wiping God's love away; remembered her mother speaking. But what had Mummy said? Elizabeth could not remember, though she was haunted by a sense that she herself had done something more than frightfully naughty: something evil. But what? In her mind was a blank space as deep and wide as the place into which she had plunged from the auto.

Gradually she became aware of her inability to move even a fraction of an inch. *I have lived,* she thought, *I have lived, and am held captive inside my body.* This was her punishment. But for what? What had she done? And, still later, she was aware of her father's near presence. "*Lizzie, my Lizzie!*" he cried, again and again, her hospital bed shaking with his sobs.

Each time she heard him voice her name it scratched her senses raw. But at last it made her mother's words come back, her face lighting up as she uttered them, "*...then say your prayers, Lizzie, we're about to take a trip to hell.*" Her crackling laughter that followed was soon eclipsed by Elizabeth's screams.

Her mother had never called her Lizzie; it was her father's special name for her. And now she wished to shed the name, as a snake will shed its skin, for it was linked with something evil and terrible that she had done with her mother in the auto. Something which her father must never know about; the reason that God did not love her anymore.

This was as much as she could tell Father Ogilvie when first he came to visit, and even though in the weeks to come, words and phrases in her mother's voice would suddenly flash through her mind, like the flames catching again, she could not put them in order, or remember her response. She was only certain that she had cast herself outside the realm of God's love.

Elizabeth wished she had burnt to death along with her mother.

Cynthia and Edward sat together on the wicker love seat beneath the pergola, in the walled garden. Edward's hands were clasped contentedly over his mid-section. The air felt light this morning and the breeze across the pergola was soothing. Spring had come early and many things were in bloom, including the wisteria Cynthia planted years ago. She looked up and around, remembering: When she left, the wisteria was a thin leafy vine, twisting up the side of the pergola from a spindly base; surely there were no more than a dozen blooms on it. But look how it had strived over the years, to show the world its beauty, its endurance. The chalky brown base of the vine was thick as a tree trunk now, and lavender blooms hung from one end of the pergola to the other, like clusters of ripening grapes. Interspersed among the blooms were tiny pink rose blossoms. What an imaginative idea! Apparently the gardener planted the climbing roses after she moved away. How long ago it seemed that her suitcases waited in the hall; and how young she was, though she certainly didn't think so then….

At first when they brought Elizabeth home from St. Martha's, Cynthia was determined to pull the child out of the doldrums quickly, and return to New York. But Elizabeth ignored Cynthia's timetable. Father Ogilvie said reassuringly, "I daresay, she's in a period of re-evaluation—it's healthy." Still, Cynthia could not leave without some sign that Elizabeth's spirits were improving. She prayed nightly. It seemed the more time that passed, the more things there were that needed praying over. She never seemed to have anything in hand anymore.

Months went by. In the end, she was forced to settle for the fact that Elizabeth was at least growing stronger physically. She would return to New York now, and go on hoping and praying for the best.

Cynthia had not told Edward she was leaving.

They had treated each other cordially since she arrived, which was a lot more than could be said for her stay back in 1923, when things were falling apart. Now and then they even reminisced about Tony and Nell as children. Being here brought back memories that Cynthia put away years ago: the birthday parties—one year a puppet show imported from London; another time, a team of clowns; a juggling act; birthday cakes as high as castles, and a surfeit of presents. Nell's first steps were taken across the terrace, from her mother to her father—that was fitting, they agreed! These memories would emerge unexpectedly in conversation, and momentarily soften her resentment toward Edward. She would imagine him reciprocating, *"I'm so dreadfully sorry for judging you, making life so hard, forcing you to leave."* Not surprisingly, he never did. It was alright; she had become resigned. She turned to him now. "I'll be leaving soon," she said.

Edward nodded. "Yes, I rather suspected that." She watched as he pulled out his pipe, filled the bowl, tamped it down and lit up. How this ritual used to annoy her when they were living together, delaying his response when she opened some vital subject for discussion—purposely, no doubt. But she didn't mind it today; in fact the aroma of his tobacco was unexpectedly pleasant.

After taking a deep, luxuriating draw on his pipe stem, Edward turned to Cynthia. At first when she came, he did not know how to deal with her. Never still, always in a spin, she made him frightfully nervous. But gradually he realized she also made him feel alive in a way he had not felt in many years. He did not want her to go, but he had no idea where to begin, to persuade her to stay. How easy it had been years ago, when he was a young man. *"Don't go back to America,"* he pleaded, three weeks after they met, and before he knew it he was saying, *"Marry me instead."* To his profound amazement, she accepted. He had not known how to deal with her then, either. She completely baffled him. But it was more complicated now, for they had a history, not all of it happy. "When will you come again?" he asked.

She was surprised not only by the question, but by his gentle, plaintive tone. What reason was there to come again? Why would he desire it? Perhaps he was only curious, after all. She could not afford trips to England nowadays, though he didn't know it. She had sworn Tony to secrecy about the losses on her investments. "I don't know," she said, and looked straight ahead at the columns of Brookhurst roses. How dazzling they were! How she had delighted in their planting; how she had welcomed their long blooming season, having arrangements around the rooms, the windows open, the breeze fluttering the curtains and stirring their fragrance.

"It has been good, having you here," Edward said with difficulty, trying hard to look as sincere as he felt, and yet wondering if he ought to add, *I adore you, I always have!* No, he was not ready to give that much, not when she might very well reject him. "Watching you with Elizabeth, one recalls how well you cared for our children, how creatively; how determined you were always, to provide opportunities." *Oh, bother! It sounded like a prepared speech.*

Cynthia felt nervous suddenly. She did not want this from Edward, or did she? "Though I was always too interfering, especially with Nell," she hurriedly disclaimed, then smiled in spite of herself. "Nell was fortunate, having you to override my ambitions."

Edward laughed. If she could be that generous, so could he. "Tony thrived on those ambitions, at least," he said.

Surprised and grateful, she looked at him tenderly. He realized he had scored a point, and wondered where to go next. Dash it! He never knew where to go next with Cynthia. He drew on his pipe and decided to venture, "It was very hard when you went away. But you did the things you needed to, got involved in things you liked. I've come to realize that was best all round, for you were miserable here."

"I had an affair in Edinburgh. He was a vocalist. It didn't mean anything. I'm sorry." Edward was turning, walking away. "Yes I was," she said, anger rising. "It was clear I could not have been lower in your estimation."

"Ah, yes…" he said sagaciously. She had simply thrown her affair in his face, given him no space whatever; what, pray, had she expected him to do with it? Still, realizing now that he could lose what little ground he had gained, he said, "You know, there are times in one's life when it seems vital to stand firm on what is *right* and *wrong.*" He looked out over the garden and went on speaking: "But then the years pass, and experience teaches one to be accepting of things, of people, as they are—" He turned to her again, "—even, I should say, to *appreciate* people as they are."

They looked at each other for a long moment. Edward's eyes were tender. Seven years with Jane for a daughter-in-law probably gave him the perspective he needed for acquiring tolerance in others who were at least decent, if not perfect. Cynthia lifted her chin. "Are you saying that you have forgiven me for what happened in Edinburgh?" she asked boldly, for if he was this close, then she intended to take him all the way.

No, you won't get away with twisting it round! After a pause, he said pridefully, "Not exactly."

Cynthia turned from him, folding her arms. What could have possessed her to ask that foolish question? How she wished she could recall it.

Slowly Edward said, "More, that I have forgiven you for telling me of it."

It was the last thing she expected, and she did not know what to make of it. She turned her eyes up to the wisteria-draped pergola ceiling; her eyes felt heavy as she did so, as if they were cups filled with water.

"Sometimes it is better—kinder—not to place the burden of one's mistake on others," he said. Then, after a long pause, he said, "Cynthia, do look at me."

She obeyed him, and found his face as young and earnest as it was on the day he proposed marriage 37 years ago. "I should like very much for you to come home to me. To us. We all need you," he said.

How ridiculous that his unexpected plea should bring a warm blush to her cheeks, making her feel…well…young again. She thought of Geneva and Emelye coming over soon, everyone together at last; of stories told to grandchildren on the Brookhurst terrace. But what about her plans? Greenwich Village? The gallery? Half of her still wanted that, even if just to show she could accomplish it.

"Edward, at this point, I simply don't know that I—"

"Only promise to consider it," he begged, interrupting her.

"Alright," she said at length. They looked at each other helplessly. He's going to say *I love you*, she thought with dread. She was not ready. But he only smiled and pressed her hand.

CHAPTER 76

On the afternoon of June 16th, while Emelye played across the street at the Youngers', Geneva knelt over the garden beds in front of the house. The ground was wet from an earlier rain. Clumps of roots dangling from green shoots in Geneva's fingers were small triumphs that made her reach down again and yet again, the taste of salty sweat on her lips as the sun burned hotter and hotter on her back. All month long she had been working to get the house ready for Rodney to put on the market. At first she concentrated on cleaning out cupboards and closets, and now the garden beds, which would help form a buyer's first impression of the house, were showing neglect.

Not that she had any firm idea of when she and Emelye would be moving, with two investigations now under way. Captain Beekman had spent several weeks in Los Angeles where he soon discovered from a receipt for a purchase of camera supplies that Benjamin was either in that city or had been there in the recent past. Yet despite an exhaustive search and a number of interviews, he found no evidence that Benjamin had been there more recently than around three weeks earlier. He returned to Springfield on the hunch that Benjamin might contact his sisters. In late May he got his first real lead: a letter addressed to Mr. Benjamin Calais in a village in the interior of Mexico. He "borrowed" it from the Maze mailbox long enough to steam it open and read it: "I hope you understand what a difficult position you have placed us in. We will not be able to get down there until after the revival June 11th through 14th, for we are very busy. Kathy." Obviously, either the sisters or maybe someone out in Los Angeles had tipped off Benjamin that he was being hunted, whereupon he fled across the border to avoid capture. Captain Beekman could only speculate why he asked his sisters to come to where he was, but apparently they had something that he needed desperately. "Could Rothby be sufferin' from some kind of illness?" "I have no idea, but the fact he fled to Mexico implicates him, doesn't it? And did you notice, he's changed his name back to Calais?" "For you and me that's enough, but not for the authorities when we ask that he be sent back across the border. I'll leave for Mexico tomorrow so I can be there when the sisters arrive, see what they're up to. Meantime I'll try and get a picture of Benjamin for Emelye to look at. If she could make a positive identification, it might be enough to get him sent back and charged."

Geneva began preparing Emelye for the ordeal of seeing the face of her captor, using a map to help her understand how far away he was from where she lived, and just for good measure, how much farther he was from England. When the picture arrived, however, Geneva was crestfallen. Benjamin had grown a full beard and put on considerable weight. Emelye said contrarily, "No, Mom, this isn't him! When will you find him?"

Four nights ago Captain Beekman called from El Paso—the closest city with long distance service. After hearing Geneva's disappointing report over the staticky line, he said drily, "I was afraid of that." A thorough search of the place where Benjamin was living—not much more than a hut, without electricity or running water—had not yielded her photographs. The typewriter on his desk was an Underwood. "He's gettin' smarter as he goes along," said Captain Beekman. "I'll be in touch after the sisters show up."

Geneva was about finished weeding the bed to the right of the porch stairs, where lantana burgeoned, thinking how much she would miss this hearty plant with each of its pink and yellow blossoms shaped like a tiny bouquet. Surely the weather in Cornwall was too chilly for lantana. Just then two pair of black lace-up shoes strolled up the front walk and entered her field of vision. She rose to her feet and found herself looking into the faces of Kathy and Virginia. Both looked weary. They wore black straw hats and dowdy clothing that made them look older than they were. "We'd like a few minutes of your time," Kathy said.

It had not occurred to her or Captain Beekman that Benjamin asked his sisters to pay her a visit, that getting "down there" meant not Mexico, but Houston. She felt very uneasy about talking to them without the advice of Captain Beekman.

Soon she was sitting across from her old roommates in the parlor, reading in amazement the Last Will and Testament of Victor Emmanuel Calais, written on the 14th day of April, 1923. There could be only one reason for Victor to leave his photograph collection and cameras to her. *Too late,* she thought bitterly. Yet, coming to the end of the brief document, she gazed for a long time at the webbed characters of Victor's handwriting: the dying man's signature closing in on itself. She felt a pang of sadness.

Abruptly, Kathy snatched the will from her hands, refolded it and slipped it into her handbag with such precision that Geneva suspected she had practiced the routine beforehand. Kathy now resembled Victor more so than when she was a child, with her high-bridged nose and strawberry blond hair. She still had that pompous air Geneva remembered; apparently finding religion had not improved her personality. Her nervousness today was almost as palpable as the summer heat outside, and in fact, though the ceiling fan whirred above, she was using a souvenir fan upon which bold letters announced: *Light of the World Church Revival—June 11–14, 1931.* As she whisked the fan back and forth to cool her face, gossamer tendrils of hair stood out like flags from her temples.

Geneva remembered Ida saying that Benjamin and his sisters quarreled after Victor's funeral over who had rights to his possessions. Yet all the time he had made his intentions quite clear. "Where has the will been all this time?" she inquired. Kathy looked at Virginia as though to cue her to speak.

Virginia's eyes were soft behind a pair of gold-rimmed eyeglasses; her hair had grown darker, though not so dark as her mother's. Her figure was tidy: a ballerina's figure, wasted in an old lady's churchy dress. "With Benjamin," she answered. "He typewrote it for Daddy, but he didn't tell us about it until—" she began, then looked uncertainly toward Kathy.

"Not long ago," Kathy finished vaguely.

Again Geneva wished Captain Beekman could have prepared her for this encounter. After some consideration, she said, "You realize that the two of you could be charged as accessories to Benjamin's crimes."

The color rose in Virginia's cheeks and her lips parted. "I—he misled me," she said in a tremulous voice.

Kathy cut in, "When he asked us to loan him money after he lost his job, he said he wanted to go overseas and make a fresh start. He promised to pay us back. I told him no, but Virginia—"

"I had a little nest egg," Virginia said. "I told him it was my sincere hope that he would recognize this loan as the Christian deed it was, to accept Jesus as Lord, and be saved."

Geneva could not help thinking, if Virginia had really been generous she would have given her brother the money, rather than using the loan as an excuse for proselytizing. It would have been more apt to change his heart.

"That savings was all I had, and now I'll never get it back," said Virginia.

"We had a feeling that Benjamin had not been honest with us when we found out he wasn't paying his debts," said Kathy.

"A man came by to collect one day—"

"But we didn't know till we had a letter from Benjamin…recently…what happened over in London," Kathy said, and with a glare at Geneva she added, "the worst of it purely unintentional." She paused to take a breath. "We were horrified. But it all started because he felt that you were to blame for everything that had gone wrong in his life, and you owed something in return."

Virginia added, "The biggest blow came when he went out to Los Angeles near the end of the war. Daddy had his hopes built up so high, and then when he finally got out there, he'd lost interest in making films. All because you refused to star in that picture he wanted to make."

I could have done that much for Victor; what would it have taken, a few months? thought Geneva. It might have changed a lot of things. Odd to realize that what initially seemed outrageous could appear reasonable in hindsight, where time is compressed….

"He told us the will was in a safe deposit box there in Springfield, and he enclosed the key in the letter," said Virginia.

"I'm sure you understand what a difficult situation you have placed us in…."

"How long has he had my pictures?" Geneva asked.

"He found them when he was doing that article for the *New American Review* a couple of years ago," said Kathy. "Just before he came down here—" (a pause; an accusatory look) "—in the *vain* hope of taking pictures of Daddy's studio, he took some shots of Daddy's cameras and so forth. He thought his favorite camera case would be interesting. It was pretty worn out. The lining had come unstitched and all. While examining it, he noticed something stuffed behind the lining. He pulled out an envelope, and what do you know?"

Geneva remembered Benjamin remarking arrogantly that day he came to photograph the studio. *"The exterior won't give a clue as to what went on in there, will it?"* All the while he had betrayed his father, who lay buried in his grave, defenseless. Well, now she understood the time lapse, at least.

"Naturally it was obvious to Benjamin what was going on when Mother was alive, and it just added insult to injury," Virginia declared. "Of course, I might add, we were shocked, too, and deeply hurt. We had trusted you."

Geneva decided not to argue that point, though she distinctly remembered that Kathy had never trusted her, and after their mother's death Virginia turned a cold shoulder as well. "Where are my photographs now?" she asked.

"In the safe deposit box," said Kathy. "My husband would not lower himself to keep such vulgarities in the parsonage. I must say, I was shocked at them, and at you."

Now Geneva's face reddened. From the moment Victor urged her to pose in the nude, the thought of being condemned for her actions was at the core of her aversion.

Kathy leaned forward. There was perspiration above her lip. Earnestly she said, "We came here in the sincere hope that you would accept a copy of the will and all the things Daddy meant for you to have...and let bygones be bygones."

That the two sisters could have so minimized Emelye's ordeal in London to a mere 'bygone' was heartless and also naive. Struggling to keep her voice even, Geneva asked, "Have you any children?"

Kathy shook her head, a strange wary look in her eyes as if she regarded the question as a threat to her privacy. "I thought not," said Geneva. "I have no intention of letting Benjamin get away with what he did to my daughter."

Kathy's eyes narrowed to blazing dots. Her chest rose as if she were about to explode. "'Vengeance is mine, saith the Lord,'" she cried, and her fan hit the magazine table with an imploring whack. "My brother has tried his best to make amends for the one and only stupid, impulsive mistake in his life," she said. "If you cannot find it in your heart to do this for him, then surely you will do it out of respect for the memory of our beloved mother, whom you betrayed."

"Think how you would feel if it was your mother," said Virginia.

My mother would not have left me in order to risk her life having an abortion. The words were right on the tip of Geneva's tongue. All that stopped her from uttering them was the knowledge that Victor had honored her request, in a manner of speaking, and she had no time to analyze how she felt about that, much less whether she might owe him the courtesy of keeping that secret from his children because of it.

She told the sisters that she would consider their proposal, while privately thinking ahead to contacting Captain Beekman for his advice.

When they were gone, Geneva felt completely drained. She found herself trying to imagine April 14th, 1923, for Victor—less than a week before his death from an agonizing disease. It must have required superhuman effort to compose a new will. But at that late hour, what else could he do? Oh, why had he not honored her request in the first place? He would have saved himself a lot of grief at the end of his life, and saved Emelye from a terrible experience.

Poor Captain Beekman. He was no doubt still awaiting Kathy and Virginia's arrival down in Mexico.

When Geneva brought Emelye home a few minutes later, she took the child on her lap and hugged her tightly. She didn't want to confuse her by telling her the whole story. Maybe when she was a little older, she would. She said simply that the man who kidnapped her in London had been caught. "So there's no need to be afraid that he'll ever bother you again," she said.

Two brown eyes looked up. "Oh Mom, I wasn't really afraid."

"Good!" said Geneva, smoothing back the blond hair that had come loose from its braid. Tentatively she said, "I have a surprise. We'll be moving to England soon, to live with your father and Elizabeth."

To her dismay, tears welled up in Emelye's eyes. "Not in London! I don't want to go there!"

"No, not in London, Honey," Geneva promised with a sigh, and kissed the top of her head. The first thought that came to mind was: *my daughter is not a cry baby. I must respect her tears.* If Emelye was still this frightened after more than a year, and despite her mother's reassurance that her captor was no longer a threat, then obviously her painful associations with London were too deep down to be reasoned away. Perhaps she should have talked to Emelye more about the details of that day so her fears would work up to the surface and could be talked through. Strangely enough, she had been concerned about frightening her.

She hugged Emelye close again. She knew she must never break her promise, even if it was years before Emelye felt at ease about going to London. Concessions in their lives with Tony would likely bring hardship and disappointment at times, but that was that. "I love you," she said, knowing that she would never love another child as she loved this one. Yet she thought sadly: *Maybe one day you'll decide you weren't so lucky to have me for a mother.*

Several days later Captain Beekman called from El Paso. After Geneva reported on the visit from Kathy and Virginia, he mused, "I'd be willin' to bet that will was typed up on the same machine as the blackmail note." After a pause, he continued, "You can always go to the Police, soon as you have the will and the photographs in your hands."

"I suppose so," she said thoughtfully.

"But if you want my opinion, I'd call it a day. Save yourself the embarrassment of goin' to court and havin' what's nobody's business written up in the newspapers. It could get real nasty for you and for Emelye."

Which would be just as bad, no, worse, than having the photographs she so despised published one day when she least expected it. And a court appearance would take up valuable time that they could be spending with Tony and Elizabeth.

CHAPTER 77

By now Sergeant Dickerson had grudgingly uncovered the fact that it was in 1923 that Houston Lumber & Paint was sold, and Mr. Scarborough requested her father's stock be reissued in his name, as trustee. Though the investigation was far from complete, it seemed obvious to Geneva, in light of this, that Ida purloined her messages to Tony in order to keep his lawyers from meddling in her business until the dust had settled around that stock transaction. Geneva had written as much to Tony, adding with caution, "Still, this is only conjecture unless I can get Ida to own up to it. I intend to talk to her if I get a chance."

With the matter of her trust account in the hands of the Police, there was nothing to keep her and Emelye here. She still had a lot to do, however, so she had not yet booked passage on a ship or given Tony an arrival date. One afternoon when she was at the kitchen table, sorting through a box of old recital pictures and programmes, trying to decide what to keep and what to throw away, the doorbell rang. Soon she was leading Sergeant Dickerson into the parlor.

In the few times she had met with the officer, he had been guarded and close-mouthed. That he was in an unusually expansive mood today puzzled her, especially when he began listing the developments in the case.

"You want the good news, or the bad news, first?" he asked. And as she admitted it might be well to get the worst over with, he told her that the stock in which her father invested had split a couple of times in the late 20's, before the crash of 1929. "At its peak, it was worth a little less than $30,000."

Geneva shrank back against the sofa cushion. This would have doubled the value of her estate. "And since the crash?" she asked gingerly.

"That I don't know. Scarborough sold it beforehand."

Her eyes watered with fury. "No one deserves to be that lucky."

Sergeant Dickerson cracked a satisfied smile. "But keep in mind, Scarborough's luck has run out," he said, and then he told her the good news. As Geneva's trust account was not of sufficient size initially to tempt any banker to cheat—she noticed Sergeant Dickerson had taken all the credit for figuring this out—he had looked elsewhere, while he waited on an answer to his inquiry into her stock's value. "I discovered that, for some time before he took over your account, Scarborough had been stealing from a widow woman with an irrevocable trust. The account had a heavy cash flow, and he got away with thousands and thousands, dipping in on a regular basis."

So that was where the money came from to buy the house in Joplin and care for Fred Scarborough. Was this supposed to be good news, that someone else was cheated worse than she was? Geneva wondered miserably.

"That's how we finally nailed him. The authorities in Joplin, Missouri will pick up the Scarborough couple and bring them back here to be charged."

For Geneva, this was the good news. She sat forward. "I want you to do me a favor, "she urged. "Arrange for me to talk with Ida when they get here."

The sergeant shook his head. "I doubt her lawyer will allow that."

"What I want to talk about may not have any direct bearing on the case for fraud," she said, "Just ask if she'll talk to me. It means an awful lot."

"I'll see what I can do," he promised, and she found herself searching in vain for a sign of his usual cocksureness.

As he walked out on the porch, she said, "Thanks for all you've done, Sergeant Dickerson."

He turned and smiled. "By the way, it's Lieutenant, now," he said, solving the riddle of his sunny mood. He tipped his hat and walked away.

Geneva hastened to report to Tony her request to speak with Ida. "How I hate to tell you that this may delay our arrival, but I'm sure you are as anxious as I am to have this matter resolved, once and for all."

CHAPTER 78

❀

Tony turned off Castle Canyke Road and drove down the narrow drive neath an archway of sycamores, which led to the Clearharbour farmhouse. Just at the end, where the drive crooked round to the left, the sunny patch of grass with its empty stone garden border opened like the palm of a hand, on the right. He angled to the left and parked the Rover near the small conservatory marking the house entrance. Stepping out on the pavement, he gazed admiringly upon the broad meadows divided by hedgerows that stretched beyond the property, as far as the eye could see. Then he turned round and looked up at the stone house with its steep-pitched roof and gables. Walter Bounds, the building contractor, was to meet him here and give him some preliminary ideas on making the improvements that he and Geneva had spoken of when first they saw the house.

Since buying Clearharbour Farm, Tony had employed a local man to look after the grounds. Once a month or so, and always following bouts of fierce weather, Merton would drive over from Brookhurst and check on things inside, to see if any maintenance problems had arisen.

Up to now, Tony had resisted the temptation to come here. It was foolish perhaps, but he feared that in so doing he might hex things for his future with Geneva. Thus it seemed he had anticipated this particular day forever. He never imagined that he would greet it not with his heart flush with the pride of ownership, but rather with a feeling of unease.

Glancing at his watch, he sat down on the stone garden border to wait for Walter Bounds to arrive. He recalled this was the first place along the tour of the property where he and Geneva paused in their steps: she to dream of growing a garden one day; and he to imagine sitting with her in the garden on fine mornings, sipping tea and reading the papers.

Had the season arrived for long-held dreams to come true, or not?

Big celebration coming up at Brookhurst on Monday night—candlelight and flowers in the formal dining room, Morey and Nell and Guy motoring over from Launceston. Lizzie—no, Elizabeth, she now insisted he call her, the new formality due to her resentment of him no doubt—would be conveyed downstairs, wearing a new party dress. Whether she would also be wearing a smile was a matter of speculation.

Tony had never seen Lord Edward as excited as he was last night when he arrived at Brookhurst; positively chatty, like a school boy. When Mother had finally returned to Manhattan after all those months following the auto crash, she learned that a buyer from out of state had made a substantial offer on her brownstone, with the intention of converting it into luxury apartments. She took this as a sign, and cabled Father at once: "I'm coming home." Tomorrow Tony would drive him to Southampton to meet her ship.

For Tony, the dream that his mother might someday return to his father had been second only to his dream that Geneva might one day return to him. And until yesterday, everything seemed to be falling into place. Wisely, Geneva had taken Captain Beekman's advice and dropped the case against Benjamin. She now awaited receipt of all the articles intended for her by Victor Calais, not least of which were those unfortunate photographs.

But then there was the other matter: when Geneva wrote him several weeks ago of her hope to question Ida Ruekauer about her stolen messages, she assumed—quite understandably—that he would be in favor of this interview.

Unfortunately, in his heart of hearts, he was not. As likely as it seemed that wretched woman was guilty of the deceit that robbed him and Geneva of eight years that could never be retrieved, what if she were not? There was that damnable receipt which always kept him wondering, no matter what else Ida and John Scarborough had been up to. Perhaps Ida's attorney would not allow her to speak with Geneva, he reasoned hopefully.

But yesterday, a letter arrived: "Darling—Ida will speak to me in the presence of her attorney sooner than I dared hope, on August 10th! This appointment will hardly delay us at all. We should be able to sail for England at least by the end of the month, if not sooner."

The 10th of August was Monday, the day of his mother's homecoming celebration.

If during that interview, Ida absolved herself of guilt, Tony would have no choice but to confront his father with the issue. How he dreaded it, and yet he owed Geneva an answer before she and Emelye sailed. If his father were to confess his guilt, Tony dare not imagine what he would say or where the relationship between them would go from that moment. He was quite sure that upon hearing of it, his mother would make a quick departure, this time for good. He was certain that Geneva would not be willing to live anywhere near his father—imagine her, seeing him Sunday after Sunday in the St. Petroc's pew, for instance—so they could say goodbye to Clearharbour Farm. And with Emelye's keen dislike of London, Geneva could hardly be expected to force her to settle there any time even in the remote future. Life would be absent all the happy family gatherings Geneva had eagerly anticipated, a series of painful and awkward episodes. Geneva and Emelye had a good life in Houston Heights. Perhaps, all things considered, they would not come to England after all.

CHAPTER 79

It was the last night of the last holiday Geneva and Emelye would spend with the Youngers on Lake Astoria: the night before Geneva's interview with Ida. Under a bright full moon and a scattering of stars, the water sparkled like a beaded evening gown. Geneva and Willa lingered outside on the terrace long after everyone else went to bed, reluctant to turn away from the spectacular view; reluctant to bid their goodnights and turn away from each other.

At supper, the Youngers presented Geneva and Emelye with a going-away present: a portrait in oils, around 12 by 14 inches in size, copied from a snapshot that Father Quanset had taken last Christmas. Geneva remembered being puzzled by his painstaking efforts to get the perfect shot, as though this picture were more important than any other. Now she knew why. Rodney stood before the Christmas tree, with Willa on one side and Geneva on the other, their arms interlocked. The children stood in front of them, with James at the center. The colors of the painting were as warm and vibrant as the smiles on all the faces. A brass plaque at the bottom of the frame stated:

Christmas Day, 1930
1204 Heights Boulevard, Houston, Texas

Upon seeing it, Geneva burst into tears: unstoppable, gushing tears, which brought Rodney's handkerchief to the rescue. Now, as she and Willa sat together out on the terrace, the mere thought of the portrait made her eyes sting. She was struck by the power of pictures, how one could force you to remember something you'd rather forget, and another could help you remember something you wished to hold forever.

Geneva and the Youngers had lived across the street from each other for ten years. They had more collective memories than Geneva and Willa could recall in one late night sitting, though they kept at it as long as they could because this would surely be their last opportunity for a very long time.

"If Emelye doesn't like it in England, she can come back and live with us," Willa said at last, and she was only half joking. For a while now, she had entertained a notion—the sheer romance of it so unlike her that she didn't breathe a word to anyone else—that James and Emelye might grow up and marry one day. Emelye had always looked up to James, probably because he was more than two years older than she was, and often when Willa saw them together, she would remark to herself what a cute pair they made. After Emelye and her mother returned from England last summer, and the neighborhood kids were being cruel to Emelye about having her mother around the playground, James stuck up for her like a champion. One day a little boy called Emelye a "titty baby." James socked him in the eye. Since then Willa noticed that Emelye was finding ways to be near her hero—sitting by him at the dinner table or riding next to him in the car.

Of course, Willa had known that one day Geneva and Emelye would move to England, and that it was the best thing that could happen to them. But only now that they were about to leave did the distance soon to stretch out between them make her notion seem utterly foolish. Within a few years, James and Emelye would hardly know each other anymore, let alone grow up and get married.

Willa's offer struck a sensitive chord with Geneva. What if Emelye was miserable in England? She said, "I guess she'll be alright as long as we keep her away from London. It's going to be hard for Tony and I to manage that. Frankly it has been on my mind a lot. But I guess we'll be figuring it out pretty soon."

Willa nodded in understanding. "What time do you need to leave for Houston in the morning?"

"My interview is at ten-thirty, so at least by six, I guess," Geneva told her. Emelye would stay behind and drive back with the Youngers later in the day.

"Are you nervous?"

Geneva took in a quick breath. "Yes I am," she admitted. She had an almost irrational dread of her meeting with Ida. It was not only that she was intimidated by the woman—as she always had been, at least during the times when Ida had the upper hand. It was the way she had put everything on the line. She had felt so sure of Ida's guilt, but now that the hour was drawing near, she was terrified that the outcome would not fulfill her expectations, and may even lead her to a conclusion she could hardly bear to think about. She conveyed all this to Willa now.

"You want me to go with you?"

Geneva's throat swelled. How many times had Willa helped her through things that were difficult? "I suppose I'd better do this one alone," she said.

Hearing this was harder than anything for Willa. Maybe she was becoming more introspective these days, but lately she figured out what had made her feel so close to Geneva for all these years was knowing that Geneva needed her. Willa had never experienced that with any other relationship. At home, Rodney was the stronghold, both for her and their children. And Willa had no other friend except Geneva. Now she was saying in so many words, *"I don't need you anymore."* And even though Willa realized she may as well get used to Geneva getting along without her, she felt an emptiness deep inside that would never be filled by anyone else. It was not unlike that wintry day long ago in Galveston, when all the questions of her birth had finally been answered, and she wound up at the burial place of her real mother. She walked up to the grave of Serena Garret feeling grateful that the blanks in her own identity were filled in at last through coming to know this tragic young woman, and grateful no less to feel emotionally bound to her with an intensity she could not have imagined. And yet, even while standing there, she knew she was losing her grip on her mother, that she could not hold on to her.

Willa grabbed Geneva's hand, raised it to her lips and kissed it. Then abruptly she rose and walked inside the house.

It was dark out on the terrace. Geneva had not realized her friend was crying until she felt the wetness of tears on her hand. Had she brought Willa to tears, by refusing her offer to go with her tomorrow? With all her heart she hoped not. Yet she knew that she must face Ida alone, for if she brought Willa, Ida would consider it a display of weakness. The last thing she wanted was to lose the woman's respect, just when she was depending on her.

CHAPTER 80

August 10th was one of the hottest days of the year in Houston. The second-floor room in which Geneva met Ida had rough plaster walls, a small window with bars, which looked out on a brick wall, and a single lamp hanging above a table with four iron chairs. The backs of her knees were sticky. Beads of perspiration formed above her mouth and on her forehead. Up in the right hand corner of the window, a spider was busily spinning a web.

Often Geneva had tried to imagine Ida's appearance when they sat across from each other for the first time in seven years. Captain Beekman's grainy photograph provided no clues. She was not surprised at the additional wrinkles around Ida's eyes and mouth, and strands of gray in her hair, cropped short—by a prison warden?—for she was in her mid-fifties, after all. Even her loss of weight seemed reasonable, for almost a month had passed since she was detained by authorities in Joplin. Yet the grayish cast of Ida's complexion alerted Geneva that she may be seriously ill. Was this what prompted her to agree to the interview? A way to ease her conscience in her last days?

Even now Ida had a defiant way of peering at people from under her pointy eyebrows, suggesting that she viewed her handcuffs and lusterless blue prison shift—and all they represented—with arrogance. She sat with her handcuffed wrists in her lap. Her attorney Gerald Wilcox sat next to her with an air of solemnity. His dark hair was neatly parted and slicked down in the way a funeral director might compose a corpse for viewing. At the beginning, he slipped a note pad and pen from his briefcase, and warned Geneva that he would bar any question which he deemed inappropriate for his client to answer.

Eager as she was to have all this behind her, she dare not put Ida on the defensive, and thus she had devised a strategy, more or less. "Who is looking after Fred Scarborough now?" she asked.

Ida gave her a surprised look. She glanced at Mr. Wilcox, but not, as it turned out, for guidance. As though some obscure signal had been worked out between them, he reached in his pocket for a pack of Lucky Strikes, put one between her lips, and lit it. She drew deeply on it, allowed her attorney to retrieve it, then exhaled out the side of her mouth.

"Fred is a ward of the State once more," she said.

Geneva thought of the benign face in the picture. "That's too bad."

"Yes. The state hospital is not a place anyone would want to be, and Fred is a gentle soul, entirely harmless. It's why John found a way to get him out."

How strange it sounded for Ida to call Mr. Scarborough by his Christian name, yet it made the relationship between them seem more real. Her husband. John. They'd slept together in a shady house in Joplin, and shared the burden of caring for John's brother. And now, because they had stolen from others, his brother was re-institutionalized. Surely that was more cruel for Fred than never having been released in the first place.

Ida was aided in another puff on her cigarette, then she said, "But you didn't come here to talk about Fred, so, out with it." *"Who is the father?...Tell me, girl, or I give you my word, I won't help you."*

So much for strategy, for leading in gently. Geneva ran her sweaty palms down the front of her skirt. She had a constricted feeling in her chest. She was not ready. "It occurred to me—when I learned about the—the stock—" she stammered, then glanced at Mr. Wilcox. *Am I on shaky ground already?* He was leaning his head back, rather absently, as if only half-listening. "—that having Tony's lawyers look over my list of assets in 1923 may have seemed threatening to you."

Ida shrugged. "We were nervous alright, because I didn't have a chance to look through things before you boxed them up to take to England. But then, next thing I knew, you were home again."

"Some of my statements vanished," Geneva accused. Mr. Wilcox became alert and touched Ida's arm. Ida whispered to him—Geneva would have given anything to know what she said. He whispered back, and Ida nodded.

She looked at Geneva. "When that envelope was returned from London, all I did was take a good look through the contents, to be sure those lawyers had not put any questions in the margins.

"Of course, that was a good while before you found out you were expecting...."

She had led Geneva right to the threshold. Now she waited.

Alright. Geneva swallowed. Her throat felt dry as cotton. "Ida, I've got to ask you something, and I cannot tell you how important it is for me to know the truth." She glanced at Mr. Wilcox. "I mean, I'm not talking about a—a punishable crime here, *per se....*"

An indolent smile crossed Ida's mouth. "I've known what you were after since I heard you wanted this interview. Would you be interested to know why I accepted?" she asked, then paused. "I didn't have to, you know," she added.

Ida's power, wielded subtly. Geneva nodded her head.

Ida's expression softened just a bit, re-composed itself. Not into a look of friendliness, certainly. Respect, perhaps. She spoke slowly and deliberately. "I owe you a favor. You could have put an end to my nursing career. In your place, I would have done it. But you didn't." She gestured for her cigarette. Mr. Wilcox put it between her lips for another puff, then stabbed the ash tray with what was left.

Geneva was thankful that she had—if inadvertently—given Ida a reason to cooperate today. She had always felt guilty for misleading Dr. Latimer. She gripped the edge of the table. "You didn't send my messages to Tony, did you?" she asked, her voice barely audible.

For a long moment, Ida gazed at her mercilessly. Then her eyes dropped. Geneva felt she could float right out of that chair and keep going all the way to England. But the next thing she knew, Ida was glancing at her attorney, then facing her again.

"You're wrong," she said, and Geneva's spirits hit the ground with a thud. "I sent them, just as I promised—by that time I felt it was safe." She shrugged. "John threw a fit when he found out. We were still waiting on that stock to be reissued. I took two or three of your annual statements from the envelope, in order to confuse matters in case Tony's lawyers got into it again.

"But I won't go to my grave with those messages on my conscience."

Mr. Wilcox's hand struck the table with the force of a judge's gavel. Geneva's shoulders flinched violently. "That's it! We hope it was helpful," he said briskly. He turned to the door and called for the guard. Geneva and Ida gave each other a long measuring look. Ida's mouth opened halfway, then closed. Would she have said more if not for her attorney? Was there anything more to be said? Soon Ida was led out of the room, her wrists bound together, with Geneva locked in the haze of her cigarette smoke, the spider spinning its web larger and larger up in the corner of the window.

As soon as Geneva got home she composed a letter to Tony, anxious to get it over with. She felt more sad than she had felt since she realized he was not going to rush to her aid when she learned she was pregnant. She had not the heart to do more than convey the astonishing result of her meeting with Ida. She would leave the rest to Tony. She was now convinced that Lord Edward was the guilty party and, remembering Tony's defensiveness when they spoke of this possibility in London, she decided that, deep down, he probably knew it as well.

CHAPTER 81

Nell stood before the large mullioned windows of her sitting room and watched her son Guy playing in the broad sloping ground behind Camellia Cottage. Now up the make-shift ladder he scampered, to disappear in the tree house Morey had built for him in one of the most accommodating of their many sweet chestnut trees, to do whatever lads of ten years do in such places. She gazed round at the overstuffed chairs with soft floral print upholstery and the huge breakfront filled with assorted knickknacks, and listened to the ticking of the longcase clock at the foot of the stairs in the hall—Father's gift to her and Morey upon their purchase of Camellia Cottage. How she adored the cluttered friendliness of her home: pictures large and small exhausting most of the wall space; potted plants in colorful porcelain urns filling in the corners of the wood plank floors. Nell had fond memories of acquiring all these furnishings, large and small, over the years—many of them presents from family and friends; some acquired on lazy afternoons strolling round village fairs.

And yet the relentless ticking away of the clock. In an hour from now Morey would be home and they would all be on their way to Brookhurst to celebrate her mother's return. Mother would not imagine, any more than the others, that Nell was in large part responsible for the fact that there was a Brookhurst for Mother to return to, not to mention a husband strong and fit, whereas but for her he might have been a broken man, may not even have survived. And Nell would much prefer that they should never have to know.

But day by day, hour by hour, her secret had been unraveling....

First of all, last year she learnt—much to her shock—that Geneva had informed her brother that they had a daughter, whom she was raising alone. Until then, Nell was unaware that Tony had been in contact with Geneva for all these years. She thought he hated her. And the daughter—well, Nell had assumed that Geneva gave up Tony's child for adoption, at birth. Upon hearing the news, Nell expected a storm of outrage from her brother. And yet, nothing. Not a letter, nor telephone call, nor a furious knock upon her door. *Tick-tock, tick-tock.* Nell did not sleep nights, waiting for it to happen. Eventually she concluded that Geneva had decided to remain silent about their arrangement.

But now Jane was dead, and Tony had announced that he and Geneva were to be married and would live in Bodmin at Clearharbour Farm.

Oh, the secret had sat heavily upon Nell's mind and heart, forever it seemed. It was quite the worst thing that one could live with, she decided years ago, even as she told herself that she had done what was best for her family at the time, the only thing that would save them. And until the crash in Dartmoor Forest, Nell felt her actions further justified by the presence in their lives of dear Elizabeth, whom Tony idolized. Of course, she knew that Jane was difficult, and the marriage was unhappy. One could easily see by the number of times that Tony brought Elizabeth to Brookhurst, leaving Jane behind, and how seldom he spoke of Jane. But Elizabeth made it all worthwhile. And then the auto crash. What if Elizabeth had lost her life? No one had prayed more fervently than Nell that Elizabeth would survive, and recover completely. She prayed as yet, nor would she give up praying until Elizabeth walked again and was in high spirits, sliding down the slope of the yard with Guy, and wading barefoot in the brook at the bottom, as they used to do, laughing all the while. And Nell would call them into the kitchen for tea and hot oatmeal scones drizzled with butter and syrup.

For years before the auto crash, Nell felt guilty for lying to Morey, and depriving him as well. One summer the roof of their home needed extensive repairs, and it was discovered the leaks in it had led to some rotting beams. *"We can pay for it with the balance of your legacy, Nellie."* Morey worked harder than ever for Tolgus Mines and traveled for part of almost every week, visiting their mining sites. Yet he was paid far less than he had earned at Selby Mines. There was not sufficient cash on hand unless they used her legacy. She had to make up an apology—she'd spent all the money on things for the house and garden. *"Just little things, here and there, and before I knew it, the money had quite got away from me somehow." "Well then, I shall pay a call on the banker and ask for a loan."*

There, it's over and done, she thought, *the first and last time I shall ever lie to my husband.* And yet, every time she sat at the desk in the sitting room and made out an installment for the bank, it was as if she were telling Morey the lie all over again. How she dreaded taking checkbook in hand! Still, she asked her-self, what other choice was there for her at the time, but the action that eventu-ally forced her to lie to her husband? She would not see her family ruined, not for Geneva, who cared so little for Tony that she abandoned him on the eve of their wedding. And that groveling letter, when she found she was pregnant. Why, Geneva was nothing but an opportunist.

Of course, Nell knew now that she had been mistaken about many things, not least of which was Geneva's character. And soon now she must look squarely into Geneva's face, and the face of the daughter she had bravely cho-sen to raise alone. Which prompted the question: why had Geneva accepted her terms so long ago? Perhaps the answer was to be found in the delay of her response. Oh how she agonized as weeks turned into months, terrified that Geneva intended to demand more money. When finally the check was returned through the bank, she assumed that Geneva had decided it would do no good to ask for more, for there wasn't any to be had. But now she envi-sioned a different rationale: Geneva struggled over whether to add to the bur-den of distress already plaguing Tony's family. Then she learned that Tony and Jane were married. She was too decent a person to interfere.

This morning when Morey kissed her goodby before going to work, he asked, "Why so glum these past few days, love?"

"Oh, just feeling a bit off." How she wished it could be over, and she could be as happy as she must pretend to be when they met at Brookhurst tonight, instead of knowing that soon Tony and her mother were going to hate her, as no doubt Geneva already did. Obviously Geneva's silence of late was not with-out purpose: she intended to force her into a confession when she arrived in England. But Nell would not wait. Tonight would be the first time in many years that their whole family sat down to a meal together. She could not bear to ruin her mother's homecoming party by confessing tonight what she had done, but tomorrow she would take her brother aside and tell him the truth. This would be harder even than confessing to her husband, and therefore it must be borne first.

CHAPTER 82

No sooner had Geneva mailed her letter to Tony than she realized she was not going to move to England, for life there would be as miserable for her and for Emelye as it would have been had she broken up Tony's marriage to Jane. She did not tell anyone, even Willa. Had she opened her mouth, she would have cried. She was surprised to find herself thinking that maybe this was a good time for her and Emelye to strike out and move to some other town. She recalled a phrase from somewhere in the Bible that advised against putting new wine into old skins. Somehow she could not help hoping for a miracle from Tony, and there were days when the notion brought her spirits up a little. But she always went to bed at night knowing this was just her way of holding on a little longer to the idea of there being a "Tony and Geneva."

Victor's things had yet to arrive, except for an envelope which came via registered mail—she had to sign a receipt, and then she grasped the envelope tightly and stared at it, her heart pounding. How often she had anticipated the act of shredding those pictures. She knew just the pair of scissors—heavy ones with very sharp blades, never before having been used for cutting paper. This was to have been a kind of ritual, a severing of the past from the future. Yet a voice in her head asked, *Are you ready to open your eyes and see yourself?* Besides, now she had no clear idea of the future. *When I have heard from Tony, I will shred the pictures,* she thought. Without unsealing the envelope, she placed it high up on a closet shelf where Emelye would not discover it.

One day Captain Beekman came by to collect his final check. When Geneva answered the door, he was standing at the porch rail, watching the scene across the street where James, Serena, and Emelye were playing with the water hose. All three were drenched, and giggling happily.

He turned to Geneva, smiling. His complexion, like the children's, was deeply tanned. "Nice to see Emelye havin' a good time with her friends, not a worry in the world," he observed.

"Thanks to you," Geneva said warmly, and invited him inside.

She told him she'd been expecting him for a long time, and thought he must have gotten busy on a new case. Sheepishly he said, "You might say my wife led me on a detour. She rented a house on the beach down in Corpus Christi for the summer, and I went straight there from Mexico. Had all the grandkids down."

"You look like the vacation agreed with you," said Geneva, thinking Corpus Christi might be a nice town to move to. Maybe they needed a good dancing school….

When she handed him the check, she said, "Thanks for all you've done. Especially, for going to Joplin." Her bottom lip started to tremble.

Captain Beekman's sleepy eyes looked off modestly. "Well, one thing you learn in this business is to expect surprises."

"I guess that's a pretty good lesson about life in general," she said with a wry smile.

Watching him retreat down the front walk, she thought, *I'll miss you, Captain Beekman. For all your surprises, wherever you are, it is safe.* Then she remembered that Tony once expressed the same sentiment about her.

On August 28th a bulky, postage-laden letter addressed by Tony's hand appeared in the mailbox. Geneva was not sure whether to be encouraged or dismayed by the thickness of it. It was not yet ten in the morning, and thankfully Emelye was still asleep. Geneva had no idea what shape she would be in after reading the letter. She sank down in a wicker chair on the porch, and opened it.

"Darling—I've just received your letter, and should have written to you sooner but for the inevitability that our letters would have crossed in transit. I am finally able to report the truth of what became of your messages to me…"

It is indeed my father who must take responsibility—

"…and though the admission comes very hard indeed, it is I myself who must finally accept the blame."

Geneva's reading came to an abrupt halt. So convinced of Lord Edward's guilt was she, that she could only wonder why Tony was taking responsibility for it. Unless…unless he extracted a confession from his father sometime after she told him they had a daughter, but kept it a secret in hopes the truth would never come to light. Yes, that seemed reasonable. It would have a been a terrible dilemma for Tony, who loved both his father and her; and she forgave him at once, though she would never forgive his father, which created a terrible dilemma for her.

She returned to the letter uneasily: "On the night of August 10th—the date on which you spoke with Mrs. Ruekauer—our family gathered at Brookhurst to celebrate my mother's return. After dinner, the party having adjourned to the drawing room for coffee, Mother mentioned the case pending against the Scarboroughs, and we talked about how matters stood. No one noticed that my sister Nell grew very quiet as the discussion progressed, and remained so for the balance of the evening. Actually she had not looked well from the outset, and only picked at her food. So we all thought she may be coming down with something, though she insisted that she was alright.

"Very late that night, after everyone had gone to bed, Nell came to my room in a state of great distress, and this is what she said to me:"

Nell.... Geneva leaned into the letter, as if it were Tony speaking to her directly; she did not take a breath.

"During that dreadful summer eight long years ago, owing to the crushing burdens he had carried for many months, Father became unwell. Nell was very concerned, and as I was away in London, she came to visit him daily. Your telegram was placed in her hands. In all innocence, she opened it. Given the fact that our family was about to be saved from financial ruin by my marriage to Jane, Nell was quite overcome by the ramifications of what she read. She told no one about it, and waited for your letter, in the meantime, struggling over what to do.

"By the time your letter came, she knew. She wrote to you and offered a settlement of £500—the entire balance of her legacy. Soon after, your second letter to me arrived, which naturally she assumed had crossed hers in transit. She waited. No reply came. Months later her canceled cheque was returned through the bank. Only then was Nell convinced that you had accepted her terms."

But what became of Nell's letter and check? Geneva wondered in bewilderment. She read on: "It seems obvious that with you safely tucked away in bed upstairs, your guardian intercepted Nell's letter and cheque, and that she and John Scarborough wound up around $2000 the richer."

Geneva felt the wind had been knocked from her. She sat back and took time to absorb Tony's conjecture in full. Ida and John must have waited to see what she would do, before depositing the money. How gleeful they must have been when she decided not to tell Tony about their child. But what if questions came up later? she wondered. Then she realized that Ida would have vanished. And no doubt, John Scarborough had fixed it so that he would not be implicated.

Just before exonerating herself, Ida dropped her gaze, as if she were guilty; later, as the guard was summoned, she half opened her mouth to speak.

Still, why did Tony feel responsible?

"It was not until the night of my mother's party that Nell came to realize you had never received her letter and cheque. She had expected the 'ax to fall,' as soon as you arrived in England, and all evening up until that point, had been dreading the confession she had already decided to make to me on the morning after. She deeply regrets the harm she did to us.

"For my part, Geneva, I have forgiven my sister, for I know she was only trying to do what was best for her family at the time. But I told Nell that she must make a personal apology to you, that I shan't do it for her.

"Yet as I mentioned earlier, when all is said and done, it is I who must take the blame, for you see, it was my own bitterness following your departure which brought this about. Everyone in the family, including Nell, was convinced that I hated you, and never wanted to see you again, that you did not love me or care about any of us. If not for this, Nell would not have taken the action she did.

"And Geneva, now as I look back I am compelled to face what is perhaps just as wrong: that I had to keep my anger towards you alive, or I could never have gone through with marrying Jane.

"In the spring of 1924, when you and I resumed corresponding, I took the utmost care that no one in the family should realize that we were deeply in love and hoping for a future, lest it somehow get back to Jane. So until last year, when we all learned about Emelye, Nell continued to believe that matters had not changed between us from the day you walked away.

"And so there you are, my dearest. I hope and pray with all my heart that you can forgive these frailties in my family—particularly my own—so that we may all come together at last.

"I must bring this letter to a close now, for I am due at the *William & Mary* in a few minutes, to meet with the contractor who will soon undertake the major job of rebuilding the stage floor. But one thing before I go. An idea occurs to me that I rather like, and hope you'll like as well: It seems to me the two of us are somewhat like the *William & Mary*: a bit weathered from having endured our share of bad times, but tempered a good deal by the experience, and looking forward to a future with our brass polished, our glass shining, and all our lights lit up again…."

CHAPTER 83

It was very late on the last night Geneva and Emelye would live at 1207 Heights Boulevard. Geneva was in the kitchen, packing utensils. The envelope with her pictures enclosed lay unopened on the dining room table. In the two weeks since Tony's letter arrived, she had been in a frenzy of packing; without Rodney and Willa lending their hands, she would not have been ready in time. But now, except for a few odd articles, the packing was done; the crates and boxes were ready to be collected by Wald Transfer & Storage Company tomorrow.

Earlier Emelye came into the kitchen, in her sleeping gown, her feet bare, to kiss her mother goodnight. She announced that she wanted to sleep this last night in her own room.

Surely this was a healthy sign of Emelye's progress in overcoming the trauma of what befell her more than a year ago. Yet Geneva had hoped to continue nuzzling up to her daughter's small body in bed until the day she married Tony, so she found herself struggling to hide her disappointment. "I'll be up in a few minutes, to tuck you in," she said, missing Emelye even as she turned back to the chore in front of her, and not just because of the different sleeping arrangement. In England their lives would change; each would have to learn to share the other. It was not going to be easy.

By the time Geneva climbed the stairs to Emelye's room and peeked around the door, she was asleep, the small lamp on the dresser dimly burning. Geneva went in and sat down beside her daughter on the bed. For a few minutes, she watched her sleeping figure: her hair tumbled around her face, and one arm thrown back over the pillow. There was not a sight more beautiful to Geneva's eyes. She brushed the fine hair from around Emelye's face and kissed her cheek, then gently brought her arm down and tucked the covers around her shoulders. "I love you," she whispered. "You'll always be my only, only child."

When she rose from Emelye's bed, her eyes were inevitably drawn to Linsky's crucifix mounted above—one of the few articles yet to be packed, for she was reluctant to take it down until the last minute. She remembered back when she was not much older than Emelye, her eyes being drawn to the crucifix each time she went into Madame Linsky's office or even passed by the open door. Though she had long ago ceased to regard the crucifix as a symbol of harsh judgment, and had come to reverence it deeply, she still did not have a firm grasp of its myriad meanings; and those oft-repeated claims about it eluded her still. But over time, at least one meaning had become absorbed in her consciousness: God's love was enduring.

Was this at the root of Madame Linsky's faith as she lived and worked within view of the crucifix? Perhaps. *Certainly it was the standard of her love for me*, Geneva thought. And as she contemplated all that awaited her inside that envelope downstairs, her knowledge of Linsky's enduring love was strengthening in itself.

She turned on the dining room light and sat down at the table, the envelope and scissors before her. *I do not really have to open that envelope before I employ the scissors,* she told herself. But then it would not count as a break with the past, and she would never be able to forgive her cowardice. She took in a deep breath, unsealed the envelope, then slid the photographs out. Who should be on top, but the *Maiden at the Window*: peering out into the future, a circlet of flowers in her voluminous hair, a thin tunic draped around her torso and revealing the shape of her hips; and her ballet slippers waiting in the shadow created by her figure?

The first glimpse of this future was revealed as she put the *Maiden* aside and viewed herself in a contemplative pose at the edge of the surf in the moonlight. She studied every detail of the position of her body and limbs, and the wild composition of her waist-length hair; the surrealistic effect created by the superimposition of one image over another. She put this aside and studied the next one, a side view in which she stood leaning against a tall iron gate pedestal, enveloped in vaporous fog; her chin tilted, her chest thrown out, her arms clasped behind her; and the next—the fairy nymph with translucent wings, kneeling in a misty field of wild flowers in the morning. In the last one, her body was stretched out in a swirl of clouds.

In looking over each picture, Geneva vividly remembered how vulnerable she felt, posing in the privacy of the studio yet knowing that she was hiding nothing from the camera's eye—most disturbing of all, the secret of her affair with Victor, which seemed to hang across her like a banner. And yet—

She lined up the photographs on the table now and looked at each one still again; then sat back, considering.

"But if you'd only look at them...."

Perhaps one might call them vulgar. It would depend upon one's perspective. It would depend on the context in which they appeared. For herself, she found nothing vulgar here, only a suggestion of what was artfully concealed by her waist-length hair, or by a soft, ethereal image, superimposed. It was clear now why Victor did not destroy the photographs, and why she should never have expected him to: they stood alongside his *Maiden at the Window* as the fruits of Victor Calais's brief foray into the world of art photography. It was not for her to judge their intrinsic value, or to prevent the world from viewing them so that the passage of time might do so.

She was only his model.

Coming in 2006
The conclusion of the *Clearharbour Trilogy*

Elizabeth's Legacy
and
Clearharbour

About the Author

Houston native **Suzanne Morris** lives with her family in Baytown, Texas, where she is writing a film adaptation of the *Clearharbour Trilogy*. Her other published novels include *Galveston*, *Keeping Secrets*, *Skychild*, and *Wives and Mistresses*.

978-0-595-67400-8
0-595-67400-3

Printed in the United States
74730LV00004B/256-282